THE LONG DARK RIDE

V. J. NICHOLAS

Ordering Information:

Prime Seven Media
518 Landmann St.
Tomah City, WI 54660

Printed in the United States of America

1

Travel at night and camp during the day. That was Henry Jaegers plan. Easier on all involved, especially the livestock. Henry's memory served him well, since he found the fording place and the water of the Rio Bravo barely came up to the shoulders of Henry's two wolves, Chani and Akila and their two children flanking Juan Mendoza riding drag on the herd. Always cross the Rio Bravo in mid-summer when the water level is low, was the long standing wisdom going back centuries.

Twenty long horns inclusive of two bulls and a remuda of eight mustang and Appaloosa horses, glanced a wary eye from time to time on each of the wolves. Over time they grew to accept each other with the wolves' job to keep them together, with merely a growl or a nip at the flanks.

Jaeger had been on the trail from Monterrey for the last two weeks, heading north back into Texas, towards San Antonio de Bexar and what had become home territory. His wagon and provisions a parting gift from the family of Don Diego de la Fuentes, the Alcalde of Monterrey and one of the ruling Hidalgo's of northern Mexico. Henry's wife of just ten months, Joselita, the daughter of Don Domingo, dead and buried as a result of giving birth to their son Rodrigo at the age of twenty.

Tears came to Henry's eyes as he thought of what he'd lost. All that he cherished vanished once again, with Joselita's passing. The past year spent recuperating from is wounds courtesy of Don Diego, his marriage to Joselita and the magic of their love, gone forever. He wanted to curse God almighty, but how can you argue with the unseen? An entity without form, Henry was afraid of no man, but out there was the unseen, just beyond his reach, granting him grace from time to time, yet being apparently absent when needed most.

Here he was, Henry Jaeger, Texian Ranger possibly the last remnant of the Mexican American War back in Texas, now that it was part of the Union. Of course his continued presence in Monterrey was impossible, with the Rancho's of the area resentful of his presence. It was common knowledge that he, 'El Diablo Texicano' had ended the life of many a good Rancho before, during and after the war. His continued presence was not to be tolerated by the locals nor anyone that provided sustenance and shelter. So Henry had to go and as part of the bargain, leave tiny Rodrigo in the care of Don Diego and his wife to raise as they saw fit. It was best not to bring ill fortune down on the Fuentes family. He owed his very life to their kindness.

Of course he had the buckskin clothes on his back, a wagon full of provisions, suitable livestock, an acquired friend in Juan Mendoza and his wolves. Things could be worse. 'Old Rough and Ready', the former General Zachary Taylor was now President and Henry had a letter of introduction, signed by the General not two years before, so that ought to be worth something. Plus General Worth was now in San Antonio as head of the Department of Texas. So that should provide some leverage in getting some two years of back pay owed to him, since he saved the bacon of each of these fine gentlemen, back in the war.

As he gazed into the heavens he noted the position of the moon and figured another three hours to sunrise. Best to concentrate on the path ahead and plan the campsite for the coming day. All those years as a Texas Ranger guaranteed that he knew all of south Texas like the back of his hand.

A well wooded glade was just an hour ahead by a stream that would give the livestock a secluded place to spend the night, off the beaten track. Ten days travel to San Antonio de Bexar and an audience with General Worth should get him off to a good start.

The livestock were bedded down, both Chani and Akila well positioned on guard at the perimeter, all had been fed and the camp was established.

The sun was now just appearing over the horizon and Juan Mendoza had just finished serving the victuals. They both would spend the next several hours getting water from the stream and filtering it through whole cloth, then boiling it prior to refilling the two fifty gallon barrels attached to the wagon, always mindful to retrieve the water, upstream from the herd.

Little needed to be said between Juan and Henry because Juan spoke little English and while Henry's fluency in Spanish was adequate, he was not in the habit of making small talk and usually spoke only when something important needed to be said. But over the past year Juan had come to know and respect Henry Jaeger and had come to know his mind. Both knew what had to be done and when. Both decided that since they were in Texas and in a secluded place that it was alright to finally remove their boots for the day's siesta. Perhaps by midafternoon they would finally take a dip in the nearby stream and remove the grime of the trail thus far.

Prior to that both Chani and Akila would be watered and fed, their fur brushed from the grime and brambles of the trail.

As the sun made its way towards mid-day both men slept fitfully, for a deep sleep was months away only to be had when they finally reached their destination. The place where roots were to be planted, a rancho started, house and barn to be built, fences to be erected. Then the work would really begin. From sun up through sun down, always with one's head on a swivel and a firearm at the ready. Ever wary of strangers, both men had a certain way with animals that defied description. An ability to put them at ease, read their moods and communicate without words. They would slowly work their way through the herd, touching each animal in turn then leave always close by. The herd was their family now and the herd would grow, providing sustenance for years to come.

The following evening, they departed the camp, leaving no direct evidence that they ever had been there.

For the next ten days they traveled north to San Antonio, engaging in the same cycle each and every morning and evening. Running a parallel course about a mile east of the Laredo, San Antonio trail, seeing the occasional rider but not being seen in return, all according to plan.

Finally on the eleventh morning they arrived at a point several miles south of San Antonio de Bexar. Then making camp by a small stream this time to stay for several days. When everything was settled down, Henry decided to clean up completely, body, boots and buckskins. For two days later, he meant to seek out and reacquaint himself with General William Worth and see what future lay ahead.

"Do joo tink da General weel remember joo, Jefe", asked Juan? For Juan Mendoza knew first hand, what Henry had done for the General as well as what Henry had done for Don Domingo, during the battle of Monterrey several years before, saving both men's lives from the retribution of the local Rancho's.

"Yeah, I think he will Juan"! I've known him to be a man of honor and a great general, during the time I've been with him. After all, he selected me and a bunch of other Rangers to go with him down to Vera Cruz and all the way up to Mexico City. He always has done right by people and I see no reason that he'll change his ways"!

Juan had selected the big brown spotted Appaloosa mare for Henry to ride into San Antonio and saw to it that it was groomed and saddled. The very last thing he put on was the two Sam Walker Colt revolvers. One on his left hand belt side and the other just under a flap holster attached to his saddle.

"Hold things together Juan for I don't know how long I'll be in town. Perhaps a day or so", said Henry as he started off towards town, in a slow gallop.

An hour later as he made his way up through town, a man called out, "Henry"! "Henry Jaeger, is that you"! Henry turned around as saw it was Seth Johntu owner of the General Store who came running over to him.

"It is you", cried Seth as he reached up to touch Henry and shake his hand. "We was tole you was killed down Mexico way"! As he shook Seth's hand, Henry replied "Well Seth as you can see, you was tole wrong".

"By god it's good to see ya Henry. Where are ya now"? "I'm camped just south of town and might need a place to park around thirty head of livestock for a few days, so can ya be any help"? "Ain't got any money yet although I'm owed two years back pay by somebody"!

"Well Henry, money is hard to come by these days all around but since it's you, I think there's someone who owes me a favor with a corral nearby, so when you're ready, let me know!"

"Seth, I'm looking for General Worth, for I heard he's now an important man as an overseer for the State of Texas, for the Government."

"Yeah, Old Rough and Ready, General Taylor appointed him in charge of the Department of Texas, a few months ago, so ya best see him if ya want anything, since the State of Texas is broke and that scallywag Governor Bell ain't worth a bucket of warm shit"!

"So where can I find General Worth these days, Seth?"

"He's taken residence in the St. Anthony Hotel, Henry and that's where he conducts his business!"

"The St. Anthony Hotel," asked Henry?

"Yeah, just got built a few months ago and it's just two blocks up the street on the left hand side, across from the old Alamo!"

"Thanks Seth, have to see the General directly and conduct some business if I can. Will look in on ya afterwards and we can have a palaver"! "You do that Henry", hollered Seth as Henry rode up the street towards his destiny. As he rode up what was now called 'Commerce Street', occasionally people would call out to him and he would acknowledge their presence. A few minutes later there it was, the St. Anthony Hotel. Here he was Almost thirty years old and this was the second hotel he'd ever entered. The only other was back in Nashville, when as a teen, he helped his Uncle build that building, but he was simply hired help then.

There it was, a three story building painted completely white with a verandah surrounding each floor, with all the gee gaws and ornamentals Henry had ever seen, with a large sign over the entrance announcing "The St. Anthony Hotel" and underneath as almost a post script in smaller lettering, 'The finest Hotel west of the Mississippi'. Henry rode up to the hitching post, dismounted and tied his horse to the hitching post, removing his revolving barreled Colt five round 12 gauge shot gun, from the saddle scabbard. Only twelve of these were ever made by Sam Colt and Henry probably had one of the very few that ever survived the war, so he wasn't about to leave it to be stolen. He climbed the steps cradling the shotgun in his left arm, frontier style and went over to the front desk and asked for the General. "The general is over there in the front parlor, but as you can see, there are several people in front of you awaiting the General's pleasure. So if you'll be kind enough to stand in line, I'm sure the general will attend to you in due course!" Jaeger thanked the desk clerk and went over to the small group of men and waited his turn. As he approached, the talkative group of men grew silent and warily gave the once over. One of them grew nervous and rose from his seat offering it to Henry. Obligingly Henry sat down and removed his wide brimmed cowhide hat. Clad in buckskin from head to boot and his presence stood silent testament that this was not a man to be trifled with. The rest of the gaggle sat or stood with their short city hats planted firmly on their heads.

One of the men approached introducing himself as the former Lt. Ulysses Grant. A smallish man he was. "Henry Jaeger I believe"? Jaeger looked at him without recognition. "We served together in the northern campaign. I was with the flying artillery. Palo Alto, the Monterrey scrape and Buena Vista?" Suddenly Henry recalled, "Yes, Lieutenant Grant, I remember now"! 'How are you Lieutenant'?

With that, both men plunged into the world of old times, with Grant bringing Jaeger up to date on events of the day economically and politically for the next hour while they both waited. Jaeger in turn gave Grant an abbreviated version of events while in the service of both General Worth and General Winfield Scot, in the southern campaign for control of Mexico proper.

"What ever became of Col. Davis of the Mississippi Rifles", asked Henry?

"Col. Davis is now a Senator from the great state of Mississippi", replied Grant! "Can any good come of that you think", asked Jaeger?

"Frankly No. Already he's thrown in with the scallywag Calhoun from South Carolina. I fear for the Union!"

As they talked the line of suitor's for the General's attention grew smaller with only Grant and Jaeger next. A man appeared and announced "Lt. Grant, the general will see you now"! Grant rose quickly shook hands with Henry, saying "Wish me luck", turned on a dime and entered the parlor for his time with the general.

From what conversation filtered out of the partially opened door, it seemed that Grant wasn't being retained in the Army for reasons unknown, besides good service as an artillery man in the Northern Campaign. He was a graduate of the Academy at West Point, yet somehow had not apparently made the right friends politically, since the federal government didn't want to retain a large costly army, General Worth was his last chance of employment, or else he'd have to become a 'feather merchant'..

Ten minutes later he emerged from the parlor, with that hang dog look of defeat on his face. "As I feared, he said to Jaeger, I'm not to be retained in the Army thanks to those in Washington!"

'Well what are you gonna do Grant?"

"I have some folks up Missouri way, so I'll have to go up there and see if I can make a livin' there, Henry!" Jaeger rose and took his hand saying, "Well Grant I wish ya the best!" With that the two separated and Jaeger watched as Grant shuffled out the front door of the hotel, with both hands in his trouser pockets and shoulders sagging with defeat.

Although small in stature, Jaeger considered Grant a good and capable military man, given his limited exposure to him. Yet he seemed somewhat diminished especially when in the company of many of the other officers Jaeger came in contact with that were 'all hat and no cattle'.

As Jaeger turned around to the parlor, the same man appeared at the door saying, 'Well sir seems you're the last of the day to see the General and you are?"

"Jaeger, Henry Jaeger of the Texas Rangers, previously seconded to General Worth during the war!"

As he turned to announce Jaeger, the General bellowed from the parlor, "Yes I know the man!"

As Henry entered, the general bellowed, "They said you were dead!

Killed by the Rancho's while you were after that renegade priest escorting Santa Ana. Did ya ever get him?"

Jaeger replied, "Well general, they were wrong as you can see and as to you second comment about the priest, (Jaeger paused for several seconds for effect) the very last thing he saw in this world was me looking at him!"

"So Jaeger, the priest Andrade is dead?" Jaeger replied, "As a doornail, Kaput and to prove it", Jaeger reached into a small leather pouch that hung from his belt, removing a gold chain running through a medium sized gold cross encrusted in diamonds, "this is his cross!"

"Seems that when someone sets you on a task it gets done no matter what", said the general sternly. "Seems that none of those who rode north with you ever made it back, except Lieutenant Bragg, who said everyone else, had been killed and that you were in pretty bad shape!"

"Well general, I cut Lieutenant Bragg loose to report back to you and General Scott, since he was of little use at the time I was better off traveling alone"..

"So the Texican Rangers always get their man, eh?

"General, it's what we do", replied Jaeger matter of factly.

"Well son, its past my lunch time and I dare say yours also, so lets you and I go across the street for some excellent Mexican food and you can fill in the blanks of your travels in the past year or so!"

Thus was spent the rest of the day, filling themselves with an assortment of Mexican delicacies and washing it all down with "Pulque". Both campaigns, the northern and southern were recanted from each man's point of view and many of the blank spaces filled in given the fog of war.

"So General, President Polk actually got congress to pay for Texas and the rest of the land all the way to the Pacific?"

"Yes he did my boy, ran it right down their throats. That's where a politician like old Winfield Scott comes in handy. Came back to Washington City all high hat and a hero. Set for life. With the likes of Zachariah Taylor elected President, with the work horses and some others like me, set aside here in this backwater to run the Department of Texas in San Antonio de Bexar! Word is they're building a Fort up north of here near the Dallas settlement and their going to put my name on it, so isn't that a nice howdy do. Well I suppose things could be worse, like the lot of that Lieutenant Grant there!" "Certainly a capable soldier, but he didn't exactly distinguish himself above his contemporaries and while at the Academy didn't achieve the high grades of, let's say, Captain Lee!" "So the man gets cut loose!" "Don't expect we'll ever hear from Mr. Grant ever again!"

"Now Mister Texas Ranger Jaeger, down to business. What exactly is it that you require?" The general had all the buttons on his uniform undone and was suitably relaxed from an abundance of food and drink. 'Well sir, as I reckon I'm due about two years of pay at about ten US dollars a month!" "Anything else Mr. Jaeger? "No sir that's about it!" "So Mr. Jaeger, have at any time in your service to The Texican Republic or the US of A, have you ever once received your pay regularly?" "No sir, not once!" "So just how have you kept things together?"

"Well General, I am a passable carpenter and once in a while I helped Captain Jack Hays do some surveying!"

"Well son, as you may have surmised, all of Texas is broke. Damn little money around, not a single bank anywhere, save for New Orleans. Largely a barter economy. Damn few Rangers are still around to keep the Indians and the rustlers at bay. Jack Hays has departed for the goldfields of California, along with some others and we're pretty thin in the law enforcement area", said the General almost absent mindedly, clearly thinking of a plan.

"Several days from now an Army platoon will arrive from Galveston with a parcel from Washington City, allowing me to do certain things. So here is what I propose, if you are agreeable;

First, a grant of land to you amounting to several sections of land. Next, Texas will need the presence of Rangers in the area of where the Waco Indian tribe is, near the upper Brazos River. Given your skills at carpentry and a familiarity with surveying and your skills as a Ranger and a tracker, if you will agree to remain in the service of the now State of Texas, as a Ranger, I will do the following. Initiate and sign the necessary documents to grant you the required carpentry implements that may be at hand locally to establish a homestead and a Ranger presence on the upper Brazos river area. Next, I will instruct those scallywags in the Austin settlement to award you the rank of Captain for the foreseeable future. Since I hold the purse strings of Texas for the time being they will have to agree. Besides, until they agree on a taxing authority for the state, they have no money to pay you and neither do I. Any future remuneration will have to be at the State's expense at such time. Besides, money is but one of many mediums of exchange.

So if you agree, you will have a place to take your livestock and set up a legal homestead and in return Texas will have a law authority in the North Central Texas Area. I'm told you are a man of great will and endurance, a man of grit. What say you?"

This had turned out far better than Jaeger had expected and he was quick to say, "Agreed! " Good, young man! I'll start on the documents first thing in the morning. By the way, I have a daughter arriving in the next few days all the way from Charleston, South Carolina. Her name is Melanie and it's certain to be a blessing".

"There is a general store a few blocks away, run by a man named Seth". "Yes sir", replied Jaeger. "Know the man well!"

"Well son, on your way back to camp, pay him a visit and select what carpentry and surveying implements you may require and have him set them aside, until I complete the appropriate documents".

"Yes sir, General". "Good, now it seems that I've over indulged and my stomach is churning. I'll return to the Hotel for a siesta and instruct my adjutant, to start on the required documents we've discussed." "Come by my office two days hence so we can complete the documents. Oh, by the way, I assume that you can read and write your name".

"Yes sir and cipher also"!

"Interesting, one of the few literate Texican Rangers I've ever met", growled the General as he made his way back to the hotel. On his way back to camp, Henry stopped by the General store to see Seth as the General directed.

"So the General put you back in service as a Captain, did he? Headed to the upper Brazos area are ya? Well seems the General is the boss, so Henry let's get to seeing what you'll need"!

"The General is running things here and has almost no money to pay for these things. Things haven't improved much from the old Texas Republic.

Oh some Army people are camped nearby well-armed, but that's about it.

Everything here has to be transported a very long way from its place of origin costs money, then there are a host of middlemen who must be paid all along the way each and every one who touches every item you see, finally it takes forever and a day for Me to get paid by the State or the Federal Government. Now since the General hasn't put a dollar limit on your requirements, select what you need, then bring the purchasing document with you when you pick things up. Should you have a dollar limit on the document then we can select what is really needed at that time. Should you not have a dollar limit, then you have no worries. I just, submit a bill to be paid along with the executed purchase document, by the generals hand and then wait for payment and trees will grow faster. Either way, you'll depart with the means to start a new life, so let's finish up with your selections before I get an ulcer"!

Henry and Seth continued on with Seth relentlessly asking, "Now Henry do you really need this",

Hand drills, screw drill bits, wood plug makers et al?"

Riding back to camp, Henry was apprehensive for things seemed to be going too well. Still, if things went as planned he was certain to count his blessings. Back at camp, he recounted to Juan all that had occurred that day, far into the night.

"So we gonna live in the upper Brazos river Jefe?"

"Sure looks like it"!

"Never been to da Upper Brazos"!

"You never been to Texas proper before Juan"! "Let's get some sleep"! With that Juan put another log on the fire and pulled his serape' over him and dropped off to sleep, while Henry made a quick round of the livestock, Chani and Akila petting each in turn as they kept a wary watch over the herd.

The following day was spent cleaning and polishing all of their equipment for the next day's events. Since gunpowder was in short supply he was fortunate enough to put aside a quantity of Salt Peter and Sulphur, the Charcoal he could make himself. The lead shot required was of the wrong caliber, but thirty pounds of lead shot could be reprocessed into the proper caliber's for his Walker Colt pistols, his Sam Colt, five shot revolving cylinder 12 gage shot gun, the Colt, five shot revolving cylinder .45 caliber rifle and of course, the hundred fifty year old Beretta .70 caliber, 40 inch long double barreled, flintlock rifle. A family heirloom.

2

As Henry worked through the day, his mind went through a constant reshuffling of the inventory of necessities he'd require from Seth the following day. The age old quandary of wants versus needs. It all depended on the largesse of the General. As he reflected, it seemed that all his life was spent in a state of constant worry. Not very different from the critters, great and small, that surrounded them all. Watch any feral creature in the wild and a few things become clear, they never sleep soundly and at all times their senses are ever on the alert. His wolves, Chani and Akila, while partially tamed and essentially predators were a constant example. If things were that way for them what could things be like for the lesser critters in this world?

He tried not to recall the fate of his baby son Rodrigo, but it was no use.

The little critter was in god's hands now, and part of the Fuentes family. They were 'Hidalgos', part of the ruling class of Northern Mexico and Dona Estella, his grandmother would have someone to devote herself to now that her daughter Joselita, was in the ground. Little Rodrigo would have available the best of everything that Northern Mexico had to offer.

Once again, he walked the camp checking on the livestock and the wolves at the sentry in silence, then made his way back to the campsite, bid a 'good night' to Juan and curled up beneath his serape, falling fast asleep.

Juan looked over at his 'Padron' and said to himself, 'Sleep well Amigo and dream….'! An hour later, Juan followed Henry into the abyss.

"Heinrich! Heinrich Jaeger! Ver bist du? Kommen ze hier" Then his Mutti, Margarita, corrected herself, speaking out again in heavily accented English, from the front porch of their log cabin, Suppers ready!"

"Coming Mutti, yelled back Henry from across the cornfield a hundred yards away!" He'd just finished digging the ditch, his father asked for so that the water coming down from the hillside could irrigate the cornfield tonight during the rain. Just in time for the clouds were rolling in signaling the coming storm.

He ran all the way back to the cabin, leaping up the steps, halted by his mother's admonishment, "Heinrich, take off your muddy boots before entering!" Already assembled at the table were his father Diet-rich at the head of the table and his two younger twin sisters Dagmar and Beatrix across from his place at the table.

He hurriedly washed then dried his hands at the communal bowl, prior to taking his place at the table for the evening meal. His mother sat down after placing the bowel of stew in front of Dietrich, then took her place at the other end of the table. All made the sign of the cross as Dietrich commenced the daily ritual of the 'Lord's Prayer' in heavily accented English with one eye on his wife, who was relentless in insisting they speak in the language of the land especially in front of their children.

"Amen", concluded Dietrich. As he spooned out generous helpings of the evening's meal, he asked, "Henry, have you completed your task for the day?

"Yes Papi, the irrigation ditch is just completed as you've directed!" Just then the first sounds of thunder came rolling across the large hollow presaging the storm that was to follow. All the livestock were under shelter, the food was on the table and the family assembled. This was how life was to be in this new land.

'Ser gute' muttered Dietrich silently to himself.

"Henry, let me see your hands", commanded his father. Henry stopped eating and placed his hands in front of him, palms up for his father's inspection. "Good, the blisters are now turning into calluses. The first sign of manhood. How do you feel son after a day's worth of hard work?"

"Very tired Papi, but as you always say we will sleep well tonight". The rest of the meal was spent in small talk and as the table was cleared a large apple pie was presented in celebration of Henry's two sister's birthday the following day. The sisters had gathered all day around their mother eagerly helping where they could in anticipation of the aftermath of the evening's meal. Tomorrow they would both be eight years old and were at an age where they were becoming their mothers little helpers. Helping clean, wash, tending to the livestock, cook, milk the cows, and churn the butter and an ever increasing myriad of skills they were eager to learn at their mother's hands.

Each day after the early morning chores, their mother would gather the children then commence to drill them in the basics of reading, writing and arithmetic, with a chalk board and the few books they had. Of course the Bible was central to their learning process. Every Sunday Morning, they would all assemble at the small grotto, that Dietrich and Henry had built down past the water well, where the family would celebrate Morning Mass, giving thanks to the eternal for all their blessings.

The past years had been difficult in this land but hard work was starting to shed their blessings on the family. If all went well, the land they had acquired from Mr. Boudinot, in the Cheviot Hills section of Harrison County Ohio, would be theirs free and clear in just a few years.

The past crops had proved bountiful each year, with Mr. Boudinot receiving a large share of each crop along with, the family's efforts in a small tannery and a seemingly endless demand for Dietrich's skills in carpentry from friends and neighbors. Of course, since money was always in short supply in the region, goods and services were in a constant state of barter. Those with needed skills, were in constant demand, those without, usually were forced by circumstance to take the low road. This is how life had been lived since the beginning of recorded time. This is how it would always be.

But since it was Saturday night, after the dinner table was cleared and the dishes cleaned, Henry and his father made the requisite trips to the water well to bring buckets of water to be heated up at the hearth to fill up the bath tub for the family bath. Part of being a carpenter required skills as a builder of barrels, and as a bath tub they always dragged out a six foot long wooden tub, large enough to hold the entire family. Washing each other with the lye soap the family had made. Disposing of the water by simply lifting a cork, from the drain and thus the water drained into a tube and out through a hole in the cabin down the hill into the creek.

In the years to come, they would have to build an add-on to the cabin for a bathing area, especially when their two daughters, started to become women. But that was several years away.

Henry was born in Baltimore the very day they arrived dockside from their homeland in Bavaria. The journey over the Cumberland was difficult, but since Dietrich proved his worth as a hunter he kept the group they were traveling with well provisioned with game. Several months later they arrived at their destination in a rapidly growing village called Cincinnati.

The year was 1820 and they had traveled by flat boat down the Ohio River.

Henry's mother had a sister who had married a merchant of the town and when they arrived they were welcomed with open arms.

Several months later a deal was struck with another merchant and land owner Charles Boudinot and the fifty acre homestead was purchased. The appropriate papers were fully executed and just prior to both parties affixing their signatures, Dietrich Jaeger spit in his hand and offered it to Mr. Boudinot.

Boudinot looked aghast at the hand offered containing a modest amount of spittle, without missing a beat Margarita's sister said, "In Bavaria, it the custom for two parties to seal a deal in a mutual manner!"

Boudinot, ever the accommodating businessman, likewise, spit in his hand and clasped Jaeger's hand. The signatures were then affixed, the town's notary seal affixed and the deal was done.

Their hasty emigration from Europe, what with Margarita being in a motherly way, did not afford them time for the necessities of a formal marriage in the Catholic Church. For the daughter of a Bavarian Ritter, could hardly be given in marriage to a mere games keeper of one's estates, no matter if he was from a family long in service of the Ritter and one of the best 'Meister Scharfschutze's in the land.

Upon their arrival in Baltimore, they found a Catholic priest that officiated a post birth abbreviated formal union and baptismal of their son Heinrich/ Henry. This was a new land and many of the old world formalities were swept aside for the time being.

In time the Jaegers began to prosper in this new land, for quite aside from Dietrich's ability as a hunter to put food on the table, his ability as a carpenter after building his home, barn, fencing and parceling off his land for livestock, grain harvesting, and tree orchards to provide fruit became well known to those in Cheviot township and all along the Harrison Pike, that led from Cincinnati to the North Western frontier.

When Henry was in his ninth year, his father decided to pay a visit to the Miami Indian tribe that had an encampment between the Big and Little Miami Rivers just a few miles away. The tribe had fallen on hard times, ever since they were coerced into joining the larger warlike Shawnee Indian Nation many years before in the latter part of the 1700's and the early part of the 1800's. The tribes were decimated in succession by the military efforts of General's "Mad Anthony Wayne "in the latter part of the 1700's and again by William Henry Harrison in the aftermath of the War of 1812.

The Miami tribes were woefully short of manpower, to hunt for the game to feed their villages. Some tried their hand at agriculture with mixed result Thus the visit by Henry and his father to the Miami the Village. After a meeting with the Shaman, early one morning, all the males of the village departed on a hunting party. The Jaeger horses were left at the village and they all were afoot. By mid-morning they came upon a herd of Elk peacefully grazing in a valley. A brief consultation resulted between Dietrich and the Shaman, with Jaeger staying on the ridge of the valley, positioned well into the trees, downwind from the herd and the Miami circling around the valley to the entrance of the valley.

Carefully positioning himself in a shooters hide, Dietrich loaded his ancient early 1700 Beretta double barreled .70 caliber flintlock rifle, with a 40 inch octagonal barrel. Henry noted his fathers every move silently whispering the movements and position of the herd to his father as preparations were made. When all was ready, it was determined that about a half an hour had elapsed and the Miami should be in position to intercept the herd with bow and arrow as they ran through the valleys entrance and chokepoint.

Noting the movement of the grass and tree branches to evaluate crosswinds, Dietrich noted the position of the two largest stags grazing just yards from each other. One just ahead of the other. If all went well, the closest could be shot and with a minor adjustment in elevation the other could be had also. After what had seems an eternity, Henry's father took the shots, with two loud explosions and the attendant smoke clouding the vision. The prey were located some 400 paces from the hide with the first going down from a shoulder shot thrashing about, unable to run and eventually expiring, while the other ran some two hundred paces with the rest of the herd towards the valleys entrance before it finally dropped in its tracks unable to move any more.

After cleaning up there hide Henry and his father went down to first the largest stag then the other to see just where each round hit.

The first hit right in the stags shoulder breaking everything the ball tearing through everything in the shoulder ending up in the lungs on a downward trajectory while the second animal was struck in the lungs missing the shoulder completely thus accounting for its ability to run a bit prior to succumbing to its wounds. Not exactly on the mark but good enough for the Master Shooter.

Several minutes later the rest of the six Miami braves that accompanied them arrived hauling two additional smaller elk and the assurances of four more elk down the trail. The Shaman sent one of the brave on the run back to the village to bring both Jaeger horses and the entire village along with all of the long poles and rawhide strips to secure all of the carcasses to both horse and man drags. Then the rest of the braves were sent back after the other elk to drag them back to the valley entrance, where they could be better guarded till the entire village returned.

Several hours later the entire village returned with the horses and immediately set to binding the carcasses to the drags and hauling them back to the village. The sun was now overhead, a good mornings work. All were tired as they entered the village with the day's largesse. The leaves were starting to turn signaling that winter was not far away. But this winter they would not go hungry. Hurriedly fires were made and the entire village set to butchering the carcasses, separating the edible meats to be immediately smoked, and the hides stored for later tanning, the bones, sinews, tendons, hooves and finally the antlers, with every part of each animal having a tangible use in the days to come The Shaman briefly stopped the activity and assembled the village offering the pipe to both Dietrich and his son and asking Dietrich what part of the kill he wanted? Henry's father looked around and pointed to the smallest of the carcasses, saying that he wanted only the edible smoked meat from that animal and nothing more.

The Shaman quickly said that Jaegers family was entitled to at least the largest of the Elk in its entirety questioned the wisdom of Jaegers selection. Dietrich suddenly recalled a lesson from his wife at their last Sunday's Mass said at their family grotto, relating to the Shaman, the quoted words of Jesus, "He who is first is last, while he who is last is first". The Shaman first seemed puzzled by that verse, but bid each member of the village to pass both Jaegers in turn and look into their eyes and touch them on the shoulder.

In this the entire village accepted the Jaeger family as their own and this was their way of saying thank you.

In the coming months as winter approached, both Henry and his father and the Shaman visited each other with Henry being taken under the wing by the Shaman and taught the Indian ways of tracking and trapping wild game of all sizes. Henry quickly learned to make and use the bow and arrow, tracking, stalking and hunting with the others, almost exclusively with the bow. He was patiently instructed in the art of not only the making of a proper bow but the art of making the arrow. While his father's Beretta flintlock had the greater range for bringing down large prey it made too much noise. The bow and arrow were silent. Both weapons had their advantages and disadvantages.

One day Henry and his father were summoned to the village by the Shaman and over the course of one day were fitted by the women of the village, with the finest buck skin trousers, shirt and coat. Made of several of the finest deerskins from recent hunts. The following week Henry's mother and his sisters were summoned to the village and made vestments suitable to their gender, again of the finest deerskin.

Upon their return the next day both sisters insisted on wearing the deerskin vestments and moccasins almost exclusively, evening in lieu of bedclothes.

"It seems Mutti, that we have a household of squaws and a brave", mused Henry's father during the evening supper.

While most of the homesteaders of the Cheviot Township questioned the Jaegers friendship with the Miami's they accepted it largely given to Dietrich's prowess as a carpenter and a hunter, and his periodic generosity to those in need.

On a winter day, at the very day of Henry's tenth year, his father and Henry decided to pay a visit to the Miami Indian encampment for a hunting expedition and to examine previously set traps for small game, especially the Beaver that were plentiful all along the Big Miami River. The large pole skids were attached to the Jaegers horses in expectation of a bounty of game. Towards early afternoon, most of the traps yielded a variety of fox, beaver and other game in such quantities to almost fill both skids when they went back to the village. Especially the beaver pelts that would fetch a handsome price back in Cincinnati. After the last trap was examined and found empty of game, the hunting party decided to turn back and take a more direct route to the village.

Directly they came to a stop, when the Miami Shaman made a hand signal to stop and listen. Henry and his father dismounted from their horses and started up a slope with the Shaman and a few other braves close behind, listening for faint sounds of what sounded like several baby animals. As Henry, now in the lead, stopped by a small cave covered by brush, he removed the brush revealing two baby wolves, one black and the other light brown suckling at their mothers lifeless teats, in vain. As Henry and the Shaman approached, they also viewed the precarious situation in silence.

Henry looked at his father in a pleading fashion, as if to say 'Father we can't let this pass'.

The Shaman then spoke, as he always did, in a combination of broken English and sign language, saying that Henry has been blessed by the Wolf spirit 'Akila' and must now become the parent of the baby cubs, or else they would soon die and the spirit in the skies would be angry. He explained that should Henry assume this responsibility, all the wolves abilities would transfer to Henry as a hunter. Sight, smell, hearing and the ability to endure great hardship that was certain to come to Henry as he matured into manhood.

Henry looked at his father in a pleading manner. Dietrich then nodded his head in agreement. In unison Henry, the Shaman and all the rest smiled, as they knew the Wolf spirit in the sky, would be appeased. Henry gently lifted the cubs, one by one away from their mother, handing one of them to his father, while the other braves lifted the mother's body gently away and secured it to one of the skids already full of carcasses. As Henry mounted his horse, with one of the cubs neatly secured within his coat for warmth, he heard his father say, "Of course you know, the keeping of the wolves will be your responsibility, Henry"!

An event like this was very rare on the frontier and the Indians of most tribes viewed this as a great blessing from above. While some of the braves were slightly envious of Henry and his father, they all knew that Akila would look down at this and bless them all for their part in the event. An hour or so later they entered the Miami encampment to a beaming and happy crowd, for the hunt had been bountiful in game of all types and soon the story about the baby wolves made the rounds of all the people and they were pleased.

After Henry and his father had left, the Shaman personally took charge of rendering the Wolves mother with great care and reverence. Holding each and every body part extracted up to the sky and reciting centuries old incantations to the heavens. He then decided in his mind to have the hide of the mother made into something fitting for Henry's mother, as a point of honor.

Henry and his father hurried as best they could in the snow back to their homestead and upon arrival an hour later, Henry's father bellowed, "Hello the house, come see what we have brought" !

Henry's mother and his sister's poured out of the house and were greeted by the sight of both baby wolf cubs, held outright them to accept. Both of Henry's sisters took a cub gently in their hands as Dietrich quickly told them of what had happened to their mother and said, "They will need milk immediately if they are to live!"

Henry and his father took the horses down to the barn to be unsaddled brushed and fed, then proceeded to the house and upon entering saw the women hard at work feeding the cubs milk fresh from one of the cows not an hour earlier and caring for both cubs. It was a bit of a task getting the milk down the cubs throats, seeing that there was no teat for them to suckle, but with patience and two baby spoons that had fed the children when they were little, the task was accomplished, by Henry's sisters with their mother close at hand in supervision.

"Seems that your sisters have taken charge Henry so there is little to do for us now"! When the cubs were full, they quickly fell asleep, in the sister's arms. Just then Henry's mother said, "But what shall we name them"? All looked at each other in askance.

Gently lifting their hind legs Henry's father exclaimed, "Well the black one is a boy" and then he examined the other, "Und the brown one is a girl, so Henry what is it to be"? Henry, now fairly well versed by the Shaman of Indian lore, slowly said, "The boy is to be 'Akila' and the girl 'Chani'!" An old box was then retrieved and a blanket was folded up and placed inside and placed near the fire place for their bed.

The cubs were then placed in the box near the warm fire and left to sleep while the family prepared supper. After the evening meal was cleaned up the girls quickly made for the box cuddling the cubs till it was time for bed. Insisting the cubs be allowed to sleep with them for the night to keep warm was a difficult argument for Henry's parents to overcome.

The girls had happily climbed into bed with their living cargo and for the very first time, went to sleep without a whimper. The very first lesson in life for parental responsibility and as time went by they adapted to their responsibility in fine fashion.

After the children went to sleep, Dietrich said to his wife, "Just one thing, the Shaman told me we must be aware of, during the period of the full moon; our new children will start to howl. Nothing to be done about it, for it's their way. So perhaps they should be kept in the house, especially during that time and the livestock should be kept securely in the barn"

As the wolves grew, they bonded readily with all members of the family as a unit and surprisingly enough, the livestock accepted them as one of their own, as the wolves mingled with them.

The ensuing months rolled by with all of the Jaeger children growing in stature and usefulness. As would be common with families of a multiple of growing children, occasional squabbles occurred. Fortunately the disagreements usually limited themselves to which child was going to spend the night with which of the wolves. The parents quickly formulated a rotation of the animals with each of the three children. Three children and two animals to embrace meant someone was to sleep alone for a given night. In short order, the plan was adopted, only to be abandoned after a few days, for it seemed the wolves had a mind of their own, starting out an evening in one bed, then sometime during the evening ending up in another.

One cold Sunday morning, the children awoke to find their beds empty of the critters, only to find both of the wolves, neatly snuggled together at the foot of their parent's bed. A finer, more agreeable family was not to be found anywhere in the entire Ohio River Valley.

In Henry's eleventh year, his father's second crop of the season, finally paid Mr. Boudinot for the deed to the family's homestead, free and clear.

From this time on, the Jaeger family could keep the entire proceeds of any crop yield, rather than only a small portion thereof.

Dietrich started to take his son more and more on every single hunt, teaching him the old world methods of game stalking while Henry taught his father the Indian methods and eventually they came up with a hybrid method of the stalk incorporating the best parts of both. Henry was gradually introduced to his fathers prized family heirloom, the .70 caliber Beretta, double barreled flintlock long rifle, that was well over a hundred years old at the time, capable of firing a lethal round over 400 yards with reasonable accuracy, given the rifled grooves in the barrel. At first glance in looked like an ordinary double barreled muzzle loading shotgun, unadorned with the usual scroll work of the day. But since this was only one of six ever produced by the Beretta factory of northern Italy and in the hands of a capable 'Meister Scarfschutzer', knowledgeable of ball trajectory and wind deflection, had been the state of the art long range fire arm for its time. Its intrinsic value was beyond calculation and it had stayed in the Jaeger family, passed down from generation to generation of Master Shooters and great hunters. As his father did for Dietrich, so he did for his son Heinrich. The stalk, construction of the hide and a secure firing platform. Endless patience and the reward of bringing down large game with a single shot. The art of estimating range or distance of the prey and thus the drop values of the round associated with distance, along with estimating wind deflection of a round as it was driven to its target. Then there was the making of gunpowder from elements of charcoal, sulphur and salt peter from scratch no different than his mother fussing over the baking of bread, or construction of a pie for the evening meal. Lastly the melting of lead into the shot ball which must be constructed without flaw being thus perfectly round. Fussy business that…

Finally after Henry had assured his father of his competence in these areas, Dietrich relented one afternoon after a bull deer had been stalked, the hide and the firing position had been constructed, Henry's father said;

"Time for you to put in practice all you've learned Henry, so you load and fire the rifle"! Slowly Henry switched places with his father; he'd prepared the weapon many times before, but never had been allowed to fire it. His father looked on in silence as Henry slowly prepared the Beretta for firing, nodding in silence as each function had been completed. They looked again at the big buck, calculating the range of approximately 250 paces. Henry put the right barrel in full cock, took careful aim, then a deep breath, slowly exhaling while gradually squeezing the front trigger, aiming for a point just a hair above the left front shoulder and fired. The big gun bucked in recoil, leaving a cloud of smoke from the flash pan, singing part of Henry's hair.

The buck lurched back as the round found its mark, falling to one knee, then the other, trying to thrash about, but discovering that neither of its front legs would work. It bellowed out in pain and as a warning to the rest of the herd, which was already on the move away from danger. Slowly Henry and his father walked down to the thrashing bull deer and as they approached the animal, they looked into the wide eyes of the animal in its death throes. Then all movement stopped.

Henry silently gave prayer to the Indian god of the hunt, thanking him for their good fortune. As they quietly inspected the animal they concluded that Henry's first shot had indeed been right on the mark, passing through one shoulder, then lodging deeply into the other as it passed through the lungs. This was why the deer went down so quickly.

"Couldn't have done better myself, if I may say so my son", said Henry's father beaming with pride!

Gradually they brought the two wolves Chani and Akila along with them as the wolves grew rapidly to maturity. At first the wolves proved more hindrance than help in stalking the game, having overcome their feral instincts by being raised with humans, but eventually their feral nature returned in part to where they grew to understand Dietrich' hand signals sensing the presence of prey where none was visible. Hearing, especially at night, sounds not audible to the human ear and smelling the presence of others, not normal in their minds, hundreds of yards off in the distance.

Whenever, something strange approached, rather than bark or howl, the two wolves were trained to shake their heads and slowly growl, standing very still, thus gaining the attention of their handlers, to any possibility of danger. Of course both Chani and Akila were amply rewarded with a cooked portion of the kill in the aftermath, growing especially fond of the smoked German sausage made with all of the spices attendant to that particular victual.

One day, terror struck the family, when Henry was out in the fields bringing in the livestock to the barn just ahead of a thunderstorm. Thunder and lightning was all around, with Chani and Akila herding the cattle into the barn, and Henry's father guiding them into the barn and Henry bringing up the rear nudging a reluctant cow. As Henry and the cow passed under the very last tree on their way to the relative safety of the barn, a bolt of lightning struck the tree, passing directly through the cow killing it instantly and Henry in close proximity caught part of the effects of the strike, throwing him to the ground a distance of five yards away. As part of a large tree branch fell to the ground, grazing Henry's head with great force, rendering him unconscious.

Henry's mother and sisters watched in horror, the event unfold, as well as Henry's father at the entrance to the barn. All shrieked in horror, then ran to the spot of the fallen tree, while the wolves, stood their ground in silent confusion, holding the livestock in the barn by force of will.

Working their way through the fallen tree limbs and past the clearly dead cow, they found Henry, unconscious. The brush was quickly cleared away and Henry was picked up by his father and carried to the houses front porch out of the rain. As he lay on the front porch, his father noted the fluttering of his eyes and the shallowness of his breathing, then yelled, "Clear away the table so I can get him inside"! This accomplished, Henry's charred clothing was cut away, to reveal the exact location of any injuries. Noting his shallow breathing and fluttering eyelids, as they rolled him over into a prone position, his back revealed, a large jagged burn, running from the base of his neck down the length of his spine tapering off to a point just above the belt line. The very image of a bolt of lightning.

Dietrich then carried Henry to his bed saying, "Clean him up while I go for the doctor". Which the mother and his sisters commenced to do stifling back tears, attending to the task at hand. Going to the barn Dietrich, finished securing the livestock. Then led the wolves to the homes front porch to sit on guard. Then he saddles one of the horses, and rode off in the direction of the Harrison Pike, at a slow gallop all the way down to the base of the hill.

Several hours later, by midafternoon Dietrich returned with the Doctor and they both hurried inside and they left the Doctor alone with Henry for examination for the next hour. Directly he emerged from the bedroom, sitting down at the dinner table, took a deep breath saying, "Well the boy has been hit by lightning sure enough. The poultice that was applied to the burns seems to be doing the trick, but it'll have to be cleaned and reapplied every day. His breathing seems to have settled down to a steady rhythm and his eyes have stopped fluttering and are gently closed. He is in a state of coma, unconscious to this world and clearly is in hands of the angels. Since its dark I'll stay the night and keep watch, returning to town in the morning. Every day he will have to be completely bathed in place, and I'll show you how to do it before I leave in the morning. For now he's clean enough and you've done a good job at that. He will have to be fed twice a day a thick broth and his bed clothes and bedding changed every day."

He then tried to explain what little was known at the time, just what a coma was concluding, "Of course medical science doesn't quite know what a coma is. Sometimes people recover very nicely; sometimes they never recover and die. Sometimes they recover changed in part in a variety of ways, sometimes they emerge from the comatose state quickly, and sometimes it takes months or longer. The good news is that your son is young and apparently fit and muscular with no apparent internal impediments. I noticed the calluses on his hands are quite similar to yours Mister Jaeger, which means he has a strong internal constitution. But no telling what internal damage or alteration had occurred. The other good news is that he wasn't hit in the head by the strike and has suffered no broken bones, but as you can see has many bruises that will heal within the week. Still as I say, there are still too many unknowns and no guarantees can be made. But I will visit every other day for the next week and will consult my medical books to see if there is anything else I can do when I return. What is necessary at this and on a daily basis is prayer to the almighty for his recovery, for he is in his hands for the moment".

At that he joined hands with the entire family and led a brief prayer for Henry. That concluded, he rose from the table and indicated that Dietrich join him outside, where they wandered over to the dead cow, in silence. "And now to the payment for my services, Mr. Jaeger. Damn little money about and your reputation as a man of his word precedes you. Yonder is a dead cow of little use to you, thus I propose that you render that critter as soon as you can, smoke the meat as I know you will and supply me with precisely half of the edible meats of that critter as payment in full regardless of the outcome! Are we agreed"?

"Yes Herr Doctor"! Both men then spit in the palm of their hands and shook hands thus sealing the bargain.

That night Henry began the long journey down the white tunnel in his mind. Passing through the arms of the most hideous creatures, reaching, grasping in desperation for his soul, the foul stench of their presence, quite sufficient to cower the hardiest of souls. Eventually he passed by a number of images of apparent friendly people who were allowed to caress him as he slowly passed by. Somehow he received the message they were long lost kinfolk that passed into the great beyond and as he progressed on down the white tunnel, their mode of clothing seemed to regress to that of men in helmets with great swords and beards. Then even they disappeared as he went along the white tunnel and he passed through a period of cold that chilled him down to his very bones. Then even that passed and he drifted through a period of gradual warmth, where he passed, a very fat man with a big belly sitting in apparent deep thought, then he passed by several faint images of people wearing strange clothes, he had never seen before, oblivious to his presence, then he passed a man with long hair wearing a white robe who seemed to recognize him as he passed, drawing a sign of a fish in the mist and finally arrived, in the presence of a great bright light. As Henry stared into the light, he felt, rather than heard a message that said; "Fear not my son of any man or beast of the earth, for your journey through this existence has not ended, but has just begun and you have a long way to travel in the service of all. Fear not, for your place beside your ancestors is assured. Go now back to your family and embrace life as it is"!

With that, it seemed that a force of some sort slowly turned him around and sped him back through a separate tunnel back to the land of the living.

Henry slowly gradually awoke from his slumber to find both Chani and Akila asleep at his feet upon his bed. As he started to pet them both awakening them to his presence, he was greeted with an abundance of great and constant licks from the wolves and small growls. He then noticed his father and the Miami Shaman asleep on the floor near his bed and awakened them both. Both men quickly arose from their slumber in amazement and wonder touching Henry repeatedly, for assurance that he was now in their midst in both body and spirit.

"Mutti, I'm hungry", muttered Henry as he sleepily walked to the front door in his night clothes. As he went outside, he was greeted by a dozen of the Indians, all rejoicing in his recovery, each in turn touching him to see that he was really in their presence once again. Henry looked at the early morning skies and saw the moon in its fullness surrounded by the star's in abundance and remembered what was told to him by the Great Spirit. The words echoing over and over in his head 'Fear not'….

Over the next several weeks, as Henry regained his strength, the story of his slumber and each family members role in his recovery was related, as well as the part played by the Miami Shaman who visited each day and spent time hovering over him, chanting ancient heathen rituals repeatedly to summon the great spirit to restore him to their presence, whole in body and spirit.

"So I was out for twenty nine days", Henry mused. "Gosh, it only seemed like a few hours!" Several days later, when pressed by the family after the evening meal, he recalled for them everything he remembered about his partially perilous journey through the alabaster tunnel. Both Chani and Akila ever at his side, as he droned on and the rest of the family in rapt attention. For Henry, like his father and mother, was not prone to telling far off tales of fancy and was generally one of few words. So each and every word that came from his lips was considered nothing less than holy writ as he knew it to be.

Whenever Henry and his father visited the Miami village, several miles away, they were now received with great reverence, by one and all. A completely new suit of buckskin clothes was made for Henry by the women of the village, to replace the one charred by the previous accident. The scar on his back was rapidly healing and as it was revealed to the women, the village Shaman was quickly summoned along with his father. The scar was a perfect replica of a lightning bolt starting from just below his neck line and tapering off to a point just above his waist.

Old tales of great warriors were now recanted and the Shaman revealed as much to Henry's father with great pride. "Your son will be a man of great strength, endurance and skills, beyond measure"! There was a brief pause before he continued, "As he grows to manhood he will be a man of great wisdom"!

As time progressed, Henry progressed into his twelfth year, noticing the normal signs of manly evolvement, like the gradual growth of hair on his bodily parts, the deepening of his voice and the gradual interests in young girls on his occasional visits into Cincinnati proper, across the Mill Creek. Something else was occurring at an even more rapid pace.

All of his natural senses, sight, sound, smell and general awareness of his surroundings became as acute as his two wolves that accompanied him everywhere. He could now smell and identify the various forms of game at great distance. His ability with the bow and arrow improved greatly, whereas his ability to stalk and now get well inside bow range for the killing shot, meant that he could now bring down several deer simultaneously before the rest of the herd sensed alarm. For the bow was almost silent as an instrument of the hunt. This he demonstrated to both his father and the Miami Shaman, who by now evolved into a secondary role as a father figure. Time spent together, served them both well, as Henry quickly learned the Miami tongue and the Shaman came to speak English better as well as the rest of the village. By the years end Henry was second to no one in the entire area in his ability to self-sustain himself and live off the land. Henry had already grown to the height of six feet and was still growing in stature.

Both the village and the Jaeger family prospered from Henry's ability as a hunter of game and a growing business in tanned hides developed for the both as well as a growing business of smoked German sausages made from the various parts of the game brought down and found a ready market for the neighbors in Cheviot township. By his fourteenth year Henry had learned all he could from his mother in the arts of reading, writing and arithmetic, so his mornings were now free to help his father in all things relaying to the Jaeger farming interests. A used wagon was purchased which now allowed them to transport things to be sold more readily to market.

His sisters were now coming into full bloom as young woman and were making trips with Henry to the Miami village to help teach the people of the village readin', writin' and arithmetic. As well as help them in a variety of ways two days a week.

From time to time, a newspaper would make its way into their hands and news of the world would trickle in. Like President Jackson's activities in Washington City and the various scandals that arose back in civilization, just over the horizon. Apparently some of the warlike Shawnee Indians, long thought put in their place, thanks to General Harrison at Tippecanoe, were starting to rear their ugly heads, with reports of settler's farms being torched and inhabitants slaughtered like cattle. Several small renegade bands of warriors began to roam the

Northwest region of Ohio and the Northeast region of Indiana, thus far eluding the efforts of several frustrated militia groups, hard in pursuit.

Further, these bands of renegades took their same vengeance out on various peaceful tribes suspected to be friendly with the white settlers. The nearest federal military outpost of any significance was in far off Detroit and reports were that shortly they would take the field in force. But that news was weeks old and no telling in which direction the renegades would travel.

Upon hearing this Dietrich and Henry's went to the Miami village and consulted with the Shaman and the tribal elders, in attempting a course of action for all concerned.

Henry's father had taken ill and was bed ridden with a fever, and the meat supplies were starting to dwindle, so Henry's father gave Henry permission, to take the Beretta hunting rifle and one of the horses an go out on a hunt for one of the big Elk reported several miles south of their farm close on to the Big Miami river. He went to the Miami village and got three of the braves to go with him as well Chani and Akila.

The stalk went well and by noon they had a large bull Elk down and on the skid pulled by one of Dietrich's horses. Certainly enough meat to get the small village and the Jaegers through the rest of winter and into spring.

Entering into the village, Henry sensed that something was wrong as he noticed strangers, in the tribes midst. Indians of a different sort, perhaps Shawnee by their markings, led by a very large man with flaming long red hair in Indian attire arguing with the village Shaman. By Henry's count there were about a dozen of the apparent Shawnee as he approached, stopping about thirty yards away from the Shamans Wigwam.

Henry made a sign to Chani and Akila, and gradually they spread out each flanking the intruders. Accompanied by one or more of the Miami braves at the ready, with bows drawn. Henry slowly dismounted, from his horse with the only thought going through his mind was 'Oh Scheist', he was in it now. That voice that has no sound whispered, 'Have no fear'. So Henry put on his brave face, and put the unloaded Beretta twin barrels on full cock and cradled the weapon in his arms, slowly approaching at the ready. He then signaled Chani and Akila to both stop, with both of the wolves now fully grown and at well over a hundred pounds each, snarling and bearing their considerable fangs at the intruders.

Henry mulling over the papers reports of what the renegade Shawnee had done to the settlers and those Indians who intermingled with them, he knew that the bringing of such a large Elk into the village, just couldn't simply be explained away. Instinctively Henry knew that these were not those who would or could be reasoned with. They were there for one thing only to kill the settlers and anyone friendly with them. Nothing more, nothing less.

Clearly these were well seasoned braves in front of him, and Henry had an empty rifle. Clearly he would have to brazen things out. The large red haired leader took several steps forward then stopped clearly flanked by Chani and Akila, their growling getting greater, tails elevated and fangs bearing.

"I have stories heard of the little white man that thinks he is a warrior and I'm not impressed"!

"What's your name", said Henry loudly, not a question but a statement. "For you little one, I have no name", the statement clearly of insult to Henry.

"What's a white man doing all gussied up as an Indian", replied Henry.

Again, not a question but a statement.

"I am a Shawnee warrior and that's all you will know," then he took one step forward and stopped as Henry quickly brought the muzzles to bear on the Red Hair's midsection, saying, "Mister, if ya heard of me then, then ya must know that I'll put a ball smack dab in your innards, if you and your friends don't git outta hereright now and never come back"! There's a number in my head, a short number and when I finish talkin', I'm gonna start countin' and when I hit that number I'm gonna start shootin' and you'll be the very first one I shoot, right in your balls"! Several seconds passed then the Red Hair turned, screaming out a Shawnee epithet and the band ran off. Henry followed them by sight up the river for several minutes as they were at full trot, until they were out of sight. He then lowered the barrel of the massive Beretta as the wolves both came to him.

He immediately removed the skid and its carcass from his horse, informing the Shaman that he was going back to his farm for a fresh horse, so he could ride into town to summon help.

As he rode into the his parents farm he yelled out to his family what the situation was at the Indian village and that he was going to change horses and go for help. As he rode down Harrison Pike through Cheviot Township, towards Cincinnati, he yelled out "Alarm, Alarm, and Indians on the warpath"! "Everyone arm yourself and go to the Jaeger farm"! Then he sped off down the pike towards town.

Several hours later he returned with a contingent of several dozen militiamen fully armed with muskets, only to find they were too late. The renegade Shawnee tribesmen had arrived at his parents doorstep not only slaying both of Henry's parents but both of his sisters and two of the unfortunate Cheviot farmers, that were the only ones to respond to his summons. All of the livestock were slain, with bow and arrow, throats cut and the arrows removed for future use. The house and barn were in the final stages of a blaze and were well past the point of saving, but the horror that confronted them all was the way all had perished. All parties were scalped, down to the bone. All parties were gutted from the throat to the genitals, with their intestines billowing forth. The final insult was that, Henry's mother and his two sisters both had gaping holes, in a place that once was occupies by their breasts.

Henry cried out at the top of his lungs as he went from place, holding each member of his family in his arms, commingling their blood on his person, clumsily trying to place their intestines back into the body cavity's and staggering from each loved one in shock.

Suddenly he thought of the Indians and mentioned them to one of the militia. Three of which departed for the Miami village and two departed back into Cincinnati proper for more help from the citizens.

An hour later the men that went to the Miami Village returned with the news that it had been burned to the ground and that all of its inhabitants had been slain and treated in a similar fashion as the Jaeger, down to the last woman and child.

One of the militiamen who years before served with General Harrison at Tippecanoe, returned with an arrow that had broken off in one of its victims and showed around with the comment, "Definitely Shawnee markings here, folks"! "Henry was right". An hour after that, a small fleet of riders and wagons arrived from town, inclusive of Henry's Aunt and husband, who upon seeing the condition of her slain sister and the children whom she doted over, fainted dead away.

Sunset would be upon them in several hours, when Henry asked that everyone that had wagons visit the Miami Indian encampment and bring all of the slain to the Jaeger farm for proper disposal. When one of the men replied that they were just Indians, he was hushed by the others and rushed away, to do as Henry had asked. Over the next several hours with the sun setting over the horizon and darkness rapidly closing in people began to drift in to the farm little by little bringing food and torches for working through the night and seeing just what in the way they could be of assistance.

An examination of the bodies on the ground revealed that one of the Shawnee had been brought down by the Miami in the brief skirmish for their village, and that two other Shawnee had been slain via bow and arrow apparently by someone in the Jaeger family, prior to their deaths.

Apparently they put up some sort of fight as best they could.

Henry, still in a state of shock moaned that if only he'd left the Beretta flintlock with his father, as his voice trailed off.

"Son", interjected his Uncle, "Then they would've been down by perhaps two more, but that wouldn't have changed the outcome"! off.

"But if I only stayed, instead of running for help", Henrys voice trailing

"Then just maybe you'd be on the ground with the rest of your family", offered another.

Henrys aunt, now recovered from her shock at least in part joined Henry on the ground and put her arms around Henry and they began to cry together.

As the torches now blazed all around, someone said, "Sure a lot of graves will have to be dug"! Remembering his trip through the spirit world and his ancestors that he passed on the way through, Henry said, "They'll be no graves dug by anyone this night"! Whereupon he directed the men to gather what combustible wood was available from the remains of the house and the barn and bring it to a cove halfway up the northern slope of the horseshoe shaped enclave that was central to the Jaeger farm. There two pyres were built, upon the slope, one for the Miami and one for the Jaeger family with both of the slain Cheviot settlers excepted by their families to be carted off for a proper Christian burial.

Several Christian ministers arrived during the interim to provide what spiritual comfort they could, but Henry would have none of it. "Where was god when he was needed the most" yelled Henry back at them when they tried to comfort him and explain the inexplicable.

By torch light Henry looked deeply into the eyes of the dead village Shaman, devoid of his scalp, as he lain upon the pyre with his people. "I will avenge you great father" whispered Henry, into the unhearing ear of the Shaman, then drew back and started into the Miami chant for the dead to the great spirit in the sky, in front of all of the settlers that, now numbering just under a hundred souls, that had gathered.

Henry then turned and grabbing a torch that was handed to him, announced to those assembled, "This is how great warriors meet the Great Spirit in the sky" and with that set the pyre ablaze.

When the pyre was in full blaze, he then turned his attention to his family, in the background, one of the Ministers had been reading aloud from the book of 'Job' in the bible all along, which all agreed had seemed the most appropriate passage from the good book, to explain the inexplicable. Yet even to those who barely knew the Jaeger family, the witnessing of the bodies and the manner in which they were all slain shook even the hardiest of those folks, down to the marrow. One couldn't merely say bad things about the native Indians, for even they had been slain like that of their white counterparts, in the most brutal of ways, without an ounce of compassion. Clearly the work of the Devil and his acolytes, in everyone's mind.

Henry then turned to the second pyre, which contained his family, whispering into each ear a message and giving each a departing kiss on the lips. Stepping back he turned to those assembled and with tears in his eyes and his voice trembling announced to one and all, "Here lays a family that didn't deserve this! A better family one could never have. All of value has been taken from me. I swear to God in heaven that I will hunt down and kill each and every one of the vermin responsible, so help me God"!

With that he, set the torch to the pyre, the flames now joining that of the Miami as they sent the departed into the night sky. All were silent save for the preacher that was till speaking the verses aloud from the book of Job. Close by Henry's side were the two Wolves, Chani and

Akila, both periodically howling into the night sky, their grief at the loss of those who loved them.

An hour later as the moon climbed into the night sky and both pyres had burned half way down to the ground, a man approached Henry knelt down joining him and said, "Henry let us help you. Your slain livestock have value. But not for long. Let us carry them away to be sold and rendered for useable food stuffs and I will bring the proceeds to you tomorrow"!

"Uh sure, mumbled Henry absently, with his mind still full of grief.

Then man departed, replaced by his Aunt, who knelt down by Henry's side and started crying once again. As the pyres continued their downward journey, they knelt there in almost silent attendance, with small groups of others, neighbors mostly; sharing their grief, for this was a family that deserved to prosper. Everyone there knew of how the Jaeger's helped others, without asking for reciprocation.

All night long Henry and his Aunt kneeled into front of the pyres, now burnt to the ground, tired to the point of exhaustion, with the wolves standing guard, until his aunt, her last reserves of energy gone, slumped to the ground. Her husband standing by patiently all night long with the wolves ran to her side, saying to Henry, come back to town with us and allows us to help you. Bring the horse and load the wolves in our wagon"!

With that Henry reluctantly agreed and with the coming dawn, the last of the wagons departed back down the Harrison Pike back to town, the still saddled horse, tethered to the wagon and Henry and his Aunt asleep in the wagons bay along with Chani and Akila. After all, wolves get tired too.

While Henry's aunt was carried into their house by others, Henry and her husband unhitched the horses from the wagon and unsaddled Henrys horse fed them and put them in the barn to rest. The wolves were fed grain and water which they eagerly consumed. He went to the Beretta flintlock and pulled it from its saddle scabbard, while Chani and Akila patiently watched him clean and fuss over the instrument of death.

Yes, he had grown almost to manhood in many ways, but still he was a child in others and he knew it.

So many things yet to learn and do before he was certain of his abilities to perform and endure. As he walked around the grounds of the home between the old Mill Creek and one of the seven hills that made up the town of Cincinnati, he felt somehow as if he didn't belong there. Upon reflection he was sorry, that he'd somehow blamed God almighty for the death of his family, when clearly it was the act of mortal man and in as much could be rectified by his action.

The Red Haired Shawnee and his now whittled down band of renegades, were making their escape and as such must be pursued, cornered and killed, by Henry's hand.

Just then his Uncle appeared from the house and walked over and stood by Henry. Strangely enough, Chani and Akila sidled up to the Uncle and rubbed against his legs as a sign of acceptance. "They must like you, because I've never seen them do that", said Henry. "Maybe it's because I've just fed them," replied his Uncle.

They talked for several hours about what plans Henry might've made, if any, for the future. All Henry could think about was going after the Red Hair and his group. It seemed to occupy his mind and there was no room for any other thought.

"I'll go ask around and see if I can get anyone to help, but in the meanwhile, you need to get some food under your belt and some rest if your dead set on your task. Go inside and see Emma the housekeeper and she'll prepare you a plate of vittles" said the Uncle.

Hours later he returned, seeing Henry asleep in the wagon's bed way, sitting down on the rear lid. Spoke, "I just couldn't get anyone interested in helping you Henry. Seems that everyone is either too busy with other necessaries or sore afraid of the Indians!"

"That's all right Uncle, think I'll set off after them in the morning and would be obliged if ya could put together some vittles enough to last me and the hounds for about a week".

"I'll get Emma to work on that right away".

"I got several urns from the store", said his Uncle and if you don't mind, your Aunt and me would like to join you as far as the farm so we, could gather the ashes of your family in separate urns"! Henry nodded his head in agreement.

"They started out as twelve as best I can reckon, two killed at the Miami village, two killed at the farm, so that means they're down to eight", said Henry almost as an afterthought. "One against eight seems fair enough to me Uncle"!

The following morning, Henry, the wolves and his Aunt and Uncle in their wagon started off, across, the old Mill Creek ferry, then followed the Harrison Pike as it made its way up the side of the western most hill of the area, then along the long stretch to the Cheviot township then turned south for a bit before drifting their way into several hundred yard long horseshoe shaped part of the Jaeger farm and down the hill. His Aunt and Uncle made their way up to the wide ledge half way up the northern most side of the hill that partially rimmed the small enclave, to parcel out what ashes could be identified as each member of the family.

Henry wandered back to the house and barn now burnt down to the ground, stopping by each of the two Shawnee braves, now bloated by the gasses now building up in each of the bodies. The ants were already gathering, as well as the flies and soon would appear the maggots. As he looked up into the sky, he saw no evidence of the turkey vultures. Perhaps they were busy elsewhere, or perhaps even they had scruples and there were some things even they wouldn't consume? In his mind it didn't matter, for it meant a bigger share for the ants and the flies.

They would be down to the bones before the month was over. He wandered through the barn and the house poking and prodding the ashes with a stick to see if there were any salvageable mementoes of his family's existence. But there was nothing. As if they had never existed, except in his mind. He hunkered down and closed his eyes and could remember just last Christmas, the joy and the laughter as they exchanged gifts. He focused his mind on both his sisters whom he cherished and then his mother, her voice, her gentle caress's when he was ill, the his father, their time together working in the fields and during their various hunting forays both with and without the Miami tribesmen.

With Akila at his side and Chani with his Aunt and Uncle up on the side of the hill gathering the ashes of the departed, Henry heard the plaintive howl of Chani's coming from the hill, followed immediately by Akila's howl by his side. Jolted back to the here and now, he rose up and made his way towards the hill.

Neither party wanted to leave the ashes of the twin pyres, but after the wolves settled down, Henry looked up to the sun, now signaling midday and said, "Well I'd better get going, if I'm gonna catch up with those bastards"! With that his Aunt broke into tears once again and sobbed, "Now Henry, you take care and come back to us"! Then they hugged, with the wolves rubbing against the legs of both Aunt and Uncle to be petted, acknowledged to be an integral part of the family.

Henry then mounted his horse and rode off down past the barn towards the Miami village to see if he could pick up any trail. As they all passed the two dead Shawnee, both of the wolves stopped for a few moments, sniffing the bodies of the bloated cadavers as if to imprint in their minds a scent to follow, then ran off to follow Henry.

After a bit, the wolves caught some sort of scent and began to lead the way straight towards the village and directly various signs of footprints began to appear leading straightaway to the Miami encampment.

Approaching the encampment, Henry could see that all of the wigwams had been burnt to the ground, along with various pools of blood where the slain had breathed their final moment. Both Henry and the wolves spent almost an hour nosing around the encampment, by the shore of the Big Miami River. Just north of the encampment Henry caught confusing moccasin footprints of both arrival and departure and as the wolves followed him northward up the rivers bank the signs began to indicate eight distinctive sets of foot prints combining with a similar number of sets of hoof prints northward towards Harrison Pike and the ferry that crossed the river into Indiana proper.

Just short of the ferry crossing the trail disappeared into the river indicating the Shawnee swam across the river, probably under the cover of darkness. So Henry went up to the ferry and crossed the river, circling back south till he picked up the scent and the trail of eight sets of foot prints heading south. From this point on he would have to be ever alert, to every possibility. Sleep could come later.

By the indications of the hoof prints, it seemed the Shawnee were traveling fast. After several miles he came upon a sign where they must have spent the night. Yet apparently it was a cold camp, for no sign of a fire pit existed. The sun was now traveling towards the earth so Henry figured just four more hours of day light, so he pressed on, traveling a considerable distance till the sunlight was no more. He noted the general direction the Shawnee were traveling and decided to make camp that evening.

He sniffed the air and concluded that rain would visit them during the night and after feeding the wolves and his unsaddling and hobbling his mount, they rested for the evening, a cold camp with no fire.

Around midnight a gentle rain visited the encampment, and Henry gathered the wolves under his big leather poncho, for the duration. Around an hour before sunup they all awoke unable to sleep no longer, so Henry saddled up and the all went in darkness in the general direction of the previous day. Now the bad thing about tracking after a rain is that the earth is cleansed and with that cleansing departs most of a scent of what is being sought after. But if they wolves were in a quandary, Henry was able to follow scant signs of human travel in numbers. So the wolves now followed Henrys lead.

By midday the trail turned again northward away from the great Ohio River, as if the prey were doubling back. Later in the afternoon the trail turned eastward, with Henry careful not to cross wide open expanses of open field and keeping wherever practicable to the tree line. As the day drew on, the wolves began to regain a scent familiar to them and they took the lead.

Several days passed and it seemed a pattern was developing of doubling back generally traveling northward and eastward when eventually they came upon the upper reaches of the Big Miami River, now not nearly so wide. A hundred yards into the trees, Henry stopped. This would be a nifty place for some dimwitted waddie to be ambushed. Follow the trail right into the river and across on the other side was sufficient coverage that a host of Shawnee could lay in wait and while still in the river rise and greet them with a hail of arrows. Yes the river was easily fordable being only about thirty yards wide at this point, but way too easy.

Thus Henry turned north and staying well into the trees traveled several miles upriver before he made his crossing. He then traveled about a mile eastward before turning south, traveling several miles back to where he reckoned they might be. He dismounted his horse and noted the wolves had caught some kind of scent and all moved forward cautiously. He decided to employ the bow and arrow, as he moved forward. The big Beretta was in its scabbard and loaded, with all that need be done to fire was prime the pan with powder, cock and fire.

He could hear the sound of the river now, so they must be close at hand.

All proceeded forward in silence, the sound of the river getting louder, when they came upon a small clearing about thirty yards from the river bank and saw signs where a number of people had made camp.

Another cold camp. But they were not there. 'Perhaps they were nearby', Henry thought. A sudden chill ran down his spine. The thought that he might've still yet have blundered into an ambush ran through his mind, he hunkered down. Chani and Akila followed his lead, lying doggo occasionally, yet ever alert.

After an hour Henry rose up and examined the quasi encampment, which seemed no different than the others. Apparently they had just missed them, so then Henry scoured the camp for signs of departure and sure enough, there were indications of a multiple of men, shod in moccasins and the hoof prints of horses traveling eastward. So leading his horse on foot, he proceeded to follow for several miles until day light played out completely. Another night, another cold camp.

He remembered all of the lessons learned from the Miami Shaman in tracking and all of the tricks one could employ to throw pursuers off your trail. As he lay down next to the wolves for the evening in silence, his thoughts ran to the Shaman and all the Shaman had meant to him. Not like his father exactly, but in many ways revered just like his father, for each in turn held a special place in his heart. Somehow he felt the spirit of the Shaman's presence and a cascade of fond memories of their time together flooded his mind as he lightly slept through the night. He recalled the Shaman's pride as he recanted in great detail Henry's accomplishments to his father, beaming as if Henry was his very own son. For the Shaman had no son. It was slain while in the service of the Shawnee many years before as they fought a losing cause against the forces of General Harrison. Also slain was the Shaman's wife during that time of strife. The Shaman for his own reasons had chosen not to take another wife and to bed none other. True to their mutual memories to the very end. But there was no doubt in Henrys mind that they were both united in that place in the sky, for all eternity.

At sunup as Henry broke camp they resumed the trek. Following signs eastward, now back in Ohio territory, of a multiple of hoof prints, rapidly on the move. He was now into his third day of his pursuit of the Shawnee and doubts began to creep into his mind as to precisely what he would do in the event he caught up with them. Did he bite off more than he could chew? Hunting a dumb animal was one thing; they could always be outsmarted, but hunting a well experienced human being, blooded in combat, being able to live off the land, resourceful and wise to the ways of the stalk and the kill himself. At that his thoughts trailed off, as he heard the distant reports of musket shots.

He then nudged the flanks of his horse into a fast trot, rising tall in the stirrups in order to see more of what lay ahead. As he topped a small ridge he saw several wagons on fire next to a small streams encampment. He stopped viewing the entire scene, being careful not to blunder headlong into an event that wasn't of his making.

Apparently it was a military contingent of approximately thirty men in train, who allowed themselves to be attacked by parties unknown. Yet Henry knew just who they were. As he stood silent on his mount, a soldier rode up to him stopping some thirty yards away and hollered, "Identify yourself young man"!

"Why I'm Henry Jaeger of Cheviot Township"! "And you sir"?

"I'm Lieutenant Hart, from Fort Detroit, down here to pursue and kill renegade Shawnee tribesmen, seconded to Captain James J. Dixon.".

"Seems that they did some damage Lieutenant," said Henry. "And to your business young man"!

"To hunt down and kill renegade Shawnee that killed my family in Cheviot Township sir"! "Been trailin' them for a few days now. There appear to be eight in the party that I've been after."

"Well, their now down to six, since we've killed two of their kind". "Well I can see that two of your three wagons are afire" said Henry.

"And Captain Dixon is on deaths doorstep with three arrows in him", the Lieutenant offered.

"Mind If'n I join ya Lieutenant, for it seems that we're both after the same thing and it looks like ya could use some help", asked Henry.

As they rode down to the encampment together, the Lieutenant said, "Seems that you're a tad young to be hunting renegade Shawnee young man"!

Jaeger replied, "Not how old ya are, its how many miles you've traveled, by my reckoning"!

As they arrived at the camp the Lieutenant was approached by a sergeant, who stated, "All four of the pickets are dead, with their throats cut, sir"!

"How about the supplies and the Captain"?

"Well sir seems we've lost some of the beef pemmican to the Indians and some of the supplies got burnt up but we save most it in the burnt wagons and as to the Captain, it appears he's on his last legs with three arrows in his chest. it's a gurgling' every time he takes a breath"!

"Very good Sergeant, carry on". Upon dismounting, the Lieutenant took full notice of the wolves at Henry's side, "Those are grown wolves are they not"?

'Why yes sir they are. Been with me since they were pups. May I introduce Chani and Akila!But I'd be careful until they get to know ya, in their own time, like not making any sudden moves while in their presence. Let em come to you and sniff ya out, then things just might be all right", offered Henry.

They went over to the remaining wagon, where Captain Dixon lay and the Lieutenant knelt down to the Captain and before he could say anything the Captain breathed his last, the death rattle rasping from his mouth, then he was still.

"Sergeant", bellowed the Lieutenant, as the Sergeant turned some yards away, "Get a burial detail and make ready five shallow graves, on the double"! "We break camp in just an hour and a half".

At the appropriate time the graves were dug, each to a depth of three feet, the bodied stripped of value, wrapped in linen and deposited forth with brief fanfare and the entire assembly heading south towards the Hamilton County Line. Henry and two of the soldiers on horse preceded the main body to see if there was any sign of the fleeing Shawnee. Several miles passed by with scant sign, before Chani perked up, barked and ran off in the direction of a scent with her nose to the ground followed by Akila and the three mounted men.

Several miles later, the wolves stopped on a high rise in the ground and about a mile ahead of them as the rise fell gradually away, were the sight of three men at a steady trot. One of the soldiers drew his mount to a halt, drawing a single lens spyglass up to his eye saying, "Three hostiles straight ahead on the run". "Any of em have red hair" asked Henry?

"Hard to tell, here you take a look" and the soldier handed Henry the spyglass. Henry not ever having looked through such an instrument took the spyglass put it up to his eye like the soldier, trying to sight on a moving mount and getting a much closer but blurry view of the fleeing Indians, agreed and handed it back to the soldier, nudging his mount ahead at full gallop followed by the two soldiers and the wolves.

Apparently the Shawnee had split into two groups, with Henry's group following one of them. Rapidly closing the gap between them, Henry signaled both of the troopers to flank either side of his mount so they would charge in line, the group of three in front of them. By chance one of the Shawnee looked back seeing the rapidly advancing riders and called out to the others. They stopped and turned, drawing their bows and placing their spears on the ground. waiting for the riders to get into bowshot range. One arrow strung and another four grasped in the bow hand, meant that fifty to sixty yards away a warrior, could shoot all five arrows in the time it took for a horse to travel the closing distance, times three bowmen.

At a hundred fifty yards distance Jaeger signaled all to halt and dismount. Just out of range of the Shawnee. As Henry dismounted, he drew the Beretta long gun from the saddle scabbard and said to the others, "Keep a keen watch on our flanks and the rear, I'll handle this", as he took up a prone firing position, quickly priming firing pans with powder and positioning the heavy barrel upon the portable crosspiece. Then he waited, the weapon at half cock, adjusting his breathing to a slow in and out rhythm.

After several minutes of standoff, a few arrows were lofted in the air in desperation, by the Shawnee all of which fell far short of the mark. Henry pulled both hammers to full cock position whispering to himself, 'this is for',…..then squeezed the trigger and then intoned silently, 'and this is for' squeezing the second trigger as both barrels bucked discharging the rifled balls down range into their targets, hitting both squarely in the chest knocking each backwards, each dead before they hit the ground. Suddenly Chani and Akila bolted forward but Henry yelled a command halting them dead in their tracks, not wanting to risk either of them to a possible arrow from the remaining Shawnee. Both came back to his side with their tail between their legs. He petted them both whispering to each a command, then stepped forward, yelling an old Miami war cry to the final Shawnee in front.

The Indian stood stock still for several moments then yelled back and started to run at them, shooting arrows as he ran. Jaeger turned to each of the mounted soldiers and said, "Gentlemen, please at your pleasure", pointing to the remaining brave. At which each sheathed their musket and drew their sabers and charged the remaining Shawnee, still firing arrows on the run. As they closed the distance one of the arrows struck one of the riders a glancing blow in the shoulder, but both of the riders drew flesh with their sabers as they passed, bringing down the Shawnee with each a single blow. They halted and turned their mounts expecting continued combat but none was given, because the Shawnee was without a head and an arm lying dead on the plains of southwestern Ohio. Henry walked his horse up to the dead Shawnee and especially the two he'd killed, stopped, hobbled his mount to graze, then examined each of the Shawnee finding the killing wound square in the middle of the chest as he'd intended.

These were his very first kills of mortal man and he felt no qualms regarding the event. For they had a hand in the death of his family. He quickly plunged the razor sharp flint knife, the Shaman had knapped for him a year ago, into the chest of each brave searching for the lead rifle ball to be re-melted at a later date for reuse, then finding each one after some indelicate digging around, took the knife to each ones scalp and removed the scalp leaving a bloody mess on the plains, then went into a Miami war chant, just like the Shaman had taught him.

By this time the rest of the party had caught up with the slain Shawnee and gathered around, Henry oblivious to the onlookers. All watched in silence as Henry concluded his dance for the vanquished, just as the Shaman had taught him, with two blood drenched, long haired scalps in hand bathed in the enemy's blood and smiling as he held them to the sky, silently intoning a message to the unseen.

Of course Henry was the talk of the camp which decided to call it a day. The Lieutenant wanted to bury the Shawnee but Henry still bloody insisted that they lay as they lay as food for the carrion the following day. After all they were heathens and the killers of innocent people an argument that resonated through each and every one of the soldiers as well as the Lieutenant, who was by now the leader of this military contingent. Then as an afterthought, he went over to the other Shawnee the riders had slain and brought them the head and arm that was theirs by right since they both had slain the warrior.

Both had declined the gift as Henry first slung the severed limb some yards distant from the encampment, then, set about removing the scalp from the last of the offenders. That done he cast the head away from the camp and went to his mount attaching the scalps to his saddle horn. His wolves ever at his side received his affection amidst a flurry of licks and growls.

"But he's just a boy", intoned one soldier to another. In reply the other soldier said, "That he may be, but a mere boy, I think not"!

Several hundred yards away, deep into the trees, Red Hair and his two survivors watched intently from high tree branches, invisible to all even the wolves since they were downwind from all the activity. 'So this was the one who had been tracking them all along', he thought to himself. Then he recalled the encounter at the Miami encampment and the boy who made him turn tail for the very first time in his life. A boy, skilled in the ways of the warrior, who would soon be a man. For the very first time in his life, Red Hair felt fear that must not be revealed to others. He had taken many scalps from both the white man and other tribes that got in his way. All stepped aside for his prowess as a warrior was known far and wide amongst the tribes and no one dared to make comment that he just might not be a true warrior, given that he was of mixed blood. But this was not a time to be foolish and perhaps heading west across the great river was the best course of action, for the time being. His skills would be in great need if the conflict was to continue. Besides, this was a big land, with glory to be sought elsewhere. Emerging from his thought, he silently summoned the others to join him on the ground and follow him westward.

The following day, the military unit and their one remaining wagon made their way south towards Cincinnati proper to engage with the town's people and summon up a militia unit under the Lieutenants command, to pursue the hostiles.

"Anybody in your unit knows anything about trackin', "asked Henry of the Lieutenant? "No young man, but when we get to town, a call will be sent to all able body men and I expect someone will show up with the appropriate abilities"!

They passed the time left in relative silence between them. The Lieutenant still disturbed by what he'd witnessed the previous day, Henry do to the hostiles. As they entered the areas outer limits, making their way down the old Mill Creek, Henry bid them goodbye and made his way to his Aunt and Uncle's house.

It was late in the day and Henry went straight to their small barn and put up his horse in one of the empty stalls, removing the saddle and tack and placing them upon one of the stall railings on his way out. He went up to the front porch and plumped down upon the wide multi person swing curling up and drifted off to sleep with the wolves at his side on the porch floor curling up just like their master. Sometime later the High Yellow house keeper emerged from the house seeing Henry asleep and the wolves in attendance, turned and went back inside without a word, coming out minutes later with two bowls brimming with leftovers for the wolves. "Ah knows jus what ya needs, heah" as she bent over and placed the bowls near the wolves. She went back in the house and reemerged with two additional bowls of water placing them in close proximity to the wolves, now greedily attacking the leftovers. Then back into the house, coming back once again with a large sandwich of roast beef and a large glass of milk for the sleeping wanderer. Then she went over to the other side of the porch and sat in one of the outside chairs, watching Henry and Chani and Akila.

After a while Henry's Aunt and Uncle returned in their horse drawn buggy, seeing the housekeeper signaling them that Henry had returned and was asleep on the porch. Henry's Aunt alit from the buggy while still in motion, the first time in anyone's memory that she had done such a thing, being a proper woman and all and ran to the porch stopping just in time, mind full of Henrys admonition to approach the wolves slowly at all times, lest their feral instincts arise. A brief huddle with the housekeeper brought her up to date as to what had occurred.

Meanwhile, her husband went to the barn, and put up the horse and buggy, seeing that his horse was taken care of for the evening. As he left the barn he noticed that Henry's mount was in one of the stalls eating some of the grain provided for and well watered and as he passed his saddle and tack he stopped and stared at the saddle.

He'd heard stories of people getting scalped by the hostiles, except for the sight of his relatives after the fact a scant week ago, but never had seen up close evidence of a post mortem scalp. Much less three of them at once, attached to Henry's saddle. The blood stains in part, on the saddle. He then joined the rest up on the front porch.

Chani and Akila now well fed and watered lay up on the swing flanking Henry, now awake and working his way through the large sandwich and milk, all the while trying to field a slew of staccato questions, from his aunt, with the housekeeper, close at hand.

"For Christ sake ladies, let Henry finish his food then he can tell us his story, "said the Uncle. Then while Henry was still working his way through the sandwich, his Uncle said, "Before I forget, here are the proceeds from the slaughtered livestock that was taken away from the farm last week", reaching into his pocket and withdrawing thirty dollars in gold coin.

"We went to Cheviot for one last visit of the farm and to say our hopefully final goodbyes and while we were in the area, made the rounds of those who benefited". Henry viewed the coinage, placed on one of the side tables. His father usually transacted all of the business of the family and Henry had never even handled coinage, in his life.

As he finished the sandwich his Uncle continued, "Then we ran into Mr. Boudinot on our way back and if you're of a mind, he says he'd be willing to buy back the acreage of your farm. So I told him I'd let him know in the event of your return. Since you're the only living direct descendent, there should be no problem in the transaction should you choose"!

The sandwich finished and the last vestiges of milk rapidly draining down Henrys gullet, his Aunt insisted that Henry relate all that had happened during the week of his absence from their midst. Chairs were pulled up and his Aunt, Uncle and their live in housekeeper all in rapt attention as Henry commenced. When he was finished, all were silent for the souvenirs attached to his saddle were mute testimony that Henry Jaeger, although barely fourteen years of age was now a man of considerable skills to be reckoned with.

He'd drawn his first blood with nary a whimper or afterthought. "It's Friday evening and you look a sight Henry" offered his Aunt. "Come inside and a bath will be prepared for you and your buckskins will be washed and we have an extra bed for you to sleep in"!

"Can Chani and Akila come in too, asked Henry in such a fashion that belied that he was still fourteen years of age? I promise they won't be a bother. Papi und Mutti always allowed them to sleep with each of us and whenever they sleep outside they tend to howl, especially during the full moon"!

Henrys aunt then relented recalling her conversations with her sister regarding the wolves sleeping habits.

3

The following day Henry awoke well-scrubbed, well fed and well rested, with nothing but time on his hands. Seemingly everyone present wanted to fawn over him, as if they were paying tribute to the misery of his loss.

Politely he accepted some of the attention and resisted others. His parents taught him that rudeness was inexcusable and to neither offer nor accept such behavior, especially with kinfolk.

As long as he could remember, his daily existence was a series of set routines, wake up, tend to the livestock, clean up, eat breakfast, spend the morning with the book learnin', eat lunch, the afternoons with his "papi", eat dinner, clean up, then go to bed. Now all of that was gone. The daily predictability and routine now 'Kaput'!

Later that afternoon, Mr. Boudinot arrived at his Uncles House, several minutes after his Uncle had closed up his business for the day. Henry sat on the front porch as they both arrived minutes apart. He had seen the land speculator and entrepreneur, but never been formally introduced.

As he climbed the steps the front porch, both Chani and Akila began to growl, an ominous signal. Henry had a fleeting thought, of how odd the senses of animals were often acutely accurate in the prejudging of others. But he silenced them both, as his Uncle made the formal introductions.

Mr. Boudinot was one of those men who always drove a hard bargain and was always on top of any given situation, especially where coin of the realm was involved. He started his offer for the farm talking to Henry's Uncle as if Henry wasn't even there, with an offer that was half of what he'd originally sold the raw land to the Jaegers some ten years before.

Never having a reason to be discussed, in Henry's presence during the years he was being raised, Henry was not privy to the land value of the family's small estate. When his Uncle raised an objection to the insultingly low amount offered, Boudinot offered that the real property improvements of the house and barn were diminished by their current condition, "Why, their burnt right down to the ground", he growled, seemingly offended. "Anyone else will have to rebuild", he offered as an afterthought, to Henry's Uncle.

"Mr. Boudinot", said Henry with firmness, "I'm over here, so please have your say with me, not my Uncle"!

"But young man, your still a boy and not understanding in the affairs of grown men"! At that, Henry stood to his full height, taking two steps towards his Uncle and Mr. Boudinot, then squatted down Indian like, looking up at Mr. Boudinot, saying "Mr. Boudinot, if you see a boy in front of you, you can kick his ass any time you'd like to try"! Next, I've killed two of the hostiles that took part in my family's murder, with in the last several days and have their skin on my saddle to prove it. Finally, you seem to omit the other improvements to the farm like the three fenced in upper fields and the lower field, already cultivated and the two other upper fields fenced in for grazing, along with an existing water well thirty feet in depth that my father dug with his own two hands when I was just a baby!"

"So, Mister Boudinot here's what you will do! You will pay me by noon tomorrow in gold not only what my father paid you as the original price of the land but an additional five hundred dollars for the improvements to the land as they exist plus an additional hundred dollars for your insult to my family's memory. You will do this Mr. Boudinot, because it will be in your best interests and that of any family you happen to have, to do so!" That said Henry rose to his full height, turned and signaled the wolves to follow him down the porch steps. As he reached the steps, he turned saying quietly, "By noon tomorrow Mr. Boudinot, in gold coin. Sleep well Mr. Boudinot," then Henry turned and slowly descended the steps with the wolves in tow and disappeared down the street.

Never in his life could the land speculator recall being dealt with in such a manner, especially by a boy. But like many who are bully's at heart, they are also cowards to the bone, using their knowledge of existing authority to extend the misery and suffering of others. Now clearly flustered, Boudinot rose up collecting his portfolio and started to go to his buggy. As he was half way down the steps, he heard Henry's uncle say, "Well, you heard the boy Boudinot, by noon tomorrow, in gold coin. Oh, and bring the appropriate paperwork pre notarized, for the sake of simplicity"!

"The boy threatened me and your witness to that fact, Simon!"

"Somehow, that's not how I recall it Boudinot, should it ever come before a magistrate"!

"I'm being placed under extreme duress, Simon and you know it," said Boudinot now clearly flustered.

"Which proves that Columbus must've been right when he claimed the world is round", said Henry's uncle with a sly grin. "Sleep well tonight", he called out in addition.

Boudinot drove off in his buggy with a sharp crack of the whip. All the way across the Mill Creek ferry and back up the Harrison Pike he was back and forth in his mind as to what he was going to do. He could go to the authorities and file a complaint, but a sum of money would have to be quietly exchanged with no firm guarantees of protection. Then he could hire some thugs to rough Henry up a bit, but in the past they had proved unreliable. Besides, this deal had to be done quickly for reasons that he alone only knew.

He would still make money on the turnaround of the property just not as much as he would've made normally. Then there was the fact that a mere boy had made him cower was almost more that he could bear. Finally, the statement of his having a good night's sleep chilled him to the core.

No, he would not sleep well this night and he had brought it all on himself.

All night long Boudinot tried his best to sleep, going to bed earlier than usual, counting the proverbial sheep, drinking warm milk, finally ingesting a sleeping potion and several hours later was still wide awake. As he passed the large grandfather clock in the vestibule it chimed 2AM. His family usually kept clear of him when he was in his occasional 'periods' and Were insulated from his occasional rages by staying in their respective rooms, then quickly finding reasons to be elsewhere until his moods had passed. He decided to walk around his property as a tribute to his business acumen. As a family provider, he had no peers in the area. The outside air provided no relief for his inability to sleep. Going back inside, he went to the jug of expensive Rum imported from the West Indies, pouring out a great draught in a clay mug. Within minutes it was consumed and all he had to do was wait for relief. But an hour later, nothing. He was as wide awake as ever and the clock had just struck 5AM. Soon the sun would be up and his time for decision would be at hand. As the clock struck 6AM, he walked out the door, with the necessary papers in hand snugly tucked away in his portfolio, his decision made. Shortly the family would arise to start their day. He had several stops to make prior to his visit to Master Henry Jaeger and he must not be tardy.

By fifteen minutes past noon all was completed for he'd arrived an hour early and concluded his business with this Jaeger fellow and departed glad to be rid of that scoundrel. As he drove his buggy off towards town to file his papers of ownership with the local authorities, his mind still raced with potential schemes of ridding that young scalley wag of his new found wealth, back into his hands. He would have to give it some considerable thought. But first to business and finally some badly needed sleep.

Several days later Henry was approached by some people from downtown. For word had gotten around by this time, of his activities in tracking and slaying the Shawnee and it seemed that no one was interested in helping the Army contingent from Ft. Detroit, in finding their way around the frontier after the hostiles. Several militia groups in the area had formed for just that purpose and while they had some modest success, they were largely ineffective.

A month later the military unit made its way back to Ft. Detroit.

One evening after dinner, they all sat quietly on the front porch watching the sun go down. After a bit Henry said, "I just can't stand this anymore Auntie, in the next few days I'll just have at leave!"

"But where will you go Henry and what will you do? You just can't go wandering about!" Her husband then chimed in, "I think I know just what's bothering you Henry. Everything here may seem cursed to you and despite our love for you it's not near enough, to lessen you misery and loss. Have I put it about right?"

"Well, yeah sort of Uncle, I feel like I just don't belong here anymore and for some reason I'd better get far away or else I'll just lose my mind!"

"Have you made up your mind Henry", asked his Uncle? "Yeah, pretty much so"!

"Well then, if you're of a mind, then you'll need a place to go", said his Uncle looking at his wife. Thereupon he revealed that he had a brother recently immigrated to the US some five years ago, who had settled in Nashville proper in Tennessee and was doing well in that growing area providing carpentry services for those in the area. "Now he isn't a blood relative, but he is my brother and that in fact ties him to you family wise." Further, his last letter complained that he could use a skilled journeyman to help him, since he's spending most of his time working on General Jackson's home, the Hermitage in Nashville".

"I'd be happy to give you a letter of introduction, to pave the way for you". Since you've been here, you've done us well by your company and the fact that you've repaired many of the things I've admittedly put off in the house and the barn".

"Nashville huh", pondered Henry for a bit? "Well I suppose it would be a possibility".

"Then please allow me several days to help you prepare for your journey Henry, for there's a great many things that you will have to learn about living with city folk. You've learned many things thus far from your father and the Shaman, but living amongst city folk is far more complicated and many just don't get the hang of it even in the best of times".

During the next several days Henry followed his Uncle around, converting a portion of his gold coinage into, smaller increments of paper money in which to make every day transactions. "Never tell anyone of your money, not even my brother, no one. For it's your business and your business alone. Shortly after you arrive, be very careful to find a place to place your coinage that only you will know about and under no circumstances reveal it to anyone for any reason. As they made their way around the city proper, his Uncle told him stories of the myriad of ways one could readily cheat his fellow man out of his hard earnings. "Trust no one, absolutely no one, for trust and confidence in others must always be earned, over time"! He further related that in one's life one makes many acquaintances, but damn few friends. "If over the span of years you make even one true friend, then you've done the Almighty's bidding, for a friendship is eternal and more precious than gold".

Thus in the span of several days, Henry eagerly soaked up the values that reinforced those of his father dark mother in the series of never ending, 'Dutch Uncle' conversations between them.

Henry decided to leave the family wagon with his Aunt and Uncle and constructed a pole sled which attached to his horse's saddle, similar to that which slain carcasses of game were transported back to the farm.

For during his pilgrimage there would be scant few roads available and many streams to cross, thus rendering a wagon of little use.

Early on the day of his departure, he embraced his teary eyed Aunt then Emma their housekeeper and finally his Uncle before climbing on his horse.

"Don't forget to write Henry", called out his Aunt as he rode off towards the Mill Creek ferry, then made his way to the Anderson ferry that would pole him across the great Ohio River to Kentucky territory and southward towards a great adventure. Any anxieties he may have had about his journey were vastly eclipsed by the excitement of what lay ahead. He'd already proved to himself that he could be self-sustaining in the wilderness for over a week and with a reasonably good map of his path to Nashville and a compass and sufficient victuals to last the month's estimated time, he was confident of his chances.

As he rode up the steep pathway of the Kentucky side of the Ohio River valley, he recalled his Uncles admonition to be wary of, and try to steer clear of any one you may encounter on the way, for who knows what their intentions may be, no matter how innocent things may appear. Further in all things, his affairs were his business only and no one else's.

Besides, he had Chani and Akila at his side, guaranteed to keep others at a distance and him good company.

As Henry made his first night camp of the trip, his mind went to the four vases that graced the fireplace mantle of his Aunt's home. Two large flanked by two smaller urns, were the only evidence of his immediate family available. They were best left with his Aunt, for they would give her comfort of sorts in the years to come. Then as he lay under the stars He recalled the wisdom of his Uncle during their relentless nonstop exchanges and he repeated every one of them in his mind, again and again, so he would not forget. As he petted both Chani and Akila, he knew for certain their bond with him was reciprocal and that in the days ahead their value would be endless.

As Henry made his way along the vast Kentucky plains, many streams were forded and little signs of native Indian activity were available.

Settlements were growing, farms sprouting up here and there. On several occasions he came upon what appeared to be a former Indian encampment long abandoned and he wondered why?

The map provided, seemed to be reasonably accurate as long as he kept track of his compass readings, with the river and streams in close approximation as indicated. What Henry didn't know was that General Jackson ordered the US Army to run off all of the tribes in the Southern States and lands and drive them across the Mississippi river. A great hue and cry came up from some members of the Congress and the Federal Judiciary. But once news of the sporadic raids of the Shawnee renegade bands on the settlements in Ohio and Indiana the protests faded away into oblivion. Without those pesky 'Injuns" around there would be peace and more land to settle.

Finally starting into his fourth week, he came across a big river, which the map indicated was the Cumberland River. Passing through the settlement of Gallatin, he now knew he was in Tennessee proper, knowing he was a bit off course, considerably up river from his destination.

Seeing a farmer tending to his fields, asked directions to the nearest fording point across the Cumberland River or the nearest ferry crossing.

The wizened old farmer, as wary of passing travelers and strangers as Henry was, slowly closed the distance between them placing a weary leg up on his fence saying, "Look sorta large for dawgs pilgrim".

"That they are mister. May I introduce you to Chani and Akila", offered Henry in a friendly off hand manner. "Raised em from pups and they won't bite, unless provoked"!

"So where ya headed"?

"Nashville City" responded Henry.

"So where ye be from"?

"Cincinnati", Henry answered.

"So what ya gonna do in Nashville"?

"Carpentry", again responded Henry, now growing impatient with the questions.

"Carpentry eh? Well ya look a wee bit young at be a carpenter", offered the farmer.

"Which doesn't tell me as the good man that you must be, just where a fording place or a ferry crossing might be, does it", said Henry with a forced smile.

"Doan see many people come down this aways from Cincinnati is all"!

Several seconds of silence stood between them before the farmer continued, "Whal I doan remember any fording points in the area, cause the rivers too deep, but as I rightly reckon," paused the farmer removing his weathered hat and scratching his head, "If'n I do recall, ye go down this road a few miles and turn right at the crossroads and go a few more miles and You'll run right inta the ferry. Hope ya got ten cents to yer name for that's just what it'll cost ya to cross"!

"Much obliged Mister and a good day to ya", offered Henry as he rode off. Not in any particular hurry to get back to his fields, the farmer watched as Henry rode off down the lane, with his hounds keeping pace. Not a runaway of any kind, and was polite and well-spoken yet he saw this large long rifle in the saddle scabbard and what appeared to be a quiver of arrows and an unstrung bow secured on his skid trailing behind his horse, along with what appeared to be supplies neatly secured. Mulling this around in his mind, he concluded that this boy was not on the run from anyone and of no further concern.

After successfully finding the ferry crossing and traversing the Cumberland, he followed the westerly course of a small road that he was certain to lead him towards Nashville and his future.

The following day he entered the Town of Nashville and made inquiries as to where General Jackson's home, "The Hermitage" lay.

As he approached the Hermitage, he saw a group of workers hard at work on part of the home performing carpentry functions. As he dismounted and secured his horse, he heard the loud bellowing sounds of someone being taken to task, by someone else in authority. "You fooking dumbkoff", he heard repeatedly along with, screeches of "Scheist", and constant muttering as this smallish man went around inspecting several workmen's efforts, in trying to hand plane several boards of siding that were off as much as a quarter inch.

"Wasted all wasted", was the exclamations from the master carpenter of his men's work. "I've shown you both how to avoid this mistake over and over, yet the both of you still make the mistakes", he bellowed. Then he went over some other work they'd performed, finding some of useful accuracy, marking them accordingly and some not. Turning to his men yet again cowed by his anger he walked up to both of them and started to berate them even further.

Completely unaware of Henrys presence, his attention elsewhere, Henry walked up to the remaining piece of siding to be planed looked at the scribed markings indicating the exact dimension's required and commenced to carefully plane the plank unbidden by anyone.

Hearing a noise behind him the Master Carpenter turned and saw a boy, dressed in buckskins working carefully on the last piece of siding to be planed.

"You there, boy, what are you doing, bellowed Barthold Fahrquar, master carpenter in charge of all carpentry at the Hermitage. He hurried over to Henry, just completing his work and inspecting the dimensions for accuracy. "I said, you, what are you doing"?

"Carpentry sir" said Henry offering his work for scrutiny. The master looked at the work Henry just completed and eyeing every inch of the finished work, looking up and said, "This work is perfect".

"Just who are you young man"?

"Why I'm Henry Jaeger just arrived from Cincinnati and I'm looking for a "Mister Barthold Fahrquar", for I've a letter of introduction!

"Who's the letter from, young man"?

"His brother in Cincinnati", said Henry!

Just then Barthold perked up, giving Henry his full attention, temporarily forgetting about the miscreants some yards away. "From Cincinnati did you say"?

"Well I'm Barthold Fahrquar and if you've a letter for me from my brother I'd say you best hand it over Master Henry Jaeger.

Reaching into his side weatherized leather pouch that hung from his shoulder, Henry extracted the letter and handed it over. "Come with me up to the porch", said his newly found Uncle Barthold, while I read this from my brother.

As they approached the porch, Uncle Bart suddenly turned to the two miscreants and yelled, "Both of you, get out of my sight and go over to where the bricks are being laid and help the foreman with the bricks"!

They both sat down on the porch, while Barthold started to open the brotherly epistle.

"Fancy yerself a carpenter do ya", muttered the Uncle as he started to read. Henry decided to remain silent as his uncle read his letter if introduction. The letter was eight pages long, going into a fair amount of detail as to just who was Henry Jaeger, what he'd experienced and his capabilities.

Upon finishing, he looked up at Henry, to hear his response, "My father was a carpenter, as was his father and the father before him. I've much to learn and your brother said that you were the best man to see"! Looking intently at Henry Barthold replied, "I hold great stock in all my brother says. And since you've already shown competence and you are kinfolk and I am in need of skilled people, how can I say no"? Just then he noticed Chani and Akila sitting patiently at the bottom of the porch steps, observing every movement of the two.

"Fooking Volves", exclaimed Barthold drawing back in his heavily accented Germanic English, stopped from any sudden movement by Henry. "They are with me, for I've raised them and trained them from pups! Once they get used to you and their surroundings and bond with you they will be all right. Until then I'd recommend slow, deliberate movements in their presence!"

"Fooking Volves", he again muttered.

"Eyes and ears and senses better than we have!"

Muttering to himself he thought out loud, "Vell, we will have to get to work building an addition to the house and of course you will do most of the work under my guidance after the normal workday is completed. Until then you will have to sleep on the floor. But you are welcome into our family Henry Jaeger".

"You will call me Uncle Bart from now on nephew Henry Jaeger"!

Then spitting in his hand and offering it to Henry, who immediately did the same sealing the bargain. As to your pay young man there will be none at first till I see the depth of your abilities. You will get room and board and food to eat and the companionship of our family. Anything else you will earn.

Agreed"?

"Zu Biefel mein Uncle", agreed Henry with a wide grin.

"It seems that you are your father's son indeed, master Heinrich".

"Are Chani and Akila part of the family", asked Henry?

Uncle Bart, now looked at the critters, the largest wolves he's ever seen, apparently in a docile state, but still Uncle Bert was apprehensive. "If they grew to love your brother and my aunt and her housekeeper in a brief time, they will grow to love and protect your family as well, Uncle"!

"Zer Gute, Henry now it is done, said his new uncle. Kommen zie hier und I will introduce you around to the others. Since the work day is almost finished, then ve will go to der house und meet your new family, including your Volves!" "Hello the House", bellowed Uncle Bart as he and his new entourage entered the Fahrquar property. As he was introduced Henry discovered that his new Aunt Marta had two young daughters several years younger that Henrys two sisters might have been and that Marta was currently 'great with child' with another arrival expected several months away. As to Chani and Akila the two children approached them as told, slowly with apprehension allowing the animals to sniff them thus imprinting their scent into their brains. When the animals began to rub up against both of the little girls, Henry said, "Looks like they are now part of their family". Then Chani and Akila sidled over to where Marta and uncle Bart sat performing the same ritual to each in kind, ending up with the rubbing against the legs of both especially Chani attaching herself to Marta, with a small whine somehow sensing that Marta was in a special condition.

Since it was suppertime and the table was set, water was set out for the wolves and the victuals were served including a new place for Henry. The evening meal was preceded by the giving of thanks to the eternal prior to consumption. Both Chani and Akila paid close attention to both of the girls, who were secreting small occasional morsels of food to their eager mouths.

As the critters made the rounds of each of them, Uncle Bart said, "Seems like the days of leftovers after each meal are over, Henry! Which means you will have to verk especially hardt to feed two extra hungry mouths", he said with a wink.

After the meal, all that was left from the table was set in two extra bowls which were consumed by the wolves in a blink of the eye. After the meal the girls were captivated by the wolves and constant affection was exchanged. But Chani somehow felt an extra affection to Marta given her condition, being her constant companion and protector in the coming months.

That evening, when all prepared for bed, Henry found a place in a corner, prepared a blanket and his saddle like always and started to curl up expecting Chani and Akila to join him. Then he went over to the girl's bedroom only to find Chani and Akila up on the girls great bed curled up at their feet. As Uncle Bart peered into the bedroom with Henry, Henry said, "It was like that before with my sisters when they were alive, Uncle! Now their sisters have seemed to have returned!"

For the next several months Henry worked with his uncle on the Hermitage each day, six days a week, and during his spare time gradually built the spare room addition to his Uncles home and an assortment of furniture inclusive of a large bed for Henry.

In each life a little rain must fall, for the individual that was in charge of General Jackson's affairs while he was in Washington City tending to the nation's affairs, was his adopted son, who had an affinity for 'Sportin' Life". Spending weekends at the Camp Town Races, with a penchant for picking the occasional loser, his ability for managing the fiscal affairs of his father was sorely lacking. Come time to pay the assortment of crafts and tradesmen that worked at the Hermitage, the payments were rarely timely, if at all. Thus work at the Hermitage, slowed to a crawl, then stopped completely.

Letters and overdue bills were submitted by post to the President in Washington, for payment which was certain to take considerable time, if at all. But everyone knew that Andy Jackson was a man of his word. Too bad his son didn't share the same values.

Henry then took charge and organized a hunt, hearing that a herd of deer had taken grazing residence in a valley not five miles distant. Utilizing his skills as a "Jaeger Meister", he staked out the valley, finding the deer sent some of the less skilled but armed men, to the valleys entrance down wind and built a hide completely flanking the herd deep into the tree line.

Selecting two of the largest Stags, he studied his aim and fired off the first shot then the second at the other Stag, felling both within seconds.

Thus driving the herd down the valley towards the other hunters and a killing zone. As he arose, Henry could see and hear the image of a large Black bear, lumbering out of the tree line to his right towards the fleeing herd. It was the largest bear Henry had ever seen and he reckoned that no good could come of things should the bear encounter the other hunters down the valley. Quickly as he could, he reloaded his Beretta, took careful aim at the swiftly moving bear at approximately two hundred yards, squeezing off the first shot then the second, dropping the bear in his tracks.

Yet between each of his shots, he heard a single gunshot, coming from across the other side of the valley. Clearly someone else was firing at the same prey. Henry quickly cleared up his hide then he and the wolves made their way out from the tree line and towards the carcasses. Half way down the ridge line he noticed a group of three hunters, clad in buckskin and beaver hats emerging from the tree line almost at the exact position across from him. Both parties approached the bear in no apparent hurry, but two of the opposing parties had their muskets at the ready, pointing at the lifeless bear just in case movement was detected. As they drew closer to each other, Henry heard the tall one in the middle say, "Shoulder yer muskets boys, the bar is kilt dead"! Heeding his words both flanking hunters put their muskets in the crook of their arm, one saying "Awright Davey"!

"Some shootin' there son" said the tall one to Henry as both parties approached. The tall one flanked by two others and Henry flanked by Chani and Akila, both at the ready with tails set horizontally and fangs barely showing. Henry then made a motion with his hands compelling the wolves to sit. The wolves slowly obeyed.

"Dem yer wolves", asked the tall hunter.

"Raised em from pups", replied Henry.

"Seems we were huntin' the same bar", said the other hunter laconically.

Ignoring the obvious Henry offered, "It was the two Stags I was huntin' as you can see over there" said Henry pointing to the two carcasses some twenty yards to his left, "the bear just came upon us after my shots and I was concerned for the other hunters down the valley, so I shot the bear." "All, by yerself," questioned the tall hunter? "I heard two shots, 'bang, bang' and there's only you in front of me". That said, Henry slowly unsheathed the double barreled Beretta from its cover, putting each barrel at half cock, never mind that he hadn't thought to reload.

"Now son, no need to be hasty, it's just that we was countin' on that bar to git us by, fer the time being", said the tall one, "An I hit him fair and square".

"As did I mister, uh…." Crockett", said the tall one, "David Crockett, from around these parts and you"?

"Jesus H. Christ", thought Henry momentarily in awe of who he was confronting. In front of him was a living breathing legend and here he was Henry Jaeger almost in a tussel with him over a kill.

Recovering his composure, he replied, "Henry Jaeger and my Uncle is Bart Fahrquar and we're currently in the service of General Jackson away in Washington City, working on the Hermitage, doing carpentry"!

"Yeah, Ah knows all about General Jackson in Washington by gawd City", spat Crockett in derision.

Just then one of the other rode up on Henry's horse, with the skid attached for transporting of the carcasses, holding the reins of two other horses similarly outfitted.

As Henry took possession of his mount, Crockett noted the three long haired scalps attached to the saddle saying, "That your horse"?

"Yessir"! "And the scalps also", asked Crockett?

"Used to belong to Shawnee hostiles" said Henry turning to Crockett. "Massacred my family up Ohio way and there are three left to go, stated Henry jaws set firm. Changing the subject slightly Crockett asked, "You set up this little huntin' party of pilgrims"?

"That I did Mr. Crockett" replied Henry looking Crockett squarely in the eye.

"Whal de well", exclaimed Crockett, "A boy doin the work of a man"! With that he put his rifle in the hands of another of his party, taking several steps forward and asked to shake Henry's hand. Henry uncocked his field piece and reciprocated, shaking the hand of a legend.

"I'm shootin' a .60 caliber Kentucky rifle and you bring them down with a double barrel shotgun, commented Crockett as he fixed his gaze on Henry's field piece. Holding it up for Crockett's inspection Henry added, "Not a shotgun Mr. Crockett, but a .70 Caliber, Beretta long rifle that's been in my family for a very long time". "Will bring down anything that moves and breathes"!

After a little small talk, all got to examining the bear to find their respective shot balls and gauge the placement of the hits that brought down the beast, with Henry eventually identifying his and Crockett retrieving and identifying his shot placements. Any of the three shots would've done the trick, but seeing that Henry had two shots to Crockets one, sealed the fate for Crockett. He had been bested, but just barely. One of his party shrugged his shoulders and with that, Crockett hung his head.

The man was a legend, having distinguishing himself in the Creek and Black Hawk Indian wars along with Sam Houston and a number of others, the hostiles inhabiting the Southern Region of the US were disinterred and de fanged, being compelled to move from their ancestral lands to across the Mississippi by presidential directive of Andrew Jackson.

Several years later, David Crockett, "King of the Wild Frontier", capitalized on his fame and ran successfully for a congressional seat in Washington City. President Jackson counted on those like Crockett, from his home state of Tennessee, to help him in his endless struggle against the likes of Henry Clay, John C. Calhoun of South Carolina and the scallywag Whigs of the eastern business establishments. Wise to the ways of the frontier, Crockett was clearly out of his element as a congressman. Barely able to read, or write a coherent sentence, he quickly assessed he was overmatched, sleeping late, tardy for meetings, carousing at the Inns in the area, even traveling to New York City to appear in exhibition of his being in badly written and performed plays. Every cent he earned flowed in and out of his grasp like water through open hands.

When he ran for reelection, General Jackson, decided to turn his back on Crockett, throwing support to his opponent, who trounced him in his bid to return to congress. Bitter and broke, Crockett wandered around Tennessee for a while undecided as to what to do next.

Henry, far too busy to tap into the gossip of his area, was nonetheless aware of the local icons situation and said, "Mr. Crockett, whereupon Crockett interrupted him by saying, "Son, my friends call me Davey"! "Davey, seems the hunt went better than expected and there will be more than enough meat around for those in need, so I'd be mighty obliged if'n y'all would help us get this all back to town and help us skin and render the critters and smoke the meat an all, and take the bear in its completeness as a token of our appreciation, "exclaimed Henry!"

"Well pilgrim that's mighty neighborly of ya and I jus doan see how we all can say no", replied Crockett, with a wide grin. With that he sent his two friends back to retrieve their horses, deep in the woods.

By midafternoon, the hunting party returned with their horse drawn skids laden, with the carcasses of game, for the working craftsmen's families. Immediately all set to work, with knives sharpened, the carcasses were all skinned and butchered down to the bone of edible meats, then fires built in the smoke houses and carcasses hung and other portions ground up for sausages and steaks cooked for one and all.

No one in this group of craftsmen and their families would starve this coming winter, with the meats of two stags, and nine other deer and one large bear gracing their dinner tables.

Of course Chani and Akila both waited patiently close at hand when a stray morsel would be tossed their way periodically, amidst all the activity, eventually wandering up to the Fahrquar front porch, laying down, bellies filled and watching the frenzied activity of all, far into the night by torchlight, those involved, through eyes now heavy with satiation.

Several days later, a letter was posted in Nashville's town square to the citizens of Tennessee written by Stephen Austin and General Sam Houston, exhorting citizens to come help the cause of Texas independence, by settling in Texas. For years, news of free land in Texas, persuaded many in the western lands who were not settled, or who failed at whatever enterprise they were involved with, to emigrate to Texas. As the years rolled by a growing number of folks, decided to roll the dice and take the risk, many of which had little left to lose, embarking on the adventure of a lifetime.

Such was the fate of one David Crockett late in the year 1835. In the months after their fated encounter, Davey Crockett ran into Henry Jaeger from time to time and together they went on a few hunts. Crockett himself an experienced woodsman, immediately came to greatly respect the skills of Henry Jaeger as a huntsman with not only the flintlock but that of the bow, having learned of his background, bit by bit and seeing firsthand the way he handled himself. Henry could track like an Indian, hear sense and see like the wolves that were his constant companion.

As they and their companions rode back from yet another successful hunt, skids laden with the large critters, Crockett mused, "Nuthin more around these parts left for me here anymore, Henry! Think me and the boys'll get some folks together and head on down Texas way an see if'n we can help General Sam! Why don't ya throw in with us, both you and those dawgs of your'in"?

Being accepted by the likes of David Crockett was about as tempting as it gets for a young man like Henry. And he must admit the sense of wanderlust was starting to involve him almost on a daily basis. However, he'd seriously bonded with his Uncle and the entire family, who'd by now, had come to depend on him in a variety of ways, with the sense of belonging running hard and deep. Besides the work on the Hermitage had just started back up, albeit on a much reduced level, with funds arriving from General Jackson in Washington City to a trusted local lawyer who then jointly released funds for work and supplies in a timely manner.

On several occasions, Uncle Bart took ill for short periods of time with Henry assuming control of the handful of workers on site, executing Uncle Bart's directives while doing his own work. Thus his new family needed him, which provided a brake against his potential wanderlust.

As they rode he patiently explained his conundrum to Davey and his reluctance to become a Texian at this time.

Christmas came and went as Crockett went round the area drumming up interest for those craving adventure for a Texian foray. Between the holidays news arrived that some Mexican troops were guilty of several massacres of American citizen settlers in Texas Territory, some months past. Then New Year's eve an announcement was posted from Sam Houston that was sent out to the various areas of Louisiana, Arkansas and Tennessee that people were needed to come at all speed to Texas to defend the American settlers, from Mexican invaders.

That was all that was needed, for David Crockett to have his ranks swell from a dozen men to just under three dozen men all bound for Texas Territory. Busy at the Hermitage one morning shortly after the new year, news reached both Henry and his Uncle that David Crockett and his men of just under three dozen 'Nere do wells', were off to Texas the previous morning with not so much as a goodbye to anyone

4

The year of 1836 kept Henry, his Uncle and the various working crafts fairly busy at the Hermitage, in preparation for General Jackson's return from the office of the Presidency, the following year. The problems that they confronted were never ending, with the sporadic arrival of funds, then the availability of appropriate construction material at a reasonable price, to the ever fluid availability of skilled craftsmen.

Thoughts of David Crockett faded in Henry's mind replaced with a myriad of other responsibilities, until reports began to trickle in to the fledgling local newspaper, of the problems in Texas. One day Henry picked up a day old paper at the Hermitage, which announced of a massacre in a place called the Alamo Mission, at a village called San Antonio de Bexar, in Texas territory. Names cropped up in the article, some he'd heard legends of and some he had never heard before, like General Sam Houston, Jim Bowie, David Crockett and a self-styled Colonel of the Militia, William B. Travis. All gone, slaughtered. A Mexican force estimated of several thousand, laid siege to the Alamo mission for almost a week, prior to the final attack. Only the few women and children were allowed to depart prior to the final days attack.

The General of the Mexican army was a person known as Antonio Lopez de Santa Anna. Further reports of a Colonel Fannin and over 300 men being executed at a settlement called Goliad Texas. With the General Santa Anna scouring all of east Texas territory to annialate the militia army led by General Sam Houston.

Henry was stunned by the announcement. Had he thrown in with Davy and his boys, no doubt he'd also be ant food like the rest of them.

Something had held him back. Then he'd thought of his new family and all the friends he's made here in Nashville and felt more than reasoned that some unseen guiding hand had restrained him, from his inner demons.

He was now regularly taking twice a month weekend hunting parties away from Nashville for big game and always they returned with their horse drawn skids laden with game to be equally parceled out to the Hermitage family workmen.

Several months later the local paper announced that Sam Houston and his boys caught up with General Santa Anna at a place called the San Jacinto Bayou. "Caught em napping' during an afternoon siesta and 'Tennessee Sam' and his boys 'whipped em all for fair'", the article continued. As Henry read on, the article mentioned that General Sam had caught a musket ball in the ankle and was in great pain, but on the mend, risking a revolt of the entire militia of Texian's when he decided to set Santa Anna free to return to Mexico, but not without signing an article of formal surrender and a pledge that the entire area of Texas north of what the Mexicans called the Rio Bravo, or what the Texians called the Rio Grande river, was hereby ceded to the "Republic of Texas".

Had the majority of the militia had their way, those who survived the "Scrape at San Jacinto" would have provided ample decoration for all the trees in the area, turning a spring day into Christmas. A just reward for the memory of those at the Alamo mission.

"The remnants of the Mexican Army were escorted back across the Rio Grande, on foot with little more than the clothes on their back, leaving a large assortment of horses, wagons and munitions in their wake", the article read.

The rest of the year of 1836, was easily predictable, going to work at the Hermitage each day, working with and learning from his Uncle the finer points of the craft of carpentry and several other aspects of construction from the other craftsmen. The goal being the complete habitability of the Hermitage upon the return of General Jackson from Washington City, at the termination of his second term the following year. From time to time General Jackson's adopted son would appear at the Hermitage, attempting to assert himself into the day to day business, usually when the general's local attorney was away on business.

Work would then cease, with everyone going home, until word of the Generals attorney's return to town. The adopted son would disappear back to Camp Town and resume his career as a 'Sportin' Man', thus allowing work to continue.

During one these lulls in construction activity, Henry and some of the craftsmen were out on one of their hunting forays and as usual were in the process of assembling the various kills, when a small group of men appeared from the tree line.

The leader of the group insisted to see the leader of the hunting party and was directed towards Henry.

"Are you the leader of this bunch", asked the leader of this lightly armed group?

"Why yes I am", replied Henry "and what business might you have with us?

"My name is John Coffee Hayes and I'm heading up this here crew of surveyors and I'd ask you to tell your boys to try and shoot straight, the next time you're out hunting. They prêt near got some of my men, not one hour ago".

Immediately concerned, Henry quickly apologized for the almost mishap and as an amends offered part of the kill to the entire surveying crew, inviting them all to a small shiveree at the Fahrquar home.

Expecting some hostility, but finding the exact opposite, John Hays responded, "Well that's right neighborly of you young man and I just don't see how we could refuse. Since we're about done here do you mind if we throsw in with ya on your way back seeing that we're goin' the same place?" At that, Henry nodded his head and offered his hand saying "Henry Jaeger am I and I'm the nephew of Bart Fahrquar and I'm working on the Hermitage with him and these here waddies are part of the family of craftsmen working for the General," as he indicated to his men working loading the various carcasses on the horse drawn skids.

As they shook hands Hays responded, "My friends call me Jack and you?"

"Henry'll, do just fine"!

The skids loaded, both party's made their way back to Nashville proper, discussing the events of the day, eventually discovering things both had in common. Principally Jack Hays current assignment surveying General Jackson's property and the adventures in dealing with his profligate, sportin' life son. Both easily chuckled at the various stories traded between them at the General's son's expense.

By the time they got back to the Fahrquar place, they appeared to be fast friends and remarked at how fortuitous it was, how a given fractious event could turn into a mutual kinship.

Hays and his crew immediately fell into the work of skinning and rendering the carcasses for the smoke house, the grinder and the tannery, knowing full well their efforts would be rewarded by a sumptuous repast later in the evening.

All of the extended families of the craftsmen came out to be involved for the aftermath always involved a complete engorgement, of spirits and meats far into the night.

In the months that followed, whenever a lull of activity occurred at the Hermitage, Henry was asked to join John Hays crew surveying a stretch of property and likewise invited both Hays and his older brother William to join him on a hunt.

Hays was constantly amazed at Henry's prowess as a tracker, marksman with both the rifle and the bow along with various, subtleties in sustaining one's life in the wild, yet the boy was still in his teens and although a few years younger was a half a head taller, well-muscled, hands as calloused as a teamster and serious of character.

As they gradually came to know one another, Henry discovered that John Coffee Hays had a significant bloodline, with his father serving with Andy Jackson, (Old Hickory) at New Orleans, just prior to his birth, and with Sam Houston and Davy Crockett in the Creek Indian Wars, coming by his middle name of 'Coffee' after General John Coffee, one of General Jackson's commanders. It was understood that his name and his father's connections would open certain doors as he grew to manhood.

His father died when he was but fifteen years of age, with he and his family being parceled out to various members of their extended family, with Jack and his younger brother and sister sent to live with an Uncle Robert Gage in Mississippi. His Uncle, being a successful merchant, selected a future for his nephew as a store clerk. But the staid life of a "Feather Merchant" was not for John, so after several years under his Uncle's wing John left to work as a chain boy on a land surveying crew and for the next two years worked on various extended surveys learning the trade, eventually running his own crew.

With his savings he departed for Nashville attending the Davison Academy, to acquire official bona fides as a surveyor, only to fall ill after a year and dropping out. Eventually upon his recovery of his health forming his own unit and contracting out work on his own, in the Nashville area.

As John and his older brother William celebrated John's 21'st birthday shortly after the New Year of 1838 at the Fahrquar residence, surrounded by a gaggle of friends, they drifted out to the front porch for a bit of fresh air, full of cake, drink and a cornucopia of vittles.

By now both had taken to an occasional smoking of the pipe, a luxury that was afforded on rare occasions. Talk about happenings in Texas, now a Republic, would surface from time to time and now that General Jackson had returned to the Hermitage to see it almost completed, Henry could see that his time with the Fahrquars was coming to an end. In spite of inconsistent cash flow from the Hermitage project the Fahrquar's family had prospered, with the lean times being filled to almost overflowing with Henry's efforts, starting a thriving business in tanned hides and smoked meats and sausages whose joint incomes exceeded that of Uncle Bart's Carpentry business.

Henry's friendship with Jack Hays had solidified to such a degree that either man had complete respect and confidence in the others skills and judgment. In the company of Henry Jaeger and his two wolves, any man could be completely confident of the unforeseen, being seen in the wilds of the frontier.

When General Jackson returned from his exertions in Washington City, for the last time, he was pleased by the efforts of the Fahrquar group and that of John Coffee Hays. Examining everything they touched with a highly caustic and critical eye yet finding no fault it the work contracted for.

One evening after meeting with a group of political suitors seeking political favors, the General asked Henry and the Hays brothers to hang back after the others had left, to discuss things of mutual interest. Neither Henry nor the Hays Brothers had any idea as to what the General had wanted, but awaited his pleasure on the front veranda being served port wine by one of the Generals darkies. He'd granted them all manumission years ago setting them free, but their loyalty to Old Hickory was beyond all human comprehension. Clearly a private affair that was no one's business but the Generals.

The loyalty of each was to exist on a reciprocal basis well beyond the grave.

As the General approached both Henry and the Hays brothers commenced to rise, but the General waved them to remain seated by saying, "As you were boys, as you were", taking a seat in their midst.

Deep into the night the General talked with the young men, discussing events that had occurred in Nashville, along with a paucity of local gossip, eventually landing on the subject of the Republic Of Texas.

Both Henry and Jack Hays glanced at each other, because their private conversations had traveled the very same path, the young men's wanderlust rising to the fore.

John Quincy Adams was now President, and while the General considered him as an inconsequential 'prig', the General was fairly secure in the certainty that Adams would continue the path of the ship of state the General had set forth. "Won't serve more than one term, but the man will keep things on an even keel. Hells Fire, I'll join Rachael in a few years and after that things won't matter"!

They shared with the General their mutual interest in immigrating to Texas to find their destiny. The General shared with them the fact that a certain cabal of folks would have him take away Texas and any and all the territories from Mexico via any means fair or foul. The manifest destiny of one land unbroken from sea to shining sea first espoused by President Jefferson, during the Louisiana Purchase.

"But god damn it," the general bellowed banging his hickory cane on the verandah's wooden floor, "I just got this country out of debt for the very first time in the nation's history, since the revolution and I'll be damned in hell if I'll see it get in deep debt again"!

"I know Sam Houston is mad at me for the present, cause he thinks I'm leaving him and his precious Texians out there twisting in the wind. Well I just might be, but fer damn good reason", he said, his voice trailing off.

"John Hays, I knew your father, he was with me at New Orleans and served damn well during the Creek Wars, but as fer you young man", he said now turning to Henry, they say your mostly Indian, a little wolf, like those critters down below", pointing to Chani and Akila sitting attentively at the foot of the verandah, having been fed by one of the generals darkies. "Yet you have light brown hair like a white man". "Those that know me well", the general continued, know damn well that I got no truck with the Indian's."

That indeed was the case, for the general was infamous for having made treaties with the natives, only to break the treaties often before the ink was dry or as situations warranted. "They saw that you move like a ghost in the woods and can track like an Indian and shoot the eyes from a movin' buzzard at a hunnert yards."

"They were wrong general", said Henry fighting to retail his composure, "someone gave you Bad information"!

"Bad information", bellowed the general, taking his frail body to its full presence while in his chair!

"Yes General bad information, a moving buzzard will be at two hundred yards and a still buzzard at three hundred"! With that, the general broke forth with a huge guffaw and slapped his knee, coughing intermittently.

"General if I may let me tell you about Henry Jaeger"! The General nodded as Jack Hays proceeded to relate all he had known about Henry Jaeger going back to his days in Ohio.

"So ya got three Shawnee scalps on yer saddle"?

"No sir, there not on my saddle anymore but tucked away. Seems they make people uneasy. Besides there are three left to go somewhere out there," offered Henry almost as an afterthought.

The general peered into Henry's eyes as he finished his sentence, "Yup, just as I thought. You're a killer alright. Seen a lot of em in my day from the British back in the revolution, to the British at New Orleans, that pirate Lafitte, the southern Indians, to those pasty skinned bastard's in Washington City."

Just then the generals pocket watch chimed midnight and his darkie, standing ever present nearby, whispered into his ear.

"Goddammit Nathan I know its past my bed time", he responded irritably.

"With that the general creakily arose with the help of his cane turning around and heeding his servant, took several steps toward the door, then stopped turning around saying to Henry and Jack both, "I'd like to see you gentlemen tomorrow after lunch, for a visit and you mister Jaeger, bring yer weapons, for I just want to see how good you are".

"With that he disappeared into the Hermitage for the evening".

At One PM, the following afternoon, both Henry and Jack Hays appeared beck at the Hermitage with General Jackson eagerly awaiting them on the front verandah. Both Chani and Akila sniffed the general as the group retired to an adjacent field to test Henry's skills.

As he unsheathed the Beretta double barreled rifle, he gave the general a brief history of its provenance going back to the early 1700's.

The next several hours were spent with Henry demonstrating just what a skilled hunter could do with both the rifle and the bow.

The general had never seen anything like it. At a distance of 450 long paces, the ancient firearm neatly exploded a cantaloupe into edible sections. With the bow, he was equally adept both on foot and on the horse at full gallop.

As they retired back to the verandah, Henry commenced to clean and care for his ancient firearm as they talked and consumed the refreshments Nathan, the general's man, provided.

"You care for that rifle better than most men care for their women", mused the general. Henry just looked up and smiled at the general's comment and with a nodding assent went back to his work, listening to the general's comments about the world at large as he saw it.

"They say that you and Davey Crockett were friends before he went to Texas", comment the general as an invite to tell the story. With that, Henry just finishing up with his rifle, put it back in the scabbard and related his brief relationship with the legendary frontiersman.

"Damn fool let me down when he was in congress", mused the general." Frittered away an opportunity that was handed to him on a silver platter, he did"! Continuing on he mused, "Well, I suppose when I meet him upstairs, they'll be plenty time to recall, just who disappointed who". Both Henry and Hays nodded in agreement. For in the presence of a former president and a legendary general one was careful of what was said.

"If the both of you will attend me two days from now I'll have prepared letters of introduction to Sam Houston since he's the President of Texas now days. Perhaps it'll open a few doors for you, perhaps not depending on just who reads the letters!" With that said he looked up at Nathan, who was at his side in an instant, helping him rise and without another word they disappeared into the bowels of the Hermitage for the general's mid afternoon nap.

The following day Henry was sleeping late when his two nieces and their little brother, bounded into his room and cried, "Uncle Heinrich, Uncle Heinrich, kommen zie heir", motioning for him to wake up and follow them outside to the porch, where right under the porch swing, was

Chani in the arms of Aunt Marta, clearly distressed, with Akila sitting silently from the other side of the porch.

"I tole everyone, that she was going to be a mother", said Marta, "but everyone was too busy to listen"!

One of Henry's nieces tugged on Henry's night shirt saying, "Uncle Henry, did Chani get a visit from the stork last night"?

Henry then cast a glance at Akila, who then lay prone on porch floor with one paw over his head.

Marta looked over at Akila saying, "If ever a party looked guilty it's Akila"!

The children, clearly in a quandary, not understanding, looked back and forth at each other.

Suddenly, Chani moved out of Marta's grasp to a corner and commenced to give birth. One by one, the little critters emerged from Chani, clad in the trappings of afterbirth.

As they emerged, Marta took each of them and cleaned off the afterbirth placing them by Chani's teats for their very first meal. As they sucked the teats hungrily, Chani did her duty and continued licking them clean, thus putting her first imprint on her children. Three young pups lay in every ones midst.

Just then one of the nieces commented, "The stork didn't visit, but some other doggie schtupped Chani"! Thus as everyone could clearly see, the pups had characteristics that clearly differed from both Chani and Akila.

Before Marta could admonish her child for using such a word, Henry winked and said, "Well what's done seems to be done, everybody"! Then he went over to Akila and sat beside him. Petting him saying "Seems you're now an Uncle Akila and you're off the hook"! Everyone then laughed, the attention temporarily shifting from Chani to Akila.

After the pups had their first meal, they curled up neatly under Chani's underbelly and all went to sleep, carefully guarded by the entire family in shifts around the clock the children, Marta and occasionally Henry taking turns during the evening ever at her side.

Several days later Jack Hays came by and sat with Henry and Chani. "Well it seems like you're gonna be delayed a bit in your departure", said Jack understandably. "Day after tomorrow, William and I are leaving for Texas"! At that he gave his route of travel to Henry, traveling overland by horse, both he and his brother would travel down to Natchez Mississippi to visit his Uncle Cage, supply up, then cross the Mississippi by ferry and make their way to Texas overland with a wagon train of future settlers. He then produced a copy of General Jackson's letter of introduction with Henry's name on it. "Of course William and I will get there ahead of you since ya clearly can't leave Chani behind while she's still suckling the pups, but you can catch up with us either in the Austin settlement or in San Antonio de Bexar".

"William and me intend to throw in with the Ranger's or the Militia and we'll save some room for ya"!

For the next several months, Henry idled by preparing for the moment of departure, clearly disturbed by the affection he would be departing from, by every member of his acquired family. He was endlessly peppered by the 'Why' questions by the children, who clearly didn't want Uncle Henry to leave.

Try as he might, he just wasn't able to muster up the appropriate explanations to make small children understand, the words "Wanderlust or Adventure", for he barely understood the why's of it himself. But going to Texas was something he was compelled to do. Besides, even though Chani and Akila were going with Henry, the pups were going to stay with the Fahrquar family, so they would need to be cared for and trained just as the kids parents cared for and trained them, until the pups were fully grown, then they would protect the family from all harm.

Later on in the day he wandered down to Pruitt Latimer's place. For Latimer was one of the craftsmen that Henry's Uncle had employed, who showed adeptness for the hunt. They spent the rest of the afternoon talking about Henry's departure for Texas, taking the occasional pull from the jug of "Old Overshoes", that was Pruitt's constant companion.

As Henry rose to leave he said, "Teach em well Pruitt".

"I'll keep an eye on em Henry", shouted Latimer as Henry walked away.

The following day Henry received an invitation to "Attend General Jackson, for a noon day brunch", the very next day. Henry told the messenger that he would.

"Young man", the crusty old general started out as they were served by Nathan his man servant, "I usually don't take a shine to someone, at least right off, for I find most people to be scallywags. But something in you is different. Can't quite put my finger on it, which gets me to no end"!

"You've no doubt, the letter of introduction I gave young Hays to give to you"! Henry nodded in assent, while chewing a mouth full of roast beef. The general continued, "You will also do me the kindness of conveying a letter to Sam Houston, the current President of the Republic of Texas. The letter is for his eyes only, with the envelope sealed with my wax seal." Whereupon, he removed the letter from his jacket and placed in front of Henry.

"Now, I understand that your probably gonna throw in with the Texas Militia, or the Rangers or whatever they are callin' themselves these days. They got no money to speak of in all of Texas. Sam Houston and anyone who comes after will be in quite a pickle for some time to come, what with reports of Comanche and Kiowa raiders hooraying' them at every turn and the damn Mexican bandits at the other and the constant threat of reinvasion for Mexico. The only godsend being that Mexico is themselves in a political mess"!

The general then coughed, taking a drink of the wine from a goblet and clearing his throat, "Now Sam Houston and his people want Texas to become part of the Union and I understand why, but not at this time. Now ole Quincy up in Washington City is the lesser of all evils, for the time being and to annex Texas, will mean a war with Mexico for fair and we are just not ready for scrape with anyone at this time and that's just how I see things.

Maybe someday in the future but not now. So Texas will have to fend for themselves for the time being!"

Henry nodded in understanding. "Now since you're gonna be a secret official courier to the State of Texas, you'll see that Sam Houston gets this letter hand to hand and no one else. Now if somethin' has happened to Houston, then this letter is to be handed to whoever is officially is the President of Texas at that time!"

Again Henry nodded in assent.

"Now for your trouble, I've taken the liberty to book you and your wolves passage on one these new Riverboats that have come up the Cumberland River, all the way down to New Orleans and from there you can make your way overland to Texas by whatever means you can!"

Reaching into one of his other pockets, he pulled out a pouch and opened it revealing a wad of federal bank notes and several gold coins. Now since you're a carpenter by trade, seems to me you're gonna need some tools and this here should cover the cost of whatever you need. Besides you're gonna need to make a livin' since bein' a militia man just isn't gonna pay well.

Now as you can see another envelope for you to show any officials of authority, that you are in the employ of the President of the United States, you'll note that I've backdated the letter from a time when I was President, and that you are not to be impeded in any way for any reason"!

Henry offered, "Well general I already have some tools from my Uncle". The general shot back angrily, "Ya got everthang ya need"? "Well no sir", replied Henry taken aback.

"Then use it to fill out the rough edges young man and no back talk ya heah", said the general.

"I like your honesty, but young man, sometimes ya can be too honest, ya heah"?

Henry meekly agreed. The balance of the time they spent together was in silence, briefly interrupted by the general's musings about a variety of events both local and national. Henry eagerly took every word in, cherishing this private moment, for reasons he didn't understand at the moment.

Eventually mid-afternoon arrived and with it arrived Nathan whispering into the general's ear. "Well young man seems Nathan says it's my nap time," said the general arising along with Henry. The General stepped forward and clasped Henrys hand with both of his saying, "America needs more men like you Henry Jaeger. We will never see each other again, for my time is close at hand, so I want these eyes to see just what the future holds"! That said, the generals eyes started to mist up as he gripped Henrys hand firmly. Then recovering his composure he blurted out, "Now get about your business, you've much to do"! With that, he turned and hobbled off to the inside of the Hermitage, helped by Nathan. As they entered the house, Nathan gave Henry a glance, accompanied with a gentle smile and a nod of his head.

As Henry rode back to the Fahrquar's he noted the Generals appearance as frail indeed, no doubt a mere shadow of the great man that many had loved and others reviled. Perhaps, Henry had seen a side of the man that no one else had noticed. He then replayed everything the general had said, in his mind, especially the part that asserted that Henry was honest, too honest.

Entering the great unknown he would have to keep that in mind. The pups now weaned and clearly bonded to the Fahrquar family the time for Henry's departure was at hand. As the riverboat pulled away from the Nashville wharf for its journey back down the Cumberland River and thence down the Ohio thence down the great Mississippi, Henry started to mist up just like the old general, seeing the entire Fahrquar family each with one of Chanis pups in their arms waving and crying over his departure. Chani appeared restless as the boat pulled away, then Henry knelt down bringing both wolves close to him for mutual assurance, once both of them reached up to lick Henrys face, he knew that all would be well, as they all ventured into the vast unknown. His thoughts then went to his parents and the cavalcade of events that were seared into his mind. Several miles downriver, his thoughts then went to the Shawnee Red Hair, his jaws becoming rigid. With a secret hope that one day their paths wound cross and the silent vow that it would take days for the Red Hair to die.

At Grand River junction, the riverboat passed into the Tennessee River and then later at the Paducah settlement, unloaded to another boat to continue on down the Ohio River, down to the Great Mississippi, stopping periodically at several settlements on its way to Memphis.

Then on to Greenville, Vicksburg and Natchez, with each stop dropping off and boarding both goods and passengers. As the boat pulled into Baton Rouge, Henry decided to leave the boat and continue overland to the Texas territory, having met a party other fellow pilgrims to the Promised Land, who could use his skills.

A party of several dozen wagons worth of settlers made their way across the southern part of Louisiana bypassing the swampy areas, thanks to a guide of mixed blood who spoke a barely understandable patois of English and French called 'Cajun'. Fording some of the many rivers and ferrying across others, weeks later the finally crossed the Louisiana frontier and ferried across the Sabine River, into Texas.

From time to time, Henry would take the wolves and a few of the men on a hunt, only to return a day later with several skids of game, which were then hurriedly prepared for consumption. Rather than use his massive Beretta, Henry, his bow, arrows and the wolves would channel the game into a killing zone where the other hunters with their smooth bore muskets could easily bring down at relatively close range.

Whatever hardships were endured by the pilgrims, lack of food wasn't one of them. Henry took his turn with several others, scouting out ahead of the main party, seeing signs and sensing the presence of native Indian parties from time, but never having a direct encounter with them. Of course the wagon train was heavily armed by serious people and their families, experiencing not one loss of man nor beast luckily during their journey towards the settlement of Austin.

After a month of careful travel in the Texas territory, the land grew away from the relative low laying lands and into the hill country and everyone sensed that their destination of Austin was close at hand.

5

Late in the afternoon Henry and the settlers pulled into the Austin settlement, recently designated as the new Capital of the Republic of Texas. They were met by the representatives of the Republic. Henry separated one of the representatives and asked where he could find the President Sam Houston. He was told that President Houston was en route from his new home at the Huntsville settlement and was expected any day now, to attend the upcoming meeting of delegates. Henry debated with himself whether or not to reveal that he had a letter from the former US President Jackson. He decided the fewer people who knew of the business between the men the better.

He further inquired as to the arrival of Jack Hays and company and was told that Mr. Hays, arrived alone some three months ago and was directed to San Antonio de Bexar, to join a company of the Texas Militia, sometimes known as the Rangers, under the command of Juan Seguin.

He joined the company of settlers on the outskirts of Austin proper as the made camp, intending to re supply as needed then press on to San Antonio and parts west and north, to stake their claims.

Each day Henry went into Austin, to make inquiries as to attend President Houston and present the letter as agreed with President Jackson. Each day he was told that Houston had not yet arrived.

After a week of refitting and supply, the rest of the settlers pushed on to San Antonio, leaving Henry and the wolves alone.

On the tenth day since his arrival, Henry arrived once again at the log building designated as the Capitol, for his daily inquiry to find that General Sam had indeed arrived, late in the previous day and was due in directly to conduct the business of the Republic. An hour later the legendary General arrived with several people hard on his heels. He was limping and with each step with the use of a cane quite similar to General Jackson's a visible cringe of pain, from the ankle wound no doubt suffered at San Jacinto. As he came into earshot he heard Houston bellow, "Goddammit Lamar, I know the Comanch are on the warpath again, up along the Uvalde, but that's what Seguin and his group are for. Send someone out to San Antonio to get with Sam Maverick and get another group of militia up and ready to scout the Fredericksburg settlements"!

At that Henry fell in with the group of men following Houston as they passed, saying "President Houston, I've just arrived from Nashville and I've a letter for you from President Jackson"!

That immediately stopped Sam Houston right in his tracks, who painfully turned around saying, "And just who you might be young man"?

"Jaeger sir, Henry Jaeger, recently arrived from Nashville with a letter for your eyes only"!

"From Jackson you say"? At that Henry nodded.

"Well then you may join us we walk to the Capitol, Mr. Henry Jaeger from Nashville"!

Henry was bidden to wait for about an hour as Sam Houston dealt with several of those who accompanied him to the Capitol, hurriedly. Then he was shown into a sparsely furnished office. "Hand me that letter from our former President young man, that you brought all this way from Tennessee, then take a seat while I read it"!

Henry did as asked then took the proffered seat watching Houston's every reaction as he slowly read each page of the letter. When he finished, Houston returned to the first page and reread the letter yet again, before putting it down and addressing Henry.

"Young man, how well did you know General Jackson"?

Thinking a second, Henry replied, "About six months ago was the first time I met him, but my Uncle and me have been working on the Hermitage for several years getting it back in shape for his arrival." "Doing just what"? "Mostly carpentry, General Houston. Carpentry's my trade"!

"Look like a damn country boy hunter, all dressed up in buckskin as ya are", mused Houston.

"I can do that too, track, shoot, skin, smoke and tan the hides, if need be".

"Were you there when the General wrote the letter"?

"No sir", answered Henry, "The General gave me the letter along with another as we dined at the Hermitage and letter of introduction for you I suppose"!

"Letter of Introduction", asked Houston? "Yessir"!

"Well hand the goddamn thing over so we can be formally introduced".

Reaching into his rucksack Henry handed to Houston his letter of introduction, which Houston promptly read.

"Letter mentions this John Coffey Hays along with you and it's by the Generals hand sure enough. I once knew a certain Mr. Hays who served with me during the Creek Wars."

"That would be Jack Hays father General", replied Henry.

'Where is this Jack Hayes"?

"One of your people told me that he came through here a few months ago and was directed to a Mr. Maverick in San Antonio, to join the militia as a Ranger.

"And your intention is to throw in with the Militia, is it not?"

"Yes General, preferably with Jack Hays"!

"Well, if he's in San Antonio, so be it and if not?"

"Still want to be any help I can be"!

"So young man, what was your overall impression of President Jackson", asked Houston, changing the subject?

Henry paused then said, "I think he's come home to die General, for he seems frail and must be helped around by his man Nathan all the time"!

"So that darkie Nathan's still with him after all these years", mused Houston absently.

Henry nodded in agreement. If you know about Nathan that guarantees that you've been in the presence of Jackson himself.

"What might not be known, is that Nathan was the Generals wife Rachel's slave and after she died, prior to General Jackson's arrival in Washington City to become the President,

The General gave him his freedom papers, yet Nathan stayed on with the General", offered Henry. "If you know that, then certainly you know the General", offered Houston.

"Know anything about the Comanche or the Kiowa Indians young'un"?

"No sir" replied Henry, but I do know about the Shawnee up Ohio way and I've three Shawnee scalps. "Don't know a lot about the Shawnee, but I heard they're a fearful bunch, but like the native Indians in the south their mostly afoot. Plains Indians are on horse and I will tell you this, never allow yourself to be captured. The only reason they will keep you alive is to extract a ransom, or keep as a slave.

Now theres more of them and they're fierce fighters on horse and on foot. Yet I'm under a lot of pressure to negotiate a peace treaty, which I'm going to try and do. If we can come to terms with them, then we can better fight the Mexican bandits down by the Rio Grande."

"Come back tomorrow and I'll give you a letter of introduction to whoever is now running the militia in San Antonio de Bexar along with a letter to the Maverick family who seems to be running things there bout's". "The Texas treasury is pret near broke so the best we can do is maybe cover your expenses, but seeing that you're a carpenter and that young Hays is a surveyor, we'll try and steer as much business you way as possible, as long as you don't get killed. Fair enough"?

Seeing that his audience with Houston was concluded, Henry arose to his full height saying "See ya tomorrow first thing General", then left.

The following day, he returned to the capital building, only to find Sam Houston busy in meetings with arriving delegates, but several sealed letters were placed in Henry's hands by a subordinate and he was sent on his way. Since the was all packed and ready to go he saw no reason to linger, thus departing for San Antonio de Bexar. Things went well on the first two nights; of course a cold camp was in order, since he was in unknown territory. Simply following the trail, heading south westerly, of the settlers that he traveled with from Louisiana, he'd no doubt that he'd catch up with them in several days.

By noon of the fifth day, he'd just crossed the summit of a rise, when he and the wolves saw faint traces of smoke on the horizon. Signaling the wolves to travel ahead to the summit of the next rise of land he followed their trail, finding them stopped and laying doggo close to the ground.

Dismounting just short of the rise and hobbling his horse, he crept up to the top of the rise and followed the wolves' line of sight.

There he saw a horrible sight, for the wagon train of settlers was a smoking ruin, with dead cattle, horses and seemingly every person in the train lying prostrate in the noon day sun. He went back to his saddle to retrieve a spy glass he'd bought back in Nashville, returning to the spot to again survey the ruins. That only made the horror of things worse. All dead they were. After a complete visual survey of the area, he returned to his horse and rode down the hill to the site of carnage. Going from body to body he discovered that each and every one was scalped and mutilated to various degrees. The wagons ransacked and partially burned and many bodies of livestock lay bloated along with the settlers in the heat of the day. He made a mental note of the livestock on the ground concluding that only a few of the horses and cattle were dead, so since the local natives were men of the horse, they must be Comanche, as he'd been told. By the trampled grass he saw he concluded that the raiders were heading due west by his compass reading.

Henry spent the next hour painfully gathering the remains of the settlers and lifting them into the partially burned wagons. Then with the help of his horse he placed the wagons in close proximity to each other prior to setting them on fire. At least the buzzards and other carrion would have the livestock to feed upon, with having to disturb the charred remains of the settlers. As the fire burned, the memories of his family up in Ohio came flooding back with a vengeance. The look on the faces of each of the settlers, men, women and children, the bloated remains, the rictus of death, exactly matched that of his family some years ago. A quiet resolve gradually took hold on Henry as he summoned the wolves to return.

He knelt down and offered a brief prayer for their eternal souls.

As he rode off in the general direction of San Antonio, he mulled over all that he'd seen and concluded that a large war party had descended on the settlers suddenly and cut them down before they had a chance to defend themselves, taking some of the livestock and most of the horses and probably some of the children to use as slaves.

Had he been traveling with them, he most likely would've suffered the same fate. Then he thought of Davy Crockett and what happened at the Alamo and again had he accompanied the Crockett party, the same result. Then he looked skyward as he rode, seeking an answer of sorts, finding none, he then looked forward to San Antonio.

Several days later, he followed a trail that indicated that his destination lay straight ahead. Coming down from the heights and seeing through the trees the settlement of San Antonio de Bexar was coming into view.

As Henry rode into the town, he asked various people as to the location of Sam Maverick, eventually finding someone of assistance. Eventually finding the Maverick residence, he dismounted, secured his mount and went up to the front door. As he climbed the steps to the porch, he noticed a woman sitting by and by who said, "Just what business do you have with us, young man"?

Henry answered, "My name is Henry Jaeger and I've come from President Houston in Austin, with a letter for a certain Sam Maverick in this city". "Well young Mr. Jaeger, I'm Missus Maverick and any business you have with my husband you can conduct with me. For he's away with the militia and Juan Seguin on a Comanche hunt out Uvalde way and I don't expect him back any time soon."

"In the absence of Mr. Maverick, President Houston instructed me that you'll do just as well"!

"If not better young man", she shot back. ""Well take your hat off, and sit have a seat and deliver whatever you have and tell me all you can about what is happening in Austin settlement"! Seeing Chani and Akila sitting at attention nearby she asked, "Are those wolves young man"?

"Oh yes Maam, may I introduce Chani and her brother Akila", with that he snapped his fingers summoning them to his side where they took up their position. "Raised em from pups I did" offered Henry. "And if you'll allow me to let them get your scent, they'll prove to be as loyal to you as they are to me".

Mrs. Maverick slowly nodded her head, then Henry made a small guttural sound and both wolves slowly approached her, taking turns sniffing all around her, imprinting her scent into their brains. As they worked their way around her she asked when it would be alright to pet them

"Not quite yet Mamm, when they're done they'll let me know." Shortly thereafter they both sat at her side, and then proceeded to lie at her feet. "Now Mrs. Maverick you're their friend and they accept you".

"So that means I can pet them and still have an arm left"? "Yes Maam, replied Henry with a smile". At that she took her first tentative attempt at petting the wolves, first one then the other, asking "Their fir is quite thick for this climate and soon the weather will be insufferably hot for them".

Henry then went to his skid and returned with a stiff metal brush saying, "Almost forgot and set about coming out and grooming each of the animals who eventually laid on their backs allowing first Henry and then Mrs. Maverick to perform the ritual.

As they worked on the animals, Henry and Mrs. Maverick started a friendly bond, conversing all along, all through the afternoon with Henry telling her his life's history and his interaction with each and every one. Sam Mavericks wife, while a bit on the abrasive side, could ooze the charm when needed and wheedle out any information she cared for from just about anyone. During the course of the afternoon's extensive narrative, Henry watered his mount and the wolves and returned to his conversation with his host while consuming endless glasses of lemonade.

"And that's about it Mamm"!

"Well, John Coffey Hays is out with my husband and Mr. Seguin after the Comanche and it seems we'll have to await their return together. Your welcome to put up your gear next to Mr. Hay's in the barn along with your critters until they all return."

"Mamm, the barn will do just fine for me and the critters, said Henry with a smile. "You all look like a hungry bunch, so I'll have my darkie Sarah, to whip y'all up some vittles"!

The following day Henry took the wolves and set out for a hunt, returning the following day, with a slain buffalo cow, that his tired horse drug all the way back to town. Mrs. Maverick summoned several people to help Henry skin and render the animal each taking a portion to be smoked and divvied up betwixt them all. Needless to say, the Maverick household was abundant in foodstuffs for quite a while after.

Several days later Juan Seguin returned with just two of his people reporting the area full of Comanche and the rest of the men likely killed. This worried her to no end especially since Seguin was bereft of details, simply saying they all got separated, during the course of events.

Several days later Mary Maverick saw her husband< Jack Hays and the rest ride down the street as casual as could be. As he and Jack Hays rode up to the hitching post, separating from the rest, he yelled out, "Well Mary I'm back"!

Standing in front of her house she replied, "What took ya so long"?

His reply a terse, "Comanche, they're thick as fleas out Uvalde way"?

"Did Seguin and his boys make it back"?

Mary nodded yes, "Two days ago".

Just then Henry emerged from the rear of the Maverick property where he was rendering the buffalo hide in preparation of tanning bellowing, "Well, de well, looks like Jack Hays"!

With that exclamation, Hays bellowed back "Henry Jaeger the big old Injun hunter" and of course Chani and Akila recognizing their masters friend sidled up to Jack for the extensive rubbing of the ears.

"Well Mr. Hays", exclaimed Mary Maverick, "We'll all be eating Buffalo sausage this evening thanks to that young buffalo hunter, so you let him be for the present for he's working' on a buffalo hide wrap to keep me warm next winter.

To keep busy during the interim Henrys skills in carpentry came to the fore and before long he organized weekly hunting parties up in the hills north of town, demonstrating his skills in tracking and bringing down wild game with both the bow and his Beretta rifle at long range.

But almost on a daily basis, he organized parties of men to travel to the same hill country and chop down a variety of trees, segmenting them into useable lumber for use back in San Antonio. All of the usable wagons and horses in town were employed in this effort.

Then months later a large contingent of militia returned to town herding several dozen cattle and approximately a hundred horses along with several children Henry recognized from the settlers he accompanied to Texas, massacred shortly before his arrival. The children were quickly parceled out to various families in town to cleanse, feed and care for.

For the most part they were in very bad shape, still in various states of shock and stupor, but in time most of them recovered quickly.

Of course Jack Hays accompanied the Militia which comprised some forty men from town, commanded by a Henry Karnes, joined by a Captain Wilson, bringing up a force of sixty five from the port of Galvez, on the Gulf of Mexico.

The cattle were apportioned out to all according to previous agreement as well as the horses which were in constant demand. But the problem remained of the horse's usefulness as mounts for humans.

Some of them were accustomed to riders, having been used by the Indians, but none of them were accustomed to the saddle or tack, required by the Texans. The normal manner of breaking in the horses, by hard riding and bucking was too time consuming and a drain upon manpower since nary a day went by where some settler had to see the local doctor for a variety of injuries.

Then one day when Jack and Henry were standing by the corral, with no one ready to jump in, Henry stepped through the fence and approached one of the wild mustangs with a bridle in hand and a small riders blanket in the other. The other horses shied away and at Henry's direction were, let out of the corral into another, leaving Henry and the mustang alone. With hand signs alone and a gentle tone Henry gradually approached the skittish mustang, bit by bit gradually closing the distance between them, until Henry was near enough to the horse to whisper into his ear.

The mustang then shied away for a bit, eventually allowing Henry to once again approach. Within minutes, Henry had the bit in the horse's mouth and the bridle attached. Then with the bridle in hand he led the still skittish mustang around the corral several times, still talking to the horse, then led the animal to the fence where he gently put on the blanket, then walked the horse around the corral whispering in the animals ear until them arrived at the place the saddle was astride the corrals fence.

Ten minutes later the saddle was on the mustang, but Henry still instinctively led the animal around the corral, getting him used to the fact that for the very first time in his life, something was on its back. Back and forth Henry led the horse gently gaining trust with the horse, as he passes a bag of grain hanging by a fence post; he stuck his hand inside removing some of the grain, gradually feeding it to the animal.

Whispering constantly to the animal in soothing tones, Henry eventually mounted the animal slowly for the very first time. By now a small crowd assembled at the corral, each and every one holding their breath as to when the animal would buck the rider off. Several bets between individuals occurred, with the odds running with the animal and against Henry.

Henry sat astride the mustang for what seemed like an eternity, waiting for the animal to make up its mind whether or not Henry was a threat or not.

All the while Henry spoke to the animal softly. Some fifteen minutes later the mustang took its very first steps with Henry on its back, allowing Henry to guide him first one way then another.

Walking around the corral for another few minutes, Henry allowed the animal to become accustomed to carrying a rider on its back and responding to directions. Then, Henry dismounted removing the bridle and saddle and putting it back on the fence. He then marked the animal with some charcoal on its flank to indicate that it had been broken. When Henry climbed through the corral fence he was approached by a smiling Jack Hays saying; "By god Henry, I didn't know that you could do that"?

"Neither did I", said Henry still smiling, glad that he was still intact, for he'd seen just what a bucking bronco could do to a rider.

"Why son, here's five dollars", offered Hays. "What's that for", asked Henry?

"Thinking that you knew what you were doing, I bet a bunch of folks that you wouldn't get bucked off and am twenty five dollars to the good, thanks to you. Doubly important since I'd only nine dollars to my name, beforehand", winced Hays. "And you've never done that before"?

"Nope".

"Just then Sam Maverick moved in having observed the events of the corral saying, "Well son, if'n ya can do that again and again, there's a lot of work ahead of you with those hundred plus mustangs in those other corrals. What do you say to a dollar a head in gentling those horses?

The rest of the day was spent gentling three more horses and identifying them for temporary homes in separate corrals from the others, with Henry handling the gentling of the mustangs and Jack Hays organizing the logistics of those mustangs gentled and apportioning them out to Captain Wilson's men for their return trip to the Port of Galvez.

The rest of the herd once gentled was apportioned to the Texas Militia in San Antonio that went on the Indian raid. All had eagerly chipped in, for now they had reasonably reliable mounts. The task took the better part of three weeks to accomplish with Henry and Jack evenly dividing the precious monies allocated for their task.

As the days and months came and went, a growing influx of settlers and men of fortune drifted into San Antonio de Bexar, seeking whatever presented itself before them either for good or for ill. The rest of 1838 came and went, with Henry accompanying Jack Hays on several surveying trips to the hill country near Austin and in the vicinity of San Antonio de Bexar. Henry quickly learned the discipline of surveying and Jack some of the varying aspects of carpentry along with the native skills of tracking and hunting. During this time the men were inseparable. The clerks at the Land Offices in Austin and San Antonio became very familiar with the sight of Jack Hays and or Henry Jaeger.

As 1839 rolled around, Henry, Jack and the wolves began to become increasingly involved in militia activities. With their other activities taking a back seat to their Rangering. Going out on various forays to seek the Comanche or their sometime allies, the Kiowa, stealing back the livestock, mostly horses, that had been stolen from the settlers. From time to time they came upon some settlers homestead only to be greeted by the dead bodies mutilated by the previous Indian raiders, and would always stop to bury the dead, thus feeding the growing hatred of all the Indians. Here is where Henry and the wolves became of supreme importance; for the other mounted units had to rely upon the friendly Lipan and Tonkawa Indians as scouts, for they also had felt the inhumanity of the Comanche and the Kiowa tribes, being very happy to see them all dead to the last. But since they were Indians they never quite had the total confidence of what had now come to be called Rangers.

Henry and the wolves proved to be excellent trailers riding just a mile ahead of the rest of the group following the trail and the scent of any raining parties, carefully scrutinizing the trail for any signs doubling back or ambush. In this there were no rules except survival. In this conflict there was no room for error.

Each and every time Henry and Jack Hays returned, they came back with horses, the Indians had lost and destroyed whatever braves chose to stay and fight, with few losses of their own, preferring to surround and attack just before sunup while they Indians were at their most vulnerable.

Some of the braves escaped into the brush followed by the women and the children. From time to time some of the white settlers kidnapped and turned into slaves by their captors were set free whenever practicable. Sometimes the slaves had turned native and fought the rangers and had to be killed, nothing to be done about it. Prisoners were never taken for a host of obvious reasons.

It was at this time that all saw a side of Henry Jaeger that was dark and murky. For every brave that he'd killed, he scalped then hung by its feet from the nearest tree to bleed out then rot, just above the height of a horses back quite out of reach from the average four legged carrion, but not the vulture. Each brave would then be gutted, with its entrails hanging down to the ground. The scalps were then nailed to the tree as a warning with Jaeger bellowing into the woods in the native tongue his cognomen and the warning that he was coming to slay every last Comanche and Kiowa that could be found.

Those who escaped being killed by finding deep woods often found other Comanche and Kiowa encampments gradually spread the word of the crazy white man that attacked at dawn with wolves that ate the young.

By this time young Henry was coming well into his own, filling the saddle with a frame well over six feet in height, thickly set with lean, hard muscle and well versed as any Comanche in the art of tracking his fellow man and killing him at short range, by bow or with his bare hands or at long range with his massive Beretta rifle. And as always, Henry Jaeger always left his message.

Of course, various folks viewed this act of overt barbarity from different angles. Some viewed it with distain, while others knowledgeable of the Comanche acts against the settlers saw Henry Jaegers acts as true justice.

Either way Jaeger was given a wide path of tolerance by those in Texas aware of his penchant for Indian suffering.

While away with Jack Hayes in the spring of 1840 down along the Rio Grande river chasing the Mexican bandits and spies operating in the area, twelve chiefs of the Comanche along with a large party of women and children reached San Antonio, to parley with the now President Mirabeau Lamar's agents for the reason of effecting a treaty and a hostage exchange. Soon after they all entered the council house, things quickly got out of hand and an order was given that all the Comanche were to be held prisoner until they showed good faith in the exchange of hostages. The Texians rising to leave the meeting were set upon by one of the chiefs who stabbed a sentry at the door with a knife. In the fight that followed all of the Comanche chiefs were slain inside the meeting house.

The other Indians out in the street wandering about the town were summoned to the council house by the sound of gunfire commencing a desperate fight. When the smoke cleared all of the Comanche warriors that accompanied the chiefs were slain, in the streets as well as the chiefs inside the council house. In the confusion that ensued, three of the Indian women and several of their children were caught in the crossfire and perished.

Seven Texians were killed, all unarmed civilians, were killed by the Comanche in the streets as they fought to leave town.

The surviving Comanche disappeared back to their various encampments vowing revenge. The Texians had to stop encroaching on lands the Comanche considered theirs and withdraw from their perspective and from the Texians perspective the Comanche would have to stop conducting raids on peaceful settlers and stealing their property. Now the Comanche had lived this way for generations and were not about to change their ways. There was no middle ground with the Indians.

Thus from this point on it was clear to all that a state of mortal conflict was in effect that would last until either one or the other parties ceased to exist.

A week later, with all of the Rangers garrisoned at one of the small missions south of town, one of the Comanche Chiefs rode into San Antonio brazenly and dared anyone to fight him. None of the citizens, shop keepers to a man, had any intention of engaging with the savages, suggesting that he seek out the Rangers in the mission south of town. Then he took his warriors to the Ranger encampment with the same challenge, but none of the Rangers wanted anything to do with this individual or his warriors.

After some six hours of standoff the Comanche departed.

In the months that followed, Comanche and Kiowa raids on out laying settlements increased with an accumulation of horses for their remudas.

In early August while Jack Hays and Henry were still chasing the bandits along the Rio Grande with some success's, the largest Comanche war party ever assembled descended down the river valleys from the hill country towards the Texas settlements in force from about six hundred to a thousand mounted warriors. As there were no Ranger units in the area, the Indians, wary of fighting in the various town streets remained on the outskirts of each settlement rounding up an immense herd of hundreds of horses and mules, in each and every town and settlement the encountered. In various areas they stole every bit of clothing and supplies they could reasonably carry advancing as far as Victoria close on to the Gulf of Mexico, driving the inhabitants into boats out into the Gulf waters.

As the various war parties returned northward in a leisurely fashion, the word of this invasion quickly spread to various settlement not touched gathering forces and scouts to chase after them. The war party was eventually caught in a pincer movement as they made their way back to the hill country laden with horses, booty and muskets. While a raiding party of militia caught up with the rear guard of the Comanche they bolted dropping much of their hard earned booty and horses behind and moving with the main body northward only to be faced head on by an inferior force of heavily armed militia. After an extended and savage battle running on for several miles, the battle turned into a route with the Comanche leaving much of the rest of their ill-gotten gains behind.

Most of the warriors escaped along with a number of horses and munitions. But a wounded Mexican agent was left on the field, later admitting under severe duress, that the plot was a product of a plan hatched by the Mexican government in Matamoras across the Rio Grande in Mexico. Now for the very first time the Comanche had muskets and powder and ball in significant numbers. Henry and Jack Hays had their own problems being down in the Rio Grande Valley while the Great Comanche Raid was in process. In pursuit of a trio of bandits numbering around three dozen, comprised of two Mexican and one Anglo leader, engaging in raids of both Mexican and Anglo ranchers and farmers along the Rio Grande Valley. Hayes and Jaeger were accompanied by a dozen Rangers at that time, the compliment including two Mexicans whose hatred of the Mexican government was boundless.

One of the Mexican bandit leaders was named Verial, while his Anglo counterpart was named Owensby. Little by little, Hayes and Jaeger whittled the band down, via Henrys marksmanship at distance. Especially important was the fact that Mexican Army regulars, were now filtering up from the valley, in small units joining up with the raiders, outnumbering Jack Hays group of Rangers. Hayes group would whittle the raiders down to a manageable size only to find that they were constantly reinforced by Mexican Army regulars, once again vastly outnumbering the Ranger unit.

When in a town, the rangers would attack the corrals driving the newly captured livestock into the surrounding bush during the night time. When in the field the Rangers would surround the encampment at some distance, with Henry setting up a hide always some several hundred yards away, in preparation of a long distance shot by the light of the raider's camp fires. At the signal of Henrys second shot the Rangers would take a lone shot at any targets that were in sight then silently disappear into the night. This eventually compelled the raiders to go to cold camps and eventually withdraw back into the protection of the various towns and villages of the Rio Grande valley.

Eventually a small unit of the Mexican Army secretly crossed the Rio Grande from Matamoras in force, working in conjunction with Owensby and Verial's raider to catch Hay's unit in a pincer movement.

Neatly done, during one raid Hay's Rangers pursued the Verial bandits across the Rio Grande back into Mexico, only to find themselves surrounded on all sides on both sides of the river, with no avenue of retreat. Whereupon they found refuge in a deserted Hacienda that had defendable walls just yards away from the river. The Mexican Commander held forth on the Texan side of the river, while the bandits formed a perimeter some three hundred yards distant on the Mexican side. With food and ammunition rapidly drawing down, the Rangers found themselves in a tight spot. As night fall arrived all parties settled down for the evening to await future events.

The Rangers came to agreement that this set of circumstances could not be drawn out for Matamoras was two days ride and no doubt Mexican re-enforcements would be on the way. At the dawn of the next day the Mexican Army commander sent out a rider with a white flag to parley with the Rangers promising good treatment if they would surrender. He returned without commitment from the Rangers. At noon an attack commenced from the Mexican side from the bandits, but the deadly fire from the Rangers beat it back with a dozen bandits lying dead under the blazing sun.

During the rest of the day Henry selected a hide on both sides of the Haciendas walls, sheltering his presence from view of either side. When night fall came both the Mexican Army on the Texas side of the river and the bandit contingent on the Mexican side, built their fires for the long evening ahead secure in the knowledge they were out of range from the Rangers rifle fire. Going from one side of the Hacienda, he employed his expandable spy glass to better see just who were the leaders and gauge the distances involved for a possible shot at someone significant. "Well Henry", said Hays continuing, "Seems we're in quite a pickle"! Continuing on he said, "Those Mexicans have us in a standoff"! Jaeger quietly figuring the distance to the bandits campfires and having placed himself in such a position that any report from his Beretta rifle would be sufficiently muzzled by the building behind him from the Mexican Army's position on the northern side of the river. As he outline his plan to Jack Hays, he planned to fire upon both Owensby and Verial should they be in close proximity with each other, figuring the bandits less likely to be disciplined of both parties and scatter into the night. Then should luck hold and the Mexican Army not be alerted by his firing, go to the Northern wall and do the same with the Mexican Army commander. That accomplished the Rangers could the escape into Mexico and circle around both groups and go back into Texas.

Around Ten PM, by one of the Rangers pocket watch, Henry carefully loaded the Beretta's barrels, placing an extra bit of powder in each charge, to compensate for the estimated distance of the targets. He quietly settled into position, adjusting his breathing and coming into an almost relaxed state. With Jack peering through the spy glass, and the air absolutely still, Henry lifted the big barrels and waited patiently. The distance was estimated at some 500 long paces from their firing position, with Henry and Jack passing the spy glass back and forth between them. Shortly thereafter Jack then saw two figures huddle down by their camp fire in a highly animated conversation, saying "Henry take a look". Sure enough both Owensby and Verial appeared in the spyglass deep in conversation by the light of the campfire. Handing the oculus back to Hays, Henry settled back into firing position saying, "Let's see if we can reach out and touch em a bit"!

Adjusting his elevation he slowly started to squeeze the front trigger, with his forefinger, while readying his middle finger on the aft trigger. Suddenly the Beretta bucked once and then a second time with a loud report. Hays peering into the spyglass quietly exclaimed, "Damn, Henry Jaeger that's the finest shootin' I ever did see", handing the glass to Jaeger, to see his handiwork first hand.

Both Bandit leaders lay slumped over into the camp fire motionless, with their clothes starting to catch fire and bandits going for their horses starting to scatter.

Then they slowly walked to Henry's hide in the north wall of the hacienda, taking position with Hays peering into the spyglass. Apparently the walls of the hacienda did their work well absorbing and reflecting the sound of gunfire southward and away from the small Army contingent across the river with no apparent sound of alarm from the hacienda. While Henry settled in his firing position and reloading his big Beretta, Jack peered through the spyglass and as luck would have it, there about three hundred long paces distant was an Army commander reaching down by the campfire for a cup of coffee and conversing with a subordinate silhouetted by the campfire before them, in their resplendent uniforms.

Henry received the spyglass from Jack, carefully seeing his targets and agreeing with Hays these were the intended targets. Going through his same ritual, he squeezed both triggers and affected the very same result, this time at a much shorter range. Didn't matter now whether or not the Army heard the sound for they all started shooting in every direction, while the Rangers quietly snuck out of the confines of the hacienda and disappeared into the night,

6

The Rangers rode all night in silence, crossing the Rio Grande some ten miles upriver and back into Texas, riding northward until sunrise. Then finding a copse of trees along a small stream, dismounted and watered their horses allowing them to rest. To a man, each was confident of a repeat of the Alamo, only to find that death was cheated just one more time. Sentries were posted and relieved every four hours allowing everyone ample rest including their mounts. There would be enough time to recount the events of the last few days once they were north of the Nueces River, deep into Texas That evening they quietly departed, with Henry and his 'Dawgs' as they'd come to be called riding point. Now was not to the time to have an encounter with anyone, with tired horses and limited food and munitions. A week's worth of traveling was ahead and careful night time travel was ahead before they would enter San Antonio to rest and refit.

The Texas Republic was rife with Mexican Army spies, Mexican Outlaws, Comanche and Kiowa raiders as well as a spate of Anglo robbers and thieves drifting westward. Gradually drifting southward were small groups of Indians of various tribes driven out of the deep south lands of Georgia, Alabama and Mississippi, on their westward Diaspora by the then President Jackson. Cherokees, Kickapoo's, Seminoles, Creeks, Caddo's and Waco's all had a reason to join forces against the Anglos.

When the group drifted into San Antonio, they went their separate ways, until the next summoning. Several days later Henry and Jack Hays had the good fortune to be employed as part of a surveying crew plotting some land two days ride north of San Antonio by Sam Maverick. Both met at his newly constructed General store and were greeted with a several new gifts, for each man was issued on of Sam Colts new .35 Caliber revolvers and five shot carbines.

"Think ya can make good use of these fellas", questioned Maverick as he handed them to the duo? "Courtesy of the Texas Navy", Maverick continued.

"Didn't know Texas had a Navy", asked Hays?

"Well, it's only a couple of sloops, out of Matagorda Bay, but they've seem to have bit the Mex's in the ass a few times, capturing stolen good from our folks at Corpus Christi and taken a few Mexican ships in return," said Maverick.

"Seems that Lamar and the boys have found some money to spend in Austin and that you and Henry here got selected to use be the very first to use these to see if they're any good. We got ten of each to distribute here in San Antonio, along with another ten for Corpus Christi and ten more for Prices boys in Victoria."

Each was issued a holster for the pistol, saddle scabbard for the short barreled five shot Carbine and bullet molds along with three extra cylinders for each weapon and several hundred firing caps, for the new cap and ball weapons.

For the next two days Henry and Jack taught themselves in the care and maintenance of the new weapons and well as test firing then to become accustomed with their use. In addition, each man was issued a newly crafted fifteen inch long single edged Bowie knife, for any close in work with the hostiles.

Now the out manned and out gunned Rangers could truly take on any group superior in numbers on rather different terms, offering a nasty surprise.

Several days later, the group of five men was laying out boundaries for several plots of land north of San Antonio when a hunting party of fifteen Kiowa Indians came upon them.

Only Jack Hays and Henry were armed with their repeating pistols, being a mile away from their encampment where Chani and Akila lay protecting the other hobbled pack mules and supplies. Emerging out of a copse of trees some hundred yards away, the Indians stopped, surveying the group of five Anglo surveyors spread out some two hundred yards, then split up into two groups, charging Henry and his two assistants and Jack and his single assistant simultaneously. Halting some fifty yards away from each party, one of each party dismounted, bringing to each shoulder a smooth bore musket and firing at a target, with the rest firing they're bows and arrows at full gallop. The assistant with Jack Hays was hit with a musket round from one of the Indians, while seven Indians charged at Jack busy dodging arrows. Hays drew his Colt Revolver and carefully selected a target, then started firing. Three braves quickly dropped from their mounts, crashing to the ground, Hays shots finding their target. Quickly switching cylinders on the run, Hays then turned and fired on the remaining four, downing two, before quickly replacing the second empty cylinder with another. Seeing their fellow braves in the dust the other two braves quickly rode away.

As he turned around he saw Henry firing at three departing braves from the group that confronted him. As he came up to Henry he could see that one of the men in his group lay dying with three arrows in his chest, bleeding out rapidly with nothing to be done about it. Several Hundred yards away the remaining Kiowa sat astride their mounts wondering just what had happened for in less than a space of a minute, they had lost over half their number.

Henry then went over to his horse, removing the new .44 caliber Colt Carbine and repeatedly fired at the rider less Kiowa horses, roaming around in the prairie. Ten Horses went down under Henrys fire thus depriving the remaining braves from retrieving valuable mounts. The rest of the horses fled in several directions out of range. Then placing his carbine back into its horse's saddle scabbard, he started to walk around to each of the fallen braves scalping each in turn, disemboweling each in turn and gouging out each braves eyes and discarding them onto the prairie. The supreme insult to each brave, all the while shouting out the old Miami Indian chant for the fallen he'd learned from the Shaman when he was young. For the remaining braves watching what was being done to their fallen braves, this was too much to bear and in unison they commenced to charge Henry and Jacks group. When the charge was finished only one brave lay on the prairie all the rest downed by Jack and Henry's accurate pistol fire. This time it was Hays that approached the wounded brave placing a round in each of his knees, thus making him a lifelong cripple should he survive. Running up to the wounded brave Henry withdrew his now bloody Bowie knife grabbing the wounded braves long hair ready to remove his scalp, but thought better of it, then leaving the remaining brave a long glance at Henry's face with the message in sign language, to remember this day and to remember what the Rangers had just done. With that Jaeger and Hays, gathered up one of the remaining Indian mounts and placed the severely wounded brave on the horses back and gave it's rump a slap, sending it away at the gallop.

Sinking to their knees watching the wounded brave depart, Henry and Jack looked at each other, then at the fourteen mutilated braves and the ten dead horses on the prairie, in wonder. Hays was the first to speak, "Henry Jaeger that was some exhibition we just put on, wasn't it?" Henry replied wearily, "Thank God for Samuel Colt and what rattles around in his head!" That said, all the men loaded up their equipment and the dead and wounded placing them upon the lone pack mule removing two arrows from its saddle noting that just inches remained from the mule joining the departed on the prairie and made their way back to their encampment and the wolves patiently guarding their supplies. After tending to the wounded survivor as best they could, all joined in digging a shallow grave to bury their dead compatriot. The following morning the other wounded man, succumbed to his wounds and joined the other in a shallow grave.

Several days later their task of surveying complete, they made their way back to San Antonio, with Henry Jaeger having secured fourteen Kiowa scalps, hanging unobtrusively from one of the pack mules. By sundown of that same day, the story of the fracas near Leon Springs and the drubbing the Indians received made its way all over town.

Over time Henry Jaeger had made many friends and acquaintances all over town and became a respected person in all things great and small, yet for some this penchant of his, bringing back long haired Indian scalps into town made a number of people uneasy. The story of his coming to pass circulated in some groups and found understanding. Here was an apparently civilized man of many skills at so early an age, with one side of him that most town folk saw, generous, friendly, quiet spoken, polite and rather literate, yet there was this other side, that a few chosen experienced, brazen, brave, unrelenting, and most of all, as bloodthirsty as any one that ever existed. Seemingly driven by some inner force that would surface when needed wreak havoc, and then gradually depart.

Most who viewed Henry Jaeger at his worst, gradually came to be grateful for his existence and had no qualms with his modest eccentricity. But no one understood him like Jack Hays. For the bond between Hays and Jaeger became that of brothers under the same skin. Jack Hays, a man who had grown into being a leader in his own right, and who's opinion was greatly respected by all, felt some ill at ease on the few times when he was compelled to ride out of San Antonio on an expedition without Henry Jaeger at his side. For he knew of all the people in this world, that in a scrape with the enemy, Jaeger would have his back.

In the spring of 1842, Jack Hays was formally made a commander of a Ranger detachment based out of San Antonio de Bexar. Other commanders would come and go over time, but from this moment on, Hays would be in the service of the Republic, with few brief interruptions of service. Since the close of 1841, reports from Texican spies all along the Rio Grande indicated increased military activity on the Mexican side and a possible invasion eminent. Thus in the spring of 1842, General Raphael Velasquez crossed the Rio Grande at Laredo, with a force of some five hundred soldiers, along with two hundred fifty armed vaqueros and a half dozen Caddo Indian scouts.

For several months the citizens of San Antonio had quietly removed much of the stores and anything of value in the town. Just before the Mexicans arrival the citizens burned anything they could not eat or drink hauling what artillery they had to Seguin. John Twohig, a leading merchant, convinced his warehouse would be looted took a powder keg and laid a trail of powder to the rest of his stored gunpowder. Waiting until most of the townsfolk had fled, he watched until the Mexican looters reached his warehouse, and calmly lit the fuse from his cigar, mounting his horse and followed the others out of town. The capitol at Austin had fled to Houston, with rumors of another invasion from Santa Fe circulating.

Vasquez and his small army stayed in San Antonio for several days and finding little of value retired back south to Mexico, with various units of Rangers and militia picking them off one by one as they rode back south.

The units never numbering more than five people moved fast and struck hard. Hays and Jaeger each commanded a unit and each took a heavy toll of the invaders. Once things had settled down and the towns people started to trickle back into both Austin and San Antonio, reconstruction had started, keeping Henry busy in town organizing lumber and construction crews in the town proper, while Hays was busy trying to reorganize a ranger contingent recently authorized by the Government in Austin.

Having little luck, Hays couldn't even muster an extra squad, much less the one hundred fifty men authorized by Austin, for many of the

Rangers who'd been serving for the last two years had become destitute, receiving little in the way of pay or mere maintenance. Losing horses weapons and clothing in the harsh frontier scouting. By the summer of "42", Hays small contingent of Rangers comprised the official army of Texas. Hays unit was constantly on the moved at this time all along the Rio Grande Valley, with constant messages being sent to Austin, informing them of a proclamation by General Adrian Woll who was gathering an even larger force of Mexicans south of the Rio Grande for a second invasion of Texas to reclaim the former province.

With little to stop him, General Woll crossed the Rio Bravo, (Rio Grande) and made his way with a force of Fifteen Hundred soldiers and made his way towards San Antonio de Bexar. The Mexican General had his spies in San Antonio informing him of every move that Jack Hays Ranger unit made. Watching the Laredo road, the route of every invasion since Santa Anna, General Woll out maneuvered Hayes unit by crossing the river west of the Laredo road, traveling north and to the west of San Antonio with a cumbersome little army of mixed infantry, cavalry and light artillery, including numerous supply wagons.

Several days prior to the arrival of General Woll's army, one of his spies, let slip the fact of the invasion while making his own incursion with one of the women of the town, during a physical transaction. Word slowly spread through town of the second invasion, with some leaving and some citizens staying.

Early on foggy September morning, the people awoke to find the town surrounded by Woll's army, with columns of infantry moving down the streets, accompanied by the sounds of the Army band marching in unison and sounds of cannon fire.

Unable to find any signs of the Mexican invasion, Hays and his contingent returned to San Antonio only to find the town completely in the hands of the enemy.

Later in the day a Mexican Army courier was captured by one of Hays Rangers, revealing that General Woll was going to fortify the town and his was part of a larger invasion force soon to come. Hays spent the rest of the day sending dispatches to every militia unit in the Republic then to Austin.

Within days, the various militia units began to quickly form, by the tens and twenties and thirties, with some led by preachers, merchants, doctors and men of every walk of life. From Houston, the port of Galvez, Victoria, Corpus Christi and Austin, units formed and were on the move.

By this time, Hays unit had grown to forty mounted militia and were constantly scouting around the perimeter of the town. Capturing another prisoner they learned of another group of Mexicans numbering some three hundred traveling up the Laredo Road. Being constantly on the move for days on end Hays unit of militia were unable to hunt for food and were perilously close to starving.

For the last few weeks Henry Jaeger and a dozen men were far north of town on a combination hunting and surveying expedition, returning with horse mounted skids of smoked meats and hides, coming across the former trail of General Wolls Invasion army and following it towards San Antonio. Eventually they crossed paths with one of Hays contingent who led them to Hays cold encampment. That night the hungry would at last be fed.

Hays and Jaeger clasped each other in embrasure with Hays blurting out, "Just in the Nick of time Henry"!

The following day they were joined by horsemen led by Caldwell and Morrell. They very day after their arrival, the men sent out yet another scouting force who reported back that a considerable force of Mexican cavalry were in the saddle and on the move. What started out as an almost daily ruse to draw out some horsemen for a little shooting practice, ended in a race to return to the shelter of the Militia encampment at Salado Creek?

The Mexican cavalry was too well trained to pursue the Texans into a trap, pulled up just out of range of the Militia's rifles and remained in formation across the creek some four hundred yards away. Word was sent to General Woll of the situation and directly he started to advance with at least four hundred infantry, several cannon, a party of forty Cherokee Indians and a hundred armed Mexican volunteers from San Antonio. All the while in spite of superiority in mounted soldiers the Mexicans made no effort to scout the flanks of the Texans.

Immediately upon the arrival of the artillery the Mexicans fired canister shot into the trees doing little harm short of spooking the horses, thus opening the conflict. Lowering their elevation, the gunners lowered their elevation, this time firing into the river bank.

When the Mexican infantry began to advance in close formation, the Texas rifles blew through their formations long before the smooth bore muskets of the enemy came into range, firing in endless relays, and then dropping below the river bank to reload. While the Mexicans charged in platoons of fifty at a time, each platoon being cut to ribbons by the accurate fire of the Texans. The Mexicans did attempt a flanking movement, but that was stopped by the contingent of a dozen men with shot guns that hurried to the exposed position, beating back the flanking movement with withering fire leaving scores of dead and wounded on the Salado Creek embankment.

The small band of Cherokees slipping around and approaching amongst the trees was the only enemy group to come close to the Texans. In a vicious hand to hand fight they were beaten back losing most of their warriors along with their leader Chief Cordaway.

For the rest of the day, the Mexicans resumed their frontal attack, by the infantry never once employing the cavalry in a flanking movement. Each charge was halted further away from the Texans encampment, the enemy dead and wounded piling up amongst the trees and the creek embankment.

Around six pm the Mexicans waved the white flag signaling truce and commenced a retreat back to San Antonio. The Mexicans tried to remove as many of the dead and wounded as they could, but several of the Texan marksmen took pot shots at the Mexicans thus ending the attempt.

The next morning all of the wounded that lay on the field of battle succumbed to their injuries and perished. During the afternoon long melee not one Texican was killed and only three received minor injuries.

Later on during the day, Wolls army made preparations to leave San Antonio, with around fifty prisoners including three rangers that were caught short in the early morning hours. For the next several days men began to stream into San Antonio from every point of the compass increasing the number of armed men from the seventy five at Salado Creek to now some five hundred, most of which were on foot.

Those who were mounted joined Hays, Jaeger, Ben McCulloch and others in pursuit of the retreating Mexican Army. General Wolls army made slow but steady progress all the way back to Laredo and beyond, never daring to stop at any time for anything, their wagons laden with wounded officers and everything of value in San Antonio. One by one as the wounded officers succumbed to their wounds; they were discarded on the trail back to Mexico. Flanked by a unit commanded by Hayes on one side and a unit commanded by Jaeger on the other and a third headed up by Ben McCulloch bring up the rear, firing all the time picking off soldiers and riders, one by one all the way back to Laredo. Never a mile went by without a Mexican invader greeting the ground of Texas never to return again to his homeland. Over the course of the invasion well over six hundred Mexican bodies were identified as gracing the soil of Texas.

Several times both Hays and Jaeger made attempts to rescue the Anglo prisoners taken back to Mexico, but rather than give them up they were heavily bound and guarded and wagons full of spoils from San Antonio were emptied along the way and packed full of the Anglo prisoners. Time and again attempts were made by the Texans to get back their prisoners, only to be met with withering fire by the Mexican soldiers.

Henry thought, 'If only they'd fought that hard at Salado Creek, things might've been different. Part of what slowed General Woll's retreat into Mexico was the fact that some two hundred families of native Mexicans in the greater area of San Antonio decided to pull up stakes and accompany him back to Mexico.

Of the native Mexicans who stayed in San Antonio de Bexar, no action of any kind was taken, even though some of them actually took part in the fighting at Salado Creek. A few of which actually continued to fight on with the Rangers, but any feeling of mutual trust and cooperation was gone, with no longer a commingling of Anglo and Spanish surnames on the Ranger muster rolls. As the rear guard of Wolls battered forces forded the Rio Grande, Henry took two final shots from the Beretta at some three hundred long paces distance, both of which were officers in their bright but dusty uniforms. No doubt each considered themselves safe and glad to be back on Mexican soil. A Lieutenant rode up to a Captain saluting, no doubt to report the final wagons crossing when as he began to speak a savage force knocked him from his saddle, while the Captain at that very instant hearing a loud report of a distant gunshot found himself thrown from his own saddle and at the very moment he hit the ground, the sound of the second gunshot was the last thing his ears ever heard. Both Jaeger and Hays, watched the retreating wagon train disappear into the bowels of Mexico wondering as to the fate of the Anglo prisoners. Wanting to pursue them but knowing they and all that were with them were simply played out and in scant condition to continue. They and Ben McCulloch's men would make camp that evening, post pickets, and then start back to San Antonio in the morning. The events of the last week had taken their toll on man and beast and all were secure in the knowledge the Mexicans would not return for the forseeable future.

Upon their return to San Antonio all the men were greeted by the town that set upon them eager to find out what happened to Wolls army and the rest.

For the moment, all the good people had to worry about were the native Indian tribes, principally the Comanche.

As the months moved on to a close of the year 1842, many Texans mourned. For the year had seen two invasions by the Mexican Army contingents, along with various Indian raids.

Many a good man had died and many others would no doubt spend a horrible time in Mexican captivity.

To a man, all considered the scales imbalanced even though they'd fought well. Most all had disbanded and returned to their respective homes for there were crops and livestock to attend to.

In early 1843, John Hays activities were almost exclusively in the service in the service of the Republic and he was now a Captain of the Rangers. Deciding to move north of town a dozen miles he built an encampment for the Ranger attachment, deciding to train and equip his men for the days ahead, with each day spent practicing their horsemanship and marksmanship, until each man was a formidable force. All the while Henry Jaeger was back in San Antonio performing his carpentry functions and organizing monthly critter hunts up country. All over south east Texas bands of Anglos made raiding trips into Mexico, while bands of Mexican bandits did likewise on the north side of the Rio Grande.

Reports that the Mexican Army we're experiencing vast desertions due to the perilous political conditions of their government were both a blessing and a curse. Given the disarray in Mexico politically the odds of a reinvasion seemed distant, yet with all the deserters seemingly ever where many were filtering northward in search of plunder no matter where it lay or just who they might happen to throw in with.

One day late in September or 1843, while Henry was in town he saw Mary Maverick at her husband's General store. While he was selecting supplies he overheard a conversation between Mary and a family that had just given up their homestead on the upper Brazos river region near a Waco Indian territory. Seems the Waco were joined up with disparate elements of Seminole, Creek, and Cree Indians that were part of the Jacksonian Diaspora in the southern states and were over starting to drift south from Arkansas and the western Oklahoma's. Listening with only half a mind, concentrating on the acquisition of supplies, his ears perked up when he heard; "And apparently the Waco's have been taken over by some great big Indian with long red hair, who they say is a Shawnee Indian. Now Mary", asked the other woman, "Have you ever heard of a tribe called the Shawnee? I haven't"! Henry slowly turned to the women, his head roaring with static. Collecting his thoughts, he approached saying, "Pardon me Mamma I don't mean to butt in but would you repeat what you just said about the Red Haired Shawnee Indian "? She then summoned her husband who was at another part of the store. "Here he comes, for he and some mounted volunteers got some of our cattle and darkies back and he has firsthand information from the darkies." Henry and the woman's husband shook hands and exchanged greetings, "Simon Hochner's the name and I'm from Mississippi so what can I do ya fer"? "Tell me if you will, everything you know about the Red Haired Shawnee Indian that's up north of here".

Simon Hochner could see by the intensity of Henry and the slow manner of his questioning, that this information was of vital importance. "A Ranger are ya, well lemme see heah," said Hochner scratching his head. "Round about a few months ago we had a spread on the upper Brazos River in Waco Injun territory and an Injun raid carried off most of our livestock and all five of our darkies. Now I paid good money for those darkies sometime back when we were in Natchez and they was good darkies. Did what they was told and t'wer no problem at all"!

"Now some months later a group of the Texican Mounted Volunteers came through and questioned us to the whereabouts of the Waco village and we told em. So I went along and lo and behold they conducted a raid and there they was my darkies and some of the cattle they stole. Never got back but two of our horses. Well not all the darkies, for several died, as a result of the treatment but two of em remained and were in pretty bad shape. Had to take real good care of em for a few months, but seems they are good as new now."

"Please Mr. Hochner, the Red Haired Shawnee if you will", asked

Henry. "Ahm getting to it young man, now lemme see heah, ah yes the Red Hair. Saw him skedaddle out with the rest of em, Waco's some Seminole, some Cherokee, a real big guy, just as big as you young man. Damn good with a bow and arrow. While the other's jumped on their horses, to make their getaway after the skirmish, this un ran on foot almost as fast as those on horse, into the brush."

"Had long red hair he did, tied in a knot in back with a single red, look like a rooster feather". "Like at tell ya more but I was jus too busy duckin' and shootin'"!

Henry ready to ask more questions, "But wait, seems this guy was a leader, and the funniest thing, yelled out in English as he ran away. "The Militia chased em alla way to the edge of the bush then pulled up. Goin into the bush after em way just plain crazy."

"How many of them escaped Mr. Hochner", asked Henry?

"Hard at say, fer as I said I was busy shootin' an duckin', but I imagine they was about thirty or so that escaped. But I imagine they'll be back cause, we spent the night at their camp and lit out the next mornin', leaving their camp mostly intact. No one ever thought about firin' the camp as we left. Reckon we should of though", Hochner mused as an afterthought.

His eyes lit up as he finished, "Some of even had muskets and shot guns". But we pulled up stakes leaving a damn good log cabin and barn we built. No use stayin' an getting kilt, so we're gonna head for Val Verde and start over. Maybe we'll be lucky there".

Hochner then gave Henry detailed instructions as to the location of his old spread on the upper Brazos and of the Waco encampment some three miles away. Thanking the man and his wife as they departed, Henry then turned to Mary Maverick, who was nearby and heard everything. Knowing Henrys story of his parents death and his journey from that point on she said, "Your goin' after em aren't ya"!

Henry staring at the floor with both fists clenched answered, "How many big Red Haired Shawnee Indians could there be"? He then returned the supplies he originally came after, adjusting his shopping to lead shot, powder and all the accoutrement one would need for an extended stay in the wild.

As he left the store, Mrs. Maverick yelled out, "Ya come back in one piece, ya hear"?

For the rest of the day and the next, Henry prepared his kit and his weapons for a long time out on the prairie. Checking that all was waterproofed, cutting new skid poles that could double as a small tee pee frame. Saddle, tack, dried pemmican, oats, water carriers and new camouflaged buckskins. During the course of the last invasion by General Woll, Henry acquired one of the new five shot repeating Colt .12 gauge shotguns from a fallen ranger at Salado Creek who wouldn't be needing it any more. That evening he brushed and combed out the wolves as a signal for what was to come.

He then recalled what some roving actor said in one of the town's Cantina's several months back prior to General Wolls invasion. Something about a playwright that lived a long time ago called Shakespeare, telling a story about an English king, in France, badly outnumbered just prior to battle, who said, "Cry Havoc and let loose the dogs of war"! Tears came to Henry's eyes as he once again recalled the carnage at Cheviot Township, seeing the empty, lifeless look of his loved ones gone forever before their time.

There was much indeed to atone for by the hostiles, all of the hostiles. He then rose to a kneeling position besides the wolves, who rose with him in unison, them making the sign of the cross, remembering what his mother taught him as a child every night before he went to bed, he silently mouthed, "And if I should die before I wake,............I pray to Lord my soul to take,...........but not before my task is done"! As he reopened his eyes, both Chani and Akila growled, and then howled. For they too were ready for what lay ahead.

The next morning Henry rode out of San Antonio da Bexar, with Chani and Akila flanking him on the northeastern road to Austin. Days later he passed through Austin settlement during midday. Several of the Texas Militia he knew, called out to him in greeting as he rode through the township, but he seemed not to hear or recognize them riding on without a word.

A day out of Austin he decided to spend the rest of the way in a cold camp each night. No use letting anyone know that he was on the way. Two days later he came upon a lone farm that had been recently burned to the ground, finding several arrows in the brush hidden from view, one with distinctive Waco Indian markings, with the other of the old memorable markings of the Shawnee. He breathed a silent 'thank you' to the eternal for his long search was about to be terminated. His unfinished business was soon at hand.

Later in the day he arrived at the sacked remnants of the Hochner place, the cabin and the barn still mostly intact. He then unleashed the skid and its contents from his saddle and remounted following the trail of the Waco raiders for several miles before turning back to the Hochner place for the night. The trail indicated the Indians were in no hurry to return to their encampment and the direction they were traveling was in line with the directions given by Hochner, indicating their camp was a few miles away, northwest of the Hochner place.

Winter was apparently arriving early this year, as cold weather was upon them all, so Henry decided to make camp at the old Hochner place for the night planning his methods of attack. He built a fire in the fireplace and settled down for the evening.

The next day Henry embarked towards his destination, the wolves once again taking up their position on either side of Henry. Ever alert were all of his senses, sniffing the air, reading the trail, he kept to the edges of visibility, always skirting around an open field, rather than crossing it, eventually rediscovering their trail, taking the long indirect route, for he was in no hurry. His prey became lax in their retreat, moving with the certainty of one not fearing retribution. Then by noon, he smelled the camp fires as he was to mount a rise in the land. Dismounting, Henry and the wolves crept up the rise, to find the Waco encampment a flurry of activity, some three hundred yards away across an open field that appeared to be some six hundred yards in length.

Six head of cattle stood peacefully grazing in a makeshift corral, while the entire village set to processing two cows that had been slaughtered.

Henry pulled out his spy glass to get a better view, scanning from his position down wind and deep into the tree line, the camp, swinging from one group of people to the next searching, searching for the one, the Red Hair. A mélange of Tee Pees and Wikiups marked the different elements of tribes assembled. As best as Henry could determine, some three dozen men, women and children comprised of several tribes that made up the encampment. Of that, perhaps twenty of them were braves. These were the ones he would contend with. Just then three braves emerged from a Wikiup shelter and there they were.

The Red Hair and his two surviving Shawnee braves. As they moved through the encampment they appeared to issue orders to the rest as it appeared they were the ones who gave the orders. Coming upon a small group that appeared to be Waco Indian natives, working on smoking the meat of one of the cattle, the Red Hair took some already cooked meat from one of the racks, prompting a response from one of the Waco Indians.

Henry couldn't hear what was said, but was surprised when the Red Hair suddenly pulled a knife and fell upon the hapless Waco stabbing him repeatedly. Then when a squaw came out of her Tee Pee and saw the brave fallen upon the ground, apparently her man, she screeched aloud and ran towards the Red Hair in anger only to meet her death at the point of his blade, silencing her at once. This action stopped all activity for a moment, with the Red Hair, barking out some orders, cowering all the rest to get back to work.

Henry while viewing the recent events, thought briefly, 'One less to worry about', then it occurred to him that perhaps the Shawnee did not have a unified group at their disposal. Gradually circling around the field to be closer to its encampment, Henry and the wolves positioned themselves just out of sight some thirty yards into the woods. Waiting for an opportunity, any opportunity. With only the bow and a quiver of arrows, his knife and the wolves, Henry waited and waited. His patience was rewarded about an hour later when one of the braves entered the woods to relieve himself, loosening his drawstrings of his winter chaps and squatted on the ground. Putting an arrow into his bow, Henry gradually took careful aim and let the arrow fly, finding its target some fifteen yards away, right into the braves throat, stifling any ability to cry out. Henry then ran to the thrashing brave and drawing his knife, slit the brave's throat, careful to avoid the gushing blood that spewed forth. Removing the arrow, and cleaning it from the braves blood in the grass he placed it back into his quiver and drug the dead brave away deeper into the brush, covering it with debris from the forest floor. He looked at the sky noting the position of the sun noting that perhaps he had three more hours of sunlight left in the day. If the gods were favorable, perhaps the encampment would send a few braves out to look for their errant brave. Sure enough, about a half hour later, three Cherokee Braves entered the woods, silent at first, searching for their fellow brave. Not finding him, they proceeded deeper into the woods after a while calling out his name as they searched. Fortunately for Henry, they passed right by where Henry had covered up his body with brush, without discovering him.

Trailing them on a parallel course, keeping them ever in his sight, Henry waited, until they were about a quarter mile away from the encampment, where the ground sunk away into a wide gully. At that he sent Chani, to his left with the hand motion to attack for the throat, and Akila to the right, to attack the brave in the very same manner. When the wolves were in position, Henry drew an arrow from the quiver, carefully placing it in his bow, taking careful aim, waiting, waiting, until the brave started to turn around. As the brave finalized his turn he was greeted by the arrival of Henry's arrow that plunged straight into his Adams Apple, severing his spinal column, trying to speak but sinking to his knees in breathless agony.

At that very moment the brave several yards to his left saw Henry's arrow plunge into his fellow braves throat but was unable to respond due to Akila's fangs plunging deep into his throat, choking off any possibility of sound, by its relentless back and forth chewing of his victim. Chani's target met the same fate at that very same instant. Again Henry, ran up to his target, still alive but just barely, removed his arrow, looked deeply into his terrified eyes as he pulled his big Bowie knife from its scabbard, and slowly cut the braves throat, again mindful of the gushing blood that gushed forth the inner essence.

Both Chani and Akila were still chewing on the throats of their lifeless prey, a brief reminder of their feral origins. Henry then approached each in turn with a low whistle, signaling the end. As the wolves stood watch at the top of the gully, Henry disposed of the three hapless victims in the same manner as the other. Buried in the brush of dead leaves and branches ready fodder for the carrion in the cold days to come. The time for scalps may come later, but for the moment his day's work was finished, for the sun was going down on the horizon. As Henry and the wolves made their way back around the clearing, back to his horse and the skid, he felt the first flakes of snow of the season.

The snow was a good omen, for it would cover any proof of his presence, for the time needed for Henry to complete his task. He would withdraw to a pre-selected spot a mile away, deep into the forest; make camp and a fire within his portable Tee Pee, whose poles doubled for the skids that carried his supplies. Luck was with him thus far and perhaps the three missing braves would be considered as deserters to Red Hair's group.

Around mid-morning of the following day, Henry arrived at the very same spot across the clearing from the hostile's encampment, to be greeted by signs of multiple foot prints in the light dusting of snow that arrived the previous evening. Apparently the inhabitants of the village were on a search for the missing braves and had scoured the immediate area for them finding nothing. As he pulled his spy glass out of his rucksack he viewed the village which appeared to be in a state of confusion. He waited and watched the activity of the village. If they appeared to be on the move, he would be compelled to act immediately, but after a while they appeared to settle down, apparently concluding those missing were simply deserters, fed up with the domination of the Red Hair and his two braves.

Then Henry commenced to construct two different shooting positions, or hides, from which to make his moves later on in the day, or the next.

Seeing that no attempt to deconstruct their Tee Pees and that all the horses of the hostiles were still in place, Henry was fairly certain, that all would be in place the following day. For they were still busy smoking the beef gleaned from the cattle and tanning the hides, all which would at least take several days to complete. Then perhaps they would be on the move. All that day he watched their movements especially that of the Red Hair and his two companions. Apparently no alarm was evident, which portended as a good omen for Henry's plans the following day. Later on in the afternoon, it started to snow once again, which again was a good omen, obliterating any sign of Henry's presence. The following morning Henry made certain that he arrived at just before sunup, hiding his horse in a hollow some fifty yard away from his first hide. With Akila and Chani flanking him at the ready, Henry settled in pulling out his spy glass surveying the area and seeing no activity went to work charging his Beretta long barrel with great care, whispering to the piece as if it were a sentient being rather than an instrument of long range death.

Now usually Indian tribes had dogs as part of their retinue in any village, to alert them to the presence of intruders, yet Henry found it strange that there were no dogs of any kind at this particular time placing them at a distinct disadvantage. Perhaps the dogs had been previously eaten, for they would never have left on their own, the villagers being a constant source of easy food, for their ever present scrutiny.

The first to arise were always the squaws, stoking the fires and getting the camp ready for the day, feeding the children, and then making certain that all was in readiness for the braves upon their awakening.

All had full bellies by this time, making them reasonably content and therefore somewhat lax regarding their environment. 'Good', thought Henry, waiting patiently for the events to unfold.

Just as the sun, first peeked over the horizon the first brave emerged from his wigwam, a Cherokee, by the look of it and walked over to the fire reaching for a piece of freshly smoked beef from a squaw. Eating and stretching as if there were no cares in the world. Then one by one various braves emerged for the day, commencing the same ritual. Six braves out and about with the rest still in their Huts and no sign of the Shawnee. Suddenly Henry froze with the feeling of unease. What if the Shawnee had not gone to sleep with the rest, waiting and watching? Henry's heart began to race as he rose up from his hide, and stepped back away from the Beretta, ever alert.

He looked to Chani and Akila for any signs of unease and they were silent. Still, there was always that feeling, difficult to describe or quantify. The air was absolutely still and cold. Ideal for a long distance shoot.

Looking slowly around for any signs of ambush, Henry found none. All was still. No birds chirping. No sound of the wind moving, with only the sound of his heart beating a staccato drumbeat.

Just to be sure, he positioned Akila some twenty yards away on one side and Chani an equal distance on the other sensing and waiting for his signal. Then he returned to his original hide, resuming his visual and calming down his heart beat for what lay ahead. He had to calm his uncertainty, concentrating on what was in front of him completely, for this was too important and he had come too far for this event to fail. His trust in the senses and the loyalty of Akila and Chani was essential. They'd never failed him yet and their eternal bond with each other was absolute.

Gradually Henry felt a calm come over him, as he once again reached for his spy glass to survey the encampment. Minutes later he recognized one of the Shawnee, emerge from a Wikiup and then a second and finally the large Red Hair.

As the trio approached the campfire they barked out something to one of the squaws indicating they wanted food right away. The squaw quietly complied as they all squatted down in front of the fire for warmth.

Henry quietly put down his spyglass without taking his eyes from the Shawnee. He pulled both hammers into full cocked position slowly grasping his fingers on both of the triggers of the Big Beretta. With his middle finger slowly pulling on the rear trigger activating the right barrel and the forefinger pulling on the front trigger, thus engaging the left barrel, seemingly independent of each other, the right barrel was the first to speak, sending its message down range towards its target, racing ahead of the sound it made.

As the round left the barrel, one of the Shawnee moved behind the other, just as the first ball arrived, passing right through the lungs of the Shawnee without obstruction and out the back finding a home through the jaw of the second Shawnee, knocking both of them over. As they both tumbled over the sound of the first ball arrived, prompting the Red Hair, to jump up just as the second ball arrived, slamming right into his hip, spinning him right around and to the ground with a look of amazement.

Red Hair looked over to his two braves only to find that one of them was bleeding out rapidly through the lungs gasping for every breath, while the other was all splayed out in the snow, his face an unrecognizable mess, jerking about for several moments before laying still.

Trying to move and finding that over half his body wasn't responding to his minds commands, Red Hair fought to gain his feet under him, constantly failing in the process. As he looked about seeing the camp in complete confusion, he looked around, crawling frantically for any cover available. Finding a log several yards away, he crawled behind it only to discover that a pain, greater than that he'd ever known was gradually taking over. He went through a quick evaluation of his condition, only to find that his entire right side was completely immobile thus useless.

Just then he heard the sounds of a horse approaching, then gunfire.

Peering over the log seeing a single rider quickly dismounting firing an odd looking scatter gun repeatedly seeing several braves fall one by one as their discharges found a home. Then the rider, now afoot, pulled a pistol, carefully taking aim and firing again many times, with still more braves falling before a hail of gunfire.

It had been a long time since Red Hair felt fear seeing two wolves attacking two other braves with their jaws firmly clamped around their throats, chewing repeatedly.

All the squaws had gathered their children fleeing for the shelter of the nearby woods, during the melee, screaming in terror. Then silence, except for the occasional moaning of the wounded warriors, soon to depart this world.

The rider, dressed in buckskin from head to toe, with a large white, wide brimmed hat, casually reloaded his revolver as he passed through the encampment. He whistled, signaling the wolves to leave their prey and return to side. Shivering in fear were two lone braves, one being the old man of the encampment with the other, a Seminole, signaling in sign language their surrender and asking for mercy.

The buckskin rider motioned for them to lie on the ground, face down with their arms out and their palms up and not to move, while each of the wolves stood guard, growling. Then the buckskin rider went through each or the remaining wounded, slitting the throats of each with his big Bowie knife, while holding his hand held firearm with his other hand, leaving just Red Hair, lying behind the log.

In great pain, Red Hair tried to gain his feet only to have the pain drag him back to the ground, with a thud. In his right hand he withdrew his knife, taken many years ago from one of the settlers he'd slaughtered back in Ohio. His mouth drawn in a grimacing hatred greeted Henry Jaeger as he slowly approached.

Hunkering down some yards away Henry said, "I'll bet you never thought you'd see me again, Mr. Red Hair of the Shawnee, did ya"?

Red Hair remained silent, twisting the knife in his hand watching this white man very carefully waiting for moment of weakness that would never arrive.

"That's my father's knife in your hands, the one you stole from him when you massacred my family up in Ohio long ago. I hope you don't have any plans for it, for you're about to give it back"!

Again, Red Hair remained silent, thinking, remembering the incident long past of the Miami Indian village and the young boy that forced him to retreat. Henry suddenly got to his feet going back to his mount, retrieving the big Beretta rifle and bringing it back to the Red Hair.

The look on Red Hairs face confirmed his thoughts, still saying nothing, then he heard Henry say, "Just wanted you to know, the last time we met, when I was just a boy, this rifle was as empty as it is now and it was I that chased you and the others all over Indiana and Ohio and I that killed your other three Shawnee, when I was just a boy"!

"Now I know you know how to speak English, so ya might as well speak your peace, and say what you will."

Henry returned to his horse sheathing the Beretta, all the while with his eyes on the Red Hair. On his way back, he summoned Chani to his side, positioning her to a place five yards distant to stand guard on the Red Hair.

Since lead shot was a very valuable commodity in Texas at the time, many hunters were accustomed to retrieving their shot whenever practicable, so Henry, as was his custom, went around to each Indian, retrieving the ball and in the process, disemboweled each brave, leaving its entrails laying in the snow. When he came to the dead Shawnee, he did the same and then almost as an afterthought, slowly scalped each one of the Shawnee in silence, his eyes ever on the Red Hair.

"'Remind you of anything", Henry asked as he worked. "Of course you know this what you did to my family and this is what's going to happen to you", he added. "But not right away". Just then the Red Hair, made a mighty lunge at Henry, now only several yards away, but was intercepted by Chain in mid lunge who clamped her jaws on the Red Hairs knife arm, with such force as to break several bones in the large man's arm dislodging the knife in his hand.

Then she picked up the knife by the handle and took it over to Henry before returning her attention back to the Red Hair. Henry looked at his father's hunting knife that was at least as old as the Beretta, passed on from generation to generation in his family. Then he drew his Colt revolver and shot a ball in each of Red Hairs knees, causing a great outcry of pain. "That ought settle you down for a while", said Henry who went to his saddle, withdrawing his lasso. With only one limb operable, the Red Hair ceased to be a danger any more, still his eyes exuded a deep undying hatred for Henry. As he approached the Red Hair, Henry drew his weapon and pistol whipped the big brave, momentarily stunning him enough to rope both of his legs together by the ankles, then ran back to his horse, leaping into the saddle, securing the rope around the pommel, and kicking the big Appaloosa into motion, dragging the hapless Indian several times around the field, finally stopping at the nearest tree near the encampment, tossing the rope over a stout limb and backing up his horse, until the Shawnee, was hanging over the ground upside down, completely unconscious with his arms hanging limply towards the ground.

By this time most all of the squaws and children of the village gradually returned, to watch this white man wreak havoc with their former Shawnee tormentors, standing meekly in awe and wonder. Clearly the White Man's anger had little to do with them. If anything he was their savior.

Seeing them gathered, by the edge of the village, he signaled Akila and Chani to his side and motioned to all the survivors to come forward and sit on the ground. For the next several minutes they communicated in sign language back and forth, each understanding that neither was a threat to the other. Then one of the other women slowly stood up and finding a stout branch went over to pick it up and went over to the Red Hair taking a mighty whack at him. Then offered it to another, who in turn, did the same until every woman in the village had taken several turns, then they offered the branch to the old man, who looked to Henry for permission and seeing Henry's head nod, performed the very same function, with a bit more force. When the second surviving Indian had a few whacks at the Shawnee, Henry signaled a halt, taking the branch and breaking it in two and tossing it away, indicating all to sit and observe.

Cutting off the remaining clothes that Red Hair had, he commenced to slowly walk around Red Hair, whispering to him for the next hour, and with each circuit made a long slice out of his skin, adding to the pain of the now conscious Shawnee. Eventually an ear would find its way to the ground, then the other. Then his nose, would succumb to gravity, slowly blood was finding its way to the ground, but not so much to be quickly fatal. All of the villagers knew that what the Red Hair was experiencing was not one whit less than what Red Hair and others had dealt out to those captured. This white man knew of the Indian way.

Finally they all watched in awe, as Henry recreated the old Miami Indian death dance he'd learned long ago from the Miami Shaman, when he was young. When Henry completed the ritual, they asked, by signing, when the Red Hair was to be scalped. Henry thought a moment, shook his head and indicated for them to gather firewood and build a fire just below where the Shawnee hung. This done, one of the squaws brought

Henry a burning piece of wood, with a nod, understanding what came next, then returned to the others.

Henry then approached the inverted Shawnee, looking straight into his now bleary eyes, saying, "As you travel to that special place, know that Henry Jaeger is the very last thing you will ever see"! At that, he placed the burning wood in the pile beneath and watched as it ignited the rest, ever staying in view of the Shawnee. As the fire grew, the Shawnee's long hair started to ignite. Holding his silence as long as he could, for to cry out would indicate weakness, a loud shout of pain left his lungs at last, the women and children cheering aloud at that exclamation.

Henry thought, 'Well it's gonna cost me a good rope possibly, but it's worth it'. As the Shawnee burned, Henry felt nothing. No elation, no joy, no sorrow, no guilt. Nothing other than the task of putting down a rabid animal.

Minutes later, both Chani and Akila started to howl, indicating that the Shawnees spirit had left the body. The squaws then approached to blanket the fire with snow then climbing up the tree to retrieve Henry's rope taking it to him with their silent thanks.

Henry then mounted his horse, viewing for the very last time the charred remains of the Red Hair, nodding to all the surviving villagers, then rode off with the wolves at his heels, disappearing into the trees.

7

A week later, Henry and his small entourage, rode into Austin to report on his activities with the Waco on the upper Brazos River, to the government. He made the acquaintance of a certain Sam Walker, an ex-military type from the Florida territory, who served fighting the Seminoles in that region. Unknown to Henry he'd been in Texas for some time attached to other mounted units of the Texas Militia. Both seemed to hit it off with each other from the start and since both were heading towards San Antonio de Bexar, they decided to throw in with each other. Once Chani and Akila imprinted Walkers scent it was like he was one of the family.

When they arrived in San Antonio together, it was like they had been lifelong friends. Walker had recently been armed with one of the Colt five shot revolvers as was most of the official Ranger force by now and was quickly taken to school by Jaeger in its care and keeping. Walker marveled at the five shot revolving cylinder Colt carbine, as well as the ever so rare five shot, Colt revolving cylinder scatter gun. When Henry showed him the dual barrel Beretta flintlock rifle, in its scabbard and related its one hundred fifty year old provenance, Walker exclaimed, "Why son, you're walking death"!

When they arrived back in San Antonio, they checked in with the Ranger unit and went their separate ways, with Walker leading a squad of mounted Militia to find R. A. Gillespie, as they were on the hunt for a Comanche hostiles operating out of the Llano River region.

For the first time in a very long time Henry was at odds with himself. His family finally avenged, with nothing apparently to do in the form of Rangering, Carpentry or Surveying, he was able to relax. For the next week he did pretty much nothing of consequence. How many times can one groom your horse, the wolves and clean ones firearms. Somehow hunting and killing the hostiles had lost its allure. He could organize a hunt for game, but even that had lost its luster.

As the year came to an end, it appeared that Texas was in for a brief respite from both the Mexicans and the Comanche. For internal politics in Mexico meant the Mexican Army units were busy quarreling with each other, or chasing after Comanche raids that had somehow shifted to Northern Mexico, devastating entire areas. Further, Jack Hays had been successful in recruiting a group of "Tejano's", or Mexican spies that had an ax to grind with the current Mexican political establishment and the Army. For the very first time the Republic of Texas had reliable information on everything that was happening south of the Rio Grande.

By this time several newspapers had sprung up in San Antonio, Austin, Corpus Christi and Laredo townships. With local folks getting a combination of local news and more distant reports, albeit months late, of events in other places. Apparently Santa Anna was forced out of office, and those vying to succeed him tore the nation apart with civil strife. Thus plans for the Reconquista of Texas were put on the shelf for the time being.

The Comanche raids into Northern Mexico were mostly after horses, to be taken back to the Texas frontier. Upon occasion, they would capture small children of the Anglo settlers as either hostages or slaves, bartering them to other Comanche bands they encountered in trade for either goods or horses. This was the period known as, "The Long Quiet".

Jack Hayes was kept busy trying to keep the Ranger Units together, fighting for funds in Austin, with which to equip and sustain the effort.

The influx of people that emigrated to Texas in 1845, gradually shifted from that of farmers, to that of the professions, doctors, teachers, lawyers and the like. People with some educational credentials. Those that arrived from the Southern States brought whatever slaves they had. Thus providing free workmen and women to get things up and running.

Late in the summer of 1845, General Zachary Taylor received orders to proceed, in force first to New Orleans, thence to Texas landing at Corpus Christi accompanied by some twelve hundred troops, comprised of Infantry and mounted Dragoons. Accompanying him were an extraordinary grouping of officers trained in the most current battle tactics, at the US Military Academy at West Point. Spit and polish types like George Gordon Meade and George B. McClellan, later to achieve command during the Civil War. While there, at Corpus Christi, other groups including those militia groups from Louisiana, Mississippi and Texas began to arrive at the Federal encampment.

By April of that year General Taylor relented in allowing Texas to send a mounted Ranger unit, Commanded by Brevet Major John Coffee Hays, thus being mustered into Federal Service and receiving their first regular pay.

By early in 1846 the Republic of Texas had been absorbed into the United States and had to be protected from the conflict everyone knew was coming and long overdue.

Sam Walker had by now been in the service of the Rangers for several years and having served in the US Military was well versed in the various logistics problems that would confront any military unit. By April he received his Commission as a Brevet Captain in the Texas Mounted Rangers forming a command and with drawing a number of revolvers, carbines and the accompanying accessories from the Armory in Austin, issuing them to selected people, thus moving south to join General Taylor's command at Corpus Christi, along with several Mounted Ranger units.

Since all of these were experienced horsemen, fighting the Comanche, their lot would principally be as the eyes and ears of the regular army, scouting units or spies and as reliable couriers between various units and commands.

In the fall of 1845, while other Mounted Ranger units were in the process of forming up to join General Taylor's forces in Corpus Christi, various Comanche bands started roaming the areas around the upper San Saba river, raiding small settlements primarily for horses, cattle, women and small children hostages that could be traded or sold to Comanchero's, for firearms or a variety of goods. Henry was given command of a unit of eleven men, by Jack Hayes with orders to try and find almost a dozen women and children and return them to their families.

Each man supplied his own mount and musket and was further issued a new Colt Revolver and adequate supplies for approximately thirty days.

Henry was supplied with one hundred US Dollars for any supplies past that.

His unit was the only force in all of Texas, responsible for the entire frontier, while all the other men were heading towards Corpus Christi to join up with General Taylor.

For months on end Henry's small unit trailed the various Comanche bands in western Texas, with Henry being taken to school by the Comanche in the art of tracking. On several occasions they came upon Comanchero traders, and being half breed Indian and Mexican, found evidence of prior occupancy by the Anglo hostages. On one occasion a fight broke out between the parties with the Comanchero survivor being compelled to reveal to whom the women and children were sold to and where. Since the survivor was badly injured, all his possessions were confiscated by the Rangers and he was left to his own devices without food or water to perish.

Comanchero traders were usually equipped with several wagons along with the appropriate horses and supplies to trade with the Indians. Thus equipped Henry's unit was able continue at some extended length. Each day, with Henry riding point, his unit pursued the trail, with Henry rapidly catching on to the various tricks the Comanche of West Texas used to divert his attention.

Encountering several small bands of Comanche, from time to time, they scouted their encampments at a distance, using Henry's spy glass, then attacking the encampment early just after the sunrise, always with the sun at their back. Killing all the braves and taking any horses available and leaving the women and children to their own devices.

When asked by one of the new Rangers if they didn't have some responsibility towards the squaws and their children, Henry turned and replied; "When Anglo women and children are captured by the 'Comanch', they are treated as badly by the 'Comanch' women as the men. Life is hard son and they brought this on to themselves. Just make it a point never to find yourself captured by the 'Comanch', for you'll wish for death"!

A month later this warning took hold by one and all, when Henry came back to camp after seeing an Indian encampment some five miles away.

Leaving three men back at camp to watch the livestock, Henry took the rest in the dark of night, to reconnoiter the Indian encampment. Being up on a mesa about a mile away and downwind from the encampment, he counted through his spyglass, thanks to a full moon that illuminated everything, about thirty Indian braves and even more important several dogs that were in camp. The presence of dogs was a problem for if this wasn't handled just right the dogs would alert the camp to the presence of intruders removing the element of surprise.

Seeing the encampment was in a long valley, he instructed three of the Rangers to slowly and carefully make their way to a choke point at the far end of the valley, several miles from the Indian encampment, to wait for Henry and the others to drive any survivors their way. While Henry would divide the remainder into two different groups attacking out of the east with the sun at their backs as they rode through the village. Of course Chani and Akila would handle the Indian dogs as they rode through.

Each group made their way carefully to their appointed positions to await the sunrise. Henry, leading one of the groups thought while he was waiting, that hunting men and herding them towards a choke point, wasn't much different than hunting any herd of beasts, especially early in the morning when their senses weren't at their keenest. Awaiting the exact moment when the sun would rise in the east over the hills at Henry's back, was one of the Rangers at the far western choke point down at the far end of the valley, equipped with a small mirror, the kind that men took when a field, to use for shaving.

The very moment the sun was able to reflect sufficient sunlight to blind the enemy, was the exact moment to flash a single brief reflective signal for other two groups to advance. With Henry at the center flanked by Chani and Akila, then flanked by the other two groups of Rangers, a brief flash of light occurred.

Both groups moved out at a deliberate trot, each some fifty yards away from the other.

After a while, sensing no alarm from the encampment, both groups accelerated, to a canter.

Seeing still no apparent alarm from the village now with movement detected by the Rangers, both groups, accelerated to a modest gallop, drawing their charged pistols, with one hand and grasping the horse's reins with the other. Now some several hundred yards distant from the camp, one of the dogs sensed an alarm,

Turning its head towards the advancing group and began to bark an alarm. One by one several of the braves turned their heads towards the morning sun, seeing nothing unusual, until, just a hundred yards away, the Rangers now accelerated to a full gallop.

At around forty yards distant the charging Rangers opened fire, each Ranger firing at will at each target that presented itself, as they made their initial charge through the camp. Coming to a halt some fifty yards away from the encampment, each Ranger quickly removed an empty cylinder and exchanged it with another. When all completed this in the space of less than fifteen seconds, Henry gave the signal to charge once again. This time the Rangers engaged in a weaving pattern as they galloped closing with the enemy, since the Comanche were now awake and armed firing what weapons they had at hand. Making their second pass through the village, as was the first, each Ranger's shot found a target, killing some instantly while wounding others. Pulling up their horses for the final time each Ranger recharged their pistols with fresh cylinders, for the final time.

Now each Ranger fired their muskets at whatever braves foolish enough to remain, while a dozen others had gained their mounts and headed away from the village westward and towards the chokepoint.

Slowly Henry's two groups approached the village and its survivors in a partial encirclement, noting the presence of four dogs lying prostrate with their throats ripped out while Chani and Akika made short work of two remaining braves unable to find a horse.

Henry whistled for the wolves to return to his side, noting the dust cloud of the remaining Comanche braves riding towards the choke-point down the valley. A minute later he and the others heard gunfire coming from that very direction. Counting the shots and noting that fifteen had been reached, then silence. They waited. Minutes later several, Comanche squaws emerged from their tee pees, each with a bound female Anglo hostage held tightly with a knife at their throat. Several more emerged with a small child also bound with a knife at its throat. As Henry looked at each Comanche squaw, he saw both looks of terror and defiance in their eyes.

Minutes passed with neither party speaking a word, and then Henry slowly dismounted with the plan to speak in sign language to the squaws, to plead with them for their hostage's lives. Signaling Chani and Akila to stay put he slowly advanced for several paces then stopped. At that point, they all heard advancing hoof beats coming from the west. Rather than the returning Comanche warriors, the appearance of three mounted Ranger's approached the camp.

Seeing no hope, one of the squaws yelled a signal to the others and at that very instant all the squaws immediately slit the throats of their hostages, from ear to ear, then charged at the nearest mounted Ranger.

Both Chani and Akila leapt into action intercepting a squaw each while the rest were shot as they advanced.

Just in time for the trio of Rangers as they came to a dusty halt. As all the Rangers were dismounted by this time, they were sickened by the sight of what had transpired. The dead Anglo hostages, two women and five children bleeding out with the look of terror in their eyes as they met their maker, beyond any mortal help. Several of the Rangers began to cry, while several others began to change the empty cylinders of their revolvers. And went from tee pee to tee pee hearing screams of small children then gunfire then more screams then gunfire then silence. All the others went from dead body to dead body slitting each braves throat, then mutilating each braves body for the afterlife, starting with the ritual scalping.

Each Ranger knew that Henry Jaeger had a sometimes penchant for scalping the fallen Comanche warrior. Thus going about their business from brave to brave. When that was completed, the continued with the squaws until that was completed.

Henry simply stood there, part of him wanting then to stop this unholy carnage, while another part seeing this as justice returned in exact kind, swiftly and without remorse.

It was sad the Comanche children had to die, but the current wisdom, hard to argue with, was simply that there was one less hostile to worry about. Henry then sent one of the Rangers back to their camp to bring up the wagons and the livestock. Then he sent two others back down the valley to make certain of the other Comanche's and gather any remaining horses, while they all gathered up the remaining mutilated Comanche bodies, in camp.

Since none of the Rangers could bring themselves to mutilate the children's corpses, all of the bodies were separated into groups with the Anglo hostages to be buried, the grown Indian women and braves to stay where they fell, as food for the vultures and other carrion that were to eventually arrive and a small funeral pyre for the Comanche children that perished.

By noon all had reassembled with the Rangers horse remuda having grown by some two dozen mustang mounts.

Several hours later all of the perished Anglo hostages lay in shallow graves, and the funerary pyre for the Comanche children was ablaze. A brief prayer was said for the dead.

Just then a motion overhead signaled the arrival of the vultures starting to circle overhead, waiting for the Rangers to depart prior to their celestial invite for dinner.

Pointing overhead at the new arrivals, Henry said, "Gentlemen it's time for us to go. I'm sorry that we failed"! One of the others said, "Henry, we didn't fail! We did all we could do, didn't we?" Henry sadly nodded his head, and then he mounted as did everyone else, leaving behind them a signal that the Anglo settlers could be every bit as savage as the Comanche, if not more.

As they rode, all agreed that it was time to return to San Antonio and that if all went well they could return, within a fortnights travel, with a remuda of some forty odd mustangs. Along the trail Henry made it a point to select several mustangs each evening, to be 'Settled Down', demonstrating his silent gradual process to everyone. By the time they pulled into San Antonio, all of the mustangs had been settled and suitable for riders, the process made simpler given that all the mustangs had previous experience with riders given that their former owners were Comanche. Within days the horses were sold to Federal Government Army people with the money equally distributed to the Rangers. It was now soon to be spring in the year 1846 and the Rio Grande River was starting to get restless.

Spring arrived and departed, with the action down around the border getting "Het up".

With a variety of skirmishing actions by the Rangers and the Mounted US Dragoons against Mexican Regular Cavalry and the Mounted Mexican Rancho's and bandits. By this time several conflicts had erupted on the northern side of the Rio Grande, with the units of General Taylor's Army along with the Texican volunteers handing the larger forces of Generals Arista and Torrejon a bloody nose at Palo Alto and at Resaca de la Palma sending the Mexican forces back across the Rio Grande licking their wounds. As the month of July came to a close, the Army of General Taylor, (known as old Rough and Ready) made the crossing of the Rio Grande from their base up river from their newly built base at Fort Brown to pursue the enemy for battle engagement. The Texican Ranger units by this time were of great value as scouts and performing messenger duties between units whereas they were accustomed to living off the land and moving fast.

Having moved into and securing the City of Matamoros almost unopposed General Taylor's Army then turned their attention to pursuing General Arista's fleeing Mexican troops towards the inland city of Monterrey, as indicated by reports of Ranger units at their heels.

Having moved his army upriver, General Taylor made camp, occupying the City of Camargo, on the Rio Grande, for the next six weeks awaiting further supplies from Port Isabel on the coast. Every town they inhabited from Matamoros inland was left with a small garrison comprised of Regular Army and Texas Mounted Rangers to act as a rear escort guard and ready express riders.

The rest of the Rangers were busy scouting out the various routes inland to Monterrey and spying on all that arrived and left Monterrey.

Which is where Henry Jaeger found himself, riding back and forth between Camargo and the Ranger units that roamed the mountainous perimeter of Monterrey, during this lull in action awaiting resupply from the coast, by steam ship? Having traversed the road on several occasions, he noted several points where ambush was sure to be certain, going off trail when need be, bypassing the point and returning to the trail. Usually traveling by night, he was delayed with a message by Ben McCulloch's Ranger unit to General William Worth, Taylor's second in command, finding himself on the road at midmorning. About to go off trail prior to one of the ambush points on his return, Henry heard gunfire just around the bend of the road. Then a great deal of shouting in Spanish. He slowed down and dismounted peering around the bend, to find a group of what appeared to be a group of bandits that roamed all over northern Mexico taking charge of a fine carriage of several women, after having killed the driver and both outriders.

Jumping into his saddle, Henry spurred his horse into a full gallop, pulling out his Colt .12 gauge revolving scatter gun, in the process. As he sped towards the open carriage everyone's attention appeared to be on the women contained within as Henry opened fire on the six men.

All of Henry's buckshot found its respective marks, dropping each in turn as Henry sped passed the surprised bandits, leaving only one left who in the process of bringing his single shot pistol to bear on Henry, painfully discovered the jaws of Chani and Akila closing on both his gun hand and crushing his neck. As Henry returned, he whistled for Chani and Akila to drop their now lifeless form on the road and return to his side.

It was all over in less than twenty seconds. As Henry approached the carriage, he viewed the Mantilla's of two finely dressed women. The one facing him, clearly older and as he approached, the other turned facing Henry with a combination of fear and relief on her face. Bringing his mount to a halt, Henry was dumbstruck at what lay ahead. Never in his life had he seen a more angelically beautiful face. Never had he thought possible a women could possess such a presence. He'd been accustomed to seeing women of the frontier, who grew old before their time and from time to time, encountering 'women of the town', who looked like they'd been "rid hard and put up wet". But never had he thought possible such beauty could exist.

Eventually coming to his senses, he dismounted approaching the carriage and asked in fractured Spanish if they were harmed in any way.

The young Senorita answered in slightly accented but well spoken English, "With the exception of my Duena, we are unharmed but as you can see the driver and our body guards have died in our service".

Continuing, she introduced herself, "I am Joselita de la Fuentes, and daughter of Domingo de la Fuentes, the Alcalde of Monterrey and you are young man"?

Capturing every syllable that came forth from that beautiful mouth and transfixed by those opalescent eyes, Henry failed to answer. As she asked once again, he came to his senses, and blurted out, "Mamm, my name is Henry Jaeger, of the Texas Rangers, in the service of General William Worth, of the US Army".

"Good Ranger Jaeger, for we have a safe conduct pass signed by the General as you can see," as she removed the paper and handed it to Henry for his scrutiny. Handing it back to her, seeing that it was indeed the General's authorization, Henry asked, "What in the world are you doing traveling this road, during a time of War"?

She replied politely, "I've just returned from completing my schooling in France, just in time for your War. We were unaware of this before arriving in Matamoros, since we've been at sea for several months. My Duena and I have traveled far and are so close to home only to find a state of war existing."

Seeing that they were in a tight spot Henry was about to speak when, she spoke again, "Senor, you have saved our lives. No doubt these bandito's were about to abduct us and hold us for ransom, for my father, being a Hidalgo is a man of considerable substance and will reward you well if you'll assist us in completing our journey home."

All Henry could do was nod his head. The report to General Worth would simply have to wait. Without further word Henry set to attaching his mount to the carriage then moved the dead bodies of the bandits to the side of the road, along with the two dead outriders.

The out riders mounts came slowly back to the carriage allowing Henry to attach their reins to the carriage also.

That done, he noticed Chani in a nervous state moving in circles indicating that she wanted Henry to follow. Several minutes later he returned with all of the bandits horses and secured them to the carriage. Then he jumped up to the dead driver's seat pushing him to the other side saying, "You'll have to tell me how to get to where you're going Senorita"!

Whence she replied, "My father's Rancho is five miles away from the city of Monterrey and there is a little known shortcut just ahead that I'll show you Senor Ranger". As Henry turned around to acknowledge her she added sweetly, "Oh and Muchas Gracias for my life Senor"!

That last dazzling smile left Henry completely undone. For from this time on, no woman on the face of the planet would ever do.

Joselita's Duena started to recover from her swoon, as the carriage lurched forward, with the wolves bringing up the rear. Through the sound of the carriage moving over a rough road, Henry could hear the breathless frantic conversation between women who had just escaped a very harrowing experience. Only making out bits and parts of the nonstop staccato conversation is their native Spanish, Henry was pleased that both women regarded him as their savior. Seems the General would have to wait, just a bit for his dispatch.

After a mile, Joselita signaled him just what to watch for as the shrouded short cut to the Rancho came into view and there it was drooping tree limbs laden with leaves partially his the angled offshoot from the main trail. As Henry slowly forced the horses through the view of the rest of the short cut trail came into view, presenting a small tree lined path; well used enough to keep from being overgrown and for the next mile and a half the path was shaded from the sun by a constant overhang of leaf laden branches. The horses followed meekly behind.

About an hour later as the carriage struggled over the rise of a hill, they were all greeted by the vista of a valley, covered with livestock of every kind and a sprawling Ranchero, with several barn's, homes and what seemed miles and miles of fences that crisscrossed the valley, some retaining horses, while others retaining cattle, while others sheep and goats.

As the carriage pulled into the Rancho several people began to gather about the carriage, to welcome Don Domingo's youngest daughter, home at last from her schooling in Europe.

Henry helped some of the ranch hands pulled the dead driver down from the carriage and with some trouble, finally communicated with the hands where the two others outriders were back on the road. Several minutes later four riders mounted up and made the ascent up the long hill they'd just descended from to retrieve the two bodies. Other hands took the other horses back into the corral.

Just then Henry felt a tug on his arm. It was the Duena, who spoke no English but pointed towards Joselita in that she appeared to be her mother's embrace as well as a host of other young men and women hovering around the duo, assuming they were family. Joselita summoned her Duena and Henry to join them.

As they approached the throng, Joselita said, in perfect English, "And this is our savior, Senor Henry Jaeger, a Texicano Ranger who killed all the bandits single handed". Then she looked behind Henry and indicated the presence of Chani and Akila sitting by the carriage in perfect attention. "But he had help of course, didn't he Senor"? Henry nodded and whistled for Chani and Akila to join his side. The entire family had seen wild wolves of course along with their cousins, foxes and coyotes, but never in their lives had seen such large ferocious creatures.

Henry bent down and whispered in the ears of the wolves and when he stood up again, Chani and Akila together presented their paws to be touched so they could sniff and imprint each one of the families scent. Indicating to the entire family to approach slowly and touch each wolves extended paw gently and allow the wolves to sniff them, each in turn approached the wolves for the formalities.

As this was occurring, Henry just couldn't seem to take his eyes off Joselita. At first she averted her eyes in embarrassment, but as the cavalcade of the extended family made their way past the wolves, both of their eyes always came back to each other, entirely oblivious to everything else. The silent bond between two hearts gradually was taking root.

Yet their obvious furtive glances, didn't escape the scrutiny of both Joselita's mother and Duena. When that was concluded Joselita said, "And Senor Jaeger may I present Dona Encarnacion, de la Fuentes, my mother and my Duena, Seniora Juanita Fuentes, whom you've already encountered with me. As they speak little English I wish to convey their eternal thanks"!

One by one she then presented each member of a very grateful family, the last being a man in his mid-thirties, clearly ex-military by his bearing. Walking about with a cane for assistance he asked, "No doubt you're here with his excellency General Taylor's army"?

Henry nodded as the two men eyed each other, each taking a small measure of the other.

"Look mister", said Henry slowly, "We didn't ask for this fight, but now that we're here it's going to happen".

The elder brother mildly interrupted by saying in heavily accented English, "Senor we are not friendly to the idiots in Mexico City. We have our own problems with the corrupt military, partisan bandits and the Comanche. Yet we must walk a fine line if we are to maintain our existence that we've fought hard to have. You are no doubt wondering if I've been in the military, well I have and have paid the price with a leg that is all but useless, thanks to some rather excellent shooting at considerable distance by one of your compadres."

Just then he noticed Henry's arms laden Horse and the holstered revolver at Henrys side, giving Henry a nodding assent of respect, from one warrior to another.

"My entire family is grateful for your intervention in behalf of our beloved sister, but may we ask your future intentions Senor"?

"Well Mister, I need to get back to my unit if you don't mind". "As to your presence here, you've my promise I won't tell anyone of the secret path to your place. The army will be along directly in strength. It is my prayer that your families lives in peace and not suffer what we in Texas have endured at the hands of your military and the Comanche"! At that he pulled out the cross that hung around his neck since he was a child, making the sign of a cross, thus sealing his solemn word for all in attendance. This alone convinced all that he was Catholic just as they were and a man of his word, as everyone else made the sign of the cross. Just then Joselita blurted out, "Senor, you are no doubt tired and in need of food and some sustenance. "Please stay awhile so we can thank you".

"Just some oats for my horse and some food and water for my wolves, then I have to go".

At that Joselita sent everyone scurrying into the larger house bringing bowls of water and food for Chani and Akila as Henry led his steed to the water trough, where servants brought a bag of oats for Henrys horse. Henry hadn't slept in two whole days and the food that was brought to him was a welcome respite to bury the pangs of hunger that were beginning to catch hold. Within the space of twenty minutes both Henry and his critters were satiated sufficiently to continue their journey.

While he ate, Henry carried on some seemingly small talk with Joselita's eldest brother, careful not to reveal anything at all that may compromise his mission, all the while stealing furtive glances at Joselita who refused to enter the house while relating to her family all that had transpired during the morning, while stealing furtive glances at the large Texicano horseman. From time to time their eyes met and certain electricity sent a shiver up each of their spines.

When Henry had finished the other horsemen had returned with the two out riders splayed out over the saddles and two of the compesino women ran to them wailing in grief.

As he mounted, Henry stole a last glance at this vision of loveliness, as she looked at him for what might've been the final time in her life. For this tall Texicano was about to ride out of her life. Well rested and full Henry and the wolves made their way at a slow canter up the long hill and when crested he stopped, turned for one final glance at what seemed to him to be paradise and disappeared. What no one mentioned was the fact that Joselita's father, Don Domingo, the Alcalde of Monterrey was summoned by the newly appointed Mexican General Ampudia, who placed the entire city under martial law, conscripting every able bodied citizens in constructing defensive earthworks to repel General Taylor's advancing Army. The family had not heard from or seen Don Domingo for days on end. Supplies and troops were arriving into Monterrey until the Mexican forces were up to approximately seven thousand infantry, artillery and cavalry, along with what armed partisan civilians could be mustered.

True to his word, Jaeger had not mentioned any word of the Fuentes ranchero, to General Worth as an adjunct to his dispatch from Ben McCulloch. As General Taylor's forces advanced upon the city, they were flanked by units of the Texas Mounted Rangers a half mile away on either side of his advancing column, with the Federal Mounted Dragoons well in advance and bringing up the rear, guarding the supply train of wagons.

The natural setting of Monterrey was easily defensible, being between the foothills of the Sierra Madre Mountains and was approached by the Cerralvo road from the north and the Saltillo road from the west, running through the Rinconada Pass, which was flanked by Independence Hill on the northern side of the narrow but swift running Santa Caterina river and Federation Hill on the southern side of the river, both which were bristling with Mexican Artillery. The approaches of the Cerralvo road from the north were well defended by artillery batteries placed upon the Citadel to the northern approaches of the road and the Devils Fort and the Tannery an old large building that defended the eastern part of this city of fifteen thousand.

An arc shaped ring of earth works was prepared in advance of these positions and even should these positions be overrun, the formidable task of breaching the inner defenses remained. Stone houses, loop holed for snipers, flat roofs with sand bagged parapets, proved a formidable problem.

In front of the Americans was a city protected by well-constructed fortifications, well supplied with victuals and ammunition defended by a force larger than anything that General Taylor could hope to muster.

Following an afternoon's reconnaissance by the Rangers, Old Rough and Ready called his senior officers to his tent for a council of war to craft a method of attack. What was agreed upon was to assign General William Worth two thousand Federals and Rangers to perform a night time flanking movement around the northern approaches of the town and Rinconada Pass, crossing the river and emerging from behind the Federation Hill, taking the heights along with the artillery. That accomplished, the city would be caught in a pincer move, then the attack would commence, with Col.

Jefferson Davis leading his Mississippi Rifles to attack the Tannery and the Devils Fort guarding the city's east and General Taylor's main force attacking the Citadel from the city's northern approaches.

All day long and well into the next the Mounted Rangers played cat and mouse, with the Mexican artillery. A similar game they learned well from the Comanche on the range. Just out of cannon range, they would make several passes at the outer edge, and then suddenly dart inside of the cannon range laughing as the cannoneer's tried desperately to adjust their cannons, which ended up having the Mexican artillery wasting a great deal ammunition with nothing to show for it.

During the early morning and evening hours the Rangers would sneak up and pick off sentries sometimes capturing them and bringing them back to Taylor's encampment for interrogation.

Henry Jaeger was assigned to the headquarters company of General Taylor. With no specific orders other than to stay close by the General, no matter where he was and to be ready for whatever the General required. By this time, both Chani and Akila has taken the scent of the crusty old general and even allowed the general to feed them at his mess.

Sam Walker and Jack Hays were both directed to accompany General Worth in his flanking move, each commanding a company of Mounted Rangers. Showing no respect for the universal day of rest General Worth decided to commence his flanking movements on cold rainy Sunday, and by eight AM the following morning secured the Saltillo road, an all-important life line for the city. After fording the shallow Santa Caterina River, drove the pickets from their position and after a sharp but brief fight, took the northern end of Federation Hill, its earthworks and its artillery, forcing the Mexican defenders to fall back on the El Soldado.

Turning the captured enemy artillery on El Soldado, General Worth directed the artillery fire on El Soldado then directed a charge of infantry sending the Mexican defenders fleeing across the river and back into the city. Yet north of his position, lay Independence Hill and the Bishops Palace, bristling with artillery, that would have to be captured before Taylor's Forces could safely advance.

Since the sun was going down, Worth decided to commence the attack the following day. All the while Taylor and his forces were harassing Ampueda's defenders throughout the day and night, with feints and minor jabs, lobbing artillery shells into the city proper, coming at the Mexican defenders from all directions.

This caused General Ampudia to concentrate the bulk of his forces, in front of him, allowing General Worth and his forces to attack his rear.

All night long, a cold steady rain persisted and at three AM the men were quietly awakened, to again cross the Santa Caterina River and commence their advance upon Independence Hill, taking advantage of the cover of night and the foul weather. By now the rain had lessened into a steady mist, with a heavy fog rolling in that muted the sounds of their advance. Worth's advancing forces were nearly at the top of the hill before being detected by the enemy sentries alarm. With a short but rapid dash, Sam Walkers Rangers seized the western most redoubts after a short but fierce hand to hand struggle with the defenders, driving them towards the Bishops Palace redoubt on the far end of the hill. The remainder of the morning the defenders of the Bishops Palace redoubt were busy fending off an artillery barrage from the Northern end of the hill by their own cannon, as well as dodging shells from their own captured artillery from El Soldato across the river on Federation Hill.

After several hours of this the Mexicans had had enough and fled pell mell, into the city leaving their artillery to the Americano's who moved into the roofless Bishops Palace without any opposition. By days end General Worth was in possession of the western approaches to the city and the heights and all the remaining artillery and supplies they contained. The morning fog had disappeared just as the American flag was being raised over the Bishops Palace. From across the entire city Worth's men could hear the immense roar of a massive cheer from the rest of the Federal troops at that sight.

During that night General Ampudia ordered his troops to abandon the earthworks the civilians had constructed and silently fall back into the city, for the house to house combat that was certain to commence the following day.

The following morning General Taylor began his assault from the northeast of the city, quickly overrunning the previously abandoned earthworks. Any gloom the troops felt because of the cold rainy weather quickly vanished for now was the time for payback.

While remaining inactive during the morning of Taylor's advance, General Worth directed a cannonade into the city with the enemies captured artillery, thus starting the second element of the pincer movement, closing in from two directions.

By nightfall both Taylor and Worth had moved relentlessly into the city and in a better position to bring their artillery to bear on the arsenal in which General Ampuedia had established in the city's principal Cathedral. All through the preceding evening and the following day, all Henry could think about was the image and the sounds of Joselita, permanently imprinted in his mind. As he advanced just behind General Taylor and his small staff into the city, observing at close hand the house to house combat between the Federal Troops, the Texas and various other Militia groups and the enemy routing them out killing them by whatever means were available, a certain feeling that all was going a bit too well.

As the group started to enter an intersection of streets, a short volley of musket fire preceded the emergence of over a dozen heavily armed civilian partisans. The musket volley made quick work of several of General Taylor's staff knocking them from their mounts. Most of the attacking partisans were armed with machetes and knives falling quickly upon the General and his few dragoons.

As they advanced Henry quickly brought to bear the scattergun and with each rapid pull of the trigger the weapon's scattershot cut almost in half every one of the citizens it was pointed at. Discarding the scatter gun, then pulling his Colt revolver, he emptied it in rapid fire at the swirling melee of horses, partisans and soldiers. As several partisans struggled to gain control of General Taylor's horse, Henry holstered his pistol and charged his horse at several partisans wielding swords and machete's, knocking a block of them down, then diving from his horse into a bunch of them, his Bowie knife cutting a wide swath. Picking up one of the many dropped swords he advanced on yet another group attempting to pull the General from his horse. This time the general's horse started to fall, with the general jumping clear, sword in hand, falling on several partisans.

Henry jumped into the fray, both knife and sword finding its mark, fending off the melee of attackers to the general. At this point the sounds of gunshots was heard, as several of the advancing troops, seeing that their general was in serious trouble turned and ran back, decimating what was left of the partisans.

A hoard of civilian partisans lay dead all over the street, along with several dying horses and badly injured members of Taylor's staff. The General observed both Chani and Akila returning to their master, covered in the blood of dead partisans, lying in the streets with their throat's ripped out. Yet both the General and Henry found their mounts skittish but relatively unharmed as Henry retrieved his scattergun, then both of their mounts, offering the reins of the Generals horse to him.

Noting the Generals sword covered in blood and his uniform in likewise condition, Henry quickly remounted his horse without a word. One of the Generals many faults was that he somehow could never bring himself to say 'thank you', or to 'apologize' to anyone for any reason, this time being no different. Yet he gave both Henry and the wolves a brief acknowledgment, with an ever so brief tip of his blood spattered hat before bellowing, "The funs over gentlemen, we still have a battle to win"! Then they all continued down the street, following the advancing units. As he followed the General, Henry recharged both of his weapons, with fresh cylinders, senses ever alert, scanning the rooftops as they passed the Alcalde's offices.

From inside his office, Don Domingo de la Fuentes observed the melee on the street with mixed emotions, noting especially the whirlwind fighting of the large buckskinned Texicano, that quickly ended the lives of so many of his constituents in so short a time. He wondered would the greed and the corruption of those in Mexico City be replaced with a different kind of greed and corruption. Clearly General Ampudia's efforts were a lost cause. This was not Don Domingo's cause and he was only a part of this enterprise because of fear for his family.

He had a very fine line to tread, if the "Familia" was to survive. If his assumptions were correct, Ampudia would make a final stand in the city's Cathedral. So typical claiming spiritual sanctuary prior to his surrender.

Keenly following the Army's progress were a gaggle of newspaper correspondents, busily scribbling down notes as they advanced on the very heels of the combatants. Most of which followed the already legendary movements of Jack Hays and Sam Walker as they served the interests of General Worth valiantly. Every evening some Ranger was selected to ride the various reports back to the Rio Grande where a regular, almost daily rotation of flat bottomed, side wheeler steam ships, brought a steady stream of supplies to Taylor's forces in Northern Mexico, from the ports of New Orleans and Corpus Christi. Then taking back what wounded survived and messengers to the Government and private enterprise.

Early the following morning, General Ampudia, entrenched in the Cathedral with a hoard of ammunition, fearful of an American bombardment, sent several of his officers out to the American forces under a flag of truce. They soon returned with Taylor's answer of unconditional surrender. Ampudia, thinking that everything is negotiable, sent the flag of truce out a second time requesting a face to face meeting with the General. What was agreed upon was a meeting of secondary officers top discuss terms, which is what Taylor relented to.

By midafternoon, the group jointly agreed to allow, an immediate surrender of Monterrey, transfer of all the public property in the immediate vicinity and the retirement of all Mexican forces to a point beyond the Rinconada Pass, with an eight week truce to be agreed upon subject to veto by either government.

This did not sit well with the Americans especially, but Taylor noting the fatigued condition of the American forces plus the fact that their ammunition and provisions were running low and that the Mexican forces, which still were quite numerous, would have to be further routed out, via house to house fighting, decided to agree to terms allowing the Mexicans to withdraw.

For the next several days the Mexican Army made ready the withdrawal or their forces, with General Ampudia being the last to depart, escorted by a joint mounted Ranger and Dragoon force to a point beyond Rinconada Pass.

As they rode back from their escort duty, Jaeger, Hays and Walker, discussed their disagreement with the General for his lack of gumption. What they couldn't know was that they were all deep into Mexico and were all vastly outnumbered. With the constant threat of another Army lurking somewhere out there, for reports of Santa Anna's return from his short lived Cuban exile, began to trickle into the American camp.

That evening when they were all back at camp, after the evening meal Hays, Walker and Jaeger, were all gathered around a campfire, where the pros and cons of the recent victory and liberal surrender terms were heatedly discussed at length, amongst the group of Rangers and American Army troops. Everyone agreed that General Worth's battle tactics and execution were such that they were singularly responsible for the victory.

"We coulda crushed em, if they'd a only let us", was a common expression of disgust. "Remember the Alamo", was mentioned by the Rangers often enough, along with "Remember Goliad and Remember Meir", whereas the Rangers brought the American soldiers up to speed with stories of what the Mexican Army had done to the Texicans repeatedly over the last decade.

Then some grumbling was heard about General Taylor for his liberal terms, when up stepped a grizzled old Sergeant, who had served under General Taylor continuously since 1812, when the general was a mere Major in the American Army on the Illinois frontier.

"General Zachariah Taylor is the man's name and I won't hear of anyone besmirching him", warned the Sergeant. "Sure he's got lotta rough edges, but none of ya know him the way I do". At that point he related to those assembled that the good General was brought up on criminal charges, by his own officers, for assault and battery by force of arms, in the beating of one Simon Bartrane. Since no one was available for trial witness, charges were dropped.

Taylor's army unit while on a mission during the War of 1812 was ambushed on the Illinois side of the Mississippi River by hostile Indians, clearly as a result of a tip from some French trappers and traders.

Presumably Simon Bartrane, who happened to have previously crossed swords with the good General Taylor, was one of the Frenchmen involved and the beating he received that almost cost him his life, leaving him a permanent cripple, was payback for the lives lost. The good Sergeant then went into some detail as to the General's efforts in tracking down and dealing with the rest of the guilty French traders. Although it took a few years, they all ended up as fish food in the mighty Mississippi river.

That seemed to quiet the group, who all agreed to give the General the benefit of the doubt. But as the group started to break up returning to each one's own bivouac, one of the Rangers was heard to say, "That all may be true, but this means that we'll just have ta tangle with them again"!

8

For the next few days after General Ampudia's evacuation, General Taylor combined forces scoured the entire city, for any contraband, weapons of ammunition, bringing all they found back to the American camp. Meanwhile the citizens of Monterrey began to clean up as best they could the wreckage, caused by the recent conflict, organized in part by the Alcalde Don Domingo de la Fuentes. After the hostilities ceased, Don Domingo was permitted through the American lines with a safe conduct pass, to visit his Rancho north of the city, where he was greeted by the return of his youngest daughter Joselita. Having to return the following day to help organize the reconstruction of the city, he hardly got any sleep, especially since his daughter related the harrowing tale of being captured by bandits on the road only to be rescued by this tall blond Texican Ranger, in the service of the Americano's. and delivered safely to the family.

The exacting way the Texan was described along with the two wolves, could only match just what Don Domingo had seen with his own eyes, as the partisans had attacked the American General Taylor and the aftermath of his peoples bloodshed. He saw how his impressionable daughters eyes lit up each time she mentioned his name, with passionate expanse.

While very grateful, this aspect could prove problematical should a future marriage arrangement be in the offing with any of the Hidalgo families in the area. For indeed his daughter had blossomed into quite a beauty, during the period of her schooling abroad, exceeding his wildest expectations. Of all his children she was indeed the fairest. Later in the evening he discussed this with his wife and her Duena Juanita. All agreed that a very close watch would have to be placed on Joselita. The following day he returned to Monterrey, to work with the Americano's in the restructuring of Monterrey. Vowing to meet them all the following Sunday at High Mass at the Cathedral.

Hearing that a special High Mass at the Cathedral was to occur at eleven that coming Sunday Morning, Henry decided to attend. Getting his shock of hair shorn by one of the soldiers in camp and face shaved to a fair thee well, as well as washing his buckskins, he prepared for Mass the following day along with a complete washing and brushing of his Appaloosa horse and Chain and Avila.

The following morning he arose early, feeding the critters and himself, then made his way into town towards the Cathedral. For you see, Henry Jaeger, although raised as a Catholic and having attended a make shift Mass conducted by his parents in the Grotto and having been taught Latin to a certain degree, had never formally attended Mass at a Cathedral, celebrated by a priest. Now in his twenties, after all he'd been through he figured that it was high time that he'd see firsthand what it all was about.

It had been awhile, but he thought he'd be able to follow along without much trouble. Arriving an hour early, he tied up his Appaloosa to the hitching post, instructing Chani and Akila to watch the horse. Anyone who touched the horse was to draw a warning growl from either or both of the wolves.

As the time for Mass drew near, the town's people started to arrive and with them were a few American soldiers that were Catholic, seeking the Universal blessing that cannot be denied. Of course some of the very last to arrive, were the Hidalgos, in their fine carriages, escorted to their assigned pews in the Cathedral. Mass would not commence until the last of the Hidalgos were seated.

As the Fuentes family arrived and exited their carriages, they all recognized the big Appaloosa, flanked by Chaini and Akila at the hitching post, indicating the presence of the big Texican Americano within. As Joselita passed Henry's horse, both wolves indicated recognition, compelling her to stoop down and allow her to briefly pet them. Then she proceeded into the Cathedral, looking resplendent in her alabaster finery, her hair topped by a gleaming mantilla, causing every man and woman to pause and wonder. Dona Joselita had returned at last.

As she made her way down the aisle, her heart felt that it would escape her chest. Her eyes darted from place to place as she made her way down the aisle seeking the visage of the Texican. Both Don Domingo and Dona Encarnacion, following close behind gave each other a glance as they went down the aisle to their assigned pew, never once considering the Americano was a Catholic.

Then they both spotted him, kneeling on the rail, deep in prayer, clasping the rosary beads, not five rows behind them. Surely Joselita would make eye contact and then…….

As she turned to her right, entering the family pew she caught a brief glimpse of the Texicano, kneeling with his head down clasping the rosary. Settling into place, Joselita glanced nervously at her parents and smiled innocently, who just at that instant were glancing at her.

Turning to each other as they kneeled to utter the preamble Mass prayer, both parents glanced at each other with that knowing look. For many years ago, when the passions ran deep, didn't they both engage in the very same ritual? Some things never change.

As the priests came down the center aisle flanked by the altar boys, everyone turned to observe them as they made their way towards the altar, from the cathedrals rear to the front. As the priests passed Henry, he turned his head to the front of the cathedral facing the altar and there not five rows ahead of her, was the vision of loveliness, Dona Josalita, As their eyes met a simultaneous chill overcame each, their gaze at each other refusing to be averted. Ever so slowly as the priests took their positions to commence the proceedings, Joselita reluctantly turned her gaze forward.

As the Mass moved forward, Henry found it difficult to pay attention to what was said. Oh he could barely understand enough Latin to follow somewhat the liturgy and when the priest delivered the Homily, in Spanish he was able to make out the gist of what was being said. But it was all just a gaggle of empty words, that a mind absorbed in other, more important things, just couldn't grasp. As the Mass lurched forward to the acceptance of communion, one by one everyone arose and took their place in line, with the Hidalgos in front accepting the eternals grace and the body and the blood of the son first, then followed by everyone else. As Joselita returned to her pew, the eternals grace firmly in her mouth, her glance again followed the large blonde buckskin clad Texicano as he made his way to the altar. Once again, as Henry returned to his place, his eyes sought out that of Joselita, finding them easily as she glanced out of the corners of her eyes, trying not to be overtly obvious to her family. As Henry again took his place, rows behind Joselita, he kneeled along with everyone else until Communion was concluded, his eyes taking in every inch of the rear of Joselita's body as if it were to be the final time, to last him for all eternity.

When the Mass was concluded, with the Monsignor offering for all to "Go in peace", signaling the celestial entourage to exit, followed by the Hidalgos then the rest, their eyes again made contact as she glided down the aisle probably forever, thought Henry.

There were times when heaven was simply out of reach and this way just one of those times. As he made his way through the throng of people exiting the assembly, Henry grew uneasy, for amongst the throng were no doubt many related to those he killed just several days before. Never considering that here amongst former and perhaps still enemies, in a house of god, were people cowed into silence, for Henry's mere audacity of presence indicated to all that here was a man, afraid of no one, yet capable of being a man of peace.

As Henry came outside, he was surprised to find Joselita petting Akila and Chani as he made his way towards his horse. Sensing he was near, she arose seeing that he was near and flashing a dazzling smile exclaimed, "Ah Senor Jaeger, my savior", as she faced her parents and a frowning Duena Juanita, whereupon she promptly reintroduced, each and every member of her family, ending with, "And finally my father Don Domingo de la Fuentes, the Alcalde of Monterrey". Compelled by civility to accept his hand, Don Domingo answered, with a bow amidst the flurry of people exiting the Cathedral, "Sir, I wish to give you my thanks for saving the precious life of my youngest daughter Joselita". Henry replied "Your very welcome senor". An awkward silence temporarily took hold, with Joselita offering, "Madre offered Senor Jaeger a place at our table when he returned us to you, but at that time he was too busy to accept. Don't you think it would be time to offer again our humble table to such a bravo as a token of your thanks father"?

Thinking quickly, ever the politician Don Domingo replied, "But of course and I would ask you to expand that offer to your General Taylor and his staff to join us at the Rancho tomorrow, since the General was kind enough to give us all favorable terms to General Ampudia thus sparing our city". "Good", chimed Joselita, offering her hand for Henry to kiss, in the European manner. Not knowing how to respond Henry clumsily took her hand, which by now was just inches from his face and gave her an inquiring look. "You may kiss my hand Senor", offered Joselita. Whereupon Henry gave her hand a chaste peck, their eyes never leaving each other for an instant.

Certain of her 'Conquista', Joselita turned and strode off in the haughty manner of one who was high born, certain of her place in the world. As the entire family entered their coaches and departed, Henry was approached by both Jack Hays and Sam Walker along with a few other officers that attended Mass in the rear of the Cathedral.

"Wahl old son, it looks like you just struck pay dirt", drawled Walker as they all approached. Just the one of the other officers said, "We'll accompany you back to General Taylor, to deliver the formal invitation".

"What", yelled General Taylor as he addressed Henry and a small coterie of staff officers including Hays and Walker. "A shindig at the mayor's ranch? Jesus H. Christ", Taylor bellowed. "We're fightin' a war in case anyone seemed not to notice"! After pacing a bit he looked at General Worth sitting at the map table in the generals tent, "Well Walker, what do you think"?

Worth rose to his full height, stretched and said, "So he wants our entire General staff to attend, does he? Well not if I have anything to say about it Taylor. Seems to me that a selected skeleton crew of officers can attend, but not all of us by god"!

"Ampudia would like that wouldn't he", mused Taylor. "By the way Mr. Jaeger, when on earth did you find the time start 'Sparkin' the mayors goddamn daughter mister"? Then the general had second thoughts saying, "Holy shit, oh never mind, that's how I met my wife back in Illinois long ago"!

"Who'd have thought it, some waddie Ranger, Indian fighter and lothario, has turned into a statesman"!

"Well so be it. Worth want to flip a coin and see who gets to go, either you or me"? Worth nodded his head and asked, "Your coin or mine"?

"Neither you scallywag, they'll be no two headed coins on this flip! Just then Lt. George McLennan brought forth a coin and after proper examination by all parties, the coin was called then flipped with General Taylor the loser.

"Shit, looks like I'm going to have to get all gussied up for the shindig tomorrow. Major Bragg, get a detail and go to the Mayors rancho and tell the good mayor that he's going to have company tomorrow at his pleasure". "McClellan", you go to Colonel Davis of the Mississippi

Rifles and tell him that his presence will be required for a little soiree' tomorrow." "Yessir", said McClellan who promptly saluted and was off.

"I suppose that you and Hayes will have to make an appearance," mused Taylor at Sam Walker each a commander of distinction in his own right. Walker nodded in affirmation.

"Well then, give my respects, to Governor Henderson, for it seems that he's gonna have to attend also".

"As for you mister Indian fighter Ranger, seems to me that since you're gonna be sparkin' this little senorita, you're gonna have to be quickly schooled in proper behavior, in order not to cause any embarrassment or cause an incident"!

Just then he said, "Where's the good Captain Lee"? "He's the very one to take you to charm school."

Just then Taylor's eyes narrowed into slits as he said, "That girls gonna be surrounded by folks all the time tomorrow, so don't get any ideas about a little 'poke in the whiskers' young man, or else they'll be sure to be gun play and we'll all be in the shits, ya get my drift"?

The following day General Taylor led the ride to the Alcalde's rancho, up over the small range of hills of the Sierra Madre range and down to the sprawling Rancho de la Fuente'. As the American's poured into the rancho's courtyard, they were greeted by a wealth of friendly compeseno's, who led their mounts to water.

Don Domingo led his family out of their encomienda to greet General Taylor and his contingent and in the formal style the Spanish were accustomed to, led the Soldiers and Rangers to be introduced to his entire family and associates. Toasts were offered all around and then Don Domingo tapped his glass with a small spoon, gaining everyone's attention.

"As some of you know, just before the battle, my precious daughter Joselita was accosted as she made her way back to us after being abroad for her schooling, by a group of the very bandits that plague our country and Texas. If it were not for the brave action of this Texas Ranger called Henry Jaeger, she might not be with us today!"

Then he turned to General Taylor saying, "I understand that he was acting as a courier for your army at the time of my daughters attempted abduction. In that I ask humbly that you may forgive him, for interrupting his important duties." With that the general nodded his assent. "I can never repay Senor Jaeger enough for what he has done for my family, but as a small token of my family's thanks and esteem, I wish to present him with," and at that he signaled one of the hands to ride up to those assembled on a mottled looking Appaloosa stallion with the finest saddle anyone had ever seen. Hand tooled leather in finest Mexican fashion with the typical large Mexican saddle horn. All assembled agreed that it was the finest horse and saddle anyone had ever seen. The mount of a Hidalgo the cost of which the average compeseno could never assemble in a lifetimes worth of work.

Handing over the reins to Henry, Don Domingo simply said with his voice trembling with emotion, "Muchas Gracias Senor", as he embraced the startled Texan.

Muttering the appropriate 'thank you', Henry walked around the horse marveling at his new found wealth, finding that Joselita had slipped in right beside him.

"I had to talk him into such a fine gift, but in the end he gave in"! As Henry turned to her, she offered her hand once again and this time Henry took her proffered had and chastely kissed it, precisely as Captain Lee had instructed him to do.

Rather than be dressed in the finery as the other ladies were, Joselita was attired in the riding trousers, leathers and boots of a ranchero. Being far taller than the average Mexican woman, she grabbed the reins and swung into the saddle of Henry's new mount, saying come join me on your other horse, so I can tell you about "El Bravo".

At that Henry looked at General Taylor and Don Domingo, both of which seemed somewhat uncomfortable at such impertinence, but neither wanting to put a damper on the occasion, both nodded their heads in assent. With that, Henry leapt into the saddle of his old Appaloosa and joined Joselita and El Bravo as the rode off at a canter down the length of the wooden fenced field where Don Domingo's fortune lay.

As they rode off down the fence line, General Taylor turned to Don Domingo saying, "Don't worry about your daughter Don Domingo, for Henry was instructed very carefully as to your ways, yesterday and the young man 'will' behave himself". Domingo nodded in assent, as they approached the buffet table laden to overflowing with victuals prepared by the family's staff, who labored all night in preparation of the event.

Changing the conversations direction, Domingo sad, "Let me tell you just what your 'Bravo' did for Joselita as it was related to me by my daughter and her Duena", whereupon he related the entire event of Jaeger's intervention to Taylor. Then he further added, "And I was at the very spot inside my office when the citizens fell upon you and your soldiers as you passed by and saw how Senor Jaeger struggled valiantly to save your life. No doubt general you were busy with others but I saw the Ranger hack off the arm of one of my citizens just short of having a machete cleave your 'Cabeza' in two. Of course your back was turned and you couldn't have seen what happened. So perhaps a commendation on your part may be something you would consider"?

"Interesting Don Domingo", very interesting said the grizzled old general. "Seems I'll have to whip something up for the young man"!

As Henry and Joselita rode along the vast fence line still in sight of the assembled family and soldiers she offered, "We'd better stay in sight of them, or else they might become suspicious of your intentions"! "Mamm, I have nothing but good and honorable intentions towards both you and your family", answered Henry meekly. He wanted to say more, to pour his heart out to her of the breadth and the depth of his emotions towards her, but his education was indeed limiting to the civilized subtleties of life. So he said, "I have no great ability with word Senorita and the life I've lived did not allow for me to become an educated man other than the ability to read and write and cipher numbers. I've read no great books, nor thought any great thoughts and I arrive before you with no great fortune to impress your family, yet every time I see you My heart seems to want to burst"! With Chani and Akila following just behind, Henry hung his head down saying, "Please forgive me, for I fear I've said too much and do not wish to offend you"!

After a moment of silence she answered, "Senor Jaeger, do you not see that I have eyes? That I see how you look at me? Do you not see how I return your glances? Do you not hear the excitement in my voice when I speak in your presence? Am I not attentive of every word that you speak? It is said that the eyes are the windows to one's soul, ones very inner essence and that all that needs to be seen is the look in my eyes, to gauge the depths of my interest"!

Looking straight ahead while they rode she continued, "In short Mr. Henry Jaeger, it gives me great pleasure to be in your company, to see you, to hear the sound of your voice, to observe your each and every move.

When you depart, my heart will be lonely, only to experience joy upon your return. And at this very moment I wish to kiss you and more, much more but I must restrain my passions. You need to be no greater a man or lesser. Your thoughts senor", she said turning to look Henry straight into his eyes?

The feeling of supreme elation grabbed hold of Henry as he tried to search for words, the right words to convey, but the look on his face spoke volumes as he blurted out, "Me amore, Te Amo", in his bastardized attempt to mix Spanish and Latin.

Laughing now, Joselita replied with flashing eyes, "And that's your final word Henry"!

Blushing now, he sputtered a meek, "Yes, until I can think of something else"! "Well, Senor Henry Jaeger, Norte' Americano, Texas Ranger and Indian fighter, a Cyrano you're not, but it seems you'll do, for you have officially captured my heart", she offered sweetly.

A bit more boldly he offered, "Joselita, how many times I say your name slowly as to bring the vision of you to my mind, which plugs a gaping hole in my heart. You have my heart for whatever its worth, for I can't imagine ever loving another"!

For several minutes, they rode on in silence, both mulling about what had quickly transpire then she said, "It would seem that as of this moment, two hearts beat as one, would not you agree"?

Henry nodded his head as he gazed deeply into her opalescent orbs.

Then they turned their horses around and slowly walked them back to the assemblage. As they rode in silence, each never took their eyes off the other, with Joselita eventually offering, "Soon I fear, you will be taken away from me by this war between our countries and I understand that you have your duties to perform, but if you don't come back to me safe and sound, my heart will be broken forever"!

There, it was sealed, the eternal bond between them, with Henry responding, "Heaven and earth could not keep me from returning, only the words from your heart, which would kill me"! That said, they stopped and switched mounts with Henry astride of his new mount and Joselita on Henry's old mount, feeling the warmth of his previous presence in his saddle and up through her loins, observing close at hand the variety of weaponry attached. This was indeed a man. After him, there could be no other. Her parents would take some working on, but in the event of his return, they would unite.

In the days ahead, General Taylor sent out Ben McCulloch and a Ranger attachment ahead to scout out the road to Saltillo, thus receiving word the road ahead was clear of threat, sent General Worth ahead to occupy Saltillo, after several brief, but ineffectual skirmishes with the locals. At the same time a smaller peripheral force led by General John Wool, moved out of San Antonio crossing the Rio Grande and headed towards the City of Chihuahua, and threaten Durango, bringing another element into play. Having done so, General Wool received orders to join the main force in Saltillo thus reinforcing Taylor, having achieved no military significance, by his long travels. By the end of 1846 all of Northern Mexico lay in the hands of the US forces with every major city containing a garrison of US troops.

During the lull in action in Northern Mexico, plans were being made to open a second front in Mexico by going after the soft underbelly of the country and follow the very same course of invasion, used by the Conquistador Cortez, centuries before against the Aztecs, via Vera Cruz. In overall command was General Worth's old mentor, Win-field Scott.

All the while, in the fall of 1846, Santa Anna now returned from his exile in Cuba, made his way towards the Capital in Mexico City, and through a variety of means both fair and foul, retook the weak government and raised the necessary funds to gather up a large twenty five thousand man army to drive the Norte' Americanos out of Mexico forever.

Early in January of 1847, Ranger Scouts brought in captured reports that Santa Anna was in San Luis Potosi mobilizing and training a large force for driving Taylor and his forces back across the Rio Grande River.

The new intelligence also informed Taylor that Santa Anna was completely aware of Winfield Scott's presence in Matamoros and his plans of invading Mexico, with siphoned off portions of Taylor's forces through Vera Cruz, thus, leaving Taylor in an inferior position to do battle. Certain that his garrison in Vera Cruz was able to hold Scott's forces at bay, Santa Anna headed north to confront and crush Taylor. Given that General Worth had distinguished himself tactically in Northern Mexico and that General Taylor was not to advance but to hold his ground,

General Scott, directed General Worth and his command to join him in his assault on Vera Cruz.

The march from San Luis Potosi wreaked a terrible toll on Santa Anna's forces, for the desert country was scarce of water and food was in short supply, with the winter weather being unusually cold and rainy. In spite of illness, exposure and an increasing number of desertions that plagued his army, he arrived in La Encarnation, some two hundred miles from where he started, still with a viable army of around twenty thousand infantry, artillery and cavalry.

Always thinking that Santa Anna would leave behind a sizeable force to defend Vera Cruz, Taylor was caught short when reports of a massive Army of twenty thousand was close at hand. Rapidly retreating in advance of Santa Anna's forces, Taylor drew up in a defensive position near the Buena Vista ranch, which had been decided upon earlier. Leaving General Wool to defend the narrows of the barely passable point on the road from San Luis Potosi, to Saltillo, General Wool placed his artillery in such a manner to defend that choke point. Messengers were sent to all of the nearby garrisons for reinforcements. For a few days both army's feinted and probed each other for weakness with Santa Anna sending Taylor an ultimatum for surrender within the hour. The time since elapsed the Mexicans cut loose with a massive barrage of cannon on the American positions. The outnumbered American forces fought valiantly, sending back wave upon wave of attacking Mexican soldiers, only being saved by the timely arrival of the flying artillery, traversing the field, which sent a hoard of grapeshot ripping through the ranks of the attackers, ripping apart their advancing columns.

By days end with both sides exhausted and their ranks thinned considerably by the dead and wounded, concluded a very unofficial truce, dictated more by sheer exhaustion, rather than tactical expediency.

As he viewed his decimated ranks at day's end Santa Anna, who's earlier confidence was now diminished, viewed the field seeing the American forces now reinforced by other who had arrived through the Rinconada Pass more than made up for the dead suffered that day.

He either had to risk another attack risking total destruction, or retreat with his forces intact, claiming a tactical victory bringing back what was captured from the Americans as symbols of victory on the field of battle.

Ordering the pickets to build and maintain campfires throughout the night, he withdrew the bulk of his forces, from the field of combat. The following morning the incredibly weary American's formed their battle lines only to discover that there were no opposing forces, a roaring cheer of exultation went up from each and every one, with the usually dour General Taylor, embracing the troops to a man.

Fortunately for both Henry Jaeger and Sam Walker, both missed this field of carnage, whereas each had been mustered out of official service as Texas Mounted Rangers, giving up their former ranks, and ordered to report to Washington City for duty. Both departing together, since by now Henry had been working under Walkers command and both were joined at the hip so to speak.

After a brief trip to the Fuentes rancho, to say his farewells to the family and have a few tearful moments with Joselita, Henry departed with one half of the previous blessed "Mispah", heart that was placed around his neck by Joselita's mother who by now had relented in her opposition. He left behind both Chani and Akila in the care of Joselita as her protector, for his eventual return. For his stay in Washington was only a temporary assignment to what lay ahead. As he rode back to camp, the howling of the wolves was still ringing in his ears while he read the inscription in Spanish which read; "May the Lord watch between me and thee, while we are absent one from another"!

Since prior to the Battle of Buena Vista and the denuding of General Taylor's forces by Scott for the planned campaign via Vera Cruz, Jack Hayes many of the Texican's who's enlistments were up made their way back to Texas and their homes to get ready for the coming winter and the spring planting afterwards. But Henry and Sam, Jack were absorbed into Army at a reduced rank, joining them in San Antonio, then traveling to Austin, then to Houston, then to the Port of Galvez, on the Gulf of Mexico, traveling by side wheel steamer along the coast then up the Mississippi, with John Hayes leaving them at Natchez for a long overdue visit with his kinfolk only to meet up with them later at the Nation's capital. Their destination, the War Department for further assignment while making a detour of several days up the Cumberland River to Nashville to visit the Fahrquar family. The duo then resumed their trip, back up the Ohio River by now stopping at Cincinnati, only to find that his Aunt and Uncle had both passed away, with no trace of their business or anyone who ever had heard of his family's existence, so long ago.

With no reason to tarry, both men continued their journey up the river towards their destination, Washington City.

aving arrived in Washington City, the nation's capital, both Walker and Jaeger presented themselves to the War Department, as their orders directed. By now Henry had acquired other suitable articles of clothing, but chose to attire himself in his frontier buckskins but with a special twist, of adorning his head with the Gaudy beaded sombrero the Fuentes family had presented him, worn in the style of the Northern Mexican Ranchero. Astride the big Appaloosa mount and the hand tooled saddle with the huge Mexican pommel horn made heads turn when they rode up to the War Department and everywhere they went.

Since Sam Walker was originally from nearby Maryland, both he and Henry were directed to mount a campaign in that state to recruit as many a man to form and train a mounted unit for General Scott's assault on Mexico through Vera Cruz. But an entire week was spent going around the War Department and giving interviews with the hoard of newspaper reporters eager for first hand reports on the campaign for northern Mexico. Sam Walker had by now emerged as a bit of a national hero, whereas the reporters that followed his every move at their risk and peril, reported his exploit's a length regarding all the battles he was involved with. Henry's gaudy appearance at his side and sometimes menacing appearance only emphasized and gave credence to what was reported. Newspaper advertisements were placed in the area newspapers for men to join a new corps to be armed with the latest word in firearms. Now Sam Colt, the inventor of the original Colt five shot revolver many of which were shipped to Texas, was bankrupt for a number of years, having found little interest in either the military of the civilian markets.

But a chance visit by Walker and Jaeger to spend an afternoon with President Polk, seemed to reverse his fortunes. For Polk, being an acolyte of the former President Jackson was known as one who trusted no one, installing himself upon occasion in the minutiae of governmental affairs whenever he saw fit. After all, the war with Mexico was of his doing, intending them to give up not only Texas but all the land they were doing nothing with all the way to the Pacific Ocean. The concept was of the natural Manifest Destiny of the nation as he saw it. As they talked at length he was surprised to hear that Henry not only worked on the Hermitage but had private conversations with Polk's mentor Andrew Jackson. Henry generously mentioned that Jack Hays was also part of that coterie, for a time. The mention of David Crockett, in his final days before the Alamo was of special interest. Finally the men retired to the outdoors to view Henry's magnificent horse and saddle. One by one Henry's firearms were examined, starting with the Colt Paterson Revolver, then the Colt revolving cylinder carbine, then the Colt, five shot revolving cylinder .12 gauge scattergun and finally Henrys family heirloom the .70 caliber dual barreled Beretta Rifle. During the course of the afternoon, Samuel Colts name was brought into the conversation, while Walker and Jaeger both heaped praise on Colt for such an invention, regaling the President with countless stories about how many was the time they might be "goner's" were it not for that revolver. "Nothing like it the whole world, Mr. President", said Walker with emphasis.

"So where is this Colt fella now Mr. Walker, asked Polk? "Well, funny you should ask, for I just received a letter from him yesterday, introducing himself to me having heard about my arrival in town, from the newspapers. Says he's in New York City and heard that I'm trying to raise a company of men to join General Scott and offered to meet with me to get a firsthand report on how well his revolver performed out on the frontier and during the war, for the purpose of equipping us with a new series of revolvers to fight the Mexicans with"!

"The both of you show me how these things work", directed the President. Whereupon both Henry and Sam Walker showed the President every aspect of the five shot Paterson revolver, the carbine and the five shot scattergun.

After several hours of Walker and Jaeger showing President Polk just what each of the weapons could do, the President said," Gentlemen this is revolutionary. I'm going to send you back to the War Department with instructions to travel to New York City, seek out Mr. Colt and bring him back to Washington, so we can get these firearms quickly into production. "Then as an afterthought, he said, "And you said these have been around for about five or so years"?

Armed with letters of introduction from the President and the

Secretary of War, Walker and Jaeger traveled to New York City to seek out Sam Colt.

"I've sent you a number of letters in Texas offering to furnish you with a new design for the Colt revolver, but it seems the letters never caught up with you, Mr. Walker", said Colt upon their eventual meeting a week later. "I've followed the news reports of the Ranger activities with my Paterson revolver, but never had the pleasure of discovering firsthand how they are received"!

"Well Mr. Colt, it seems providence has brought us together at last", answered Walker. "May I introduce you to Mr. Henry Jaeger who was the one who taught me about the idiosyncrasies of your weapon, out on the Texas plains fighting the Comanche"! At that Jaeger and Sam Colt heartily shook hands and commenced to exchange views about the strengths and weakness of the Colt firearms.

Rather than celebrate the Christmas holidays, all three men threw themselves into the redesign of the Colt revolver, then hurrying to meet with lawyers and meeting with the Eli Whitney Company to design and contract for two thousand of the new Walker .44 caliber six shot cap and ball revolver, then meeting with the Federal Ordinance Department, utilizing the Presidents name, in cutting through mountains paperwork usually involved in the acquisition of new firearms.

The new Colt .44 caliber was to be the largest hand gun ever made in the United States. The increased size of the bullet, from the undersized Paterson revolver added one more round to each cylinder, thus making the weapon more suitable for combat. Each chamber in the cylinder was enlarged to provide a larger powder charge, to propel the larger bullet with much greater force, thus making it the equal of any musket at any given range, but with an increased capacity for rounds on target.

When the first hand made trial pistols were presented to Walker and Jaeger for testing, several weeks later, they were huge in comparison to the old Colt Paterson, with a brass trigger guard, a larger hand grip and a longer barrel. Each weapon was furnished with the newly invented conical bullet design designed to provide greater accuracy, than the standard round ball design.

As they met with the Whiney people in design meetings, one of the Whitney Company's arms designers commented on Henry's heirloom saying, "I've heard legends about the old Beretta muskets, whereas they were the very first to invent rifling. I thought this weapon was a myth, because few of with were ever made but, this piece is a work of art. Twin barreled .70 caliber with a forty inch barrel." With that he eagerly drew Henry aside, offering to improve the weapon, from the flintlock design to the cap and ball design, fired with a fulminate of mercury cap, driving a new .70 caliber conical ball down range for even greater accuracy than before. "Sir this of course will be without charge and I insist that you be close at hand for each and every step of the process". The gunsmith continued, "To work on such a weapon, the superior metals involved that have lasted well over a hundred years, would be an honor and our company's gift to you".

Henry looked first at Walker then at Colt, then back at Walker who replied, "Henry, these folks are the finest gunsmiths in America and one should never look a gift horse in the mouth, should one?"

Jaeger then spit in his hand and clasped the gunsmith hand thus sealing the bargain. The following day as one group of gunsmiths were working on the new Colt revolvers, Henry was at the gunsmiths shoulder following his every move in converting his treasure into a far more deadly and accurate weapon, all the while filling in the blanks of Henry's firearms knowledge with the exacting science of ballistics. Day and night they worked and when the conversion was completed, the addition of a new adjustable sight graced the firearm with incremental gradations out to six hundred yards.

Eager to test the conversion, the duo went out to the company firing range and spent the entire day charting each shot fired down range and the angle of drop, with the new conical bullet. The Beretta was now accurate to a range of six hundred yards and a bit beyond. The company metallurgist commented to Henry, "That there Beretta was made of the finest steel available at the time Mr. Jaeger and the workmanship, as I'm sure you know, is the equal if not greater than anything, then or now"!

The following day both men tested the second batch of the new Colt Revolvers, marveling at their stopping power, accuracy at distance and much more, the balance of the new weapon. For a weapon of such great heft, had one hell of a kick when fired from the hand, that it seemed to buck like a mule each time it was fired, yet was easily twirled, coming into the hand as if it were a long lost lover.

"Damn things as heavy as a hog's leg", jibed one of the gunsmiths.

Thus the unofficial 'nom de guerre', "Hog Leg" stuck. While Sam Colt traveled down to Washington City to spread a little 'Lagniappe' around to the various people, in the form of gift samples of his latest invention to grease the wheels of payment and production politically, Jaeger and Walker returned to Baltimore to see to the enlistment and training of the newly formed Mounted rifle unit, each armed with the latest Colt .44

Even with the gifts to the War Department and key ordinance decision makers, while production was proceeding apace at the Whitney plant, the agonizingly slow pace of paperwork, in providing ancillary equipment like spares, powder flasks, bullets and bullet molds, wrenches, etc. continued.

They eventually crossed paths with Jack Hays since directed by the Governor of Texas to travel to Washington City to talk to everyone from the President on down about a nationwide recruiting drive.

Both Walker and Jaeger with the Maryland mounted units now trained and partially outfitted, with the exception of the new Colt revolvers, departed for New Orleans as did other groups, in fits and starts. Eventually with the exception of Walker and Jaeger, the mounted units would arrive at Vera Cruz far ahead if the deadly .44 Colt revolvers. As for Jack Hays, his recruitment efforts largely falling on deaf ears back east was directed to return to Texas, thence southward to join General Taylor in Mexico. Shortly after arriving in back under Taylor's command, General Taylor received orders from the War Department directed Jack Hays to be reassigned to General Winfield Scott, for the specific assignment of fighting the guerillas on the southern sector of the war. The southern campaign under General Scott was already several months under way, when Walker and Jaeger finally united once again, at Vera Cruz.

The Mounted Rangers were assigned the role of keeping the road free of guerilla activity between the towns of Jalapa and Petote. Since the Mexican guerillas never were in the habit of capturing prisoners, those that served in patrolling the roads adopted the very same tactics, with Henry running afoul with some of the regular army officers who found that his penchant for scalping and disemboweling captured Mexican guerillas who ambushed the supply wagons that traversed the road, doing many of the same things to the Americans who drove the wagons, not in keeping with the rules of warfare.

In short order the guerilla activity in this area ceased to be a problem, when wagon trains traversed those very roads. Having missed the early stages of the Scott's southern campaign for the heartland of Mexico and the various battles at Cerro Gordo, Jalapa and Perote, Jaeger and Walker found themselves in the thankless task of sheparding supply convoys and playing cat and mouse games with the variety of bandit gangs and Guerilla Groups that dogged the Army's every move. Those American soldiers, who were found to be careless in their everyday activities, were later found dead, their bodies stripped and mutilated beyond recognition. Upon several occasions, Jaeger was sent back to escort to the front lines, several military observers, from the various European powers, such as England, France and several of the German and Prussian Duchy's, amongst which was the second Duke of Wellington. As the American forces and their entourage of reporters and official observers, made their way overland from the coast, in fits and starts, trudging up through the mountain passes ten thousand feet in height, they came upon the crest of the mountains viewing the beautiful former Valley of the Aztec's below them, containing the prize of Mexico City. The army paused for several days to scout reconnoiter what lay ahead and assemble the baggage train.

All wondered just how such a relatively puny force, could capture a well-fortified city of over two hundred thousand inhabitants defended by an Army three times the size of the American forces. The Americans then came down into the Valley of Mexico in force, allotting their forces into four separate groups, each responsible for a sector of activity. By the middle of August, 1847 Winfield Scott commenced operations for the battle of Mexico City. For slightly over a week, the American and Mexican forces engaged in a series of seemingly endless small skirmishes and battles of maneuver and counter maneuver, each side fighting valiantly and bravely, but with each engagement the Mexican forces suffering far superior casualties. During these engagements scant consideration was given to capturing prisoners by either ride. After a week of almost continuous fighting, Santa Anna found that his forces had been whittled down by almost a third of what he started with, by virtue of casualties, desertion and the occasional capture by American forces. The American forces were now within three miles of Mexico City, forcing General Scott to halt and rest his weary troops plagued by sickness, battle fatigue and dwindling supplies, despite their successes.

General Scott sent an emissary to the city demanding their immediate and unconditional surrender, after placing his artillery batteries in strategic positions around the city threatening an unrelenting bombardment. Panic and riots started to spread throughout the city, with the emissary driven back to the American lines barely escaping with his life. What followed were the battles of Molino Del Rey and then later the Chapultepec Castle that closed the vise grip upon the city.

By nightfall of the 13th of September after several more weeks of intense fighting, General Worth informed General Scott, that two of the city's gates had been taken and the city proper was open to attack.

Unknown to Santa Anna, was the condition of the American forces. For their position was indeed desperate. Weary, with casualties increasing, with supplies again running low, with an inferior force numerically, divided against a still numerically superior force, they still faced a daunting task of wresting a city, house by house, street by street, from its defenders.

Inexplicably, Santa Anna came to the Americans rescue, with an army demoralized by constant defeat and a panicky population rapidly getting out of control he decided to evacuate his forces from the city via the northern gates he still held, as General Worth directed his artillery against the city.

After several attempts by civilian authorities to bargain for the surrender of the city as Santa Anna rapidly retreated, met with a resounding "No" from the Americans reminding them that the city was now at their mercy, the City of Mexico formally surrendered as the last of Santa Anna's troops fled in disgrace, vowing to fight another day.

The following day General Scott entered the now cowed and defeated city, occupying the Grand Plaza, and General Worth was given the honor of raising the American flag over the enemy's capital. Scarcely an hour after this happened, trouble again commenced when American troops were fired upon just off the plaza, causing rioting that spread throughout the entire city. For the next three seemingly endless days, a pitiless irregular warfare gripped the city, despite of endless efforts of the city officials, the Catholic Church, and the American forces to quell the insurrection. Armed patrols were sent against the mobs that roamed the streets with orders to shoot to kill anyone that came into view.

Areas, such as flat rooftops, that served snipers well were leveled by roving artillery battalions, with no quarter to be given.

After three constant days of nonstop fighting, quiet once again fell upon the city, with martial law having been declared by the Americans. In short order, courts were reopened to hear cases, newspapers resumed their printing, along with stores, shops and cantinas reopening for business. The streets were eventually cleaned of debris and the heart of Mexico beat once again.

Santa Anna had again fallen on hard times of his own making. All of his efforts to control Mexico had brought nothing but defeat and disaster to the country bankrupting the country. In one last desperate effort to restore his honor, he brought a dispirited Army to attack the American garrison at Puebla, Mexico's second city. Unable to force them out, he then tried to capture a supply train to the Capital from Vera Cruz, failing in that he was removed from command by his subordinates and fled in exile to Jamaica. The remnants of his command then disappeared into the country side, shedding their uniforms, blending in with the populace joining with and forming their own bands of banditry, for purpose of private gain. Jack Hays now fresh from Texas with a battalion of mounted Rangers joined Walker and Jaeger who were busy guarding the supply trains from Vera Cruz to Scott's forces in Mexico City. Each member of the mounted Rangers brought along the new Colt .44 Revolvers and were thusly equipped, each with the brand new weapon, thus increasing their firepower. Attached to a Brigadier General Lane, commanding 2500 fresh troops heading for the Mexican interior. Guarding a slow moving supply train of well over two hundred wagons, Walker and Jaeger each commanded a mounted rifle unit scouring the country side searching for the various gangs of banditry, on various quick, out and back forays. The soldiers and the wagons moved slowly with more than ample warning of their units.

Amongst the various units of banditry was one led by a notorious defrocked Catholic priest, formerly of the order of Jesuits, known as Cisco Andrade. Declared 'Anathema' by the Church and driven from their ranks, Andrade was a former army officer and participant of the massacre at the Alamo in 1836, who came from a family of Hidalgo's in northern Mexico, opting to leave the service of Santa Anna and eventually becoming a priest for a number of years. A skilled horseman, swordsman and pistol shot, his tenure in the service of Jesus, eventually turned to boredom, with an increasing failure to conducting himself as a man of god, spending days on end in dissipation and in the company of those of ill repute, he was eventually found out as a result of his forcible entry into the virginal daughter of a prominent family of Ranchers.

Tried under Canon Law, by the bishops of the church, he was found guilty and driven from the church. His name read at the following Sundays Mass, signaling all believer's in the land to turn their back on him, for as long as he lived. After his verdict was read aloud, he slew the priests who approached him in an attempt to remove his vestments, with a hidden dagger, then drew and cocked two hidden pistols and fired upon both of the presiding Bishop's killing them both before running out of the Cathedral and stealing a nearby mount and disappearing into the country side.

Thus embracing the darkness, he became one of Mexico's premier bandit Chieftain's traversing the land, stealing from anyone who crossed his bands path. All the while still wearing the vestments of a priest where ever he went. He would make temporary alliances with not only the government, but other bands of guerillas as the war progressed, only to break them whenever it proved expedient.

His favorite enterprise was to capture an enemy then drag that poor soul to his death behind his horse until he was unrecognizable, leaving him for the creatures of the ground to dispose of.

As General Lane and his vulnerable supply train of wagons, moved towards Puebla and hearing that a force of mounted Mexican Dragoon's were in the area guided by some renegade priest named Andrade, Lane halted his column sending ahead Walker's mounted Rifles, to survey the area ahead to a small town called "Humantla", which lay some twenty five miles from Puebla. With Henry and a dozen mounted men riding ahead of the main body of mounted rifles, Henry felt uneasy as they progressed through the small town of huts, with a single Cathedral in the towns Plaza. As they reached the other side of town Henry could see no evidence of an ambush, but feeling very uneasy about the absolute silence and absence of any activity in the town, he reluctantly signaled Walker to proceed into the main body of the town.

The main body of infantry was a half a mile away from Walkers rear as his mounted unit proceeded into the town's center. As they slowly reached the plaza, they saw that Henry's unit ahead was coming under attack by a larger force of mounted Mexican Dragoons. Spurring their mounts to join Jaeger, they suddenly ground to a halt finding themselve's surrounded by a superior force of civilian guerillas and uniformed mounted Army Dragoons. Heavily fighting ensued with Walkers group heavily outnumbered and surrounded, falling like leaves in a storm, with bullets going in all directions. His mount shot out from under him, Walker emptied his new Colt revolver, while struggling desperately to free himself from under his horse, while quickly reloading a fresh cylinder in his revolver. Just as he was able to free himself and gain his feet, he fired upon two mounted guerillas dropping both from their saddles and as he cocked his Colt drawing a bead on a third, he felt a huge bump from the rear and a sharp pain in his firing arm, seeing the remnants of his arm dropping to the earth with the revolver still firmly clasped in its hand, the gun firing harmlessly into the dust. As he whirled around to see just who had done such a thing, the pain still not having arrived to his brain, he caught a glimpse of a mounted man in black priestly vestments, wearing the large Mexican sombrero, with a huge devilish smile, as the large machete came down splitting his head in two.

Sam Walker fell to the earth, in silence, while a wild melee still surrounded him. Henry not fifty yards distant wheeled his horse around just in time to see his friend fall to earth at the hands of someone on a horse in the garb of a priest. The horseman looked at Henry for a brief moment then, with a roar of musket fire coming from the rapidly advancing American foot soldiers from his rear and seeing this Americano rapidly riding upon him reaching for a musket in his mounts scabbard, yelled loudly for his horsemen to ride into the Cathedral and out the rear, disappearing into the woods to the rear of the church.

The rapidly advancing foot soldiers destroyed the bulk of the mounted guerillas while what was left of Henrys advance horsemen chased off the Army mounted Dragoons. All over the streets of Humantla, lay the dead and the dying of both men and horses, of mounted rangers Mexican Dragoons and the guerillas. As Henry jumped from his horse, he knelt over the slain body of his friend Samuel Walker and broke into tears. As the American foot soldiers arrived to secure the town, all the Mounted

Rangers surrounded the stricken duo, with Henry cradling the fallen warrior's cleaved head in his arms. Screaming in solemn grief to the heavens repeatedly, Henry seemed to summon the clouds which let loose a misty rain on those assembled below.

A comrade had bravely gone down in battle. A leader of men beloved by all. Just then as the gentle rain misted down from the heavens, one of the Rangers looked up and said, "Henry, look up. Even God is crying"! Then even to a man all the Rangers started to shed tears. Even men hardened by years of fighting the Comanche, who made it a point of never shedding a tear for any reason, found it impossible to withhold their grief. As the American General Lane approached he yelled, "What's going on here"?

Now dismounted he made his way into the center of the crush of soldiers and Rangers, seeing the cleaved skull of Sam Walker, in the arms of Henry Jaeger, just as one of the Rangers addressed the General, "You want to know what's going on General, I'll tell ya. Today a man died"! Seeing the carnage and the manner of Walkers death and having just met him days before and impressed by his manner and the stories that grew from newspaper reports about his activities. General lane agreed, "Yes it seems that this day a man amongst men has indeed died"! Then addressing the Rangers he said, "Gentlemen, seems a military funeral for a brave warrior is in order, are we agreed"? A loud shout came from the Rangers. "Then if you will be kind enough to see to it and find a suitable place for burial" I will halt the column for several hours to accomplish this. Rangers and Common foot soldiers gathered together to secure the town, and find a suitable place for burial.

While all this was occurring, Walkers heart was still pouring out his blood onto the ground bit by bit, and Henry thought he could see some faint eye movement by Walker and said, "I know who this man is Sam and I swear he'll die by my hand". With that Sam Walkers lone eye closed its last.

Just then one of the American troop's, picked up Walkers severed arm laying just feet away, still clutching the big Colt revolver in a tight grip saying to Henry, "Here sir, I believe this is his"! After thanking the soldier, Henry gradually laid Sam Walker on the dusty street, wrenching the Colt from Walker's lifeless grip and went to Walkers dead horse, removing the saddlebags and Saddle and tack, directing several of the troopers to place them in one of the supply wagons. He removed all of Walkers personal effects, along with all the accoutrements, that would belong to Walkers former sidearm, now in the custody of Jaeger.

Now armed with two .44 Colts, Henry made a silent promise as Walker was lowered into the ground, that both of the firearms would be put to good use and soon. Walkers Grave was separate from the long trench the troopers dug for the Americans that perished and all great care was made to hide the grave site with suitable brush so the locals wouldn't be able to find it. No grave markers for brave men who died.

The killing of Walker, though an act of combat, made all the troops extremely bitter along with General Lane, for many of them considered him a national hero, by virtue of the numerous newspaper reports and their personal contacts with the man.

The enemy forces now duly scattered, he directed the town be turned over for immediate plunder, by saying to one of his Captains saying, "Lets light this whole place up". Within the hour, the last of the long supply train headed for Mexico City, completed its passage, through the former blazing town of Humantla, that was no more, leaving scores of dead animals and partisans lying in the streets.

Henry was now the commander of both the remnants of his mounted unit but that of Walkers in addition. This was the very last thing he wanted to do, for the renegade priest was getting away and Henry was eager to get after him while the scent was fresh. Yet his duty and obligation to see the re supply mission to Mexico City through to its ultimate conclusion was vital. Later that night, during his few moments of solitude by the light of the campfire, he brought out his weatherproofed writing tablets, and began writing yet another of the series of letters, he'd been writing to his precious Joselita, since they were parted. The letters now grew to about fifty, all as of yet un mailed, since no reliable service was available between wherever he was and the Fuentes rancho near Monterrey. Many night he poured his heart out to her, telling her of the events at hand and even more important the innermost feelings he had, something he'd relate to no man, even his best friends.

The death of Sam Walker struck him so deeply, that in many ways it was the equal to the death of his family, long ago by the Shawnee Red Hair. But in the course of time, Henry had learned one basic thing. Whereas most of us are led to believe that we should have faith in the eternal father, faith was very hard to get ones hands around, seeing that it had no form, or history. Yet an even greater thing replaced the concept of 'faith' and that was the concept of 'confidence'.

For years Henry periodically prayed to God, that one day his path would cross that of the Red Hair, relying on faith alone, with no guarantees that this event would occur. Then one day his prayers were answered and eternal justice was indeed meted out. As Henry's abilities increased, he often wondered why others had suffered injuries and death at the hands of the enemies and he had not. Was it pure luck, or something else?

But now the concept of faith, while still important was replaced by the concept of confidence. He now had a body of evidence with which to draw from, which he could measure, gauge and rely upon. In his entire event filled life, the eternal had never once failed him. Not once. Allowing him sufficient time to grow in a host of ways and hone the variety of skills he would need to survive and then ultimately prosper. Many obstacles had been placed in his path, with each and every time he surmounted. Perhaps there was a purpose for his family's slaughter. Perhaps there was even a purpose in Sam Walkers death.

In both cases the solution eluded him. What was certain, was a comment once by Ranger Mike Chevallie, long ago in a saloon in San Antonio, when he said; "Never become close friends with someone when in battle, for if they get killed its every bit as bad as if one of your own blood got killed"! Those words now echoed this truth.

Several days later Jack Hays, now a Colonel and in command of his own unit of Mounted Rangers, caught up with General Lanes supply column and after hearing word of Major Walkers death, from the General, sought out Henry, where the two men commiserated the entire afternoon. At the very least glad to see that each other was in one piece, Henry turned over the command to Hays.

Early in December the Texans entered Mexico City at the head of the supply column.

The altitude, cold weather and the sheer size of the city refused to inhibit the Rangers.

In a uniform column, replete with rifles, pistols, knives, wide brimmed hats and every kind of coat and serape'; the bearded men rode in silence, their reputation as fierce fighters having preceded them. They moved their mounts at a slow walk proceeding to the city's main plaza, while they awaited assigned quarters. Only Henry Jaeger, stood out amongst the others, sitting tall on his large Appaloosa with the serape' covering, the overly wide sombrero, the gaudy Mexican saddle, and his long blonde hair and short beard, was indicative of a Castilian heritage.

What caught everyone's immediate attention as Henry rode past was that his horse was bristling with an array of weaponry that could and had killed at any range. This big Norte' Americano's silent presence caused fear upon all that dared to glance his way.

Until the arrival of the Texans, the city, now at peace was usually in an uneasy calm. With constant reports of American troops being assaulted by roving bands of civilians, thieves were running rampant. Those who doubted the reputation of the Rangers were in for a very nasty time. For the Rangers methods, while Draconian, were effective.

When one of the Rangers was buying some sweets from a street vendor and haggling price the vendor grew angry and picked up some stones and started to throw them at the Ranger who drew his long Colt revolver and shot the man dead. He then took his sweets and placed several coins on the man's dead body before walking off. On another occasion, one of the street people, snatched the hat off the head of a Ranger and ran. The Ranger shouted for him to halt in Spanish, and seeing that he wasn't going to stop pulled his Colt and shot the fleeing robber dead, recovering his hat. You just didn't knock the hat off a Texan. General Scott, a few weeks before Christmas, directed that each post in the city commence active street patrols with the purpose of pushing out of the city, the partisan guerilla bands that plagued the city, by whatever means available. Many officers of Santa Anna, simply shed their uniforms and blended in with the population wherever possible. Many of the Rangers accompanied the regular army patrols; seasoned in the assault of Monterrey they shared their knowledge of urban combat with the regulars on patrol. Whenever they came upon a bandit or a partisan, they killed him outright, or questioned him harshly to glean information, then killed him.

While Hays stayed behind in Mexico City to lead the Rangers, Jaeger was directed to take a contingent of Ranger's back down the road, to Puebla, to join up with some regular army mounted dragoons. Information had arrived that the former Mexican General Mariano Parades, was the leader of a band of former soldiers that were now mounted partisans and bandits. What was particularly interesting was that this man had joined forces with another bandit chieftain. A former army officer and priest called Cisco Andrade.

Hearing that, Henry stood up immediately along with Mike Chevallie, and with so much as another word waved good bye and saddled up a company of Rangers departing for Puebla which was on the road back to Vera Cruz. Once at Puebla they presented orders from General Worth directing the local commander to assign a troop of mounted Dragoons to accompany the Rangers commanded by a Captain John Daggett, while at the direction of either Jaeger and/or Chevallie.

With Jaeger and a few others riding ahead, the unit traveled mostly at night to minimize their exposure to the locals. Hearing that the former General Paredes and his group was in a town called Otumba a day's ride away. The unit rode in that direction, all night reaching Otumba around daylight. Resting and tending to their mounts, they questioned a local who said that both Paredes and El Diablo (Andrade) now known as the "Devil Priest", had left for San Juan Teotihuacan, a small village about thirty mile away back towards Mexico City.

Awaiting nightfall, and seeing that both Paredes and Andrade had stripped the town clean of supplies for their own purposes, leaving the occupants destitute, Jaeger and Chevallie departed. Riding all night with Jaeger at the head of the column they approached San Juan Teotihuacan early in the morning. Surrounding the town, they awaited sunrise, noting that like all Mexican towns there were entrance and exit roads that always led to the main square. In this case there were three exit points away from the center of town and Henry mounting a small hill some two hundred yards distant from the square, with a clear view of everything, directed both Chevallie and Captain Daggett to have a contingent to block every exit. Counting some eighty odd horses in the town square and knowing that he had fifty nine other souls with him, most of which now were armed with the new Colt 'hog leg' revolvers, the odds were considered better than even.

The plan of battle was agreed upon, with the hearing of the second rifle shot from Henry, Chevallie's men would enter the plaza choking off one method of retreat commencing fire on anyone in the main square, while the other two groups would hold fast to their positions and fire upon anyone that rode their way. An hour later as the sun crested one of the hills; the town awoke to the sounds of two rifle shots that rang out bringing down two sentries in the town square. As men came out of the stone built buildings that ringed the central square still groggy from their sleep Chevallie's men started to open fire on anyone in the street. As still more men emerged from the buildings heading for their horses, sporadic gunfire echoed from the square and those lucky enough to find a mount did so and made for the other two exits away from Chevallie's withering fire, only to find a yet another withering barrage awaiting that route, their luck had run its course. Slowly all groups converged on the town square firing at will at any target that presented itself. As each approached the town square, everyone started counting bodies, counting over seventy five bodies out of eighty horses, left five unaccounted for. An immediate house to house search commenced and several minutes' later gunfire erupted from one of the buildings ringing the plaza. Then silence, other than the sounds of those dying in the towns square.

Then several Dragoons drug out the final five, from one of the buildings, three of which were dead and one well on his way, with the only survivor was a man in the partial uniform of a Mexican General, without his boots.

By now Henry had made his way to the central plaza joining Chevallie.

Captain Daggett spoke to the General through an interpreter saying, "General Parades I presume", before he could answer Daggett, grabbed a single shot scatter gun from one of his Dragoons, bringing it to full cock and pointed it at the now sobbing and cowering General saying, "Where is Andrade, the priest"?

This caused Paredes to throw himself prostrate at Captain Daggetts feet saying in Spanish, that he didn't know. That Andrade and his twenty horsemen, left the previous day, heading north towards probably Tampico on the Gulf Coast.

Surveying the carnage in the towns square Daggett, Chevallie and Jaeger all agreed that the operation would have been a complete success had they bagged Andrade the priest. With the only casualty a Ranger and as the building to building search had uncovered only cowering towns people with no signs of Andrade or any of his people, separate interrogation of the towns folk confirmed Paredes claim that El Diablo and his men had left the day before after only a six hour stay, heading north.

With Paredes guerilla unit obliterated completely and a cache of arms and ammunition discovered the Dragoons decided to return to the garrison in Pueblo bringing along General Paredes to present him to General Scott to suffer any fate Scott deemed appropriate.

Now the question as to what to do about Andrade the priest murderer of the beloved Sam Walker, who was probably just a day or so ride ahead of them.

Before Chevallie could say anything Henry said; "Mike, this is my task and mine alone and I need to travel light and fast if I'm to ever catch up with the bastard". At that several other Rangers who had known and rode with both Henry and Walker ever since the days of fighting the Comanche, said "Henry don't leave us out of this please, we're coming along to the bitter end, no matter what you say"! Y'all know me and my conditions are this, once in never out, even to the death and whatever I say is to be done immediately, even to the death"! Another Ranger then added, "If not sooner"! With grim determined faces all around everyone nodded in agreement, then Henry said, "We're gonna need an extra mount per man and supplies for a few weeks, Captain Daggett"!

Daggett nodded in agreement saying, "We've a plaza full of mounts gentlemen, take your pick". An hour later, as he prepared to depart with his men Henry took Mike Chevallie's hand saying, "Don't know if our paths will ever cross again Mike, but if they never do, it's been good knowing you". Both men shook hands then Henry mounted his horse, adjusted his sombrero and rode out of the plaza, leading his men north, following tracks at a measured pace. Not a several hundred yards from town, the mottled tracks of a large body of men were not difficult to follow. With the men and mounts well fed, watered and rested and extra mounts that could be switched every other hour, Henry was certain that he could make up for lost time.

What he didn't count on was that Cisco Andrade was also a man on a mission. A mission to sow misery and discord amongst the citizenry. The nation was in a shambles, with no viable political entity in charge and the remnants of Santa Anna's vaunted military were scattered to the four winds, in fragmented groups of bandits and guerilla's which really were no different from each other, living off the land by whatever means were available.

With the Norte' Americanos still occupying Northern Mexico and Southern Mexico, Central Mexico was relatively untouched by the conflicts, with only the pitiful local governments in charge. If Andrade moved hard and fast he could concentrate on the Cathedrals and the few banks in the area for supplies and cash. If anyone had the money in this country it was the church. For rumors had it that when Santa Anna, returning from exile, tried to raise the money for an Army to go North and do battle with the Americano's, the government was unable to comply and he had to go hat in hand to the Catholic Church, for a loan or a grant for the funds to raise and equip the army.

But as he'd heard the churches in central Mexico were relatively untouched. Every sanctuary was built in the pretty much the same manner and their hiding places were generally the same all over. So each town and village he would enter he would allot no more than one hour to enter, usually in midafternoon when everyone was at siesta, hitting the Alcalde's offices, any bank in the town and the local Cathedral, killing anyone who got in their way, taking anything of value.

Henry and his small group of Rangers had to pace themselves, rather than riding flat out in pursuit of their quarry, they settled into a canter, changing mounts every other hour, stopping at a stream to water and graze the horses, then moving on. From the look of things, Andrade's band was not taking any steps towards hiding their trail and by the looks of their tracks were driving their mounts to the limit and beyond.

Eventually the trail led into the foothills of the Sierra Madre Oriental Mountains. The trail led them to a small path up through the mountains no wider than that of a mule, compelling them to ride single file, eventually traversing the crest and heading down into one of the valleys.

The following day they entered Sequalteplan at midday, their horses at a walk and tied them up at the Cathedral. Quickly noticing the square was occupied by a number of dead bodies, starting to bloat under the midday sun. Several buildings had been set on fire. Most notably were the horses, wandering around looking for food, rider less without saddles.

Encountering a withered old man, Henry spoke through one of the other Rangers fluent in Spanish asking him what happened. Just an old compesino, and one of few words, he took Henry and two others, first to the Cathedral, showing where they'd murdered the priest, then around to the rear of the sacristy, to where they'd pried open the stone hiding spot for sacred relics. Plus all of the golden artifacts were missing. Soon they would be melted down into gold bars. Then he led them across the plaza to the Alcalde's office, finding the Alcalde sitting at his desk with a bullet hole high on his forehead, like a misplaced third eye.

Then a small strong box was wide open and empty. As the old man made a swiping motion with his hands saying, "Dinero, Vamanos"! Then pointing in the northern direction they'd ridden out of town. From time to time some women and children would enter into the plazawith donkey driven carts and a slew of children, finding a bloated body of a loved one, wailing in grief, then loading the body into the cart and disappearing down an alleyway.

The old man said that all the horses in the town were taken by the El Diablo and his men, who left their played out mounts behind, which explained the presence in the Plaza of so many played out horses, some so exhausted they were soon to die, but clearly fine horses at another time.

After an hour of reconnoitering the town and finding nothing useful, the men all mounted up and rode off following the trail of Andrade's bunch.

Still heading in a northerly direction, Henry decided to camp for the evening and rest the mounts, sensing no signs of rain that might wash out the trail. Now up in the Mountains of the Sierra Madre, the nights grew cold and their encampment was in a small tree lined arroyo which shielded the glow of the fire. After each man had fed and tended to their mounts, they set to examining their weapons as was their custom for the following day. For without a good mount or a useful weapon a man wasn't of much use when amongst enemies.

Heading north the following day, they discovered a wreckage of several wagons as they'd just completed the fording of the Rio Santa Maria. No horses, one dead body, three empty wagons and a lot of horse tracks all in a muddle, then a single set of wagon wheel tracks along with a horde of other horse tracks indicated yet another encounter, with prisoner's very real possibility.

Still traveling north they entered the village of Antiquo Morelas, only to discover the same scenario as before. The town and church authorities murdered the village completely pillaged, with the dead staring at the noon day sun. By now the Andrade band was traveling in a zig zag manner, staying away from the large towns and preying only on the small villages.

When they came upon one of the few of Andrade's campsites they examined each site with great care, finding where a great fire had been built and small droplets of gold mingled in the dust, telling all that the gold religious implements stolen from the Cathedral's, had been melted down and probably distributed amongst the bandits.

By the look of things it appeared that the Rangers were now getting very close to Andrade and his bunch. They had been after them now going onto two weeks and were now far away from their fellow Americans with their supplies running low. All had been dedicated to a single sparse meal a day and had husbanded their animals as best as could be practicable, but soon they would be compelled to live off the land. Hunting of any kind was out of the question, for a gunshot might alert the enemy of their presence.

Having ridden along the banks of the Rio Tamesi and bypassed the large town of Ciudad Victoria, Henry was told of the village of Hidalgo was just a few miles ahead by a Shepard, leading his flock of goats, who saw a large group of mounted riders leading a wagon heading in that direction, not an hour before.

"Well boys, it looks like they're just up ahead", said Henry as they rode off in pursuit. As they approached Hidalgo, the sounds of gunfire reached their ears, with Henry bypassing the town riding to the wooded heights that overlooked the town. In a secluded spot they all dismounted, at about a hundred yards away from the towns square, as Henry pulled his spy glass from his saddlebags. As he surveyed the towns square, taking a count of those he encountered he noted that there appeared two men that appeared in the dark garb of Catholic priest, on horse yelling directions at men pillaging buildings on the main square. As usual, the village had a church, but this time it was rather small in comparison with others. Seeing that all were busy in the village and that there were only two ways in or out of the town, Henry directed two of the Rangers to cover the northern exit of the town, while the other two to cover the southern entrance and to be at the ready once the heard two rifle shots from Henry's Beretta rifle. Within fifteen minutes both groups signaled

Henry they were ready by a single flash of a small mirror each man had, as part of their general issue pack.

Observing through the spyglass, the central plaza Henry went through his standard pre shoot ritual, slowing his breathing and settling into his firing position. Again looking through the spyglass, his intent was to shoot both of the the priest's mounts, then quickly reload and if luck was on his side Andrade would be stuck under the horse, then he would put a ball in him, joining his men to finish off the others.

Carefully placing the second loads of powder, caps and ball close at hand for the quick reload, he again viewed the town square. At two hundred fifty yards or so this shouldn't be a difficult shot, but since both mounts were in constant movement, it just added another problem. He was well concealed and had a good field of view, yet he thought, which was which, not that it mattered just so long as both went down. He made a mental note, two men at either end of town, each with the long Colt revolver and each with three six shot cylinders at the ready, for reloads. Henry would see to it that at least two possibly three or four went down by his Beretta, plus he had both his and Walkers Colt revolver with six charged cylinders against twenty riders with single shot muskets and knives and swords.

A fair fight if there ever was one, he thought. As he took a deep breath, holding it then slowly exhaled, one of the black riders came into view as the big rifle spoke, then as the second rider came into view, the Beretta spoke again, with both horses falling. Henry quickly reloaded, taking some thirty seconds in the process. Then reacquiring his targets, he noticed that one of the bandits was not in view but the second was and he shot the one in view, then reloading again this time in a hurry, he selected two of the horses that were at one of the hitching posts, where riders were just about to mount and again the big rifle spoke twice, bringing both mounts down. As he reloaded for a final time, Henry could hear a fusillade of firing coming from both ends of town and taking a final view shot two horses with their riders going for the town's south entrance.

He then sheathed his Beretta and jumped on his horse, heading for the towns north entrance. Still hearing sporadic gunfire, he slowed his mount, securing it to a bush out of sight of the square and grabbed his Colt revolving scatter gun.

He heard firing just ahead yelling out for the two Rangers just ahead, seeing several horses lying on the ground, in their death throes, their riders and several others either dead or dying. Then he saw one of the Rangers lying dead his Colt in his hand and an empty cylinder close by indicating that he'd done his job and took several with him. Just then he saw the other Ranger on his left some thirty yards away and was about to yell at him when from three different houses, a hoard of bandits rushed them both with knives and swords, and from Henry his scatter gun roared each time bringing down a bandit stopping him in his tracks Then Henry brought to bear both his and the other Rangers Colt, knocking down each one who came after him. As he went to reload, there was still one who charged Henry, with a sword, ducking the blow, the sword knocking Henry's big sombrero' from his head, Henry pistol whipped the bandit as he ran past, knocking him senseless.

His pistols now recharged with fresh cylinders, Henry looked around to see the other Ranger of the duo, in a death struggle with two smaller bandits, each of which had a knife struck deep in the bowels of the Ranger, while he had each of his large hands around their throats, in a struggle to see who would be the first to drop. The bandits were thrashing about moving their knives in repeated motions devastating the Rangers innards while the big Ranger squeezed his large hands around each ones throat, crushing their windpipes strangling them to death.

Henry's Colt fired twice with each bandit going immediately limp. The big Ranger turned to Henry, saying with his last breath, "Thanks, Henry for I was fadin' fast"! Then he dropped to the dust, still with a death grip on each of the bandit's throats.

With the dead all around him, Henry hollered for the other Rangers, hearing no response, he yelled again. Still hearing nothing he started a building to building search, for Cisco Andrade, making occasional forays into the plaza, especially viewing one of the bandits in a cassock, whom was the first to go down courtesy of his big Beretta. Finding him very dead, he moved on around the plaza ducking into a building then back out, keeping the square under vigilance he got down to the other end of the square seeing the last two Rangers that were with him dead, with the still bodies of horses mules and bandits.

Still making his way towards the center of the square in a similar manner, he came upon the small church, quickly entering it with his back against the wall. His eyes and every one of his senses alert to any possibility. Suddenly from the rear of the church he heard a loud explosion and felt a pain in his shoulder. He ducked for cover behind one of the pews.

Since there were only thirty yards distance from the front of the church to the rear the musket ball should've knocked Henry off his feet, but as he surveyed the painful wound high up on his left side, the ball barely penetrated the skin, meaning that whoever shot him didn't put enough powder in the musket. Henry had never been shot before and the wound was starting to hurt like hell as he rose to his feet, finding a priest with a gleaming cavalry saber in his hand battle ready. This must be the real Cisco Andrade, Henry thought as he started to approach down the churches main aisle, stopping ten yards away.

"Habla Englese", Henry asked?

"Better than you Vato", sneered the priest, his sword in his trembling hand, signaling defiance. "So then you must be Cisco Andrade, eh"?

"I am Cisco Andrade, and I will soon kill you", he spat in heavily accented but precise English.

"So you're the one who cut off the arm of a Ranger in Puebla, then cleaved his head in two"?

"So you were there to see that eh"?

"And I suppose that is the sword in your hand, that did the evil deed", stated Henry!

At that, Andrade stood erect, bringing the saber to a salute than back at the ready, saying this is the hand and the sword that performed the glorious deed"!

At that, Henry brought the big Colt revolver up and as it rose his firing thumb brought the hammer to full cock and fired off a round into the priests leg, spinning him around and knocking the priest off his feet, the sword spinning out of his grip, clattering to the stone floor. As Henry slowly approached, he saw the folds of the priest's vestments open up and again the big Colt revolver bucked in his hand, shattering the knee of the priest, who tried not to, but bellowed, forth with a mighty scream of pain.

Henry was in pain, but he wouldn't for a moment trade his pain for that of the priest And as Henrys pain would eventually subside in time the priest's pain was only just beginning. Henry went over to retrieve, the sword, then returned and grabbed the priest's pony tail that secured his long black locks, dragging the wailing priest out of the church by his hair and out into the main plaza. Only to be greeted by some of the towns people who somehow emerged from hiding, to view the carnage. In broken Spanish Henry directed several of the men to bring back his Rangers from both ends of the square. Then somehow some of the women came forth and made motions they wanted to look at Henrys wound. Horses were retrieved as well as all of the weapons by the villagers. Henry retrieved the Rangers firearms and gave the others to the villagers for their own defense.

One of the old peasant women with a well weathered face seemed to take charge signaling several others to return with some implements.

Minutes later a bowl was brought out and the others returned with the things she asked for. With the priest Andrade writhing in agony on the ground with Henry watching him with his big Colt following his every move and sitting on the edge, of the central squares fountain the old woman cleansed Henrys wound with water. Peering into the would she brought forth a small pointed instrument looked into Henrys eyes, nodded, then gently probed the wound eventually bringing forth the large musket ball that hadn't penetrated too far in, along with some modest detria and blood. Henry gritted his teeth against the pain.

The assembled crowd was growing restless, watching for the slightest wavering in the big Rangers resolve as the old woman removed the bullet. Henry grimaced in pain, his eyes scanning those preening to gain a view. He knew it was all for show to demonstrate a superiority of his existence surrounded by potential enemies. As Andrade, the renegade priest, still writhing in agony from his shattered leg tried to move in a more comfortable position, Henry squeezed of another shot this time shattering the priests foot, as his cried of pain and anguish intensified.

This caused the rest of the crowd to move back some distance, but the old woman didn't seem to notice, continuing to cleanse the wound with the squares fountain water, then gently applying a poultice into the wound, then reaching for a needle and thread that had been prepared. Looking again into Jaegers eyes, she said, "No Muerte' Senor", then winked pinching the edges of the wound together stitching the skin together. Those crowding around, marveled at the stoic way the Norte' Americano grunted each time the needle penetrated his skin. When the task was completed, one of the village women offered Henry, an earthen jar of 'Pulque', with which to quench his thirst and lessen the pain. Painfully Henry stood up, showing the crowd, that not only was he still alive, but bristling with an assortment of weaponry, causing them again to draw back and give him space. He then approached the lone wagon laden with the booty gained by the bandits, directing several of the villagers, to rummage through the lot. Eventually discovering the gold bars that were inside some sealed boxes, he indicated to the villagers for them to keep the bars as well as all that was in the wagon, plus the horses, saddles, trappings, in return for the proper burial of the Rangers. Gathering up all of the Colt revolvers along with the holsters, powder, spare cylinders and ball, they were bundled up into a package and placed on one of the Rangers horses along with all of the private possessions in the saddlebags of each Ranger and loaded onto the spare Ranger horse that Henry took with him. Turning his full attention to the renegade Andrade, still writhing in pain in the dust of the town square, Henry walked around him slowly several times, wondering just what to do with this murderer. Torn between killing him outright, thus putting him out of his misery and pain, wanting something more. Clearly Henry would leave him as a cripple for life, should he leave him as he was. On the other hand, killing him here and now would guarantee that he could cause no further harm to anyone else ever. This seemed to be the only course of action that a rational man would consider. Then a third course of action came to mind as he continued his slow journey of encirclement of Andrade. For the seemingly modest cost of just a few more caps, powder and balls, a round in each shoulder and the as of yet remaining uninjured knee, would cause immeasurable pain and guaranteed suffering for the rest of his life and possibly a slow and lingering death.

As Henry still circled Andrade, considering the possibilities, he looked to the crowd, searching for an answer. Then as he looked back at Andrade, he saw a look of defiance and concluded the best course of action would be to remove any possibility of Andrade being a burden to anyone ever again. Then bringing his weapon to bear, shot Andrade, in one shoulder, then the other and finally in the knee as he continued his encirclement.

The villagers cowed by the Rangers presence, in spite of his wound and wondering why a priest would bring bandits into their village, only to be rescued by Americano's who clearly gave their lives for strangers, could only stand in mute silence as this event worked its way towards conclusion.

For anyone to do this to a priest indicated a revenge motive that was of supreme importance.

As Henry made his final circuit, he brought the big Colt to a point between Andrade's eyes, then pulled the trigger as the big hog leg blew apart Andrade's head, his jerking body coming still. He would trouble people no more.

Then Henry turned to one of the old men and asked, "Donde esta Matamoras", Whereupon the man pointed down the road in a northerly direction a cross road, thus going in one direction would take him to Matamoras, then added if he went in the other direction, he would arrive in Monterrey.

At that Henry placed the big sombrero on his head and painfully climbed into his saddle and taking the reins of the spare mount gave a tip of his hat, spurring his mount to a slow canter as he left the town square. As he passed each person in turn, they made the sign of the cross as he gradually faded from view.

In the days and weeks to come, the villagers learned of what terror they narrowly missed, by the arrival of Andrade's renegades. Of events that occurred in the villages he visited south of them. Of what he was and what he and his people did. More important was the gold, horses and weapons that had been placed before them, of which they would all benefit and of which they would remain silent. For a time, the village would prosper. The dead Americanos would be buried some with dignity, while others would be dumped in a common trench far away from the village proper and thinly covered so the carrion could eat their fill of the remains. Ashes to ashes....

10

As Henry made his way northward, having taken the fork in the road leading towards Matamoras, he reflected on the small fortune that he left behind, in horses, saddles firearms and most important the melted down gold that Andrade had stolen from the others. A snap decision to be sure, but one that went a far distance in purchasing goodwill and his life. Besides, he had his all of his personal things, plus four other Colt .44's which counted for a great deal. Prior to his departure one he'd seen of the Compesino's, rip the cross that hung from Andrade's neck along with the string of Rosary Beads, pressing them into Henry's hands. He supposed that the peasant wanted to make certain that Andrade arrived for his meeting with his maker, completely naked and alone.

Bringing to mind the old Latin adage, "We are born alone and die alone"!In the coming days, he'd srt through the personal effects of those who rode with him that final time and try to find any relatives to the best of his abilities to return his personals. Not normally aware of the way he appeared to others, Henry took stock. On the surface, if he kept his head low and mumbled he could probably pass for one of the locals, what with his overall external appearance, of the big sombrero, the serape, the saddle and his horses bristling with weaponry.

After an hour of riding on the road that would lead to Matamoras, Henry decided to cut trail to his left and cross country to the Monterrey Road. He felt the change in atmosphere that indicated the arrival of rain before too much longer, which would erase any hoof prints left on the dusty trail.

He just had to see her again. Joselita! Her image flooded into his brain. The distinct sound of her voice, echoed through his head. It had been almost a year since Henry had seen or heard from her. His many letters to her still in his saddle bags undelivered. Her last message echoing, "Come back to me"!

He wondered if he'd ever see any of his old Ranger friends ever again and the answer just hung there. 'Probably not', he thought. For the only thing that mattered was Joselita. That evening he made camp and rested his horses, starting to go through the effects of the former Rangers that rode with him. Although they had not been with him very long, he should've been able to remember their names, but he couldn't. They had ridden a very long way, very fast with little time for trivial conversation. As he went through their personal effects, he couldn't find a single thing that connected any of them to anyone else. So certain he was that they'd receive a decent burial he'd purchased by the villagers, he decided to bury their personal scant personal effects, in a small hole he dug. Never to be seen again.' Small blessings', he thought, 'one less thing he had to attend to'.

Then he thought of Chani and Akila, for the first time since he left them in Joseilta's care. For most of his life they had been with him, never away from his side. Much of what Henry was about was drawn from them and never had he spent a night away from them, except for the last year. Then his eyes were drawn to his big Appaloosa mount. The horse had been with him through many a scrape with the Comanch and had been up and down northern and the southern campaign, with nary a scratch. The gift horse presented by Joselita's family was lost in the northern campaign. He's taken great care of his horse and the horse had rewarded him with reliability. It didn't get much better than that.

His left shoulder was starting to stiffen up from his wound and Henry gently removed his arm from the sling the old woman had made for him, opening his shirt and peering at the wound, still fresh with the stitched up skin all puckered up. The pain was starting to return. So Henry reapplied some of the poultice the old woman had given him, eventually lessening the throbbing pain to a manageable ache. As the small fire started to diminish, Henry gradually drifted off to a light sleep, his right hand loosely clasping the big Colt revolver.

The following morning it took him well over twice as long to saddle the horses as it normally would have, since he had only one useful arm to bring into play, careful not to engage the other, so as to allow time for the wound to heal. Besides it hurt like hell when even modestly stressed.

Not in any great hurry, he decided to ride a path some distance north of the road to Monterrey paralleling the road to his left, taking notice of everything that traveled the road. Bypassing several villages, he noticed the road traffic of farm goods was starting to increase, which told him that Monterrey must be close at hand.

The next day he drifted into Monterrey noticing that some evidence of an American Garrison was still at hand, he decided to skirt the town via the many back streets and alleys, emerging on the road to Camargo which led to the Rio Grande. By the look of things the American forces were starting to pull out of Mexico and head north, spotting several groups of infantry interspersed by a few squadrons of mounted dragoons, trailing after slow moving supply wagons.

Waiting for the column to pass from sight, Henry crossed the road, riding through the brush towards the road that led to the De la Fuente rancho, north of the city. Riding through the brush and along a narrow arroyo, he emerged on the road and as he approached a sharp right hand turn on the road he heard gunfire ahead. He brought his horse to a halt and listened. Just a few brief shots were heard, in rapid succession as he edged his horse slowly ahead peering around the bend of the road seeing, four horses, three of which were mounted with Mexican Rancho's, one of which was dismounted rummaging through the fallen bodies of three other people on the ground.

Part of Henry said to him, 'stay out of this, you've done enough,' but since they party was just forty yards away and their collective attention was away from him and in the direction of the fallen. Just then his horse gave a nervous snort, taking any course of action other than straight ahead away from him. Just as the thieving Rancho's turned their heads in Henry's direction, he spurred his mount straight ahead, leaving the other where it was, placing the reins of his horse in his stiff and painful left hand and reaching for the fully charged Colt revolver in his right, charging right into the horses as the started to wheel around, getting off two shots in rapid fire each hitting a rider knocking them from the saddles, the third horse was knocked to the ground rolling over its rider as Henrys horse got tangled up and came crashing down, throwing Henry to the ground, separating him from his horse and his Colt revolver.

The pain in Henry's wounded shoulder ran through his body like a bolt of lightning as he rolled and struggled to regain his feet. The fourth rider was rushing towards him with a drawn knife, and took a sweeping swipe at Henry as he rushed by, with Henry leaping out of the way, but not fast enough to avoid the knife completely seeing that a crimson stripe suddenly appeared in a wide diagonal stripe from his right shoulder across his chest to his hip. His Colt revolver some distance away on the ground, Henry instinctively drew his big Bowie knife as the Rancho turned and leapt back at Henry with a vengeance. Now in great pain Henry manage to parry the bandits thrust. For several moments they both circled each other, Henry could see an element of fear in the other man's eyes. This was indeed the moment of supreme truth for both of them. The other smaller but very fast and relatively fresh and Henry larger but now with multiple wounds and starting to tire. Yet something deep inside said that he'd come too far and done too much to have things end with at the hands of a common thief.

Henry the sneered, "Andale' Vato" and as the thief charged him again, this time feinting left then right, Henry countered his feints, side stepping the thief, as their knives touched with a dull clang, getting their legs tangled up Henry pivoted around and with his left arm still in the sling, brought it around the bandits neck and drove the big Bowie knife straight into his back, emerging out his chest as both fell to the ground. For a brief moment, the bandit tried to struggle out of Henry's grasp, but a twist of Henry's knife stopped all movement.

In great pain from both of his wounds Jaeger struggled to feet, only to see the that the one he'd not had time to shoot was crushed by his horse as it fell to the ground. By now all of the downed horses had regained their feet and Henry went around to everyone to see if anyone had survived. As he approached one of the men who were not the bandits, he saw that the man was clearly older and well dressed, and apparently suffered nothing more than a blow to the head and the two men that had accompanied him were shot dead, clearly by the bandits.

Henry gathered his revolver and holstered it as he approached the older man and helped him to his feet. He went to his saddle and got his canteen returning to the older well-dressed man offering him a drink, saying "Agua Senor". Without looking up the older man reached out and deeply drank, the water overlapping his lips, returning the container to Henry who joined him in a deep draught.

His senses starting to return, the older man, clearly dressed and with the superior manor of one born to privilege, took the measure of the one who saved him. Dressed like a Rancho, but clearly an Anglo and asked in broken English, "Anglo senor". Henry responded, "Henry Jaeger at your service Senor".

"And what brought you to Mexico if I may ask"?

"You don't want to know that Senor for my affairs are my own business and no one else's", said Jaeger slight annoyed by the imperious manner of the man whose life he'd just saved.

"I would think it would be a common courtesy to know the name of the person who's life I've just saved", said Henry.

"Perdonna Me Senor", said the Hidalgo with a nod, continuing in halting heavily accented English "I am Don Francisco Andrade. I've come from Saltillo and I have business with Don Domingo de la Fuentes, when we were set upon by these animals and I ask your pardon for my ill manners"!

"Andrade eh", answered Jaeger slightly taken aback? 'The world was getting to be too small a place', he thought.

"You have heard of my family's name senor"?

Thinking quickly, Henry replied, "Who hasn't heard of the Andrade name", he stated with a wry smile and a nod. Then continuing on he said, "Seems we're both heading in the same direction"!

"You have business with Don Domingo", Andrade asked incredulously? "In a manner of speaking", answered Henry grimacing, the pain returning to his wounded shoulder. Henry then changing the subject said, "Let's get your people on their horses, and collect the other horses, then we can go on to the Fuentes rancho. The others can stay here and rot"!

Whereupon they struggled to get Andrade's men draped over their mounts and secured, gathered the others and Henry struggled to regain his Appaloosa, finally saddled upright and they proceeded to complete their journey, both worse for wear, but still alive.

Joselita, was out in the pasture when she heard both Chani and Akila start to howl. Usually the only did this during the period of the full moon and it indeed disturb the livestock, to such a degree that she had to come outside in her night clothes and gather them inside for the duration of the full moon period. Other than that, they would roam the edges of the pasture at night keeping the other predators at bay. Several months previous, they even teamed up on a Jaguar who thought he'd get an easy night meal of one of the calves, only to get a nasty final surprise, courtesy of Chani and Akila.

The following morning the vaqueros discovered the dead Jaguar in the middle of the pasture with its throat ripped out with the cattle giving the dead cat a wide berth.

Only later in the day when Chani and Akila were in the barn nursing their wounds was Don Domingo summoned by the head Vaquero who related what happened. Joselita was immediately summoned whereas she was the only one Chani and Akila would allow to nurse their wounds. Now the wolves each weighed in at well over a hundred pounds each with Akila the male, standing almost to the hips of Joselita, who was in her own right a tall slender woman. But both were almost dwarfed by the big Jaguar, whose claws fully extended were well over an inch long.

Rushing to the center of the pasture, seeing the dead male Jaguar, the Vaqueros all made the sign of the cross, and immediately sensed from the disturbed ground and the multiplicity of wounds on both the dead cat and the wolves, that a monumental struggle had occurred amongst two feral breeds for survival. For a hungry male Jaguar could do a great deal of damage to a herd of cattle and horses.

It was early afternoon when the wolves began to howl, summoning Joselita to come out of the main house and approach them, calming them down sensing their nervousness, uncharacteristic except in the period of the full moon. She sat with them for several hours, their presence reminding her of the big Ranger. It had been almost a year and she'd heard not a word from him. As of late her father and mother were making suggestions that Jaeger probably wasn't going to return. For reports had filtered north of the heavy fighting in southern Mexico and the eventual fall of the capital and the embarrassing defeats suffered by their superior forces against inferior numbers of the invading Americans. Reports of Santa Anna, again in exile, this time in Jamaica, were abundant. The vast lands lost to the Americano's, were a festering sore in the soul of every Hidalgo. Even worse, if that was possible was the feckless government in Mexico City. Yet the martial law of the Americanos was coming to an end, with their current withdrawal across the Rio Grande. Signaling a time for all of her father's Vaqueros, to go armed once again. For the bandits were to soon roam the land, with a vengeance. With the lack of news as to whether Henry was alive or dead, her parents were starting to make plans for an arranged wedding with any number of the sons, of the high born families in northern Mexico, chief of which was the Andrade family of Saltillo. Don Francisco had two sons, recently returned from the southern military wars with the Americanos.

Both of which had been formally introduced to her recently. Normally either one of them would provide a modest interest, which might serve as a basis to proceed. But the more they preened and displayed their male dominance, the less interested she became. Her heart, hopelessly the property of the big Americano.

Memories of the story of Cyrano de Bergerac, flooded into her mind, with the ardor between the beautiful but hopelessly inarticulate Christian and the beautiful Roxanne, their love never fully consummated. Christian's heroic death in her arms and her grief so massive that only the walls of a Parisian convent and the daily vespers where she could silently converse with her distant lover, could keep one day marching into the rest. But there in the wings, was the one, the only one, the ever faithful Cyrano. The old warrior poet, the gruff, profane, yet gentle silent knight, her guardian till his final breath.

Henry Jaeger was her Cyrano. Anyone could learn artful words, but this was a man amongst men. The very moment she saw him at High Mass long ago, kneeling in silent prayer, oblivious to all but the eternal, she then knew, she knew……. She would wait. For his wolves were her constant reminder and their very presence were beyond price.

Joselita softly drew Chani and Akila to her as they all joined together.

For a while they seemed to calm down, but eventually their restlessness grew in intensity. They gently nudged her and nipped her arm to come with them around to the front entrance of the rancho.

As Henry and Don Francisco came over a rise in the road, they could see the entrance to the Fuentes encomienda. There, they would be assured that aid for the elder Andrade's head wound and Henry's extensive wounds would be forthcoming. As Henry looked down he could see the front of his shirt was stained with blood and was gradually growing in size. As he hadn't taken the time to examine his wounds, he assumed that the bandits knife slash wasn't all that bad. Apparently he was wrong, for he started to feel light headed and instinct told him that he was fading fast.

As the main house came into view, he saw both Chani and Akila running towards him in advance of what seemed like an angelic vision. He felt another hand grasp him as he weaved in the saddle and turned to see Don Francisco leaning over in the saddle holding him upright as they rode up to the rancho. Then he slumped forward, draped over the big Appaloosa's neck. Screaming at the top of her lungs, Joselita summoned everyone from the house and as many of the Vaqueros were available, to help the wounded form their horses and into the house, while seeing to the other mounts in tow. Sometimes prayers are answered in rather strange ways. Joselita was both elated and angry at the same moment, for Henry seemed to be in terrible shape and unable to even stand upright much less having to recognize Joselita. Her fondest wish granted via celestial intervention, only to be taken away at the very cusp of her happiness. Then the thought entered he mind of the old adage, "The Lord giveth and the Lord taketh away"! 'What kind of God would play such a cruel joke', she thought as she directed the Vaqueros to place Henry on her bed then go summon the doctor in Monterrey, Muy Pronto. While her father and some of the servants saw to Don Francisco, Joselita and her mother and two of her sisters, removed Henry's blood sodden clothes and began the task of cleansing his body and wounds in advance of the doctors arrival which was at least several hours away, if he was available.

The horses were put up and fed, with Henry's personals all brought to Joselita's bedroom for now began her vigil. Just before sundown, the Vaquero's returned with the doctor and were immediately ushered up to Joselita's bedroom. There, all prepared and cleaned by the women, an ashen faced Henry was laying, at last in the pristine bed linens of the high born.

The doctor quickly went to work, discovering what the problems were, and issued instructions to the women of the house as what to bring immediately, which sent them scurrying about with a purpose of immediacy.

As he worked the Doctor explained what was wrong, to those assembled in the bedroom. First the musket ball wound seemed to be several days old and was rudimentarily sewn up, but an infection was just starting to take hold and as Henry's recent apparent activity had ripped open many of the stitches the wound would have to be reopened and recleaned and be allowed to drain naturally.

Next and almost equally important, the knife wound he suffered defending Don Francisco, was almost two feet long from his shoulder slashing down across his breast bone and his ribs, slashing deep into his musculature, which was considerable. As he worked the doctor said, "While this is serious, I think we can heal him, while a less robust man would have been cut to the bone and have bled out"! Whereupon he cleaned the long open wound and began to properly apply stitches to Henry's wounds while he was still unconscious. Seeing that his patient had apparently stabilized he allowed himself to be led to the dining room and bed fed a sumptuous feast. As he ate, he and Don Francisco exchanged views with Don Domingo, who added to their knowledge of what Senor Jaeger had done for not only Don Domingo, but his daughter and the General Taylor during the battle of Monterrey. Don Francisco, seeing that his counterpart's daughter was clearly in the thrall of the Americano said, "Seems that our plans for your daughter and any of my sons will have to be put on the shelf, my friend"

In reply Domingo said, "The heart of a woman is a precious thing never to be tampered with or amended"! Pondering a bit he continued, "An Americano he may be, but a 'Bravo' he is and after all he is Catholic"...... The doctor stayed the night and half the next day, having also tended to Don Francisco. After having been remunerated the doctor was led back to Monterrey where he went to an apothecary and procured certain medicines and sent them back with the vaqueros, with precise instructions as to their use for Senor Jaeger. Chani and Akila were permitted to enter Joselita's bed room to attend their master, periodically during the day, then apparently satisfied their master was going to recover, went down upon the advent of sundown, were well fed by Juan Mendoza one of the vaqueros they'd had apparently taken a liking to, them went about their business making the periodic rounds of the various herds of livestock in the various pastures and corrals. Interestingly enough, in any given year, the vaqueros would report several of the livestock were missing and their carcasses eventually discovered victims of the predators in the wilds. But since Chani and Akila, started making their rounds each and every night, no matter what the weather, not one of the livestock met an untimely death.

Every night, Joselita stood vigil, at Henry's side tending to him, whispering to him, praying for him and every morning the wolves arrived on time after being fed by the vaquero Mendoza and relieved her, standing vigil at the foot of the bed along with a steady stream of others while Joselita slept on a small settee.

On the third day, Henry briefly awoke, still weak from the loss of blood, his eyes caught sight of Joselita and he asked weakly, "Am I dreaming"?

Joselita softly responded with tears starting to well up in her eyes, "No, me Amor, you are not dreaming", beaming with a gentle smile. "You have but one thing to do now is rest and get better so we can be as one, so close your eyes and dream good dreams". At that she gently lifted Henrys head, reaching for the small goblet of water at the bed stand and helped him to drink, then placed his head gently back on the pillow as he drifted back to sleep.

The following morning, he again woke up and was joined upon the bed by Chain and Kaila, eager to shower their still ailing master with unrestrained licks of joy, when they were gently but forcibly removed from the bed. Suitably chastised, they assumed their position of watchfulness at the foot of the bed.

For the first time in his adult life, Henry was treated almost as an infant, cleansed daily from head to toe, by the family servants, fed by both Joselita and her mother Encarnacion.

Little by little, Henry's Spanish began to improve, as he made his basic needs known to everyone. Eventually he was able to use the bedroom chamber pot, to evacuate his daily waste's, always with the keen attendance of Chani and Akila. Henry was visited weekly by the doctor, who examined him finding that his wounds were gradually on the mend but that he must not leave the comforts of this bed for at least several more weeks.

Of course this met with Joselita's immediate approval, for what better way could her dreams be answered. She would sleep on the uncomfortable bedroom settee for an entire year if need be, if it would help Henry recover. Such was the depth of her ardor for him.

She took great delight fussing over him and insisted in handling the bulk of the feeding personally, depositing with great care each and every morsel of food and every drop of liquid he consumed as if he were a small child. All the while they conversed endlessly, engaging in subjects both great and trivial.

After a month in bed, a decision was made, by the doctor that Henry was permitted to rise and attend his meals with the rest of the family and that his wounds had sufficiently healed to permit daily walks. Of course, during their daily walks, the family Duena, Tante' Juanita, was ever discreetly at a distance, to ensure that the proprieties were to be observed.

After an inspection of Henry's property, Henry decided to present gifts to his benefactors. After the evening meal, he presented to Don Domingo, his eldest son and the Chief Vaquero and Juan Mendoza who took it upon himself to look after Henry's Appaloosa horse personally on a daily basis in addition to his other duties, as well as tending to Chani and Akila, the four Walker Colt .44 pistols along with their accoutrements.

The following day, he instructed them in the care and maintenance of such a state of the art weapon. Of course they would end up being unaccounted for by the US Government but so would many others, due to the fog of war, Henry reasoned. In all of Mexico, no one but the Fuente family had such a prized weapon. Henry took great care in instructing them in its use and its limitations. Joselita and her family observed these efforts at a distance, noting that Henry was a great marksman, without his equal from where they reckoned. The following day, Henry mounted his big Appaloosa horse for the first time, with some difficulty, due to the soreness still in his mending muscles. But wearing all of the trappings, of a Vaquero, he rode the horse, with the attitude of a true Caballero. The sombrero wore in a rakish manner, slightly tilted on his head, the head straps tied tightly behind his head. As he rode around the rancho, Henry encountered vaqueros with great skills of horsemanship, equaling anything he'd seen from the Comanche of the Kiowa Indians. Of course, Henry's horsemanship was not quite of their caliber, but more than sufficient to serve his needs. He saw little needs to take the risks they did, by driving their mounts almost to the edge of revolt and exhaustion. His prized Appaloosa's had served him well in the Comanche conflicts and the encounters in southern Mexico. More important it had never failed him.

One evening, after the meal, Don Domingo sat with Henry out on the rear verandah, smoking cigars and making small talk when the subject of Joselita arose. Whereupon, he related in some detail, that she was of such an age that it was time she took a husband and added, "While you were gone in the service of the Americano's, she pined each day for your return. At Mass, she kept a perpetual candle lit for your safe return and as it is our custom and the candles were kept lit in the shrine to the Madonna, in our home. Many suitors are in the wings, from the families of Hidalgos Senor Jaeger. Also I see the way you look at each other, neither able to tear your eyes away from the other."

Henry abruptly interrupted, "And I suppose that you want to know my intentions, is that right Don Domingo"?

He nodded for Henry to continue. Henry then asked the Don, "Perdonna me, I'll be right back", returning minutes later, bringing with him, his writing packet, brimming with all the letters he'd written to Joselita, but hadn't the means to deliver.

He'd explained the burgeoning packet of letters to the Don's daughter and why they hadn't been delivered saying if you read these then you'll know what's accumulated in my heart, all this time. What Henry forgot in his writing tablet were the written commendations for bravery from General Taylor and the letter of introduction from President Jackson.

"The only thing I'd ever have to offer your daughter Senor is my word of honor. Either I am worthy of your daughter, in your eyes or I am not.

Here are almost a year's worth of letters to Joselita for your inspection and hers if you so deem"!

Pausing he continued, "Muy permisso Senor, I would like to ask for the hand of Joselita, for the honor of being her husband. I have no family for they were murdered many years ago, so there is no political gain from this for the Fuentes family. Should you say no, then I shall have to depart and respect your wishes, with sadness yet gratitude for saving my live".

With that Henry departed for the barn, and to walk a bit.

Over the next hours, Joselita read aloud to her father and mother, the chronicalization of Henry's past year, of those he'd met and many of the things he'd done, of things both trivial and of importance. Intertwined in this narrative was his personal story. From his early days, his family origins, his time with the Miami Indians and the Shaman, his emigration to Nashville and the family he found there, then his pilgrimage to Texas.

Most men lead dull and uneventful lives, but Henry Jaeger had lived an extremely full life up to this point. Yet from the tone of his writing, his life was empty spiritually, until he laid eyes on Joselita de la Fuentes. Yet as his daughter droned on with the letters, by the light of the accumulation of candles, Henry was willing to walk away from happiness, should anyone object to the Union. Domingo thought back to the time that he was to be wed to Encarnation, his wife. Of course the union was an arrangement between families to unite them. When he first laid his eyes upon her, seeing her beauty he felt blessed by God. Therefore once the betrothal was settled, should anyone have changed their minds, he would have willingly kidnapped her. Thus was his unrestrained passion. so he found difficulty in understanding why this Norte' Americano would willingly accept a negative response, since his passion for Joselita was so obvious. Just then he heard the sound of sobbing amongst the women as Joselita read a passage, regarding the savagery of the Comanche and the Kiowa Indians in Texas, towards the settler families. Domingo had seen evidence of their activities, from various raids on the Rancho's along the Rio Bravo, in recent years.

The sound of the front door closing brought everyone's attention to Henry as he entered the room. Joselita in a flash, threw down the letters and ran to him throwing her arms around him, with tears in her eyes saying, "I've read the letters to me to my family, 'me amor', while she was kissing him furiously.

Henry was pleasantly taken aback, for this overwhelming display was the very first time her lips touched him. Then she turned to her family and with a defiant attitude said, "He is my Cyrano, who has my heart if he wants it"!

Then silence. With the only sounds coming from her mother and her Tante' Duena, who by this time were fighting back tears, but losing the battle. They all looked at the Patriarch Don Domingo in relative silence.

"Have you, been formally baptized into the faith, my son"?

Henry thought then answered, "I don't think so. The very first time I attended Mass, at a Cathedral was a year ago, in Monterrey"!

As everyone held their breath, Domingo thought a moment then said, "The first thing in the morning Encarnation will go into town accompanied by the vaquero Juan Mendoza." Turning to his wife he said, "You will seek out the Monsignor and make the necessary arrangements for a proper baptism at the earliest opportunity. Then it appears that the proper rings will be necessary, so you will tend to that if you please. Then a wedding will have to be arranged and that is women's work. Finally take your daughter with you so she will have something to occupy her time"!

"Oh one thing more. We seem to have forgotten Senor Jaeger. Are you in agreement Senor"?

Literally dumbstruck by the rapid chain of events, Henry mumbled something unintelligible and nodded his head in agreement with a huge smile.

The Fuentes women all screamed in delight as Don Domingo broke through the joy saying, "But my son, you will have to relinquish your sleeping quarters back to my daughter and join the Vaqueros in the bunk house, for the time being."

Henry nodded in agreement, then Tante' Juanita made for the bunkhouse, seeking out Mendoza and informed him of what was occurring and his duties for the following day. As they both came back to the main house, Mendoza turned to Juanita saying, "It has been too long since we have been together Me Amor"!

"Why you old goat, haven't you seen that I've been busy as of late"? "But if you'll be a little patient, until Joselita and Jaeger are as one, then perhaps we can find some time to be together", as she flicked his nose gently in a coquettish manner. Even passion can occur between the older people, where Tante' Juanita had been Joselita's Duena almost since birth, accompanying her abroad for her schooling these many years, while interrupting a passionate relationship with Juan Mendoza. Since Juanita was of a Castilian bloodline and an Hidalgo from birth and Mendoza was a Mestizo with an Indian bloodline, marriage was an impossibility for their time. Yet both agreed that the occasional 'stolen moment', would have to suffice. During her absence abroad, Juanita had to satisfy herself with the receipt of letters written by Mendoza, who dispatched them secretly and whenever she wrote the family letters in return ostensibly about Joselita and how she was doing, she would always sent Mendoza a secret message in the body of the letter that only they understood. Since Mendoza was one of the top Vaqueros he accompanied the women everywhere they went when they departed the Rancho. The women in the carriage and Mendoza as an outrider riding tall in the saddle in a haughty manner whenever she was around.

Seemingly to all, they conducted themselves in a circumspect fashion, but from time to time, their exchange of glances would linger a little too long, to be strictly the business of the family.

The only one to detect this was Juanita's sister, Dona Encarnacion, who was wise enough to see that her sister conducted herself above reproach at all times. Besides, she was her sister and a guardian of her daughter and there were some secrets that should always be kept.

As is usually the case amongst the young, the time prior to Henrys baptism passed at a snail's pace, the event occurring with little fanfare. Now as the women made their way into town, they kept the news of the new entry into the De la Fuentes family to a chosen few for the memories of the battle of Monterrey and the occupation by the Americanos, were still fresh in the minds of many of the locals and Don Domingo was still the Alcalde and Chief Magistrate of the area.

Henry stayed busy during the time between his baptism and his nuptials, keeping a respectful distance between himself and Joselita during that sixty day time frame, spending the bulk of his daily time with Juan Mendoza as they made their way around the rancho gathering the livestock, repairing the wooden fences and various roof leaks the plagued the bunkhouse and the several barns, impressing the vaqueros with his carpentry skills. Henry took the bulk of his meals with the vaqueros in the bunk house, only relenting to join the family every Sunday after High Mass, for the afternoon meal prior to siesta. During Mass he always sat in the row just ahead the family proper, with Juan Mendoza and served as one of the outriders accompanying the family who rode in the carriage. During Mass the family observed the precise way he celebrated the services, finding no fault in his manner and marveled, that this man of the prairie would be as fluent in Latin that he was. When his letters to Joselita were reread it became clear that Henry's family took great care to educate him as well as possible under the primitive conditions that existed.

Two days prior to the wedding, when Joselita read the final letters that Henry had sent her to her mother and Tante' Juanita, she came to the part in his last letters where he was tasked to hunt down a man who killed his best friend, tracking him northward. The man was a renegade priest and a former mounted Dragoon for Santa Anna with the cognomen of Cisco Andrade. Thankfully no exacting description of Andrade's demise was evident, but everyone knew of Cisco Andrade, the black sheep of the Andrade family. Who eagerly took part in Santa Anna's very first venture into Texas, the massacre at the Alamo, his survival of San Jacinto. His bragging at length of what had been done in the aftermath at the Alamo, with the men of the town. His two ventures into Texas as deep as San Antonio de Bexar and back with the Mexican Army and his convenient joining of the clergy just prior to the war. Plus his subsequent excommunication, after a brief stint in the service of the Jesuits from the order and the church.

The embarrassment his very existence caused a proud family of Castilian Hidalgos, with bloodlines going back hundreds of years. Only in the months ahead would the final fate of Cisco Andrade be revealed.

Promptly Dona Encarnacion said, "This must never leave this room". "It must never be spoken of again". Immediately, Joselita and Tante' Juanita nodded their heads in agreement, swearing a solemn oath. News of this could be misinterpreted in these troubled times. The Andrade family had other brothers that might have different feelings towards Cisco. Never mind that Henry had saved their father life, for such things are quickly forgotten in troubled times, by men driven by false loyalties.

The day of the wedding was a day of supreme celebration, with Jaeger and Mendoza in the city and at the Cathedral well in advance of the De la Fuentes, having previously rehearsed just what their role would be, which would simply be follow the priest's lead at all times. Pretty simple really.

All of the families in the region were invited to the wedding and brought the appropriate gifts for the celebration to occur after the wedding.

As each family entered the Cathedral, the men were all directed to deposit whatever weapons they had on them in the sacristy for retrieval after the wedding. Of course each family had accompanying them a retinue of Vaquero body guards, who dutifully took their place outside of the Cathedral.

As Joselita entered the Cathedral in all her pristine alabaster finery, she literally sparkled as none other since the erection of that edifice, a monument to the beauty of a woman who waited until the very day of her wedding, to consummate their union. As she made her way down the center aisle, escorted by her father, all eyes lit upon her, drawn like a magnet to her radiant countenance.

Seeing her slowly and majestically glide down the aisle, Henry's knees began to weaken, struck as he was by her beauty, enhanced of course for the solemn occasion, but even without her various enhancements, she radiated an elegance heretofore unknown in the history of mankind.

The question that ran through his mind was, "Am I worth all this trouble"? Of course the resolve was that every single day of his life he would make certain that he was worth it, by thought, word and deed. As the celebration progressed he hardly heard a word the priest had said, but just barely, the priest speaking in Spanish and Henry's well-rehearsed responses on queue and of a deeply and audibly resonate tone.

Finally when the priest pronounced them both man and wife and they drew together in a celestial embrace, the applause almost drowned out the priest who had to bring the proceedings to an end by shouting, "The Mass is concluded, go ye all in peace" As they both proceeded down the aisle, Henry noted Don Francisco Andrade and his entire family, who nodded his head regally in silent acknowledgement of this day of days.

During the post wedding proceedings the various families were introduced to Henry and his new bride, with Henry saying little other than the obvious banalities. His chief thoughts of the nights he'd recently spent amongst the Vaqueros and what awaited him in Joselita's bedroom. Yet he forced himself to endure the long line of Hidalgo's who were kind enough to attend, giving scant thought of the political implications each family brought and the obligatory gifts to get them through the early days.

From time to time, Henry and Joselita's eyes briefly met and she appeared to be disciplined sufficiently to let the ceremony's play out.

Henry thought, 'If she can wait, then so can I'…

When they all returned to the Hacienda, Henry was drawn aside by his new father in law, Don Domingo for cigars and a goblet of his finest Andalusian wine, to allow the women sufficient time to prepare the bride for her husband. Eventually Don Domingo said to Henry, "Well my son, it is now time for you to do your duty. Give me a grandson", he said with a wink. As Henry finished his wine and climbed the stairs, he gave thanks to god for allowing him to experience his grace.

Opening the door to Joselita's bedroom, he was greeted with the scent of jasmine all around, with the room dimly lit by carefully placed candles, and of course by the vision of Joselita adorned in the briefest of gossamer night clothes, which revealed everything, concealing nothing. "The only argument my mother and I had was over this, which I brought back from Paris". When I selected this, I didn't know you but I hoped that someday this would be worn for someone exactly like you. As Henry slowly approached the bed, he sat on its edge with great care, taking in every visual of Joselita as if it had to last him a thousand years. Her long slender legs, her proud full breasts, replete with just a bit of a sag, the fullness of her femininity laying thus within, with her nipples pointing upward at an angle towards the ceiling.

Without a word he gently kissed her, their lips coming together at first gently, then gradually, her tongue parted his lips, sucking his back into hers as she sampled the wine her father had plied him with. With a rush she pushed him away, removing the gossamer covering displaying her in all her virginal glory. Then she pushed Henry down on the bed, and set to work removing all his clothes, throwing each and every article on the floor, in every direction. Finally seeing that his engorged member was fully erect she descended upon it, with a series of gentle kisses, taking it into her mouth gently moving the length and the breadth of the shaft, as Henry was helpless to do anything to disturb her, with waves of pleasure confronting him at every level. Then she positioned herself upon him in such a way that she still had full control of his burgeoning member, but with her vaginal area, sweetly fragranced, awaiting his lips and tongue to gently explore her inner sanctum to the fullest. As his tongue explored the sweet folds of her labia, she gently directed him with wordless positioning as to where he was to travel on his journey towards the inner heavens. For what seemed to be an eternity they, gently rolled around the vestigial bed, with her relinquishing her efforts on his member, so not as to have him come to completion too soon, while Henry obediently remained true to his task, bringing her to heights of ecstasy she'd only read about while in school.

When she stiffened, stifling a muffled groan, Henry could feel could feel a barrier deep inside with his tongue. As he pulled away, he rained kisses over every blessed inch of her body. Breathing heavily, she climbed over Henry, straddling his middle and reached for his erect member, slowly guiding it towards her inner sanctum. As Henry entered her he could see a brief grimace on her face, then a brief gushing of liquid from her now breached womb and then smile as she swayed her ample nipples across his face, her pounding rhythms gathering in tempo and in force. A slight breeze coming from a partially opened window cooled the fevered pounding of two ardent lover's intent on the process of creation. Like two medieval chargers intent on eternal impalement, the duo finally completed with a muffled spasmodic jerking of their intertwined torso's, neither desirous of parting. As Joselita lay on top of her eternal love, panting and flushed with her first experience with man, feeling the rising and falling of his chest, she heard him ask, "Please Joselita pinch me and pinch me as hard as you can"!

As she lay straddled on top of him, his erect member still deep inside her she replied, "Now why would I want to hurt you me amour"! Henry replied breathlessly, "Because I need to know whether or not I'm dreaming"!

After Henry ascended the stairs, Dona Encarnacion, discretely waved Tante' Juanita away from their presence as she started to put out the candles from the main dining area, leaving just one lit, she approached her husband saying, "Now that your daughter is doing her duty to her husband, don't you think it's time that you returned to yours"? Then after a brief pause she concluded with a whisper, flicking her tongue ever so lightly on his ear, "Me Amor"?

Deep in thought as to what might lie ahead, Don Domingo looked at his wife, a single candle secured in a silver holder and that look in her eye he'd not seen in a long time, and replied, "Me Amor, your lightest touch is but a command"! Whereupon he rose from his chair, extinguished the cigar and finished the last of the wine, then grabbed his wife by one of her ample buttocks, never relinquishing his grip, as she led the way up the stairs.

Her work done, Tante' Juanita approached the Vaquero bunk house, finding her sometime lover Juan Mendoza, smoking a small Cigarro and working his way through a fresh carafe of the potent and milky Pulque, watching the stars roll by, joining him as she placed a foot up on the lower railing of the corral.

"Will you offer a thirsty woman a drink Senor", she asked huskily. He replied, "Perdonna Me, but of course", as he placed the carafe in her hands. She then drank two lusty swallows of Pulque, some of which spilled out over her blouse. As she handed back the carafe to Mendoza, she remarked "How do you people love this peasant drink"?

Mendoza replied, "No doubt the same way that some women are attracted to simple men with simple needs"!

"Well senor, Joselita is hard at work at the moment, and I imagine my sister Dona Encarnacion is doing her duty as well"! With that, she untied the drawstring of her peasant blouse, shrugging her shoulders allowing it to fall down partially exposing her breasts, as she drew his eager lips toward her ample bosom.

Soon they would search for a clean and empty stall with an appropriate pile of fresh hay, to once again resume their duties to each other.

All over the greater area of Monterrey, those that attended the wedding and the festivities thereafter, found it necessary to consummate with either a loved one, or love the one they found themselves with, for the evening.

Thus, for a moment in time, all was well with the world.

11

Over the days and weeks ahead, Henry was brought into the fold of the Rancho de la Fuentes and all of its various aspects, cattle and horses, agave plantations and distillery, tannery operations, the raising of prime bulls for the Corrida in Mexico City and finally politics.

For many years, even before Mexico won their independence from Spain in 1820, regional Governors and Alcalde's were appointments, usually for life, from the Spanish Crown. Of course, they always were from the high born, the educated, the Castilian or Hidalgo elements of societal class. Family and social connections were everything and political stability was vital. No matter that the Central Government was ineffectual or unjust, things must remain as they are, so from time to time an areas ruling class would keep an oligarchy ongoing for the preservation of areas status quo.

The period of time after the Americanos had gone back north was especially difficult for, Mexicans of every class. The poorest would remain poor, for after all, they were usually of native Indian blood, without benefit of education of any kind. The shop keepers would muddle along fragmented, peddling their skills and goods as best they could in spite of the various inconsistencies economically. Out in the country side, there were always the thieves and the Indians, be they either Comanche, or the Apache.

The Indians would always maintain their way of life and their way of live was always at the expense of others.

Keen were the senses of the various Hidalgos, for alliances were always shifting depending upon expediencies of the moment in time. Today's allies were often tomorrow's enemy.

On several occasions, Henry was asked to lead a group of selected Vaqueros from the various families, to track down and destroy various groups of cattle thieves, be they Indian, Mexican or the occasional Americano's that came over the to steal cattle and horses and retrieve whatever livestock possible and return it to the owner.

From time to time Henry had to cross the Rio Grande in pursuit and then back south. He always proved successful in his task, getting back across the river by moving fast, hitting hard, leaving no survivors, then returning south in force, with the property well in hand.

His return was always greeted by a celebration and an evening of passion between him and his wife. After almost a year of this, he was greeted by the news that he was to be a father. Recognizing the politics of the region, Henry gladly ceded the responsibility of naming the child to Don Domingo. Should it be a boy, it would be named "Rodrigo", after Rodrigo de Bevar, the mythical, "El Cid", who fought the infidel in Spain over a thousand years ago. Should it be a girl, then it would be named "Maria", after the Virgin Mary.

Either name was just fine with Henry, for the Jaeger name would be maintained in any case. He would render unto Caesar what was Caesar and Don Domingo was the local Caesar.

When he was not out running down rustlers and thieves, with the other Vaqueros, Henry stayed busy learning the cattle business or breaking in horses with his unique kind of settling, which proved to be not only faster, but less injurious on the Vaqueros. Many were the evenings they gathered him around a campfire and he told tales of his adventures against the Comanche. The only thing he refused to talk about was his service in the War, which was a sticky subject with many of the Vaqueros still. Eventually his first Christmas as a member of the family, he was presented with a complete set of buckskins, Chaps, pants, shirt, jacket and rain slicker. Over time he'd adjusted to wearing the local clothes, since his normal buck skins were long discarded when he first arrived. This new suit of clothing seemed more at home to Henry and he wore them from time to time, especially in the winter months, putting them up during the long hot summer.

Never in his life was Henry more comfortable or happy. His family and his wonderful Joselita treated him with acceptance and respect. Both Chani and Akila were well fed and cared for by everyone. Every Sunday when the family assembled for the hours ride into Monterrey, to attend Mass at the Main Cathedral, Henry always rode point with Mendoza and Joselita's eldest brother Miguel, the men leading the way into town in all their finery.

After Mass, a large meal, and the conversations between the men, then the siesta, this in Henrys case never involved sleep, but lovemaking that always ended in a sweaty pile of limbs.

As Joselita's pregnancy progressed, plans were made for the day of birth, usually by the women, calculating on when the date of birth would occur and visits with the doctor for periodic progress reports. Plans were afoot for a midwife to be in attendance in case of either the doctor's absence or to provide assistance in any case. Since this was the first child of Joselita, their youngest, no expense was to be overlooked.

When Henry allowed himself to think about things, he concluded that he was indeed blessed, with an overwhelming series of circumstances, perhaps the 'eternals' grace, that was mentioned, from time to time during the weekly Mass homily. He was blessed with a family that was just as loving and accepting as his "Muti und Papi" would've been, yet of a far different culture. He had learned much from Don Domingo, in the areas of business and politics, by just being in his company and seeing how he operated and why. Yet each time he rode into Monterrey for any reason, people would always look at him as if he were an intruder in their midst. As his grasp of Spanish slowly improved with use, he was able to understand many others when they spoke of him thinking they were out of earshot.

He had adopted many of their customs and ways thus assimilating into their community, or so he thought. But whenever he was in the company of the town's folk or other Hidalgo's, he always felt their unease by his presence. His dirty blond hair was a rarity in the area, but other men of Castilian origins had light hair and were readily accepted, but not Henry.

He made it a point never to mention this to either Joselita or her father, for with the coming birth of their first child, everyone had about all they could say grace over.

Then a month before the birth, in the early hours before the family awoke sounds of gunfire came from the south pasture as the eastern skies started to brighten. Henry hurriedly put on his clothes and grabbed his pistols, running to the pasture, along with several other Vaqueros, to see Mendoza laying on the ground wounded, with a number of other Mexicans dead and their horses scattered over the pasture, while Chani and Akila were standing over several dead men, with one of them still alive, frozen in terror while Mendoza had his Colt trained on him and the wolves growling. The one left alive was simply the victim of some serious wolf bites.

As the other Vaqueros rushed to the scene, Henry directed one them to ride into town to fetch the doctor and the others to return to the bunkhouse to get a litter for Mendoza. While several of the others stood up the intruder and at gunpoint marched him to the corral railing soundly binding him to one of the posts. His wounds could wait.

The women of the house ran to meet the men as the returned from the pasture, with the prostrate Mendoza. Immediately Tante' Juanita took charge, directing the men to boil water and bring what supplies the doctor would need upon his arrival. As she took charge, Dona Encarnacion, nodded her head in understanding, for not only was Juanita her sister, but she had silently known of her secret with Mendoza since almost from its inception, yet saying nothing, yielding to the class differences of their society. Often women had to take their pleasures and find their level of happiness whenever and wherever they could.

The intruder was tied up to one of the fence railings to await the pleasure of Don Domingo, by several of the Vaquero's at gunpoint. The dead were collected and placed in the center corral and their horses were sequestered in yet another corral. One by one the Vaqueros recognized the dead as being in the employ of the Andrade family as vaqueros, on the family rancho between Monterrey and Saltillo.

Rumor had it that the Andrade family fortunes were suffering from a variety of events, starting with bad political investments in Mexico City, then the periodic Comanche raids thinned his herds of some of the finest imported Andalusian horses, to be bred with some pure breeds, coupled with the gambling problems of the male heirs of the family.

Don Domingo had known Francisco Andrade, since before the time of Independence from Spanish rule, some thirty years. Always known to be a hard and shrewd businessman and politician, but with a sense of Castilian honor and a man of the Church.

Badly planned common horse thievery didn't seem to fit his bag of tricks. Yet reports of financial ruin could be such to turn the most righteous of men, to men of dishonor.

Several hours later the doctor arrived from Monterrey, and immediately went to work, removing the bullet from Mendoza, re cleansing and cauterizing the wound. As the doctor placed the white hot iron upon the wound, Mendoza looked into the eyes of Tante' Juanita, clenching his teeth as he gripped her arm, clenching his teeth over a piece of wood that had been placed in his mouth. All the vaqueros were gathered around to observe Mendoza's trial of pain and when he didn't cry out, they all nodded to each other, glad that a man was in their midst who could endure, as they knew he would.

Weak from the loss of blood and in great pain from the searing of the wound, Mendoza, shakily stood up and smiled saying with great bravado, "It takes more than bullets from Andrade horse thieves, to put an end to Juan Mendoza"!

"Someone bring me some Pulque", he bellowed, whereupon he refused to move, until one of the female servants brought a mug of the highly toxic milky liquid, which he drank greedily in a single gulp, to the cheers of all the Vaqueros.

Then Tante' Juanita, throwing all caution to the wind, signaled several of the Vaqueros, to bring him into the main house and up to her room, and a change of clothes, whereupon she bathed and cared for him in the days to come just as Joselita had done for Henry a year earlier.

So now the secret was out and even the lowliest vaquero, could figure out that something was between the two. But as everyone on the rancho was considered as "Family", to greater and lesser degrees, the blind eye was turned. For good and loyal men were hard to find.

Their collective attentions were then turned to the thief who lay tightly bound and stretched out on the corral fence. All the women were directed to go inside and not emerge until summoned.

The doctor was asked to stay for lunch as the men all took their turns in the grand inquisition of their captor and the only reason the good doctor was retained for the day was to see, to the viability of the prisoner. He had to reveal what he knew and all that he knew, for a dead man was of no use to them. About noon he'd revealed, albeit grudgingly, all that he knew, about the raid on the rancho. At that time the doctor was permitted to attend him, but the captive was now deeply in shock, from not only the wolves injuries, but from the series of skillfully broken bones administered by the Vaqueros in their quest for truth.

Turning to Don Domingo the doctor said, "There is nothing I can do for him Senor. He is in shock and is on his way to his maker"! At that all the Vaqueros grudgingly made the sign of the cross, looking to Don Domingo for further instructions.

Apparently, according to the surviving captive, Don Francisco had no knowledge of the abortive incursion. The entire idea was the result of his two sons, who were desperate enough to plan, but not to lead the raid, trusting the task to others.

Then Don Domingo spoke: "Of this we will do nothing to avenge our Honor." Thinking things through he continued, all the bodies will be stripped clean, their clothes washed and distributed amongst you, or given to the poor in Monterrey. The horses with the marks of the Andrade family will be returned, the saddles will remain here for our use. Any horses without markings will be kept here. All weapons will be retained. The stripped bodies of the thieves will loaded onto a wagon and driven through Monterrey tonight when everyone is asleep, and placed at the side of the road half way to Saltillo every quarter mile, to rot in the sun as a sign for all. Then you are to return here in silence"!

Orders thus given, Don Domingo thanked the Doctor for his services, and paid him accordingly with the instructions that what he observed here was to be kept under the tongue.

Before the doctor left he once again looked in on Joselita, just to reassure both him and the family that all was progressing well. As well as anyone could determine, the blessed day of birth was two weeks off, perhaps three at the most.

Late the following morning, the vaqueros returned in the now empty wagon, the deed done, to await future developments.

The following day the Monterrey newspaper was full of the news of seven unidentified dead men being discovered just outside of the town of Saltillo, lying neatly lay on the side of the road, stripped clean of all possessions probably by robbers. Yet the article posed the question, 'what robber would go to the trouble to lay the victims neatly at the side of the road'?

Further, the article went on about for horses belonging to the Andrade family were discovered grazing in a field not far from the discovered bodies.

Don Domingo thought, as he put the paper aside, 'The Andrade family lives closer to Saltillo than to Monterrey, let the disposal of their remains be Saltillo's problem'..

Every day Henry spent more and more time with Joselita, tending to her every need as the magic day approached. During the cool evenings he sat with her on the verandah and they talked about the future, about their love for each other, while a few of the vaqueros who could play the guitar serenaded them at a distance…He insisted on carrying her up the long stairs each evening, as the stars made their way across the heavens. As Henry placed his treasure upon the bed and adjusted her bed linens and pillows, he whispered a silent 'Thank you' each might into her ear. She would always reply, "Porque, me Amor" and he would whisper simply; "For being you and none other"! The each night Joselita would close her eyes thanking the almighty for her wonderful Cyrano, before drifting off to sleep.

The following week went by without incident, with Don Domingo noticing the mood of Monterrey somehow altered to a certain degree, as he tended to his affairs as the City's Alcalde. The bodies of what appeared to be several of the dead Vaqueros, had been identified as in the employ of Don Francisco Andrade, were seen by many to have been murdered, by parties unknown.

Yet there were two men, who knew the truth of it, the sons of Don Francisco. Their little venture squashed like a bug. Yet there was yet one card left to play. There was no question as to why, or what tangible profit could accrue from what they were about to do, just simply that it had to be done.

For you see, Don Domingo had insulted the entire Andrade family, by allowing his prized daughter to marry an Americano, rather than either one of them. Then there was the business of their brother Cisco and the manner of his death, apparently fighting a partisan fight south of Saltillo. Reports of his passing at the hand of a big Americano attired as a vaquero and the sudden prosperity the town enjoyed, pointed to the handiwork of this villain, Jaeger, the hunter. They could see that he was a formidable individual, and far their superior in all things combative, but as the event of the emergence of his first born drew near, the key element was the family doctor. Knowing the approximate time of the blessed event, if the something should delay or impede the doctor, to prevent his attendance…….?

A scant week later as the time for the blessed event approached, Henry was up country with several other vaqueros retrieving some of the long horn cattle that had escaped into the country side. It was supposed to be a two day, out and back, with plenty of time to spare to be on hand for the blessed event.

The day Henry left with the vaqueros, the doctors wife stayed up late awaiting her husband to return home for the evening, for he had received a message from one of the Hidalgo's to visit their home, in the country side, for she was reported to be suffering from, "The Vapors". Since the doctor was visiting one of the Hidalgo families, it was assumed that he spent the night at their encomienda. Often this came up and no one wanted to travel the roads at night. The following day when the doctor didn't return by midday, his wife fearing something amiss sent a messenger to the encomienda. By nightfall, the messenger returned saying the family in question was perfectly all right and had sent no such message. The following morning Don Domingo was notified of the doctor's absence, sending searchers out to find him. That evening his carriage was retrieved from a copse of trees, without the horse and with no sign of the doctor.

Since Henry was up country retrieving the Don's cattle, no one with his tracking ability was available, except possibly Juan Mendoza, who had ridden with Jaeger on some expeditions. Mendoza arrived hours later, examining the apparent scene of the abduction, knowing full well how important the retrieval of the doctor was to Don Domingo and Henry. Being helped from his horse and still weak from his wound, he looked for signs of a struggle and finding none, tried to glean signs of hoof tracks, but since other horses had trampled over the area, it was impossible to make a determination. Eventually widening his field of examination he thought he saw signs of some tracks and followed them on foot for several miles, the sun now fading fast in the west and his reserves of strength starting to wane, he made out four sets of hoof prints heading in the general direction of the Andrade rancho. Just as he was to give up and call it an evening, Mendoza thought he saw a foot sticking out of the bushes.

As he summoned the others, they pulled out a body from the brush. It was the doctor. "Muerte", whispered one and all almost simultaneously, all making the sign of the cross. For the good doctor had met an untimely end having his throat slit from ear to ear a victim of an apparent robbery.

His watch, money and wedding ring were all missing, so what else could it be?

The others hoisted the remains of the doctor back on his one of the vaqueros horses and rode back to Monterrey, to notify the authorities especially Don Domingo, who was still in town finishing up some business germane to his duties as Alcalde. He briefly visited the doctor's wife to deliver the untimely news only to discover that someone else has done preceded him in that regard. As he made his way back out of town with Mendoza and the others, a vaquero from his rancho met them en route with the message that Joselita was in labor and things were not apparently going well, to summon the doctor and the Cathedrals priest.

Don Domingo told the vaquero of the doctor's death, redirecting him to the Monsignor to hurry fast, to the rancho.

Riding as fast as they could, all the men pulled up, running into the main house, with Don Domingo running up the stairs two at a time.

A half hour later the Priest and the Vaquero arrived with the Priest being hurriedly escorted to Joselita's bedroom.

Mendoza, sat down on one of the chairs in the dining room, just as Tante' Juanita came running down the stairs and into the kitchen fetching something for the midwife in attendance. As she ran by she said breathlessly, "The baby is arriving a week early. It's not supposed to come a week early. Where, oh where is the doctor, she yelled from the kitchen area?

Mendoza didn't have the words to answer. As she ran back past him on the way upstairs, carrying some clean towels, she repeated the question, to a mute Mendoza, "Where is the doctor"?

Mendoza looked up then said, "Muerte"! "Asesino"! "Now please go back upstairs woman", he responded briskly. He then reached inside his shirt, kissing the cross that hung around his neck, then to the little bag that was always attached to his belt, withdrawing the rosary beads that were always with him. He then went out to the verandah, sat wearily down on one of the steps next to Chani and Akila petting them both in the process, then went into the endless ritual chant, "Hail Mary, full of grace, the Lord is with thee. Blessed are thou amongst women and blessed is the fruit of thy womb Jesus"! Endlessly, he prayed, for the blessing of life for Dona Joselita, his fingers pressing each and every bead as they made their way through his hands, going so far to add,

"And remove from my allotted span of life as many years as you deem necessary, just save Joselita and her child from the ferry man this night. As Mendoza relentlessly strove to continue his plea to the eternal, he heard periodic sound of people rushing up and down the stairs. In the back of his compartmentalized mind he reasoned, 'They are doing all that they can and the least I can do is all that I can'. Eventually he looked up at the stars and from somewhere deep in his heart, he felt the words, 'Into your hands I deliver my spirit'.

Just then he was startled by the plaintive howl of first Chani then Akila, who stood up and walked to the edge of the verandah and commenced their relentless announcement of grief.

Mendoza thought, 'So they both felt it too'.

Then he heard a shout and a wailing from upstairs in the house.

Joselita had now crossed over. She was but a memory. Her soul was now with the angels.

Hurrying back as fast as he could with the Don's cattle along with a few of the Vaqueros, Henry came over the rise of land viewing the Don's Rancho in the valley below, leading the small herd. In the distance he could hear the faint howling of Chani and Akila, from far off. At first he thought they sensed his coming since they usually roved the herd at night driving off intruders. But how could this be since Henry was clearly downwind from them, and too far away for them to gain his scent? A gentle breeze was blowing in his face from the direction of the rancho. He looked up into the sky and reckoned by the stars and the position of the moon, which was entering its phase of fullness, that it was around three AM.

Suddenly as the wolves howling increased in intensity from far off, he remembered the precise way the wolves howled, when his parents were murdered. The howl of the dearly departed.

Henry turned to one of the Vaqueros instructing him to take over and that he was going to ride ahead.

He spurred the big Appaloosa on into a slow gallop, down the gradual decline into the valley below, not knowing what to think, but sensing something, something very bad. After several miles he spurred on his horse to increase its speed, now pacing at a full gallop. As he approached the main house, he could see that most of the rooms were lit and that people were mulling around. This time of the evening everyone was supposed to be asleep with no candles lit.

As he rode up to the house, he could see that on the porch there were people crying. As he reined his horse to a halt, he jumped from the saddle and ran into the house, still more people crying. He ran up the stairs two at a time, pressing his way through the members of the family. As he entered into Joselita's bed chamber he saw the Monsignor in the process of giving his beloved her last rights, sprinkling the holy water on her serene and lifeless body. He approached the bed slowly, sinking to his knees as he came to the head of the bed.

There lay his precious jewel; her eyes closed forever, her arms placed in front of her clasping her icon of the Holy Mother Mary. His breath seemed to leave him as he turned to Don Domingo with pleading and questioning eyes, seeing Dona Encarnacion holding a bundle in her arms that contained the family's new son Rodrigo.

Then Don Domingo spoke haltingly with tears in his eyes almost apologetically saying, "Our precious Joselita is in heaven, having given her life for your new son Rodrigo," nodding in the direction of his wife carrying his son bundled up with swaddling clothes. Finding it hard to catch his breath, Jaeger stood up looking around as if to say, 'How could this be'? Then he again knelt beside Joselita, gently touching her as he heard Don Domingo say; "Her last words were of you my son, she spoke you name as she passed "Henry me Amor"! Continuing, the Don said, it was a difficult birth and the doctor was not here because he was murdered by people unknown, yesterday while you were away and the midwife just didn't have the ability to stop the bleeding inside, after the child was born"! Henry then looked at the blood soaked bed linens and the pile of blood soaked towels that lay at the foot of the bed, seeing the truth of it. After a lifetime of struggle, finally to find happiness, then this...........He began to sob uncontrollably as he clutched her lifeless hands, then suddenly everyone began to enter in yet another round of crying. As Tante' Juanita came forward to comfort him, he shrugged her off, standing up he could hear the wolves howling outside, commencing with a huge bellow from the very depths of his being, then joined them in a primordial howl of grief for several moments. Then catching his breath he turned to everyone and said calmly, "I would like some time alone with my wife". At first everyone stood still as if they couldn't believe what they were hearing, then when no one responded, Henry bellowed; "Get Out"!

Within seconds the bedroom emptied and the door was closed, offering Henry precious final moments alone with his beloved.

Down stairs Tante' Juanita, herself as overcome with grief as anyone said, "Those wolves are driving me crazy with the incessant howling. Can't anyone shut them up"? The wolves were expressing their grief in the ancient ways passed down through the millennia. Then Mendoza, himself almost crazy with grief said, "Dona Juanita, they loved her as much as any one of us in their own special way. They are announcing to God that she is coming and to welcome her with open arms. Besides, which one of us is crazy enough to try and stop them?"

Suddenly he had an idea and went outside sitting down on the verandah steps and joined in with them announcing the demise of Joselita. After several minutes of this, he stopped and signaled to them to follow him inside of the house and up the stairs and as he knocked on the door to Joselita's bed chamber, he opened it just enough to allow Chani and Akila, to enter. They did so and gathered at the foot of the bed, in silence to see their master kneeling beside her mistress. Henry at last summoned them to climb on the bed, whereupon they did, showering her with licks and sniffs nuzzling her gently as they said their goodbyes as only they could. After a short time of this, they descended from the bed and slowly approached the door signaling Henry that they were ready to leave him to grieve alone.

Henry arose from Joselita and let the wolves out.

The wolves slowly went down the stairs and sat erectly flanking the foot of the stars as if standing guard, to the privacy required above them all. Lost in all of this was little Rodrigo, who lay clutched in the arms of one of the family maids, suckling at her unabashedly proffered breast, eagerly attending to his first meal. The fact that she was of Mestizo blood, didn't seem to matter in the wee hours of the morning. An hour later the Vaqueros arrived with the errant livestock and were informed of the tragedy that lay within.

As the sun peeked over the mountains signaling another day, the business of ranching still continued with the appropriate members of the rancho enduring their daily routine, because it had to be done. Meals were prepared and partially eaten although without the normal gusto of another day. Still, the sun rose, the sun set and the world kept turning. Henry emerged from the bedroom, descending the stairs slowly painfully, sitting on the bottom stair, as the wolves came up to him flanking each knee as he pet them, staring at the floor with empty eyes. He had no more tears to shed; he'd said his goodbyes and was as empty as a man could be. His heart still beat, his lungs still drew breath, but not because he wished it or willed it. Then after a while, while the family members stood silent, muffling their grief, the peasant servant that was suckling little Rodrigo, slowly came forth and kneeled before the big Texan bringing his son into his field of view.

"Senor Jaeger, Tuya Hijo Rodrigo", introducing him to his son and offering him to Henry.

Recently fed and tended to, little Rodrigo looked up at his father, with the trusting gaze of the newly born. This was either the moment of acceptance or rejection, as each member of the family held their breath. As Henry held his child in his arms, the wolves were also eager to greet the newborn, sniffing his swaddling clothes. Then Henry lowered his son for their inspection and as they sniffed him eagerly it was if all the pain of the recent hours were forgotten as they imprinted his scent into their brains, then pulled back as if one and looked at Henry signaling their acceptance.

He then looked up at the family saying, "Well if they can accept him, then so can I. Joselita would have wanted it that way"! With that said, the entire family gathered around Henry in solidarity.

His eyes puffed out from hours of grief and a lack of sleep, Henry asked the Monsignor what was to be done as far as funeral arrangements? The priest answered, "My son if you will, please allow Don Domingo and me to handle everything"! Henry nodded in agreement as he handed over his son to Dona Encarnacion and rose from the bottom stair step slowly walking outside followed by Chani and Akila.

12

Mendoza and several of the Vaqueros escorted the Monsignor back into Monterrey along with Don Domingo, to make the appropriate arrangements with the town mortician. While waiting outside for Don Domingo and the priest to conduct their business arrangements, Mendoza noticed the entry into town of a man he'd not seen for many years, riding down the street with both of the surviving Andrade brothers.

That man was the bandit Chuey Medrano, leading around a dozen hardened, heavily armed bandits. Each man with a musket secured in the horses scabbard and a brace of dueling pistols, hanging under their armpits via shoulder holsters, along with the requisite knives, which adorned each man's body.

The last Medrano heard of them, they were fighting the American troops in a guerilla action, after they settled into Mexico City, going from house to house at night setting up ambushes to ensnare and take a heavy toll on the American's. Then other rumors had him escorting Santa Anna as he made next escape into Cuban exile. He was reported to be from Culiacan, a small town on the pacific coast, in the state of Sinaloa. From an early age, Chuey Medrano had sold his muscle to anyone who needed protection, or someone kidnapped, or killed, or tortured, or maimed. Of course the standard cattle and horse thievery were but a necessary sideline, to further his ends.

He and his cadre of each possessed a brace of scalps, hung plainly from their saddles, taken as proof of a bounty, paid by the government whenever a pogrom was announced on whatever troublesome Indian tribes the government required putting pressure upon.

No good could come from their presence.

As he passed Mendoza, Chuey Medrano recognized him from long ago, and yelled out, "Mendoza, you old bastard, you still alive"?

Leaning upon the hitching post, Mendoza simply drew aside his coat revealing his .44 Colt revolver, without saying a word, letting the image of the deadly revolver do the talking. As Medrano passed, upon seeing the revolver on Mendoza's hip, drew aside his coat revealing a similar

Colt revolver in his holster yelling out, "Perhaps our little friends will be talking to each other very soon,……no"? As he passed both men never took their eyes off each other until Medrano was long past.

Minutes later as the Don and the priest emerged from the Morticians, Mendoza told the Don of Medrano's presence with his gang and the Andrade brothers. His face went white, the blood draining from his face as he listened to Mendoza. What with all that has happened this insult was just about more than he could stand. For he too had heard the stories and legends regarding Chuey Medrano and his men. Then he went back in to the morticians, changing plans rather than bringing Joselita into town for the mortician to work his will with he insisted the mortician bring what equipment needed out to the rancho and perform his art there. Then two days hence, they would bring her into town just hours before the funeral.

An hour later, the Fuentes entourage accompanied the mortician out to the rancho. As they passed one of the towns Cantina's, they could see a bevy of horses tied to the hitching posts outside, and hear the raucous celebrations from within.

Henry had gone back upstairs to be with Joselita, unable to leave her for long or remove her serene visage from his gaze. He let the image of her sear itself into his memory, like a hot iron searing a brand into a cows hide.

Forever, she would own his heart. He lay next to her, silently. Wanting to touch her, to caress her, to feel the softness of her skin, but seeing the white pallor of her skin, told him the spirit that was uniquely hers had gone to the great beyond. The Elysian Fields, Heaven, wherever it was, now had complete possession of her soul for all time. Henry struggled to accept reality, hoping all this time that it was all a bad dream.

He recalled the aftermath of their wedding night, when completely flushed with celestial bliss, he asked her to pinch him, which she laughingly did, so he pinched himself, with the same result. Pain and the resultant reality.

As he heard the Don and the riders return, he got up from the bed and went down stairs.

The Don introduced the mortician to Henry, explaining the change in plans while the mortician was guided to Joselita's bed chambers and promptly went to work. As he worked all the key men of the Fuentes family discussed the presence of Chuey Medrano in town, in the company of the Andrade brothers.

Henry then turned to Juan Mendoza asking, "Juan, tell me everything you know about this Chuey Medrano. No thing is too great or too small."!

For the next twenty minutes, Mendoza searched his memory revealing all that was known or suspected about Chuey Medrano, his lieutenants and his men.

"How do you come to know Chuey Medrano, Juan"?

"I am also from Culiacan, Senor", he replied with embarrassment. "I rode with him, many years ago, for a brief time, before I knew better"!

"Thank you Juan, for I know you to be a man of honor and what's done, is done"!

Then Henry turned to Don Domingo asking, "Muy Permisso Senor"?

The Don nodded his head to continue.

Jaeger then embarked on a series of directives for all assembled, which entailed rounding up all of the livestock and sequestering them in the various corrals, under heavy nonstop around the clock guard, thus putting the entire rancho on a war footing. He went into meticulous detail as to what was to be done and how to do it. Then he speculated as to the precise whys and wherefores.

After every sequence, he asked if they all understood and all replied, "Si Jefe"! Then he said; "They will be back, to night and every night, until every last one of us is dead" Then he continued adding, "The most vulnerable points will be at the funeral while some of us are gone, two days from now and each and every night".

"Chani will accompany Mendoza for half the night and I'll take Akila, till and past sunrise and make our rounds of the rancho. What our eyes and ears and senses may miss, will not evade their senses"! Continuing on he said, "This will be over when all of them are Muerte"!

Every man understood as to the heart of darkness that lay deep within their fellow countrymen. Every man understood this was to be a struggle that would be over when the other was no more. Thus without further ado, everyone arose and immediately went to their tasks.

As evening approached they Vaqueros tasked with rounding up the livestock from their various pastures, herded the last of them into the various corrals, separating into their various groupings, getting their meals, grabbing some rest, until the women aroused them to make their rounds.

At midnight the mortician had completed his task, placing Joselita into the temporary wooden casket, Henry crafted with his own hands, whereupon she would be transferred to the permanent casket selected by Don Domingo earlier in the day, when they arrived at the Cathedral. His work duly completed the Mortician was fed a full meal the paid as agreed for his efforts and shown to a spare bedroom to sleep. The next morning he would be escorted into town by Mendoza and a few Vaqueros to complete the arrangements for the funeral.

Sentries were posted in shifts around the two dozen packed corrals, moving stealthily from preselected position to position on a random basis. Looking and listening for the slightest sound or movement. Henry had spent time with the men, teaching them the basics of what to look and listen for.

At approximately one in the morning, one shift of men gradually evolved into the next in a smooth transition. Back at the Main House, all the candles were extinguished, to give the impression that all were asleep, even though everyone was fully clothed unable to sleep. Sleep could come afterwards.

The vaqueros of the earlier shifts, found it difficult to sleep, a victim of both fear and the ever present supply of black coffee. Sleep for them would also arrive later.

Henry had suspected that around two in the morning, when most people were fast asleep, the attack would begin, for that's exactly what he would do. That's exactly what the Comanche would do and have done.

As Henry silently moved from place to place, with Akila, he sensed something just at the same time Akila stopped behind him, sniffing the night air. He turned slightly to see what the matter was. From the position of his body Akila was searching the night movements and through Akila's posture, Henry could sense something was near. He signaled Akila to join him in the deep brush and wait.

A short time later Henry could see the movements of several men on foot making their way past him through the edge of the tree line, heading towards the corral. Clearly it was the others, for his men moved about alone. Then across the pasture he saw in the moonlight several other mounted intruders, moving in a parallel course at the edge of the tree line in the direction of the house and the corrals.

Henry decided that he would follow behind the group that was closest to him and as he moved to within bowshot range, he withdrew four arrows from his quiver, fitting one of them into the bow, holding the other three in his teeth. Being not ten yards behind the last of them he shot an arrow which entered into the back of his neck and out his front, dropping the man grasping his throat unable to draw breath much less cry out. As the man in front of him turned to see what the noise was behind him, he was greeted with yet another arrow entering into a place just below his chin line, with the same result. The leader of the trio unaware of what had happened behind him, pressed on for a bit, then turned to see where his men were, only to be greeted with the point of Henry's razor sharp Bowie knife, which drove through his throat emerging out the back severing his spinal column, dropping him immediately to the ground silently.

Henry hoped that his people on the other side of the wide pasture were aware of the mounted intruders, who he could still barely make out.

Suddenly he felt the presence of others behind him and fading into the brush could make out a half dozen riders on his side of the pasture, hugging the tree line heading towards the corrals. The plan was clear now, for the men afoot, now dead, were to open the corral gates Moving the livestock out, while several more mounted vaqueros were to stampede the livestock, while an even larger force were to fire upon anyone who tried to stop them.

As the half dozen riders on Henry's side passed him, Henry could see yet another half dozen a hundred yards behind them.

A quick count in his head told Henry that three of his Vaqueros should be on the other side of the pasture, with another three on his side of the pasture, each armed with a single shot pistol, a musket and a knife. Of course Henry had both of his Walker Colt revolvers, with six fully charged cylinders on his belt and his bow and arrows.

There were five other vaqueros covering the corrals each eager to end things with intruders, along with the other ten and Mendoza in the bunk house hopefully still awake.

Henrys instructions to the vaqueros were to shoot the horses that were moving with riders on them, so hopefully the riders would suffer injuries as the horses fell making their killing much easier. Since the vaqueros loved their horses and horses were vital to their lifestyle Henry had to drive the point home, that this was a life or death moment for them all and a moving horse made an easier target than the rider. After all there would be other horses, but if one got himself killed, by the rider? The point appeared to ring true to each and every one.

"Besides", Henry continued, "they're not our horses"!

Just then, gunshots appeared to come from the direction of the main house, prompting several musket shots, to come from across the pasture, causing, several musket shots to come from the corrals and some musket shots to come from just ahead of Henry on his side of the pasture.

Both men and horses dropped in the pasture, as several of the horsemen on Henrys side wheeled their mounts only to find a lone man behind them with a pistol in each hand firing repeatedly into their ranks as he advanced on foot. Akila, not to be out done, raced ahead for the riders in front leaping upon one of the horses sinking his fangs into the shoulder of the rider knocking him off the horse and landing on him as he hit the ground crushing the live from him in an instant.

Where Henry had a clear shot of the rider, he shot the rider. Where the target wasn't so easy and the rider was on the move, he shot the horse, in the front withers, bring both the horse and rider down in a heap.

As Henry reached for the spare cylinders to reload his Colts, several riders, their weapons quickly emptied, made a break past Henry and raced across the field as fast as their horses could carry them.

As Henry brought one of his big Colts to bear on the back of a fleeing rider, the big Colt bucked once, then again and again., with one horse going down and one other rider unhorsed.

Henry looked across the field only to see a vaquero fleeing on foot rapidly being pursued by a rider who ended his effort with one swipe of a machete'. Several more shots to finish off, those reaching for their weapons, then silence except for the lowing of restless livestock, hurriedly being calmed by a few of the vaqueros.

Within the space of about a minute all of the firing was done, with the main pasture littered with both dead, or dying horses and dead or dying riders. The death toll, a dozen horses, three seriously wounded intruders, fourteen intruders dead, plus three of Don Domingo's cattle having met an early end.

Miraculously, none of Don Domingo's vaqueros suffered as much as a scratch. Later it was discovered the cause of the gunshot that started it all came from Don Domingo, perched as he was in the recesses of his bedroom window brought down a rider with one of the family muskets approaching the front of the main house.

Few people ever survive the massive blow of .60, or .70 caliber musket ball, for if it can bring down a horse, just think of what it can do to a man.

Yet later there they were three vaqueros, unknown to any of the Fuentes crew except one, who was recognized as being in the employ of the Andrade family.

Despite of a broken leg on one of the intruders, a broken collarbone on another and a smashed shoulder courtesy of a musket ball on the third, all were stripped clean and drug to a corral and string up and spread eagled on the fence. They were going nowhere.

Several of the vaqueros set about distributing hay to the livestock, for they could not be let loose from the corrals until all were certain the threat was past and the pasture cleared of all the dead.

Yet one had escaped, just one. Henry could see him frantically whipping his mount as he went out of range.

Saddles were removed from dead horses, several oxen were brought forth to drag back the horses to a central point whereupon the woman servants fell to the task, along with a few of the men to render the carcasses immediately for the smoke house. All the vaquero's fell to it and by noon all the bodies had been cleared from the pasture, while Henry set about the task of gleaning information from the survivors.

By noon Mendoza departed with a few of the Vaqueros to escort the mortician back to town along with Don Domingo. By noon all was known with regard to the involvement of a certain Chuey Medrano in the affairs of the Andrade family. As he walked away from the captives secured as they were on the corral railings he heard the plaintive sounds of, "Agua, Agua", coming from them. He went to the verandah and sat down in one of the chairs. Henry was certain that he, nor the Fuentes family had not heard the last of Chuey Medrano or the Andrade family.

As one of the servants brought him a mug of Pulque, to quench his thirst, he ran through his mind just what they could have been thinking that they thought they could get away with this? This Medrano was supposed to be a "Muy Malo", professional thief. Two of his people had led this abortive attempt; with the rest of them were Andrade vaqueros. One of the two, died as Henry shot his horse out from under him and the horse rolled over him crushing him immediately. One of the Medrano people led the attempt the other night, when Henry was away and one of the men hanging on the corral belonged to Medrano. He watched as the livestock were finally allowed to leave the confines of the corral, gradually populating the vast main pasture.

Once again Chani and Akila had done their work well, as they waited patiently by the women and the vaqueros rendering the horses and cattle, eagerly accepting the various cuts of meat tossed their way, till they could eat no more and slowly came to Henry on the verandah, laying at his feet, one on either side and falling quickly to sleep. He thought, 'The dogs of war, have earned their rest'.

Then his mind went back to Joselita and the funeral, the day after tomorrow. According to Don Domingo, the City's Sheriff and Magistrate were worthless, as far as averting any problems that might arise, the former being too old and toothless, while the other, a political appointee just like the Don, was morally corrupt, doing nothing without "Mordida".

Henry mulled over in his mind just what Mendoza had told him about this Medrano, when he rode with him briefly long ago, concluding the man was a bully and a coward, only making a move when the odds were on his side. Mulling over in his mind the layout of the city square and the various buildings that surrounded the Cathedral, he decided on just what to do in advance of the funeral.

There were three rifles in the Don's possession, family heirlooms, and gifts from the Spanish Crown for services rendered long ago. He waited for the Don to arrive back from town, then explaining his plan, he took each one of the rifles and several of the vaqueros, the Don had selected as his best shots. They all were flintlocks and as he inspected and cleaned them, he set targets in the pasture to gauge their accuracy. Finding them suitable, he then instructed the selected men as to the subtleties or a rifled barrel as opposed to a smooth bore musket.

Within an hour he had his men and off they were along with Don Domingo, towards town. Entering the Cathedral he sought out the Monsignor asking him to escort them to the bell tower. Finding a suitable place in the shadows where a shooting position could be having a full traverse of the square, he assigned one of the men to that position. Then they selected two other locations both of which were higher than the rest of the buildings that surrounded the square and with the help of the Don, money changed hands, with the clear understanding that at a certain time an individual will be let in to occupy a defensive position on that roof. That accomplished, Henry explained to his selected vaqueros various other spots an assassin could occupy, in the employ of the Andrade's.

With the preparations made, with a minimum of visual exposure, the men left Monterrey and rode back to the Rancho. As they returned, some of the men, clearly fatigued, commented about the graves that might have to be dug for the "Vato's". Understanding their complaints, Henry said, "We're all tired and need sleep and they'll be no graves dug for them tomorrow. Instead, they will be sent to Hell"!

The following morning he and a dozen others loaded the dead bodies stripped bare, onto a wagon and driven to one of the upper pastures, where trees were felled and a pyre was built and the bodies unceremoniously loaded upon the pyre and set afire. At around two in the afternoon the pyre had mostly burned to the ground and the corpses rendered to mostly white ash and some random bones. All was raked into a pile until the last embers were snuffed out and dirt shoveled upon it. No last rites were given. No signs of the cross were made. No prayers offered. Some are born to this world, and then take a certain path in life, thus reaping the appropriate rewards. At two AM in the morning of Joselita's funeral, the selected Vaqueros were awakened, fed a proper breakfast and sent on their way into Monterrey, to their assigned positions in the city, passing the horse drawn hearse driven by the city's mortician, on its way to deliver Joselita to her final resting place. By half past four each one was in position, sequestered from external view, one in the Cathedral bell tower high above and the other two atop the other two largest buildings ringing the square. By six AM, they all noticed two riders approach the square, there looking around at the few early risers that signaled the start of the day, separated and disappeared, only to reappear, on the roofs of two other buildings, below them in height, but with a clear view of the front of the Cathedral. Now all the parties settled in to wait. Starting at ten AM those attending the funeral Mass of Dona Joselita Fuentes Jaeger commenced their arrival, for the High Funeral Mass, that was to occur at Noon. One by one all of the Hidalgo families in the greater Monterrey and Saltillo area arrived in all their finery, as a sign of respect for one of their own. The town square was cleared of all that was not representative, of the services soon to begin. Each family had a place where their carriages and horses were to be placed and attended by their attendant vaqueros, with the Fuentes family placed at the very front of the Cathedral.

As the Fuentes family cortege arrived with Henry and Juan Mendoza riding in front, followed by the Funeral Hearse, followed by the Fuentes family carriage, and six of their vaqueros, bringing up the rear, some took notice that all of the men were armed and attired appropriately for such an occasion.

As the carriage came to rest, Mendoza took charge of all the horses and tied them to the family carriage, which was secured to a ring in the small wall surrounding the Cathedral. Both Chani and Akila took their place beside Mendoza at Henry's direction. The Don's Vaqueros all took their places and lifted the ornate coffin with great care, slowly making their way up the steps and into the Cathedral, as the Cathedrals bells tolled.

In spite of the cotton the vaquero stuffed into his ears in the bell tower, he prayed the bells would soon stop their ringing, for his head was starting to hurt, from the pressure of the bells.

As the coffin entered the Cathedral, the bells ceased their ringing, answering his prayers. This was not the time to have an unsteady hand.

The coffin in place, the lid was opened for everyone to pass by and see the serene look on Joselita's face as she lay in quiet repose. That eventually accomplished the pipe organs opened with the Ave Maria and the celebration began.

The Andrade family was across the aisle from the Fuentes, yet a few rows back, yet somehow the two elder brothers were missing from the celebration. Francisco Andrade noticed that Henry Jaeger was in the church armed with his two Colt revolvers and the big Bowie knife, something the church policies never had permitted. Andrade's eyes flitted back and forth between the altar and Jaeger. He wished that his sons were with him, but he feared they were with the bandit Chuey Medrano. A number of Andrade's vaqueros had gone missing as of late and they would be needed in the coming days.

Suddenly there was a commotion from outside the Cathedral and one of Don Domingo's vaqueros came running unceremoniously down the aisle and whispered into Henry's ear, causing to rise, quickly kneel, making the sign of the cross and slowly walk out of the Cathedral into the sunlight. As he went down the aisle, he unhooked the leather loops on his holsters that secured his revolvers, for ready access. He'd cleaned and reloaded each revolver the previous night in anticipation. Emerging from the Cathedral his eyes beheld a dozen Vaqueros surrounding the Andrade brothers with one with his leg thrown over his horse's saddle horn, facing Mendoza and Chani and Akila snarling, but kept in place by Mendoza, who kept his eyes locked on the casually mounted rider, with his right hand resting on his big Colt holstered high on his left hand side of his belt. The restraining strap was off.

As Henry approached he touched the wolves quieting them saying, 'What this about someone wanting my horse'?

The rider looked at Henry saying, "Ah, joo mus be Senor Jaeger, the Americano peeg"!

As Henry fixed his eyes on the rider, he said a silent prayer and realized that he was looking into the empty eyes of the beast. Then after a brief pause he answered, "And you must be that thieving "Cabrone" from the rat infested Culiacan, who calls himself Chuey Medrano"! The words rolled casually from his lips with as much distain as he could muster.

Unfazed, Medrano said, "I hab fallen in love weed jor horse, the Appaloosa an I weesh to buy her"!

"The horse is not for sale at any price to anyone"!

"But senor", Medrano continued, perhops joo deed not hear me, I weesh to buy joor horse! And Chuey Medrano weel hab your horse, one way or da odder! I weel gib joo a veddy good price, for joor horse"!

As their eyes fixed on each other as a matter of wills, Henry said, "Today is the celebration of my wife's funeral and your presence here and now is an insult. The only thing you're gonna give is a headache"!

Just then, a smiling Medrano gradually started to inch his gun hand close to his big Colt revolver and Henry said, "If that hand moves one more inch, it and you will be gone"!

"But Senor", Medrano slowly retorted as he slowly removed his sombrero to mop his brow, "Joo hab me all wrong"! Just then a rifle shot rang out, then another as bullet ricocheted into the front door of the Cathedral, then another, then a forth, with two men falling from the roofs of buildings flanking the square.

In a flash both Jaeger and Mendoza had their Colts in hand and pointed at Medrano. Then another shot rang out, this time from the bell tower as one of the Andrade brothers fell from his saddle, his single shot dueling pistol just barely out of his holster. As he fell from the saddle his pistol discharged into the cobblestones, ricocheting into one of Medrano's horses, which reared up throwing its rider to the cobblestone pavement.

Still at the ready were all six of Don Domingo's vaqueros single shot pistols at the ready as well as the riders with Medrano, all pointed at each other.

By this time both of Henry's pistols were in hand and Medrano's hand was on his, but it was still in the holster. "Your shooters are dead and in addition to Medrano and me there are three rifles pointed at you, the very same three that took your men on the roofs out. Now everybody's got their guns out and there are more of you than us, but right this moment I wouldn't give a centavo for your life if anyone twitches!"

"I'm gonna count to a number I have in my head, and if that holster of yours hasn't hit the ground with its weapon by then, you'll be the first to die"! "Que sabe Vato"? "Uno, dos, tres", then Henry counted in silence, his fingers tightening on the trigger.

Gradually Medrano unbuckled his holster, it dropping to the ground, with the Colt it contained. As he wheeled his horse around he cried aloud, "I weel hab jour horse" and whipped his mount as fast as the cobblestone streets could permit, followed closely by his men. Just then a loud shriek came from inside the Cathedral, when it was discovered that Tante' Juanita had been struck by the errant ricocheting bullet by Medrano's assassin.

Dead on the cobblestones was the youngest of the Andrade brothers, still with his empty pistol in his hand staring blindly into the noon day sun. After the last of the riders left the plaza, Henry went back inside the Cathedral only to find the celebration of the Mass had stopped and a throng of people had gathered around the Fuentes family. Forcing his way through the crowd, Henry discovered that Tante' Juanita was slumped over in the pew, lifeless and in the arms of her sister Encarnacion. He went immediately to the casket as he heard the shrieks of grief from his mother in law, to view Joselita, as she lay in quiet repose. As he turned he could see the elder Andrade standing in his place in his pew with his wife. Then he walked over to him saying, "I think you need to go out in the Plaza and tend to your son. He was riding with Medrano along with his brother!"

Just then Don Domingo approached the duo. Henry asked, "Tante Juanita"? The Don answered, "Muerte", following after Don Andrade and his wife as they ran down the center aisle.

Henry then turned back to Tante' Juanita and tried to approach the throng. There were those who were fleeing the Cathedral, then those closer to the Fuentes family who watched and waited, seeing if they would be needed.

One of the assistant priests helped them to lay Tante' Juanita on the floor, her mouth gaping open, he lifeless eyes, staring at the ceiling seeing nothing. Finding no pulse in her wrist the priest looked up and declared, "Muerte' "! At that moment, all heard screams come from the outside of the Cathedral, closely joined by Dona Encarnacion who went to her sister once again, clutching her to her breast.

Seeing that there was nothing he could do for the moment, Henry went back outside to see Mendoza and Don Domingo standing together observing the grief the Andrade's displayed as they groveled on the cobblestones, cradling their dead son.

Henry looked at Mendoza saying, "I think you'd better go inside Juan"? Quizzically Mendoza looked at him asking, "Porque"? Henry replied "Just go inside Juan, you will be needed more there. I'll take care of things here"!

He watched as Mendoza entered the Church, then turning to the Don asking, "What now"?

This was all almost too much to bear for the Don as a crowd of the towns people began to gather. Just then, the shooters Henry placed upon the roofs approached, leading their mounts, rifles in hand, joined by the shooter in the belfry. Both acknowledged that the other shooters were indeed men in the service of the Andrade family. Don Francisco then approached Henry and Don Domingo yelling, "My son is dead! The both of you are responsible for this"! Henry interceded saying, "There are two dead shooters in this plaza that are in your employ Don Francisco" and he pointed to where they lay. "I think you might want to see if I'm not right then ask yourself why they were here, before saying anything else"? The Don walked over to each of the dead bodies, rolling them over and staring at them, before slowly walking back to the Fuentes gathered in the plaza. Don Andrade stood still, his mind reeling. He looked over to where his youngest lay, in the arms of his grieving mother, then back to Henry and Don Domingo and started to speak, when Henry put his finger to his lips and said, "Just listen. Why is Chuey Medrano associating with your sons? Eating at your table trying to steal the livestock belonging to Don Domingo. Why are vaqueros in your employ along with several of Chuey Medrano's men, dead on Don Domingo's rancho? You and your family are considered people of honor and yet you associate with known banditry. We can only assume that you mean the Fuentes family harm. Are not those men in your employ", asked Henry? "Are not the arms they carried, bearing the mark of your family? And is not the musket ball in the head of Tante' Juanita, done by your men? Ask yourself these things Don Andrade, before you ask anything else"! Don Andrade looked at his keening wife, holding her son in her embrace.

"I cannot speak for Don Domingo, but your remaining son should be somewhere else! I now have to complete the burial of my wife"! With that Henry reentered the Cathedral. As he approached the crowd gathered around Tante' Juanita, he could see Mendoza, his eyes filled with grief holding his sombrero with both hands, wanting to embrace his lovely Juanita, taken from him by a fluke of nature, an errant musket ball that found its way into her head by the hand of fate.

He sobbed, "Our time together was all too short! Yet she will live in my heart forever"! Just then Don Domingo approached and Henry asked, "Would you approach Dona Encarnacion and ask her permission to permit Mendoza some private time with Tante' Juanita"? The Don knowing of their secret ardor for each other and the loyalty Mendoza had for his family nodded his head and went to his wife, bending over and whispering into her ear. She looked up at Mendoza and nodded her head for him to approach, relinquishing her position with Mendoza, who now with his darling in his arms broke down in a torrent of tears.

At this point, class distinctions did not matter. At the point of dying, when faced with eternity, social niceties are of scant consideration. Henry and the Don asked the people to join them outside, while Mendoza said his good byes. Mendoza had grown close to Henry over the course of the last year and had grieved with him silently by being of service to such a man at his moment of grief. But not before this very moment was he completely aware of the depth of his sorrow. Now he knew completely what was deep within.

Henry walked back inside past Mendoza and his grief, kneeling at the casket of his inamorata and started to converse with the departed. At the door to the Cathedral Don Domingo and his wife were joined by Chani and Akila, both of which looked up at them with pleading eyes. Both the Don and Encarnacion reached down to pet them both, and then nodded towards the front of the church signaling them that it was permissible to approach.

As the wolves walked down the center aisle, they stopped at where Mendoza sat with Juanita cradled in his arms and sniffed them both, then approached Henry and sat on either side of him and began to howl to the heavens, their announcement that another good and kind soul was about to enter. Within the hour the mortician was summoned to the Cathedral to perform his ritual on Tante' Juanita for the now dual services to be performed the following day. The following day he was summoned to the Andrade compound to do likewise. The Don and his wife returned to the ranch that evening only to return the following morning, leaving Henry, Mendoza and several vaqueros to perform an all-night vigil. The services were conducted, the words were read, the bodies interred and the ordeal was over. The time for healing was now at hand, or was it? The day after, services were conducted for Andrade's dead son at the main Cathedral.

Attendance was sparse, with only the immediate Andrade family and the Medrano riders in attendance. Later in the day was the burial, with the surviving male member of the family now clearly in charge and Don Francisco left at the rancho incapacitated and under guard.

As the funeral cortege returned to the Andrade rancho, the eldest son stopped his horse, then turning to his mother as if to say something, when he was struck by something knocking him from his horse dead before he hit the ground, with the sound of a rifle shot arriving a split second later. The hacienda was on a flat expanse of ground with no significant foliage of any kind within a hundred yards. Once again his mother screamed to see her last son dead before her very eyes. The remaining Andrade vaqueros gathered around their dead 'Jefe', weapons at the ready. Chuey Medrano emerged from the hacienda, seeing what had happened and thought, 'Saves me the effort', for he'd planned to do away with the entire Andrade family anyway and take over what was left of their rancho. Only just repayment for the gambling debts their sons had run up.

Soon Chuey Medrano would be a Hidalgo, a land owner and a man of respect, for a week earlier, he had a Last Will and Testament crafted by a master forger in San Luis Potosi, with the signature of Don Francisco a perfect likeness. Three more funerals then some respect.

Tonight the Andrade family would meet an untimely end, and the City Sheriff and the Magistrate, already in his pocket since each one of their relatives had been kidnapped the previous evening and were secreted safely away in small line cabin miles away. The whole affair would be blamed on the Americano and the Fuentes. Of course the City Sheriff would require additional deputies and who better that the Medrano people.

Then there was this business of someone lurking about. He would send Obregon with a few of his men out to kill this one.

Minutes later Dona Andrade was led into the house, her dress a bloody mess and was greeted by the sight of her husband bound and sitting in a chair. Medrano had her similarly bound and set in a chair right next to her husband.

With her eyes filled with both grief and terror, she looked at her husband who was drugged and incoherent, then glanced back at a smiling Chuey Medrano, just in time to see the blade as it slashed her throat almost to the back of her neck. She tried to cry out only to find that no sound came other than a bloody gurgling sound, as blood spurted and oozed from her severed neck. Then all went black as he head sank to her chest.

Trying to feel some emotion, all he could think to say was, "Vaya con dios Madre"! Then he went over to the Don, who witnessed the entire thing, yet showing nothing but tears as he was incapable of movement, being drugged and bound securely to his chair.

Medrano looked down at him, holding his head by his sparse hair and kissed both of his cheeks saying, "I geev thanks to joo pour gibbing birt to two veddy bad gomblers", then with yet another swipe of his blade, Francisco Andrade followed his family into the great beyond.

Just then Obregon entered into the house saying, "The last of the Andrade vaqueros have ridden away, Jefe"! "Muy Bueno", Medrano said absently, still admiring his handiwork peering deeply into the Don's eyes as he died. "Take some bravos and fine da one who shoot the brodder and keel him". Obregon turned and went to the door and as he passed through it he glanced back at Medrano, still fixated on the rapidly dying Don Andrade.

Medrano thought, 'good now they're all gone, which saves me the effort of killing them."

Henry saw four of the Medrano men spread out as the headed in his general direction, with weapons at the ready. He motioned to Chani and Akila where to lay in wait, as he climbed a tree in readiness. The big Beretta lay hidden at the base of the tree, covered by brush. Hidden by the branches Henry waited, an arrow mounted in his bow with two more at the ready. As Obregon and his men entered the brush they waited and listened, before moving further. They as one they advanced, deeper and deeper into the dark and bristly brush.

Henry saw two men advance in his general direction, their heads on a constant swivel and their muskets at the ready. As one passed directly below him, he shot his arrow almost straight down, piercing his upper back just behind his neck and disappeared completely into the body cavity. As the man fell, unable to move or cry out, Henry strung another arrow and made out the outline of another, just as one of the wolves went into action to his left, a noisy affair, which summoned the shadowy one who ran at the noise revealing himself. Henry let fly with the second arrow which found its mark in the vaquero's chest, sending him to his knees. As Henry dropped down from the trees, he heard the attack of the other wolf.

Pulling his Bowie knife he finished the hapless vaquero off, slitting his throat. As he looked up he saw both Chani and Akila, trotting towards him, their mouths containing what was left of the vaqueros throats. Which they laid at Henry's feet.

Retrieving his Beretta and the bow, he moved on around the perimeter of the brush line to the other side of the hacienda. There, he saw three of Medrano's men drinking and laughing, smoking cigars. He calculated the range at slightly over a hundred yards, adjusting the elevation devise on the Beretta, settling into position, deep into the brush, pulling back both hammers into full cock position, slowly taking aim and squeezed the first trigger. As the big barrel came to rest after the first shot, he readjusted his aim and fired again; sending two of the three tumbling backwards and the third diving to take cover.

Henry quickly moved to another hide he selected. As he moved he saw four other of Medrano's men emerging from the hacienda, joining their compadres. Then all of them fired their weapons in the general direction of where Henry had been. Quickly all of them started to reload their muskets and pistols.

Now at slightly an angle, Henry reloaded the Beretta and settled into position, waiting for the first head to pop up from behind the small retaining wall. They waited along with Henry, eventually after some minutes and hearing no more firing two of them rose up to see what was out there. Each one was greeted with a rifle ball entering their chest driving them back against the house.

Henry the pulled one of his Colt's from his holster. At a hundred yards distant the range should be should be more than the Colt was designed for, but when the other two decided to rise as one and make for the house, Henry took aim and fired all six rounds. Amazingly one of the rounds found a mortal mark dropping a vaquero instantly and the other one wounded, made it back into the house just barely.

Taking a brief head count, Henry made it to be ten down including the eldest son and unless Medrano was squirreling some of his people away, he was down to his last vaquero and that one was wounded.

All of the Andrade men had made tracks a short time ago. This left Henry alone with Medrano and one other who was probably wounded to some degree Henry reckoned. Now all he had to do was wait. As he looked up to the sky the sun indicated something around midafternoon. About five hour or so of daylight left. An hour later the side door opened and Henry heard from within a bellow, "Eh Puto, Aye steel wan joor Appaloosa an aye weel hab eet"! Then the door slammed shut. Henry thought, 'If I were Medrano and I was down to my final man, I think I would try and get a rise from him, insult him, compelling him to fire on me, revealing his location, then my man would fire upon him'.. Seemed like a possibility, except Henry wasn't Medrano, holding his fire and moving to a third location, where he had a good view of both the main and side entrance of the encomienda.

Chani and Akila both flanked him at thirty yards distance, so he knew no one was going to flank him. So he waited.

Inside the house, the last of Medrano's men writhed in agony, gasping for breath, the luck shot by Jaeger, entering his torso just under his right armpit and lodging in his chest puncturing his right lung. He was starting to cough up blood and the pallor of his skin indicated to Medrano that he would soon be of little use leaving Chuey Medrano all alone to confront this Jaeger.

He fought back the feelings of fear for the first time in his memory. He was Chuey Medrano, from Culiacan and always went where he wanted, took what he wanted, killed who he wanted and he wanted a lot. He wanted everything. Men from Culiacan were bravos, known and feared far and wide and he was the best of them all. Yet here he was cowering in this house, when on the verge of having everything he wanted, this 'Vato', this 'Son of a whore' was ruining everything. For the very first time in his life he thought about dying. Before, others thought about dying, never Chuey Medrano. But now, the thoughts of pending death had invaded his mind and his entire being. He'd seen many men and women die mostly of his own hand, taking great pleasure as he looked into their eyes as they faded away.

He'd seen many bravos calling for their mothers at the moment of leaving, with others still uttering the names of loved ones with their final breath.

He'd led a hard life and had no regrets, about what he'd done of who it was done to. Yet he had a last card to play, before he checked out. He whispered into his dying vaquero a plan and received a head nod, positioning him with his musket out the window and told him to fire at the last spot he could remember where Medrano would position himself in another place and as Jaeger fired back he would fire on him. So he'd pointed the Vaquero's musket out the side window and when Medrano was ready he would signal. The vaquero waited, his vision starting to dim, then he heard from Chuey the signal and pulled the trigger. As the flint struck the pan of the musket, a bullet struck his barrel ricocheting into his head ending his misery. A scant second after Henry fired he rolled to his left seeing a second barrel emerge from another window and fired at where he just was, as the barrel withdrew Henry quickly brought the big Beretta to bear on the window and pulled the trigger moving again quickly from where he was, coming to rest behind a small tree ten yards into the bush. Dame fortune can arrive in silence and depart the same way; whether with a whimper or a roar it doesn't matter. Sometime it can linger, even amongst the unworthy, for years or decades, so when it suddenly departs, as it often will, the pain will be more keenly felt. Such was the fate of Chuey Medrano, Jaeger's lucky shot ripping through the wooden window sill, driving shards of wood deep into his right eye. Dropping his musket, Medrano screamed in pain as he fell to the floor, his eye hanging out of the socket, the pain, ever more than he could bear. Forcing himself to his feet, he pulled his stiletto knife from its scabbard, lurching for the door, tearing it open he emerged from the house bellowing, "Eh Vato show moor sell, for Aye still weal hob joor horse"! As he lurched around in the open still bellowing insults in every direction. Henry slowly came out of the brush, very carefully, wondering who if anyone was left. Seeing the condition of Medrano he was assured they were alone, with the possibility of Don Andrade. Still he had to see Medrano dead so he took the risk. With a Colt revolver in each hand he approached the lurching Medrano. Yards away now he placed a bullet in each knee, bringing the man to the ground in even greater pain which was now overwhelming his being. Then as Jaeger walked around the writhing Medrano, he placed a bullet in each shoulder saying, "There, that oughtta slow ya down a tad"! With Medrano rolling around on the ground roiling in pain, Henry decided to enter the house with Akila, leaving Chani behind to watch Medrano. He entered cautiously and coming into the main room of the hacienda, he saw Don Medrano and his wife sitting bound in separate chairs, covered in blood that was freshly pooled around their feet. The agony of a swift and painful death apparent as their heads hung precariously from their torsos. He went from room to room searching for any remainders and finding none he returned to the main room and was about to leave and get his horse hidden deep in the brush, when he spied a document on the table. Picking it up he tried to read it with his spotty understanding of Spanish making out that it was a last Will and Testament. Not having any legal training, he made out two names, Don Andrade and Chuey Medrano. He decided to take it back to Don Domingo for translation. Then he saw a map on the same table, with directions and made out the words 'Detener Rehen', "Held Hostage".

Something deep within told him to follow a hunch and he picked up the map, retrieved his horse, and rode past Medrano stopping briefly as Medrano now prostrate unable to move and apparently fading fast from his wounds, saying "Joo wan my horse, Senor"? Then he rode off. A half hour later he came across a small cabin and rode up to it with the Colt in his hand and entered the cabin, to find two women bound lying on the floor. He quickly untied them, amidst the grateful thanks and placed them on his horse, walking them back to the Andrade Hacienda. The old wife of the Magistrate could speak a little English and as they made their way back to the Andrade Hacienda they told Henry the harrowing tale of their abduction by Medrano's people. As they approached the hacienda they saw Medrano now dead from his extensive wounds and Henry helped them from the horse and they went into the house where Henry related to them what happened as best as he could.

Seeing that only an hour of day light was remaining, he retrieved two of the vaquero's horses and helped the women to mount. Within the remaining daylight, Henry escorted both women to their respective homes quickly departing for the Fuentes rancho and some food for his horse, the wolves and him. Then sleep.

Joselita and her Tante' were in the sanctified ground, all known threats to the Fuentes were done and gone and his spiritual emptiness still remained.

As he went inside the main house, everyone was surprised and dismayed to see him and as he sat at the dining table food and drink were served as he related to everyone all that had taken place. Taking the document from his shirt he handed it to Don Domingo to read to all.

It was indeed a Will, from Don Andrade, granting his entire estate upon his death to Chuey Medrano. What nobody could figure out was precisely why? Both sons were known to be gamblers, yet how could such a prominent family get entangled with the likes of Medrano?

"I will take the will to the Sheriff and the Magistrate tomorrow and I think I know what Medrano had in mind for us using them and the law.

After what you've done I think none of us will see a bit of trouble from either one of them. Now you need your rest my son, your bed awaits", offered the Don pointing up the stairs. "Tomorrow, you can become a father to your son". During the night, Henry went downstairs and went to sleep on hard floor of the verandah. Joselita's bed contained too many fond memories, keeping him awake. As Henry finally drifted off to sleep, Chani and Akila went over to him and lay side by side flanking his prostrate body Early at the crack of dawn Don Domingo went out on the veranda with his eldest son, seeing Henry curled up on the floor next to his wolves both who were awakened by the sound of his departure, then went back to sleep. He immediately understood Henry's dilemma. Perhaps peace would come to his heart, in time.

The Don had a Sheriff and a Magistrate to see and affairs of his jurisdiction to manage and manage them he would. As the sun peeked over the Sierra Madre Oriental, the rancho came to life. The Rancho's Encargado barking out orders to the vaqueros, after their morning breakfast, the women going about their business, a veritable anthill of activity. Marta, the one who took to nursing little Rodrigo, came out onto the verandah, sitting down in one of the rocking chairs and commenced to start nursing her new charge followed by Dona Encarnacion, still weak in body and spirit from her dual tragedies. Seeing Henry still asleep on the verandah with his wolves, rather than upstairs in Joselita's bed and Marta busy offering her teat to a hungry baby, spoke volumes to her spiritual recovery. She joined Marta and the child as they both kept a vigil on Henry and his wolves.

Eventually Henry awoke, to hear Encarnacion ask, "When is the last time you bathed senor"? Still groggy from his sleep, Henry was befuddled saying, "I don't know"? Just then she said as she arose,"You will eat a hearty breakfast then we will prepare your bath". Marta started to rise as she was the head cook for the family, but Encarnacion chided her saying, "Marta, sit down please, you are busy with more important things. I can still remember how to prepare a proper meal"!

Henry arose and allowed the women to boss him around as Akila was busy following him around. By late in the morning Henry was fed and washed feeling slightly better as he went out on the veranda only to see Mendoza sitting by an apparent ailing Chani who seemed listless and ill at ease, still laid out on the verandah. Just then one of the Compesina's came up on the verandah took one look at Chani and her condition and spoke to Mendoza in Spanish, walking inside with an armful of finished laundry.

Henry looked at Mendoza who said. "Looks like Chani is going to be a mother". Minutes later Marta and the servant returned to the porch to gently examine Chani, in her distress. When they were finished Marta said to Henry, "Senor, looks like you're gonna be a father again"! Then she departed to prepare for another birth. In the past year the wolves more than proved their worth around the rancho. So every effort would be made to insure a proper birth of the offspring.

And Henry wondered if Akila was the father, yet Akila wandered back on the verandah, seemingly uninterested by Chani's discomfort lying down on the other side of the verandah, just watching.

At midafternoon Don Domingo and his son returned, his affairs in town completed, just as Chani started her birthing process. One by one, the little creatures emerged and were promptly cleaned by the women and the afterbirth cleaned from the floor. After the last little doggie was birthed it became clear that Akila was not the father. Then Akila got up and came over to Chani who by now was busy suckling her newborns as she lay on her side. He sniffed each one of them, and then took his place by Chani's side, sitting down. Henry related all that she'd done in recent days and all marveled at her toughness and endurance while carrying newborns within. One by one as the vaqueros came in from their duties at days end, they paid their respects to the new family members. Six new mouths to feed, life would now start to improve.

Both Jaeger and Mendoza threw themselves into the work of the rancho, gentling horses and preparing them for mounts, branding cattle, rounding up strays and training Chani's newborns as to be comfortable around humans. Growing fast, it became abundantly clear the newborns were not a product from Akila, but some other large breed, for one had red fur; two of them were of a blondish hue, while the other three were brown. Within six months they became almost as adept at herding livestock as their mother and Akila, eagerly joining them on their daily outings and eventually their nightly vigils.

The Don joined them all one afternoon while some of the cattle were being branded by the vaqueros and after observing the animals in action, commented to Mendoza, "In many ways, they are the equal of Vaqueros and cheaper"! Mendoza replied sardonically, "Por favor Jefe, but can they brand the cattle and horses"?

Chuckling, the Don nodded saying, "You have a point my friend. You have a point"!

It had been slightly over two and a half years since Henry had left

Texas, had Joselita still been alive, he would've been content spending the rest of his days in Mexico, growing into old age, nurturing their children to maturity. His life at the rancho was about as good as anyone could hope for and his acceptance by the entire family, vaqueros and servants was complete.

As his grasp of Spanish began to improve, little thought was given to the fact that he was one of the dreaded Americano's. He was in fact every bit the Sombrero clad Vaquero and much more. Being everywhere when needed, taking part of every aspect of the rancho life, be it great or small.

From time to time he would get bits and pieces of news north of the Border. Gold had been discovered in California, which struck a massive blow to all the Hidalgos, since just the previous year California was a province of Mexico. Yet the government in Mexico City was in such a complete shambles, nothing could be done about it. An everlasting thorn in the side of every Mexican, from Hidalgo to the Compesino's.

Governmental bickering in the Nation's capital had grown to such a degree, that governments rose and fell seemingly every other month, with the bulk of governance administered mostly at the State level and every state was staffed by either incompetents or thieves. For anything to occur 'Mordida', (the bite) had to be satisfied. Then one day, the Monterrey newspaper announced that "His Excellency General Zachary Taylor had been elected President of the United States", in banner headlines. The news struck all of the Hidalgo class as the supreme insult. The very man who made mincemeat of Santa Anna's army from even before he invaded Mexico, was now grandly rewarded. Yet there was nothing that could be done. As news of this invaded the evening meal, with the Don's family, Henry was asked his opinion. His responses were muted and noncommittal.

The Don's eldest son, Alejandro asked Henry point blank, "Did you not serve with and save the life of the General"? His father quickly added, "He also saved the life of your sister Joselita, may she rest in peace", whereupon everyone quickly made the sign of the cross "and mine also, even before he knew who I was and Don Francisco"!

"Most fortuitous", answered Alejandro! "The Lord giveth and the Lord taketh away", he continued almost as an afterthought.

The comment stood like a brick through a church window at the table, when the Don offered, "Alejandro, look at me! I don't like the tone this conversation is taking. True, our family has been visited by tragedy. Also true is that Henry has been a blessing in so many ways that they are uncountable. Had it not been for his intervention this rancho just might be in the hands of Chuey Medrano. Then ask yourself where would your inheritance be"?

The Don often had a way of cutting right through all of the pretension, that lay just under the level of truth and this was it. With Henry's presence at the rancho and the accomplishments he'd displayed and would continue to display in the coming years, there would be little doubt who would be more worthy of the family inheritance, when the time came. In every aspect of life Henry was his superior and he wasn't even of their blood, but a former invader. Try as some did to paper over it, there it was.

The table was silent for a time after the Don had spoken, just then Marta appeared with little Rodrigo all dressed in his new bed clothes, freshly fed and bathed, now ready for bed and ready to be placed in the arms of his father, as was done every evening after the meal.

Henry gladly accepted his child into his arms and once again he could see Joselita's face in the little boy. Her eyes her nose, her ears, yet his chubby but solidly growing frame. He fought back tears as he gently hugged the boy, loving him as he did a living extension of Joselita. Perhaps in time, the pain of her untimely departure would lessen, but that time was far in the distant future.

Her gave little Rodrigo back to Marta, who disappeared from view.

Then Alejandro spoke, what was clearly evident in everyone mind saying, "Henry, what my father says is true and I humbly apologize to you.

For you are every bit as much as a Fuentes as I am, perhaps more"! Just then his wife visibly stiffened at that comment, for that was an admission that could interfere with the legal bloodline, should Don Domingo find Henry more worthy in time.

Henry accepted the apology in the spirit with which it was apparently given. Then the conversation at the table turned more to the Comanche raids visited upon Nuevo Laredo, penetrating down as far as Monclova, taking not only horses but captives to be sold as slaves or held for ransom, which ever proved more profitable. Little children plucked from their homes in the dead of night, often never to be seen again.

Then everyone rose up from the table with Henry going outside to enjoy one of the Don's finest Cuban cigars. After a while, the Don joined him outside offering a snifter of brandy and said, "Henry, you know you are most welcome here and are considered a part of the family, by one and all"!

Thinking before he spoke, Henry said, "You know what your son Alejandro implies is true.

Apparently my presence is viewed as a threat to his inheritance, in years to come. Now I've gotten along with Alejandro very well, but I sense there will come a time when my presence will prove to be a problem for the both of us forcing you into a decision. Alejandro is a good man. My affection for your family must not get in the way"!

"You sound like you're going to leave us Henry"! "What about little Rodrigo"? Henry thought a bit then said, "Whatever is done must keep in mind what's best for Rodrigo and the Fuentes family. I just must think on it awhile, if it is alright with you Don Domingo"?

"Do what you must my son, but whatever you do, you must know that you have more than earned our family's respect and an important place at the Fuentes table." Then the Don went inside. Henry then sat down on the front steps as the Chani's family came up to him eagerly vying for his attention, with Mendoza and Akila bringing up the rear. After a flurry of licking jumping and petting, Chani's brood, one by one climbed the steps and settled in to their various places on the verandah, for the night ahead.

"They have already said goodnight to the vaqueros", said Mendoza as he took his place besides Henry. As they talked, Henry became aware of the restlessness in Mendoza that started to match his. Everywhere Mendoza went there were the memories of time spent with his precious Juanita, as he chronicled the various places on the rancho, where they secretly made love.

The longing he felt when, Juanita accompanied Joselita off to France to receive her schooling for four long years. The utter joy he felt upon her return, during the most unlikely and perilous of times, then an all too brief reunion, taking their pleasures with each other, knowing full well, they could never wake up in each other's arms. She was Castilian, while he was of Mestizo blood from of all places Culiacan, a known pit of vipers throughout all of Mexico. Now she too was gone. The pain that was felt every single day was almost too much to bear. Almost every single thing Henry had felt for Joselita, was equally felt by Mendoza, with one exception, legitimacy and a child born from love. As to who's loss was greater, was a question without an answer.

As they talked, Henry related all that had been said at the Don's table to Mendoza, with Mendoza offering, "But what the Don says is true. Many are the time that he has marveled at your bravery and leadership. But if it were not for you, all of this might be in ashes"!

"There is the subject of little Rodrigo, that hangs out there", said Henry! "Other than my time in Nashville, this is the only place I've ever known happiness and contentment! One must think of him before one's self. What I could offer him against what the Fuentes family could offer."

With that, Mendoza slowly arose from the step, stretched and moved towards the bunkhouse to join the other vaqueros. Then he stopped, turned and said, "We both have ghosts lingering about and our fates hang in the balance. If you decide to depart, then if you don't mind I'd like to accompany you senor"! Then he turned and made his way to the bunkhouse. Several days later, Henry and Mendoza accompanied the Don into Monterrey for supplies, for the ranch, dropping the Don off at the Municipal Hall, so he could attend to the affairs of the City while they went around to various shops procuring the rancho's supplies.

As the wagon made its way down the cobblestone streets, with Mendoza riding besides the wagon, they passed one of the larger Cantina's in the City, only to see three horses tied to the hitching post, with a lone vaquero standing guard near the entrance. They vaquero watch them as they passed by and around the corner, coming to a halt in front of a small Tiende'. Henry and Mendoza went inside to transact some purchases in behalf of the Don, only to find the shopkeeper would not talk to or accept payment from Henry, even though it was in behalf of the Fuentes rancho.

Mendoza took over and completed the selections and transactions and they departed with their goods. At the second Tiende the very same thing happened, with the shop owner not even acknowledging Henry at all, with Mendoza once again, having to complete the transaction. With two placed down and three to go, they again stopped at another establishment with the same result.

As they emerged with the supplies, both Henry and Mendoza noticed the very same trio of horses just down the street, but now the saddles were filled with strange men eying the duo with apparent keen interest.

Entering the final establishment Henry told Mendoza to make the purchases, while Henry went out the rear door and circled around the building, just in time to see that their shadows were already at the hitching post, while two of the men went inside and the third was wandering around the wagon peering inside at the purchases. Henry waited until the man had his back to him and approached, withdrawing the long Colt revolver.

Sensing that some was approaching his rear, the vaquero turned around just in time to see the butt of Henry's pistol crash into his face sending him to the ground. Henry quickly disarmed the man, throwing the weapons into the wagon, then giving him a swift kick in the head, climbed the steps to join Mendoza inside.

Mendoza noticed the two men as they entered the store, yet still went on with his transactions. As the men made to look like they were shopping, Mendoza slipped the rawhide strap that was looped over the hammer of his revolver. As one of them came into view, he noticed that one of the men was similarly armed with the Colt .44.

Slowly the one of men started to approach Mendoza from behind, not seeing Jaeger enter the store. The other man was at the rear of the store looking for something or someone. As the man near Mendoza approached finally standing right next to him he said in Spanish, "You remind me of someone I once knew in Culiacan, Senor"!

Mendoza quickly swerved to his left, narrowly missing the slim stiletto, knife that was drawn, pulling his big Colt from his holster as he turned and pulled the trigger as the barrel came to bear. From a distance of three feet, it was impossible for the big Colt to miss, the impact of the bullet driving the other back knocking him off his feet, with a deafening sound that left ears ringing in its aftermath. The bullet drove right through its target slicing right through the spine leaving the man paralyzed before he hit the floor.

The other man came running up the aisle, with his weapon drawn towards Mendoza as Mendoza was taking aim on him and suddenly was driven to the floor, by Henry who seemingly came out of nowhere. The man, being of a spare build, was knocked senseless as Henry drug both men out of the premises and onto the street, while Mendoza calmly completed his transaction, saying to the proprietor, "Muy Permisso Senor, Perdonna me", walking out with his purchases. As he loaded the purchases into the wagon, he saw that Henry was in the process of stripping each horse of its saddle and tack, after stripping each man of all his clothes and boots and after a severe beating of the two remaining men, loaded each man on a horse, face up and tying them to the back of their horse with their own lariat and whipping the horse down the street. It was near noon and the commotion began to draw a crowd. Mendoza simply stood by as Henry did his work, in silence whipping each horse in turn down the street, carrying its cargoes of the dead and severely beaten men, dishonored and naked.

As the last horse galloped down the cobblestone streets, Henry turned to the assembled crowd, yelling in his fractured Spanish, "I am Heinrich Jaeger, the Norte' Americano, who took part in the Battle of Monterrey, who none of you seem to want! Well so be it"! He then leapt onto the wagon and taking the reins started the wagon back up the street to his rendezvous with Don Domingo, with Mendoza alongside.

The crowd started to disburse, some with quizzical looks in their eyes while others, swept their hands together in a sign that they were glad the Americano would not be a presence on their streets ever again. For well over the past year, stories began to circulate regarding his activities, with scant attention being paid to the lives he'd saved, just the lives he'd taken.

Later as they drove to the rancho, the Don looked at Henry, who was uncharacteristically silent as well as Mendoza. "What is wrong my son", asked the Don. Henry was silent as the Don asked yet again. Henry replied, "Ask Mendoza, he'll tell ya"!

With the question directed this time at Mendoza, he responded, leaving out some of the more salacious details, telling him of the interim events, with both the shop keepers and the additional bandits from Culiacan and their ultimate disposal.

As they continued their journey, the Don tried to dissuade Henry from leaving for he'd grown to love Henry as well as his own son, which brought up yet another reason for his departure, blood loyalty with his eldest son Alejandro. "I'm not of your bloodline Don. Mendoza and me will always be in the way of your family's harmony", offered Henry!

And there it was, irreconcilable, the nexus of human nature.

The Don turned to Mendoza saying, "And you Juan"? After a moment he replied, "As long as Henry is here, there will always be someone from Culiacan coming for him. It stands to reason that eventually some of this will affect the Fuentes family in some way. Remove this as a reason then you remove a reason for further visits. I'm from there and I know those people."

Continuing he said, "Every single day, I'm reminded of Henry's loss, for every single day everything I touch, everywhere I go I see, Juanita and my heart grows unbearably heavy and that it how it is with Henry! So with great reluctance I must accompany Senor Jaeger wherever he goes"! The Don asked Henry, "So you and Juan my son"?

"If Juan wants to go, it will be of his free will and I can't think of anyone better that I'd like to have along"! They talked further with the Don discussing little Rodrigo's future and Henry acceding that he would be better off with the Don and the Fuentes family than with Henry. "He will bear the Jaeger name proudly. We will see to it that he receives the finest education, in all things, before he comes to the age of majority. He will be known as Rodrigo de la Fuentes Jaeger, muy permiso"! Henry nodded in agreement. The Don went even further by adding, "You both will be given your pick of two of my finest Bulls and as many of the cows as you think you'll require, plus horses. Of course Chani and Akila would depart, but since the brood was almost fully grown, Henry agreed to leave behind their mixed breed wolves behind at the rancho, where they were already proving their worth in helping the vaqueros herding and guarding the livestock, having bonded with some of them. That evening the announcement was made, amidst tears and it was agreed that they would celebrate Mass together, for the final time at the Main Cathedral in Monterrey, departing after sundown the very same evening. In discussing his future prospects, Henry allowed that he was aware that General Worth was now in charge of the Texas District and since Henry was never formally mustered out of the Rangers, he must be due some back pay and that he would present himself to the General, in San Antonio de Bexar, with the letter of recommendation from the now President Taylor, for further assignment and hopefully a homestead in Texas.

The Don stressed that Henry try and keep in touch with the family as best as possible and as soon as he was settled, let him know where, so he could keep him appraised of his son's progress. When Rodrigo's schooling was finished and he was of the age of majority, he would be given a choice to either stay with the Fuentes of join his father, wherever he may be. The Don, being a man of honor and aware of Henry's manner of sealing a bargain, then spit in his hand offering it to Henry. Henry then smiled and did likewise, thus sealing the bargain.

The evening of Henry and the Juan's departure, all were sad, except the wife of Alejandro, who was relieved that the last impediment to her husband accession was fading away.

As the sun was setting in the west, Jaeger and company were heading in a northerly direction. Chani, Akila and two of her offspring were bringing up the rear of the herd as they cleared the rise. They stopped and turned gazing at the rancho for the final time, with Chani giving forth a final long and plaintive howl, only to receive a multitude of separate howls from the valley below. Then she turned to Akila and with a snort they joined Henry and his entourage.

13

As Henry awoke the following morning, he rubbed his eyes as Akila licked his face signaling that it was time the wolves be fed. Either that or they would make their way into the brush, eventually returning with blood on their faces from reverting to their feral nature.

Today was the day when he would go into San Antonio de Bexar and do two things, dig up the small water tight box, left under a tree, north of town by the buffalo camp, for it still contained some memento's from his parents, the letter of introduction from General Jackson and the monies he'd earned all the way back to his days in Cheviot.

Mendoza was up and stoking the campfire, in preparation of the of the morning coffee saying, "Our chugar is almost gone Jefe", a reminder to add yet another item to his shopping list at Seth's emporium. As for the cream, well there were the cows, fresh from the source.

He wanted to bring Mendoza into town with him, but someone had to watch the herd with the wolves and besides, for a vaquero fresh from Mexico with all the trappings and a Walker Colt sidearm would take too much explaining to a population still with raw memories of the Mexican invasions. So Mendoza agreed to stay put.

Henry wanted to make some time to look in on the Maverick family and let them know he was still a part of the world. Over time they'd expanded from their origins as 'feather merchants', having started in town the first general store and expanding into the town's first newspaper, might be good to let the people know.

By mid-morning, Henry mounted his big Appaloosa, bid Mendoza goodbye and headed into town, for his meeting with General Worth. As he rode down the dusty Market Street, he saw Mary Maverick, who was shocked to see him and yelled out, "Well Lordy lord, if it isn't Henry Jaeger", which prompted Henry to ride over and dismount, hugging the woman as if she were family.

"When nobody heard from you, everyone assumed you were a goner", she offered holding him at arm's length in admiration.

"Seems General Worth said the same thing several days ago when I came to town for a meeting"!

"You met with the General", asked Mary? "Yes Maam", replied Henry.

"Well, it seems the General is in a bad way", she offered! "A bad way"?

"Yes. They say it's Cholera". Then continued, "The waters been bad in town as of late, what with all the newcomers and their horses shitting in the San Antonio River upstream north of town. It our only source of water and it's too expensive to dig wells, so everyone's gone to boiling our drinking water except for the few Mexicans in town and it seems they're mostly coming down with Cholera. So now everyone's starting to boil their drinking water.

Then Henry told her of his lunch with the General at the Mexican Cantina.

"You didn't drink the water did ya"?

"No Mamm, just Pulque"! But now that I think of it the General did have a mug of water to wash down the heat in his mouth.

"Pulque, eh? Horrible tasting stuff, but there you are! That what must've done in the General!

Henry asked, "Have you seen Captain Jack Hays? Did he make it back from Mexico"?

"Make it back he did it fine fettle with nary a scratch, but many a tale to tell he did. Soon as the news of the Gold Strike in California arrived, he and some waddies lit out and headed west to make their fortune. Don't imagine we'll ever see their likes again. Too bad since there are damn few men like you and him to hold things together. But you better git along to the Hotel and finish your business with the General, while you can. But I just gotta tell ya that he had a daughter that nobody knew about. A real looker, blonde she is, from Charleston South Carolina and she brought her 'darkies' with her, so things might be a tad crowded what with all the commotion there"!

She gave Henry a hug and said, "Now you come around and visit with Sam and me before ya leave and we'll make ya a meal, so git along little dogie" and gave him a slap on the rump.

As Henry approached the Hotel he had to hitch his horse to a post a block away, since there was not room at the hitching posts in front of the Hotel. As he entered the hotel he was greeted by the sight of a swarm of people, all wanting something from the general. 'How can the general tend to all these people if his condition is as perilous as Mary Maverick dictated', Henry thought. Overhearing some conversations, Henry gleaned that the general's suite of rooms was on the second floor and that his newly arrived daughter was helping tend to him along with her darkies.

After almost an hour it seemed that no one was being summoned to the second floor and the crowd or petitioners grew restless. Just then the Generals adjutant came running down the stairs on his way to the office and on his way saw Henry waiting patiently by the general's office on the first floor.

"Ranger Jaeger, Henry Jaeger I believe", called out the adjutant as he ran by, "Please stand by and when I come out follow me up the stairs to see the General. Henry could see the adjutant scurrying about the generals desk, through the open door for sheaves of documents, then gathering up what was needed, hurriedly exited the office summoning Henry to follow him up the stairs.

As the ascended the stairs the adjutant said, "Since you were with the general last seems he's been stricken by Cholera, as well as a host of others here in town and is in a bad way, according to the doctor. But he's been expecting you and has ordered me to bring you to him, upon your arrival."

"Have the people from Austin arrived as the General has said", asked Henry as they walked down the hallway?

"Not as of the moment. Seems a wagon wheel fell off, near New Braunfels settlement and they had to spend the night. But we're assured of the wheels repair and their arrival this very day"!

As they came to the room, the adjutant asked Henry to wait in the hallway, while some business was concluded with another. Fifteen minutes later the door open and someone attired like a businessman emerged, stuffing what appeared to be a contract into a bulging portfolio while hurrying down the hallway.

Then the adjutant emerged, "The General will see you now, Captain Jaeger", he said with a smile. Henry entered the suite of rooms following the adjutant, announcing his arrival. "Sir, Captain Jaeger is here to attend you"! As Henry entered the bedroom he saw General Worth lying in his bed, still in his nightgown, attended by a blond woman with her back turned to him, wiping the perspiration from the general's brow.

"Captain Jaeger, so good of you to come, said the general weakly, no longer with the robust voice of a military commander of line rank. May I introduce you to my daughter, Miss Melanie Swanson, of the Charleston Swanson's who, has traveled a great distance to be by my side"!

As she got up from her bed, Henry was struck by the radiant beauty of a woman that every bit rivaled his departed Joselita. He nervously reached out his hand and said, "Pleased to meet you Maam"! She took his hand briefly, nodding her head, her eyes puffy with either an overabundance of tears, or a lack of sleep, or both.

For the second time in his life Henry was confronted with the presence of a woman, of which it was very difficult to tear his eyes from, even in apparent grief or distress.

As the general cleared his voice, they both turned to him as he said, "As you may have surmised, you are hereby appointed to a Captaincy in the newly constructed Texas Rangers law enforcement enterprise. My adjutant has the necessary paperwork for your signature when we're concluded.

Next an amount of diminished back pay in the form of warrants and credits redeemable in any local store in town for the supplies you'll require, as we've discussed the other afternoon"!

The general then stopped briefly to cough up some phlegm, before continuing, "Finally the adjutant has the documents authorizing you to establish a homestead, on the upper Brazos river region, near where the Waco Indians have an encampment, as we've discussed.

For the purpose of clearing out what native Waco tribesmen for a contingent of settlers expected to arrive in the coming years. Since you have some experience in surveying you will have to register your homestead in Austin at your earliest opportunity, lest some other waddie beat you to it, then lawyers will have to get involved and that'll muddy things up. Now since you have a possible location in mind that should simplify things"!

At that, the general went into yet another spasm of coughing, before continuing. "Now on your way to the upper Brazo's you'll need to stop in Austin at the Governor's Mansion, presenting a letter of introduction from me regarding my decision to the sitting Governor, just a formality for his sub approval, since he answers to me, for the time being. Then you'll have to visit the Commanding officer of the Rangers, and report to him thus establishing your bona fides, presenting him with the letter of your commission, which is a life time appointment"!

"Let me see", the general pondered, while enduring yet another coughing spasm. When he looked up he said weakly, "The Cholera's got me boy", looking first at Henry then his daughter. "Now to a personal favor. I've directed my adjutant to see to my personal affairs after my departure and my remains will be escorted by him back to my family in New York City, for burial by my son."

"But as fate would have it, my daughter here has suffered the loss of her mother in Charleston and wrote me months ago about joining me here in San Antonio. I eagerly agreed, not foreseeing my current state of affairs. So here she is in my final days soon to be without anyone in the world to look after her, on the frontier in Texas. Now here son, here is where the difficulty lays", again yet another coughing spasm overtook the general, before he continued.

"The difficulty is that neither my family in New York, nor anyone in the military knows of her relationship to me, if you catch my drift young man"!

As he let that sentence hang in the air a bit, Henry was perplexed, not being accustomed to the myriad ways of city life. Then it struck him all at once, with the force of a lightening bolt, the importance of the unspoken word. His eyebrows rose as he went to speak, "General I think I understand what you're getting at. You're telling me that she'll need looking after"!

The general nodded in agreement. The just as his daughter started to speak the general interrupted her by saying, through coughing spells, "Now Melanie we've been all over this last night. I'm dying and there's no two ways around it. I've been a military man all my life and had hoped to die in combat, but instead here I am bedridden like a common feather merchant.

My innards are about done in. I was not there when you were born, nor at any time that you were growing up. I've been greatly remiss in my duties as a father, pursuing fame and glory, missing out on the finer things in life. At this very moment I feel like St. Paul must've felt as the lightning bolt knocked him on his keester on the road to Damascus. I see how beautiful you've become and in the here and now I see no one in this town worthy of your consideration. It's being overrun by brigands and vagabonds with every arrival."

"Now in this Henry Jaeger, is a man I've come to know, intermittently, a bit rough around the edges, but he is literate and wholly capable of taking care of himself and others which is why I've appointed him as a Captain of the Rangers. Fortunately you both are of the same religion and all the both of you need is time to get to know each other"!

Then he turned to Henry saying after another bout of coughing, he wheezed, "She's an educated woman Henry and has taught school in Charleston. The Waco settlement will need school teachers"! Then the general lay back on the bed asking for them both to leave for a while and asking the adjutant to be sent in.

Passing the generals adjutant in the doorway, the duo just stood there both clearly uncomfortable, in each other's presence given the situation. Henry had not old the general of his previous marriage to Joselita and of his son still in Monterrey and the fact that he was still in mourning. The conflict and the guilt of feeling an inkling of desire for another woman, so soon after the departure of his lifes love was an impediment to any future relationships. Yet here she was, a beautiful woman out on the edge of civilization, soon to be alone. The general was right. Someone had to take care of her.

Suddenly he blurted out, "I think I know what a shock all of this can be for you as it is for me. I just met up with the general two days ago and he was healthy and now, "His voice just trailed away. "Is there anything I can do for you"? Then she broke down in tears. For life does have its way of playing little tricks on us all, providing apparent disaster, then an apparent reprieve from life's difficulties, only to find that it was all a ruse and one is once again hanging over the deep abyss by their fingernails.

"Let's take a walk outside in the fresh air", Henry said as he gently guided her down the stairs and out of the hotel. For several blocks they walked aimlessly, saying nothing to each other.

Then, "Just so you know, my father the General had an ever so brief relationship with my mother, when he was stationed in Charleston long ago. My mother was married at the time, to my father, who was gracious enough to die from malaria a week after the good General left. Of course he was married to a woman in New York and has a legitimate son by her.

My mother later discovered that my father was carrying on with one of our servants", she said in a rush of words.

"Of course as the years rolled by my mother and the General, she always referred to him as the General, kept in periodic correspondence. Just prior to her death, she wrote to the General telling him of her situation and asked if I could come to him. He said yes and here I am, Mister Henry Jaeger", with a shred of defiance in her voice. I seek not your pity or the charity of anyone and I am confident that I can make my own way"!

They walked for another block in silence, before Henry said, "There is someone I'd like you to meet, if you'll accompany me a few more blocks"!

Melanie nodded her head and they walked on, until they came to the Maverick house. After knocking on the door, Henry was greeted by Mary Maverick with a beaming smile, "Well, I never expected you so soon Henry and who is this young lady". Taking his hat off, Henry said, "Mary Maverick, I'd like to introduce you to General Worth's daughter Melanie, and thought a visit with you would do some good. As you can understand her father is in a grievous way and she's traveled far and been through a lot"!

True to Mary Maverick's nature, she fully embraced the Generals daughter saying, "Well come inside child so we can visit", inviting them both inside.

After several minutes Henry asked, "Miss Melanie, your people, your uh, darkies, where are they"? She replied, "They're staying in a boarding house on the edge of town!" Then she put her hands to her mouth and said, "Oh my god what with all that is going on, I forgot all about them"!

Mary Maverick butted in saying, "Henry, you go an get her darkies and bring em on over here and we'll make a place for em. Melanie and me will stay and visit awhile. Now go git Ranger"!

Henry went back to the hotel and mounted his horse for a little trip just north of town to that shade tree where his necessaries lay buried.

Several hours later he returned, this time going to the boarding house and retrieved the Miss Melanie's servants and led them to the Maverick home, just in time for the evening meal.

Henry watched as Melanie interacted with her darkies, for the way she would treat them indicated to him whether or not she would be worth the trouble, regardless of her obvious charms. There were four of them, Elijah, Mattie, Little Joe and his sister Beulah.

After the introductions Mattie and Elijah were enlisted to help Mary Maverick and her servant to prepare the evening meal and the children were well behaved and set the places at the dining table for everyone, taking their meal in the kitchen with the Maverick servant.

Finding nothing apparently objectionable, when supper time arrived and Sam Maverick arriving home from his day at the towns newspaper as he entered the house to find Henry there bellowed in exclamation, "Well, Jesus Mary and Joseph, if it isn't Henry Jaeger himself", then coming up to Henry with a bear hug of an embrace he almost forgot himself when his wife Mary brought forth Melanie for an introduction.

Sam then looked at Henry, then back at Melanie saying "Never knew ya got married, boy"?

Then seeing the look on everyone's face he looked to his wife who said, "There ya go Sam, putting your foot in your mouth again! Let's all sit down to supper and we can fill in the blanks"! During the course of the meal, all was made clear, regarding Melanie Swanson's presence in San Antonio, Henry's lost years, with the exception of his marriage and his son in Monterrey. "So ya gonna set shop on the upper Brazos, Rangering and raising cattle eh Henry"?

"Well that's my orders from General Worth and the plan"!

"Before ya leave town, see me so I can provide you with a letter of recommendation to those waddies up in Austin, said Maverick. My word must be worth something' still"!

All through the meal, both Henry and Melanie paid close attention and took stock of each other, via what was said and the manner in which it was said.

Melanie assessed Henry as an overly large man, who walked with a light step, not overtly overbearing, but appropriately affable in the company of others, but deep behind the eyes she suspected a sinister darkness existed. He was sufficiently mannered and polite, but she could plainly see that he would not fit in well with the big city dandy's she was normally accustomed to. Thus man clearly suffered no fools. Yet he bore all the trimmings of one who was civilized.

On the other hand, Henry sized up Melanie as being quite apart from the type most associated with the women of the frontier he was normally familiar with. His mind quickly traveled back to his times in Ohio, Tennessee, Texas and Mexico. Different places at different times in his life, with different cultures, each a new experience and the attendant period of adjustment. As the evening progressed he tried to assess whether or not this particular woman had the sand to be a survivor and make a life on the frontier. Would she retain her regal like femininity in the face of the unknown? Was she reliable? Could she be counted on?

In the end it was all a roll of the dice, Henry concluded. Besides, she showed no apparent interest in Henry, unlike his precious Joselita, who early on made her feeling known. 'Jesus', he thought, 'why did life have to be so complicated'?

After supper, it was agreed that Melanie's darkies would be housed temporarily with the Maverick family while Melanie went back to the hotel to spend the night with her father the General and Henry went back to his encampment south of town.

Henry lifted Melanie up on the back of his Appaloosa side saddle, then vaulted into the saddle, leg over the mane style like the vaqueros.

As they rode back to the Hotel, Melanie wrapped her arms around Henrys waist, feeling that just perhaps, life might not have dealt her such a bad hand after all. Everything seemed to be happening too fast, decisions had to be made that could either bear fruit, or portend disaster. Rounding the corner of the hotel she quickly made a decision and said, "Mr. Jaeger should my father die, what say you to his proposition"?

For several moments Henry said nothing, then arriving at the hitching post in front of the Hotel, he dismounted and held his arms up for Melanie to fall into and as she slowly was lowered to the ground, Henry surmised that she was as tall as Joselita, and just as attractive and her eyes were the kind that drew one into them like a magnet, her southern voice distinct and with a special lilt and charm. Then he slowly held her at arm's length as he felt himself begin to grow.

Unable to take his eyes from her and searching for something intelligent to say, he blurted out, "Well the clothes you're wearing will not serve you well out on the frontier, Miss Melanie"!

With a toss of her head, she said "I think I have a few things that will get me along, Captain Jaeger. I shall attend my father; can I count on you to attend me on the morrow"?

"I reckon so Miss Melanie", said Henry. Then she turned and

ascended the Hotels front entrance, looking back ever so briefly at the Ranger in the street.

All the way back to the encampment Henry was trying to make sense of the current developments. Wary of the way fate could hold something precious out just beyond ones grasp, and then suddenly jerk it back, while the sounds of raucous laughter permeated down from the heavens. He concluded that he was no more than a grain of sand on the shore of life and that he must hold himself open to all options, trusting to his instincts which had thus far served him well over time.

He then again felt some guilt feeling an attraction to this beautiful Melanie, who was presented out of the blue and under normal circumstances might find another more suitable.

Then again, perhaps it was the celestial wisdom that transcended all mortal understanding, trying to even up accounts, 'the almighty taketh away and the almighty giveth! He would present himself to Miss Melanie on the morrow and allow the chips to fall whichever way they wished.

As he approached the encampment Chani and her children approached him and he acknowledged their presence and as he looked up to the heavens he silently asked, "Muy Permisso me amor"?

The Appaloosa unsaddled and fed, Henry sat down by the campfire and said "Looks like we're gonna have company Juan", telling him all that had gone on that day.

At sunrise the following morning, Henry was again off towards town this time in the wagon, to retrieve the supplies and equipment needed for his new homestead from Seth's General store. After providing the appropriate document authorizing the purchase he was on his way back to the camp site, when he noticed a military column arriving in town. 'Must be the delayed column from Austin the general and his adjutant mentioned.

Shortly before noon he was back at the camp site and left the wagon with Mendoza, immediately saddling up his Appaloosa and returned to town.

As he arrived at the Hotel, he immediately sought out the adjutant who was busy with the newly arrived visitors from Austin. Recognizing Henry, he directed him to go to the Generals room where he saw Melanie at the Generals side along with the doctor, both of which were looking haggard having kept vigil over the General throughout the night. Henry stood with the mostly military officers somewhat away from the bedstead, when the doctor came to them saying, "Gentlemen I've done all I can do and it seems that the General will not be with us too much longer"! Then recognizing Henry, he said, "The General wants to see you" and grabbed his arm directing him to the bed stead.

Melanie was sitting on the bed, holding the Generals hand, her eyes puffy from a lack of sleep and looked up as Henry approached. The doctor whispered into the Generals ear, when the General's eyes opened as he croaked in a weak raspy voice. "Well young man, have you conducted your business"!

"Yes sir, already done", he replied!

"And that other matter we talked about", glancing at his daughter and then back at Henry? "Yes sir and I don't think you need to worry yourself about that other matter at all sir", glancing briefly at Melanie, then back at the General.

"Your word on it", wheezed the general? "My word on it sir"!

Then General Worth looked upon his daughter, with pleading eyes, for perhaps the final time wheezing with difficult," My life has had a great many regrets, chief of which is my absence from you, but if possible in the afterlife I hope you don't mind if I look in on you and perhaps we can then make up for lost time and get to know each other"!

Tears once again started to well up in her eyes as she nodded her head kissing his hand. Their eyes never left each other for the longest time, as if to imprint a vision that must last for eternity when finally the Generals grip on his daughters hand lessened as his eyes closed for the final time.

Without looking, Henry could feel the others in the room draw nearer to the bed as the doctor felt for a pulse. Finding none he said, "It is finished"! Then from amongst the others in the room someone said, "A great man has passed to his maker", as all bowed their heads in silence.

The Generals adjutant then brought the man forward to Melanie saying, 'Miss Melanie, may I introduce you to Major Robert E. Lee who the General has invited to Command those of us to accompany him back to New York for his final burial.

Her eyes briefly acknowledged the gentlemanly man with graying hair who gave her a brief bow. Who said, "We will be leaving for the Port of Galvez on the coast at sunup with your approval Maam"!

Once again Melanie nodded in agreement, still holding the hand of her father. Then the doctor asked all the military men to leave the room and in came someone from the hallway bearing the resemblance of a dour man dressed in formal black attire.

"This is Mr. Voorhees, the towns newly arrived mortician, from New Orleans, who will need access to the General to prepare him for his final trip home, if you please Miss Melanie"!

Taking that as a sign for her departure, she arose from the bed and slowly walked out of the room, turning at the doorway for one last glimpse of her father, then walked down the hall way.

As Henry and Melanie walked outside of the Hotel, Major Lee approached them both saying to Melanie, "Miss Walker you," she then interrupted him by saying, "It's Swanson Major and my presence at the Generals side must never be known, for it's a matter of great discretion, in regards to his memory and the family he has up north, if you catch my meaning Sir"!

Major Lee, being a man of the world was briefly taken aback by that statement, then seeing the truth of it, or his perception thereof said, "Your existence here will be kept under the tongue, my good woman and I was about to say that General was indeed a great man and was one of my instructors at West Point in my youth and a man of great vigor and vision. And it was my great pleasure to serve under his command in both the northern campaign, but again with General Scott in the southern campaign for the heart of Mexico.

Just then Major Lee, turned to Henry saying, "Sir it seems that our paths have crossed before, but your cognomen eludes me for the moment"! "Jaeger sir. Henry Jaeger formally of the Texas Mounted Rifles and the Texas Rangers.

We served together at the battle of Monterrey when I was under the command of Captain John Coffey Hays, doing a bit of scouting, then again when I came ashore just after the capture of Mexico City while I was under the command of Lieutenant Bragg and General Lane". "OH yes, now I recall, you were one of those Rangers that kept the Rancho's off our backs on the road to Vera Cruz and back. Didn't you have a sort of nickname the Rancho's gave you, something to do with Diablo"? "Yes Major. Something like that"! Continuing on he inquired, "I hear General Taylor has been elected President"?

"That was months ago, but since then we've received word that he's been taken ill. Rumors bound that he was poisoned, by those loyal to Senator Calhoun, but those are rumors that fly about Washington all the time. After I get back up north I expect I'll hear the truth of it"!

"But what about you Mr. Jaeger", inquired Major Lee?

"Well sir, the General just appointed me as a Captain of the newly reformed Texas Rangers and I am to report to Austin, to present my bona fides then be assigned to the upper Brazos river and try and civilize the area thereabouts"!

"Good and I wish you ever bit of good fortune", said Major Lee formally!

"Now I must bid you both a good afternoon for I've much ahead to prepare for our long journey ahead"!

As he departed, Mary Maverick approached them in front of the Hotel saying to Melanie, "How is your father child"?

"He's with the angels now Mrs. Maverick" answered Melanie. Just then Mary noticed, "Why you're still wearing the same clothes you wore yesterday child. Have you had any sleep?

"No Maam, I've been at vigil all through the night"!

Then Mary turned to Henry saying, "Stay right here young man, you're going to accompany us to my house shortly", whereupon she escorted Melanie up to her room for a change of clothes and as they walked back to the Maverick house, Mary kept fussing, you're gonna have a bath then a long rest this afternoon then a great big meal tonight with us all again and I'll not take a 'No' for an answer".

As they walked to her home Mary Maverick caught Henry's eye and gave him an imperceptible wink, and a nod that he was to tag along and be at the ready if needed. He went back to the Hotel retrieved his horse, following after them at a discrete distance.

The following day Henry arrived back in town, just in time to see Major Lee and his detachment depart, with the embalmed General casketed on their way to the coast and the Port of Galvez. As the detachment passed the Maverick home with the flag of Texas at half-mast in the front yard, Henry still mounted on his horse, removed his wide white straw hat as Mary and Melanie stood on the porch, with Major Lee barking out the orders, "Detachment, Eyes Right", with that directive, all the foot soldiers in company strength, removed their muskets from their shoulders in unison and placed them in the 'Present Arms' position as they passed, with every mounted officer, unsheathing their sabers and giving the military salute.

When the last of the column passed the house, all heard Major Lee give the order, "Shoulder Arms", and the column resumed their previous positions continuing their way down the street and out of town.

"Well Captain Jaeger, I expect that you'll be eager to head up Austin way, present yourself to the powers that be and then onto the upper Brazos directly"!

"As soon as Miss Melanie is ready, if she hasn't changed her mind", offered Henry in response. Melanie looked up at Henry as he was repositioning his hat saying, "Off on yet another leg of the grand adventure, with a man I barely know." Then she looked at Henry and nodded her head in agreement. "Good" offered Mary Maverick, "I've a number of Mexican saddles and tack back in the barn your welcome to that was left by the Mexican Army last time they were in town, that your welcome to so Miss Melanie's Darkies won't have to use up their shoe leather"! "I'll be back early in the morning with the horses, tipping his hat towards Melanie and Mary,

Then he rode back down the street towards his encampment south of town. While he was gone Mary sent her husband and Melanie back to the Hotel to retrieve he things and bring them to the Maverick house, spending the rest of the day examining her wardrobe, most of which was suitable for city living only but not at all appropriate for life in the wilds. Then they went to her husband's store and fitted her with a bare bones wardrobe that would serve her well over the course of time.

Later in the afternoon Mary and Melanie sat on the Mavericks front porch and over the course of several glasses of Port wine Mary gave Melanie Swanson of the Charleston Swanson's, a picture of what lay ahead for her as a woman of the frontier and completed the picture of one Henry Jaeger as she knew him to be over the course of time.

"Never seen the man angry, he's not prone to be boastful, if'n he tells ya he's gonna do a thing, it gets done 'Muy Pronto', he doesn't suffer fools with grace, his memory of a slight or an insult by mortal man is eternal, with many a man who's done him wrong, gone from the face of the earth, yet he's slow to anger and I have seen him, not often mind you, in moments of prayer.

"Ya know child, as we say in Texas, it's not how old ya are, but how many miles you've traveled, and that man has lived several lifetimes and has been through more than would've broken lesser men"!

Then she continued, "I've seen him work from dawn to dusk helping people build and repair things around town and Jack Hayes taught him how to survey a stretch of land and get it legalized. So if'n you were my child I'd say, you couldn't do much better and probably could do a whole lots worse. Now as he might be as a lover, I can't rightly say cause I never seen him in the company of a woman before you, but he does seem awfully keen on ya and after all, it's always been completely up to us women folk to gentle our men some"!

Both of them were quiet as they sipped their Port, when Mary added, "But what we need, in these parts are women who have grit, sand, and the ability to endure everything. To be reliable, dependable, able to work with their man together, without expectations of any kind, to give till its hurts, then give some more and if'n their man is of the same mind and ya can stay out of the way of misfortune, then your life together can be wonderful."

"Take my man Sam for instance" she continued in the monolog,

"Isn't a good Hunter, ain't good at fixin things, but he's great at a poker table, taught himself the newspaper business, and is a damn good feather merchant. Damn Mexican Army ran us all off twice and stole everything that wasn't nailed down, but every time Sam Maverick came back bigger and better than ever. The man has grit and the very least I can do is match him. Now if'n he could only lick his eyebrows", she concluded with a saucy wink, upon which both women giggled the wine having loosened up their spirits.

The following morning Henry arrived with his loaded wagon with two triangular contraptions atop the wagon, with three horses following behind secured to the wagon. He promptly selected three sets of the Mexican saddles and bridles for Melanie and her entourage, from those in the Maverick barn. Attaching the two triangular skids to her servant's saddles, he loaded all their baggage onto the skids and helped them up on their mounts.

As they prepared to leave, Sam Maverick emerged from the house and said, "Now y'all be careful, ya heah"! With tears in her eyes, Mary Maverick said, "Now I know you're going far away remember, everything in Texas is just up the road apiece"!

Within a half hour the entourage met up with Mendoza and the herd on the outskirts of town and they made their way around San Antonio and eventually by noon were well on their way towards Austin.

With Henry riding point and Mendoza driving the wagon and the herd in between them flanked by the wolves on either side, Chani with one of her siblings and Akila with the other, Mendoza gave Melanie a running commentary in his broken English interspersed with the occasional Spanish word or phrase, on the do's and don'ts regarding the wolves and their off spring along with much of their history as he knew it.

"Look at Chani and her Nino over there, she give a small bark and the little one runs up to the steer and herds him back into place when he wants to lag behind. Soon he will know, without having to be told just as your Padre and Madre do for you", he said addressing the two children of Miss Melanie's servant's.

Shortly before sundown, Henry selected a spot near a stream for their first camp site, unsaddling the horses and leading all the livestock and the wolves to the stream for a well-earned drink and then to a spot nearby where he made a corral of sorts by stakes driven into the ground, encompassed with rope. With the livestock busy grazing he saw to it that Chani, Akila and their brood were fed then led them to their spots to spend the night on guard of the herd.

When he returned, Henry poured himself a mug of coffee form the campfire pot and served himself some of the carne and beans and entered into the conversation of the evening, relating his vision of where they were going and what was to be done when they got there.

Bedding down on the bare ground, with the stars overhead, the saddle blanket to give her comfort and a Mexican army saddle for her pillow, Melanie fell immediately asleep. She and her servants had done a day's work. As Henry settled into his place around the camp fire, he noticed that Mendoza had slipped into the same habit that he had, by removing the big Colt Revolver from its holster and slipping it under his saddle blanket that covered him. As their eyes met just prior to going to sleep, Mendoza gave a slow wink, nodding in the direction of Melanie and her brood, indicating that in his mind they would all be just fine.

The following days on the trail to Austin, this routine was practiced five more times and by the fifth evening everyone knew their task at sunrise as well as sunset, the safety of the herd being the priority before all else.

By noon of the fifth day as they came over a rise in the land they saw the outskirts of Austin and selected another campsite. As they talked over the evening meal, Henry told them of who he had to see in town, to present his bona fides and when to expect him back.

After his business in Austin was concluded, he knew just the trail he was going on to reach the banks of the upper Brazos; to a cabin site he'd visited long ago to settle the score with the Red Hair. As he went to sleep, memories of his Mutti und his Papi and his siblings came into view, this time only the good and pleasant times surfaced in his head, along with the memory of the old Shawnee Shaman and all that he'd ever taught him and said.

The following morning Henry was up and away from the camp site, with the fire built up and the coffee made for the rest of them all as he rode off towards town. In the growing dawn approached, the morning chill being replaced by the gradual warmth of sunlight, he made for the building where the Governor conducted the business of the state, to present himself. Attired in his nominal buckskin attire he always worn as a Ranger, he'd hoped that someone was in residence that would recognize him from his days as a Ranger. As he was the first one to arrive he hitched his horse to the post in front of the building and waited. An hour later the first of the clerks arrived still partially asleep as they made their way into the building, with Henry in their wake.

Henry asked where he could find the Governor from one of the clerks, who sleepily answered, "Wahl, Governor Bell usually doesn't mosey on in until nine in the morning!" At the mention of that name Henry asked, "That wouldn't be Peter Hansford Bell would it"?

"The very same", answered the clerk who then saw the Governors secretary enter the building, yelling out "Oh George, George, this man has business with Governor Bell". A tall willow thin man approached introducing himself to Henry looking him up and down as he approached and asked, "You have business with the Governor"?

"Yes sir I do", replied Henry standing to his full height, usually an imposing sight upon lesser men, "If the Governor is the same man who served under John Hays then he will know me for we served together, for some time and I bear correspondence from General Worth in San

Antonio"! "I understand the good General is doing poorly", the Secretary said.

"The General has been done under by his illness and is being borne to the Port of Galvez on the coast, by Major Lee and I have his last official correspondence to the Governor and the State for the Governors eyes only", Henry added with a flourish.

The Secretary removed his pocket watch from his vest and said, "Well, the Governor should be around directly, so if you will be so kind to follow me I'll place you in one of the antirooms and you can be his first order of business of the day.

One of the things Henry could never get used to, was waiting for important people in places of comfort. Now lying in wait, for game or other two legged forms somehow never seemed to bother him, just waiting in civilized surroundings was unnerving.

However sometimes the gods are favorable, and not too many minutes later, he heard a familiar bellow, "Henry goddamn Jaeger, why where is he"? Just then the door flew open and a familiar face from the past came to light, "I heard that you died going after some goddamn renegade priest in Mexico Henry", as the Governor ran up to Henry and shook his hand vigorously.

"Well, as you can see, they were wrong" said Henry.

"And the priest", asked Governor Bell? "Dead and his rosary beads are mine".

"I should've known", said the Governor as he tilted his head slightly in wonderment. "Man crosses Henry by gawd Jaeger he's soon to greet the ferry man."

"Jesus H. Christ it's good to see ya, why come on into my office".

As usual in the south between two men they have to settle into the business of the day gradually, before getting down to brass tacks, briefly covering all the scrapes they'd been through together, touching on the fact that John Coffee Hays had gone to California the previous year in search of long denied wealth. Then Henry gave the Governor a thumb nail recanting of his adventures during the Southern Campaign in the war, his time with the Fuentes family and his final days with General Worth, plus General Worth's final declarations as a regent of the US Government in the Department of Texas, handing over his final declarations in writing, to the governor, plus his letter from the then

General Taylor and finally the letter of introduction from the dearly departed President Jackson. As Governor Bell silently read all of the correspondence, he then looked up when finished and said, "Jesus Henry I didn't know you at all did I? Seems the General forgot that as soon as the War with the Mexicans was over the state disbanded the Ranger units officially and sent everyone on their way. There are no Rangers anymore. There should be but there aren't. Seems the Federals in Washington in all their wisdom can defend us from the Comanche and the Kiowa, so they say, but without the Rangers", his voice trailing off to nothing.

Henry breathed a heavy sigh, wondering when the other shoe was about to drop and so it apparently had. Bell then looked up and said, "But I find no fault in the Generals reasoning. We need someone of your capabilities, especially up north in the Upper Brazos area to hold things together. So here's what I'm gonna do"!

The governor then called in his secretary to dictate the following directives from the office of the governor, granting Henry Jaeger approximately twenty sections of land, more or less, by both the State of Texas and the Federal Government pursuant to the authority of General Worth, Commander of the Department of Texas. Then he dictated another letter authorizing the loan of such land surveying equipment as was available to one Henry Jaeger, Special Captain of the Texas Rangers, answerable only to the Governor of Texas.

Lastly he dictated and directed the secretary to enlist such legislation appointing one Henry Jaeger as Special Captain of the Texas Rangers for the Upper Brazos river region with jurisdiction state wide at a salary of seventy five US dollars a month, with a per diem of one dollar a day any time he is away on State business. The appointment to be for the duration of his life or until he voluntarily resigns in writing.

"Two months from now the legislature will be in session and I'll see to it that this is quietly inserted as an addendum to the first piece of legislation that crosses my desk for signature Henry. Probably will take some months for the back pay to arrive so how are ya fixed for funds"?

"Oh, we're probably all right for about six months", said Henry.

"As soon as the legislation is signed I'll see to it that you receive a letter under my hand officially authorizing your appointment. Leave the documents from General Worth with my secretary to serve as authorization. When things are concluded they will be returned"!

"Now I just have to say that it's important that you get the land in questioned surveyed soonest, so some scallywag doesn't get in there ahead of you. And one final thing, what this will mean is that you are the law for the Brazos river area. We got railroads coming to Texas someday, like they have back east, in the far distant future and with that I'm told will be a host of problems called civilization. So if you're summoned to solve a problem, you're have to drop hat and git gone".

"Jesus Henry, it is certainly good to see you again", said Governor Bell as Henry departed for the State Land Office to procure the surveying equipment.

Just around noon Henry returned to camp laden with a surveying transit and an assortment of ancillary equipment. Dropping the equipment off he rode back into town, only to return with an entire bolt of flaming red cotton cloth.

Then he explained all that had gone on with the Governor and the State Land Office and finally the red cloth, "Reckon it'll take me the better part of a week and I'll need Elijah to go on with me to help to survey the land grant I have from the State. Gonna need Elijah's help holding the stakes and the red cloth cut up in strips will serve to highlight the stake markers"!

He wondered in his mind just how good a shape the old Hochner spread was still in. While he was at the State Land Office, he could see by examination of the records that a small settlement of Waco was laid out, but not yet incorporated and due east of the land Hochner spread he had in mind.

Henry had been granted as much land as he could ride in from sun up to sundown in all four points of the compass. This would be his first order of business within days of arrival at the old Hochner place.

A week later Henry and his pilgrims came upon the old Hochner place, and as he'd remembered from the last time he spent the night there just prior to his business with the Red Hair. The cabin was indeed habitable, needing some work in the roof and the long shed could work for a time to shelter the herd in a storm and the log fences needed some maintaining and extension into separate corrals and he had the approximate dimensions rolling up un his mind's eye as he went along with his inspection. The following day after everything had been sorted out and unloaded from the two skids and the wagon. He then took Juan and Elijah spending the day repairing the small smokehouse on the property, for the following day they were both off at the crack of dawn taking the wagon and several other horses for a hunting party leaving Melanie and her entourage to fend for themselve's.

On the evening of the third day the hunting party returned, with the wagon laden with felled deer and assorted other game. The smoke house fire was set alight and all parties fell to the task of dismembering the game and rendering the carcasses. Of course for Melanie and her darkies the task seemed an onerous chore, especially by the light of night time fire, but by the morning sunrise, all of the carcasses were rendered, and separated into the various, sections needed for future usage, skins in one pile, tendons in another, the entrails in yet another and the intestines cleaned repeatedly of their waist down by the small stream, then briefly boiled in order to contain the sausage that was repeatedly made by little Beulah who manned the meat grinder, while her brother and her mother mixed the newly ground meat with the assorted herbs and spices, then repeatedly stuffed the mixture into the intestines, twisting them into long string fat links, ready for the smoke house.

As the sun came up, a decision was made to have everyone go to the adjacent stream in shifts to wash the filth and grime from their tired bodies and clothes, the women first, then the men, just to preserve the proprieties of common decency.

All through the day everyone slept, except for Henry and Mendoza who slept in shifts, with Henry till noon, the Mendoza till suppertime.

The following day, Henry instructed all to urinate in the large container that contained the games entrails and brains that would be then be used to provide, them with the medium with which the hides would be tanned. Late in the afternoon Chani came up to Henry making signs for him to follow her to the pasture where it was discovered that three of the cows were about to drop their calves any moment, whereupon they were led to the long shed to complete the task.

As Melanie looked on to the miracle of life she muttered," Now more blood and entrails"!

When Henry jibed in, "Save the umbilical cords, in a container of clean water, for they will make fine containers for more sausage, that'll get us through the winter"! That evening the herd increased by five newly birthed future longhorns, a very good omen, according to Elijah's wife

Maddie who took great stock in signs and premonitions. Only ten years older than her mistress, Maddie had helped raise Melanie ever since she was born and a silent bond ran between them, with Melanie taking great stock in all that Mattie said.

Between them as they worked together Melanie said absently, "Mattie I swear, I don't ever know if I'm gonna get used to country life, what with the smell of the animals and all"?

Thinking a bit, Mattie replied, "Chile, I just feel it in my bones that we're all in about as good a place as we could be given what's happened"! Then she continued, "That man of yours, is a good provider and I suspect that we will see even more as time goes on, so y'all just be patient, ya heah"?

Several days later, Henry and Elijah loaded up the wagon with supplies for a week along with some four hundred odd, stakes that had been cut from tree branches and the red cotton cloth cut in strips, to periodically mark their way as they surveyed the land Henry intended to register in the State Land Office, in Austin.

Six days later they returned tired, but with the look of completion with the wagon containing nothing but the surveying equipment. With Elijah commenting, "Sure looks pretty, all those red streamers all in a straight line over every hill and valley".

Then Henry announced that the following day he would take his readings and measurements back down to Austin for registration, then maybe pay a brief visit to the governor before returning.

"Ya know we've got a whole lotta pine trees around here", whereupon he took everyone to a spread of pine tree's noting some of the cones that had fallen on the ground. Then he picked one of them up saying, "When I come back, I'll need that that there wagon almost full of pine cones just like this one"! "Then he took pains to show them why a pine cone had to be a certain kind.

"When I return, every ten yards one of these will be planted in a straight line, North, South, East and West and in five years or so, this'll be the formal property line of our place"! "Then eventually, if the creek don't rise too high, I'll have two lines of wood fence that'll connect the trees and just maybe a gate every mile or so"!

The next morning Henry departed for Austin, with his survey calculations tucked neatly away in his saddlebags, and the borrowed

State survey equipment, lashed securely to the skid pulled by the second horse he rode with. Two days later he arrived in Austin and made his way directly to the State Land Office registering his claim. When the registering agent asked what the name of the ranch will be, Henry was flummoxed, for he never considered a cognomen for the ranch.

"Just a minute and let me think on it", Henry said. For agonizing minutes he thought then he looked up and said, "The MHM ranch".

"And the way the brand will look that will be affixed to each of your livestock, Captain Jaeger", asked the agent.

Again Henry thought a moment then said, "Just like it reads, with a Capital 'M', then a Capital 'H', then a Capital 'M'..."

"Very good sir then if you'll please wait, I'll get everything registered and reviewed by the commissioner, then back to you with the appropriate document".

An hour later the agent returned and said "Here sir is your document of deed, En Toto, granting to you in return, for special services rendered to the Republic and the State of Texas as well as the United States of America Twenty sections of land northwest of the unincorporated township of Waco in the State of Texas, for the rest of your natural life and that of your heirs and/ or designated assignees. Keep this in a safe place Captain. Thus I trust our business is concluded"!

"That it is sir", said Henry as he tucked the document into its leather folder and then into his saddlebag, donning his wide brimmed hat and departing.

Henry's next stop was to see the Governors secretary and see if the paperwork for his appointment as Special Ranger was completed and to his great luck it was along with an unexpected benefit.

The Governors secretary said, "We have a post office of sorts in the General Store in the settlement of Waco and have sent word that you are going to have a place set aside in their store for an office of sorts while you are conducting States Business which the state will recompense the proprietor for. Your monthly salary and any correspondence will be delivered to a special post office box that only you can access, via a key.

Further, in this envelope is a month's pay in US Currency for your sustenance."

With that accomplished, he departed for the Waco settlement to meet with the town fathers and to make him self acquainted.

His arrival in the village of Waco that straddled the upper Brazos River, separated by a small horse drawn ferry, was without fanfare and after making himself known to the proprietor via his bona fides, he was glad to discover the village had the services of a blacksmith.

Within a short period of time, he outlined the type of branding iron that his livestock were to sport on their flanks, with the 'MHM', cognomen.

After agreeing on a price he said he'd return within the week.

Finally he returned to the general store, to purchase a small gift for each of his people back at the homestead, soon to be the MHM ranch. Starting with a wide brimmed straw hat similar to his for Mendoza for his occasional trips to Waco. Then a bonnet for both Miss Melanie, one for Maddie and finally a bag of crystal candy for Maddies children. Then thinking about Elijah, he knew that he needed some new foot ware since his were soon to give out. Guessing as to his size, he crossed his fingers and selected some high topped lace up brogans, thinking, 'There, that ought to last him awhile'.

Then he looked at his boots that had been with him for the longest while, and it occurred that he'd never had store bought boots in his entire life. After some modest haggling with the proprietor over the price of each purchase, he departed for the ranch.

As he returned, he gathered everyone around and dispensed the gifts to each and every one declaring an early Merry Christmas to one and all.

14

The following day after Henry returned, he set everyone to cutting wood. He placed little Joseph the task of making the thousands of wooden plugs of various sizes and depths that would be needed in the building that was soon to come. Iron nails were in short supply in Texas and very expensive.

He set the women the task of making a water resistant glue from the entrails of the bones from every animal rendered in the MHM ranch. As was going on, Henry and the men set about cutting down the trees and segmenting them into the various sizes and depths needed to construct the various projects he had in mind. Within a week he and the others had constructed a variety of barrels to bathe in and to transport water. Two of the water barrels were attached to the wagon, for his tree planting project in the weeks to come.

From time to time, people from the Waco settlement would arrive with their children to welcome the newcomers. In many cases they brought their children and as soon as it was known that Miss Melanie, as she was soon to become known, was a school teacher with books. Discussions around the area centered on her becoming the town school teacher. As new settlers started to arrive and staking their claims, Henry became involved in the job of surveying their claim and registering it in Austin. This entailed a separate trip back to Austin to more or less permanently borrow the equipment necessary. Of course since little money was to be had in the area, a continuation of a barter economy took hold with neighbors exchanging services with each other on a 'Quid Pro Quo' basis.

Talk of construction a school house took hold and a group of people approached Henry, to see what could be done in that regard. Thus a convenient location was located and surveyed with Henry taking charge of several land clearing and wood cutting brigades, in preparation to the event. In the passage of time, once all was assembled, a party of families assembled and had the small building built in a single day.

As further people settled in the area, a doctor and a lawyer and a traveling pastor arrived to set up shop, each lending their skills in exchange from help from neighbors and new found friends, with the settlement of Waco taking on all the trappings of becoming a town. Months passed with Henry becoming diverted from the task of setting forth the formal boundaries of the MHM ranch by the planting of pine trees every ten yards along the line he had surveyed and marked previously.

Winter came and passed with the seeming birth of multiples of livestock being birthed and by the six month anniversary of his arrival the size of his livestock more than doubled in size, with no losses. As the livestock gradually grew used to the presence and the daily prodding by the wolves, entering the corrals each evening and being led to pastures each morning and back, the herd grew in size without concern of predators that constantly circled the perimeter. Ever on the alert, one morning Mendoza noticed the bodies of two Kiowa scouts, apparently taken down by one of the wolves thus stripping them of all they possessed, hung them feet first from the limbs of trees, in a highly visible place naked, with their throats having been torn out as a sign to all that the MHM ranch wasn't a very hospitable place. As he returned, Mendoza showed everyone what he'd encountered, drawing an approving nod from Henry. In time the carrion would dispose of the Indians in their way allowing nature to run its course. Then a discussion of the branding of the all newborns in the herd, the following month and it was agreed that Mendoza would take the lead in the branding since that was his métier, being an experienced Vaquero most of his adult life. But first the long delayed planting party was a must with Henry. It was decided that Henry, Elijah, Joseph and Miss Melanie would take part, with an estimated time of several weeks to complete.

Along the lines of where Henry had surveyed, the red cloth markers still in place, pointing out clearly the lines of demarcation, Joseph would pace off ten large steps, then Henry would dig a hole a foot deep, with Elijah bringing one of the pine cones with a measure of water, positioning it in the ground then covering it up with soil and the measure of water.

At sundown of the first day Henry estimated that they had gone some three plus miles, with Henry spending an hour digging then Elijah digging for an hour and so on. They ate as they worked, for Henry was eager to complete this task prior to the oncoming of the expected spring rains.

That evening Melanie tended to both Henry and Elijah's hands with a poultice then wrapped the hands with cotton strips. As the evening progressed Elijah stoked the fire, and made certain that sufficient fuel was available throughout the evening, curling up with his son under the rear of the wagon, with the Mexican musket between them on half cock, while Miss Melanie decided that it was high time, Captain Jaeger started to tend to his duties as a potential mate and keep her warm for the evening placing her saddle blanket on the ground under the front of the wagon and summoning Henry to join her, curling up before him with the fire in front of them keeping her warm and Henry's buffalo robe draped over them with him curled up around her.

She loosened her blouse and gently grabbed his hands guiding them to her ample breasts, saying, "These also need to be kept warm Henry"!

At that very moment, she felt the growth of his manhood, press against her spine, as she turned her head and whispered, "At some point we will have to find some time to be alone, don't you agree"?

Henry responded, "I've been waiting for you to let me know when, but we've had a lot to do and not a lot of time to do it in. But your right, we must have some time to ourselves and soon"!

At that he started to gently massage her breasts in emphasis that better thing were just over the horizon. It is said that actions speak louder than words, but often the words are vital at just the right moment, to provide the proper cement to bind the intent. After Henrys words and the resultant touch of his hands Melanie had all that she needed to give her comfort, that this was her man, the right man at the right time and drifted off to sleep, with Henrys hands on her person in a very personal and welcome way.

Just shy of two weeks later the wagon approached the ranch pretty much empty of its cargo of pine cones and Henry had that look of relief on his face. Both he and Elijah had the beginnings of massive calluses on their hands, with all welcomed by the rest. "You have had several visitors while you were gone", said Mendoza, asking as to your return, with some requests to survey the village". "You and I can go into Waco tomorrow and see what they have in mind. It's about time the people of Waco got used to you, so don't forget to wear your town hat, implying that Juan was to wear the same white wide brimmed straw hat as Henry, but when on the ranch and elsewhere the wide brimmed sombrero would do just fine.

During the evenings, Melanie would break out one of her books from her trunk and read toeveryone from the light of the fire, all of Shakespeare's works, playing the part of all of the participants. When she had the time she worked with Mendoza, in his attempts to become more conversant in the language of the land, noting that his conversant abilities were improving, "Muy Rapido".

The following week was taken up with Henry and Juan working the surveyor's transits with the township founders in laying out the metes and the bounds of Waco proper as it existed and the planned look of how the township was to grow. The calculations were handed to the newly arrived town lawyer, who the traveled down to Austin to complete the procedure.

Henry and Melanie were never able to find a moment to be alone with each other, to consummate their relationship, the ranch being a beehive of activity, with always the next task, the next project, taking precious time away from them.

With Texas now becoming a resting place for immigrants from seemingly every point on the compass, outlaws fleeing just ahead of the law, came with the others, to join the native Comanche and the Kiowa Indians in bringing grief to this land.

Every week or so, newspapers from Austin and San Antonio would arrive, to a ready market eager to find out what was happening elsewhere in the world. As he read, Henry was grateful that he'd decided to settle in the Waco area, for the rest of Texas, especially west and north of San Antonio as well as the Rio Grande Valley was a constant beehive of activity as far as robberies and livestock rustling. Never mind the news being a week in arrears, it was news.

Fortunately his Rangering duties took scant little of his time, perhaps two or three days a month, with the occasional conflict to resolve between farmers and ranchers in the area and with Henry serving as a temporary magistrate for the area until Waco grew to such importance and size where they merited an appointment from Austin. He was grateful that his little part of the world was relatively quiet, for the time being. He wondered just how long that would last.

Miss Melanie's days were usually taken up schooling the children that arrived daily at the school house, until the end of May. Then the long summer when it was empty, with the children helping their respective families at their respective homesteads, then after the fall harvest, they were cut loose once again to get their schooling.

Every month Henry and Mendoza would take a few days off from ranching, and head up country to seek and find game to kill, always bringing a wagon load of deer and the occasional buffalo, and even once landing several bears, which was why his hunting trips required a four horse rig to haul the freight rather than the normal two.

Then upon their return, everyone fell to the task of rendering the meat and the hides from the carcasses and the entrails, with each and every part of the animal having a vital use, whether to clothe, or provide sustenance or of a variety of other uses.

Henry and Juan even found time to construct a religious grotto, similar to that Henry had grown up with, down by the stream that served the ranch, where every Sunday Henry said the order of Mass from memory. One Sunday they all woke up early and snuck out of the house before Henry and Melanie woke up, leaving a note saying they were all going into Waco for the First Annual Waco Fair and that Henry and Miss Melanie were not invited, hoping that the both of them would make good use of everybody's absence. At least the smell of the morning coffee came from the fireplace, as Henry brought a cup of coffee for Melanie as she woke up. He sat there on her bed as she started to awaken with two cups at the ready, looking at her still with sleep in her eyes and said, "Seems the others have left us alone for the day", as he offered her the cup of hot coffee. "Any idea what we could do to pass the time", asked Henry with a wink?

"Just a moment let me think", said Melanie, faking an inquisitive look then asking several innocuous questions relating to work or chores, then slowly arising and shedding her plain cloth night gown, revealing a tall, slender, full breasted, blonde woman, in the full bloom of her femininity.

Henry marveled that he'd let so much time pass prior to this moment. As she approached him with a mug of hot coffee in her hand, she was standing on the top of her bed and with her free hand, she pressed his face into her neither regions, so Henry could take in the full odor of her musk. She felt his free hand grab her buttocks repeatedly then soon joined by his other hand kneading her hind quarters as if it were a fresh loaf of sourdough soon to bloom in the oven.

Melanie then opened her legs as an invitation to Henry to seek release and eternal salvation that was certain to be deep within. As his tongue found its way inside her, she felt her legs grow weak, as she held onto his head as he lifted her up and gently lowered her to her bed, both cups of coffee neatly finding a resting place on the night stand. As his tongue relentlessly worked its way waxing and waning then exploring every nook and crease, that lay within, Melanie writhed in ecstasy refusing to relinquishing her hold on Henry's head until at last a sudden gush of liquid burst forth, covering him in her bodily fluids. As she jerked and writhed in celestial bliss, Henry briefly recalled that his beloved Joselita had the very same reaction to his ministering, revealing that it was something quite apart from her normal daily bodily excretions.

Then she reached for his burgeoning member and inserted it in her to its full depth, groaning in bliss as he made his way, towards that eternal pilgrimage for salvation. Starting out slowly he gradually increased his tempo as she matched his in intensity, both surging towards that moment of divine release, the sounds of hips clashing together in an ever increasing tempo, until both stiffened in unison, her legs tightly wrapped around his hips, their body's both convulsing in release.

As she lay with her legs still surrounding his hips with his knees clasping her hips, she felt him gradually diminish in size, yet neither one of them agreed to release each other. Each gently covering the other with a flurry of gentle kisses and stokes, every so often gazing into each other's eyes, with a look of wonderment.

For the second time in his life Henry uttered the words, "Me Amor", without a second thought. Bringing a smile to Melanie's eyes, who responded, "J'taime Mon Amour", almost in a hoarse whisper! For almost an hour they lay together, neither one uttering a word, for the eternal bond was sealed between them both. Both at peace with the world, for the time being, each dedicating what future lay ahead for them both without any expectation of the other. For each one knew in their very bones, the other would give to the other, over and over repeatedly, for that was their way. In return the other would reap untold future benefits as a result of their mutual dedication. No matter what lay ahead, each would treat the other with dignity and grace, constantly striving each day to earn the respect of the other. Their gaze upon each other cemented the celestial bargain.

In the lingering afterglow of their long overdue union, Henry got up, grabbing both mugs over to the fireplace to refill them with coffee. As he made his way over then back, naked and unashamed, Melanie lay up on one elbow leaving one of her breasts exposed, as Henry sat down beside her giving her his cup, Melanie could readily see the effect her exposed breast had on his already re-engorged member. As they both sipped their coffee quietly Melanie began to slowly stroke his erection, her head slowly being drawn by gravity and by curiosity to the throbbing that pulsated from within with each passing of her delicate touch. As her mouth slowly enveloped his member, she could slightly taste the remnants of her ardor. As Henry groaned in supreme pleasure, he relieved Melanie of the burden of her coffee mug, so she could apply all of her energies to the depletion of his inner essences.

In due course, he stiffened, groaned then burst forth with an eruption, which she promptly consumed in its entirety, still languidly mouthing his now shrinking member, refusing to relinquish it until the wellspring was declared, "Hors de Combat". Then she retrieved her coffee and sipped it enjoying its warmth in the chill morning while gathering Henry's free hand and placing it between her satiated thighs.

Just then, thoughts of Joselita invaded Henry's bliss and he silently fought back feelings of guilt, by having another woman intrude on what was supposed to be the memory of what they had together for an all too brief time. He had served his period of mourning to a fairtheewell, observing all the proprieties in due course and now it was time to get on with his life.

While the almighty had deprived him of a wonderful life mate, in time he was provided with another equal in almost every way and perhaps superior in some.

Suddenly his reverie was broken by Melanie as she said, "Ya know, eventually we will need help around here, for there's just too much to do and not enough hands or hours in the day to get things done."

"We got fences to build, a barn, cattle and horses to tend, branding next year, hides to cure, food to make, then corn and wheat to plant and maybe some cotton," her voice trailing off into a whisper.

"We're gonna have to pray on things Mel, just gonna have at pray on it".

Later on in the afternoon when everyone returned, secret winks were traded between everyone, by observing the obvious natural change in mannerisms between Miss Melanie and Massa Henry, as they went about their business.

That evening as Melanie climbed into Henry's bed for the very first time, Maddie and Elijah nudged each other in the knowing that things were now official. From now on it would be Miss Melanie and Massa Henry. The following day, seeing that their meat supply was in need of replenishment, Henry took the wagon and an extra horse along with Akila to ride the perimeter of the property to see how his tree markers had grown and in the process keep an eye out for some game. Leaving just after sunrise, followed the trail that his efforts had yielded finding that every ten yards, sure enough a tiny pine tree was growing, most of which had already achieved a height of just over a foot and a half tall, in a straight line over hill and dale, as far as Henry could see. This was his land and he was going to do whatever it took to bring it to full yield. By noon he noted that Akila was making signs that something was near and he stopped the wagon, taking his big Beretta rifle out of the scabbard and noting that the wind was gently blowing in his face. As he crawled over the rise he could see a large herd of deer just a hundred or so yards in the distance, completely unaware of his presence. With measured speed, he loaded both barrels of the Beretta, then applied the firing caps on the nibs, placing both hammers at half cock and gradually peeked through the tall grass at the herd just below. Much to his surprise the herd was wandering in his direction. Then he decided to exchange the Beretta for his bow and arrows quickly going back to the wagon still out of sight of the slowly advancing herd.

A celestial gift if there ever was one. Taking out a slew of arrows from the quiver placing them between the fingers of his left hand for quick retrieval he peeked through the tall grass once again, noting the wind was still blowing in his face and seeing they had advanced some twenty yards in his direction.

Now it was time to wait. Wait for them to come to him. After a long interval he could see that they'd now come within thirty yards range of his position and it was time for a selection. Still unaware of the danger that lay ahead, Henry had made his selections as he slowly rose up loosing the first arrow, then the next, then the next in three quick successive shots aiming for the area of the lungs just behind the front withers. Each arrow silently found its mark, as the now stricken large bucks bolted and bleated loudly as they started to flee in all directions alerting the herd rest of the herd to danger.

Henry, as quick as he could, shot three successive arrows into the three wounded bucks, as they fled, each finding their mark within inches of their previous shot. As Henry watched the herd fleeing he saw that, one by one the stricken animals started to falter after about a hundred or so yards, coming to a stop and sinking to their knees then crashing to the earth.

Within a distance of a hundred and fifty yards between them, all of the prey lay still panting their last breath's as they jerked and spasm's their way to their death. As Henry approached, he thought of the Shawnee Shaman would so generously provided Henry with the skills of the hunt.

He inspected the first buck as it lay in its final throes of life and gave thanks to its spirit along with the apology for its death. Satisfied, Henry then went back to the wagon leaving Akila in charge temporarily. Passing Akila, he pulled up to the second and third bucks, some twenty yards from each other, securing the wagon then jumped down to inspect the kills. Then he started back to the wagon when he heard the sound of a distant gunshot, coming from the vicinity of a grove of trees just around a small hillock.

He unhitched the spare mount from his wagon, directing Akila to stand guard of the kills.

Akila knew full well that this evening he would eat well for his simple efforts as he always had. Mounting his big Appaloosa, Henry rode in a measured trot towards the direction of the gunfire, securing his mount just out of sight from the end of the hillock. As Henry peered around the hill and through the tall grass he could see that not fifty yards away was a wagon and chained to that wagon were a large number of darkies all chained together and another Negro male astride a horse, bound with his hands behind him, with a noose in the process of being tossed over a low hanging tree limb. Quickly running back to his horse Henry grabbed the Beretta, returning quickly to his previous position, quickly taking aim and fired first at the man struggling to get the male darkie to mount the horse, then the other one holding the reins, dropping them both where they stood. Then he pulled the big Colt .44 and took aim at the third man sitting on the driver's seat as the man was reaching for a musket, his first shot hitting the man in the shoulder, spinning him around and the second shot, knocking him forward into the horses, still with a death grip on the reins.

As Henry approached he got hold of the reins of the horse and secured them to the wagon, then he gentled the partially spooked horses that were to pull the wagon, removing the reins from the dead driver and dragged him out from under the wagon. Finally he inspected the two others he'd shot and as he expected they were goners, soon to be fodder for the critters. At fifty yards from the Beretta, of course they were dead.

Then Henry turned his attention to the darkies, all of which were chained by the neck to each other, with heavy Iron chain. Immediately he could see that they were slaves owned by someone and as he inspected the long line he counted some thirty poor souls as badly clad, their clothes almost in rags, most of which were bare foot and poorly fed if at all.

Then he said, "Any of ya know jus where these men keep the keys to the locks"? Just then one of the women pointed to the wagon driver and Henry went to where the driver lay and came up with a set of keys and one by one went to each of the darkies and unlocked their chains freeing them. Then he bade then to sit in front of and said, "My name is Henry Jaeger and I'm the law around these parts and a Texas Ranger duly appointed by the Governor. Now y'all are on my land. I know ya didn't mean to be and were placed here by others but ya all are. I assume ya all are slaves and property of someone somewhere and I can see that whoever owned you treated you worse that just about anything.

Now I don't hold with slavery, but being the way things are there's nothing I can do about it. I unchained you all to prove a point. As far as I'm concerned you're all free as of this very moment. Now with Indians and the variety of white son of a bitches like these all around", he said pointing to their former captors, "Ya all need food clothes and shelter, while I need some people to help me with my ranch. I can't pay y'all anything at first, except good food every day and clothes and shelter if y'all let me teach ya how to do things to help out"?

"Any of y'all know how to read, write and do yer numbers?" One woman raised her hand meekly. "Good", announced Henry. "Any one wanna learn how to read and write"? That said everyone just looked at each other Can any of you drive a team of horses"; asked Henry and four of the men meekly raised their hands?

"Any of y'all paired up family together here"? Several hands went up, with Henry saying "Well then ya better get with each other right now for they's gonna be no more separation."

"How long has it been since anybody had eaten", asked Henry." "Two days Massa Henry", came a voice from the crowd. Then Henry looked into the wagon and saw a variety of food stuffs and began to distribute it out amongst those that started to gather around, providing for the children first then the women, lastly the men. As they ate, Henry pulled out his big Bowie knife, first retrieving the lead bullets, then removing the scalps from the dead, then removing all the clothes and boots from them loaded the dead up on the wagon with the help of several of the men who seemed to relish in the task. Then driving the wagon under some of the trees hoisted the dead up onto several of the low hanging branches saying, "The critters got to eat, just wanna make em work for it".

Then driving back to the others Henry said, "Anyone who wants a warm meal and shelter tonight can follow me for we gotta pick up supper"?

Just then one of the men rose up and jumped up on the driver's seat as Henry said, "Maybe the women and the children would like to ride awhile" inviting them up on the wagon. Ten minutes later they came upon Akila, standing guard over the fallen bucks and Henry said, "If some of you will kindly help me get these bucks loaded up then we can have food and other things in the days and weeks to come"! The Henry introduced them all to Akila with the standard admonitions as how to behave around the wolves, "Make no attempt to pet them, until they invite you" and he instructed them as to what signs to look for before it was alright.

At that, Henry directed the men as to the backing up of the wagon and with a series of leveraged loops by his lariats hoisted the big bucks up onto the wagon with two in one wagon, and the third in the other. With both wagons loaded the younger women got off and walked alongside the wagons.

By late in the afternoon Henry and his cavalcade approached one of the corrals, when Mendoza looked up to see the parade of wanderers yelling, "Jefe, que paso"?

As the wagons pulled up to the old cabin, everyone came out to see what the commotion was, with Henry struggling to remove the bucks from the wagon yelling, "Light the fires, Miss Melanie, we got company and work to do"!

With Henry directing them all and giving introductions all around on the fly, the entire group had the animals rendered by nine PM and the smoke house was in full fetter, pregnant with edible meat on the smoke while the rest of the newly enlarged family engorged themselves, with sausages made from other prior visitors to the smoke house.

As Henry sat next to Elijah, Melanie and Mattie, eating Mendoza sat down and said, "Well Jefe, it seems that we are to be farmers also", eating with a wink.

Thinking out loud Henry said "Tomorrow we start on the barn but with some additions", directing Elijah to get a wood cutting crew together with some axes, then adding," We're gonna need a plow, harness, needles, thread, cotton cloth, seed, and listed a slew of things needed from the store in Waco.

Thirty days later, the frame of the giant two and a half story barn was formed with each side of the barn having living quarters on the perimeter of the barn with access from the barn and from without. Each set of quarters had its own stone fire place and the barn was sufficient to house fifty separate stalls around a large central area, sectioned off into a dozen more stalls all for temporary birthing quarters. Each side of the barn was provided with a large stone fireplace that would remain constantly lit during bad weather. The following thirty days saw the barn completed and habituated by everyone with Henry and Melanie finally alone.

Without a single nail, just endless amounts of glue and a variety of pegs the barn was up and running. Widows shuttered all the way around Just then Melanie revealed just what she had done in behalf of each of the arrivals, by giving them new names and conjuring up official looking documents, granting each of the darkie's ownership papers via an official looking notary seal that belonged to her mother while she was alive. "I just kept it as a memento, never thinking that one day it would be of any use", she offered with a wink.

Thinking ahead Henry said, "Got to get them all shod and clothed before winter", and suggested that Melanie start up a sewing brigade amongst the women, while Henry would show several of the men how to make a full set of workable boots out of the growing stock of hides and pelts most of which were already tanned and processed ready for manufacture. During the winter months Melanie taught the townships children in the little school house in the mornings for three hours, then went back to the ranch to teach the children and some of the adults the very same lessons as previously in the afternoon, for another three hours.

Several days a week, everyone would gather in the barn while she would read aloud and act the parts of the complete works of Shakespeare, while explaining the entire story and subtext in advance. After one of her performances one of the brightest children asked aloud, "Miss Melanie, are ya sayin' that those rich white folk of olden times are actin' as bad as everyone else"?

Melanie smiled as she said, "Excellent question, young lady. I'm not saying it but the author who mostly lived in those times long ago, William Shakespeare wrote it all down. The lessons it teaches are as plain as day to everyone with eyes to see, ears to hear and a mind to think with"! Then she walked over to the little girl and gave her a hug and said, "Let's all think about these things that happened long ago as we go about our daily work and in the coming months we shall all hear from the words of the Bible and see examples of where good and evil take their place and the rewards that come from our actions."

In the course of time the literacy of the ranch started to grow in fits and starts, with some learning at a faster rate than others, yet no one was felt to be inferior to anyone else.

Some worked harder than others, some worked smarter than others, yet in time everyone discovered what they enjoyed doing the best and settled into their daily tasks with relish.

For it was clear to everyone that outside of their cloistered environment, the world at large was a dangerous and clearly unfair place. The men were all rotated for training in the arts of the bow and arrow and took turns on Henrys every other week hunting outings, each time returning with two wagon loads of game of all sizes. Before the year was out each man could hunt and track almost as well as any Indian and Henry grew proud of them all.

His herds were growing at a record rate and eventually livestock was traded and sold to other members of the community.

By the end of the second year of operation Juan Mendoza, has assumed the duties of the ranch foreman, escorting a number of the men on forays go gather the livestock with the help of the wolves and commence with the arduous chore of branding. Mendoza smiled just as Henry had as his men learned quickly the arts of the Vaquero.

Then one evening Mendoza called everyone together after branding and suggested that it was time that Henry and Miss Melanie had a fine home of their own. The fields had been planted with their very first crops of Corn, Wheat and Alfalfa, and since everyone had built the barn and the ancillary living quarters for all, it was time to build a 'Hacienda' for the Jaegers.

Taking the rest of the summer before Fall harvest everyone took turns in the building of the Jaeger Hacienda, employing the skills they'd been taught and working in unison to achieve the monument for their benefactors. The smokehouse was in a constant state of operation, the leather tanning operation was humming along nicely, the crops were growing and the herds were expanding. And the Lord was indeed their Shepard, for no one was in a state of want or need.

Just a week before the harvest the two floor Hacienda was completed, with a fireplace on two sides of the house, and the entire second floor, surrounded with a ring of bedrooms intended for the children yet to arrive. A complete verandah surrounded not only the first floor but the second as well. Since glass was not readily accessible in the area, shutters would suffice to keep the weather at bay. As an added factor in all of the buildings, a chest high wooden reinforced berm was dug around every building just in case of an Indian attack.

The very first evening after the Hacienda was completed Henry and Melanie took great pains to see to it that the first of the upstairs bedrooms were occupied and they fell to that task with almost reckless abandon. It was agreed the task of naming the issue of Melanie's loins fell to her to decide the names of the wee bairns.

After the fall Harvest was completed, Miss Melanie announced to one and all that she was "Great with Child", deep within, to the great happiness of all. Of course the several darkie families had gone ahead in the normal course of events in increasing the population of the ranch, which in time would need all the help it could get.

The township of Waco was now growing at a measured pace, with now a second General store, a saloon, a barber, church, doctor, lawyer and with news that a newspaper and a bank were in the offing. For several years news of Railroads coming to Texas came and went with most never getting off the ground past the planning stages and going bankrupt, while the others that seemed to get built were mostly short lines in distance serving the Houston and the Port of Galvez on the Gulf of Mexico. Rarely was a steam powered boat seen on the upper Brazos River and then only after the spring rains when the water level was certain to be high enough so the boat wouldn't run aground. Life for Henry was not a pressing thing for his duties as far as Rangering were concerned required only a visit to town every other week, to consult with the town fathers as to the problems that were arising and the settling of disputes. But after several incidents in the local saloon that required some pistol whipping of a number of drunken miscreants it was decided that the town now had to erect a proper office, for Henry and a jail in which to sequester law breakers and well as a court house in which the newly arrived Magistrate appointed by Austin was to ply his judicial pronouncements. Since Henry had the only available supply of harvested wood around, he struck a deal with the town fathers that if they would fund a water driven saw mill, owned by Henry, on the banks of the Brazos, Henry would supply all the wood necessary to build not only the jail but the court house and serve as Contractor for no fee during the course of its building. Contracts were duly executed and funds expended to construct and provide all of the equipment required to build the saw mill.

So the MHM ranch was now expanded into the construction and the sawmill business. Thinking that all his harvest was sold as was to others as is, Henry reasoned milled grain ready to use would fetch a better price than that that of non-milled grain, saw to it that a Grain Mill was built a hundred yards upstream from the saw mill and ready to mill not only the products harvested from his fields but that of others as well, for a modest fee. By Spring of the following year, the Saw Mill was completed, followed closely by the Court House, then the Jail and finally, a scant week before the fall harvest the Grain Mill. Elijah was placed in charge of both milling operations which required two men each to be siphoned from the ranch duties to help run each mill. Since Elijah's son was of such an age he was elevated to the rank of Vaquero as well as several other of the young boys recently entering into their teens. Still growing to maturity they learned their lessons well from the master Vaquero Juan Mendoza, horsemanship, roping, herding, cutting, branding and the like, as well as helping birth the young when necessary, for every single critter had value.

By the spring of the following year, Melanie has rewarded Henry with the gift of a young son and a daughter, twins that were promptly named Zachary and Josie and was again pregnant with what would turn out to be another boy named William. The sons each named after a famous general and the daughter named after one of Melanie's favorite aunts back in Charleston.

As fate would have it, when Josie was first placed into Henrys arms moments after her birth and her name announced as "Josie", unexplained tears started to well up in Henrys eyes as he immediately thought of his Joselita of long ago, then briefly wondered about Rodrigo as to how he was progressing.

Gaining control of his emotions, everyone thought that Henry was overcome by the birth of his daughter, which he was, but as Henry glanced at Mendoza, he was greeted with a knowingly silent nod, and a warm smile.

One day Henry would have to tell Melanie of his life before her, but that day was hopefully a long time off.

As Henry read the news that intermittently arrived by the weekly newspapers, he was greeted with the fact that seemingly all of Texas was in a state of perpetual turmoil with Indian raids occurring with increasing regularity north by the Red River and west of San Antonio, by varying bands of Comanche and some Apache near the Val Verde area of the Rio Grande. Then there was the constant hectoring by the Mexican bandits along the Southern border with periodic forays into Texas to steal what cattle and horses could be had and murder anyone that got in their way.

Since the Rangers had been officially disbanded since the end of the War by the Federal Government defense and law enforcement in the state, out in the country at large, was effected only by the formation of bands of Militia for a single purpose of the retrieval of stolen livestock or women and children as slaves sold and bartered by various tribes and worked almost to the point of death, for their lives weren't seen as worth much by the native Indians.

The longer they survived with the Indians, on those few instances where they were rescued; they seemed to almost to a person as having suffered an irreversible injury to their mind and spirit, giving the overly harsh treatment as the hands of their captors. Henry was repeatedly approached to form a group of men to pay a visit to the tribes up along the Canadian river well into the Oklahoma Indian territory and wipe out the hostiles once and for all.

Jaegers constant reply was that since he was a duly appointed Ranger he was obligated by the legislature in Austin, to stay put until he was directed by Austin to do otherwise. Secretly he had little stomach for any more killing of the Comanche, since over time he had done well more than his share of ridding the world of those savages. Further, things at the ranch were progressing well and the Indians were keeping well north of the Waco area. He had lost not one of his livestock in the years and his fields were bountiful, thus he saw little need to stir the pot. Besides over the years, he had been successful in erecting a string of wood fencing that had surrounded almost half of the perimeter of his land, with his string of pine trees pointing in a straight line over hill and dale.

The Country Magistrate and the town lawyer agreed with Henry's point of view, plus the fact that word had gotten out that the township of Waco wasn't a healthy place to be if one had mayhem in mind. For Henry was well known to meet out Draconian Justice upon occasion to those who transgressed. He was not above hanging miscreants naked by their feet, with their hands bound behind them, for days on end from a tree at the edge of town, without sustenance, finally cutting them down and leaving them with only their clothes on the ground to find their way out of town never to return.

They always found it in their best interests never to return, their survival was of no concern to Henry Jaeger. Once when a drunk was threatening the County Magistrate when Henry was in town, thus knocking the Judge from his horse to the ground, Henry calmly walked out of his office, pulling both of his vaunted "Hog Legs" from his holster and commenced to open fire on the four horsemen that accompanied him, killing three and seriously wounding another and they tried to open fire on Henry. Henry then ran up to the offender and clubbed him senseless with one of his Colt revolvers, then grabbing one of the horses, grabbed the lasso from the saddle and tied it around to poor souls legs mounting the horse and rode up and down the streets for five minutes dragging the miscreant almost to the point of death. Leaving him some distance from the edge of town, removing his boots and declaring that his mount and all his belongings were now the property of McClendon County.

Riding back to town, he collected all of the weapons depositing them in the jail and then directed several of the town's people to strip the dead of their personal property dividing it amongst themselves and bury them in the deep pit a mile east of town.

While his brand of justice was indeed Draconian, it was always viewed as fair and since it was duly observed by the town lawyer and the Magistrate, and objections they may have had at another time, in another place remained unspoken, for Waco was largely a peaceful place and it was in every ones best interests to have it remain that way.

Later when the Judge was recovering in his residence Henry said to the doctor, "How is he"? The doctor scratched his head and said, "Well Henry he ain't a gonna be liftin' his drinkin' arm for quite a spell, cause its broken and I'm gonna have to come back and set it, and he's got this terrible bump on his head, but there'll be enough towns women to look after him and the bump will pain him some but I reckon, he'll recover. Might be a good idea to double up on your visits to town for a spell, just till he gets back on his feet, ya think"?

Henry nodded his head in agreement. Even the women around town noted that Henry Jaeger was a nice and polite man who went out of his way to help others, "Just don't git him all fired up, for it just ain't healthy', they whispered amongst themselves always out of earshot. Months later when Henry and Mendoza were making the rounds of the northern most fence line trying to determine what manpower they could glean temporarily to get more fences up, they took notice that nearly all of the tree's planted years ago along the perimeter were around ten feet tall, thus providing a clear demarcation as to the ranch's boundary's . They talked about how well the livestock were multiplying, with both the bulls and the stallions doing their work well, with nary a day going by when at least one of the livestock giving birth. The latest census of the herd was around a thousand head of longhorn cattle alone, along with another four hundred horse. In the following weeks a representative of the US Army would be paying them a visit as to purchases from their herd. As they rode on they saw four male Indians astride their horses just outside of the tree line waiting for them. As they approached, the Indians dismounted and sat on the ground, a clear signal for a palaver. Henry and Mendoza came to a halt with Henry handing Mendoza his reins and sliding down from his horse, giving the peace sign, which was returned by each of the others. By the looks of things, each warrior represented the Cherokee, Tonkawa, Shawnee and Waco tribes. The pipe was brought forth and a small fire was quickly prepared and after the pipe was passed around signaling that trade was to be discussed, the Indians quickly noted that Henrys herds have grown greatly while theirs diminished, thus they were prepared to trade hides of every kind for cattle and perhaps a few of Henrys horses. Since sign language was employed in the transaction it took a considerable time in which to convey precisely the terms of the agreement.

All the while, Mendoza sat impassively on his mount with a hand loosely near the Old Colt Horse Pistol, occasionally scanning the surroundings in a casual manner for any nasty surprises, without unduly alarming the transaction.

When Henry arose with the others, Mendoza saw Henry spit in his hand, then reach out for one of the braves hands and indicated for him to do likewise. At first the braves all looked at each other askance, but one of them finally spit in his hand and offered it to Henry whereupon he grasped the hand nodding his head and shaking it with two pumps before releasing it. Then seeing what had gone before the others did likewise, one by one till the deal was finalized.

As they rode away from each other, Henry told Juan what had just transacted. "In ten days when the New Moon is in the heavens, we will be visited by twenty skids full of buffalo hides and it'll cost us four bulls and eight cows." That said Mendoza immediately knew what had to be done, being that within the next week he needed to cull out eight cows, as yet unbranded, just out of their lactation and place them in a corral. And the day they departed cull out four bulls to accompany them.

Henry would bring the appropriate pen and paper to fill out bills of sale for the Indians just in case anyone should question the transaction.

Ten days later Henry set out with ten of his Buffalo Vaqueros, as he now called them, with two extra horses each, for transporting of the hide skids and Chani and Akila for the day and a half trip to the northern perimeter. Upon arrival the inspection of the hides commenced taking several hours with Henry pleased at the quality of the Hides. Then some more time as Henry patiently filled out the requisite bills of sale to each tribe, taking time to tell them about the importance of these documents for each one should they ever be questioned.

Thus concluded Henry repeated the ritual of the handshake with each of the braves, prior to their parting. Then he was greeted with yet another offer of another trade to occur within two month's time at the very same place, during the period of the new moon, this time with an equal number of horses and cattle involved.

Thinking a moment Henry agreed nodding in the direction of each, followed with the ritual of the hand shake.

As they returned he mentioned to Mendoza, "Well Senor it seems we're in the hide tanning business in a big way, for we'll have to part with some four stallions and eight mares and four more bulls and eight more cows, but in return we'll be getting forty skids of hides for our trouble. Now if those hides are as good as these here are then we'll be in high cotton. The reason being is that there's a merchant down Houston way that'll pay top dollar to get the finished product and ship it back east. Better yet he'll come and get em"!

So for the next year and a half, the Jaeger herds stood dormant in size with the Army making demands of his horses and the Indians trading primarily for the cattle. Of course horses that were already saddle broken brought a much higher premium and since Henry had taken the time to teach his special talent to two of his youngest Buffalo Vaqueros, ten horses per week were prepared to be 'saddle ready', when the need arose.

At the behest of Miss Melanie a quiet decision was reached to share with the others a significant portion of the now flowing income of the ranch with all of their family. Each and every one was loyal to the enterprise of the ranch. Therefore in the aftermath of the evening meal it was announced that each and every member of the ranch family, male and female and every single child would receive an initial fifty US dollar annual stipend, set aside in a separate account in the bank that was due to be open for business in Waco, in the coming months ahead. Both mills were now in almost a daily business, with the wood mill cutting wood brought to it in various lengths and sizes for a fee, as well as the grain mill that was mostly a seasonal operation, operating in almost a nonstop fashion, during the fall harvest and eventually in the spring months after the winter wheat harvest.

With the advent of a steady supply of hides from the Indians, the tannery operation was in full swing, churning out high quality tanned hides for, the multiplicity of uses on the frontier and in the cities back east.

In spite of the steady demand for horses and cattle by the Army, in Fort Worth and the friendly Indian tribes, the Jaeger herds continue to multiply, for the Bulls and the Stallions were kept very busy by the demands of their counterparts, coming into season on an almost daily basis, multiple times a year.

These were the good years, a time to be fruitful and multiply, with the shield of good fortune over them all.

Then by lot, every year a family of the darkies was chosen, to receive their very own house, built by all the rest from the supply of lumber the mill constantly churned out. Once a year a plot of ground within walking distance of the corrals was selected and everyone pitched in to erect the home in its entirety dependent on its needs, with a separate well dug and a covered latrine set well away from the well to provide for each family's needs.

In time everyone wore the mantle of the Buffalo Vaqueros, old and young, great and small, with Henry being the chief Vaquero and Mendoza, still in the cups for his lost love of time gone past, in his private moments. But Henry knew of his loss first hand and made it a point to have Mendoza an important part of the family, as he became known as Uncle Juan by one and all.

As time passed, they all took part in firing practice, of both the musket and the bow and arrow, both men and women and periodically drilled as to what to do in the event of an attack. Thus in time all achieved a degree in proficiency the arts of musketry along with the bow and the arrow, for the day when peace would take a holiday.

Everyone had a variety of clothes and was well shod, mostly by virtue of their own industry, with a well-made roof over their head, a warm place to sleep a full belly and a unity of purpose, that all were an important part of the whole.

15

We all have a tendency to take certain things for granted in our lives, such was the case of Henry Jaeger. Chan, Akila and their two children, had been with him for so long and the service and unquestioned loyalty exhibited went far to assure his safety and success in almost every venture he'd undertaken. Not able to reason like humans, they exhibited another intelligence that defied measure, their heightened senses. Their sense of smell, vision, hearing and the innate ability to sense danger on the continuum, when no evidence to the contrary was apparent, was beyond any human sense of worth. Further their constant reliability was as apparent as the sun rising in the east each morning. Guarding rather than eating the herds was their task. Guiding the herds at the behest of their masters was as ingrained in them as breathing.

Therefore it came as a shock to Mendoza when at midmorning he could find them nowhere in sight as he made his morning rounds of the pastures to inspect the herds. No signs of foul play, no signs of any tracks of wild animals or traveling marauders. Greatly disturbed, he spurred his horse back towards the ranch to alert Henry, before he left for town.

But as he arrived, he also saw none of the normal activity of the ranch by the people. Drawing his weapon, he placed in on half cock as his horse approached the barn complex. Rounding the corner he saw several of the people hurrying towards the barn, disappearing inside. Pulling up to the hitching post he secured his weapon and went inside to see everyone gathered around at the far end by one of the stalls. All were peering intently into the stall, craning their necks to get a view and as Mendoza approached he discovered why. For there, in the stall lay Chani's daughter nursing four little additions to the family. Nearby lay Chani with her head lain upon her paws in front of her looking keenly intent on her daughters blessed event, with Akila and his step son standing alertly nearby.

Now when Chani gave birth it was clear the father was not Akila, given the general appearance of the little critters, but from the look of things Chani's son was clearly the father, issuing forth one with light brown fur, one with jet black fur, another with a chestnut color and the last with dark brown fur all eagerly suckling from a proffered teat.

The Lord may clearly be the ultimate Shepard, but his agents on earth just multiplied. One by one the youngsters gently approached to sit quietly beside Chani, Akila and the new father, petting them gently, freely giving the never ending bond of love between a human and its protectors. For over time, the wolves grew to be the most beloved of all the creatures on the ranch. In every sort of weather they never grew weary of their task, always on guard and ever alert to danger.

Standing just behind Henry and his wife, Mendoza noted that each had one of their children in their arms to witness the blessed event. In his mind he calculated that in about a year they would be a tremendous help in managing the herds. But for now, at this very moment there was no one guarding the herds and someone had to be redirected from their duties for the time being.

As he whispered his concerns to Henry, Henry quietly exclaimed "Scheist", "that's right Juan".

"Jefe, I will handle this por favor", as he caught the attention of four of the youngsters in the neighborhood of their twelfth year, weary of the menial tasks assigned them and trained in the ways of the vaquero, he caught their attention and motioned for them to follow him.

When he got them aside, he explained that now was the time for them to put in practice temporarily all they'd been taught at least until Chani and Akila were back in full form. Eagerly each one went to the nearest corral and selected a mount bringing it back to the barn to get saddled and then when Mendoza inspected each one he reminded them that they forgot their muskets and sent them over to the section of the barn that served as an armory.

Within minutes each one returned, to present their selection for 'Uncle Juan's' inspection. Full canteens, muskets in their scabbards they all mounted to follow Juan out to the herds, to gather them up for the time being and consolidate them into a tighter, less spread out mass, thus easier to watch over. No wolves to help them, for the responsibility was all theirs.

Periodically during the day a rider would be sent out to feed them and bring the necessaries as required, with Juan an ever present factor for the duration.

When he got back to the barn, he saw that everyone was returning to their daily tasks with Henry late for his twice a week visit to town. As Henry and Miss Melanie exited the barn Mendoza hitched his mount on the post as Melanie said, "Well Juan, you might as well hear this along with Henry"! Then she stopped and said "Henry, you're gonna be a father again"!

Henry met this news with a turn of his head almost unbelievably and said, "When did you know"?

"Just this morning when it was confirmed by Maddie and Juan you're gonna be the Uncle and once again, a god father of another little Jaeger"!

Juan beamed almost as much as Henry as the addition to the Jaeger clan required his attention and responsibility to yet another. As little Zack and his sister Josie were just starting to talk, addressing him as Uncle Juan, yet another would be arrived to continue this bond. In many ways this helped to gradually ease the still evident pain of his loss of Juanita, a love that could never be. And he was approaching his fortieth year, never expecting to live even this long, given his origins, he vowed to be careful in all things, for there was much responsibility on his shoulders.

He thought about the budding Buffalo Vaqueros and how quickly they appeared to take to his teachings in the fine arts of the Vaquero, and he smiled for their success was his reward.

Kissing Melanie and hugging his children Henry quickly mounted his horse and rode off towards town. For it was clear that Henry was now in need of a deputy since the little village was now growing rapidly in size and the town had to find someone that Henry could deputize to be there full time. Henry's services were paid for by Austin, but the deputy would have to be paid for by the town.

Stopping by the Court House, Henry paid his respects to the County Judge, just recently returned to health, before going to his office. As Henry entered the Judges office, he was greeted by a scowling countenance as he peered over his glasses. The Judge, never known to be an overly affable man, was particularly disturbed when Henry greeted him. "Well good to see to up and around Judge"! "Bull Shit", bellowed the Judge! "Just got a visit by that scallywag, Amos Ledbetter. Seems, all his Nigra's ran off on him the other day and he's raisin' holy hell by wantin' you to run em down and return his propitty"!

"Well Judge, what did ya tell him"?

"Told the Sumbitch, that he's gotta tend to his own and that we're not in the Nigger chasin' business"!

"Well Judge, since that's what ya said, then that's the way it'll be"! Then as an afterthought, Henry asked, "How many hands ran off"?

"All of em", the Judge bellowed. "Around fifty so Amos says, bought and paid for"! "He's angry cause his cotton crop is about three weeks away from harvest and he's screamin' bout how he'll be wiped out lessen we gat em back."

"Seems like a Federal problem to me Judge, did ya refer him to Ft. Worth and the troops up there"?

"As everyone knows those Federals don't know their asshole from their elbow and unless they got some friendly Indian scouts they can't trail anyone"!

"Amos is right about one thing, you're the only white man around that can bring em back"!

"Still seems to me that it's a Federal problem and if he comes back send him on to me and I'll set him straight"! "Won't have ta wait that long Henry, since he and some of his boys are camped out on your doorstep waitin' for ya"!

"How many of em Judge"?

"Amos and his three sons and they're all in a foul mood"!

"Four of em eh, seems about right. Thanks for the warning"! At that Henry tipped his sombrero and left.

As he turned the corner of the street, he could see Amos Ledbetter and his sons all angrily pacing in front of Henrys small Ranger office. As he pulled up his mount and secured it to the hitching post, he noticed several onlookers from across the street, apparently curious as to what was going to happen next. Human nature, it seemed to Henry every time something was to occur to break the monotony of everyday life, someone would have to be there to see the blood flow and if it didn't they'd be disappointed.

"Good Mornin' Amos" offered Henry as he climbed the steps to his office, "What can I do for ya"?

"My Niggers all ran off a while back an", cutting him off Henry said, "Yeah I heard, from the Judge just minutes ago".

"Well I gotta get em back Henry"!

"The Judge says ya got the proper papers for all of em, that right Amos"?

"Damn right", Amos fumed!

"Probably across the county line by now, so it seems like you're gonna have at make a trip to Ft. Worth and get the Army to get em back for ya"!

"Gawdammit Henry, that's the same thing the Judge told me", bellowed Ledbetter.

Just then Henry said, "Tell your boys to stay within my eyesight or else I'll not take kindly to your visit and you start speaking to me in a more respectful tone".

With that said, one of the boys that started slowly to move behind Henry reversed his course.

"Do ya know why all of your darkies ran off Amos"? With that Ledbetter stood silent, "Cause I heard stories that ya treated em somthin' horrible, not feedin' em enough, beatin' em, none of em with shoes and all of em in rags and ya work em till they drop, then work em some more"!

"Henry, they be my propitty and I can do withem what I want, it's the law"!

"That may be Amos, but their also free to decide when they've had enough. Why you've got three times the darkies Miss Melanie has and not a one of em would ever consider running off and ya wanna know why?

Because we don't treat them like animals! They all got good clean clothes on their back, shoes on their feet, food in their bellies and a good roof over their heads. All of em knows that we care for them each and every one and ya wanna know what else, they all know that each and every one of em is important. We can turn our backs on them and never once worry that a job won't get done or that they'll run off. So it seems that you've taken another path in the way y'all treat your darkies. Seems to me it didn't work so well did it?"

"But my cotton crop needs to be picked soon", moaned Amos. "Then I see that y'all have three choices, either track em down your selves, or ride to Ft Worth and see if the Federal Troops'll help ya, or pick the cotton your own selves"!

As Henry made the last statement, he noticed that one of Amos's sons's moved around to the rear of one of their horses, near its saddlebag.

"Now Amos, tell that son of yours that if'n he reaches into that saddlebag and comes out with anything other than a chaw of tobacco, he's gonna be without a father Muy Pronto like, ya sabe"!

"Luke, step back now", Amos bellowed shaking with anger for he was accustomed to having his way all his life and up till now no one ever stood up to him, ever. His slaves all run off and the bankers in Shreveport wanting their money or the crop advanced for seed victuals and the other necessaries to run a plantation, for the crop to rot in the fields would ruin him. He knew that and his son's knew that. It made him no never mind that he was standing up to a man who was almost a legend in these parts, he was determined to have his way, no matter what. Henry's argument that his actions had brought all of this to pass, had fallen on deaf ears, the solution to his problem lay just in front of him and his mind quickly raced to come up with an immediate solution as to compel Henry Jaeger, Texas Ranger to get his niggers back for him and now.

Almost thirty seconds of what seemed like an eternal silence lay between the two men, with Henry staring right into the eyes of a desperate Amos Ledbetter and his three sons. He noted the positioning of his three sons in the street, with Luke still with in reaching range of whatever was in that saddlebag and the Judge hobbling down the street, escorted by the town lawyer and the town doctor carrying his medicine bag as he always did.

"Amos, my position is clear, now if'n you'll excuse me I've work to do and if you don't leave right now, I just might think that ya wanna kiss me and that dog won't hunt"!

Just then Amos's eyes grew big and he lunged at Henry in sheer desperation. Quickly he sidestepped Amos bringing his big Colt revolver down hard on Ledbetter's head then whirling around, his hand brought the big Bowie knife out of its sheath and throwing it the fifteen feet to one of the sons as he started to bring his musket to bear upon Henry with the blade sinking squarely into his chest as his finger pulled the trigger, the musket ball whistling past Henrys ear.

As Henry suspected, Luke came out of the saddle bag with one of the pepperbox, multi barreled pistols, and as he came out from behind his horse for a clear shot, Henry's "Hog Leg" spoke just once, knocking Luke backwards to the ground never to rise again. Seeing that both of his brothers were killed in the space of a few moments, the remaining brother, threw all caution to the wind and took aim at Henry with the musket ball passing through Henrys sombrero knocking it off his head, coming to rest on his back, hanging by virtue of the rawhide head strap. In the space of about two very slow seconds in time, Henry calculated as to whether to spare Amos's last son's life of not. After all he had tried to kill Henry and missed, just barely and if he were to live, Henry would never get a good nights sleep worrying about where he was.

His decision made, the big hog leg spoke once again, the bullet finding its new home in the last of the Ledbetter's male heirs, knocking him well of his feet and out of his boots by the force of its impact.

As Henry went down the steps to the street to inspect his handiwork, he felt the movement from behind from the last of the Ledbetter's, as well as heard the Judge bellow, "Henry, look out"! Jumping quickly to the side and whirling around just as Amos Ledbetter, now partially recovered from Henrys blow, blew past him with his own knife drawn, the tip catching a half inch of Henrys ear, falling down into the street.

As Amos struggled to regain his feet for a second chance, Henry didn't have to take a second or two for consideration as the big Colt roared for the final time of the day, spinning Amos around, with spittle flinging from his soon to be lifeless lips as he came to his eternal rest on the dusty streets.

The body jerked once then lay still.

As the crowd gathered, everyone whispered to each other, "It was a righteous shoot, I seen it, didn't you"? And in every case the recipient of the comment nodded or said, "Uh Huh"!

The doctor gave scant attention to the Ledbetter's who lay in the street, for they were well beyond his help and went straight to Henry, finding a bleeding left ear with a half inch slice that would need attention and bade Henry to sit on the steps while he tended to him.

As the Judge approached he echoed everyone's comments that it was an unprovoked attack on his life. As Henry sat on the Jail house steps with the doctor tending to his sliced ear staunching the flow of blood, Henry asked, "Other than what lay in the street, does Amos have any family back at his place, wife, and small children"? The Judge thought a second then said, "As far as I know, you're looking at the entire Ledbetter family". Then almost as an afterthought, he said, "Apparently he's a crop of cotton that has to be gotten in"! Then the Judge spoke, "Henry you go with the doctor and get your ear taken care of and we'll all tend to this and later on get on out to the Ledbetter spread to see what has to be done. The cotton will get picked somehow". Then he directed the townsmen to strip all the weapons from the dead and grabbed the keys to the jail from Henry and made certain they were all placed inside the jail as local ordinance stated.

An hour later Henry emerged from the doctor's house, his ear stitched up and looking ugly with a half pint of the Ledbetter's corn whiskey in his innards to dull the pain and then accompanied him back to the ranch.

'Now that the Ledbetter' were no more who on earth was going to supply cheap corn whiskey for the town', thought Henry as he slowly rode towards the ranch? Not being a teetotaler, but recognizing the occasional value of a stout shot when the occasion called for it, for its medicinal value mind you, Henry realized that he just might require a supply for a brief while and expressed his concerns to the doctor who told him not to worry.

As they approached the ranch by what was now the middle of the afternoon, Henry heard the plaintive howling of Akila. Then after a while he realized that what was missing was the howl of Chani. Spurring his horse on he arrived at the ranch, seeing that all were gathered in front of the barn around Akila as he howled. As Henry pressed his way through the crowd he saw Chani lying still in front of the entrance to the barn and removed his sombrero and unhitched his holster letting it fall to the ground approaching with great reverence, his cherished Chani. He slowly fell to his knees, as tears flooded into his eyes, realizing that her time had come. Akila had once again started that long plaintive howl to announce to the heavens the pending arrival of his sister Chani. They had both traveled far and had seen and done much and now their work was finished. At this point Henry broke down and cried like a wounded creature, for in many ways they were of his blood as well as he was theirs. Memories of his life with them flooded into his consciousness. Then he looked at Akila and knew that his time was soon at hand and approached Akila, looking into his eyes and thought the words that were not to be spoken. Memories of his parents and his long lost family and the Shawnee Shaman, his other father came yet again to the front of his mind as he nuzzled next to Akila.

He heard as well as felt everyone assembled start to cry for in each ones way Chani and Akila was as much a part of them as they were to Massa Henry. The doctor, usually a taciturn man, started to tear up, knowing scant little of what passed between Henry, the darkies and a dead wolf, he was taken by the complete change in Henrys personality. In the late morning Henry was the angel of death, a whirling dervish, ending lives of the unworthy with scant regard for personal safety, his judgment final and complete, while hours later his compassion for an animal was the equal if not greater than any that he'd seen for mortal man.

Henry then unashamedly joined Akila in announcing the new visitors to the great beyond, via the long plaintive howl giving little care for how it may seem to others for as he nuzzled Akila and made little animal noises, he then heard two additional howls from deep within the barn. For the children knew that a time had passed. Then something told Henry to release Akila as he rose and walked the three steps to the dead Chani, licked her lifeless muzzle then lay down beside her, slowly looking around at a small sea of grief stricken faces and finally at Mendoza, then Henry, giving a weak bark then put his head down next to Chani, closing his eyes then lay still forever.

Suddenly the flood gate of grief opened, washing over everyone and as Henry looked around, he saw Melanie holding one of his children and Maddie the other. Then Mendoza kneeled down saying, "Jefe, at noon, she got up from her children and moved away slowly walking out to the front of the barn, the sat down for awhile then lay down. I went to her and somehow knew right away that her time had come somehow and she looked at me and somehow seemed to search for you, then seeing that my presence would have to do, looked at me the very same way that Akila looked at you then peacefully closed her eyes"!

"Muy Gracias Juan", uttered Henry slowly! Then with swollen eyes he looked at Melanie, his precious Melanie, who mouthed silently 'Je Taime Amour' as she had said hundreds of times before sensing the depths of his grief but not fully understanding the why's of it. Henry nodded in assent.

Then Juan rose up and summoned some of the men to saddle up and go out to replace the vaqueros in the pastures for the night taking all of the appropriate precautions. As they rode off, Melanie led everyone in the recitation of the biblical, "The Lord is my Shepard, I shall not want…"

When the prayer was completed Melanie went over to Henry, summoning Maddie to follow her, both of the women placing Henry's children into his arms as a silent reminder of the many blessings Henry had received over time saying, "Lately Chani has been moving sorta slow and has started to look kinda puny as has Akila also. Then I remembered you saying that you grew up with them. They were a blessing in every way possible, to all of us, but it seems to me that Chani held on long enough to see her daughter bring on her replacements. That done, then it was time to die. She went peacefully and was surrounded by those who loved her. A far better fate than what might have awaited her had she not met up with you Henry.

As for Akila, his sister gone and his replacements delivered, his work was done also and I guess I could make an argument that he wanted to follow her to that Happy Hunting Ground soon, lest he lose her scent, ya follow"?

Somehow all of this made perfectly good sense to Henry. Melanie had put her finger right on it. As he looked at her, with each one of their children in his arms, he renewed his respect for the woman as being wise as well as resourceful. Suddenly, with the day rapidly on the wane, and her hair all undone and smudges of dirt both here and there, she never looked more beautiful.

Then Henry looked up and said to one of the young budding Buffalo Vaqueros, we need to build a funeral pyre to say good bye to them, so gather the wood and put it in the west pasture.

Since they were unaccustomed to what he wanted, he went with them directing them as to how the pyre was to be built and where. Within the hour, the pyre was built to a height of eight feet, with Chani and Akila gently placed atop of the wooden edifice.

As the fire grew in height Henry gave a brief explanation of the old Shawnee way of saying good bye to a warrior, then started into his relentless chant, announcing to the eternal spirit that celebrated visitors were coming to stay.

This was a side of Henry Jaeger, that not even Mendoza had seen and as a professed Christian and Catholic, his exhibition at first seemed extraordinary and heathen at first, but when everyone started to mull over the many facets of the man, it gradually started to make sense.

Later in the evening when the embers of the pyre started to wane, all had gone to their homes, for an early evening for the following day's work could not wait.

As they walked back to their home Melanie asked Henry, "And when were ya gonna tell me about that big slice out of your ear Henry? It appears that the good Doctor has stitched it up right and proper. Does it hurt much?"

"Matter of fact it does now and I'll need a good portion of that Jug we got in the kitchen before I get to sleep"!

It was later that she discovered a neat hole two inches from the top of the crown of Henry's prized sombrero. Even to her untrained eye this had the appearance of a freshly earned musket ball hole. Since Henry refused to enlighten her, she reckoned the good doctor would provide the answers in due time. If Henry could live with the hole then so could she, but she would get to the bottom of this. The following morning as she made her way into the barn to visit the newborns finding them busily feeding on their mothers teats, she gathered one of the darkies to get two small earthen containers for the ashes of Chani and Akila so they could be placed on the fireplace mantle. It would be a fine surprise for Henry when he returned later in the day with Mendoza, from inspections of the herds.

As she emerged from the barn, she was greeted by the sight of Henry gathering several of the darkies to hitch up some of the horses to the wagons and gather water pouches. Within minutes both wagons were off with Henry explaining exactly why, to a mildly hectoring Melanie who was insistent that she go along.

"Seems that we have fifty or so slaves a mile away in the northern pasture, who are just about played out after wandering for days and I'll bet that these are the same darkies that fled Old Amos's plantation a few days ago", was Henry's brief explanation.

"Won't Amos be wanting you to return em", asked Melanie?

"Uh, No"?

"And why not"?

"Because he's dead"!

"What about those sons of his"?

"Because they followed their father"!

"Followed their father", asked Melanie bent upon squeezing the information out of a reluctant husband?

"They're all dead too", said Henry reluctantly.

"Something tells me this has something to do with that horrible slice out of your ear", said Melanie as Henry looked straight ahead as he drove.

"Well, I'm waiting"!

"Jesus, Mary and Joseph, you sure can be an exasperatin' woman at times"!

"I'm still waiting Henry"!

Seeing that she was like a hound dawg on the scent, Henry relented explaining to her the events in town, leaving out some of the less pleasant details, not suitable for a lady's ears.

Minutes later they came upon Mendoza and two of the Buffalo Vaqueros that stood over the escaped Ledbetter slaves that were indeed played out. Parched with what passed for clothes, but in reality were rags and all of them unshod. Melanie quickly leapt into action taking charge, going around with the water bags to each and every one, asking questions and separating people into what she thought were family units, calming their fears.

She pointed to Henrys prominent ear and said "Your former Master Amos Ledbetter and every one of his sons are dead and can no longer do you any harm".

"This man is my husband Henry Jaeger, the Texas Ranger in this territory and he will see to it personally that no harm of any kind will visit any of you as long as he draws breath! Isn't that right Henry", she offered turning towards him.

Henry nodded in agreement, for his wife had committed him to his word. Just then he looked at Mendoza and as their eyes met they nodded together in the knowledge the ranch could use the addition man power.

Then he and Mendoza went to the poor darkies and loaded the women, children and those too weak to continue into the wagons and returned to the ranch depositing all of them into the barn, gathering everyone else about them to feed bathe and share clothing with all of the new comers. In the coming days, Miss Melanie's darkies would share stories about how much better life was here at the MHM ranch that anywhere else, putting fears mostly to rest.

Now all Henry had to do was figure out a way to settle the accounts. As usual Melanie, contributed much to the discussion as to the most logical direction during the evening meal.

The following day, Henry visited town again, this time gathering the town lawyer and the County Judge for a meeting. It started out with the Judge and the relating his visit to the now deserted Ledbetter Plantation, "If one can call it that" said the Judge. That place is a rundown piece of pure tee shit. The house that old Amos and his boys is so run down and little better that that pitiful string of sheds he kept his nigra's in. But since they're all long gone the man has at least seventy five acres of cotton that is indeed just scant weeks from harvest, with no one to get it done".

"Asked around to some of the other land owners and they got all they can say grace over, and none can spare the help".

"Just for the sake of argument what if the cotton could be harvested Judge, then who would benefit, what with Amos and his sons all gone and no relatives to be found."?

"Well, lemmeseeheah", pondered the Judge. "No last will and testament is on file so I suppose the property would revert to the State and in this case the County, so any monies gathered from an 'In testate' estate would revert into the County's treasury."

"So all of the Ledbetter property including the land and any improvements would become county property, is that about it Judge", asked Henry?

"Yep son that's about it"!

"And what about Amos's bought and paid for slaves, are they considered his property"?

"But of course", replied the Judge. "But their long gone, all spread out to parts unknown".

"But if they could be found and the Ledbetter's fields harvested, what would happen to his walking property", asked Henry?

"Well then the ambulatory property would then have to be sold to the highest bidder", said the Judge.

"How would this sale take place"?

"Usually on the court house steps on the very first Tuesday of each month", replied the Judge in an arching eyebrow.

"Henry Jaeger seems that you have something in mind, that you're not revealing so just spit it out, young man".

"One more question Judge, if some, shall we say, a friend of the court could find a way to greatly benefit the county, could a way be legally found reimburse the friend of the court and the county, on a "Sub Rosa" basis"?

"Henry, when I was a young buck studying the law, I asked a wise man why men become lawyers and he said to me the following; 'To study the law and become conversant and a master of its various intricacies, is the secret to manipulating the law to exact a certain outcome, hopefully for the common good and if not that for the benefit of those involved'"!

"So I take it that a way can be found to benefit those directly involved. The county and its administrators, the darkies if they can be produced and various peoples involved in effecting a positive outcome for the common good"!

"Henry what is it you have up your sleeve? You've no people to spare and no one else does either"! "Please just answer the question Judge" asked Henry.

"Well yes" said the Judge.

"And could a special price be put on the walking property of the Ledbetter estate, during a closed bidding, for a friend of the court, should the county's needs be met", asked Henry?

The Judge nodded in agreement. "Then for the price of ten dollars and other considerations it just might be possible that the Ledbetter cotton can be harvested on time with the proceeds of the crop being placed into the county's coffers and the walking property of the Ledbetter Estate being awarded to Melanie Jaeger and part of her estate for the agreed upon price, of ten dollars and other considerations"!

"Do we have a deal Judge", asked Henry reaching out his hand? "Why Henry Jaeger you old son of a bitch, you just danced all around me didn't ya"!

"Do we have a deal Judge", Henry repeated with his hand still outstretched.

"Henry we have a deal", answered the Judge as he spit in his hand, as Henry spit in his to seal the bargain. While their hand were still joined, Henry added, "They're in pretty bad shape out in my ranch and yesterday my Buffalo Vaqueros found em all wandering just about played out and we had to feed em, burn their clothes, clothe them wash them and it'll be at least two weeks for them to be ready"!

"Mind if I take a look Henry and oh by the way we do have a deal"!

Turning to the town lawyer said "Ambrose, suppose you tag along with us seeing that you're gonna have to be the one engaged by the county for a fee of course", thus Ambrose Womble nodded his head and eagerly joined them for the trip to the MHM ranch. An hour later Henry and the town duo were in the barn inspecting the poor souls gathered therein seeing for himself the remains of bad ownership of human resources. Men women and children were all in an emaciated state, the rags gathered, that were once their cloths were still in a pile at the barns entrance ready to be burned. Then as a contrast Henry showed the Judge, the rest of the ranch, built from the ground up over the course of time and the condition of Miss Melanie's help, men, women and children.

"I've seen enough", said the Judge. "Let's go back to the barn and assemble as many of your people as you can for I've something to say to everyone"!

"The Judge being raised in the Alabama and schooled in New Orleans was well accustomed to the concept of slavery and in agreement with its necessity for the white man's progress and he'd seen human property mistreated before, but never to the degree he'd just witnessed".

As he entered the barn he was shortly joined by a dozen of the other of Miss Melanie's darkies and quietly said "Gather round everybody. I've something to tell y'all. Amos Ledbetter is dead and so are all of his sons"! For a moment he was silent, then one by one the former slaves began to cheer as best they could in their condition.

"Now as I've seen for myself you've all been treated very badly but this is going to change, as of now, but to effect this change I'm going to need your help and I've several questions to ask". The Judge was silent for several moments seeking everyone's attention. "Henry Jaeger is the duly appointed Texas Ranger for these parts, appointed by the Governor for life.

And he has willingly agreed to take y'all in and feed and clothe y'all and make you an important part of the MHM ranch and all of its other enterprises, but to have this happen I first need to know is that is this what y'all want to happen?"

The darkies all looked at each other wondering what to do, when the Judge said, "Everyone that wants this to happen raise your hands" and one by one, every hand was raised.

"Good said the Judge, but Henry's gonna need your help, because he committed y'all to harvesting the Ledbetter cotton in exchange for your being a part of the ranch and there's no one that can get it done but y'all, now that all the Ledbetter's are gone. Who amongst you knows anything about harvesting cotton raise your hands"! At that just about everyone raised their hands, men, women and children.

"Good" said the Judge. "Now in two weeks' time we'll need a goodly number of you to be ready to harvest the crop and it looks like some of you just won't be ready and will need more time to get better, so Henry what about your people pitching in as much as possible"?

As Henry looked around he saw every hand raised.

Just then the Judge turned around and asked one of the new darkies, "How long might it take to get the Harvest done"?

The man stood up and meekly said, scratching his head, "Well Judge ah spect it'll take about two or three weeks if'n it doan rain"!

The Judge then put his arm around the man and said, "Well son, just rest up for in two weeks you're gonna be picken cotton most likely for the last time if I know Henry Jaeger".

For the next two weeks, the whole of the enterprise was busy making shoes for fifty people, making clothes for fifty people, with needle and thread along with broad cloth being in short supply sending Henry to town for the necessaries, along with weekly hot bath's for the new people and a bounty of food that started to put meat on their bones.

At the end of two week's time, all but two of the fifty were in sufficient shape to tackle the Ledbetter's fields. All of the myths of darkies being lazy and non-industrious were put to rest as Henry joined in with the rest. Being used to hard work Henry joined everyone each evening more tired than he ever had been.

Every other day the Judge let a small train of wagons to the Ledbetter land to cart off bales of freshly picked cotton, in exchange for loads of fresh victuals for the work. Finally after the fifteenth straight day the fields were bare, with no more cotton to be picked and the worn but happy hands stuffed into the four extra wagons sent to transport them back to the MHM ranch.

Since cotton was in short supply that year, the Judge was able to fetch a high price for the cotton by a broker in Houston, receiving an appropriate commission, in the form of a little Lagniappe for his exertions. Henry was engaged to survey the Ledbetter property into the various sections parceled off by the Judge at public auction and Ambrose Womble as the only lawyer in town was kept busy gathering legal fees for every transaction. Finally in a meeting that lasted a total of ten minutes, Henry Jaeger spent all of ten US dollars of Miss Melanie's money.

With a week off from the new recruits to rest up, Henry and Mendoza started into the building of three new homes for the older members of the expanding clan to make room for the rest of the people in the barns surrounding living spaces. By the end of November, the wheat and corn fields were harvested and the grain stored in the two silos's recently erected on the ranch. All summer long the livestock were busy grazing and multiplying happily with additions made on almost a daily basis.

During the evenings Melanie was busy secretly teaching her young charges to read and write for an hour and a half six nights a week in addition to her mornings at the school house for the white county children. For state law forbade the teaching of slaves to read or write.

After each evening, she would entertain the children and the few adults in her class, with tales straight out of Shakespeare, acting out all of the parts for the evenings entertainment. Every other month, a delegation of either Tonkawa, Cherokee or Anadarko Indians traveled down to the ranch to sell their surplus hides to Henry, in exchange for long horn cattle and or saddle ready horses, both of which Henry had a ready supply. Twice a year, Indian agents and the Army would travel down from Upper Brazos reservation and Ft. Worth to inspect and purchase livestock as needed, paying in hard currency.

Crops were grown in such varieties, that everyone had their bellies full at all times. Trees were felled, the sawmill and the grain mill rolled along and the financial coffers grew at an amazing rate. The ranch was completely self-sustaining by the close of 1856.

A small bank was started in town that had as one of its first depositors the MHM ranch at least in part, with Henry depositing an initial Five Hundred Dollars, the rest well secured in his ranch house via a small underground vault.

Every month Miss Melanie would travel into town with a list of items from each and every family, for purchase with their own monies, silently paid for by the semiannual stipend each working family earned, for the gee gaws, the variety of extras. One could almost call it a communal existence except, values were fixed and periodically adjusted. Henry was tempted to open and account for every one of his people, except for the fact that he wasn't certain of the security of the bank and even more important, he was keenly aware of the sentiments of his neighbors what with all this abolitionist talk running around via the newspapers. His business was his business and he impressed that upon all of the members of his ranch, especially those that worked in the two mills, who interacted daily with outsiders.

Without his people, Henry could not have made the progress that was evident in the previous years and he completely understood the attitudes of his neighbors regarding slavery, but he kept his views on the matter under wraps, never engaging in an exchange of views on the matter and when pressed always quickly averting the discussion to another subject.

As the necessity for additional crops grew, additional fields were carved out of the land scape, with certain folks placed in charge of these fields, which were several miles distant from the main ranch complex, so the necessity for building additional homes came to the fore, in which all were put to work to accomplish that task, ever mindful of the homes security from hostile attack and its self-sustainability.

When harvest time came each year, all were engaged in the gleaning of the various fields, into the various silos erected. Selling part to various traders and retaining part for the use of the ranch. Yet from deep in the recesses of Henrys mind grew the notion, that in spite of the Lord being his Shepard, things were going too well. Yes he now had a contingent of twenty odd Buffalo Vaqueros that could function every bit as well as those of Don Fuentes long ago, thanks to the efforts of Juan Mendoza and of these better than half, had shown a real ability with firearms when on the hunt with Henry and could function as a decent tracker if needed. His love, Miss Melanie had gifted him with another son, which she named Michael, after the biblical Angel of the Lord responsible for "Putting the Whack on the agents of Satan", as she was wont to often say. From time to time Henry would roll around the name in his head, 'Michael Jaeger, The hunter and slayer of the demons'. Time would tell if he would live up to his name, but Henry was certain to afford any of his children the knowledge gleaned from his many years in this world. From his perspective, his children were expected to exceed him in everything possible.

Last year he sent a letter to Don Domingo telling him of where he was and what he was doing and inquired as to how little Rodrigo was progressing. But given the still tense state of affairs down along the Rio Grande Valley, he had little expectation of the letter reaching its destination, and if so its ability to be returned. Every so often he thought of little Rodrigo, but that immediately brought of his time with Joselita and he felt immediate guilt, for his heart now belonged to Melanie and the bond was total and complete.

From time to time he wanted to tell Melanie of his marriage to Joselita and of her death in childbirth, but cowardice took hold every time. Odd how in his entire life he was afraid of no mortal in a physical sense, but when dealing with the unseen, the deep abyss of a woman's feelings and emotions, he was the prince of reluctance. Yet since he'd come to know her Miss Melanie, never once exhibited the typical emotional ebb and flow that he'd seen in other women. Hers was an even handed flow, generally cheerful and helpful, giving to all initially and eventually being rewarded by others in ways both great and small. Praising in public and mildly admonishing in private in an even handed manner. Using anger only when it was called for, yet even then never being critical or demeaning of others, except in only the rarest and most well-earned occasions. All of this and wrapped in such a package that it was impossible for anyone to but cherish her very existence. A walking, talking example of that of Latin saying; "To be loved, first, one must be loveable"!

She truly loved every one of her darkies, tending to them when they were sick, making certain they had all they needed and often being a whirlwind of activity. For certain, one could make an argument of her simply taking care of an investment, but it went far beyond that, for even at the evening dinner table she was truly expressive of each and every birth and malady for one and all. As hard as Henry worked, he truly believed she worked harder. She always set the example. Perhaps it was the correspondence she carried on with Mary Maverick in San Antonio several times a year that instilled in her a sense of grit and sand, while being wrought with a sense of gentile style and graciousness.

He vowed that when he returned this evening he would surprise her with simple affection that was long overdue.

From time to time Henry's skill at surveying was called upon by the newly arrived settlers to survey and register their homesteads for the county and the state. Whereupon he would siphon off a few of the workers, who achieved a semblance of writing and ciphering skills for a simple and welcomed vacation from their daily toils, thus training them in the rudimentary aspects of surveying. Never gone from the ranch for more than three days at a time, Henry would always deliver the results of his work to either the County Judge or Lawyer Womble, for full registration. Then usually a visit to the general store to spend the entire fee for his efforts for candy, tobacco, snuff and an assortment of minor baubles for one and all.

The darkies would follow him where ever he went thus giving the towns people an opportunity to become accustomed to them in the event they visited them on an errand. Then he would visit the newly hired town Constable to see if he were needed. While the Constable was technically paid for and under the aegis of the County Judge, and Henry, as a Ranger was in effect, a State employee, with overlapping responsibilities, Henry's reputation was such that no one questioned his word in any given thing. The respect for his history and skills was a known quantity in these parts.

Besides Wiley Rudiger was a former Army Sergeant, with the field artillery, who served in the Northern Campaign, with some moderate distinction, with his own weapons and the skills. At a stipend of thirty US dollars a month, he seemed competent to function within the confines of the town and most of all, was sober and reliable. Taking over the office and the town jail, there was a desk for Henry to work from and full access to the jail at any time of the day or night.

As the winter of 1857 was coming to a close, Henry was returning to town, from one of his surveying forays with two of his people, when a rider approached in a hurry coming to an abrupt halt. "Mr. Jaeger, something terrible has happened", shouted the rider. "The Bank has been robbed and Constable Rudiger has been shot, so ya gots ta come quick".

Covering the last mile town at full gallop, Henry stopped at the bank to survey the scene, seeing the crowd that assembled he pulled to a halt and ran into the bank to see the doctor, ministering to Wiley and another laying wounded by the front door with several of the town's people holding guns on him.

Seeing Jaeger as he knelt down Wiley said, "Sorry Henry there was just too many of em, but I got a bullet into two of em, with one of em being over there", pointing at the fallen miscreant, being held at bay"?

"How many in total", asked Henry?

"Four of em Henry, but one of em is wounded so that oughtta slow em down"!

"How long ago Wiley"?

"Bout a half hour start they's got".

"Just then the banks president Fortune Boudine, came forward holding his head saying, "And they got all of the money Henry"?

"How much"?

"I'd say about seventy six hundred dollars, more or less"! "Which is it more or less"?

"Seventy six hundred dollars Henry"! "Which way'd they go", asked Henry?

"Headin south", came an answer from someone in the crowd.

"You all right Fortune".

"Nothing' a right smart pistol whippin wouldn't give me", Boudine answered holding a bloody handkerchief to his head.

"Ya gonna go git em Henry"?

"Fortune, a good bit of that money is mine ain't it?

Just then Henry turned his attention to the wounded robber on the floor, walking over to him and grabbing him by the shirt collar and dragging him to the streets, summoning his two darkies to haul the hapless robber over the hitching post as Henry removed the bull whip from his saddle. As the darkies stepped aside, with the robber tied upon the post Henry said, in full view of the crowd, "I'm gonna ask you this just once, what direction are your boys headed"?

Groaning from the bullet wound to his side, the robber said, "Like the man inside said" and before another word came out, he felt the jolt from the bull whip lash across his back, ripping a wide path tearing both the shirt and a large gouge out of his skin. Never in his life did he believe such pain could happen. So great was the blow that it took the breath away, leaving him gasping.

"Wrong answer", whispered Henry. "I'll give ya one last chance to come clean then it won't matter for I'll get em no matter what".

"Five miles down the road there's a cutoff through the woods and they'll be headin' west, into Injun country cause they didn't reckon nobody's follow em there"! "Well they reckoned wrong", said Henry.

"You better be right hombre', for if you told me wrong your live won't be worth a plug nickel" Then he looked at the crowd and said, "This man stays where he is till I return and lord help the man or woman that tries to help him in any way".

"Now pilgrim I'm gonna leave ya something to remember me by", and with that said he administered a dozen mighty lashes with the bull whip, each one with the full force of every muscle in his body. Each one, bringing untold pain and leaving a deep wound through the skin and down to the under laying muscle. By the sixth blow the man hung limp, from the hitching post.

"No one comes close to him until I return", bellowed Henry as he swung up to his saddle, and followed by his two Buffalo Vaqueros who followed him out of town at full gallop.

Slowing down to a canter, Henry could plainly follow the tracks in the trail softened by the pre spring rains. Four fresh sets of tracks, with one of them less indented than the rest indicating the horse was without a rider and another set of tracks, trailing off erratically back and forth, indicating the rider was not in charge of the horse, but otherwise.

'That rider must've been the one who caught one of Wiley's bullets,' thought Henry as the trio trudged forward, with Henry providing a running commentary for his vaqueros to learn from. He could further tell by the length of the strides and the depth of the tracks, the riders were pushing their mounts for all they were worth, in the effort to put as much distance between them and any pursuers. At that rate if they weren't careful they would ride their horses into the ground, thus making their capture all the easier.

True to his word, five miles down the trail, the tracks took an abrupt right hand turn into the brush, which all followed, with Henry saying, "Stay alert boys, the fun is about to begin"!

The Vaqueros eyes became wide with fright, for nothing in their life were had prepared them for a situation such as this. All they had to go by was their faith and confidence in Henry Jaeger to guide them as to what to do. For slaves to pursue free white men in the south was unheard of, no matter what the provocation.

Henry directed his men to see well into the trees and by a series of pre rehearsed chirps and hand signs alert him to anything that looked out of place, while he concentrated on the tracks.

An hour later, they came upon a lone horse, wandering in a clearing and minutes later a horseless rider crawling in his last moments of life.

Henry dismounted, and turned the robber over on his back, so wounded he was through the lungs that it was a miracle he even got this far. He looked into the man's eyes which were growing dim and decided that he was not any longer the issue and reached for his bowie knife, looking into the man's eyes and said, "Good bye sport" and plunged the knife deep into the man's throat, then tightly secured the man's horses reins to his belt and said, "That'll keep em in this spot for awhile", then jumped into his saddle and continued the pursuit.

A few hours later the trio cautiously saw movements of two riders with a trailing horse high on a ridge about a mile away. The horses were moving slowly indicating that they were just about played out. Henry passed the eyeglass to each one of his Vaqueros as to fix their quarry. Then he directed both of his Vaqueros to carefully ride around and ahead of the remaining robbers, noting the straight on direction they were taking and Henry would dog them from behind catching them in a pincer movement.

"Keep them in your sight, but also keep me in your sight and I'll drive them to you. If they even twitch kill em both"!

"But Massa Henry, a nigger killing a white man", questioned one of them?

Henry answered, "Have I ever treated you like a nigger? Have I ever lied to you? As long as I draw breath, no man ever will in my presence or that'll be the last thing he ever does! Besides y'all are my unofficial deputies and will be getting back all of the money from the robbers. I'll wager those in town won't give a care just who pulled the trigger should it ever come to that"! Then as an afterthought said, "And it probably will, so now get along now". As the ridge riders continued never once looking back, Henry kept both of his men in sight as they rode fast in the encircling moment around the now slow moving robbers.

Then as his men disappeared from sight, the robbers likewise moved over the ridge out of sight, prompting him to move forward. As he neared the top of the ridge he dismounted and pulled out his spy glass and saw the slowly fleeing duo making their way across a wide valley towards a tree line about a mile distant from them. Hoping that his men were in that tree line somewhere ahead of the robbers, he decided to press the issue and mounted his horse and rode down the side of the ridge in an oblique right angle to the robbers, hoping that at some point they would look back, but not too soon. Perhaps when he got within a quarter mile of them. Then that would drive them right towards his men and their destiny with the devil.

Now at a three quarter gallop, his Colt revolver in his right hand and the reins in his left, He spurred his horse into a full gallop, then just as they were about fifty yards from the brush, both of them stopped, turned pulled their weapons started to take aim and Henry heard two musket shots in quick succession ring out and both robbers were jerked from their saddles by the driving force of two sixty caliber musket balls slamming into them.

As Henry approached the duo he could see they were both dead even before they hit the ground, tightly holding the reins of their mounts in a death grip, with their mouths both agape and their eyes wide open. Both of them had US Army issue Colt revolvers, which Henry could tell was of recent issue and of perhaps even better quality than he possessed, the latest issue. He quickly made note that they would both soon be his.

As the two Buffalo Vaqueros approached, and dismounted they were both in a state of wonderment, for there both of them were, the first men they ever had killed and to boot they both were white.

As Henry arose from the two slain robbers, he looked at his men and said, "Ya done real good today boys! This day is a righteous day for everybody", as he opened the large satchel and showed them the loot the robbers had made off with. "A lotta folks are gonna be real happy with us when we get back to town. A hour after sundown, with the town brightly lit by torch light, the trio wearily came back to town with three naked robbers tied face down on their four horses, all of their belongings bundled into a bunch and hanging from each man's saddle horn as they pulled up to the bank. There, hanging still in place was the first robber, limply secured to the hitching post where Henry had left him and a small crowd gathered around the now dead man from his beating, even though he wasn't about to go anywhere.

The crowd started to cheer as Henry and his men approached, of which the commotion drew out even a larger throng into the street.

Henry dismounted handing the reins of his horse to one of his men and went up the banks steps to hand the large satchel containing all of the county's money to a weary Fortune Boudine, saying "Ya better count it all, but since they had no place to spend it, it's all probably here". Then turning to all the towns folk assembled he yelled out, "And all you fine citizens of Waco, can thank these here two darkies of mine for bringing down the last two robbers and gittin our money back, every last dollar, for it was their bullets that brung down the last two, and Constable Rudiger's bullets that brought down the first two"!

That said at first met with silence, then from somewhere in the crowd came the shout, "Hip, hip, hooray,……hip, hip, hoo ray", with a continuous swell as all assembled in the streets began to pat the still mounted riders with great appreciation and affection as the saviors of their funds.

Henrys men at first didn't know how to respond, but with each successive pat on their legs, and "Huzzah" and "Well done" and "Thank you", they looked at Henry for guidance and he shrugged back at them as if to say, 'You've earned it so enjoy it while it lasts'…

An hour later as they wearily made their way back to the ranch, Henry asked, "Did I lie"?

"No sir ya didn't".

The following morning Henry took position of two newly minted state of the art, 1856 Colt .44 caliber hog legs, as well as two more for a surprised Juan Mendoza and finally the presentation of their older Walker Colt revolvers to the two men that accompanied Henry and two other of the now Senior Buffalo Vaqueros. With a little practice and some training the Vaqueros would probably be the equal of any man, given the 'sand' they showed this day.

The following day, both of the Buffalo Vaqueros that accompanied Henry were the talk of everyone on the ranch, with endless recantations of their great adventure, with Massa Henry in capturing and killing the bank robbers.

Of course with the admonition that they be worn at all times when on the ranch, set aside, whenever they were sent off the ranch, for any given task the way things were, slavery and all, it wouldn't be wise to spook the white folks. Henry traveled into town the next day to see how Constable Rudiger was and after consultation with the town doctor and a visit to the town jail, discovered Wiley behind his desk with his left leg elevated and his left arm in a sling, with several of the towns ladies feeding him freshly baked cherry pie and milk.

"Shouldn't you be in bed restin' up", asked Henry? "Well gotta keep up appearances don't I"?

"You'd be in sad shape if any bank robbers made an appearance any time soon"!

"Well Henry, at least they didn't get my shootin' hand any! Besides, the Judge's temporarily deputized some of the towns folk who're prowlin' around with shot guns till I'm up and around. Besides don't expect any robber's any time soon, once word gets out"!

"Yeah Wiley and lightning' never strikes twice in the same place," said Henry absently.

"The judge ever get them robbers buried"?

"Yeah, and he's angry causin' no one wanted to do it and it cost the county five US dollars for each grave, but I don't expect the graves to be the regulation six feet deep"!

"Well, I expect the wild animals gotta eat too", said Henry.

"You get to keep the horses, Henry"?

"Yeah and the saddles and everything they owned! Gotta get something' for my trouble. Miss Melanie's darkies'll get the clothes after they get washed proper as well as the boots if'n they fit proper, but I expect that they'll fit someone out there. I'll be there very first store bought boots".

"Sorta reminds me of what happened after Buena Vista", offered Wiley, "when old 'Rough an Ready' detailed us all to get up several burial details and those that went into the ground went in buck nekkid and the shoes and boots were the first things to end up as booty. Took a look at some of the dead Mexicans, but the soldiers were all in sandals and the dead officers we saw all had their boots stolen already"!

"Same thing at Monterrey town", Henry replied!

"Anybody make any comments about Miss Melanie's darkies killin' the robbers"?

"Nothin' I heard Henry! Seems that everyone is so grateful and relieved that someone took out those snakes, that it didn't make no never mind who it was, just that it got done"!

'Well, I just wanna make sure that the credit goes to the righteous and in this case, it's you and Miss Melanie's Darkies"!

"Gotta go over to the General Store and pick up some things for the ranch. I'll be back in a couple of days to look in on ya and if ya need anything let me know Wiley"!

"Sure will Henry"!

As Jaeger reached the door, he turned and said, "Oh and good shootin' Wiley"!

16

As the year of 1857 came to a close, Henry was receiving more and more reports of incursions and raids by hostile Comanche and Kiowa Indians, mostly in the areas of western Texas and the southern Indian Territory known as Oklahoma, which was set aside by treaty to be the repository of all misplaced Indian tribes, driven out of the south by President Jackson, years earlier. The territory was not to be settled by white settlers and in no case were state militias to enter the territory for any reason.

Thus this land was set aside as a refuge for all of the Indians who were to settle there, including the war like Comanche and the Kiowa.

The Comanche occupied an area located east of the Edwards plateau on the upper Canadian River in western Oklahoma which became known as 'Comancheria', safe in the knowledge the US Army would not pursue them north of the Red River, the boundary between Texas and Oklahoma, for any reason.

At any rate the Army proved hapless in their feeble attempts to bring the hostiles to justice, responding with far too little and way too late to reports of settler's massacres that were on the rise. Thus proving to be little more than burial parties for the dead. The combined forces of the Comanche and Kiowa tribes would venture south of the Red River and raid not only the white settlements but those tribes friendly to white settlers including their mortal enemy the Tonkawa, who served as scouts for the Texas Rangers on many occasions, as well as the Anadarko, Waco, Cherokee and peaceful Shawnee tribes.

Those tribes north of the Red River that adopted the white man's ways, engaged in peaceful, farming and the raising of livestock met a similar fate as the white settlers. Particularly the Tonkawa tribe, the Comanche's mortal enemy, which was known to dismember and consume the body parts of captured enemies and display them from their ponies as they rode, as part of their long established tribal ritual.

With the sudden transfer of the US Second Cavalry to Utah from Ft Worth, to keep the Mormon settlers in line, the northern border of Texas was without a defense from the marauding hostiles. Now they could freely enter Texas at will, without any concern for their safety.

The Comanche made no distinction between their victims and the treatment of the settlers, with the exception that men old enough to fight were expected never to be captured and to fight to their death. Surrender was considered as an act of cowardice amongst most Indian tribes and so those men who surrendered were usually brutally tortured for a long period always ending in their death.

Young children were tested and should they prove to be healthy, strong and resourceful were adopted into the tribe, while the women were repeatedly and brutally raped then turned over to the other women to be used as slaves. Almost no records exist of women lasting more than a year under those conditions.

In the Gubernatorial elections of 1857 Harden Runnels, was elected Governor of Texas, vowing to bring to an end the Comanche and the Kiowa campaign of terror. Once he had the entire legislature behind him he authorized the recreation of the Texas Ranger Militia, appointing John S. "RIP" Ford as its Captain and Commander of the Rangers and any Allied Indian Forces he could recruit.

The reason for John Ford was simple; The man was never known to take a prisoner. Men women and children all met the same fate. His directives were simple, "To carry the fight to the Comanche's deep into heart of their homeland of the Comancheria on the upper Canadian River. He was further directed to "follow any and all trails of hostile, or suspected hostile tribes discovered, overtake them and chastise them if unfriendly"!

The very first person he was to summon was Henry Jaeger, for he'd not only ridden with Jaeger during the days as a Ranger in the Texas Republic but respected all of his skills in every aspect and knew they could work well together.

Thus in the last week of January 1858, Henry received two letters, one from his old friend John Ford inviting him to meet with him in one week's time at the now largely abandoned Ft. Worth and the second from Governor Runnels placing him as second in command under John Ford and direction him to meet Ford in Ft. Worth to assist Captain Ford in any and every way practicable in the coming venture, bringing to an end the activities of the Chief Iron Jacket and his son Peta Nocona.

Henry called the County fathers together at the ranch to announce to them of his recent assignment by the Governor and to make suggestions as to the safety of the county during the time of his absence. Since Henry was to take two of the slaves with him, on his venture with the Rangers, he suggested that Juan Mendoza along with two of Miss Melanie's darkies be authorized to serve if deemed necessary by the County Magistrate as deputy town Rangers under Wiley. Since they carried side arms on the private property of the MHM ranch, they would be authorized by the authority of the Judge to do the same in the service of the county.

Then he hastily prepared a will, leaving the bulk of his estate to his acknowledged wife Melanie and their children and twenty percent to his trusted associate Juan Mendoza. The will was promptly witnessed by the Judge and placed in Melanie's hand for safe keeping. Since the wolves were needed at the ranch to assist with the livestock and there would be some Indians to assist in the tracking he decided to keep them at home. There were at least a dozen men under Juan's supervision competent in firearms that should be sufficient during Henrys absence, to watch over things.

Later that evening, after all the children went to sleep, Henry awoke and went downstairs, to stoke the fire in the fireplace, since he couldn't seem to sleep. He noticed something attached to his holsters and as he examined the little leather pouch he was about to toss it into the fire, when he saw the inscription that had been skillfully etched into the leather. It was the old Santeria Voodoo symbol of strength and good fortune and immediately knew that it was Melanie's Maddie that was looking after him in her own way. Silently Melanie came down the stairs in her night clothes, to join Henry in front of the fire that he'd built up and sat next to him watching the flames.

"I can't sleep either and its gonna be a rough go for me with you gone and all", mused Melanie. "Besides, I sorta got used to you hanging around" she said holding his hand.

Henry turned his gaze away from the flames of the fire place and looked deeply into her eyes, drinking up every scintilla of her visage.

As he looked at her she asked, "Is anything wrong Henry"?

"No, just that this image of you is going to have to last me awhile and will be the last thing that enters my mind when I fall asleep on the trail each night, for you see I've gotten used to you hanging around"!

Just then as lovers often do when one of them is going to be away in a dangerous place, they came together with a slowly building passion, in front of the fire, lifting their bedclothes to have access to the vital necessaries performing that age old ritual of complete bonding. Passing their hands over each other to cement the image in each other's memory as if it would have to last to eternity. When they were completed Melanie relished in the feel of his rough hands over her. As they lay there together in front of the fire she could feel Henry starting to fall asleep and nudged him saying, "Our bed would be more comfortable Henry, wouldn't it? Might be the very last soft spot you'll feel for a while"!

Henry nodded and allowed her to escort him up the stairs. As she followed him up the stairs, Melanie wanted to cry but repelled that emotion until much after Henry had left.

The man had all he could say grace over for the time being and had to concentrate on what lay ahead without a single concern of what lay behind him. Henry would return as he always had, and everything would be fine.

As Henry rode north with his darkies, he was joined, upon occasion by several people on their way to the big Pow Wow in Ft. Worth, some of which he knew and had ridden with in the past, with an ongoing palaver of old stories adventures and close calls told once again. As each party joined Henry on the trail, they gave a nominal glance at Henry regarding his negro compadre's, but since they rode with Henry Jaeger, they must be all right.

Now numbering over twenty well-armed men, half of which were former Rangers, Henry and his group slowly rode into Ft. Worth, to be greeted with but a squad of US soldiers, commanded by a Sergeant Landingham accompanied by the State appointed Indian Agent for the Upper Brazos Reservation, Captain L.S. Ross.

As Henry dismounted, he saw that out of the Agents Office stepped John Ford, his new Commander and former fellow Ranger going back to the days of the Republic. A thin but wiry, ruddy faced fellow, RIP Ford wasn't a man to be trifled with just like Henry, sporting his Walker Colt revolver along with the requisite Bowie knife on his left hip in cross draw fashion.

As he approached Henry he bellowed, "Gawddamn Henry Jaeger it sure is good to see you again", shaking his hand furiously, then adding, "Good of you to bring some folks along for our little trip up north"!

"Good to see you again John, but these pilgrims and me just fell in together on the here"!

Then Captain Ford made his way around to those, introducing himself to the new fellows and reacquainting himself with those he rode with before. Then directed them all to go up to the Commanders office and sign their name or make their mark so they all could be enrolled and thus paid by the State when this was all over. Henry followed the group sheparding Miss Melanie's darkies in the process to see that nothing went amiss, other than an occasional raised eyebrow, no dissent was proffered by their presence.

When completed the men gathered in the main quadrangle to be fed from the Forts Mess, while Henry was made aware of the situation at hand. As Indian Agent, Captain Ross was the one closest to the events of the day and took charge of informing Henry as to the situation at hand.

"One thing everyone agrees on is that during the winter months, the Comanche and the Kiowa lay low on the Upper Canadian River, puttin' the meat on their bones so when spring comes their war parties can head back into Texas and have their way with us", said Captain Ross. "So we want to hit them hard when the weathers still cold before spring, burn their camps take back the herds that were stolen or as much of it as can be had, and kill every last one of those heathen devils, so that no one's left to head south no more. So just how does that sit with you Henry"?

"Kill every last one of them, including the women and the children", asked Henry?

"The livestock can live", offered Ford.

Over the course of time Henry had mellowed a bit, for that's what being a husband and having children will do to some folks, but he has seen far too much of what the Comanche and the Kiowa had done to the settlers.

Recalling the many graves that were dug and the many children abducted and decided that it was finally time for these Indians to pay the piper.

"So I'm told we're gonna have some friendlies to join us! When's that gonna happen"?

Ford smiled and said, "The three of us are gonna have a palaver with

Chief Placido of the Tonkawa, tomorrow at his camp upstream from here.

The States gonna have to pay us, but Placido and his tribe should be with us since they've been on the receiving end of things just like the settlers and we just might get em for free, if we play our cards right."

"Gonna be some Cherokee and Anadarko there too". Continuing he said, "Counting y'all's arrival we number around eighty armed men, but we're up against the entire Comanche and most of the Kiowa nations, so no telling how many they got. One thing though, some of em are armed with Muskets, but they use em most for Buffalo huntin'"!

"Gonna try and get as many of the Indians to ride with us and they should be up for a good tussle with the Comanche"!

"So no one has a problem with the Tonkawa being Cannibals", asked Henry?

"Nope, as long as all they eat are Comanche, I'll be fine", said Ford seeing a grin of agreement by Henry.

"The Army was nice enough to leave considerable shot and powder along with vittles for the trail and I've the assurance from Sergeant Landingham that we've access to all that we need, just as long as he and his men don't have at come along", said Captain Ross.

"Ya know after all the time I spent in Mexico I developed a taste for that thing they drink called 'Pulque'", mused Henry, sorta hit's the spot when it comes to gittin rid of the trail dust from a man's throat"!

"Well, don't know about no Pulque, but I think a jug of Old Overshoes just might be available to suit your needs Captain Jaeger", offered Captain Ross and he rose up to retrieve the jug from a shelf.

Turning to Ford Henry asked, "What role do you want me to play in this John"?

"Well Henry, I'd like you to head up the Indians along with whoever they send to run them on their side. Keep em in line as much as possible. They all know you by reputation, and since none of us can read trail like you and upon occasion, you've been known to be just as vicious as them if not more so, I figure your just the man to give them orders. For if'n they'll listen to anyone they'll listen to you"!

"Then that's the way it'll be John. Just one thing, if ever our units get split up and we both know that's possible, I'll want to send one or both of my darkies to you as messenger. Their as reliable as anyone I've known and if they tell you anything, consider that it's come from my mouth directly".

"Then that's the way it'll be Henry", replied Ford who then spit in his hand and offered it to Jaeger, who did likewise and they sealed the agreement. The following morning Ford, Jaeger and Ross along with six others rode out to the Tonkawan encampment for the big War Council with Chief Placido and the chiefs of the Anadarko, Cherokee and the Shawnee. Captain Ross took the lead in stirring up the various chiefs anger against their mutual traditional enemy, the Comanche Nation, reminding them of the scores of raids and women and children killed along with the countless livestock stolen. The Comanche and the Kiowa prospered at the expense of others.

When he concluded, over a hundred Tonkawan warriors jumped up along with another forty Cherokee, Anadarko and Shawnee. It was agreed that all of the tribes would serve under and answer to Chief Placido of the Tonkawa who would be guided by and serve under Captain Henry Jaeger, of the Rangers, known by the Shawnee as the "Ghost Dancer".

The head of the small contingent of Shawnee stood up and told of Henrys pursuit of the dreaded renegade Red Hair who slew Henry's family as a child then each and every one who took part in that action was slain by the "Ghost Dancer". Further he related that on the very spot that the Red Hair was slain, Henry built his ranch which thrives to this very day. Finally he turned to Henry and thanked him for erasing the stain on a small but proud people, asking him for his forgiveness. Then he turned to all assembled and proclaimed that his ten braves would be proud to join Chief Placido and the "Ghost Dancer", in their war against the Comanche.

When he had finished, the braves all stood up as one and shouted. The pipe was then passed around to all the chiefs and they agreed to assemble in three days' time for the trip to Comancheria.

But as usually is the case, the very nature of their cause was certain to summon a hoard of reasons not to depart as planned. Starting with the tardy arrival of sufficient members to form the militia unit, arriving in twos and threes, then a seemingly minor dispute amongst the tribes as to the leadership required the State Indian Agent Captain Ross, to go to their camp to resolve the problem. So upon his return he fell from his horse breaking his arm, requiring his being left behind, this signaled an ill omen for the campaign.

But several days later, the Rangers ranks swelled to a hundred and twenty five competent men accompanied by a hundred and fifty members of the coalition of the tribes. As they made their way overland towards the Red River, they were accompanied by a reporter from the State Times a newspaper in Austin, whose purpose was to act as a chronicler of the venture as well as a reporter for his newspaper.

As Ford led his column across the Red River in the dead of winter, into Indian Territory, he was peppered with questions about his willful violations of federal laws and treaties, finally spitting out testily, "Young man, the job is to fight the hostiles where ever they may be, not learn about geography"!

Henry took an advance contingent of Cherokee, Shawnee and Anadarko scouts out ahead to follow the trail towards Comancheria on the Upper Canadian River. The trail was well worn by each successive raid made into Texas and its resultant return with significant numbers of horses and cattle in their wake.

Henry thought to himself, 'Even a blind man could follow this trail', yet as the days went by and they grew closer to Comancheria, crossing the Washita River, Henry insisted on cold camps at night and drawing his scouts to hang a little closer to the tree line, lest they be seen by a Comanche hunting party. When greeted by some questions about the need of the cold camp at night, in the winter, Henry responded, "Don't hear the Indians complainin' do ya"?

"This is supposed to be a surprise party and I'm not about givin' the heathens an invite"! After three weeks on the trail, the scouts could see signs of hunting parties of Comanche and Kiowa far in the distance, which apparently didn't expect anyone this far from Texas and were intent on hunting game to feed their tribes.

Lying very still in the tall grass, of Northwest Oklahoma Territory, Henry was grateful for the company of scouts for they were as patient as Henry had long ago learned to be when stalking prey. Hunting wild animals that have no apparent ability to reason is one thing, but hunting human beings, who are savvy to the ways of the stalk, is an entirely different matter. Five miles back was the main party of Rangers and

Indians and Henry sent one of his darkies back to Captain Ford to tell him of his discoveries.

Two more difficult days of reconnoitering were necessary to get a feel for where the various Comanche and Kiowa camps lay on the Upper Bend of the Canadian river in the Antelope Hills. The river as it faced them flowed in a south easterly direction, buy as they approached it bent north for about ten miles then west for another five miles, then finally southwesterly for another five miles presenting them with an inverted horseshoe grouping of four of five camps each around five miles distant from each other all around the northern bend of the horseshoe. The Comanche Chief Iron Jacket was sighted at the third camp in line at the top of the Canadian River horseshoe and his son Peta Nocona was sighted at the far western encampment.

The nearest encampment in the line of attack was the smallest, with but only two dozen Winter Lodges and the second encampment had double that many being five miles distant, with herds of horses and cattle grazing nearby at each. The first camp was for some reason, placed a mile west of the river, while the other camps were close on to the river.

Going back to the main encampment Henry set out his pickets at sundown authorizing several fires to be built in the tree copses during the night to warm the men and the horses for the coming day's battle.

The hostiles, being completely unaware of the invading force of Texican's and Indians went to sleep that night certain of the sunrise the following morning. As Henry drew a diagram of the enemy encampments on the ground in front of the campfire he offered the plan of attack to Ford and the accompanying lieutenants of the tribes.

Attacking out of the east at sunrise he suggested the Tonkawa have the honor of attacking the village first, silently with bows and arrows and in silence with no war cries and that the village be surrounded by the other tribes to eliminate any that might escape to warn the others. That quickly accomplished they would assemble and ride northward to the second village attacking from the south the larger village of about fifty Lodges, with the same plan. That accomplished they would ride to the third village of about a hundred and fifty lodges where he was certain Iron Jacket was encamped.

There they would attack in force with the Tonkawa in the center and the Rangers on each wing of the attack.

Chief Placido of the Tonkawa grunted his approval as everyone broke up to join their respective contingents to get some sleep.

"Great plan Henry. Attack them with the sun at your rear and in silence.

Sorta reminds me of how we did it years ago when we were after the Comanch way west of Hondo and we were after the white children. A lot less of us then", said John Ford!

"Yeah, but I don't recall us getting the children back John"!

"Well that's just one less thing we gotta worry about now Henry. Just hope the Tonkawa Don't go off half-cocked and keep quiet for the initial attacks." "I'm thinking about splitting off Jim Pockmark and having him ride with us for he's the only one of the Tonkawa with a Buffalo Gun and I hear he's a pretty fair shot, for when we get Iron Jacket in sight. Then we can maybe reach out and touch him together and put to rest the myth that his breath can blow bullets away", Said Henry!

"As I hear he likes to show off and ride in front of the enemy and rally his warriors by daring us to waist our ammunition by shooting at him, the moving target. Well between Pockmark and me, one of us will shoot the horse, bringing him down, then the other will plug him for fair as he gets up"!

"Henry Jaeger, I certainly do like how you think", scoffed Ford as he folded the saddle blanket over him.

Very early the following morning, Henry woke up the camp, putting his fingers to his lips indicating that from here on out silence was to be observed. Sign language and whispers only, until indicated otherwise. He went to Chief Placidio and asked that Jim Pockmark be allowed to ride with him, explaining his reasons to the chief who agreed.

Within a half hours' time, both groups were on their mounts, the morning's pemmican being chewed for sustenance and they were off in the direction of the first and smallest village of their targets. A small rise separated the groups from the first village, as a scout went up to the summit then returned signaling the village was all asleep. The wind was coming straight out of the north so the village dogs would not gain their scent. Both groups then split up, with Henry leading the Tonkawa east towards the Canadian river and Captain Ford taking the rest around the rise west of the encampment to stop any that tried to escape. Bows and arrows only for the first two villages. No war hoops or shouting. No stopping to take scalps or souvenir body parts. No immediate torching of the village. For there would be plenty of time for that upon their return. In and out quickly inflicting maximum casualties.

A half hour before sunrise all elements were in place and the horses were all made to lie down and wait in silence. As the sun started to rise in the east, Henry correctly noted that a vast shadow would mask the Tonkawa's approach as the sun rose above the hills behind them shining in the eyes of the Comanche. That and the north wind should provide them with complete surprise in their attack. John Ford lay on the ground west of the Comanche encampment with his small shaving mirror in hand as he'd done once before, waiting for the precise time when half of the morning sun was above the horizon. At that very moment he could see a few of the men and women emerge from their Tee Pees, starting their morning ritual, when he flicked the mirror once then a second time. Then put it away and waited. Just then one of the squaws in the camp trying to rekindle the morning fire from the previous night's embers, noted out of the corner of her eye a brief flash of light, pausing for a moment, then seeing nothing else, returned to her task.

Seeing the dual flashes from Fords shaving mirror, Henry arose with his mount signaling all the others to do the same. He then rode along the length of the hundred warrior skirmish line holding his finger to his lips, reminding all of silence. Then he turned his mount westward and started off in a canter, as the entire skirmish line of mounted warriors followed en masse. After the line went a half mile Henry picked up the pace followed by the warriors. As they rode, they could see people emerging from their shelters rubbing the sleep from their eyes oblivious of what was shortly to come, then a quarter mile from the encampment, Henry broke into a full gallop again followed by the Tonkawa in full discipline thus far. One by one, the encampment could feel the rumbling of the ground made by approaching horses, but looking in all directions for what felt like a stampeding herd saw nothing until it was too late as arrows started to one by one find their mark in the startled Comanche.

Henry, his two Buffalo Vaqueros and Jim Pockmark, pulled up at the edge of the village allowing the Tonkawa to do their grisly work. Arrows found their mark, bringing down everyone in a matter of a few minutes, and then the warriors dismounted and went around silently finishing off each and every one. Men, women and children all were dispatched in a matter of minutes.

The Tonkawa quickly remounted and followed Henry north where the second encampment was closer on to the Canadian river, requiring them to attack from the south and surround from the west. The second encampment was twice the size of the first, but the battle plan was the same, Tonkawans in the lead and everyone else to contain.

All the arrows were removed from the first victims for reuse on the second and again and again. The more bloody arrows a warrior had in his quiver, the greater his respect by others.

A half hour later, the sun still in the ascendancy Henry again gave the signal and the Tonkawan warriors again moved out following Henrys every move. When he speeded up they followed in his wake.

This time the surprise wasn't so complete for they were finally sighted a half mile from the sleepy encampment and some of the warriors started to break for their horses, yet the end result was the same as the first encampment. Yet this time some of the Cherokee and Anadarko on the north and west made their arrows speak for them brining down escaping warriors as they fled to alert the other encampments of attack.

This time some of the Tonkawa were foolish enough to dismount and finish things before they were certain the Comanche was fully disabled. As they kneeled to deliver the Coup de grace, they were surprised to find a Comanche knife disemboweling them. One of which even with four arrows in him was covered in the foolish Tonkawans blood when three additional arrows arrived to silence him before he could cry out. It took longer this time to complete the task, but in the space of slightly less than twenty minutes, two Comanche encampments were obliterated completely without a shot being fired and with only two casualties. The Tonkawa were ecstatic, for years they had suffered at the hands of the Comanche and in a very short time had brought to an end, the lives of over a hundred warriors and well over twice that amount in women and children, never to grow up to savage the Tonkawans ever again. Much coup was achieved this day. There was not one Tonkawan warrior that did not have the blood of another warrior and their family not on him. As they mounted their horses they were all beaming in delight. As they followed Jaeger and Ford northward they would now face their stiffest task, the village of Iron Jacket, with well over a hundred Tee Pees surrounded by a well-guarded herd of horses and cattle that ran into the hundreds. The village lay right on the banks of the northern most bend of the Canadian River, split in two by the shallow Little Robe Creek, which flowed north into the Canadian River. This time the sun was well into mid-morning, yet the wind was still coming out of the north and in their faces. The elements of complete surprise were now gone, yet from appearances Iron Jackets encampment was unaware of the danger that was about to befall him.

Still and all what had worked still might be a viable plan for the larger camp of Iron Jacket. What worried both Ford and Jaeger was the even larger encampment of Iron Jackets son Peta Nocona that lay some fifteen miles southwest, upriver from Iron Jackets camp. Twice the size of Iron Jackets, with twice the warriors. While the first two attacks went smoothly, what lay ahead would prove a problem and if Peta Nocona was alerted and arrived to his father's rescue with yet hundreds more warriors, then other encampments upstream on the Canadian river, if they were ever alerted, Jaeger and Ford agreed they had not sufficient ammunition.

Helping their situation, were the small hillocks and their attendant trees that ringed both banks of the Little Robe Creek which provided cover. Yet again dividing his forces Ford decided to place half of the Tonkawa with him and transfer half of the Rangers to Jaeger providing equal fire power to both groups, ceding the frontal attack to Jaeger and his group-which was to attack from the south east with some of the suns shielding benefits while Fords contingent was primarily to contain from the south and west.

Given the bulk of the herds were on the east side of Little Robe Creek, Henry decided that to start a stampede of livestock into the Comanche camp and follow his attack on the heels of the stampede.

It came to the Anadarko scouts to arrive upon a solution of how to quietly stampede. In minutes, the entire herd of peacefully grazing livestock turned and charged northward into the Comanche village, through campfires, Tee Pees, trampling women, children and some unsuspecting warriors. Followed close at hand by the Rangers and the Tonkawan's firing as they rode on targets as they came to bear. Unfortunately Iron Jacket was camped on the western side of Little Robe Creek, hearing the commotion ran from his tent already dressed in his flowing war bonnet and the Chain Mail Cuirassier, he'd taken from a slain Spanish soldier some forty years earlier. For decades he'd fostered the idea and myth of his apparent supernatural invincibility amongst the other tribes and to both Anglo and Mexican victims of his numerous raids. He would ride back and forth in front of his warriors just within firing range of those he was attacking daring them to fire on him, the moving and weaving target and on those rare occasions a bullet did find its way to his torso it was usually in the final throes of its impactability and running into the chain mail provided little more than a small bruise.

The live stocks initial charge, now petering out found the, entering Little Robe Creek and heading into the western half of the village. Iron Jacket mustered his braves to divert the frightened animals away from the shelters, while his brethren across the creek were having a hard time of it, for the moment.

On their own initiative, several of Iron Jackets warriors rode westward to alert Peta Nocona two of which were gunned down by the Rangers, while one escaped unseen by anyone riding hard on the banks of the Canadian River downstream ten miles to alert Peta Nocona and the other encampments. In several hours, some five hundred or more Comanche and Kiowa mounted tribesmen would arrive.

The surviving Comanche on the eastern side of Little Robe Creek put up a stiff resistance, with their arrows finding targets of the Tonkawa and several Rangers alike and it took some fifteen minutes of sometimes hand to hand fighting until the very last of them fell. With dead bodies everywhere, there was no time to count the dead, for as Henry looked westward he could see trouble.

For on the west bank of the creek, Iron Jacket had rallied his remaining warriors numbering well over a hundred and started to attack John Ford's contingent rather than Henrys, who was by now whittled down by twenty or more riders.

Yet Henry in striving to make quick work of the Comanche rallied his forces and crossed the creek to present Iron Jacket with a hammer and anvil fighting problem, since the Comanche were giving Fords people several kinds of fits.

Their ability to fire numerous arrows from a bare backed horse while at full gallop and hit a target astounded the most hardened Indian fighter.

"Fire at the horses", yelled Captain Ford and while many did, their marksmanship came into question, with more bullets that not missing their targets. Every once in a while a horse would tumble and a cheer would go up and once in a while the warrior would stay put. But quite often the brave would struggle to get up, fire several arrows before succumbing to a hail of bullets.

Out in the open plains, it was a matter of time before Iron Jackets warriors were whittled down, as time and again Iron Jacket rode through a hail of gunfire only to emerge seemingly unscathed.

As Henry and Jim Pockmark, the Tonkawan buffalo hunter dismounted, they set up their rifles on firing sticks to steady their aim. He was armed with a .60 caliber Hawken Buffalo rifle, which never failed to bring down a buffalo. By previous agreement Pockmark agreed to aim for Iron Jackets horse while Henry would finish him off should he ever arise.

"You know they say that Iron Jacket is a man in his sixties", said Pockmark as he set up his firing position.

"Ya ready Jim," asked Henry as he followed Iron Jacket. Pockmark nodded his head, took a deep breath, letting it out slowly, then the big Buffalo Gun roared and bucked back. Iron Horse's mount staggered then continued on for Pockmark had hit the horse yet in its hind quarters.

Quickly at a range of seventy yards Henry's Beretta spoke, hitting the struggling horse in the front shoulder, bringing it crashing to the ground.

For a moment all were stunned, then slowly Iron Jacket somehow slowly rose up, clearly dazed from the fall as several of his warriors tried to ride to his rescue.

Just before they arrived and Iron Jacket turned towards Henry, the second barrel of the big Beretta .70 caliber spoke for the final time, knocking Iron Jacket backwards, dead before he ever hit the ground.

Cheers arose from every corner of the battlefield, yet the Comanche now without their sacred leader were now a shadow of their former selves, dispirited and confused.

Rather than rally, the Comanche fled the field for a large, thickly populated copse of trees, where they could find a brief respite from the murderous gunfire of the Texans. Yet rather than quickly follow up, the Tonkawan tribesmen fell upon the dead body of Iron Jacket as well as several Rangers eager for a souvenir. Iron Jackets chain mail cuirass was taken by the Rangers and parceled out while Iron Jacket was immediately dismembered and his body parts were amply distributed and consumed as war booty to the eager Tonkawan warriors.

Both Jaeger and Ford on both sides of the battlefield came to the conclusion that discipline for some can only carry so far. Henry became increasingly concerned as the fight drug on with a large number of the surviving Comanche warriors making repeated attempts to retrieve what was left of the body of Iron Jacket, but beaten back each time by both the Rangers and the Tonkawan warriors, both eager for their souvenirs. He sought out Placido, Chief of the Tonkawa, to rein his warriors in and to attack the survivor.

But as they spoke Henry spotted additional horsemen, Comanche by the look of it, starting to join the fray, then a shout as all the Comanche left the field in the direction of the deep copse of trees.

Just then a Cherokee scout rode up alerting them all to the arrival of Chief Peta Nocona, Iron Jackets son, with reinforcements from the other villages along the Canadian River. Captain Ford then ordered all of the Rangers to array themselves in a picket line by laying down their horses as well as all the Tonkawan warriors in a long defensive line. The only ones still mounted were Ford, Jaeger and Chief Placido who rode along the picket line both calming and alerting their respective forces.

Emerging from the forest some two hundred yards away, was a single Comanche rider and then another, riding his pony several yards behind him. Handing his spy glass to Jim Pockmark, the Tonkawan buffalo hunter Henry asked, "Is that Peta Nocona"? Pockmark took the spy glass and peered through it saying, "Yes and his grandson, little Quanah Parker is at his side and they are soon to be joined by others if my guess is right"!

From across the wide expanse of the field of battle he could hear Chief Nocona shout for all of 'them' to come and get them.

But Captain Ford, recalling all of the mistakes made by the Rangers during their numerous encounters, with the Comanche during his time with the Rangers during the Texas Republic, grabbed Chief Placido and rode up and down the line exhorting the Rangers and Tonkawan tribesmen to "Hold Fast"!

The forests would give the Comanche the advantage of putting their bows and arrows into play, negating the firepower of the Rangers with their repeating weapons and single shot rifles.

Then after several minutes, Peta Nocona issued a plea to allow his men to retrieve the mutilated body of his father, Pobishequasho, 'Iron Jacket', who lay between them. When no reply was received a lone Comanche brave rode slowly out of the forest and toward the body of Iron Jacket.

Suddenly a shout came from one of the Tonkowan warriors and up came his horse with the warrior on it and charged towards the Comanche to do single combat battle over Iron Jackets remains.

After several intense minutes of hand to hand battle on horseback, the Tonkowan warrior, fell from his mount, just yards away from Iron Jacket to join him on his eternal journey. As this happened, the victorious Comanche Warrior withdrew and was immediately replaced by another to greet yet a second charging Tonkowan Warrior to do single combat. For this was their way.

After the second Tonkowan Warrior fell in eternal disgrace, the second victorious Comanche withdrew, immediately replaced by another. Then went on repeatedly and each time a Tonkowan Warrior came up short and by the seventh combat, a Tonkowan Warrior finally proved victorious, riding back to his fellows, passing his replacement, who eagerly charged forth, to a tumultuous shouting.

"Well, at least we got one of em," commented Ford sardonically, to Chief Placido who was content to allow the combat continue, for it was their way. "My folks were German immigrants", said Henry to John Ford continuing, "and while I was growing up, my 'Papi' used to have a favorite word whenever he took delight in someone else's misfortune and the word was "Schadenfreude", which means "Better them than us"!

"Schadenfreude eh", replied Ford? "I'll have to keep that in mind"! As the eighth combat began a female squaw emerged from the Comanche glade charging at full speed at the Tonkowan, who cut loose with two arrows from his bow in quick succession, each missing their target by a whisker and as they passed each other her lance found a home deep in the Tonkawans midsection penetrating completely through. As she passed, the force of the thrust tore the lance from her hands and she turned her horse quickly around in triumph and rode up to the now stopped Tonkowan warrior, who stubbornly refused to fall from his mount and pulled her lance slowly from his midst, speaking inaudible words of distain for his abilities, then kicking him from his horse as she rode triumphantly back to her shouting people.

When no other Tonkowans charged forward Henry said to Chief Placido, "I think it's time to take our winnings and depart. Then he directed Placido to have his men burn each Tee Pee and Hogan to the ground in all the villages they visited in advance of their retreat. Soon a dozen Tonkowan braves departed, to affect that task.

To cover their efforts a steady but intermittent covering fire came from the Rangers for the next half hour, while another dozen Tonkowan warriors risked their lives in retrieving Iron Jackets mutilated body back to their lines. After all that had happened, this would be proof positive of their Warrior Coup.

With additional Comanche warriors certain to be arriving, Jaeger and Ford quickly agreed that complete retrieval of the livestock was probably not in the cards. And as the first Tee Pee's west of the creek went up in flames, enough of the Rangers and Cherokee scouts drove what livestock was west of the creek, back across the creek to join the herds mulling around the east side.

Minutes later when the flames of the eastern Comanche encampment began to be visible the remainder of Rangers and Tonkowans retreated slowly across the Little Robe Creek and joined the others in a huge stampede of livestock back from whence they came, passing the second encampment, setting fire to it and then the first. As they passed the first, what was left of the horses and cattle were now all played out and slowed to a crawl. While horses can run on for some ten miles before tiring, cattle are just not built that way and while a number of exhausted cattle still were with them, a long line of cattle moved slowly, mounds of steam, streaming from their exhausted bodies, on this chill winter day.

As they rode south, with the sun indicating high noon overhead, they placed a line of Anadarko scouts in their rear to cover their retreat. While the objective was not completely reached, all in all they had a rather good day. A huge bite had been taken out of the Comanche hide, with hundreds of warriors slain and an innumerable number of women and children following in their wake. Far less to give birth to future warriors and those future warriors in training, ceased to exist.

As far as Ford could see, a dozen Rangers were not going to make it back, while the Tonkawan's suffered the most with their numbers literally cut in half as they licked their wounds. Still, for the moment they had possession of the remains of Iron Jacket and for them that counted for a lot. Things would be very dicey for several weeks as they rode south slowed by the progress of the cattle and horses but in a pinch they could always cut loose some of the cattle for any pursuing Comanche and skedaddle. If they all crossed the Red River in one piece then this foray could be called a success. For the first few nights they held a cold camp, but as the successive days came and went the weather became colder, and fires were lit each night to warm the Rangers and the Indians. With each passing day the herd was joined by a few additional cattle that apparently trudged on valiantly to catch up with family members in the large herd.

Yet with each passing day the rear guard of Anadarko scouts, reported no signs of pursuing Comanche. Apparently the beating they suffered along with last the cold weather of the winter dissuaded them of pursuit. As they finally crossed the Red River, at Jonas Ford, the Tonkawa suffered their last indignity thanks to Comanche Providence. As the horse carrying the remains of Iron Jacket struggled to swim across the river the body of Iron Jacket somehow broke loose of its apparently less than secure bindings and floated away downstream. Everyone was tired and the weather was cold and the Tonkawan followed the body downstream as far as they could, hoping the body would come near shore, but the body stayed in mid-stream as if tethered by some celestial rope and after some ten miles sank in the middle of an eddy current never to be seen again.

Across the Red River and back in Texas, with a larger than expected herd and the Comanche in apparent disarray for the foreseen future, all agreed it was a very good venture.

Ten days later the entire group entered the Fort Worth, greeted by Captain Ross. Most important was the parceling out of cattle and horses to the surviving Indians of the war party, with over three hundred cattle and two hundred mustang horses, it was agreed that seventy five head of long horns and fifty mustangs should be apportioned to the Indians for their efforts, while the rest be held in stasis for the various claimants of stolen cattle registered in Austin.

As Captains Ford and Jaeger were debriefed by Captain Ross in behalf of the Governor, the slayer of Iron Jacket was attributed to Jim Pockmark by Henry Jaeger. When Henry was challenged by Ford who said, "Why

Henry, that's not how I remember it at all"! Henry responded, "John, you were a hundred yards away tending to your flock and had all you could handle at the time as I recall, while I was right there and I'm sayin', that Pockmark was the one who put the horns to the old chief and that's just the way it is"!

"Well Henry, I suppose your right and if'n that's the way you said it went down, then that's the way it went down", said Ford with a slow wink and a nod.

Several days later, Jaeger and Ford would go their separate ways, with Ford going down to Austin with an official report for the Governor stating that over five hundred Comanche Warriors met an untimely end along with complete elimination of their immediate families. While Henry and his two compatriots parceled out eight mustang stallions to breed with his herd back at the ranch. They were a hardy lot, the mustangs and they apparently listened to Henry as he spoke to them. His mares just might be pleased with the new arrivals.

<h1 style="text-align:center">17</h1>

As Henry and his two vaqueros approached one of the northern pastures they saw on a distant hillock one of his horse herds grazing in the late morning sun. With eight eager mustang stallions following along, he could see their noses in the air scenting the possibility of several mares just entering their season as the spring approached North Texas. There guarding the herd was the second reincarnation of Chani, sensing the approaching riders even though she was up wind of them, turned her head and rose up suddenly with a certain knowing of who approached that defied description.

She held her ground, then barked, then howled. Henry answered her with a howl of his own as the riders slowly approached. Just yards away she ran up to his horse, compelling him to dismount as she sniffed and licked him excitedly as he ruffled her fur, forcing Henry to exclaim; "Boys its official, we are now home"!

Without any needed encouragement his newly acquired Mustangs, eagerly blended right in with the wealth of mares in the pasture. Of course there would be some sorting out of just who would be who, amongst the stallions already at hand, but since there was an abundance of mares, Henry was fairly certain the fuss would be minimal.

Each rider's horse pulled a skid that when they departed was laden with supplies, but as the houses of the ranch complex came into view the skids were almost empty except for the rawhide skins made for their portable lodges on the trail. As Henry looked up, noticing the position of the sun in the late morning, he surmised that Melanie would be busy with the town children at the one room school house, teaching them reading, writing and their numbers.

He was joined by Juan Mendoza who rode up from one of the west pastures, hollering, "Buena's Dias Jefe", waving his overly large sombrero. After exchanging greetings the first thing Henry asked was, "How's the herd Juan"? Thus compelling a long exchange between the men which met with Henrys approval. It seemed that in his absence the cattle had expanded by well over a hundred head and the horses by almost the same number in spite of an unusually cold winter. Right around the corner was branding time, which meant that completion of the final phase of the fencing would have to be put off awhile. Since the Army was now in Utah territory keeping the Mormons in line, another market for his horses and cattle would have to be found, which is what he discussed with Mendoza as they rode on in. A trip to Austin and then perhaps San Antonio would have to be made to rub shoulders with the ones who mattered.

His reunion with his children would have to wait since all but the wee one were with their mother in school, but that would come in due time before sundown. He cut loose his two associates telling them to get some much needed rest for tomorrow it was back to their normal routine. Quickly following up with, "Thank you gents, ya done good", which brought a huge smile on each of their faces.

Later in the afternoon upon Melanie's return, he was sound asleep when he was brutally awakened by his children jumping on him screaming, "Paw paw's home", smothering him with kisses, while his wife looked on with a smile of regal grace. Her time of welcoming would arrive well after sundown while the children were fast asleep. For now a simple kiss and a hug would have to suffice.

That evening, after dinner all the darkies were gathered around the two Buffalo Vaqueros that accompanied Henry on his journey as they recounted as best they could their perilous adventures on the high plains of Comancheria with Massa Henry. While at the very same time Melanie formally welcomed her husband in the time worn tradition of women who found their men back from the wars and under their spell once again.

There's always something significant to do on a ranch no matter what the season and Henry was certainly thankful for the presence of Mendoza to run things in his absence. For here was a Vaquero Supremo, who knew what to do and when on all matter's in running a cattle and horse ranchero. In Henry's absence, the affairs of the ranch ran smoothly and efficiently. Sure Mendoza was an integral partner in the ranch, but there seemed to be something more he could do to reward him. He would think on it on his journey to Austin the following week.

All through the week, as he rode around the ranch with Mendoza, he recanted his time amongst the hostiles. Part of Mendoza wished he could've been a part of it, while the practicality of things dictated that it was best that Henry do what he did best, and Mendoza do what he did best, for his days as a pistolero and bandito were but an embarrassing memory and life was good here and at this very place he was accepted and needed.

Before his trip to Austin, he rode into town to check on things meeting up with the key citizens who just now were receiving reports from the newspapers about the 'Great Battles of Little Robe Creek', asking seemingly endless questions about every aspect of the great adventure amongst the hostiles.

While Iron Jacket was dead, they still had the worry about Peta Nocona, perhaps not this year or even the next, but at some point down the road the Comanche would regroup, find a leader and become a problem once again.

When Henry arrived in Austin, he made the rounds of those who mattered in State Governance reminding them of a huge herd of horse's saddle ready along with an even larger herd of long horn cattle ready for sale.

Since no one was at war at that time and the King Ranch in South Texas also was overflowing with livestock there appeared to be a temporary glut on the market with livestock. However as Henry caught up on the news coming from the other states via weeks old newspapers, he was certain that would change, for those rascals back in Washington City were stirring things up. Talks of succession of the Southern States were in the air. Not only slavery being imported into the western states and violent unrest in Missouri and Kansas, filling the headlines, but a newfangled tariff, placed on all imports and exports favoring the northern industrial states gradually placed the southern states in dire financial need. The price of imports climbed while the price of southern cotton became less competitive. The Southern Planters that concentrated on King Cotton were going to take it up the ass for fair.

While Henry never was partial to slavery, the arrival of the fifty or so slave's years ago made possible his ranch as it existed this very day. As he read the plethora of articles from back newspapers he could see and understand the points of view of the Northern as well as the Southern States, but could see no middle ground between them. Unless divine intersession occurred there would be war on the horizon, but when and for how long? Henry would have to walk a fine line politically in Texas for a long while.

Just when they have dealt a heavy blow to the Indians and the Mexican Rustlers were seemingly on the wane for the time being, things politically were starting to heat up. Would Henry's friends of today become his enemies of tomorrow? Keeping working capital of five hundred US dollars in Waco's only bank, Henry decided that he would withdraw much of that capital and invest it in the latest farm machinery, forsaking cotton for the time being and concentrating in wheat and corn which were certain to be in great demand in the years to come. He ordered the latest horse drawn planting and harvesting machinery along with updated implements for the saw mill and iron nails in a wide variety of sizes and in great quantity for the building of more silos to store grain.

Then he rode down to San Antonio to look up the Mavericks were so good to both him and Melanie years ago. Regaling them with countless stories of Melanie, the children and the ranch, along with his view of the recent raid on the hostiles in the Comancheria, he provided Sam Maverick with an eye witness viewpoint of the Texican Ranger Militia that was certain to sell a lot of newspapers for at least a little while. While he was there he placed additional orders for the basics, cloth, thread, and a newfangled foot powered sewing machine with Sam at his general store. Finally he ordered a large quantity of Salt Petre, Sulphur and lead shot for his plan to make his own gunpowder, for the days ahead.

With any luck at all, just maybe he could sit out the conflict he sensed that was just over the horizon, for he had no dog in that fight. His only true loyalty was to his family, his servants and to the MHM ranch that he'd crafted out of practically nothing.

With some working capital of almost six thousand Federal dollars in gold and silver back at the ranch perhaps, just perhaps, he could sit this out and emerge on the other side in good shape.

The ranchers and the farmers were not about to let loose their darkies no matter what anyone in Washington said of did, thus it appeared the "Dogs of War", would make yet another appearance.

Several days later he bid a tearful Mary Maverick a fond farewell, and started on his journey back to Waco, stopping by for just a day visit with the Governor and some of the State Senators while in session, to report and take measure of the events of the day to reinforce his recent decisions and help him plan for the future.

When asked what his plans were for the coming conflict? Henry neatly sidestepped the issue by reminding them that he had been at war in one fashion or the other since the latter 1830's in behalf of Texas as an Indian fighter mostly, and that as a lifelong Ranger he could better serve the State of Texas as a source of livestock and grain as well as gunpowder if he'd a steady supply of the makings.

He was assured that he would find a ready market from Austin in the coming days for all of his output. Remembering what his 'Papi' once told him not one week before he was killed back in Ohio, "Son, while one should always strive to be truthful remember this, Lies are the lubricants of society, while Truth can oft times be abrasive. It just depends upon the occasion, which is to be done"!

As he entered Austin, it started to rain, so Henry decided to spend the night at the newly built hostelry and stable his horse. As he entered a local saloon that was across the street from a similar establishment that he thought made General Worth sick, he went to an open table, unencumbering himself of his outer garments settling in for quiet evening of victuals and beer imported from New Orleans. The waiter came took his order and returned with the day's newspaper from the local press and a draught of beer. The citizens of Waco prohibited the evil brew even though it was probably better to drink that the local water. As he started to read the local paper and dry out, letting the deluge outside run its course, he heard the rapturous melody of the Spanish Guitar coming from the balcony that surrounded the main floor of the establishment. The guitar player whoever he was was very good as Henry had developed a taste for the music during his time with Joselita and the Fuentes. The sound of the music seemed to be coming from a source that was in motion, as it passed overhead around the balcony of the establishment. Then he heard the dulcet tones of the lyrics coming from what was clearly a female voice.

She was singing about a lover that went off to the wars and never came back, leaving her heart in limbo, for her memory of him was ever present, every single day especially during the long, cold nights. As one song ended and another began, Henry was impressed by her skill as her fingers literally danced upon the strings, sending a well-crafted cornucopia of notes, waxing and waning, climbing and descending the music scale, interspersed with the crisp vocals of the singer.

Then she came into view, an attractively mature, full bodied woman attired in the peasant blouse, showing the glistening of her shoulders, and the promise of a pair of bosoms that would set any man afire with desire. Her face matched her voice, with sharply defined features with deep set flashing eyes, high cheekbones and perfectly formed lips with not a hint of the wear and tear that usually takes its toll in the women of the plains. As she came down the stairs slowly she continued with yet another song singing of a lover who disappointed a virgin on the very night of their wedding. What was she to do? As the lyrics continued, they moaned of her anguish in discovering the love of her life, the one she was saving herself for, the one her family schemed to find as a lifelong lover, preferred men rather than women. The joke was upon everyone, his family, her family and especially on her.

She went to confession telling the priest all and yet the priest was of no help. She went to her family, yet they pleaded for her to keep silent and endure for the family fortunes were at stake. From the bowels of the Hidalgos fled a refugee of love.

The lyrics pleaded for an answer to the question, of how such a man could be so stunningly beautiful, riding on his horse, a true Caballero, one who set hearts all a flutter and be a Cabrone? Those on earth were silent and the heavens were mute. Then the song begged the audience to answer the question, what is to be done?

The music then ended in a flourish of chords of notes. With the singer holding her head up high, a vow that she would endure, whatever was ahead. As the place was filling up with patrons for the evenings dinner hour, Henry put aside his paper as his food arrived, with hunger gaining the upper hand.

Wandering around the main floor of the Saloon, she kept up a steady strumming for the patrons, reminiscent of old gypsy encampments that Henry had seen while in central Mexico.

The singer gradually wandered around the floor gradually passing Henry's table, noticing his overly large sombrero sitting in an adjacent chair. Sombrero's of this type were very expensive and only came from central Mexico and usually only worn by Hidalgos. Since she had been in Texas, she had never seen a sombrero like that one. The Texican's wore a variety of head gear, the wider the brim the better to shield them from the blazing sun. For an Anglo to wear such a hat meant that he was either a 'Bravo', or stupid. Curiosity got the better of her and she decided to ask as she played, "Muy permisso senor, but your Sombrero, it is from Mexico, is it not", she asked in heavily accented but precise English? Henry looked up and said "Buena's Tardes Senora, Yes it is from Mexico, a gift from a very old friend"!

"An Hildago no doubt"?

"Yes senora, a certain Don Domingo de la Fuentes from Monterrey, if you must know?

As she continued with her music she kept in motion slowly walking around Henry's table as he asked her, "You play and sing very well Senora indicating that you are very talented but educated in the art of the Flamenco guitar"!

"You have spent much time in Mexico Senor"?

"A very long time ago yes. I have many memories of Mexico, some of them even good"!

"And your name Senor"?

"Henry Jaeger at your service Senora, and yours?"

"Juanita Magdalena Andrade", she said proudly! At that Henry did an ever so slight double take, thinking this must be a coincidence. Names from the distant past.

As she continued slowly circling Henrys table and playing she asked, "You know of the Andrade name"?

"A name from long ago, with harsh memories of the past, from a time spent in Monterrey, almost forgotten until this very moment. And you Senora", asked Henry? "My family, long ago was from Culiacan, but so long ago it disappears in the mists of time".

Yet another name from the past and Henry asked, "Have you ever heard of a certain Chuey Medrano, from Culiacan"?

Suddenly her playing stopped, a visible chill coming over her.

Seeing her distress, Henry said, "Por favor, pardonna me Senora, I did not mean to startle you, please continue playing".

The guitar resumed its playing and she appeared to quickly recover her senses as she said," Senor Jaeger, I would wish to talk to you some more.

Shortly I will be able to stop playing for a while and would like to join you and ask you some questions if you will permit it"? "Well Senora, seeing that it's raining outside, how could I say No"!

That said Juanita smiled and wandered off, continuing her playing for yet another hour, nonstop, before concluding her soiree and announcing a brief intermezzo.

As he disappeared for a time, then reappeared coming toward his table Henry noted that she didn't move like a peasant woman, she walked in an elegant fashion reminiscent of the high born ruling class of Hidalgos, Henry had observed, in Mexico, gliding rather than walking, something that had to be taught not inherited. By her manner of speaking, it suggested a once educated woman, who spoke in the elegant fashion of the Castilian, with the letter 'S' almost disappearing from her speech patterns, replaced by the letters 'TH', thus signaling that she was anything but low born.

As she approached, Henry rose and drew her chair, for as she sat down both of them had a flurry of questions for each other recognizing a confluence of similarities in such a distant place, that sheer coincidence was out of the question. Carefully avoiding the depths of his relationship with the Fuentes and Adrade families, he gave her a brief explanation of his time south of the border, yet discovering that while she was born and partially raised in Culiacan, she was somehow adopted by the Andrade family in Monterrey and sent off to Spain to be schooled in all the ways of the Castilian Hidalgos and upon her return to Monterrey to find that her entire family had been murdered by Chuey Medrano and his gang who was in turn killed by this mysterious Americano who was living with the Fuentes family. Then one night was gone never to be heard from again. It appeared that Juanita Magdalena Andrade could connect the dots just as well as Henry Jaeger as she asked him with pleading eyes, "Senor Jaeger, are you that Americano"?

With all the commotion that surrounded the duo, a bubble of silence surrounded them as Henry slowly nodded his head saying, "It would appear so Senora"!

Her expression was a blank slate as she showed no emotion at her recent discovery. For a woman with her education at the hands of all aspects of the worldly experience, living by her wits, making what compromises she had to make, enduring the difficulties of a woman alone, but retaining a sense of dignity, had to view the world as a stage and play whatever role was called for.

Just then a large burly man appeared at Henrys table grabbing Juanita by the arm and jerking her from her seat saying, "Goddammit you fuckin' whore, I pay you to play for the customers, not set up dates, unlessen' I tell ya"! No go git yer guitar an git at playin' before I kick your ass again"!

As Juanita started to rise the man started to raise his hand again, this time as it started to descend it stopped, held fast in place with an iron grip. As he turned to see what was the matter a huge fist appeared crashing into his face, dislodging teeth and rendering him immediately "Hors de Combat", as he sank limply to the floor. Just then a chair flew in Henrys general direction and as Henry caught sight of it from the corner of his eye, he drew the big Colt and followed its path back to yet another burly man charging at him.

The Colt revolver bucked in Henry's hand, with a deafening explosion as the charging man was not only stopped in his tracks, but flipped backwards and turned around the force of the .44 round shattering his shoulder, forcing shouts of agony. As the wounded man writhed on the floor screaming in pain, Henry dragged the other towards him then brought barrel of the revolver down on his head, silencing him for the moment.

He then let his first victim drop and turned to see it anyone else was eager to play, and then bellowed as everyone stood still, "My name is Henry Jaeger and I'm a Captain in the Texas Mounted Ranger Militia. I answer only to the Governor of Texas. My authority is state wide"!

Then he asked "Who knows where the town doctor is"? One man meekly raised his hand, "You there go get the doctor now, ya got fifteen minutes to return. I don't see ya back here in fifteen minutes with the doctor, you better hope I never seen your face again. Now git"!

Then he bellowed, "Who knows where the town Sheriff is"? Another patron raised his hand, only to hear, "You there go git the Sheriff and the same goes for you for I got a good memory for faces, now git"!

Then Henry looked at the bartender and bellowed, "You there, draw me another beer and bring it to me and be quick about it". The bartender flew into action, running around the bar and carefully bringing it to

Henry, as he was yelling, "Everybody take a seat for nobody's leaving till either I or the Sheriff says so".

Juanita gathered her wits about her rising from the floor and silently sitting in the seat formerly occupied by this 'Bravo', this Henry Jaeger Capitano of the Texican Rangers. She now knew in her soul this was indeed the very man who took the full measure of the dreaded Chuey Medrano, her deepest secret.

As the bartender arrived and offered Henry the beer, Henry said "You take the first drink and drink half the glass". The bartender did as he was told emptying half the glass then handing the remainder to Jaeger, who promptly drained it then said, "Refill the mug".

Then addressing the entire saloon, he asked who are the people he'd just dispatched, when one patron willingly answered, "Well sir, that there one ya smashed his face in, is the owner, a Mister Beau Mortimer and some say he's from Algiers Louisiana, cross da river from New Orleans"!

"And the other", asked Henry? "That one there, who ya shot, everyone calls Buster, on accounta he busts heads of anyone Mortimer says to. And as far as where he's from, nobody rightly knows, 'Parts unknown' maybe"?

As he finished and sat down the bartender approached with the refill offering it to Henry, who said, "Same as before", this time the bartender was only able to drink a quarter of the mug when he offered it to Henry. Then he asked "What the deal with the singer", pointing to Juanita sitting silently nearby?

"Well sir as far as I knows, Mr. Mortimer purchased her contract for three years a year ago, from a Mister Wiley Sanchez in Galveston Texas and that's all I rightly know sir"? Just then the town doctor entered and was immediately put to work on Buster who was bleeding profusely from his gunshot wound and the gash that Henry had placed across his brow.

Then the town sheriff entered on the heels of the second terrified patron. Although he'd never met Henry, he knew him by reputation and by sight, being pointed out by another leaving the Governor's office."

You the town Sheriff" asked Henry seeing the badge on is belt"? "Yessir", Seth Parker, answered seeing the Ranger badge placed unobtrusively on Henry's belt.

Henry then spent the next few minutes telling Sheriff Parker what had occurred and suggested the he verify his testimony with the others held in place. Unawares to either of them Beau Mortimer slowly came to from the head busting he received. Seeing his teeth on the barroom floor and feeling the dull pain in his head, he became enraged and started to rise seeing Jaeger talking to the Sheriff, he removed a knife from his inside waistband and started to charge Henry and the Sheriff.

As he passed Juanita she screamed alerting Henry and the Sheriff who whirled around drawing their revolvers and placing several shots each into the charging Mortimer who fell dead at their feet.

Placing his weapon back in the holster, Sheriff Parker said, 'Well that simplifies things a tad bit Captain Jaeger, doesn't it"?

"I'd say it does Sheriff". Then he turned to the bartender and said, "Looks like you're the new owner of this establishment Mister Barkeep, wouldn't ya say Sheriff"?

"I suppose, but only if he wants it? Carl do ya want this place"?

"Well sir, I guess I do"!

The town Judge'll have some paperwork to do and I suppose that Captain Jaeger'll have to eventually sign an affidavit at some point but that'll have at be sometime down the road.

Then Henry turned to Juanita, and then turned back to the bartender asking, "Her contract Carl, where is it"?

"In Mortimer's safe"! "Go get the contract Carl and do it now", said Jaeger!

Minutes later Carl returned with Juanita's contract, offering it to Jaeger, who briefly scanned it then handed it to Juanita saying to the bartender, "Carl do you hold this here woman to this contract one minute longer"?

In plain eyesight and earshot of every patron in the saloon, Carl said "No sir I do not hold this here woman to this contract"!

Henry turned to everyone and said, "Everyone in agreement as to what they just saw and heard"?

The entire saloon gave a resounding "Yes"!

"Well Senora Juanita, I suppose you're now a free woman. Do with that contract what you will"! For the first time in a very long time Juanita Andrade was free from the influence of any man. But here in Austin Texas, where would she go and what would she do? For years she had been an entertainer, along with several other things she had to do to survive, but here in Austin Texas, what other option did she have? New

Orleans was a world away. Mexico was out of the question, San Antonio not much better.

Just then Henry sat down with a visibly stunned Juanita saying, "Muy permisso Senora, but things and fortunes have happened so fast and putting myself in your shoes I'm wondering what next and if I may be so bold I have a suggestion. Now to start out I'm a happily married man with a wife and children. I have a rancho north of here and on that ranch is a man, a Vaquero Supremo who runs things for me when I'm away. From what I've just gathered, the both of you just might have many things in common.

Most of all, both of you are from Culiacan and both of you hated Chuey Medrano along with a host of other things. The man has never been married and has no children. The man's name is Juan Mendoza and I trust him with my family's life. So if you have nothing better to do, please accompany me to my rancho, where I will find private accommodations for you and perhaps........... at any rate a woman of your talents will have gainful employment with me"!

Then Henry stood up offering his hand. Juanita nodded her head and took Henrys hand and rose.

"Muy Bueno", said Henry turning and said to the Sheriff, "I'm taking custody of this woman to my ranch in Waco and I'm going to need to borrow a horse and saddle for the trip which will be returned, when the affidavit is delivered and signed"!

Then he turned to the bartender who was close at hand saying, "Carl, did Mortimer have any horses and saddles"?

"Yessir, a couple of em"!

"Then I need to borrow one of em, so get someone to bring one of Mortimer's horses, which are now your horses, around pretty quick saddled up and do it now.

Then Henry asked those assembled, "Who's gonna be good enough to help this lady to pack her duds and bring em back here"? Just then two hands shot up, and Henry added "Carl will make sure that drinks are on the house for those that helped, is that not true Carl". The bartender cheerfully nodded his head, for why not? For the price of a few drinks, he was going to get a going concern, absolutely free of any encumbrances. Not to mention be out from under one of the most horrible people one could ever work for.

Then he left to retrieve his horse and skid, returning some fifteen minutes later all saddled up.

He walked up to the bar and asked the new owner, "Carl, what do I owe you for the steak and the beers"? "Captain Jaeger, not a blessed thing. Your money's no good here"!

"Just the same Carl, your horse will be returned in due time".

Then Juanita reappeared with her retinue and Henry directed them to secure her few belongings to the Indian skid, attached to his horse. As Henry went outside with his leather slicker on, he shook hand with the Sheriff and the doctor who said that "Buster" had died from his wounds caused by Henrys Colt revolver.

"Life is getting simpler and simpler", offered the Sheriff as Henry and Juanita rode away into the foggy night, for the rain had stopped a half hour ago.

As they made their way up the trail from Austin towards Waco, Henry brought Juanita up to date on everything he knew about Juan Mendoza, acknowledging that he knew nothing of him before he met him at the Fuentes rancho years before. He left blank any mention of the depths of his relationship with the Fuentes and the marriage to their daughter, knowing full well that it would surface someday but that day was far off and it would be a time of his choosing. He also intentionally omitted the fact that Juanita was the name of Juan's lover, a member of the Fuentes family. Simply stating that Juanita was the name of the love of his life, of whose death Chuey Medina was responsible.

As Juanita rode along part of her was concerned about the unknown she was riding into, but as the miles rolled by and as Henry told her of his family, her concerns slowly began to evaporate as rapidly as the early morning fog. Perhaps, just perhaps, this would be a day of days, a good time to remember, when the chains of ill fortune fell away at long last.

18

The trip home took three days, as Henry and his recent acquisition approached the ranch he exclaimed, "Well there it is. The 'MHM' in all its glory"!

Although not exactly fraught with the finery of many of the ranchos in Mexico, the complex seemed to be well tended and fairly new, with people going about their day, tending to their tasks.

Just how Henry was going to introduce Juanita Andrade to Juan Mendoza, Henry had yet to figure out. He would just have to play things by ear. Then as they pulled up to the house, he saw Maddie with his youngest child Michael, perched on her hip.

The introductions made, he asked Maddie to help Juanita to settle into one of the temporary quarters attached to the barn complex. That completed, he shed the Indian skid, and mounted his horse and sought out Mendoza, to tell him that a guest was coming to dinner tonight and that he was to clean up and dine with the family. The only information Juan would receive was that Henry's guest was hopefully here to stay awhile and that she was from the place of his birth.

By early afternoon Melanie had returned from her teaching chores at the little school house and met saw the Henry had returned. Delighted to see her husband she and her children ran to him for the standard hugs, kisses and the standard invocations that "Paw Paw's Home". Yet within minutes the joy of his return gave way to running to Maddie and their little brother to play the afternoon away.

Melanie fell into Henry's arms with the softness only a wife can give, with few words exchanged. Suddenly Henry exclaimed, "Melanie we're going to have a guest for dinner"!

The he explained his trip and the aftermath of encountering Juanita Andrade in Austin.

Of course, he chose to omit the draconian aspects of his encounter, but entered into the aspect of his plan.

"And they'll meet right here under our noses for supper tonight", said Henry eagerly.

"What if they don't take a shine to each other right away", asked Melanie?

"Well, didn't we turn out all right"?

"Not right off Henry if'n you'll recall. We took a little gettin' used to each other, but once it took, it took", mused Melanie. "And I wouldn't trade you for a thousand head of cattle"!

"You ever meet any Jewish people Henry, asked Melanie straight away?

"No, can't say that I have".

"Well, growing up in Charleston, there were a few Jewish families there, not many but they all lived in town. They were seemingly folks just like us, but they were a doctor, a banker and lemmesee, a pawn shop owner. My folks told me they were God's chosen people, but when I asked them why them above anyone else, they couldn't answer".

"Now there was this widow woman, who made a living as a marriage broker and folks from all over would come to her to select them a mate. And I'm given to understand that she made a pretty fair living out of this"!

"So just what does that all mean"?

"Henry, are you Jewish", asked Melanie.

"I'm Catholic, Melanie"!

That said, she arched an eyebrow and grabbed his hand and escorted him into the house, when she could formally welcome him home in a way that would take up several hours of the afternoon.

Mendoza was not exactly himself, for the rest of the afternoon after hearing that a woman, from Culiacan of all places, he was to meet this evening at Henrys table. He was quite aware that he had few of the social graces of the Hidalgos and although a vaquero, was little more than a compesino. His ever so brief affectations for his Juanita were about as close as he was to come to dignity and grace and he would marvel how she could bring style and grace to a simple horse stall and a bale of hay.

He decided to not take this event seriously as he entered the barn to put up his horse for the day. Henry was home and with his family and Juan had made his rounds, with every one busily at work.

As he finished brushing off his horse, he faintly heard the almost long forgotten strings of the flamenco guitar somewhere nearby. As he followed the music outside, the sound made him wander around the barn complex and as he went, the sound became louder. Rounding the rear corner of the barn, he discovered the origin of the music. There under a shady oak tree, was the form of a woman playing the flamenco guitar. In a fashion he hadn't heard for many years. The music was played with passion, with the notes pouring forth in a hard driving staccato rhythm. He approached with great caution, stopping then moving forward again as he circled to see her face. If she turned her head just a little bit she would see him watching, but her concentration was on the strings as her fingers danced upon the strings almost at war with them, forcing the strings to adhere to her will.

Suddenly she ended with a flourish, taking a deep and well-earned breath. Then looking up at last, she caught sight out of the corner of her eye a tall mustachioed man, with a similar Sombrero worn in the way of the Vaquero, the side arm worn at a rakish angle at his belt leaning against a tree watching and apparently listening in silence.

At first neither spoke for what seemed like an eternity, each staring at each other. Then Mendoza apparently embarrassed for his voyeuristic enterprise spoke; "Muy permisso Senorita, I did not mean to startle you. It's just that I had not heard the guitar played so well for many years and that here in Texas to hear such a thing is a rare treat.

Please continue playing if you so wish"!

As her startled look gradually transformed into a smile, her fingers went back into motion almost automatically, caressing the strings in a slow, rhythmic sonata. She sized up the Vaquero that stood a distance away, signaling with her head that it was permissible to approach.

She thought, 'This must be the Juan Mendoza that Captain Jaeger was talking about'. Not a bad looking man for his age. In his eyes she could see that he'd led a hard life and knew instinctively that he would possess a wealth of calluses on his rough hands and perhaps elsewhere. But also in his eyes she could see a longing, a need for a good woman. Rough around the edges he must be, but as she took stock of what was before her she could sense a man of great depth of character and that was what mattered most of all. For in all her travels she had encountered men of every kind and the great teacher of life taught her the subtle differences and it all lay in the eyes.

As Juan approached cautiously, he removed his hat and sat leaning against another tree yards away, peering deeply into the eyes of someone that was indeed captivating. For this must be the new arrival Henry was talking about. Not meaning to give her reason to pause, he closed his eyes, listening to the slow captivating rhythms of the guitar, while fixing the image of her in his mind. She was 'Muy Linda' to behold.

Suddenly the music stopped and she asked, "Senor you bear the appearance of one who must be a certain Juan Mendoza, would that not be true"?

"At your service Senorita", said Juan.

It was many years since she could actually answer to the polite term 'Senorita', but she decided not to quibble and she asked, "The very same Juan Mendoza from Culiacan"?

Mendoza nodded and asked, "Perhaps you are from Culiacan also? But how can that be? While famous for the guitar it has never produced such a virtuoso of the craft and certainly being a den of robbers and thieves, never one of such beauty such as yourself"!

Never exactly famous for having a smooth tongue with the fair sex, the very right words somehow flowed from Mendoza's mouth perhaps with the guidance of some celestial source.

"But I do not know your name Senorita", stated Mendoza.

She started playing again as she said, "Juanita Andrade is who I am, from Culiacan". As he continued her playing, they began the dance. Well not really a dance, but verbally began circling around each other, exchanging information, discovering commonalities. Yes it was a dance as they encircled each other, with much delicacy and grace, instinctively knowing that just one misplaced word or phrase could break the spell each other was casting upon the other.

While Juanita was thinking that Mendoza was an older man than she might've wanted, he was nevertheless one who was a man of depth and if he was partnered with Capitan Jaeger, then he was a man to be reckoned with and respected. Juanita had only known two men in her life that had earned her respect and they were both long in their graves. Yes this man would do and very well he would do.

Mendoza was disturbed somewhat by the confluence of events. Here was a woman from Culiacan, who exuded all of the graces of a Castilian yet so much a reminder of his Juanita of long ago yet much younger and her name was Juanita. Either the angles were playing a sad joke, or they were bestowing a precious gift at his feet. He decided to continue with the small talk and enjoy the wonderful music and put everything in the Almighty's hands.

Then as Mendoza noted, the sun was on its downward journey and he left coming back with a bucket of water from the well and told Juanita that he would see her at Henry's table within the hour.

An hour later as Juan left his cabin, he had bathed, shaved very closely and performed his ablutions with such great care that he was looking forward to the event. As he approached the house, there she was serenading Henry and the children. As he approached the children ran up to him screaming, "Uncle Juan, Buenos Tardes" and attacking his legs begging him to lift them into his arms.

As he climbed the steps, Henry rose up from his rocker and said, "I understand the two of you need no introduction"! "Yes, it seems that we have Henry. We've talked about many things and have many things yet to talk about". As he gazed fondly upon Juanita, he noticed something different, something wonderful. Earlier in the day, when under the trees, she was quite beautiful, but not yet at her visual best having traveled far and not all cleaned up. Yet now an hour later she was radiantly lovely and completely captivating. Her hair done, different clothes and yes what Henry always described as artfully done "War Paint", to highlight her obvious charms. Not since his time with the Fuentes and the other Juanita has Juan experienced this close at hand. His eyes could not nor would not leave the visage of Juanita Andrade. All through the meal Juan tried his best not to be too obvious, enjoying the camaraderie of the Jaeger family and the glorious meal, playing with the children and noticing that Miss Melanie and Juanita were fast becoming friends. Two educated women finding much in common no doubt for days and years to come.

As the mantle clock struck nine PM, Juan said "Well, I think it is time for us to go for we all have a busy day ahead of us tomorrow." Then turning to Juanita he asked, "May I escort you to your quarters"? As she nodded and they departed walking away towards the barn complex, Melanie gave a gentle poke of Henry's ribs saying, "Well Pilgrim, just might be that you got a little bit of Jewish in your own self"!

Minutes later, as Mendoza and Juanita arrived at her quarters he helped her find and light the candle providing sufficient illumination of her quarters and as he made ready to depart, she stopped him rising to her full height, planting an not so innocent kiss on his cheek, close to his mouth saying,"Perhaps muy Bravo I may return the favor and soon"! The kiss provided a jolt to his system, followed by the sweetly mouthed seemingly innocent words that conveyed a not so innocent message that even Juan Mendoza could ignore. As he walked back to his cabin Juan looked up at the heavens noticing the complete fullness of the moon and hearing the distant howling of the wolves, ever on sentry watching after the herds.

Days later Mendoza awoke to the summoning of the rooster as he had on countless mornings before, except on this particular morning his bed was partially occupied by a wonderful 'Chulita', who had transferred all of her belongings to his quarters the night before. After she settled in, several hours were spent as his long unruly hair was cut to a more desirable length, his drooping moustache was trimmed, revealing that he indeed had a mouth and his face was shaved with great care. Stepping back and admiring her work, Juanita produced a mirror from her belongings and displayed her results to Juan.

"Now there is a 'Bravo' that one could adore", she exclaimed!

Then she slowly straddled him as he sat in the chair by the firelight of the evening. Lowering her peasant blouse to her waist, revealing a set of full breasts, in the bloom of their femininity and buried his head in them, while slowly grinding her hips against his groin in that age old ritual of 'Amour'. The rest of the evening blended into a whirl of relentless lovemaking such as never thought possible by the average vaquero. She was the teacher and he was but a willing student, allowing her to mold him to her will. In the end came a crescendo that stiffened them both as if cadavers at a funeral.

Finally as he softened, they drew slightly apart and she held his face in her hands asking, "Can you hear Juanito? The Angels, they are singing at long last"!

As Juan opened his eyes he could barely speak uttering, "I'm looking at an Angel right now and find it difficult to cast my eyes elsewhere"! "I will give you children, Juanito", she said softly kissing his face.

Then as the fire gradually diminished in the fireplace they both fell victims of a much needed sleep. From the very first morning Juanita was at the ranch, before even having to be told, she made her way into the barn complex and fell to the task of milking the cows along with the children that were brought before her by the others, then taking the heavy buckets of milk to still other children who separated the buckets to either be churned into butter or cheese products. For as a child of a poor family in Culiacan that was one of her many tasks. As time went by she revealed many of the mysteries of her past. Her family as well as she could remember, had sold her to the Andrade family in Monterrey who raised her as their own, even to the point of imparting their cognomen to her. As time went by, when she reached the age of menstruation, Don Francisco Andrade accompanied her to Valencia Spain and enrolled her in a private school, to train her for a life as a Hidalgo, in the Mexican ruling class. Upon returning from Spain after her schooling was completed, now a young woman, she was confronted by the fact the fact that the Andrade family was no more. All killed by the Medrano clan, was the way the story was told. The very same Medrano clan that had a long standing relationship of murky origins with the Andrade family. For she too had known of Chuey Medrano a "Muy Malo" man who often cast his eyes upon her as a child.

Then came the time of wandering, making her way in a man's world as best she could, mostly as an entertainer, yet forced by circumstance to engage in many less savory acts of skull duggery.

Then one stormy evening, in a saloon in Austin Texas entered Henry Jaeger and her life changed forever. She was right where she wanted to be, seemingly escorted by some celestial power, firmly in the bosom of those who grew to love and respect her and right where she was needed most in this world. Juanita Andrade Mendoza would make it a point to be needed and bring every talent to bear to earn her place. Here she was safe at last.

Henry went into Waco the following week and was sought out by the County Judge where they discussed coming events germane to Texas and the big tussle booming in Washington City.

"That feckless idiot in the White House, Buchanan, isn't worth a bucket of warm shit", exclaimed the Judge! "Why there's already rumblings of 'Succession', coming out of Louisiana and the rest of the Southern States, cause the Yankees wanna take away our darkies. Hells fire the tariffs they laid on our imports have almost destroyed our cotton exports. The Cotton exchange people down in Houston, say that our cotton exports to England have almost dried up and that Egyptian cotton is being bought up almost completely"!

"Which is why I decided to grow corn and wheat, since there will always be a demand in Texas for those crops, one way or the other", replied Henry.

"Hell Henry, the Texas is even short of gunpowder and rifle shot", offered the Judge.

Seeing an opening as to advance the fortunes of the ranch Henry said, "Gunpowder, short ya say".

"Why, for years I always made my own and made my own my own lead shot from molds. I make my own charcoal and all I need is Sulphur and Salt Petre and I'm off to the races." Then Henry added," Now if had several wagon loads of Sulphur and Salt Petre and lead bars along with enough bullet molds of the caliber Austin might need then I would be willing to take some of my darkies and get em to make enough munitions to satisfy Austin for a modest price."?

"You can do that Henry", asked the Judge?

"Certainly can and I've the people that can do it"! "There's some people in Austin that owe me some favors and can get things done in a hurry Henry", the Judge offered.

"I'll get a letter, off to Austin this evening and we'll see just what's what"! Two weeks later some representatives from Austin appeared at the ranch, escorted by the County Judge asking to see Henry's processing of gunpowder. Duly impressed they asked to see the entire ranch including both of the mills. After seeing the extent of Henry's operations they all hunkered down to outline the terms of an agreement between the MHM Ranch and the State of Texas for not only munitions supply, but saddle ready horses and ground corn and wheat at a fixed price that was agreeable by all.

The Judge immediately went to work as all were invited to dine at Henry's table that evening and find comfort in his quarters at the barn complex. After dinner, while everyone was serenaded by the gentle music of Juanita with Juan sitting closely by. Henry was discreetly asked by one of the visitors of the State, "They say you have no trouble at all from your Darkies Captain Jaeger! Just how do you do it"?

After thinking about the question a few seconds, Henry replied, "Pretty simple really as far as I can see. I treat em well, feed em well, see to it that they're all well clothed and shod. When they are sick the doctor comes, when they have babies everybody takes a turn. Juan and me have trained em all in the tasks they have to do. Everybody knows that their important and needed. But even more important I think, is that nowhere else will they be better off"!

"Ever have to raise your hand to any of em, Captain Jaeger"? "Not yet", replied Henry "and I don't expect I'll ever have to"!

"Why, two of my Buffalo Vaqueros rode with me all the way up to Comancheria a while back and did as well anyone else, so they can hold their own water"!

"Slaves at Little Robe Creek", exclaimed one of the States Agents? "Yessir and they killed their share of Comanche's", mused Henry.

The following morning after breakfast, the County Judge concluded the contract between Henrys newly founded company and the State of Texas for the variety of goods and munitions at the agreed upon price.

A month later, four wagon loads of materials arrived all the way from the Port of Galveston on the Texas Gulf Coast, forcing Henry to exclaim to Melanie, "Seems were in the gunpowder business my dear"!

During the interim a special building was constructed, away from the rest well ventilated and with space to store the raw material as well as the finished product and a month later five hundred pounds of gunpowder was loaded on the wagons sent by Austin, along with five thousand rounds of ball of varying calibers.

Thus came the cycle, arrival of raw material from Galveston and the following month the finished product sent back to Austin with an invoice for services rendered. As the year of 1858 came to a close, Henry was introduced to a water diviner who claimed he could find water on his property. With his divining rod he accompanied Henry around his ranch, identifying the places where wells could be dug, where water was close to the surface. Previously he'd read of an invention by a man named Halliday where a wind powered water pump could pump water out of the ground.

Since he had the carpentry skills to build the derrick required, he contracted with the general store in town for the equipment needed. Then he contracted with a water well driller in Houston to drill the wells in the places previously determined. After the first well hit water, Henry proceeded to drill two more. By the time the wind powered equipment had arrived he'd prepared enough wooden timbers to erect and build the first wind powered water well, which pumped the water into a large round wooden, above ground cistern. By the spring of 1859 the first water well was pumping water in sufficient quantities to supply the needs of everyone on the ranch.

The bulk of 1859 was spent building tall wooden silos to store harvested grain and erect two additional wind powered water wells to provide water for the herds and when needed additional water for the fields of grain.

Saddle ready mounts were always in demand thus requiring Henry's presence in the corrals as well as in the fields supervising the various construction projects. The various aspects of the Ranch's enterprises rolled on with people and wagons arriving and departing on a weekly basis.

Yet with few exceptions, on the seventh day all rested, from their exertions, except for the wolves, who were now multiplying yet again. As they matured they were trained by Henry and several of the hands now skilled in the gentling of the feral nature of the beast, into watching and protecting the herds as well as under the watchful eyes of their parents.

As the calendar turned over into 1860, general anxiety all over the southern states grew as the election campaigns for the Presidency took hold. As far as Texas was concerned it was clear where their sympathy's lay, yet Missouri, Kansas and some of the Border States were busy within themselves sorting things out.

Henry had no interest in either side of the tussle. While he was in the company of those who were clearly partisan to the southern point of view, he could understand their concern, for they had mostly been raised in the southern states and that is what they knew to be true, so he played along when in conversation, giving no indication on which side he was favoring. Everyone knew he was supplying Austin with all that he could and rarely the question arose as to his sympathies.

He would tell Melanie and Mendoza his deepest thoughts and no one else. His loyalties were to his family, his ranch and Texas if the creek didn't rise too much.

As 1860 came to a close, it was clear that unless some divine intersession occurred the nation would be split in two. Lincoln had been elected and the lines had been drawn in the sand. Henry put several more people to the task of turning out more gunpowder and shot for the needs of the South for as long as they lasted.

He had stockpiled enough Yankee dollars and goods to last awhile. As the children grew everyone had the responsibility to become proficient in the art of the bow and arrow as well as the cap and ball musket of which he had sufficient supply. Several of the children were of such an age to be taught in the art of the Vaquero and became as good a horseman as existed in the territory.

Of course any news of politics was not shared with the darkies for the obvious reason. But Henry knew that something would happen to bust the bubble of slavery forever and discussed with Melanie on many occasions just what to do if the South lost the conflict.

Then a week after the event Ft. Sumter was fired upon and subsequently taken by the secessionist forces and the "Dogs of War", finally bared their teeth once again. Henry wondered about those he'd met in the War of 47, in Mexico. Some were clearly political scallywags while others seemed to be effective commanders. Then he somehow recalled the image of that little man, while waiting for General Worth. Yes, Grant was his name. Seemed the Army had turned its back on him after the War in Mexico. General Worth had related all the reasons at that time in the Cantina. Destined to a life of mediocrity, while Major Lee, seemed to be one who was born to lead a company of men into a very perilous place, for he had apparently acquitted himself very well in Mexico.

By 1862 the War was still in its early stages and the Southern forces were appearing to do well on the field of battle, by all reports. Then one day a mention of a General Ulysses Grant taking Vicksburg jolted Henry as he read newspaper reports of the battle. Of course Robert E. Lee was now a General of the forces of Northern Virginia and was giving the Union forces all they could say grace over and seventeen kinds of fits on the battlefield.

When George McClellan was dismissed as Commander of the Union forces, Henry wasn't surprised at all, for the man was not a soldier but a martinet, a preening dandy it seemed to Henry. All hat and no cattle.

When the Emancipation Proclamation was issued by Lincoln, none of the Southern newspapers printed the story, but eventually spies began to distribute leaflets throughout the south especially in plantations of Lincolns freeing the slaves. The nightmare had now arrived for all plantation owners. Who would work the fields and the farms?

By the end of 1863, the State of Texas Treasury which had been paying for things in Southern Script was virtually broke and traffic at the MHM ranch came to a standstill. Many of the town merchants were having a difficult time keeping their business's afloat and the few farmers and ranchers that were still in existence were having a rough go of things.

News of the war, by the open of 1864 was hard to come by. Confederate forces in Texas were still viable within the state, but elsewhere it was another question altogether. Deserters of the Confederate forces began to filter back into Texas from all over, but when they arrived back to their homes, they found then almost destitute. Although the terrible forces of the conflict had mostly eluded Texas, the economy of the state was laid bare of any sustenance. The southern money was worthless and a barter economy had long taken hold, with scant difference than that of the old Texas Republic.

By the close of the war, Henry had long since come to terms with the slavery issue and had gathered his darkies around him one evening in the barn and made the announcement of the war being over with the Southern forces on the short end of the stick. Then he produced a letter of manumission for each and every one, signed some two years ago freeing every darkie on the ranch. "But Cap'n Henry", a voice rang out "Who's agonna tend to things round heah"? "Where we gonna go? What we gonna do"?

"Well seems to me that y'all can go anywhere ya want and do anything ya want and now it's the law of the land"! "Well Capn' Henry, do ya want us to go? Do we have at go"?

"Of course not. Me and Miss Melanie consider all of you family and have tried to treat you as such. All I'm saying is that you all are now free to do whatever ya want, for the rest of your natural lives, and as y'all know, I've put aside money for each and every one of you that you each have earned, man woman and child, in Federal dollars for just such a day.

Then a period of silence occurred amongst everyone assembled as they looked at each other, with Elijah standing up and saying, Capn' Henry, I and my family have been with Miss Melanie since she was a chile an she and then you have treated us very well and if'n ya don't mind and I think I speak for everyone," as he looked around, "That we all'd like to stay on as before"!

Henry looked around and asked, "Does everyone feel the same way"?

He was met with a resounding "Yes"!

"Then that's it. Everyone stays. Welcome everyone. I'd say it's time for a celebration. Fire up the pit, we're gonna have a celebration! But I gotta warn ya, there are gonna be tough times ahead for all of us, but if we all keep our wits about us, we'll all come out on the other side of this better off"!

During the prewar years, Henry invested in a variety of farm implements that served him well, allowing increased acreage of wheat and corn to be planted and harvested. After the war the State was under martial law for a while, while reports of horror stories flooded into the state of northern carpetbaggers appropriating southern plantations for the back taxes not paid during the war to the federal coffers. It was all very legal, sort of.

Early in 1867, the carpetbaggers came to Henry's part of the world, scooping up at county auction farms and plantations from southern sympathizers. They even made the mistake of approaching Henry, while in Waco. Insisting that Henry allow them to inspect his ranch for auditing purposes, Henry met with the men the following day at the ranch and escorted them around the entire vastness of the ranch, which was to take a week to assess.

Four days later Henry and Mendoza rode into town, with the quartet of federal tax assessors strapped over their horses with arrows clearly still protruding from their bodies.

In his report, attested to by the County Judge their contingent came under attack while inspecting the northern boundary of the MHM ranch, by a band of renegade Kiowa Indians, estimated to be fifty or more in size.

Ignoring Henry's advice to stay with the party who were in a well defensible position, they panicked and mounted their houses and while attempting to flee, were pursued and slain. The fact that that each of the men were scalped and their government issued horses were stolen along with the issue of arrows still in place that clearly had the markings of the Kiowa tribe, quickly put the issue to rest. The entire county was never visited again by Federal tax assessors. For since the hostiles were clearly on the warpath, it was agreed that easier pickings were available elsewhere in the state.

From time to time Henry wondered about his first born child Rodrigo in Monterrey. Not once had he received a response from the several letters he'd sent to Don Domingo over the years. Of course any interchange between Texas and Mexico was always an iffy thing at best, certainly one of the letters was sure to get through. In time he had to force this thing from his mind, relegating to a certain place deep within. He thanked the eternal every day, that at least the issues from Melanie's loins were doing just fine, with every one of them healthy and as well educated in the letters and numbers as Melanie could. Mendoza educated them in the arts of the Vaquero while Henry took everyone on a quarterly hunting trip for game, teaching them along with several others the art of the stalk. In time every aspect of ranch life and its ancillary affairs was deeply ingrained with his children. When anything was built, there they were, eagerly watching their father teach them the arts and crafts of carpentry. Henry was especially proud of the accomplishments of his middle child Josie, who could shoot, rope and ride with the best of them.

One day coming back from town with Mendoza, Henry's oldest Michael couldn't wait to teach his father the latest thing he saw, "The Road Agent Spin", one evening after dinner.

Using two unloaded Colt .44's he handed one to Henry and stick the other into his belt and asked Henry to point it at him and demand that Michael hand him his weapon, butt first. Michael, already a very good hand with both the pistol and the rifle, slowly retrieved the weapon from his waist band, offering it to his father as directed and as Henry reached for it, flipped it around in less than a blink of the eye, holding it on his father, it full cock position, ready to fire. Henry was indeed startled and surprised saying, "Show me that again son".

Within the month after much trial and error, all of the family became adept in performing the "Spin", even developing several offshoots of the spin, depending on the situation, for the world was a dangerous place and in time everyone became gradually proficient in performing the "Spin" and its variations with either hand.

From time to time small cattle herds coming from southern Texas, on their way to the Dallas markets, approached the MHM ranch and were escorted around the ranch, to streams nearby for watering. One day

Henry was alerted that a small herd in the general area heading north, skirting the towns and traveling at night while resting during the day. Thinking nothing of it at first, something nagged at Henry. Something deep in his memory, that he couldn't quite put his finger on. Then the fact that there was but one rider pushing twenty head of strange looking cattle, struck Henry as unique and he asked "How far out is this herd"?

"About a day's ride as best as I can reckon Captain Henry" answered one of his Buffalo Vaqueros.

On a hunch, Henry asked Mendoza to accompany him to meet this wandering pilgrim to see if any assistance could be rendered. The following morning, while the children were at school with their mother, Henry, Juan and one of the Buffalo Vaqueros rode out to meet the new arrival.

At a steady gallop they rode to where Henry thought they might intercept them. Instinct was driving Henry rather than logic as he rode. 'No it couldn't be', was the thought that kept coursing through his mind as he rode south. Then some ten miles south of the ranch's property line as they rode over a small ridge, Henry thought he saw a glint of some reflection of the sun overhead from a large wooded area to his left.

Halting the riders, he withdrew his spy glass and peered into the wooded glade and sure enough he saw several cows settled in for a day long siesta. Then a closer glance revealed a pair of eyes, scrutinizing his every move.

As Henry and his group drew closer, they stopped about several hundred yards away from the trees as Henry again peered into the wooded glade, this time revealing short horned cattle, some of which had large humps on their backs, relaxing in the shade from the late morning sun, while every fifty feet or so, just at the trees edge a set of eyes, watched in silence.

Henry dismounted, handing the reins of his Appaloosa to Mendoza and approached the wood line afoot, stopping fifty yards from the tree line, kneeling and started to whistle in a low tone. Eventually causing a large chestnut furred wolf like creature to rise up and take two steps out of the tree line. As the first wolf stopped, a second emerged and then a third and then the fourth.

The Henry offered the muted whistle again making a certain hand signal, he learned long ago from his Shawnee Indian mentor. One by one the wolves slowly came to him. Not exactly as large as the original Akila had been long ago, what with interbreeding of species, but still by the wary way they moved, Wolves none the less. The first wolf, clearly the leader, stopped scant yards away from the kneeing Henry its eyes and nose working at their own pace, every wary of that sudden move that would signal attack, the seeing none approached Henry close up scenting him, thus imprinting his scent almost deciding that while he may not be foe, that friendship was still in question. Then he gave a small bark and one by one the others approached, as the first drew a short distance away, engaging in the same ritual, yhen joining the others, finally in a small semicircle they sat erect waiting. Then from the wooded area ahead, came a deep voice speaking in heavily Spanish accented English, saying "What do you want Senor"?

Henry said back, "We were alerted to the fact that a small herd was heading towards the MHM ranch and wanted to see if we could be of help"!

"I need no help Senor", came the sound from deep within the woods.

"How do I know that the cattle you have in the woods ain't rustled cattle", asked Henry trying to gauge the location of the voice for whoever was speaking was well hidden?

"How do I know that you are not trying to steal my cattle Senor"? Slowly standing, ever cognizant of the wolves that surrounded him, Henry drew aside his long white trail duster indicating his Rangers badge fastened to the front of his holster. "I'm a Texas Ranger, duly empowered by the governor of the state to enforce the law. Now a whole lotta folks around here are trying to steal cattle and I'm gonna ask you only once to put down whatever gun you have on me, and show yourself, or else some of your wolves are gonna meet their maker".

A long minute passed, before a tall young man partially emerged from the shadows of the trees, saying "Senor, make one false move and my wolves will tear you to pieces and I am a very good shot and I will shoot the horses out from under your men from here"!

Continuing on he said, "My business is with a certain Henry Jaeger in Waco Texas. I understand he is the owner of the MHM rancho and I am here to bring him some cattle"!

The barrel of Rodrigo's rifle was pointing towards the ground but could be brought to bear in a target in an instant.

Trying not to hope for or believe, Henry then asked one final question, "And then who exactly are you"?

"I am Rodrigo Fuentes Jaeger and you Senor"?

Try as he might not to believe, there it was, all the elements fit together right down to the ground, the manner of his travels, his bearing in the face of potential danger, his size, those eyes, his mother's eyes, the wolves.

Try as he might, tears came to Henrys eyes as he tried to catch his breath, finally saying, "Then young pilgrim, it looks like your long trip is soon at an end, for I am Henry Jaeger"!

Taking several steps forward, then several more coming from the woods, Rodrigo was too young to remember just what his father looked like, asking "If you are indeed Henry Jaeger, then you will know the name of my mother and the manner of her death"!

"Your blessed mothers name was Joselita. You're the grandson of Don Domingo de la Fuentes. Your grandmother is Encarnacion. There is more, much more"!

At that, Rodrigo gave his own slow whistle for his wolves to stand down as he approached his father. Yes he could see the resemblance as he approached; perhaps his journey was at an end. Now as far as Henry was concerned there was no doubt, this was Rodrigo Jaeger. As Rodrigo approached he could see tears in the eyes of the other man. This wonderful twist of fate had brought them together at long last, as they came together in a long embrace both with tears in their eyes. Slowly Henry held Rodrigo's face in his hands saying, "Let me look at you son. Yes, you have your mother's eye's", and then he clasped him once again to his chest.

As the other two riders slowly approached, Henry turned and yelled, "Juan, cast your eyes upon little Rodrigo, for he's not so little any more"! Mendoza slowly dismounted approaching Rodrigo almost with disbelief saying, "The last time I saw you, you were, this big", hold both hands about a foot from each other. "A little 'nino' and now look at you"!

By now the wolves were all gathered around wanting to be part of the crowd, with Rodrigo saying, "And to think I came all this way to join you and I almost shot you"!

"Damn glad ya didn't son, damn glad"!

It was clear at a glance that Rodrigo had traveled far and with a lot less than Henry had when he and Mendoza left Mexico.

"The ranch is about ten miles away son, what say we all get back to your new home and get you cleaned up, your cattle settled and the wolves fed"!

The cattle were awakened from their slumber by a simple signal from Rodrigo which sent the wolves back to work as the entire group made their way northward, the wolves following drag, hampering the recalcitrant cattle from their slumber pushing them ever northward for the final phase of their journey, with Henry, Mendoza, Joseph and Rodrigo leading the way.

As they worked their way to the ranch, Rodrigo revealed that over the course of time Don Domingo and his wife succumbed to old age five years ago when he was but eleven years old and his Uncle inherited the entire rancho.

Over the years, his Aunt and Uncle had intercepted the letters from Henry and hid them from his grandparents. But over the passage of time, Don Domingo and his wife had told him wonderful stories about his mother and Henry and his Tante' Juanita and Juan Mendoza and the manner of their departure.

One day he by chance discovered a box of letters, hidden in one of the barns he was cleaning and discovered his uncle's duplicity.

One night when his uncle was away in Saltillo on business for a week, he made off with a dozen head of the newly acquired Brahma and Hereford, short horned cattle to follow the route of his father to Texas, the purloined letters showing the way. Traveling by night sleeping by day, avoiding towns and settlements, living off the land.

"So I'm afraid father, you were right. I am a cattle thief!" "Son, did ya take all the new breed cattle?

"No father, the rancho has two dozen left to breed with their longhorns."

"Good, then all ya took was your birthright! Besides, you're in Texas now and that's all there is to it"! "Then I gather", Henry continued, "that you know I've remarried and you have two brothers and a little sister".

"And your Uncle Juan here, we got him hitched up and he's got two little ones who are practically family, and Joseph here, he's a Buffalo Vaquero so he's just about family, so your about to jump right into a big family"! "The thing is you know about them, continued Henry, "But they don't know about you" Just then he could feel the stare of Mendoza and said, "Now don't you say a word Juan"!

Several minutes later Mendoza asked, "Jefe, may I say four words"? Henry nodded, with Mendoza saying, "Bueno, I tole you so"! "That five words Juan"! It seemed that Henry would have to throw himself at the mercy of his relationship to Melanie. He'd meant to tell her of Joselita and the Fuentes years back but every time he got the nerve up, something always got in the way. But Rodrigo was the oldest and where There was a will, there was, by god, gonna be a way. He would somehow find a way. He was determined that what happened to the Fuentes family never happen to his if he had anything to say about things.

Later in the day as they entered the ranch proper, the Herefords and the Brahmas were fed and watered and Rodrigo was shown quarters by the barn complex to relax and clean up as best he could for tonight he was to join the family at supper.

They talked together for a time, then Henry left him just in time to see Melanie deposit the children as they all made their way eagerly to their afternoon chores, for the chores were one hell of a lot more fun than the schooling they all had to endure and useful too.

As Henry caught up with Melanie as she struggled to climb the steps into the house carrying several skeins of broadcloth she'd ordered from town, Henry took the burden from her kissing her cheek in the process saying, "Mel, there's something' I gotta tell ya".

"All right so tell me, Henry"! "Something I shouldda tole ya long ago"!

"All right so tell me Henry", she repeated! "Somebody's coming to dinner tonight"!

"So, somebody's coming to dinner tonight. Is that what you should've told me long ago, or should I wait for the other shoe to drop"!

"Please sit down Mel for this just might get complicated". Then he poured his heart out to Melanie, head down droning on telling her about his every so brief life with the Fuentes family of Monterrey and of his love and marriage to their daughter Joselita and of the birth of his son Rodrigo and the death of his mother during childbirth while he was away. "And every year I meant to tell ya of this but as the years went by and my letters weren't answered by Don Domingo I thought I'd never see him again, ever. And as time went on, well I just guess I put things off, because you and the children were what mattered most", as his voice seemed to trail away.

For several brief moments Melanie thought Henry had really bad news for her, but as his tale unfolded, she really felt sorry for him. She long ago took the measure of this man and had a solid history of events to go to reinforce every day of her life his eternal love for her and their children.

She could clearly see that he was truly distressed by this minor, venial, sin of omission of his past.

When he had finished, she asked him a question, "Henry Jaeger do you believe in God"?

"Yes Mel, you know I do"!

"And what do you say during the saying of the 'Apostles Creed' every Sunday at the Grotto"?

"I believe in one God, the father almighty, maker of heaven and earth and in all things seen and unseen", then before he could utter another world Melanie said, "Stop right there Henry"! "In all things seen and unseen" and she let that turn of phrase hang out there for a moment, then continued, "As you so often say, 'the spirit in the sky', almost every day, do you not"? Just then Henry started to see the wisdom of what this wonderful woman was pointing at. "Now Henry you were right in thinking that I'd probably be angry for your hiding this from me, but for all the wrong reasons. Your oldest son, who clearly had a piece of your heart all these years, has made a pilgrimage to this home we have and you place him near the barn as a mere guest, when he is of your blood and a member of this family"?

"Henry Jaeger, shame on you for thinking me so callous. Now if ya really want to really make amends, your remember that we have five bedrooms upstairs and use only four and as providence has somehow dictated awhile back there's one left over ready to occupy and its occupant is out by the barn"? By the look of things Melanie could see that she had her husband completely flummoxed and bewildered.

"Now if ya want to stay in my good graces, you'll get your great big ass over to where your son, no, our son is and bring him here to this house and settle him into the last bedroom upstairs and make him to home. For now this is his home as well. Besides, I want to get a good look at him my own self."

"Now git"!

As Henry hurriedly went out the door to do her bidding, Melanie looked upward and silently whispered, 'Thank You', to anyone who might be listening. Besides another man around the house simply meant someone else to love and there was still plenty of room in her heart, especially if it came from the loins of one Henry Jaeger.

Later on in the evening after supper, Rodrigo was overwhelmed by the immediate acceptance by his new family and later when the Mendoza family came by, Juan's wife, Juanita, serenaded them all with endless melodies from her guitar as it began to draw a crowd from all the families of the ranch, each eager to make the acquaintance of Captain Jaeger's son Rodrigo.

Before the month was out, the entire family went on a buffalo hunt, each bagging a bison in turn and Rodrigo riding with Mendoza and the Buffalo Vaquero's performing all the tasks required, each meeting with approval by Mendoza, who would expect no less."

Then each evening, endless drilling by Henry's other son Zachary, of the fine arts of the pistolero, especially the "Road Agent Spin".

The family was now complete, not to mention that the new Brahmas and Hereford cattle would vastly improve the quality of the longhorn herds. New pastures would have to be cordoned off for separation, which meant more lumber would have to be harvested and trails cut, but that was not a bad thing, just more to be done.

As for the additional wolf pack brought into the family, in the initial meeting both Akila's being the Alpha's of their brood, had the initial tendency to be standoffish and even snappish upon their initial meeting, even briefly snapping and growling at each other as they circled each other warily sniffing and taking the measure of each other, but several days later when Henry, Zack and Rodrigo came back one evening from inspecting the herds, both Akila's were seen laying in close proximity of each other, both gorged from their evening meal prior to heading out to each one herds, guarding them for the evening.

19

or a number of years, Henry would every three months or so, cull out around fifty head of cattle fattened up by his grass on his expansive ranges and drive them to the Ferry point on the upper Brazos river, and if the water level was high enough sell them to a New Orleans cattle Agent named August DeHeloussey, for the going price of between Eight and Twelve Federal Dollars in Gold Coin. Even during the first two years of the Civil War, Henry secretly sold his cattle to August DeHeloussey but was paid in Confederate Script. One the cattle were loaded upon the river boat, Henry got paid and the cattle were the responsibility of the New Orleans Cattle broker. The script was immediately spent on essentials for the ranch as long as it reasonably held value.

But in 1862, when New Orleans was taken by Union Forces, Henry's relationship with the New Orleans broker evaporated. Still, the ranch was fairly self-sufficient and the herds were prospering. Half of the corn Henry harvested was stored for fattening up the cattle prior to transshipment, while a quarter was sequestered for replanting, the rest either consumed by the ranch or sold locally. Nothing went to waste, not even the manure from the livestock, which was readily used to fertilize the fields each spring for replanting.

After the war, were the lean years, but Henry was keen enough to maintain relationships in Austin, Houston, Galveston and Ft. Worth. Keeping his head down politically, serving the Southern interests, whenever possible, went far amongst the locals in proving where his interests lay, from the Texans point of view.

But at wars end, the MHM ranch was in far better shape financially than most of his contemporaries who wore their loyalties to the Confederate cause on their sleeves. The demand for saddle ready horses was such that with a herd of several thousand horses on his spread and the ability to produce an average of eight to ten saddle ready horses a day, consistently Henry had a ready market for his mounts both by the government and the locals.

His flour and wood mill operated six days a week to satisfy demand

and his munitions shed, churned out gunpowder that was contracted for far in advance of production while his tannery operation had to be expanded to satisfy demand. When coin of the realm was not readily available to effect a transaction, physical services or good in kind were bartered in equal measure.

The only time that Henry or one of the local officials had to get involved was either the theft of livestock, or when one party to a transaction didn't hold up his end as agreed. Since the services of a lawyer were costly and a goodly number of the citizens were at best partially literate, most transactions were concluded by a simple handshake and hostage of a mutual memory.

While most of the transactions between parties' occurred as agreed, history is silent as to the number of them that went awry for any number of reasons, with only the ones that turned deadly being revealed by the light of day and the intercession of Henry Jaeger and the County Judge.

At the wars end and even before, men started to drift back into Texas with no means to make a living. Since Henry had sequestered sufficient funds during the war years he was one of the few that had any work that went at a going rate of a dollar a day. Digging ditches, erecting fences, herding livestock, working at either of the mills, harvesting lumber or any of the myriad of jobs were quickly filled by men tired of the endless fear of war. Each man signed, or made his mark, for a six month contract, renewable and if at the end of twelve months work, if a man decided to depart, he would be provided a saddle ready horse and saddle if needed and a serviceable firearm, from the armory Henry had assembled over time. In addition each man was provided a warm and dry roof over his head, three square meals a day and repairs of any and all personal needs, clothes, boots, hats, et al.

Now since all the hands Henry employed were former Confederate soldiers, and Henry employed some eighty or more former slaves full time, he had each man agree to get along in every possible way with his 'Darkies'. Nothing short of complete compliance in this regard was tolerated. At the first sign of an offense in this regard the offender was "Run off" the premises for good, the contract null and void.

Since nowhere else was any work as good as this and all that Henry hired on, willingly agreed. Even those who still had misgivings about working with the darkies found that the necessities of life often trumped lifelong prejudices. A dry roof and a full belly in times of want can go a long way to change minds. Only twice during this time, did Henry have to run anyone off with due cause and each time they left with all their accumulated earnings, a horse and a saddle and a weapon with which to make their way in this world. And each time the recipient would discover before sundown they were worse off than before.

As the ranch expanded, more wells were drilled, more homes were built, more trails were expanded into roads, more fields put into production for grain for harvest, more wooden fences erected into corrals and grazing areas and of course the relentless expansions of the herds still droned on.

Upon Rodrigo's arrival with the Hereford and Brahma cattle for cross breeding, separate areas for each were erected for their sequestration of each breed that evolved. For the Long Horn Cattle, being derived from the old Criollo Mexican breed of long ago, were better able to be self-sufficient by themselves and were a heartier breed than other cattle. The new breeds being less hearty yet tastier required more manpower.

After the war August Deheloussey resurfaced and Henry was again shipping livestock, but this time it required a week or so drive to Shreveport Louisiana, where Henry would be met by August or his agent, the cattle inspected and counted and payment made right on the spot in Federal gold coin and currency. This worked out better for all, since Shreveport was on the Red River that ran through Louisiana intersecting the Mississippi River.

The Red River was navigable almost the year round and bigger river steamers could travel upon its channels and a hundred cattle at a time could be shipped downstream to New Orleans quicker. Thus every ninety days, a hundred long horns were culled out by the Buffalo Vaqueros and headed east to Shreveport. As 1867 opened for business, news of a Trans Continental railroad came to Waco and all Texas Cattlemen were looking for markets for their cattle back east. With the Indian threat of invasion a thing of the past in east Texas the cattle herds grew. Some drives headed west over the years to California while some headed to New Mexico and Colorado, but since the rail road was heading to the heart of Kansas, Henry and the family decided that a little trip with some five thousand head of cattle, to the rail yards of Abilene Kansas, where stock yards were just being built for the transshipment of livestock to points east by railroad at prices of upwards of Thirty US Dollars a head at the rail head, payable in cold, hard, train ridin' cash money.

Reading a week old newspaper Henry gleaned that Cattle buyers were traveling to the stockyards with ready cash waiting for the herds.

Preparations were made and additional hands were hired at the going rate of a dollar a day, per man payable upon delivery of cattle at the rail head. The drive was estimated to take some three months and it took some thirty days to cull out only the oldest and the fattest of the Long Horns only to make the long and hazardous journey, but when all was finished some fifteen thousand fully grown and prime Long Horn Cattle were left milling around in one of the northern pastures in late April of "67". What remained were still some twelve thousand head of Longhorns back at the ranch, still ready to yet multiply.

Henry left Mendoza behind to run things and took a dozen of his Buffalo Vaqueros along with another dozen of the newly hired cowboys and four of the wolves to keep a watchful eye on the herd. Two wagons of supplies went along to provide for the drive. Rodrigo and Michael were taken along to gain experience and help out wherever needed. Some days riding point and some days riding drag at the very rear of the vast herd.

With no guide, but a compass and a map Henry navigated his way overland crossing the Red River with a minimal loss of livestock traveling at a rate of fifteen miles a day, with scouts riding five miles ahead and on either side of the herd, the herd made its way north with the precision of a military campaign.

Having crossed the Oklahoma Indian territory without incident and staying away from any towns and settlements, often traveling by night and resting the stock during the day, the herd relentlessly made its way north. Crossing rivers and streams, Henry was glad that he took the time to cull out any cows that were visibly pregnant for should they deliver while in route, the calf would have to be taken from her and killed lest it slow down the herd.

On two occasions rain storms and lightning spooked the herd causing it to stampede, but each time Rodrigo and Michael working hand and glove together took it upon themselves to turn the herd right in a circle, after a four mile or so run and turn the herd upon itself in a circle until the tired steers came to a stop.

On the second occasion Henry was right there with them as they all performed their heroic deeds for just one misplaced step by their ponies would case their mounts to come crashing to the ground at night and the herds to trample any and all of them to death.

Every day, Henry said several prayers to the almighty for the safety of everyone on this venture. Above all he was the only one to never allow him self a good night's sleep or afternoon siesta, for there was just too much to keep track of every minute of every waking hour. He would sleep later after all the business at hand was completed.

As the herd approached the town of Wichita in southern Kansas, he sent one of his new men along with his son Michael to see if the rail head made its way to Wichita yet and if any cow pens had been erected. Six hours later they returned with the news that the rail road was yet a week away from having tracks in Wichita and that cow pens were just starting construction. So Henry decided that Wichita was probably good for the following year but as for this drive Abilene it would have to be.

Ten days later, the herd encamped within sight of the Abilene rail head and stock yards. Henry went into town with Rodrigo and came back with several cattle buyers in tow, for his was the very first herd of the season to arrive at the new rail head. The buyers, flush with cash, eagerly inspected the herd and when they were finished one by one met with Henry giving their bids for the entire herd. The prices started out at fifteen dollars a head and before the sun went down the final bid ended at Thirty Eight Yankee Dollars a head.

Since, the stock yards could only hold six thousand head of cattle, telegraphs were sent for additional trains to transport the cattle and funds with which to complete the agreed transaction.

Henry explained to his men the situation and after the first portion of the contract was paid, assembled the men to tell them that work was not yet completed and paid each one of them a portion of their wages not exceeding ten dollars and that they were still necessary to help herd the cattle through town and to the stockyards and on to the trains as they arrived until the last cow was delivered.

For each man that stayed clean and sober until the bitter end, his total wages would be doubled. For each man that ran afoul of the law, then he would be paid off in full and told to leave. The whores and the whiskey could wait a little while if they wanted their wages doubled. If not, then good bye.

"Just one thing more, all firearms and knives will be left at camp for anyone going into town, to spend your initial ten dollars. If you want to purchase a bottle of rotgut then go ahead as long as every drop is consumed right back here at camp. Any man that returns with a hint of liquor on his breath will be immediately paid off in full then run off, without his bonus.

Gentlemen, am I understood completely", Henry asked?

To a man they all agreed and followed his dictates to the letter, for the bonus that hung out there the doubling of their wages was just too much to turn down. So they would have to wait just a little while longer to dip their wicks and be lied to by the whores and gamble with the card sharps and whoop it up.

Two weeks later and ten train loads later the last of Henrys herd made its way into the cattle pens and Henry gathered his men together paying each in turn their full wages inclusive of the bonus he promised including his sons. Then he commandeered the largest saloon in town throwing a party and hired two off duty deputy sheriff's to ride herd on the all-night party he threw and hired the finest whores in town to service the cowboys.

Since all of his Buffalo Vaqueros were all married and had families and were church going folk, all they did was get drunk and listen to the piano player. Henry and his sons stayed above the fray joining into the celebration and taking the occasional drink of rotgut whiskey, but in general following the lead of their father.

At midnight Henry and his sons and the Vaqueros bid a fond adieu and made their way back to camp carrying on a makeshift Indian skid a newly purchased strong box full of Gold coins and paper money exceeding more money than anyone thought possible that existed.

Yet they would have to keep their wits about them Henry concluded.

At sunrise the following day they all broke camp and made their way south, but this time taking another trail back to Texas. There were still two states to cross, Indian territory and the possibility of thieves and robbers at every turn of the bend. A day later one of the hired cattle drovers Henry hired, rode up from behind rejoining the group, telling him about one of his men left behind who lost all his trail driving wages to tin horn gamblers and whores and finding himself in great debt to some very serious men, decided to save his life and reveal the cattle route from Texas the Jaeger herd took.

The group of desperados surrounding him silently concluded this was going to be their return route.

"Exactly how many head of cattle did y'all drive up from Texas", the gambler who the debt was owed, demanded to know?

"Around fifteen thousand head of Longhorns is what we left Texas with", answered the scared drover, now that fear was gradually starting to sober him up. They all knew that the rumor around town was that Cattle buyers were flush with cash to such a degree that armed and nasty Pinkerton detectives were their round the clock body guards and that the going price per head of cattle was to exceed twenty dollars a head. Within an hour the a group of men had assembled numbering no less than twenty in number, all mounted and ready to catch up with the Jaeger group who was estimated to be but a day's ride ahead of them. "Yeah, they don't impress me at all", said one of the town desperados. "Come into town not packin' iron is just askin' for trouble and I mean to give it to em"!

Henry's instincts were well founded and Leander McNelly's rejoining of the group and informing the Captain of his fears, just confirmed what Henry surmised. Further it reinforced a hunch he had about the young man when he hired him on. Rising to the rank of Brevet Captain in the Texas Confederate Army, he was said to distinguish himself repeatedly by his leadership abilities in the conflict, despite his rather small size and his consumptive lung condition. On the trail north he took on every single task asked, often with considerable difficulty. After day riding drag at the rear of the vast herd, eating no end of dust that made his breathing difficult, Henry decided to put him on one of the wings for the duration of the drive. The young man had the grit to work his way through his breathing problems, still coughing up a storm, but several days later he seemed to recover, ever watchful of the condition of the herd. He always did what he was told without complaint.

Eventually they came to a stream and noting that a storm was coming in from the north, Henry decided to cross the stream and rather than complete the crossing travel down the opposite bank for some five miles, before coming up on the opposite side. All this was done at night and by the sunrise of the following day rather than make camp, they pushed on for the entire following day, heading south. The desperados not being used to the rigors of the trail, rode their horses hard following the clear trail the Jaeger party made, covering some forty miles before sundown. With the horses just about ready to give out, decided to make camp. No one thought that they'd be out more than a few days, so provisions were few. As each man fell asleep around the camp fire, thoughts of big money coursed through every one mind. No doubt there would be a shoot out of sorts and some of them wouldn't make it back. So each man's share would be greater. The recalcitrant cowboy who owed the gambler was taken along to point out the trail southward and if he was lying he wasn't to make it back either. In fact the Gambler had no interest in seeing to the cowboys' safety at all. Visions of whores and whiskey danced through every ones dreams as they slept, never thinking to place a guard on duty while they slept. Never once aware of the band of Kiowa Indians, some fifty in number that had caught sight of them riding south, looking for easy pickings before heading back to Comancheria in Oklahoma territory. Twenty of the braves slid off their horses, sneaking up and surrounding the sleeping desperados and surrounding them. Each and every one desperados had upholstered their weapons and removed their boots, never once considering the perils of the trail.

At a signal the Indians rose up and each one taking a target silently, let loose with a shower of arrows and in less than fifteen seconds each and every desperado from the town had a very painful ending to his dream never to be realized. The others rode up with their ponies and stripped the bodies of all they contained, starting with the scalps, clothes, weapons, boots and of course their horses and saddles, for the desperados would have no need of them any longer. By noon the following day, all that lay there were the fallen, being consumed by the carrion overhead and on the ground.

Traveling by a different route home Henry made no less than forty miles a day, in a zig zag pattern always with a scout several miles ahead and a scout in the rear. Two weeks later he was crossing the Red River back into Texas. Five days after that, he entered the Northern gate of the MHM ranch. Just one more day and he would embrace his family once again.

Henry pointed to the barn complex, for Leander McNelly saying, young man you have a place here as long as you want. Time to rest for you've earned it. We all have earned it.

Since it was the summer season and Henrys foresight had paid great dividends in more ways than one, he's started his drive well before the torrid heat of the plains summer and as they all made their way south he caught sight of a few sizeable herds heading north. They were in for a time and in a way he felt sorry for them all. But the word "Schadenfreude" came to mind and that of his parents long ago in southern Ohio. Oh how he would've loved to have them at his side, he thought.

As he rode up to the house, Melanie came running out to embrace him and welcome him home asking, "Well I see that you came home in one piece. Did you get a good price for the Longhorns"?

Without saying a word, Henry removed the strong box from the wagon and muscled it up the steps and into the house placing it on the table.

"Melanie, will you take a seat", asked Henry?

Upon her compliance, Henry placed the key into the lock and opened the metal banded wooden box revealing it full of neatly arranged bank notes and gold coinage. His wife fainted straight away at the sight, with Henry barely able to catch her before she hit the floor.

Minutes later as her swoon subsided she said, "Henry you're not supposed to rob banks", weakly.

As he helped her to her chair, he pointed out the notarized Bills of Sale to the Cattle Broker and pointed out the prices and the sum total. "As you said my good woman, I'm not supposed to rob banks"!

Right there on their kitchen table was probably more money than existed in the entire county. No Correct that, in ten surrounding counties. No correct that……. Melanie simply muttered, "Tell me I'm dreaming Henry and that I'll be all better when I wake up"!

He gently pinched her, saying "It's not a dream Mel"! "Do the boys know"!

"Oh I suppose they have an idea, but not an exact amount and they shouldn't know at this time. Just you and me, ya follow"? She silently nodded saying, "Well I best get along and make supper and you nest secure that fortune in the place, ya follow"?

Melanie then went to the cabinet and reached for the Jug of 'Old

Overshoes' that was locally produced pouring a large shot in a mug and downing it in one gulp bringing a grimace and several coughs.

"I thought you were a wine drinker".

"Well pilgrim, there's a time and place for everything ain't it", she jibed back! As Henry disappeared up the stairs, with the strongbox, her two sons Zachary and Rodrigo came running in after putting up the horses and the wagons, pestering her with tales of their very first cattle drive.

The following day everyone was assembled as Henry called out each and every family and presenting them with two hundred Yankee dollars per family and an extra hundred dollars per every single Vaquero whether or not they stayed behind or made the drive north.

Privately he presented Juan Mendoza with a Thousand Dollars, for being there holding things together. Then everyone celebrated for the day, with Harmonica's, banjo's and Juanita's guitar providing the proper background for the festivities.

Every single one involved with the entire enterprise, whether great or small, directly or indirectly, received a reward commensurate with their involvement.

Now the thing was what to do now with his family's sudden wealth?

One thing became clear in all his travels, cheats and charlatans were everywhere. Henry had indeed been fortunate and to a degree his hard work and dedication went a very long way towards making his luck happen. His intuitive nature, no matter where ever it came from, guided him. Did it come from his parents, the Old Shawnee Shaman, or from years of hard work, or the sum total of the events of his life? Is this what 'Common Sense' was? For the very first time in his life he was overly reflective. He'd seen overly reflective people before and concluded they were thinkers, not doer's. So fearful of error, that action of any kind never occurred.

He once heard a legislator say, "When I don't know what to do, I don't do nothing"! Thus it was people like this that more than earned his disrespect. When out on the range, a Texican fighting the hostiles was not afforded all the information he's like prior to attack, he would take what he knew to be the case, factor in his experience then make a quick decision and leave the outcome to the almighty, while fighting like hell.

Yet one thing was certain, he was not about to do a single thing to draw undue attention to himself, his family, or any aspect of the ranch. Not only did he have himself to consider but that of a host of good people that respected and depended on him. Yes there was a bank in town, but Henry never kept more money in that tin horn emporium than he could afford to lose, especially given all the banks that were being robbed lately. Reading all of the newspapers from out of town that he could get his hands on, he concluded that men, a lot smarter and better educated than he, were gaining and losing fortunes at the drop of a hat. Scallywags were everywhere. The only thing that mattered was cold, hard, train ridin' cash money. Over time, he concluded that, 'the flashier one was, the less one had of substance', "All hat and no Cattle", was how the saying went! Guarantees were almost worthless in the after math of the war years, with each man looking after his own self, with precious little charity towards others a rarity, except in certain areas. In the end he decided to make no investment that he was not directly a part of or have a controlling interest in. He had done fairly well since he returned from Mexico with Mendoza and little more than twenty head of Longhorns and a lesser amount of Horses. No doubt the Almighty or one of his agents was keeping a watchful eye on him and his family, the least he could do was to be ever watchful, of his family's largesse. As he rode around the ranch one day with Mendoza, exchanging ideas as to what to do, he'd decided to invite a select group of share croppers onto his land, for even with his vast herds of livestock and farming, barely a third of his land was being used constructively. The complete northern fence line hadn't been touched since he'd arrived years ago. It was well wooded, well watered and five well sites were there to sink water wells on powered by the wind. He still knew how to survey property and he decided to plot out fifty acre plots for share croppers covering the entire northern line of his property. Timber would have to be harvested and processed, water wells drilled, homes and barns built, fences built and Grain bins erected.

So the following day, Henry and his sons set out to survey and mark out all of the plat lines for the new venture. Subdividing land controlled by Henry and the ranch for the purpose of renting to selected people to sharecrop. As each family was selected, Henry persuaded the town banker to lend the new tenant the money to pay for the enterprise. The following day Henry would deposit a given amount of money in the bank, somewhat in excess of the loan amount, secured by Preferred

Shares in the bank. Each prospective tenant brought to the enterprise a certain amount of expertise and livestock, with which to bring to bear a successful effort.

By the end of two years' time eleven farmers lined the entire northern third of the Ranch. Homes and barns built, water wells up and pumping into wooden elevated water towers, wooden fences erected, road's made and grain planted and harvested. By Thanksgiving, eleven families, all victims of the war in one fashion or the other, saw a beginning of a glimmer of prosperity.

Unofficially, the ranch was now in the banking business, with Henry now owning a forty percent interest in the town's bank. Henry would see to it that no one ever robbed this bank and lived to tell about it.

Two years later he was approached by some Cattle brokers to drive a substantial herd to Dallas since a rail head had been built and stockyards were almost ready for livestock for shipment.

Since Henry was busy running down local desperados, he designated Mendoza and his three sons, Zachary, Michael and Rodrigo to head up the drive. Since Dallas was only a fortnight's drive away with the cattle, the drive should not prove to be a problem. The drive would take place in the spring, after the rains and all traveling would occur at night.

All the while Henry and Melanie worried each and every day about their family of cattle drovers, but five weeks later when Mendoza safely returned with their brood with but few scratches on them and a strong box full of Yankee Cash, the stories abounded, since all did not exactly go as planned. Oh the transaction went well enough, the cattle agents and their bodyguards were there, the count of livestock made, the paperwork completed as to the notarized bill of sale and the accounting transacted as to half in US Gold Coin and half in Federal Notes, each one scrutinized for validity. But when the story emerged, out of earshot of their mother of course, of how Michael got the best of a man reported to be none other than the killer, John Wesley Hardin, via Flawless execution of the "Road Agent Spin", while in a minor dispute in a saloon. Henry's heart almost stopped. "Juan, did you have a hand in this", Henry asked? And before he could answer Rodrigo butted in, "Father, Juan was across the street making purchases at the general store and we were thirsty after all the time on the trail. So without his knowledge we went into this saloon. We found a table and had a drink of beer, when another waiter could not be found for a refill, Zachary went up to the bar to get replenish our mugs. This other 'Vato' was drunk and was playing cards and he then went up to bar and lurched into Zachary just as he was getting our beer spilling it all over him. While he still had the mugs in his hands the 'Puto' drew is gun on Michael demanding that he apologize, the telling him to put down the mugs and give his Navy Colt to him.

As all this was happening the man had his back to Michael and me and we slowly drew our guns and flanked him. Zack put the beers down on the counter and drew his Colt slowly from his holster and handed it to him butt first. As this cowboy reached for Zack's gun, Zack did the spin faster than the eye could see, and now each man was just feet away from the other with their fingers on the trigger when Zack said, "Look around and see the last thing of your life"!

"So this 'Puto' looks around and sees us with our guns drawn down on him. Then Zack says, quietly, "Put the gun down on the bar and leave now" and the man does.

"He knew that if he didn't he'd never leave alive"!

"We were only told later who he was"!

Oh and as he left he passed Juan who had just arrived and had his gun drawn.

"Rumor has it that John Wesley Hardin is a stone cold killer with almost twenty men dead by his hand", said Juan!

'We still have his weapon in the saddle bags"!

"Say nothing of this to your mother, any of you! Do I have your word each and every one"! Without another word, each one went forward spit in their hand and shook it with Henry. For a man's word was his bond and the only thing of value that could never be taken away, by mortal man.

In spite of the swirl of activities occurring at the ranch on a daily basis, the business of Rangering went on nonstop. For in the aftermath of the war swarms of seemingly changed men were almost everywhere, willing to take uncalculated risks for scant rewards. When news of a robbery came to Henry's attention, he'd grab one of his son's and several vaqueros and set out after the miscreants. Often they'd retreat into Louisiana and more often than not, were not well skilled in eluding a seasoned tracker. Sometimes weeks would go by before Henry and his deputies would catch up with them. Usually ending up in a rather unfair scuffle with the robbers on the short end of the stick. Depending on the nature of the theft, drew exactly on whether or not the thieves would survive their flight. Often the thieves met an early end at the end of the rangers, who would always return the stolen goods and of course there was always horses and saddles to consider along with the latest assortment of firearms. Yes, a Henry repeating rifle was the state of the art firearm of its day, but if you didn't allow the owner to get his hands on it, it was useless.

Once Henry and Rodrigo trailed four robbers all the way to Shreveport Louisiana only to miss them as the river steamer just pulled away from the wharf, completely unaware of the two Rangers tracking them. Riding at full gallop, the duo got ahead of the bandits, riding cross country, whereas the steam boat had to follow the river's many twists and turns, arriving well ahead of the boats first stop downstream, waiting. Given an approximate description of the bandits and the horses they were riding, Henry was able to catch sight of them all together as the boat pulled away from the dock in Shreveport heading no doubt for a high time in New Orleans, with whores and whiskey in abundance. But the money they had in their sacks belonged to a host of farmers and ranchers in Texas and Henry, by gawd Jaeger would see to it that they never had the opportunity to spend their ill-gotten gains.

Besides they busted the skull of one of the bank clerks and shot a deputy sheriff on their way out of town. Unnecessary, by Henry's lights.

As the River steamer pulled into its first stop at Taylor Town, some twenty miles downstream, on the Red River to take on a load of cotton destined for New Orleans, Henry and his son boarded the boat, finding their quarry busy spending their ill-gotten gains in the boats saloon catching up on their drinking. Immediately Henry drew down on the, catching them all in a drunken stupor, disarming them and dragging them all out on the deck.

After identifying himself to the ship's captain, he demanded that their horses be brought forward.

As he forced his prisoners to all lay down on the deck face down and their arms spread out, palms upward, the local sheriff boarded the boat wondering what the ruckus was all about. As the Sheriff approached he drew his weapon seeing Henry and his son holding a quartet of men on the deck, face down at gunpoint.

"Hold it right there and surrender your weapon", yelled the Sheriff.

Henry turned to see just who was yelling at him and seeing an older, portly man, clearly past his prime wearing a badge of the local constabulary, slowly uncocked the trigger of his old Navy Colt horse pistol and offered it to the sheriff butt first. As the Sheriff drew near and reached for the weapon Henry engaged in "The Spin", in a blink of the eye, the butt of his weapon finding its way back into his hand once again at full cock position ready to fire, while with the other hand he swiped at the sheriff's pistol sending it spinning into the river water.

"Sheriff, my name is Henry Jaeger and as you can see from the badge on my belt, I'm a Captain in the Texican by gawd Rangers. Now my associate here has the draw on four desperadoes' that not a week ago robbed the Bank in Mexia Texas, beating one of the tellers within an inch of his life and shooting a sheriff's deputy, who was doing his duty. Now we been trailing these rascals for over a week and are in just no mood for any interruptions, for we mean to take them back to Texas to stand tall before a Judge. Over there are their mounts and inside the saddle bags is the loot still in the bank bags marked "Bank of Mexia Texas. So look for your own self"! The portly Sheriff waddled over to one of the horses and sure enough, there in the saddlebags were the loot still in the bank bags. "But you're in Louisiana now Ranger and clearly out of your jurisdiction", said the Sheriff full of indignation at being so rudely and easily disarmed. Stepping over to the Sheriff he whispered into his ear, "These men are coming with us back to Texas, to stand trial and there is nothing you will do about it. After we depart, should we see any attempt to pursue us, we will kill the robbers, then kill every single one who is after us and take their scalps, horses, and leave them naked where they lay. They will not return to their families and should you be with them, then you will be fed to the gators bound and alive"!

"Slowly nod your head if you completely understand what lies ahead", whispered Henry! All the while Henry has a warm smile on his face and he spoke, which underscored to the Sheriff that this man knew what he was about and was a stone cold killer should the situation warrant.

"Now I'm gonna ask your help in putting these robbers on their horses well secured so we can all ride away peaceable like. So nod your head if you understand Sheriff"?

Again the Sheriff grudgingly nodded his head. "One last thing Sheriff,

I insist that you smile and say a few words aloud that you completely understand and will be happy to help us enforce the law for the benefit of all the onlookers"!

Just then the Sheriff burst forth in feigned laughter and started to place each robber on his horse, taking measured pieces of rope and tying their hands behind their backs and securing their feet under the horse's belly.

This required the each rider to make it a point to stay on his saddle for if he didn't, he would slide under the horses belly and horses just don't like that, all the while mouthing nonstop staccato words of praise for the Rangers, by the Serriff.

By now Henry and Rodrigo were on their mounts with the horses reins all tied up to Rodrigo's horse as he started out of town back to Texas. Henry reached for his wallet and withdrew ten Yankee dollars and gave it to the Sheriff saying, "I deeply apologize for disarming you, but this ought to by you another firearm Sheriff, but in the future it might be wise if'n ya thought twice before drawin' down on any Texas Ranger doin' his job"!

"Oh and just one more thing, I heah the gators are mighty hongry round heah, this time of year Sheriff", and with a wink turned his big Appaloosa around and quickly joined his son as they rode away with their prisoners, still in a partial stupor wondering just what had happened.

Rather than travel due west, the way they came, they traveled in a southwesterly direction and with a day's worth of steady riding came to the upper reaches of the Sabine river basin, which dissected Louisiana from Texas. The robbers now fully sobered up demanded to be fed and were all so strident in their complaints as the sextet made their way around the estuary and into Texas that Henry looked at Rodrigo and asked, "Do you think these men need a bath, Rodrigo"?

"Well, they sure stink a lot Capitan", said Rodrigo as he drew his pistol.

At that Henry dismounted and dragged each robber down from his mount pistol whipping them each in turn to a state of unconsciousness, then he undid their bindings and stripped them of all they had, rebinding each of then securely and then waited for them to recover.

Seeing a few gators some fifty yards from the estuary's bank, Henry threw each robber into the water making a loud splash, which drew the gators attention to the newly arrived dinner splashing frantically in their bindings. Within a few minutes a hoard of hungry reptiles descended upon the hapless, desperately splashing thieves and as soon as each in turn was involved in the gators swirling dance of death, Henry looked at his eldest son saying, "Well it seems our work here is done Rodrigo. Let's go home"!

As they rode silently northward Rodrigo was very proud of his father and made a mental note of all that had occurred and was thankful that his father was a man to be feared and respected. As a father, he reckoned, he couldn't have done much better and could've done a whole lot worse.

Besides, after what these men had done, he figured they'd saved the State of Texas a great deal of money and themselves a lot of aggravation.

A week later they rode into Mexia Texas and returned the bulk of money they'd recovered to the Bank of Mexia and reported to the local Sheriff. The local town's people treated them to a sumptuous meal and a night in the local hostelry and the following day they departed for the ranch and a life of normalcy.

20

In the ensuing years, one by one the Jaeger children grew to full maturity and met others, courted them and got married. Each time the appropriate wedding and honeymoon took hold and upon their return a home of their own and a thousand acres set aside for their own enterprise along with the assorted livestock duly culled from the existing herds.

Thus by the mid 70's the Jaeger house was back to just two inhabitants. Soon the first wave of grandchildren came one by one leaving Melanie far busier than she'd ever been tending to her flock. The little school house near town had been expanded and several teachers were imported and paid for by county funds, thus taking the load off her as far as her daily teaching requirements involved. Each teacher had a home built for them near the MHM ranch.

Henry made quarterly visits to Austin to stay in touch politically with the State Government, with his ear always to the ground to stay ahead of current events. Always the trips were made on horseback, eschewing the current stagecoach service that had been in operation for some time as that for city folk, never trusting his fate to be in the hands of others.

He discovered that Leander McNelly had led a contingent of Rangers down to the Rio Grande Valley to clean out several gangs of rustlers, both Anglo and Mexican that had been terrorizing the area for years and was proud to see that this young man, though small in stature and fighting a consumptive lung condition all his life had proven to have more grit about than many of his contemporaries. Although he was greatly criticized by some by his draconian tactics, he always got results and those who rode with him would follow him into the jaws of hell willingly without a second thought. He never put his foot wrong once he decided on a course of action, but in the course of time, the consumption got the better of him and he passed away into obscurity alone and forgotten. For a brief time Henry tried to find out where he was spending his final moments but no one knew.

Still he would remember him, along with a cavalcade of others, who made this part of the country secure for civilization to take root.

However the newspapers reported an endless string of events relating to the lawlessness that swirled about the entire western region. The native Indians were ceasing to be a problem to those settlers in Texas, replaced by a home grown threat of those still displaced by the War of Succession some years earlier. The land was full of those who were long on clever, yet short on smarts, which kept Henry and the members of his family, now duly deputized as Texas Rangers and Constables of the Peace, constantly busy as they split their time enforcing the law and tracking down desperados and pistoleer's all over Texas, while trying to keep their personal enterprises thriving.

One early spring afternoon, while riding outside the ranches perimeter he spied a lone rider driving up some hundred head of cattle, around his ranch heading north and rode up to him recollecting his earlier days heading north from Mexico with Mendoza. Yet this pilgrim was all alone with some hundred head of Long horns.

Keeping out the possibility this was a lone rustler who'd bitten off more than he could chew, he rode up to the wary rider and identified himself.

Now the man was riding around his property and looked fairly much like he was all played out.

"Henry Jaegers the name and I'm a Texas Ranger," said Henry as he drew aside his long white duster showing his badge affixed to his gun belt.

"I hope you have a bill of sale for these here cattle you're driving", said Henry his hand lightly leaning on the butt of his Navy Colt revolver.

Noting the badge and the easy position of the one opposite him the man said, "I'm Charlie Siringo of Matagorda county and if you'll stand easy Ranger Jaeger, the ownership of these here long horns are in my saddlebag", whereupon he slowly reached back into his bag never taking his eyes from Henry. After fishing out a waterproofed leather folio, he ruffled through his papers producing a weathered bill of sale indicating that the cattle were indeed his.

"Where ya headed son" asked Henry handing back his papers?

"Well, I been on the trail from Matagorda, down by the coast and am headed up to Dallas to the stock yards" so I can sell these critters"!

"How long has it been since you've eaten, Mr Siringo"? "Well sir it's been awhile"!

"Your cattle look awfully puny to ever bring a good price at the stock yards son", offered Henry as he scanned the herd.

"Well I reckoned I could fatten em up on the trail if I didn't drive em too hard, but it seems that I was wrong what with the drought an all", said Siringo sadly.

"Well young man, seeing that you're all but played out, let me make you an offer I hope you'll accept. About a half mile ahead is the west gate to my ranch and if you'll let me help you, we'll find a fenced off pasture that's well watered and full of prairie grass that your herd can rest and fatten up for a spell, for in their current condition I can't see you getting any decent price for them. In addition I'm needin' a wrangler who knows his way around a cattle operation who can help with the branding and I'm willing to pay Thirty US Dollars a month including your own place to sleep and three square meals a day. Stay with me through branding season and after that if things work out as long as you like or you can move on as you please young man and your cattle will have their very own place to fatten up, without mingling with my herd"!

"You'd do that for me Ranger Jaeger", exclaimed Siringo. "Why you don't even know me"!

"Let's say I'm a pretty good judge of men and what you were trying to do take's a lotta sand and it reminded me of someone long ago who did a similar thing. So what ya say", said Henry spitting in his hand and offering it to tired cowboy. Quickly Charlie Siringo did the same shaking it with Captain Jaeger.

At that, they both started to move the cattle to the gate some distance ahead with Henry opening the gate and allowing the livestock to enter, closing the gate afterwards. One of the things that slowed Siringo down was the fact that a number of his cattle had given birth and that many heifers had young calves moving with them slowly. Now these calves would have a fairly safe place to mature.

After Henry had selected a certain pasture, fenced in surrounded by other fenced in pastures, Henry explained the role of his wolves that kept constant patrol of the pasture areas and the various herds. "And they don't eat the cows", asked a surprised Siringo?

"Nope, bred that out of them and trained them to be a horse and cattle friend and protector. Besides we make it a point to keep them well fed.

Once the wolves and you get properly introduced and they imprint your image and your scent in their heads, you'll be safe from any harm coming from them and if in trouble, once they get to know ya, they'll rip the throat out of anyone who tries to bring you harm. Of course it'll help a whole lots if ya bring food to each of them a few times at first, so that'll be one of your duties for the first few weeks, as a getting to know ya chores. It'll yield benefits down the road"!

As they neared the barn complex Henry showed Siringo to one of the empty places surrounding the barn and then showed him the common area where meals were always served to the unattached help by the darkies, and then said "Get yourself cleaned up and rest a bit for tonight you'll be having supper with me and my wife"!

The following day Henry made the rounds with Charlie introducing him to each of his sons and Mendoza, then made the feeding rounds of the wolves eager to gorge themselves and take the scent of the new arrival.

Thus for several more days Siringo made the rounds with each of Henry's sons, each in turn taking the measure of the new arrival. After ten straight days, the chore was handed off to another when all of the wolves began to recognize Siringo by sight.

Now he was ready to show his worth joining everybody else in the tasks of cutting out the recalcitrant cattle, roping and securing them for the one with the branding iron. Siringo didn't miss a beat, as Jaeger and Mendoza observed him easily segmenting each of the livestock out of the herd, then guiding his mount with little more than the occasional spurs on the flanks, finally deftly laying the lariat around the neck of the fleering critter and sliding off his mount as easy as you please, grabbing the flailing legs and winding the rope around them, with but a few twirls of his wrists then stepping away holding on to the rope taut so the another could close in and apply the red hot branding iron to the struggling cow.

Mendoza then commented to Henry, "He has a certain style of roping not often seen north of the border and clearly Jefe, he knows his business"!

Later on in the day, Mendoza with Henry in tow asked Siringo just where he learned his roping technique.

"Down at the King Ranch, from a Mister Brucelino Dominguez, a very old man who taught me when I was ten years old", answered Siringo.

"Brucelino Dominguez, I know this man, for he was the very one who taught me when I was young, back in Mexico! I met him when I worked with the Andrade family", he let slip.

As they walked away Henry asked, "I never knew that you worked for the Francisco Andrade family Juan"?

Sheepishly he responded, "I never wanted you to know, for as a young boy I was taken from my family in Culiacan, just as Juanita was but at an earlier time by Chuey Medrano's people and put to work for Don Francisco doing everything at the rancho. When I proved able to perform as a Vaquero, we rode far and wide stealing cattle from where ever we could and driving them to the Andrade rancho, then changed the brand to resemble Don Francisco's brand. For years no one found out or wanted to find out. Those who tried were killed and their bodies cut up and fed to the coyotes."

"That is where I met Dominguez who was a maestro with the lariat. One night I left and was lucky enough to have Don Fuentes take me in and apparently Dominguez was able to get away and join the King family"!

"Well never you mind Juan. Hey I got me some secrets even you don't know about. So we're even I suppose"!

"Besides after all that you and I have been through, and the fact that you're part owner and that we're both God parents of each other's children", at that Henrys voice trailed off, his point being made. Much is often made of friendship. For many claim to have friends, but are they around when truly needed? Are they really reliable? Can they be counted on, no matter what? Will they require repayment in kind at some future date? Will they have to arrive at your doorstep with a long list of bona fides?

What had been Henry's guiding star was really quite simple. He always remembered what his father told him while helping him plow a that field in Cheviot. His father was a simple man and always broke things down to their base elements before making a decision, saying that; "All that is simple is useful, while much of what is complex is not useful"! "Never look for trouble for trouble will always find a way to cross your path, but when it does act quickly and decisively and without fear, for fear is the mind killer, it immobilizes"! He always remembered what his father meant by what a real 'Man' is. "A real Mench is someone who will always be counted on to do what is necessary, at precisely the time it is necessary, without having to be told and never to expect compensation of even a thank you for ones efforts"! Often it did not require heroic feats, just timely help and direction.

In this Henry was truly blessed, for in Juan Mendoza was a man, barely literate, who had a certain depth of character, that given his origins, was inexplicable. Yet through the history of time, his bona fides as a true 'Mench' were rock solid. As Henry looked out at his family, each and every one of them, made him proud, they conducted themselves with dignity and grace yet could rise to the occasion at a moment's notice to defend what was theirs and the weak and downtrodden.

Each and every one of them had their dark side, but it lay deep within, bound by their will, surfacing only when needed swiftly and without remorse, then willingly submitting to the bonds of civility and returning to that place in the deep abyss, laying doggo in the tall grass. "Firmitas et Honorare'", was the family motto that lay etched over every fireplace mantle.

The "Eternal" was their Shepard and they shall not want, with each and every family member seeing to that very fact. Which wass why Henry started to grow uneasy every time he went to town to tend to either Ranch or Rangering Business. A growing movement was taking hold certain elements of the community at large and Henry could understand the source of most people's discontent. For while his affaires had prospered during the war because he'd stayed at home and out of the war, many of his neighbors who had cast their lot with the Secessionist Cause had not fared so well.

Husbands who went off to war often never came back leaving their wives at the mercy of life in general and many times when a husband did return, he was either physically or emotionally not the same man the wives had once known and grown to love. Often when Henry or Melanie discovered that a family was in need, a year's worth of smoked meats suddenly appeared and help with the planting or harvest came out of nowhere.

Then there was the Republican Administrators sent down from Washington to bring the Reconstruction and all of its strange new laws to the conquered Southern States, especially the laws that freed all the slaves. Forty Acres and a mule, was now the law of the land and the slaves fled their former masters with a vengeance, casting their grateful lot with their new Republican Masters every time it came to vote.

Of course the Darkies that had occupied Henry's land led lives free of fear, for each family was, granted a full 'Fee Simple' title to fifty acres of land to work any way they wished, with access to livestock or implements, never a problem.

There was a growing movement called the "White Knights of the Golden Circle" that had existed for some years, never really amounting to anything significant, usually malcontents staying busy chasing down slaves who fled from their masters. Since they had the good sense not to come around the Waco area< Henry paid them no mind. But the newspapers brought reports of various groups in Houston, San Antonio and Dallas with a variety of names all dedicated to "Keeping the Nigger under the thumb", employing tactics of terror and intimidation on those poor souls largely ignorant and unskilled, highly superstitious, just trying to make a life for themselves. Torch light parades of the faithful were reported in Houston and Galveston, for the purpose of gathering people to their banner.

Random hangings of the 'Darkies' were reported all over the south principally in Louisiana and a few near Houston.

One day when Henry was in town, he noticed that a sudden influx of heavily armed strangers were arriving gradually in small groups and the rumor was that they called themselves the "Red Legs", implying that underneath their boots were legs stained red with the river of blood they trod through, usually the blood of anyone not white, or Catholic or Republican.

Since they had not broken any laws or stolen any livestock Henry had no cause to question them. But he knew the type and he just knew that trouble was on the stove and it was fixin', to simmer.

As they would pass through town, they would always keep a wary eye on Henry as he would on them as if they knew each other from a former existence. Hardened men they were. Hardened by life's circumstance and sheer hate for anyone who was just not like them. As long as they behaved in this part of Texas, Henry and his people had no cause to ruffle their feathers.

But in his bone Jaeger just knew thing were about to get out of hand. In various meetings with the County Judge, a learned man and well-seasoned lawyer, the term 'Probable Cause' kept echoing over and over. With the Judge saying, "Henry both you and I know these waddies are up to no good, but seems that they've got on with some of the farmers and ranchers in these parts and their gainfully employed. So the law says that there's nothing we can do until and when they get outta hand"! Several months passed, when one night an entire Negro family was discovered hanged by the neck from various limbs on a single oak tree and under each and every body a fire was built to make the slow strangulation more painful. Clearly the act was performed in the dark of night and by torchlight, to send a signal to all of the newly freed slaves to stay away from the polls come election time two months away. As Henry, the Judge and several towns' people, came upon them several days later chasing away the coyotes and buzzards circling overhead, both were deeply saddened by the brutality of the event, noting the expressions of painful terror on the faces of the father, the mother and the three small children as they went to their maker.

Henry immediately sent one of the townsmen to his ranch to summon his son's to come to this place immediately. Three hours later, they arrived with Mendoza and several of the Buffalo Vaqueros in tow all heavily armed and in tow was Charlie Siringo who flat insisted that he be included. The partially charred lower half of the bodies were all cut down and placed neatly in a row to await burial, while Henry looked around for the various hoof prints signaling just where the murderers had gone. Returning minutes later Henry had disclosed to the Judge, "Seems they were awful confident of themselves, cause they left a trail that anyone could follow". All were duly deputized after the dead were partially buried and the graves covered in large stones to keep the critters away, then away they all went including the Judge, just to ensure that all the legalities were observed as the guilty were brought to justice.

As the group followed Henry, more out of respect than anything because even though each one in the party, except for the judge, could read trail as well as any Indian, being taught by Henry himself, the trail the killers left.

Several hours later as the sun was setting in the west the group came upon a farm house where it appeared an early supper was being served. "Why that's Randall Webster's place", exclaimed the Judge"!

Webster had just settled into the Waco territory about a year ago and no one seemed to know just where he came from. Didn't appear to do much in the way of ranching or farming and always paid for everything in gold Yankee dollars.

The entourage spread out and as Henry made his way stealthily to the barn returning some tem minutes later saying to the Judge, "Yup, inside the barn are the very horses that visited the Darkies a few days ago".

"Well Henry I suspect it's time we interrupt their supper, don't cha think", offered the Judge. Whereupon Henry shouted, "Randall Webster and everyone in the house, come out immediately, unarmed with your hands up!"

From inside the came the answer, "Who wants to know"? The Judge whispered to Henry, "That's the voice of Randall Webster Henry"!

"My Name is Henry Jaeger, Captain of the Texas Rangers and I mean to bring to justice you and everyone in the house for the lynching of the Negro family on Jasper Creek a few nights back"!

Several minutes went by with no sign of movement from the house when a brief volley of gunshots rang out from the opposite side of the house and then more silence, before a door opened and Webster and two others emerged from the house with their hands up.

Henry, threw the trio face down on the ground and as they were being held at gunpoint by Siringo and the Judge went around the other side of the house to see what all the commotion was, only to find one man on the ground clearly trying to escape and another stuck hanging from the window, for as he was shot apparently the window sash came down on him making him an easy target, for Mendoza and his Vaqueros.

The dead were dragged around to the front to join the others.

In short order they all were securely bound and lifted over their unsaddled horses, with bridles only and secured face down and with the rope tightly bound around the horses belly. To be taken back to town along with the two other dead accomplices similarly bound for trial and subsequent burial. "I'd make sure that you boys stay on top of the horses, for if ya slide down around their belly the nags just ain't gonna like it", said Henry. As they all rode off with the three prisoners and the two dead, they were unaware of another who was fortunate enough to be late for supper with Randall Webster and seeing the shoot out and arrest of Webster and the others waited deep in the trees, for at least an hour then rode off to tell others. Hours later as the sun was setting, Henry made certain that Webster and his two murderers were safely in the county jail, he said to Wiley, who was by now the town Sheriff,

"Don't worry about getting em fed tonight, they already had supper and don't make a sweat over them tomorrow for it appears they been livin' high on the hog and could use to miss a few meals, their own selves"!

An hour later as Henry and his men returned to the ranch, everyone went to their own habitat, secure in the knowledge that Justice had been done.

Charlie Siringo made his way to the feeding hall where all the single Vaqueros gathered to get their meals, finding some scraps of leftovers sufficient to last him until morning when he would make the rounds of the pastures and feed the wolves.

He rolled a cigarette and lit it up taking the soothing smoke deep into his lungs and when it would be finished he'd try and get some sleep for the next day's work would await no man, but since the excitement of the day was still coursing through his body he was certain that sleep was not to arrive any time soon.

As his last puff made its way into his lungs, he thought he heard the faint sounds of gunfire coming from one of the northern pastures. He put out the remainder of the cigarette and then heard it again, a brief volley of gun fire, coming in from the northerly gentle breeze in his face. One by one, lights came on from the nearby homes and from the quarters for the single vaqueros around the barn. Then Henry came out from his house and like many others still in his night clothes with a side arm in his hand. "Captain Jaeger", yelled Siringo pointing northward, "Gunfire from the northern pasture"!

Siringo ran to the barn and as he finished saddling up his horse and twenty others came running into the barn, some still hitching up their breeches carrying their rifles and side arms. One by one the mounts were selected and hurriedly saddled and within fifteen minutes Jaeger and the rest of the vaqueros followed Siringo at full gallop towards where he though the sounds came from. Ten minutes later they came to a halt at as they entered a fenced pasture, through an already opened gate, in a pasture that should've been full of peacefully sleeping livestock but was now almost empty with just a few frightened strays hugging the wooden fence line and eventually coming upon a rider less saddled horse wandering aimlessly and then upon a duo of bodies in deaths embrace, There lay one of Chani's progeny with his massive fangs embedded in a death grip in the neck of his assailant, while his hand was still gripped around a knife deeply embedded to the hilt in the wolves body. Henry had seen this before and was certain the man had met his maker first but his sheer will power at the moment of dying kept firm grip on the knife assuring the wolves demise would follow.

Before he had time to grieve, they all heard the cry of one of the wolves and rode off to yet another pasture over a far off ridge. Minutes later as they crossed into another pasture through a broken fence that could only result from a massive stampede, the came upon yet another scene an exact copy of the previous one with another of Chani's offspring dead, its fangs locked in a death grip crushing the neck of its assailant, the only difference being that this time the wolf was riddled with bullets which made no difference for once the fangs entered the throat of its prey, with their viselike grip, only the breaking of the jaw or sweet moral suasion could make the jaws open. The wolves had died well, in combat as was their birthright, doing their duty. Henry would grieve later. As the group followed the trampled grass over hill and down dales they passed other empty pastures the herd which by now should be pretty well played out, passing exhausted cattle standing there unable to move another step after five or more miles of running. Then they came upon two more wandering horses and eventually what had been their former riders slain by gunshot and then finally one of the Buffalo Vaqueros riding night duty who'd apparently coming upon the rustlers and had a running gun battle with them, taking down two of them before he was himself killed. He also had died a warrior's death.

As they kept on at a steady pace through the night Siringo was at grateful for a quarter moon and the presence of one of the wolves at Henrys side. His sons homes were far away on the other side of the ranch, as was Mendoza's, so it looked he would substitute as one of Captain Jaegers son's for at least a little while.

As they easily rode in pursuit, it appeared that few if any of the cattle would make it outside the property line as more played out cattle appeared standing stock still exhausted by their night's efforts. Then as they approached a rise just a mile away from the eastern fence line Henry signaled for them to stop and he dismounted running at a crouch peering over the top of the ridge then running back to the rest mounting up saying, "Boys, looks like their horses aren't in much better shape than the cattle they left behind and are in no condition to either jump of bust through the fences. Now there are just seven of them and they're milling around at the property fence line with some of em starting to slowly ride north along the fence line on mostly played out horses. Now I'm gonna take five of ya and Siringo you get to come with me, while Nathan you take the Vaqueros and then ride north for a mile then make a skirmish line all the way to the fence line and walk it back south. Siringo and I will get just ahead of em, then head back towards you and we'll squeeze em a tad"!

Within fifteen minutes of steady riding Jaeger, Siringo and his crew got ahead of the would be rustlers and murderers and strung out a skirmish line and headed north towards the rustlers, with weapons at the ready and well in hand.

All Siringo could think of as the forces slowly came together was, "Hammer and Anvil, Hammer and Anvil" and he almost started to feel sorry for their quarry, almost.

Minutes later Henry's group heading north saw the some stragglers up ahead following the wooden fence line heading north, along the line of pine trees that Henry planted years ago when he first started up this spread.

The riders ahead were completely unaware of anyone following them and only paid attention to what was in front of them, looking for a gate to bust open and escape into the open prairie west of them. Cresting a ridge with their quarry ahead of them on played out horses, they saw the men ahead, almost in a single line hugging the fence line which went from one pine tree to another. Then across a small depression in the land appeared Henry and the rest of the Vaqueros blocking the way, spread out in a skirmish line across the ridge some twenty yards separating the riders from each other.

The quarry seeing their way ahead blocked, turned around and discovered Nathan and his riders blocking any possibility of retreat.

Outnumbered and desperate to escape the entire group spurred on their tired mounts and headed east back into the ranch proper. After riding a half mile on flagging horses they were about to crest a small hill when ahead of them, completely unexpected was, Juan Mendoza and all of Henrys sons coming to a halt with weapons drawn.

Fear and desperation does many things to many people. Some will fight against all odds while others will give up the ghost and surrender, falling on the mercy of their captors.

Those closest to Mendoza and his group drew their pistols and before they could be brought to bear fell in a hail of bullets by those right in front of them. Those trailing seeing the fate of the three ahead of them brought their mounts to a halt and threw their hands in the air.

As Henry and Siringo's men closed with the remainder surrounding them, they could hear Rodrigo and Zachary yelling to the captives to throw down their guns, dismount and lay on the ground face down.

Weapons collected, Henry set about the task of finding out who had put them up to this. Several of the others set about the task of collecting the dead and placing them on their mounts for the trip back.

With his riding crop Henry set about to flailing each and every one, noticing that all of them were attired in white trail riding dusters and then set about searching the duster pockets coming up with white pointed hoods in each of their pockets. Every one of them had the white pointed hoods, indicating membership in the order of the 'Knights of the Golden Circle', just like Randall Webster and his bunch that lynched the Negro family, several days ago.

The very last thing one wanted to see, was an angry Henry Jaeger, for once he saw the white pointed hoods, he reached for his Bowie and grabbed the long hair of the nearest captive and brought the butt of his knife down hard on his head knocking him senseless, the proceeded to employ with the swiftness of one well-practiced in the art, to remove the bulk of the scalp of the poor miscreant, with several well placed strokes from a razor sharp blade. Only Mendoza had seen Henry do this before, while everyone else had now witnessed the beginning of Henry Jaegers darkness. The entrance into the hell that waited.

All were quiet as Henry swiftly went about his business, removing the scalp from each and every one then attaching the four scalps to his saddle.

Then as an afterthought went about to the three that met their fate at the hands of Mendoza and Henrys sons, tossing a scalp to each one with the terse comment, "Here, you earned it"!

As they made their way back to the inner pastures of the ranch they were met by others who were in the process of rounding up tired cattle that survived the stampede and gathering up the dead livestock that littered the plains, into the wagons without having to be told. For each represented a value in either meat on the hoof or the hides that could be processed. Not one thing went to waste.

Then wagons came back for the dead, the lone Buffalo Vaquero and the two wolves. Henry decided that both of them were to be afforded burials with all the honors of a human at a secluded glade, while he sent Mendoza and Rodrigo into town escorting the four survivors without their scalps to be held in the town jail, for trial with the rest of the murderers. Sitting astride their mounts the four captives entered Waco wailing in great pain drawing a crowd that followed in dismay seeing that here were four bound captives, secured to their horses without their scalps. Few had ever seen such a sight and all had cringed at the visage, but followed the slow parade of the hopeless through town and to the jail for incarceration. The town doctor followed in the wake, but there was little he could do since each and every one was cut right down to the bone and the skin tissue was staring to shrink. None could imagine the pain that each of the murderers was going through and finally the town pharmacist ran over from the apothecary with several bottle of the opiate Laudanum that would go some ways towards alleviating the pain so at least the doctor could clean and bandage the missing scalps.

The Judge arrived on the scene at the court house and was told of all of the events that befell those at the ranch. When he asked about how the prisoners came to be scalped, Mendoza and Zachary looked at each other, then back at the Judge and shrugged their shoulders.

"Not talkin' eh", said the Judge.

Then Zachary spoke up saying, "Judge, men came onto our property, killed one of our people and two of our wolves, in an attempt to steal our cattle. They do this at their own risk. We can connect these men with Randall Webster's fella's, the Knights of the Golden Circle who strung up the Negro family several nights ago, and here's the proof taken from the guilty"! Then he pulled out one of the white pointed hoods made of sack cloth with eyeholes cut in the front.

"Every one who owns one of these will be out to murder and steal from the citizens here about", continued Zack.

"We demand a quick trial and a hanging thereafter, Judge"! Then Zack and Mendoza left the jail and as they got outside were confronted with a restless crowd, being verbally swept up by the rantings of the firebrand Minister, Otha Rudibaugh who every Sunday could be heard shouting out his outrage at the existence of Catholics, Niggers, Mexicans and other nonbelievers in their midst to a small, but growing congregation of the faithful.

As Zack and Mendoza left for the ranch, the doctor approached the county Judge saying, "These men are experiencing pain that exceeds anything I've experienced and are in need of better care that we have anywhere in the state. All I can do is keep them in Laudanum, but that's expensive and since you're the county judge I think you should know this, for I just don't know how they could ever be brought to trial Judge. Do you"?

Continuing on he said, "Captain Jaeger and his people, dropped them on us, when it might've been better to take care of them privately on his ranch without trotting out his methods of Justice given to the hostiles back in the time of the Republic"!

All the while, the obsequious owner of the area newspaper was close at hand, making furious notes on the back of anything with a paper value, of the events as they occurred. Something told Jared Millpond, that he would get precious little sleep this night. On his way back to the small office that served as the press room, he passed one of the town's saloons hearing a ruckus occurring betwixt some angry citizens. Sliding unseen between the swinging doors he made his way towards a corner table as the good reverend Otha Rudibaugh loudly exhorted a rapidly exercised crowd of men, towards action.

"We all need to free our poor brothers from that jail tonight during a torchlight event, when the White Camellias will bloom"! Which was codespeak for all those assembled to don the white robes and the peaked hoods of the dreaded Klan. Then march on the jail where Wiley the sheriff, was sitting duty all by himself.

"Go on out to the countryside and hearken a call to arms, so we can be free to march down the streets, this very evening by torchlight", exhorted Reverend Rudibaugh to the crowd of men well on their way to a drunken evening.

Playing the part of a drunk leaning on the table face down, the town reporter heard Reverend Rudibaugh say to another as they all left the saloon, "Soon as we get enough folks together in the Robes and the Klavern, we'll all assemble after dark on the edge of town by torchlight and march on the jail. Just Wiley will be there and he'll pose no big problem.

Then we'll bust the boys out and set fire to the jail. Anybody gets in the way and we'll send em early to their maker", as they passed through the swinging doors.

The newspaper man thought a moment and agreed with all he'd heard that Sheriff Wiley would be overwhelmed, but the Jaeger Clan wouldn't. He could see the headlines now, "The Klan battles the Clan in Waco"!

Looking for the coast to be clear he slipped out the side door and made his way towards his office and hurriedly hitched up his buggy for a ride out to the MHM ranch. As sunrise approached, the buggy went through the overly large wooden gate, wide enough for two large wagons that served as the formal entrance to the MHM ranch. Erected some five years ago, the entrance was covered by an immense wooden archway that strongly implied that Henry Jaeger and family lived here. He was impressed by the long, well-manicureddrive, showing nary a rut covered by a long copse of Pin Oak trees that covered the long entrance way, providing complete shade, that some say was planted some twenty years ago.

The entrance way snaked about a half mile before the tree line ended as the Jaeger house and the main barn complex came into view.

He rode up to the house and there on the main porch that surrounded the house was Henry Jaeger, napping in his rocking chair, still fully clothed unable to sleep after his nights efforts. "Captain Jaeger", he yelled several times alerting him to his coming as he dismounted securing his buggy to the hitching post, then running up the steps, breathlessly relating what he'd seen and heard at the saloon.

"Captain Jaeger, they mean to secure the release of all the prisoners, this very night and burn down the jail, with the Sheriff in it", revealed the newspaperman as he tried to catch his breath.

"Helluva way to wake a man up don't ya think", mumbled Henry as he stretched his arms and legs trying to will tired limbs to a state of alertness. "Looks like you after a story, so follow me and you'll have all the story and then some.

Henry quickly went down the steps and over to the main barn complex and started to ring the big bell, usually rang to alert everyone for meals or emergencies. Within minutes people came running to the source of the ringing from the nearby pastures.

When about twenty had arrived, Henry the asked the reporter to repeat to those assembled what he'd told Jaeger about the coming events of the evening in town. When he concluded, Henry directed one of the men to ride to alert Mendoza and his sons to meet up at the barn complex, by midafternoon, well-armed, then to alert all the tenant farmers of what was happening and light torches and patrol the entire northern fence line. Then he directed seven of his Buffalo Vaqueros to prepare for an evening in town and to meet back at the barn heavily armed by midafternoon. Finally he directed yet another dozen of his Vaqueros for picket duty on various sections of the ranch, to prevent a repeat of the prior evening's incursions.

When everyone went about their tasks, Henry turned to the reporter saying, "You must be hungry, why don't you come up to the house and join me and my wife for the noon meal?"

Given the events of recent hours, Henry trusted no one not of the ranch. If the reporter was indeed after a story and interested in the common peace then he'd want to stick like glue to Henry for the duration. If there was a more sinister plot afoot, the reporter would find a reason to be elsewhere soon enough, thus bringing his career to a sudden and violent ending.

Within the hour Charlie Siringo and his sons rode up to the main barn complex, followed close at hand by Mendoza and several of the Vaqueros.

When everyone was assembled Henry asked the reporter to once again relate what he'd overheard to everyone while Henry put the finishing touches to a plan he rolled around in his mind.

"Men, if any of ya hadn't eaten then get on over to the eatin' hall and get your fill, for in an hour we all leave for town. As the men took their meals, Henry sat down with each group of men and directed them as to how they were to disperse and where in town quietly and what signals were to be given and what to do. Then he met with two of the younger Vaquero half breeds, half Cherokee and half Negro skilled with the bow and arrow directing each of them to lay in wait at either end of town where it was likely men would assemble and the horses would be sequestered.

This evening's activities were to be accompanied by shotguns and pistols and a nasty surprise was in store for any attired in white robes and hoods. By late in the day, all were in their places in town, at either end and on roofs with firing lanes all charted out in every one's mind. Their mounts were placed well back and out of sight in several wooded areas.

Charlie Siringo was well placed on a roof across the street and some distance away from the Sheriff's office and Henry's sons were well placed on roofs on either side of the street.

Inside the Sheriff's office was Henry, the reporter and Mendoza who gained entrance by the rear door. Now all everyone had to do was wait, for the sun to go down so the roofs could cool off.

All his young life in Matagorda County, Charlie Siringo was indifferent towards the law and those who enforced it. Most cow-hands has little use for Sheriffs and their deputies, for it limited their fun and many of them where either incompetent, relatives of authorities or dishonest or both. But in his time working for Captain Jaeger, he gained a different view, for the man had never put his foot wrong as far as Siringo could see. He'd a way of sensing if someone was lying to him and heaven help the person who tried to steer him wrong. Probably a product of his time fighting the Comanche during the Republic, tracking them, then in a scrape no one was better at long range or up close than Captain Jaeger.

He'd seen the darkness in his eyes when danger was on the horizon, the cold and serious manner with which he went about his business. The even tone in his voice, warning that death was just around the corner.

His ways with the critters were beyond comprehension, within an hour he'd seen him gentle a wild mustang to that of a saddle ready beast ready and willing to carry a rider some distance as long as the rider treated the animal with respect. Somehow Mendoza and the Captain's sons and some of the half breed Vaqueros had learned this skill.

He could scalp a man, within an inch of his life, yet be as gentle as any grandparent with the young babies, all in the span of a single day.

Siringo took a swig of water from his canteen and reexamined the array of ammunition lain out on the roof top. As he looked around he could see Michael on one side of him on a rooftop and Zachary several buildings away on another roof top and across the street he knew that Rodrigo and others were lying doggo ready and waiting.

Inside the Jail Henry saw the Doctor trying to tend to the seriously scalped prisoners as best he could. Henry drew aside the doctor saying, "Think its best you fill em up with that Laudanum stuff as best ya can Doc, for they just might not last the night, ya follow"?

As the Klansmen donned their pointed hoods over their long white robes and lit the torches setting off towards town Otha Rudibaugh was certain this would be a glorious night with his two dozen hooded Klansmen approaching from the south side of town and an equal number approaching from the north end with lit torches and that special touch of a few of his waddies climbing up on roofs across the street from the Sheriff's office where it was shielded from the torch light in the streets.

'They would never know what hit them', thought Rudibaugh with smug satisfaction.

All the while as the Klansmen marched out of sight, the skinny teen age boy left behind to guard the mounts, grew quickly bored and hunkered down opening his new pocket knife and flipped it into the ground endlessly, while behind him moved stealthily the half breed with an arrow in his bow, moving to the boys right to get a better shot not ten yards away.

While both boys were about the same approximate age, the difference in experience and motivation was soon to be apparent as the horse guardian felt the silent pressure of an arrow penetrate his neck, slicing his voice box in two. Unable to breathe, much less cry out, he next felt himself being roughly thrown to the ground and saw the dark image of someone quickly astride him, slicing his neck deeply from ear to ear.

His last fleeting thoughts were about 'how unfair this attack was', as he started to feel the faint pressure of his scalp being separated from his head and then nothingness.....

Henrys young half breed Vaquero, thought about how the Jaeger family was now not the only ones who would sport a scalp taken in battle, hanging from his saddle horn. Then he silently gathered all of the two dozen horses, soothing them with secret touches and tethering their reins one to another to lead them back to the ranch the long way around town, for his nights work was completed, as he was sure his opposite number on the other side of town was heading in the same direction, with many horses and saddles counting much "coup", in the process.

Both Michael and Zachary could hear noises from the rear of the buildings they were atop of and moving silently behind an abutment in the rear of their buildings, drew their knives as movement was detected with someone climbing onto the roof. Waiting, as they could hear whispers of the assailants to another with the shadow of the one who reached the top bent over the roofs edge to lend a hand to another trying to climb up behind them.

As both men reached the summit of the rooftop, they made the mistake of turning their backs to Michael and Zack who leapt from the shadows quickly plunging their blades deeply and quickly into the backs of the others then grabbing them both quickly and with two swift swipes of the blades, sliced right through their necks and gently placed them on the slightly slanted roofs with only the last rattling of breath's burgling from four dead throats.

Peering over the roof tops and seeing no one else anywhere behind them, the two brothers looked over at each other across the roofline and gave each other a brief nod. Then they both disarmed the dead and brought the additional firepower to their original positions.

Between them lay Charlie Siringo who witnessed it all, thankful that he was flanked by the sons of Captain Jaeger. For should any of them failed Siringo would've have to shoot the remaining assailants throwing the entire surprise party in a hell of a mess.

Further, he was grateful these were his friends and would make it a point to keep it that way. In the distance, up the streets, they all could see the torches of two separate groups of men closing in from two directions. 'Best we keep our heads low and listen very carefully', thought Siringo as he brought the hammer of his Navy Colt back to half cock position. Soon enough the crowd of Klansmen's attention would be elsewhere.

As Otha Rudibaugh and his hooded Klansmen marched up the street by torchlight, he peered out of his eye slits seeing the other marchers closing in from the north part of town to join him in front of the Sheriff's office and jail. He looked up at the roofs of the two buildings across the street from the jail, hoping that he wouldn't see the heads of the four others he was sure was on top of the buildings. When the good Sheriff Wiley came out they were to hold their fire, as Rudibaugh would try and talk the Sheriff into surrendering his prisoners. At a given verbal signal the men were to stand up and open fire, killing the Sheriff thus allowing the Klansmen to rush the jail and free the prisoners. But they must be quiet as a mouse and not visible until signaled.

Seeing no sign of those waddies peering over the roof top Rudibaugh was pleased, for the Klan would triumph this very night. But then he had his backup plan, of one man behind the jail with an unlit torch, should his rooftop boys fail, or the good Sheriff not emerge with the prisoners. They would set fire to the rear of the jail, forcing out the Sheriff and the prisoners. The Sheriff would certainly come out rather than be burnt to a crisp. A little risk was involved, but the Klan was there to save their own.

The news reporter shrank back as the sounds from the street grew louder and louder. For this was the very last place he ever wanted to be in gathering news. Yet this was probably going to be the greatest news story he would ever get, even selling it to the other newspapers and probably to the eastern papers as well.

Henry gathered up his old Colt revolving cylinder, cap and ball shotgun and said to the Sheriff to watch the rear of the jail, while Mendoza and he would take care of the front.

Mendoza had both of his Navy Colt revolvers in his hands, cylinders charged and ready to fire as Henry opened the door stepping outside to confront the crowd of hooded Klansmen, right as Otha Rudibaugh bellowed, "Sheriff, come out for we want to have a talk".

As Henry stepped outside, he cradled his shotgun in his left arm, as Mendoza left the door slightly ajar just in case he was called upon to come to Henrys rescue with both guns blazing.

In the torchlight Henry looked around and bellowed disdainfully to one and all, "Jesus H. Christ, I didn't know Halloween came early this year"!

Rudibaugh took a step forward saying, "You may make light of our presence here Ranger Jaeger, but we mean to free those there prisoners in your jail this night as God is our judge"! He hadn't counted on Henry

Jaeger making an appearance this night, but 'no matter', he thought, 'the man could bleed like anyone else'.

"So you all mean to break out these murdering thieves as if they were righteous pilgrims eh"? Before Otha could respond, Henry then bellowed to the crowd, "Brave men every one, so brave they have to hide their cowardly faces from one and all and ya think that nobody can recognize any of ya", said Henry as he leaned against the buildings support column, lighting a fresh Cheroot from a single wooden match, apparently unconcerned.

"Hells fire, the good Reverend Rudibaugh can be recognized by the way he bellows like a wounded cow and Harley Race over there with his Mexican spurs that jingle like Christmas and you Marcus Carpenter, how on earth could you ever hope to hide that hump on your back? Y'all want the prisoners out do ya? Well, come on", Henry bellowed as he brought to bear his old Colt revolving cylinder shot gun, "but understand this, five of you will die this very instant starting with you Otha"!

"I certainly hope you're a righteous man because", as he drew back the hammer on full cock position, this here scattergun will blow you to smithereens unless all of you right now remove your hoods and drop your weapons to the ground right now"!

That was the signal for all of Henrys men on the roofs to rise and fire warning shots on the ground around the perimeter of all those assembled by torchlight, forcing everyone to look up and around them. "As you can see gentlemen you're surrounded and outnumbered by my people on the roofs. Now I just don't give a care whether or not y'all surrender peaceably or not, for I just as soon shoot the lot of ya. But drop your gun belts to the ground and do it now"!

As the last gun belt met the ground, Henry then bellowed, "Now remove your hoods and robes and do it now"!

Reluctantly everyone did as they were told, when Henry added, "Now everyone who doesn't want to be arrested and go before the Judge tomorrow, remove all of your clothes including your boots and do it now"!

Again with great reluctance most of the men started to disrobe, complaining all the while, as they worked their way down to their long underwear, the stopping, all but completely naked save for their long woolies.

Then Henry bellowed, "Gentlemen I said all of your clothes, which means everything, flat down to the skin and do it now"!

One by one the men started to reluctantly comply, driven by the fear of certain embarrassment versus jail time, versus the certainty of immediate death on the streets. Yet there were but three holdouts driven by rage, dove for their firearms, struggling to get them from their holsters finally emerging in their hands and starting to fire wildly in Henrys direction.

Which suddenly drew fire from the roof tops upon the confused crowd down below. Henrys eyes were concentrated on the form of Otha Rudibaugh who upon hearing the firing commence dove for his weapon. As his hand found the handle of his pistol he felt the full force of Henrys Colt shot gun, slam into his side as his bloated naked body rolled over with his gun held in a death grip.

Hearing the firing in front of the jail Wiley came running to join Henry and Mendoza on the jails front porch as the firing started to diminish.

Arriving late to the game was Otha Rudibaugh's ace in the hole, the torch bearer who hearing the gunfire in front of the jail, took it as a signal to light the torch and set fire to the kerosene soaked pile of brush, piled up against at the rear of the jail, then flee, his simple task finished.

As the gunfire abated, Henry's men came down from their positions on the roofs, one by one, to hold at gunpoint the terrified Klansmen survivors in the street below. The reporter emerged furtively, from his crouched position inside the jail to witness the carnage in the street, taking a body count of those assembled, to find out of fifty some now naked men nineteen lay dead in the streets, including the bloated corpse of the Reverend Otha Rudibaugh, his hand tightly clutching his pistol. He started taking notes as townsmen emerged from their hiding places, all a wonder at such a thing happening in their community.

The town doctor, wisely concealed under the Sheriffs desk emerged, from the jail behind the town reporter wondering where to start first circling the dead and sorting out the wounded to treat.

Calmly walking down the street came the County Judge to inspect and put his legal imprimatur on the events at hand. While wandering around the assembled naked Klansmen all hunkered down on the ground held at gunpoint fearing for their lives now unmasked, everyone attention was turned back to the jail, by the screams of the prisoners held captive in cells located in the rear of the building, now all aflame. As Henry ran back to the jail, he stuck his head inside the door, only to be driven out back again by the heat and the flames of the rapidly advancing fire that while started in the back of the building raced to the front consuming all within.

The town's people who gradually gathered quickly formed bucket brigades, bringing water from the horses water troughs, to dowse the adjoining buildings to keep them from going up in flames.

As the fire reached the jails ammunition magazine, stores of shells started to explode causing everyone to fall to the ground lest they be shot by an errant shell. As the townspeople frantically fought the flames to keep them from spreading to other structures, several of them were felled by errant bullets, exploding from the conflagration; still they worked frantically to save the town.

While most of the attention of the town's people was towards the jail, one by one the naked Klansmen left all their belongings in the street and started to flee in the direction of where they left their horses.

One of the Vaqueros was about to fire upon the desperately fleeing Klansmen, when Henry put his hand on his arm saying, "Joseph, where is he gonna go? His horse is long gone, he's naked, unarmed, thoroughly discredited and will have to walk back to wherever he came from and will have some tall explainin' to do to somebody most likely. So do you think he worth a single bullet? Besides, there's no jail left to keep him in"!

As Henry turned to the flames that were engulfing the jail and the frantic town's people he was approached by the County Judge who absently muttered, while watching the now dying flames and the walls of the structure fall into each other, sending a shower of sparks into the air, "Bad Barbeque", over and over.

The bodies of the four Klansmen on the roofs of the building across the street were retrieved and placed alongside the dead in the streets, stripped of their clothes and weapons. All the clothes were thrown into the fire, the bodies covered with sheets from the town and the firearms loaded on to the saddle horns of Henrys horses gathered and brought into town. The boots of the Klansmen were neatly paired up and placed alongside one of the wooden sidewalks.

The County Judge quickly met with one of the town's merchants to find a temporary office, for the Sheriff, as Henry agreed to provide all of the lumber and wood products free of charge for the quick rebuilding of the town jail. As Henry and his family of men slowly rode back to the ranch the hour approaching midnight, he was secure in the knowledge that a night's work had been achieved. It would be a very long time, if ever; the areas darkies would have to fear a Klansman's terror. Further as he and his proud men rode back in one direction, laden with firearms of every description, they all chuckled at the thought of a fool's parade of naked men, afoot, walking back to, wherever they came from in every direction but theirs.

Their respective horses and saddles now the property of the MHM ranch. Late at night the town's lone news reporter was busy crafting a story line that would be printed in the next day's paper, by the light of his kerosene lamp when the door opened and the County Judge entered.

Sitting next to the reporter, the Judge said, "Herman that sure was something out there on the streets tonight wasn't it"?

Feverishly working on his text, the reporter uttered a mumbled< "Uh yeah Judge" and kept writing, when the Judge put his hand on the pencil stopping the reporters writing, "But the story just can't be told the way it happened Herman"!

Then he went into a brief legal description of just why the story of Henry Jaegers involvement would place him at risk legally with the state if the real story emerged. "A very good man who has served this state and the county well could be placed at legal risk by some up and coming scallywag lawyer intent on bringing a good man low and I just won't allow that Herman"!

"But Judge, what about freedom of the press, freedom of speech and freedom of"! Just then the Judge cut him short by saying, "Round here, I'm the very last word on what 'freedom' is and I suggest in the strongest of terms that you go along to get along, or else!

Now you're gonna have a story to tell but tonight I'm gonna help you to edit that story, for public consumption. Now if ya don't do as I say, I'll see to it that Henry Jaeger tracks you down wherever you go and you will simply disappear and your bones will be found somewhere out on the prairie gnawed bare by the critters of the wilds. Now are ya gonna cooperate or what"?

Tearing up his previous writing and handing the torn papers to the

Judge, Herman said, "Now how do you suggest we begin Judge"? For the next two hours the Judge slowly dictated the edited tale of "The Night the Klansmen Marched through Waco"! As he rose to leave he said, "After you set the type on the press, bring me the first tear sheet before ya get to printing, for I'll be at the Court House all night working. Then when ya print up the first batch of papers, I'll need to see the first copy of the paper before I approve them for sale. Any funny business, any at all and I 'will' have your ass, ya follow"!

Gritting his teeth the reporter, raised as a city boy and not accustomed to the ways of the frontier agreed to meet the Judges requirements. As he reread what the Judge had dictated, he grudgingly acknowledged the story was not half bad as it was. Not entirely the truth, but not half bad as it was.

After all, Herman was a practical man and practical men stayed alive and some even prospered.

21

onths later, Charlie Siringo sadly departed the ranch after almost a year with Henry and the family. Noting that some of his cattle were pregnant and ready to give birth to calves, Henry traded them with a like number of his cows not pregnant and provided documents to verify ownership. In addition, he provided a letter of introduction for Siringo to a cattle broker he knew at the Dallas stockyards.

He sent Juan and some of his men with three hundred head of livestock to accompany Siringos herd on the drive to Dallas. Riding back from the northern property fence line where the final goodbyes were said, he looked up to see two eagles high up in the sky doing their mating ritual. Shielding his eyes from the afternoon's sun he stopped his horse to look up and remember a time long ago, when the Shawnee Shaman stopped them on a hunt in mid-winter, to observe nature's vital ritual.

When spawning time arrives for the young eagles, the female instinctively will swoop to the ground, grabbing a sizeable twig in her talons then ascend to a high altitude, with a male suitor in close pursuit, then fly back up to the same altitude, once reached she will release the twig for the suitor to snatch in midair with his talons.

That accomplished, she will swoop back to the ground, grabbing a larger stick or branch and fly back up to a slightly lower altitude, again with her suitor in close pursuit. Once there she will release her recently acquired stick. Then the suitor will release his stick and swoop down to snatch the second stick in midair with his talons.

This action will be repeated several more times by the eagles, each time the stick getting increasingly larger and the altitude lower. At any time during this ritual should the male eagle fail to snatch the stick in midair and the stick fall to the ground, the female will immediately lose interest and fly away, determining her suitor unworthy to be her mate.

But should the suitor, be successful at every turn, then both will fly to an even greater altitude, with the suitor dropping the last stick and both eagle will embrace intertwined with their talons, falling to earth in a spiral, disengaging just before hitting the ground, quickly spreading their wings, coming to a soft landing.

That completed, both eagles were matched for life with each other.

Their courtship completed, both worthy of each other. Should either of them die at any time during their time together the survivor never takes another partner, choosing solitude till their death.

That was the honor, eagles kept amongst each other. Henry remembered the old Shaman explaining as best he could in broken English and sign language, conducting a running narrative of the events as they unfolded.

He remembered the final phase, of the ritual as both eagles plummeted to earth intertwined with each other, pulling out at the very last instant to come to a soft landing, with Henry asking, "But have they ever crashed".

"The Shaman responded as he put his hand on Henry's shoulder, "No one has ever seen the eagle's crash, during the ritual, ever"!

Several months later, the Shaman, his Avatar was slain by the Red Hair.

This was but the second time in Henry's life, in all these years, that he'd seen the eagle courtship ritual and true to form after almost an hour of aerial activity, here were two eagles plummeting to earth like a stone, disengaging at the very last second, spreading their wings and coming to a soft landing, scant yards away from each other. Not a sound emerged from either of them as the fell, but once on the ground, they paraded around each other, screeching in triumph for all the prairie dogs and critters to hear, while walking around each other several times viewing their new life partner, then taking wing together and flying off till they were out of sight.

Nature was sending Henry a message, but as to just what it was, he was uncertain. He would think about it on his way back to Melanie. By late afternoon, he pulled up to the barn, unsaddling and brushing down his horse and joined Melanie sitting on the porch, taking in the warm sun on a mild fall day, while knitting some new baby clothes for their son, Michaels newborn.

He gently took her hand in his, stopping her work momentarily saying nothing for a while, then related the dance of the eagle's ritual he'd observed earlier in the day. None of his children had undergone such a ritual of courtship and neither had he. Yet it seemed the eagles had their own truth, while humans had theirs also.

Melanie coming up from the environs of the old south in Charleston, then related a swirl of stories, about how the elite of southern society belles, made life sheer hell for a great many of their suitors and how her mother had done the same. More often than not, the rituals had their weeding out of the unworthy, process resulting in solid relationships, but more often than anyone cared to admit, precisely the opposite took place. Marital treachery and infidelity from both the husband and the wife often broke apart great families ending in scandal.

Henry listened with great interest, for even on those rare occasions when Melanie chose to engage in gossip, her manner and style of oral delivery of the narrative never failed to capture his interest.

"Seems to me, that eagles live a far simpler life than we do and their rituals make good sense on a certain level for them. But in any case I'd say it's all a roll of the dice, with no guarantees. Take us for example; when we got together I had no other options. My father had just died and I was practically on the other side of the world I'd always known. The General had gotten us together and I accepted, rolling the dice"!

"Life was hard for me at first and every night I fell asleep wondering if I'd done the right thing. But I was lucky, only you would've sufficed. Both you and Mendoza were honorable men, skilled and hardworking. As time went on, I grew to realize my endless prayers were answered, over and over"!

"At first I wondered if you ever were going to take an interest in me, but later when I discovered that you were married to Joselita and that she died in childbirth, the truth came clear, that you were still in mourning, an honorable thing. Over the years I discovered that I had made the right decision to take up with you at that time. For Henry Jaeger, you're an honorable, smart, hardworking man with an abundance of common sense. You've made a wonderful life for all of us!"

Their eyes were locked on each other as Melanie spoke from the heart and when she concluded, Henry asked, "I was wondering, the only Catholic church around here is down San Antonio way and we could take a stage coach there and be there in a few days and get married in the Cathedral, so Melanie will you marry me so I can make an honest woman of you"!

Thinking very carefully before answering, with tears starting to well in her eyes, she said, "Henry Jaeger, you adorable scallywag, I have to decline and before you get all het up about my answer, understand this. I am already an honorable woman and have brought into this family three wonderful children all of who assume that we did the appropriate thing years ago and to do this now would lend an air of illegitimacy to their existence, can't have that at all. But most important Henry, I know where your heart is and it's with me and just like the eagles I just happy the way things are and don't need the trappings of society to tell me what's right and what's wrong. Besides with all the times you've said to me that you loved me and what with all the things you've done, its cast in stone, we love each other. That's it and there it tis"! "My god woman you've sure got a lotta sand"! Melanie put her knitting down, got up from her chair and sat in Henry's lap embracing him and kissed him saying, "A man coming off the trail could sure use a bath, don't cha think", she asked with a wink, the signal between them that heaven awaited in the aftermath.

"Besides I know where your heart is, right next to mine pilgrim"! They embraced for what seemed like an eternity, neither wanting to let the other go, the odor of sweat and livestock somehow not mattering at all to Melanie. As they embraced she tried to recall what she had read from some ancient philosopher, which roughly put was that, "In every one's life all one could reasonably expect was a sea of misery, which every so often was interrupted by a spate of dry land and that land was called happiness."!

Holding Henry close, she reflected that she had experienced more happiness with this man than was ever her right to expect. When she compared her life to the lot of many others, she always came away eternally grateful and blessed. She had a wonderful man in her life, wonderful and honorable children and was blessed with wonderful grandchildren. Her life just couldn't be much better, but it could've been a great deal worse. She had dedicated her life to this man in every possible way and had been rewarded many times over. It was impossible to know what lay ahead, but she always prayed to that unseen image, 'To keep all that she's worked for and yielded safe from harm and should the unforeseen calamity arrive at their doorstep, let her "Melanie Jaeger", be the sacrificial lamb. Short of that, old age with her man, sitting on the front porch holding hands, looking at each other's greying hair, wrinkles and infirmities, was just fine with her. As the sun set in the west, she finally rose up saying, "Henry, you need a bath and while ya get that done, I'll go and whip ya up a great big steak made just how ya like it"! Then with a wink she turned on a dime and disappeared into the house.

Several months later, the town jail now rebuilt after the fire, Henry was tasked to transport some fugitives from justice, from Austin, handed off to Henry in Waco, to be escorted by special Stage Coach to Dallas, where they were to be handed off to one of the Territorial US Marshall's for further transport to Ft. Smith Arkansas. Henry and one of the newly hired town deputies accepted custody of the prisoners in Waco and replaced the guards who were to catch the next stage back to Austin later in the day. The Deputy was to ride up top with his scattergun while Henry rode inside with the three other prisoners.

"When we gonna get fed Ranger", complained one of the prisoners? "Whenever it suits me pilgrim", said Henry casually!

"Well, when's that gonna be you son of a bitch", growled the prisoner angrily! "Just then, quick as a wink, Henry drew the fifteen inch long, razor sharp Bowie knife that always accompanied him wherever he went, grasping it by its flat edge and brought the heavy handle down upon the prisoners head, laying it open knocking the prisoner senseless. The other prisoners looked on in horror as their partner in crime was out cold, with a big bloody gash upon his head and a slow stream of blood working his way down to his chest while his head lolled back in forth with the swaying of the coach over the uneven road north.

"Any other questions about food being served", asked Henry wryly as he cleaned the blood off his blade on the prisoner's shirt and sheathed the knife.

In talking to one of the guards back in Waco, he was told of the prisoners being part of a gang working the entire Rio Grande Valley area as far north as Corpus Christi, involved in livestock rustling, kidnapping and standard road agent work, robbing stage coaches, as well as anything that might make a dollar. It was the remnants of Leander McNelly's, Texas Ranger Police bunch that put a dent in them. Always elusive and varying in numbers, this un named gang got by more by sheer luck, rather than skill in having their way and eluding the law. Yet one night, by sheer misfortune they all were at a whorehouse in Galveston, when Leander's boys swooped down on them catching them mostly by surprise, several of which died with their boots on and little else, as they foolishly went for their guns rather than serve time.

Five of them died, three were captured, thanks to the fact they were passed out drunk at the time, while the rest rode off on their horses in the dead of night. Their ranks cut in half and their leader captured, the Rangers decided not to task their horses any further, settling in for the evening, courtesy of the establishment's proprietor.

Signs of the gang heading north following their leader, served as every indication that a rescue was in the offing. So Henry looked at the other two prisoners as the Coach made its way to Dallas over a rough and rutted roadway.

"Now I don't take sass from anyone, especially road agents and rustlers. So you boys are gonna be nice aren't ya", Henry stated! "I know your boys are comin' after ya, so if you two know just where they're gonna make a stand ya better let me know 'muy rapido', cause at the first sign of gunfire each of you are gonna earn a bullet first, before anything else"!

The other two remained silent, holding out hope that their men would have a fool proof plan. But no one had foreseen of someone like this, not exactly your standard law dog, as their escort. With every passing mile, their hopes began to dim.

An hour out of Waco, Henry called up to the driver to halt the coach directing the guard up top to come down and keep an eye on the prisoners while Henry climbed up to the top of the coach. He'd made this this trip several times before, driving cattle, so he knew the lay of the land. The Coach was atop of a ridge of land with a full view of the landscape for miles around and it had been several weeks since the last rainfall, so anyone following would raise up a cloud of dust, just as his coach was as it made its way north. As he pulled out his spyglass, he took in the long view of the way behind them and sure enough, a cloud of dust was showing just over the horizon, he figured some five miles back. 'It could be anyone', Henry thought, then again it could be the road agents fixin' to close the trap.

Henry strained his memory of the trail ahead wondering where just the right spot to spring a trap was. Then the answer came, just ahead some ten miles distant, where the roadway came briefly between two densely wooded areas was the perfect spot to spring a trap.

He directed the guard to stay in the cab trading places and stayed with the driver up top. As the coach made its way forward, he found the very spot for a detour around the anticipated ambush area some five miles distant, where the roadway hit a patch of very hard ground and ordered the driver to veer left off the road, into the tall buffalo grass. He stopped the coach and ran back to examine the presence of tracks and finding none made his way back through the high grass, straightening the tall grass some ten yards into it. It would have to do. Only an experienced tracker could see the deception. Rejoining the driver, he guided the coach in a roundabout detour some ten miles out of their way around the ambush area and proceeded northward to their destination.

The remnants of the gang were reported to be only a half dozen in number and Henry reasoned that if he was to spring a trap, he'd have two men hid in the tree's on either side of the road getting the coach in a crossfire, with one just ahead to fire on the driver and maybe catch the horses, with three bringing up the rear close by. That's what Henry would do, if he had a mind to. As the coach rolled north the driver commented to Henry that driving the Coach off road was tiring the horses and that if they were to be of any use, the coach best find its way back to the road and soon.

Not being a good option Henry decided to stop the coach and feed the horses grain and water from the emergency supply each driver kept on hand and rest them for an hour still in their traces, then proceed north to the crossroads where the road split in two, the left hand going to Ft. Worth, while the right hand went on to Dallas and the end of his travels. He'd read about the telegraph lines that were springing up all over the nation and were to come to Texas the following year. Too bad they weren't in use now, for he could've sure used them to alert the US Marshall Deputy in Dallas of his time of arrival. An hour later the horses rested, watered and fed, the driver cracked his whip, over the lead horses and the Coach lurched forward, with Henry still riding with the driver, his ancient Colt, revolving cylinder scatter gun at the ready, while a Henry repeating rifle sat in the drivers well and a brace of Colt Navy cap and ball revolvers sat fully charged at his side. The driver was directed to proceed across country in the direction of the crossroads at a steady pace as to not overly tire the horses. Anticipating trouble, he instructed the guard down below to pistol whip all of the prisoners at the very first sounds of gunfire, then to join him in firing upon anyone who tried to stop the coach. The road way north provided a few wooden bridges to cross the streams that intersected their path, whereas the roundabout way presented them with the problems of finding the right fording places where a wagon could safely cross during the dry season.

Fortunately Henry was aware of the various fords in their travels northward. This of course put a further strain on the horses causing Henry to stop the coach just a mile from the cross roads in a copse of tree's for yet another hour. Seeing that it was growing late in the day the horses were yet again fed the last of the emergency grain and water still in harness. The hour up, the coach once again lurched forward and within a mile rejoined the road way with the Dallas, Ft. Worth crossroads within sight. The stage coach horses, while not exactly fresh, should be able to make the rest of the trip in good order. As Henry looked at the setting sun, he figured that an hour and a half of sunlight remained in the day, when something caught the corner of his eye, a glint from behind. He pushed the large sombrero from his head and reached inside his vest pulling out the spyglass and extended it to its full length. Hard to see anything clearly from the top of a stage coach going down a rough road, but what he could make out about a mile away was a cloud of dust and the occasional glint, from some of the fancy traces on a horse that one would never find on the horse of a poor working vaquero. Only the wealthy or road agents had such glitter. Henry turned around and said to the driver, "We have company and they're closing fast about a mile away"!

"Well Captain Jaeger, well see just how much these nags have left," as he stood up in the drivers well, cracked the bull whip just over the lead horses and hollered, "Hee Yawww", snapping the reins and the cruising coach, lurched forward.

Henry leaned down alerting the guard inside the coach of the rapidly closing riders saying, "At the first signs of gunfire you know what to do"! Then as an afterthought, he leaned back down and yelled, "Your scatter gun is only good for close work, use your pistol on the pursuers only shoot for the horses. If they can't ride, they can't follow."

As Henry drew up he could see the driver was taking his mounts just at a point below flat out as the driver said, "Dallas should be just ten miles ahead just over that here small rise up ahead, then after that everything is mostly downhill"!

In his mind as he drew up his spyglass once again to look to his rear, he could now barely make out the riders pursuing them. As he took a rough count he could make out about ten riders kicking up a cloud of dust coming hard. It could only be one thing. His instincts were correct and these were the people, who somehow grew their ranks, riding hard meaning to rescue their leader. Desperados of the worst kind.

The stage coach slowed a bit as the horses made a mighty effort to climb over the rise in the road, the driver skillfully prodding his charges, while saving just enough of them for a final sprint to the finish.

Henry looked at the driver, then back at the rapidly closing riders, he decided the driver knew best how to glean the very last ounce of energy from his horses as the Carriage came over the rise with the town of Dallas on the distant horizon. Gaining momentum now the carriage gathered speed as the driver steered his chargers down the gradual grade towards its destination.

Henry looked back once again, he could see the riders now almost a third of a mile behind them. He briefly wished for his Beretta rifle to bring down the lead riders, but it required a steady hand and what with this bumpy road it was out of the question. He reached down for the Henry Rifle and cocked the lever, putting a cartridge in the chamber, yelling to the driver, "Tell me when there's a smooth patch road ahead so I can get off a few well-placed shots". A half mile ahead the driver yelled, "Get ready... Now"! As he said that Henry ripped off a few shots at the lead horses now only about a quarter mile behind them causing one of the horses to stumble, tossing the rider to the ground, while the second horse veered into another causing both to veer off the roadway slowing down.

Just then Henry warned the driver, "Duck down, their pulling their pistols"! Just as the words left his mouth the sound of several bullets came careening all around them. The driver had the horses going flat out now, while Henry could hear the guard down below starting to fire his weapon at the riders apparently unsuccessfully, still keeping up a measured rate of fire at those in pursuit, making them pause a bit and think twice about closing in. As the Carriage careened down the road towards Dallas,

Henry saw several riders try and leave the road and parallel the road way in order to get a firing angle on the coach's horses. Hit just one horse and have it go down and the coach would come to a very brutal halt, the momentum of the coach crushing the horses and ending up in a heap.

Henry took aim, leading the rider to his right and fired off two shots, one bullet hitting the horse in the fetlocks and the other in the riders hip, then quickly turning to the other side he saw the rider now had a firing angle on the coaches horses as it started to aim his pistol, Henry quickly fired two bullets his way, both seeming to miss their mark, but causing the rider to duck down as he rode, then he fired two more bullets from his Henry rifle, from the swaying platform, one of which luckily hit the riders gun arm just as he fired causing the bullet to hit off the mark of the lead coach horse, yet as Henry's bullet found its mark the rider fell from his horse, crashing in a heap, head first.

A hail of gunfire from behind whizzed past Henry, one bullet tearing into his earlobe and yet another tearing off a piece of his shoulder. The riders were now only fifty yards away, their numbers now somewhat diminished, still Henry crouched down in the drivers well and as he took aim, he heard a resuming of gunfire from down below and saw a rider fall from his horse.

Well, at least the guard could always say he plugged one of the bad guys.

Henry slightly stood up as the carriage swayed back and forth and rapid fired the last six rounds from his rifle. Then tossed it in the well empty, drawing his Navy Colts in each hand and started firing at the riders behind him, three of which fell from their horses, while Henry felt the sting of a bullet enter his left side and the pressure of yet another bullet hit the thick leather of his holster.

The riders behind them, four in number had reloaded their pistols in their dogged relentless pursuit of their friends. The Coach driver had all he could say grace over driving the flagging horses to and past their limits and was no help in the fight.

Rather than reload his now empty pistols, Henry holstered them and reached for the ancient Colt revolving cylinder scattergun down in the drivers well bringing it to bear on the pursuers now two of which had closed in on each side of the coach close enough for shot guns. He heard the roar on the scattergun from the cab below, just as he fired from above always aiming for the horse and at this range Henry fired at both riders at the very same time they fired at him, both parties some fifteen yards away from each other. Both of Henry's riders fell from their now tiring horses, dead before they hit the ground, while one of the bullets grazed Henry's shoulder, while the other tore a nice gash across his cheek.

The final rider made a fatal error, in which he carried on his pursuit far too long as Henry, brought the Colt scattergun to bear, blasting him from the saddle. Just then he heard the sounds of gunfire coming in front of him, with a half dozen riders closing fast from Dallas with their guns blazing. As Henry whirled around to bring his final shot to bear, he saw the riders from Dallas were briefly firing at what was left of their pursuers. All of which were dead.

As the coach came to a gradual stop the driver, after putting on the break, looked at Henry saying, "Their all but played out. Don't think they had another mile left in em at all"!

As he went forward to inspect his horses, Henry climbed down from the front of the coach, going around to the cab and opened the door only to find that all of his prisoners were dead as a result of being secured facing forward in the cab and apparently their own people firing at the stage coach sending enough rounds that entered the coach from the rear killing those they tried to save. The guard riding inside the cab was dead, from an errant gunshot that entered into one of his eyes.

One just might say it was a lucky shot, but since the shooter himself was getting friendly with the prairie dogs, it seems that luck for him, was on a holiday.

A man approached wearing the badge of a US Marshall Deputy and said as he offered his hand, "I'm Jack Vermillion the US Deputy Territorial Marshall. The one who you were supposed to hand over the prisoners"!

"Henry Jaeger, Texas Rangers. Glad to make your acquaintance"! "So it seems you been in a pretty fierce scrape Ranger"!

"Ya might say that", responded Henry.

"Have your people ride back a ways, and you'll find some dead or dying horses and some ten pistoleers layin' alongside of the road. Most of em should be dead but to tell ya the truth been a tad busy and the lead was flyin'!"

"From the look of those prisoners in the cab, seems those waddies back shot the very folks they were tryin' to rescue", said Vermillion in an offhand manner. "So it seems that I'll have at either drag them back to Ft. Smith or telegraph the Judge tell him what happened and wait for instructions"!

Then Vermillion took a good look at Henry in the fading light saying, "Seems you are in need of a doctor before too long, what with part of your ear shot, the wound in your side and all"!

The he went up to the driver and asked about the horses, only to discover that one of the lead horses has a bullet in one of its fetlocks and still ran. But now with all of the excitement gone down and six of the pursuers horses brought back, the carriage horses were set free of their traces, gathered up and replaced by others and the Stagecoach slowly entered Dallas, with its cargo..

What Henry wasn't told and had no way of knowing, was that a shipment of gold, silver and US Currency was being transferred from a repository in Austin to a federal repository in Dallas as the Coach was met by special agents of the Pinkerton's authorized with the proper paperwork and the keys to the two strongboxes hidden away in the cab under the front seat.

As the Pinkerton operatives asked Henry questions as to the trip north from Waco and the running shootout, he commented as the doctor worked on his wounds, "Sure would've been nice if someone had told me about the other cargo we was haulin', to Dallas"! "Looks like y'all got yourself a security leak somewhere in the Austin repository, Henry continued.

The Pinkerton agent said, "We try not to get involved in politics whenever possible"!

"Politics Hell, you're duly contracted agents of the Federal Government aren't ya? Normally cash shipments carry a pretty sizeable guard, don't they? I'm supposed to transport prisoners to a Federal Marshall and get damn little information in return. We get waylaid and a running shootout happens. Now I'm not blaming you gentlemen, but I expect to get answers and damn soon as to just who authorized this. I understand there's a new telegraph station in Dallas and it's connected directly with Austin. So I'm holdin' you responsible for sending a message in Austin at the highest level and do some detecting. The doc's telling me to stay put a few days before traveling back to Waco, so my wounds get a good start in healing and I intend to do just that at government expense. So sometime before I leave I expect some answers or they'll be hell to pay"! "I'll get on it right away Captain Jaeger", said the Pinkerton Agent noting from other explanations of the survivors the role played by this Ranger.

By the end of the following day, the Pinkerton's and the Federal Marshall went back down the road to Waco, picking up the dead and rounding up what horses were available from the bandits, grazing in the fields. In the aftermath, the story of the running shootout began to unfold, especially as the telegraph wires were under a constant load of inquiries, between Dallas and the State and Federal authorities in Austin.

By the end of the second day in the hotel and growing restless from the confinement to bed and the constant room service, Henry had a visitor. Jack Vermillion had gone with the Pinkerton's down the road and reviewed the scene of the gunfight and as he sat in the chair adjacent to the bed recanting the events of previous days, he said, "Those Pinkerton boys want little to do with you after the Hoorah you gave em. But in reality they weren't the problem. Seems like some clerk, in Austin took it upon himself to cut corners and have a two fer, thinking that a shipment of money under the guise of a prisoner transfer would go un noticed"!

"You believe that, Vermillion", Henry shot back?

"I dunno, cause on the surface it sounds like a clever plan, but I see where you're goin' with that and a certain part of my mind says that it stinks like fresh buffalo shit"!

"You or the Pinks have anything better to do for the next few days"? Jack Vermillion shook his head from side to side.

"Then here's what I want ya to do", sad Henry. "Send a telegram down to Jake Rathman at the Governor's mansion down in Austin and tell him to keep a sharp eye on the clerk involved. Either he's in on something bigger or I'll bet he's on the hook somehow to some desperados.

I'm planning to leave back to Waco on tomorrows stage and I'd like you and the Pink's to accompany me to Austin because, my nose tells me that something's afoot and ya just might have someone examine the books to see if what's supposed to be there is there, ya follow"?

"Y'all can spend the night at my ranch as my guest's then go one down to Austin and I'll follow ya the very next day"!

The following day, as the Stage Coach followed its way back south towards Waco, Henry with his left arm in a sling and moving gingerly so as not to reopen the wound in his side, regaled Jack Vermillion and the Pinkerton Detectives as to the when's and where's of his hallowing trip and running gunfight.

"Used to be hostile Comanche and Kiowa roam these parts", mused Henry. "Used to be herds of Buffalo almost as far as the eye could see, but no more I suppose, just assassins, desperados and other scallywags roamin' the roads"! All the way to Waco, Henry was peppered with questions as how it was, back in the days of the Texas Republic? He summed it up by saying, "It was a close run thing, what with the Comanche and the Kiowa raiders, on one hand keeping everyone busy, then the Mexican's along the border stealing our livestock, then elements of the Mexican Army invading from time to time. Lotta good men never saw old age. Nobody had any money to speak of, so all and all it was a close run thing. But I guess us Texians had enough grit and sand to see things through"!

Then a discussion of the Civil War took hold, with the Pinkerton's being former Unionists and Vermillion having served under J.E.B. Stuart's command a bit of friction started to arise, when Henry said, "Gentlemen, take hold of yourselves. It's all over and no doubt everyone did their part in what seemed to be a righteous cause on either side. With what I've seen it would be very easy for me to hate all Indians, but I don't and I'll guarantee ya that for every tale of woe any of ya have in your hip pocket I have ten or more, so there's more than enough bad memories to go around. As for me, I did my bit in the War or Forty Seven and in the service of the Republic and the War of Succession was just not my fight. Had a family to keep track of.

Several hours later as they pulled into Waco, the driver made a detour to the MHM ranch dropping off Henry and his visitors just in time for dinner. Now normally when one brings home visitors unannounced for dinner one just has to expect some pointed words from the wife of the house, but Melanie, hardly expecting company and discovering that her life's love had been injured several times over in a shootout with desperate men, stayed true to her genteel upbringing sending for Maddie and several others to help prepare a Texican repast' for their newly arrived guests, while she made herself more presentable. While Henry moving slowly, showed the visitors to the available guest quarters around the barn complex.

Messengers were sent to invite all of Henry's sons and Juan Mendoza to join them. Several hours later as all assembled at the main house, Melanie saw to it that a glass of pre-dinner wine was served while the introductions were made and the men gathered around the front verandah admiring the ranch and the life that Henry Jaeger had carved out of the Texas country side. For all this is what kept the man busy before and during the conflict between the states.

Melanie was now approaching her fiftieth year and while flitting about seeing to the dinner needs of her guests was viewed by one and all as still a formidable looking woman, who the years had not, served her ill at all. In fact the years had been very kind to this attractive looking woman, who clearly was a woman of quality and grace. It had been a very long time since her visitors, long accustomed to the seedier side of life, had cause to practice the manners taught them as children.

But after an inch thick Hereford steak, done to a turn with all of the trimmings, each man famished from either the trip or his exertions of the day, had to loosen their belts and stifle a belch or two.

Then ale, brewed at the ranch was served along with the appropriate cheroots for the after dinner digestives. Each man recounted his origins for the group as the talk and fellowship traded back and forth. As the evening progressed, even Jack Vermillion decided the Yankee Pinkerton's were all right fellows, a far cry from his previous attitude on the stage coach previously in the day. Discussing the events of the coming days, it was agreed that Henry was to follow them to Austin the following day accompanied by his three sons, which he had the authority to deputize for the occasion. "My sons are as good with a firearm as anyone you may have known and have been around all the elements of perfidy", offered Henry. "Hopefully they will not be needed but some extra help never hurts"!

The following morning, everyone had a monumental breakfast and we're put on a buckboard wagon into town to get on the noon stage coach for Austin. Accompanying them was Henry's youngest son Michael, barely out of his teen years but the best gun hand of any of them. During the previous evening Henry had an opportunity to gain the measure of the two Pinkerton operatives as well as Jack Vermillion and decided they all knew what they were about and that on this little foray Michael could learn much very quickly.

The following day, when Henry had some time to rest up and be examined by the town doctor.

He, Rodrigo and Zachary would follow on the same noon stage coach to Austin. The stage pulling into Austin later that evening was met by Jack Vermillion who brought them up to date on the previous day's activities after he checked them into the hotel and during a late night dinner.

"Those two Pinkerton boys are pretty slick. They took your suspicions and figured that a counterfeit money operation was going on, so we all went to the Governor's Mansion and after Michael mentioned your name, the doors opened shortly thereafter and there he was the Governor, big as life. Well sir the Pinkerton's being experienced in this, out lined their suspicions and the Governor got out the State Treasurer and the Federal Repository official and over to the mansion pretty damn quick.

It was narrowed down to this clerk in the Federal Depository Office, who was the one who authorized the shipment to Dallas that the Captain here rode shotgun on. Now the clerk was apparently the one who forged the Federal Official's signature on the paperwork authorizing the shipment. A telegraph message was sent to the Federal official in Dallas, to examine very carefully the recent arrival of cash, coin and the bullion.

We all kept a round the clock check on the clerk at his home checking the comings and goings in case anyone else was involved and discovered that the lights were on in the barn behind his house all night long.

Early this morning the Governor gets a message from the local Federal Treasury official telling him that all of the transported money was counterfeit and that the Gold and Silver coins and bars were all lead coated in gold silver cladding.

Then Henry interjected, "Seems like the Pistolero's had this clerk in a vise, of some kind and the clerk devised this plan to double cross the thieves, or else it was simple serendipity and the robbers bad luck"!

Just then Rodrigo spoke up saying, "Now if I were the clerk and I knew someone here in the Marshall's office, like a fellow clerk and knew that some of the robbers friends were being transported to Dallas and I wanted to double cross them, I'd hand them some information they couldn't refuse. Then I'd make sure to wrap things up and get out of town for parts unknown 'Muy Pronto', don't you think"?

Then as an afterthought he added, "Has anyone thought to examine the Paper money and the bullion here in Austin"?

Vermillion's eyes grew wide as the thought just never occurred to anyone saying, "Uh, No"! "Seems like some people will have to be wakened from a sound sleep this night"! "Well Jack, take Rodrigo and Zack along with ya, I'm goin upstairs and get a little shut eye and let this meal digest. Call me if ya need me"!

Early the following morning while Henry was just sitting down to a breakfast of steak and eggs, the Pinkerton's entered the hotel accompanied by Henry's sons and Jack Vermillion. Seeing Henry just starting his meal in the overly large table, they all joined him placing a similar order with the waiter. One of the Pinkerton's then spoke saying, "Well seems like the cow shit has spread through a windstorm. Your son Rodrigo was right, for once we got everyone out of bed and went to the Repository and examined the currency coin and bullion, seems like a hundred thousand dollars was not legitimate. Gold and Silver bars, were lead clad in Silver and Gold and a large portion of currency was counterfeit. Your son Zack and Jack here were watching the clerks barn when it looked like he was about to leave in the dark of night driving a buckboard containing bullion, coin and real money as it turned out. As it turned out the clerk at the repository and the clerk at the Marshall's office were in cahoots with each other and apparently hung out a carrot the thieves just couldn't refuse. In addition the barn was the place where the clerk and another printer working for the local newspaper and an engraver working for a local jeweler did their work. We found one of the stalls in the barn with bags of lead shot, covered with straw. The lead shot was melted down into bars similar to those the treasury stores, then the bars are dipped into already molten gold or silver and what do you have?" He let the obvious message hang for a moment before continuing, "The very same was accomplished with the coinage, of the twenty and fifty dollar denominations"!

"So where is the rest of their ill-gotten gains buried", asked Henry? "They ain't talking, said Vermillion. Then he added, "They know they're going to prison and I suppose when they get out they'll go get it and head for Mexico and live the rest of their days high on the hog"!

"Not in Mexico they won't", added Henry wryly. "My guess is that the Federal clerk is the only one who knows where the loot is buried and that it's highly unlikely he'll get out of prison before his partner and he's never gonna tell his partner or anyone where it's all buried"! Then he said, "It'll probably be buried within a half a day's ride from Austin, somewhere up in the high country near a wagon trail. Figure that clerks aren't big on ridin' horseback, besides one would need a buckboard to haul the loot and a shovel. Riding out of town with a shovel tied to your horse just is something anyone would remember and the very last thing this one'll do is want to draw attention to himself"!

"But how will ya get them to talk legally", asked one of the Pinkerton's working his way through a well-earned steak?

"Where are they now, asked Henry wiping the last of his breakfast from his lips?

"In the local jail", answered Vermillion

"How soon can they be transferred to Federal custody, namely both of you Pinkerton's"?

"We should have the paperwork done by noon", answered one of the detectives.

"Good, said Henry. "Ya might wanna get their buck board all horsed up and one of the clerks shovels so we all can take a little trip this afternoon.

Oh and one more thing, see to it that the clerk in question is not fed anything until you take him in custody".

"That's all well and good Captain Jaeger, but just how are ya gonna get this man to talk", asked one of the detectives.

Zachary then added wryly, "Once this man meets my father he will 'want' to tell all, for my father has the power of persuasion. It will be good for his soul"!

Henry and his son's spent the rest of the morning shopping for their wife's and loved ones, making purchases not readily found in the few stores in Waco. As Henry often told them, "Happy wife, happy life" and every once in a while one just had to spoil the one you loved. By noon their purchases made inclusive of things for Mendoza and his wife, everyone met at the hotel for a meal and to plan the trip to parts yet unknown.

"I've the orders of transfer right here inside my vest, a shovel and two buckboards are outside and the prisoner in question hasn't been fed a thing, since we put him in custody. Looks like he could miss a few meals anyway", offered one of the Pinkerton's!

"Then let's all sit down for some steak and taters and when we're all finished we'll accompany you on your duties", said Henry.

When the meal was completed, everyone drove over to the jail facility and retrieved the prisoner, who emerged from the jail shackled with leg irons and handcuffs placed behind him, with a small burlap bag placed over his head as he hobbled out to be placed in the buckboard and driven out of town with little fanfare. About a mile from the town limits, the wagons pulled over into a small copse of trees, well off the main road. Henry ordered the wagon carrying Zachary and the prisoner to pull under a tree and a rope was tossed over a low hanging stout limb and secured to the chains that bound the prisoners hands behind them, then the prisoner's hood was taken off his head and he was raised up to eye ball height and secured hanging there, with his arms stretched behind him in sheer terror.

Henry said to the others, "Why don't all you all go way over there", pointing to a place just out of earshot, "and relax awhile while me and this clerk can have a reasonable conversation"!

When everyone was out of earshot Henry approached the prisoner saying, "Son, I'm goin' to lay it all out for ya plain as day. You're in quite a pickle as you've no doubt figured out by now".

As he calmly walked around the swaying prisoner, giving him a little nudge every so often causing him to swing in constant motion he said, "A few of those pistoleer's that had you in a bind, that you sent after that stage coach escaped and when they find out that what you sent was phony money they're not gonna take very kindly to you. Now you've got some others in trouble, the printer and the engraver are already in custody and are singing like a bird. The pistoleer's get hold of ya they just might not care about the money and when ya get to jail, it'll be made known that you're sittin on a stash of loot. Now while I've never been in prison, I'm told that time in the Huntsville repository is just sheer hell especially for a puny little thing like you with a precious secret"!

Hearing no response from the prisoner, Henry walked around to the front of him pulling out the razor sharp big Bowie knife from his sheath slowly so the prisoner could see it, then slowly turned him around without a word and letting the weight of the knife guide him drew it down the length of his back several times, leaving a small trail of blood each time for the blade was so sharp, the pain of its passing wasn't felt till minutes later when the blood started to congeal. "What, what are you doing to me", stammered the prisoner after some minutes and a dozen passes of the blade took hold?

"The Comanche and the Apache have a thing they called the 'death of a thousand cuts', they use to make a person talk, or just to have some fun with. This usually can go on for days. It'll eventually sting to high heaven and over time you'll lose all your blood"!

Henry then started to remove the hapless prisoners shoes, then cut all of his clothes away from his body, leaving them fall in a heap below him. "There", said Henry satisfied with his work. "It must be painful, hanging there, buck naked, hongry, completely alone, with your arms feeling like they're gonna come outta their sockets and with no possibility of rescue in sight. Now I don't know if you were aware of my part in this, but I was the one guarding those waddies and your phony money on the stage to Dallas and I was the one in the shootout and I've a few fresh bullet holes to prove it, so I got a real good reason to be right here, right now", as Henry let the blade continue its journey, slowly crisscrossing the clerks hanging body. An hour into it, the clerk still was not talking as Henry would stop awhile then resume the journey of the blade. He could see the poor soul was in great pain by now, with his thin arms alone straining at its sockets, the tendons screaming for release and if time wasn't an issue Henry would continue this all day and deep into the night and the following day, just like the Shawnee or the Comanche or the Comanche when they had some poor soul in their clutches.

Just then he noticed a way to accelerate the procedure, seeing the dangling member of the naked prisoner, swaying helplessly, Henry decided to adjust his target, the shriveled member pointing to the ground then, gently passing his knife up and down the length, leaving a red trail in its wake. The man's back alone had well over a hundred minute red trails on it and in time they would heal leaving a host of scars, but a man's privates, were his sacred trust and without them? With each pass of the knife, the member grew.

"Son, in a precious few minutes, my knife is gonna get very hungry and will demand to be fed if ya catch my drift", whispered Henry making his point with a sharp intrusion into the very base of the prisoners personal business. Hearing not a sound but the stifled painful groaning from the prisoner, Henry grabbed the man's sack with one hand and with the blade in the other began the pass to oblivion, as he mused, "I wonder how long it's gonna take ya to bleed out and after your dead, when the vultures arrive, the eyes are the very first think they'll eat"!

Just then his hanging prisoner the last vestige of his willpower exhausted screamed out, "Oh please not any more, I'll tell ya where it's all buried, just cut me down, and I swear I'll tell ya"!

Henry summoned the others to come quickly and the prisoner was lowered to the ground whereupon he was loaded into the back of the buckboard and directed them to the very place he buried the real gold and currency.

An hour later they arrived at the spot atop a small heavily forested hill some fifty yards off an old wagon trail, hoisting the prisoner from the buckboard and following his weakening directions to the very spot of the buried treasure.

As one of the Pinkerton's started digging Henry mused, "Strip a man of his dignity, remove any hope, add a little pain, then sprinkle in a major loss of one's manhood", as his voice trailed off, with the shovel hitting something solid.

Not two feet down in the dusty soil of the hill side near the base of an old oak, emerged a small leather steamer trunk that took the combined efforts of two men to bring to the surface was all of the purloined efforts of the clerks work. One almost felt sorry for the poor man, all of his scheming, all of his work down the drain and all he could look for was a very long time in the hell of a federal prison.

The steamer trunk was loaded into one of the buck boards while the naked and shackled prisoner, occupied the other and everyone made their way back into Austin to redeposit the prisoner in the local jail, just in time for the evening meal while the leather steamer trunk was returned to the Federal Depository, just in time to see the Governor and his entourage dressing down the Federal Authority responsible for the misdeeds.

The Pinkerton detectives struggling with the steamer trunk brought it up the steps and into the facility laying it down at the Governors feet, huffing from the exertions, with Henry in their wake saying, "Ya just might want to count this before anyone gets to bed tonight, and ya can thank these here two detectives for their fine work"!

The entire party was ecstatic at the unexpected arrival of the stolen real gold, with a flurry of verbal appreciation showered upon the new arrivals.

"Just one thing", offered Henry, 'Ya just might wanna keep this whole thing under wraps, because if the public ever found out about this, well gentlemen, your all intelligent men and you know what I mean"! Then Henry feeling tired begged their leave and joined his sons and Jack Vermillion back at the hotel for a hearty dinner and a good night's sleep.

As the dinner progressed Jack Vermillion grew envious of Henry Jaeger and his family, seeing that they were an impenetrable unit. Many separate parts, all moving together in lockstep in almost every endeavor imaginable. As the dinner conversation's conviviality, passed back and forth, something deep inside Jack Vermillion wanted to become part of their enterprise. He'd come from a large family in Virginia, mostly fractious not unlike many families, but here in the midst of the Jaegers was something he'd like to become a part of.

He was certain that he could carry his weight when it came to ranching and he'd served as a deputy US Marshall quite long enough, what with the low pay and the myriad restrictions and all. All he had to do was ask to be put on, free grub and a roof over his head each night and the standard dollar a day wage paid to cowpokes and little risk of getting shot each day.

Yet there was something getting in the way of asking to join the ranch.

Then during the after dinner cheroots and whiskey it came to him. The regimentation of ranch life was quite different of that in the military or working as a Marshall, but it was regimentation none the less. Things had to be done at a certain time, all the time and that was at the root of Jack Vermillion's discomfort.

He yearned for freedom, to come and go as he pleased, to take wild risks, realizing that there was scant difference between his attitudes as a Marshall and of those robbing thieving scoundrels he brought to justice.

He would travel back to Ft. Smith and present his resignation to the area magistrate, get his back pay and head for Dodge City or Abilene or parts unknown as soon as it would be practicable. He was handy with a gun and would pick his fights carefully, so in his mind, he said silently, 'Thanks gents, but I gotta move on'.

The following morning Henry visited the government doctor to clean and examine his wounds and have the bandages reapplied prior to the stage coach trip back to Waco and his family.

"Seems that the two bullets that caught up with you passed right through and didn't hit any vital organs, or else you wouldn't be on the mend like you are. Just tell that goddamn driver to take it slow and avoid any undue jostling, sleep late as you can for at least a few weeks allowing your body to mend. Then start walking to build your strength then maybe in about six weeks' time, you'll be ready for a horse again. Any sooner than that and your just askin' for all the good mother nature is doing healing your body to be quickly undone and none to the good. Now for the pain I know is there, here's a prescription for Laudanum, which I suggest you only take prior to bed, for it'll alleviate your pain and help you to sleep. Now it's an opiate and too much of this stuff is a very bad thing. A half teaspoon, an hour before bed will get you through this!"

The coach driver duly warned by Henry's children wended his way around the road ruts at half speed as the stage worked its way northward.

His mind was telling him that maybe; just maybe his Rangering days were pretty much done. He was, after all getting on in years and the older one got the longer it took to heal up. His boys and Juan could run things as well as anyone, in fact maybe it was time for Juan Mendoza to join him on the front porch, for he'd worked as hard as anyone and no one could've been more loyal.

But then he came to his senses as the landscape slowly rolled by.

Neither he nor Mendoza were one's to be simply let out to pasture. Sure they would, turn more and more of the day to day management over to the children and eventually fade out, but to stop work now and retire? Out of the question, still much to do and time for rest can be when the white hair started showing. But in the meantime, Henry would allow himself to be tended to by his wife and the entire family, for after all, he'd earned it.

But sometime in the next several months he would send his letter of resignation to the Governor in Austin. After all he didn't exactly need the seventy five dollars a month the State paid him for his Rangering anymore. There were other capable men around to do the hard and dirty. But in the event he was ever needed to track down some desperate men… Something deep inside, just couldn't completely let go. Perhaps in time when his hair turned white. But then again…

22

For the second time in his life, Henry Jaeger found himself incapacitated by wounds. While some patients do what their told by their doctors, others serve their convalescent time in an ornery fashion. Henry was the latter, eager to get back in the saddle before his body mended properly, and bristling at the constant attention he was given as if he were not a grown man but a child, it took Mendoza to remind him privately of a time long ago when he was almost at deaths door, yet yielded to the ministrations of his former wife, Joselita and the Fuentes family.

"Jefe, does your family and Miss Melanie love you any less, than Dona Joselita did", asked Mendoza? "They all want to have you around to see your hair grow white, so accept what they offer and be at peace with yourself. The rancho is running well and its time your family assumed leadership"!

Later on in the afternoon, when the family doctor relented and allowed Henry to get dressed and wander downstairs, taking his meals at the dinner table rather than be fed in bed. Following each meal, he would retire to the front porch and watch the comings and goings of the people of the ranch performing their daily routines.

Several weeks earlier, he'd dictated a letter of resignation to the governor in Austin of his Ranger duties. After nine years in the old Texas Republic, a year and a half during the War of '47' and the only continuous official Ranger in the employ of the State of Texas since almost 1850, it was time that Henry called it a day.

A month later, a communication came back from the sitting governor, returning his badge, and containing commissions for Henry's three sons as Texas Rangers. Henry's resignation was accepted, but placed in stasis, by the governor. An official 'Son of Texas', was a lifelong obligation, that yielded no pay but callable for duty at any time the governor deemed necessary for the public good, at the then going rate of remuneration.

His son's appointments, also meant they were in the very same auxiliary status as he, but the wearing of the badge meant they were able to effect legal enforcements throughout the entire state, not under any constraint of jurisdictions.

Henry had his sons sign and notarize the official documents and be sworn in by the local magistrate, sending the documents back by the next mail to Austin.

As the doctors' visits evolved from a daily to a weekly basis, Henry apologized to each and every one he spoke harshly to while in his confinement of healing.

"Don't mind telling you Henry, that it was a close run thing", said the doctor. "Your wounds had opened up and you were suffering a tad bit of internal bleeding, but as you decided to stay put and let nature do its healing work, your fevers have passed and you appear to be on the mend"!

The doctor rose up from the swing couch on the verandah and descended the stairs for his buggy, saying "I'll drop by next week to look at ya and if you continue to mend the way you're doin', you'll be on top of a horse within the next six weeks"!

The afternoon sun started to shine upon Henry's face as he sat there watching the good doctor drive back to town to see to his afternoon appointments. Just then Melanie came out of the house with a fresh glass of lemonade, from the glade of citrus trees planted years ago sheltered from the north winds and placed it in front of Henry on the wicker table beside him. Just as she was about to reenter the house, Henry called out to her, "Melanie, would you sit with me a moment"? She turned and took her place next to Henry's side on the swing couch, sensing that he'd something important to say. Ever the cheerful soul, she smiled and looked Henry straight in the eyes saying, "What is it Henry"?

"I just wanted to say that I'm sorry for treating you and everyone else so badly while you all were tryin' to do your best to help me heal up"!

"Apology accepted Henry but as for everyone else, they're all coming here for supper tonight so you can apologize to them all in person including the Mendoza's and the grandchildren. Seems to me since the grand children all love you so, that you oughtta make more time for them, each and every one cause you've got a lot to teach em all. I'll do my share teaching them there letters and numbers, but there's a whole lot more to learn than that, if they're gonna be the next generation running things around here"!

Then Melanie's smile faded as she added, "Over the years I've noticed that you've the heart of the wolf pack and the soul of the eagle. Now however that came about doesn't matter. What matters is that it's there as plain as day. A brief time of you bein' cranky is nothing when placed in the balance of your life. So don't y'all go getting' all down in the mouth, just cause you went out and got yourself all shot up. What matters are that you're on the mend and I'll have you all to myself for the first time in a long while won't I", she ended as a statement not as a question"!

"Well since you're the boss around here, I best mind my manners, Missy"!

"Yes you should", whereupon Melanie sat next to Henry and kissed him deeply, not in the manner of eliciting his prurient nature, but in the exchange of pure affection. Then she rose saying "Maddie and Beulah are coming to help me prepare for supper and their family will also join us", then turned with a flourish and went inside.

It was difficult for Henry to let go of the day to day management of the various aspects of ranch life, but during his convalescence the entire family rose as one to assume command of the family business seamlessly. Even Juan Mendoza cut loose the bulk of his supervision of the vaqueros, gradually turning things over to Rodrigo, who now made all of the salient decisions as to the livestock, which still was the main cash earner for the ranch. Zachary took over the supervision duties of their planting operations, alternating the various fields to be cleared, plowed and planted, as well as both Milling operations, the grain and well as the wood mill. Providing milled grain for the area as well as finished wood products for a growing population.

Melanie's former slave's family, headed up by Elijah and his son Joseph, were responsible for the reforesting of the cut timber as well as the day to day maintenance of the wooden fences that surrounded and segmented the vast enterprise.

Michael the youngest, served as Rodrigo's 'Segundo', regarding the livestock, concentrating on the horses, breeding and making saddle ready in the ways taught by Henry. Yet when time came for the seasonal branding of the calves all joined in for the task at hand.

Chani and Akila's progeny were selectively bred to other canine breeds to improve their capacities and as usual each birthing proved successful in yielding a breed that stood strong in their task in protecting the livestock, much to the dismay to the occasional rustlers, that would breach the fence line, gaining access to the interior of the ranch property, always at night, only to find a rather nasty and deadly surprise awaiting them laying doggo in the dark of the tall grass, leaping en masse upon the backs of the horses bringing down the riders, with their fangs sunk deep in their throats, till all movement ceased.

A joint howling would always alert the entire ranch at the termination of each event, with many riders converging on the point of attack, seeing frightened rider less horses wandering nearby and eventually coming upon the dead guarded by their respective assailants who were always lavishly rewarded for their efforts. By the end of the following day, the bodies would be stripped and quietly buried in out of the way places, the fences mended and new horses and saddles would join the family.

Very efficient whereupon, the disappearance of such vaga-bonds were of no consequence, for they would not practice their craft on anyone else, the courts would not be burdened by the effort of prosecution, nor the prison down in Huntsville tasked with their incarceration, for they simply disappeared.

Rodrigo's wife 'Esme', trained in accountancy by an exclusively private Woman's College back east, took charge of integrating all of the various accounting and record keeping activities of the family enterprise, eventually at Henry's request performing quarterly auditing functions at the bank in town which Henry had long ago acquired a majority interest. When in the course of her internal audits of the banks books, various financial discrepancies were unearthed, the Bank President and original founder was urged to quietly sign over all of his stock and retire due to a certain matter of his health, which required his hasty leaving from the State of Texas, never to return, of course for the reasons of his health.

Of course, all transfer documents were duly witnessed by the County Magistrate, given the caveat that 'Time', was indeed of the essence.

"Well Esme, looks like you're runnin' a bank", quipped Henry, the following day as the Bank opened for business. Now that Henry had a great deal of time on his hands and his health and vigor had returned, he decided to venture forth down to Austin, to try his hand at some glad handing, with the boys in Austin, taking along with him the County Magistrate, for the railroads were to finally to work their way down from Dallas into the interior of Texas and the Rail Road tracks right of way was of great importance to both the Ranch operations and the City of Waco if it were to grow.

After several weeks of meetings with both legislators and representatives from the railroads, decisions were reached, minor legislation was rushed through the legislature, contracts were let and certain minor sections of land were ceded to the railroads as track right of ways, with a spur line right into the eastern portion of the ranch, built at the railroads expense. Never again would the ranch have to drive their livestock to the Dallas stockyards. They could load them right on the railroad and the very next day they would arrive at their destination, saving manpower and time.

The following year Henry purchased additional harvesting equipment and built new grain silos, near the railroad spur, to ship the overabundance of raw grain the ranch produced, to market. The family fortunes gradually increased as all aspect of the family enterprise turned a tidy profit year after year.

As the 1870's gradually drew to a close, the family gradually withdrew from the day to day interactions with the citizens of Waco, whereas the attitudes towards outsiders of any kind not in tune with the majority grew less and less tolerant, once again. Since a large portion of the family business employed Negro's and the Klan once again started to make inroads into the county, it was made clear that anyone not White or Protestant was not welcome.

The Jaeger family was of the Catholic faith through and through and every Sunday they celebrated Mass, at first at a small grotto Henry had built in the ranch's early days, then as time went by at a small chapel that Henry and the boys had built. Whenever possible Henry conducted the order of the Mass himself, reciting the Mass in Latin that he learned from his parents as a child. When he was away, Melanie took over the task. For in those days the nearest Catholic Church was in Austin serving a small but growing Mexican community. Therefore almost everyone in the county was ignorant of the family's religious leanings, for it was none of their business.

All of the children born on the ranch were duly baptized by either Henry or Melanie as soon as was practicable. Never mind that neither was ordained nor authorized by the church; it was the intent and the exact process that counted most to them.

Henry and Melanie were both keen on insuring that each and every member of the ranch benefited in kind from their labors on a pro rata basis and as the yearly accounting of the profits rolled in, separate family accounts were set up in the bank that accrued interest, accessed only by the members of each family. All of the ranch's children were educated in the three "R's", to each individual capacity, by Melanie and whenever they took ill, Henry saw to it they received the best medical care the area was to provide. Henry and Melanie were if nothing else, very practical people, for not only was it the moral thing to do, it was just good business.

As soon as children were of a given age, they were all given daily chores to do well within their capacities, as part of their learning curriculum, as well as the daily grind of book learning taught by Miss Melanie after the fall harvest and before the spring planting. Needless to say, every single youngster was an expert in the art of milking cows prior to their tenth birthday.

The very year after the railroad came to town amidst of great jubilation, tragedy visited the ranching operations, whereas Juan Mendoza had a heart attack in the middle of the annual branding of the calves. Clutching his chest, he directed his horse in the direction of a tree and started to dismount.

Henry noticed his withdrawal from the gathering and branding, never seen before, for this was the very essence of the Vaquero. Sensing a problem he leapt on his horse and rushed to his side, the horse coming to a sliding halt and Henry leaping from the saddle just in time to catch Mendoza as he fell from the saddle.

Laying him under a tree, shielding him from the spring day sun, Henry could see that his lifelong partner was in severe distress, gasping for breath and clutching his heart. Unaware of just what to do, Henry felt helpless as he did what he could to loosen Mendoza's clothing and after a short while Juan seemed to be able to breathe once again.

Then Juan said, "I see the end of things for me is just over there", as he pointed to some distant spot on the horizon. "I want you to promise me that you'll take care of Juanita and the children, Jefe"!

"I'm the godfather of your children aren't I Juan? But of course", said Henry! Henry had looked into the eyes of many just before they were to pass away and he recognized that certain look of inevitability. Juan knew he was dying and the time of his passing was near, so no use to argue or go for help, for he would be dead before any doctor could arrive and a lifelong friend such as he didn't deserve to die alone or amongst strangers.

As Henry cradled Juan's head in his arms he could see that pain was returning to him, as he cradled his head in his arms, feeling the arrival of several riders, then seeing that it was his three sons, all nearby having removed their sombreros in quiet reverence as they slowly approached.

As they all came into view, Juan said with great effort, "Thank you for all coming, for the thing I always feared most was dying alone and without friends"!

The passing of a revered friend and teacher is always a serious thing for grown men, as each of them started to mist up, trying their best not to cry.

As Mendoza slowly passed his eyes past each and every one for the last time, imprinting their visage in his rapidly fading brain, for all eternity, his eyes met those of Henry, clearly now, silently overflowing with grief and said, "Por favor Jefe, tell Juanita and the children that I'm sorry that I'll not be home for dinner, but that I'll be waiting for them in the garden when they arrive"!

Then a great pain caused him to grow rigid, and then he slowly exhaled, with a forced smile upon his well-weathered face, his sightless eyes staring into emptiness. Just then Henry felt Juan's body grow noticeably lighter, as he closed his eyes saying, "He is gone"!

The branding would just have to wait a few days, as Rodrigo was the first to rise saying, "I'll go get a wagon" and departed. Then Michael rose up saying, "I'll go wrap things up with the branding and tell the Vaqueros of what happened and that we'll resume in three days. Is that alright father"?

Henry looked up and sadly nodded his head, still reluctant to give up a man that just an hour ago was a vibrant individual doing what he loved best, and in almost an instant, he was gone. But he had his memories of his time with Juan and as his children grew to maturity, he would make certain that their memory of him was enriched with the many stories of his time with Juan Mendoza and as important to him as any of his blood children. At the very least he owed that to Juan's Memory.

He saw to it that the town mortician was brought to the ranch to prepare Juan for the funeral the following day, which was to occur under this very tree where Juan Mendoza had breathed his last.

The site and the burial grounds were prepared with great care by all the members of the ranch and even the tenant farmers arrived to pay their respects, as Henry read the Funeral Mass in Latin from the Book of the Masses, he'd rescued from the burned down family farm in Cheviot township, long ago. As part of the litany, he recanted what he knew of the history of the man, being as brief as possible, in the recalling of a man's life.

In closing he added, "Here was a man who did what was necessary, just when it was necessary, without ever having to be told, because it was the right thing to do! A lesson for us all", he added.

After all had departed, each and every one in attendance taking part in the refilling up of the grave, the only ones that remained were Henry and all of the family wolves, now numbering some two dozen, all howling to the heavens the arrival of Juan Mendoza as Henry tidied up the gravesite.

After sometime spent talking privately to the grave, amidst the din of the wolves, Henry rose up and made a sign quieting the wolves then released them to return to their duties. An hour later he arrived back at the main house, to see Melanie comforting a distraught Juanita and her children, just into their teens. As he sat in his easy chair he made a sign for everyone to approach saying, "Juanita, I am the godfather to your children and I will see to it that, 'Muy Permisso', they are raised as if they were of my blood. As you know he is in heaven for the wolves have alerted those above. You are not to worry about anything in the least, for you are family and that is all there is to say"! Then Henry told Juanita of his very last words saying, "And he'll be waiting for all of you, in the garden, in your own good time"!

Then Juanita dried her tears and took a deep breath saying, "The very best day in my life was when your united me with Juan Mendoza. I didn't know it exactly at that time, but with each passing day, of our time together my love for that man grew and grew and now I must be strong for the children and grateful for your blessing Jefe"!

"Please Juanita, do not call me Jefe again, for I am not nor ever have been your Boss. I only permitted Juan to call me that because it was a habit with him. He was a partner in every way and you and the children are family in every way. Is that not the case Melanie"?

Melanie quickly nodded embracing the two children, saying "Yes, in every way"!

Then one by one, the family members started to arrive, along with all the others in subdued homage to the fallen, with Rodrigo having stopped by to retrieve Juanita's guitar so she could gently play the vast repertoire of Mexican Ballads for the gathering throng as if Juan was still in attendance.

Grudgingly she took up the instrument, for at that very moment she felt a vast emptiness, but as she began to play, she felt uplifted in spirit just as if her life's love was there before her, a great smile emitting from out under that vast drooping mustache. As she played she closed her eyes, imagining his visage of a Haughty Vaquero, with his overly large sombrero tilted forward, his hand on his pistol ever at the ready, astride his horse. Yes, this was the image she would carry with her of Juan Mendoza, till the time her eyes closed for the final time, when they would have eternity together.

Although a wake had not been planned, since everyone was here, the women all hurriedly banded together to prepare victuals for those in in attendance, breaking out glasses and the assortment of hard whiskies and wines and the wide assortment of foodstuffs hurriedly prepared for one and all. One by one everyone seemed to have a significant story about some aspect of Juan Mendoza that affected them. Toward the end of things when people started to depart, Henry gathered Mendoza's children about him just before they piled into Rodrigo's wagon to take them home, saying, "Children, never fear, for I have some real stories about your father, that in time I will tell you that will make you proud and that you will really like"!

After the last of the mourners had left, Melanie joined Henry on the front verandah as he sat there, sipping his whiskey, and nursing a lit cheroot, staring at the almost full moon. Holding a similar whiskey glass half full of "Old Whatchamacallit", she absently said, "Seems like death is gonna visit us all someday and all we can do is cherish each moment together"!

Henry reached for her hand, gently clasping it in his hand, feeling every aspect of its curvature. Relishing the very fact that it was not as young as it used to be showing the weathering of the years in the lamp light that covered the verandah. He opened his mouth as if to speak, when she put her forefinger on his lips saying, "Henry, remember, I know what's in your heart and you know what's in mine, with every touch and glance, don't you"!

He nodded his head saying, "Seems like our immediate family just grew didn't it"?

The problems with having a vast tract of land, other than the eventual annual remission to the State in the form of taxation, was that one had a great many things to keep track of.

In the early days, the monumental erection of a wooden fence all along the perimeter was but one of many priorities to be addressed, along with the internal sectioning off of land for pasturing and tilling. Then the fact of providing sufficient shelter for those employed in the tasks. All along the way, at crucial intervals, Henry received the help he needed, often from out of the blue.

Many of his neighbors did not. Yet he started out no better than any of them. His spate of land oft times, seemed like an island of prosperity in the midst of a sea of inconsistency. Some of the settlers prospered, while others did not. Henry's tenant settlers that covered the entire northern perimeter of the ranch were in the very same boat. Some prospered while others seemed to struggle. Each had their own source of water plenty of land for the livestock to graze in and each with fifty acres could plant what they wanted and commingle their harvest with Henry's at the railroad spur line, as well as their cattle shipped to market. The one thing they never had to worry about was security, with the well fed sons and daughters of Akila and Chani defending the perimeter.

Oh sure, every period of the full moon, the wolves would always signal to each other, but eventually the livestock grew used to them. From time to time other wolves would arrive at the fence line, to see just what was available in the form of easy prey, only to be intercepted before they penetrated too deeply into the ranch proper, by the ranch's wolves and after a brief but often brutal struggle, the others accepted that an easy meal had to be sought elsewhere.

Hard to explain just why Henry's wolves acted completely out of character, acting not as predators, but as defenders of all that lay within the perimeter of the ranch. One thing was certain, Henry always saw to it the wolves were well fed. Going back to his days as a young boy living with his parents in Cheviot, the Shaman of the Miami always taught him to feed the wolf cubs always before he took food and with each successive generation of Chani and Akila's progeny he maintained that rule and over time it served him and his family well.

A story he would often tell with great relish, was of his youngest, Michael who as just a baby was laying on the ground under a tree in a small bassinette, in the middle of the afternoon and one of Chani's daughters, who had just given birth herself to a small fleet of cubs and was still lactating, wandered over to him as he was crying, placed herself over him with her teats hanging within reach and patiently waited for little Michael to make a selection. Once he had, he suckled peacefully until satisfied, with Henry, Melanie and the rest of the family standing a discrete distance away, quietly watching in wonder.

Of his three boys, Michael, while the youngest, was just slightly more aggressive than Rodrigo or Zack and Henry from time to time always wondered if it were that very moment if the spirit of the wolf pack took hold.

His daughter Josie had taken to helping her mother run the little school on the ranch property for the families of the rancheros and anyone else working on the ranch in helping them acquire basic reading, writing and numerical skills. When time permitted she joined Rodrigo's wife Esme with the family accounts, or at the bank in town, conducting audits or in any other activity the bank required.

As is usually the case, just when life has settled down for a period of quietude and prosperity, the forces of darkness always working, scheming, out of sight of mortal beings, surfaces to wreak havoc on society. Such was the situation with a certain Mortimer Ermy, the longtime clerk at the Jaeger's bank. A fastidious and quiet little man, he was always Neatly and modestly attired, never seen without his signature gray spats and neck tie, with nose glasses precariously perched on the bridge of his nose, his hair neatly parted down the middle as was the fashion of the time. Lifelong bachelors with no apparent vises save one. In his off hours, with no known hobbies to while the time away, he was known to frequent several of the saloons in town, where he could upon occasion acquire the services of one of the "Women of the Town", whenever he had a good night at the poker tables. He fancied himself a better than average poker player, being rather good with numbers and odds, as a man of his education and avocation would expect. Dealing with money and numbers all day long, almost wasn't work but interesting to him. He prided himself with of never having to cheat, always watching the cards as they were played and the various tells the players always exhibited to greater or lesser degrees. Once a month when some of the farm workers or cowboys got their pay, he always did well, never winning too big and from time to time tossing in a modestly winning hand to some drunken pistolero, lest there be an incident. His cash till always balanced out down to the penny at the end of each day and since he was a man of modest visible requirements, as honest a pilgrim as could be found and completely reliable, he was the very last man one could expect would bring trouble anywhere for any reason.

Until Fabian DuLesseps, came to town. A man of intemperate habits and a master of all the varieties of the game called Poker; he made a rather good living at the tables. Of course it didn't hurt that his main hobby was magic tricks and sleight of hand, for while at the tables he'd never had an occasion where he'd been caught cheating, in over fifteen years living the 'Sportin' Life'. Of course, whenever his apparent overwhelming luck seemed too good to be true, he was always a keen observer of when it was appropriate to be somewhere else in a hurry. For timing was everything.

He wore the finest clothes, ate the finest food, smoked the most expensive cigars, drank the finest whiskey and wine available and never lost at the tables, always walking away a winner, to greater or lesser degrees. Of course a man of his ilk guaranteed that money always flowed in and out of his hands, bedding the very finest women available at the time and always paying in cold, hard, train ridin' cash money.

He'd worn out his welcome all up and around the gulf coast, from Mobile to Corpus Christi, spending an entire year in New Orleans, then having worn out his welcome there, emigrated by ferryboat across the river to Algiers, where he could delicately fleece all those long generational inbred Cajuns with long black hair tied in a ponytail, with ear rings like a pirate and the constant odor of dead fish and Jambalaya. Never was there night that a foot long razor sharp bowie knife wasn't in evidence. These were all serious men, who did their share of laughin' an sportin', but never turned their back on a scrape, with or without due cause. Everything was legal, exceptin' if it went against ya, then hell would be paid by someone. When the walls started to close in on DuLessups, he folded his proverbial tent like the Arabs of old in the dead of night and silently stole away, surfacing the following day, up river in Baton Rouge, for yet another run of good fortune. Then he spent the next several years plying his trade up and down the Mississippi and Ohio Rivers and all its tributaries, working the riverboats, fleecing the unwary along with a gaggle of other professional gamblers and Sportin' men that roamed the river. After his welcome was worn out there, he worked his way back down the river to Baton Rouge, where he decided that out west was the place to be, for no one knew him there.

The river boat took him up the Red River to Alexandria, then after a few months to Shreveport, where he quickly learned that a more lax attitude towards Sportin' Men, was to be found across the river in Bossier City, where all the action was for that part of the country. Now the Red River became too shallow much past Shreveport for the flat bottomed River Boats, so any exit from Bossier City would have to be across country by stage coach service to Dallas.

And it was right there in Bossier City that Fabian DuLesseps killed his first man. He always went around 'heeled', with two small shoulder holster derringer, .38 cap and ball pistols which were good for four well placed shots, if need be, for the close up work of the poker table. But Fabian had always been able to avoid, circumvent, or talk himself out of uncomfortable situations at the table. Now when a man has a fully charged .44 Navy Colt hog leg pointed at you from just scant feet away, it takes a man with a cool head and quick wits to turn things around.

Now even if things got turned around on Fabian and he was disarmed, he always had a last line of defense, for on each forearm was a tightly strapped, spring loaded razor sharp stiletto knife, that would jump out when triggered, twelve inches from his wrist. This required no strength to engage, but if it could penetrate un tanned buffalo hide, then the human body didn't stand a chance.

One glorious evening, after an afternoon of the finest pussy available in Bossier City, drawn and quartered by this dusky looking octoroon, of Mestiza origins, bled dry of his bodily inner essence's, he tidied up for a night at the saloons poker tables. It was the end of the month and the stupid 'Waddies' would be wandering into town just to try their luck, get drunk and if they still had any money left, get a little 'Poontang', from one of the 'Working Girls', that always lingered close at hand.

A little after nine PM, a group of cowpokes wandered in and Fabian busying himself with a lone game of solitaire sat alone at one of the tables. It was a Saturday night and the moon was indeed full. Flush with their monthly earnings, the boys got a bottle of mighty bad whiskey and seeing that most of the other tables were full and several games in progress, eyed warily the table where Fabian sat alone with a drink on one side and a stack of greenbacks on the other.

The largest of the bunch, named Luke slowly walked over to where Fabian sat and asked, "Ya in for a night of cards mister"?

"What's yer poison", asked Fabian?

"Aw most anything, but five card draw is my favorite"!

"Then slow yer money boys and welcome to the table for five card draw you shall have", said Fabian trying to stifle is eagerness, for there was room at the table for six more souls and six there were, all eager and flush with their hard earned money, which he intended to separate them from, to greater and lesser degrees before the sun came up.

The big guy who spoke to him called Luke, was a better than average player, but Fabian had learned his tells early on and kept him in the game, winning small whenever he was in and dropping a few winners, all night long for of all the guys that came and went in the game, this Luke seemed the most volatile. One by one his friends dropped out as their modest bank rolls diminished in size. "Well folks seem this just ain't my night", said one of Luke's friends, rising from the table. "Need just enough for some of dat 'Boojun' over there", motioning to several of the whores, sipping their colored tea, as if it were whiskey, standing at the bar eyeing the tables, looking for a summons, a too long glance in their direction, signifying interest.

"Which one of em meets your fancy", asked Fabian innocently?

"Well sir, I think that one with the fancy bow on her shoulder just might be the one to milk my cow", offered the cowpoke.

"Louise", yelled Fabian over the din of the crowd, "Come hither", motioning her over to the table. As she bent over the table, giving all the players an ample view of not only her generous bosoms, but the nipples for fair, Fabian stuck ten dollars in between her glistening globes saying, "See to it that this well deserving cowboy has a night he'll never forget"! Louise then gave Fabian a discrete kiss on the cheek, and lifted one of her legs on the table, opening her thighs and lifting her dress, revealing the finest shaved pussy any of them had ever seen. Since no one had ever seen a real live twat unshaved except Fabian, it proved to be a real show stopper, leaving all of the men's jaws agape.

Then Louise slowly lowered her dress saying, "Shows over boys! But if'n y'all ever git a hankerin' for the real thing", then her voice trailed off, the message sent loud and clear, her availability and price being a thing of dreams. She then grabbed the cowboy by his neck bandana, dragging him bewildered and gape jawed out of his chair saying sweetly, "Come on Cowboy, the stairway to heaven is this way"!

As he led the pliant cowpoke up the stairs, the saloon was as quiet as a mouse, watching the duo as they ascended the stairs and disappeared into one of the rooms. Slowly the noise level of the room rose to its former level, led by the tinny sound of the piano player.

"Ten Yankee dollars for the 'Quiff' like that", mumbled one of the players like that! "Yeah", offered Fabian, "But you boys never seen a finer 'Quiff' like that! What say we continue with our gambling', and let our cowpoke get his milkin' upstairs"?

Fabian could afford to be generous, for since he started playing he was over seven hundred dollars ahead and it wasn't even midnight yet. He wasn't surprised at all how eagerly the cowboy jumped at the chance for some easy pussy, for the ignorant sold their souls at the drop of the hat. Besides, should anything go awry with the cowboys, he'd made at least one temporary friend. One by one the cowboys that started the game, dropped out replaced by others, with only Luke left at the table.

Fabian had let him win some sizeable hands over the course of the evening, for a reason. He'd seen no reason to deal seconds, or bottoms during the course of play, letting the cards and the other player's incompetence, determine his winnings which gradually grew.

But as he dropped out of a hand, he checked his silver pocket watch, noting that two AM was close at hand and that Luke had just taken a sizeable hand with a King high flush. As the other started to rise from the table grumbling, Fabian said to Luke, "Seems like the deal is mine and there's just you and me Luke, so what you say this be the last hand of the evening since you seem to have done fairly well"!

By his quick count Luke was up almost eight hundred dollars and Fabian some fourteen hundred to the good. Louise had long since returned to the action and was standing by Fabians shoulder, while her former temporary lover was at the bar, recanting to all who would listen how great a piece of ass the legendary Louise is. "She milked me dry for fair boys and it sure looks like I'll be walkin' bowlegged fer a while"! Better advertising could not be had for a service to mankind, at any price. Business for Louise was certain to see an increase, soon as the boy's put together the entrance fee. "Name the game sport", said Fabian!

"Five card stud", answered Luke confidently, for he'd been on a streak the last few hands and was feeling invincible. Then he looked at Louise saying, "Show me the way to heaven once more Louise, so's after I clean Fabian out you and me can celebrate, till dawn"!

Knowing full well what was to happen next, she had no reason not to comply, for Fabian would deal the boy seconds, giving him a monster hand, which he would bet all his teeth on, but in the process, he'd be certain to deal himself a slightly better hand, thus winning the table. Her confidence in Fabian was well earned for their paths had crossed many times over the years, with her acting as the bait and him cleaning out the suckers. So she lifted her dress slowly and placed her leg once again on the table saying, I'm thinking about getting a tattoo on top of my entrance saying, "Welcome Y'all! Whadda ya'll think"?

At that the crowd roared in laughter, as they gathered around the table as Louise stepped back and Fabian said, "Five card stud poker it is, straight up and began to shuffle the cards with no less than a dozen eager onlookers at hand to see that no shenanigans went on. This never bothered Fabian one bit, for over time he'd developed the skill of the shuffle, being able to miraculously place a hand of cards neatly in the deck and no matter how intently people witnessed, the various sleight of hand maneuverings always went undetected.

He selected an Aces over Jack's full house for Luke to whet his whistle on, while he would draw to an two to six clubs straight flush. As the cards rolled out, Luke kept on eyeing Louise and winking every so often as to say 'Get ready for the poke of your life'.

With almost everyone gathered around the table, no one noticed the town Sheriff's deputy enter walk up to the bar and grab a beer. For working the graveyard shift in Bossier City was thirsty work.

As the cards rolled out from the deck, Luke was feeling supreme and eager to clean this dandy gambler out, started to increase his bets with an incautionary fervor. As the third card rolled out for each of them, Luke was holding two Aces and a Jack showing. Seeing Fabian's card, he was blind to what that Fabian was evidently trying for. So he increased his bet significantly and when Fabian raised him, he just knew that he was trying to bluff him out, so he raised back and Fabian called. As the last card rolled out, Luke drew the third Ace, thus completing his triumph. An Aces over Jacks Full House. The very moment Luke looked at the card, he showed his unconsciouses tell to Fabian and he knew the hook was set, for he'd received the Ace. It was Luke's bet and he immediately pushed in all his money, save what he started out with, the fifty dollars. Fabian, glanced at his cards, and matched the bet, knowing that he could've raised and driven the poor sucker out, but with so many witnesses hanging about, it would've been unseemly.

Luke turned over the King and visibly licked his lips at Louise, prompting Fabian to slowly turn over the three of clubs completing the low- ball straight flush. An immediate gasp went up from the crowd as one commented, "He'd drawn it on the very last card, lucky sonofabitch"! Just the kind of response Fabian wanted. Immediately Luke shot up from his chair with his pistol in his hand fully cocked yelling, "You bastard you cheated me"! Just then the Sheriff bullied his way through the throng with his pistol in his hand as the people fell to the floor yelling, 'Put that hog leg away right now and git, or else I'll drop ya where ya stand. I saw it all and sure didn't appear that you were cheated. Anyone here see it otherwise"?

When none answered, the Deputy again said "Take yourself and your boys right out of town right now or else"!

Slowly Luke put his weapon back in his holster, finished his drink, took a final glance at Louise, then gathered his friends and stormed out of the saloon, jumping on their horses and rode down the street.

Taking a deep breath, Fabian gathered his winnings, placed fifty dollars in Louise's hands and then placed another fifty dollars all rolled up, up her dress between her thighs all the way up to the top between the folds of her lips, with a wink saying," Follow her to the bar boys, ya got some drinking to do"!

Louise was a working woman and expected to receive a share of his night's labors. A little Lagniappe now and then always made life easier.

Fabian gathered his winnings up neatly and placed them in his portmanteau and decided that perhaps it was time to take the morning stage for Dallas. As he left by the side door into the adjoining alleyway, he looked both ways and pausing for several moments so his eyes could adjust to the darkness, before proceeding. The hotel he was staying at was just a block away, several turns of the alleyway. As he made the final turn he stopped, for right in front of him was Luke with his gun drawn saying, "Drop the bag and raise your hands"!

Fabian quietly did as he was told, measuring the distance between him and his assailant, just feet away, yet the size of the fellow and the fact that his revolver was just right up against him precluded any idea of going for his derringers. Just as he thought this, Luke was lifting the bulging wallet from Fabians inner coat pocket and in the process said, "Now what is this"? Lifting both derringers right from Fabians shoulder holster, tossing them on the ground saying, "You were gonna shoot with these pea shooters"?

As he started going through Fabians wallet, Fabians arms slowly went down as Luke was eager to find his money, which took his attention for an instant from his quarry. With two swift motions, Fabian twisted his wrists back striking a pin, which released a razor sharp stiletto blade that shot forward twelve inches straight into Luke's midsection just below his breastbone slicing in twain the main artery to his heart. The blade from Fabians other forearm found a home sliding effortlessly into Luke's throat as Luke sank to his knees unable to breathe.

As Fabian held both blades in place, he looked into Luke's eyes and said, "Son your fadin' fast and I just want you to know that if ya wanted some poke time with Louise, I'd a been happy to pay for it just like the other, but it just doesn't look like that's gonna happen now isn't it! See what ya missed"? He wiped both blades clean, resetting them back.

As Luke's eyes went shut and his body sank to the ground, Fabian bid him goodbye. Then retrieving his two derringers and placing them back in his holsters along with his bulging wallet intact. He struggled to place the cowboy between two piles of trash. With some luck it would be at least several days until someone discovered him. Looking around in the scant light of the alley he saw that nothing seemed to be amiss, and picked up his bag and made his way to the hotel, entering from the rear he went to his room, to lay down and freshen up until the morning stage coach out of town.

Louise would no doubt be busy this very moment performing her dairy duties and he was sorry that he wouldn't have time to bid her a proper goodbye. But she'd understand, for this had happened before and they had always eventually crossed paths again. He looked at his pocket watch and since it was almost three AM he decided a brief nap was in order.

Having arrived in Dallas two days later, Fabian checked into a hotel, got and a shave and a bath, having his clothes cleaned and slept the rest of the day away for the days on the stage coach were a far cry from the luxury of a riverboat suite, still it got him here. His efforts in the past few weeks yielded him some five thousand dollars to the good and since here he was on the edge of what seemed like civilization, it was unlikely he'd run into anyone he'd fleeced before, he felt rejuvenated. While eating breakfast the following morning he briefly thought of his last night in Bossier City. A close run thing it was. The very first time in all the years he'd gambled that he'd had to take a life. He decided that he didn't feel at all bad about it, just one of those things that were bound to happen someday and now that it had so what?

He sauntered around town, seeing what there was to see which wasn't much, just a dusty cow town, not much different from the portrayal by the dime novellas of the era. Surrounded by simple people with simple tastes, but he'd not be quick to prejudge, for Bossier City was a far cry from bustling New Orleans and he'd done well there.

Settling into first one saloon then another, he'd sit for hours on end playing solitaire hoping for some wandering minstrel to sit down and challenge his abilities. He entered into a few small games after people got to know him, making it a point to break even each time or deliberately win small. As the weeks rolled by he discovered the rail roads had worked their way from Dallas south to a place he'd never heard of called Waco, then to Austin and on to San Antonio and Houston in the latter part of the year.

The cow towns of Kansas were promising territory for the taking, but Oklahoma was the province of Indians and thieves and he wasn't about to ride across country, for he was a city boy at heart, so after things started to dry up in Dallas, he'd get on the train and work his way south.

Cow towns seemed to always have a way of attracting hard men, eager to find an easy pathand in tis Dallas in its early days, was no different.

Anglos, darkies and half breeds, made their way into and through this dusty cow town, south of the upper reaches of the Red River.

Patiently waiting for the big game certain to wander in by months end when all the locals 'Pokes' would be flush with their meager wages, Fabian wiled his days away getting his morning shave, then parking himself in one of the saloons, reading the local rag and playing endless game of solitaire. When just prior to months end a dozen cowboys walked into the saloon he was then frequenting, led by what appeared to be an overly large half breed, he eventually came to know as "One Eye". The brown leather eye patch, the man sported said it all. Disdainful of head covering of any kind, he was dressed in an assortment of clothing, part Indian, part Cowboy, with long greasy hair tied in a ponytail, sporting a single long feather drooping down of unknown origins, announcing proudly that Indian blood flowed through his veins and to hell with anyone that had a problem with that.

Taller than most, with a deep brown skin tone that covered clearly Anglo features, his lower coverings consisted of two leg chaps that flanked a loin cloth in all kinds of weather. Rather than high heeled cowboy boots he wore handmade calf high, laced up heavy moccasins. At his side was the latest nickel plated break front Smith & Wesson revolver riding high on the hip, with a foot long pig sticker on the other hip. Just one look told most mortals, that this man was not worth the time for acquaintance and it would be wise to give him a wide berth, hoping that fortune would lure him elsewhere and quickly.

However Fabian DuLesseps was not cut from the same cloth as most and somehow saw that this man as he stood at the bar just might be useful some day in some way. So he just sat there, pretending to read his newspaper and taking an occasional sip of his chicory coffee, studying the man and his entourage, quickly arriving at the conclusion that here were those who made a living the easy way, rather than doing the hard work that only suckers engaged in.

Eventually he put his paper away and pulled out a deck of cards from his vest and started playing solitaire, hoping that it would catch the big half breed's eye. True to his instincts, 'One Eye', wandered over and sat down in front of Fabian unannounced and asked directly "What cha doin' there"?

"Playin' Solitaire", said Fabian without looking up directly, in a matter of fact manner.

"What's Solitaire", asked the half breed? Whereupon Fabian gave the 'breed' a quick and simple primer as to how the game was played.

"How often do ya play"?

"Almost every day", said Fabian.

How often do ya win"?

Not very often sad to say, in fact the last time I won a game was, hmmm, lemmesee, about five months ago"!

"What do ya get if'n ya win?

"Not a blessed thing except maybe satisfaction".

"Then why do ya waste your time playin' that dumb game", asked the breed?

"Pilgrim, I play the game to keep me humble", said Fabian still eyeing his cards not looking at his visitor directly. He guessed that his visitor was sizing him up just as Fabian was doing to him, seeing if there was any fear there and seeing nothing but an easy confidence in this man, decided that there was something worth wile in his presence.

While Fabian wagered with himself that here was someone, at best marginally literate, if that, who would take life as easily as taking a breath and never give it another thought. Which reminded him of an old associate now long dead that was of Cajun origins from the deep swamps of southern Louisiana who made a living in a host of ways, who was a very reliable sort when it came to the taking of a life as long as he was paid well and all in advance. He took great relish in taking a life, often for the sport of it and just to watch the man or woman in their death throes. Now since it paid well, so much the better, but once the victim was pointed out to "Leroy", the person was as good as dead. Might take a week or even a month or more, but Leroy was indeed reliable, until one sad evening Leroy, drunk and full of cash money had the misfortune to fall off the Ferry from New Orleans across the Mississippi to Algiers. Poor guy, raised in the swamps, had never bothered to learn to swim.

Everybody had their Achilles heel and Fabian was determined to find One Eye's, chink.

"Wanna play some real poker", asked the breed?

"Well as long as its friendly like just to pass the time", offered Fabian.

"I'll order a fresh deck from the bartender"!

"No need, your deck'll do just fine"!

"Just as you say", said Fabian. "So what'll it be"?

"Five card draw" said the breed.

"Cut the cards to see who deals", offered Fabian?

The breed nodded his head and Fabian drew a five of clubs while his visitor drew a Jack of Spades thus winning the deal. As the breed shuffled the cards, Fabian suggested the modest rules of the stakes they were playing for and seeing agreement the game began. Just a friendly game to while the time away. After an hour or so, Fabian was able to spot the various "tells' One Eye exhibited on any given hand and only prudence kept him from gaining advantage, so back and forth the fortunes of each traveled. A few hours later with Fabian still dealing, several of his boys joined in making a foursome, with the same results as before. Any monies won or lost stayed well within their influence and by supper time Fabian was ahead a scant five dollars.

Then the boys decided they had business elsewhere, gathering up their cash and bidding Fabian a friendly good bye, with 'One Eye' saying as he left, "See ya around sport"! Fabian silently acknowledged their departure and watched with a keen eye as the leapt upon their ponies rode out of town with a flourish.

For several days things were quiet around the old saloon, but in three days the end of the month would roll by and then the boys of the range would be Johnny on the spot, to relive the "Sportin' Life". He wondered where the One Eye and his bunch had gotten off to when news of a stage coach robbery between Dallas and Texarkana arrived via an empty Stage Coach arriving into town, with just the driver, long dead, caught between the horses traces, shot and no doubt pummeled to death by the charging horses. Hours late, the horses simply walked into town, tired from their labors, knowing that a bag full of oats was at the end of the trail. The Sheriff led a group of riders east of town, returning with a buck board of slain men and women, shot through and through apparently by road agents. The strong box and its contents were missing only to be discovered days later, empty. The mail bag was discovered a mile away, by a small stream, its contents strewn all over the place. Of course, the slain were devoid of any jewelry and monies. They wouldn't have any use for them, where they were going.

Successive Sheriff's posse's, were unable to track the robbers, the trail always disappearing into a stream somewhere and with no experienced trackers close at hand the Sheriff just gave up trying to apprehend the villains.

Soon as the news of the robbery reached Fabians ears, he instinctively who was involved. The second last day of the month, in walked One Eye, all by himself into the saloon, seemingly happy and seeing Fabian sitting there all by himself at a table, paid for a bottle of 'Red Eye' and walked over and sat right down without a word.

Pouring himself a drink, the breed looked at Fabian as he said softly, "Well Hello there, I trust the road proved profitable to you"?

"Just what do you think you know about my business", asked One Eye with a hint of suspicion?

"Nothing, nothing at all. At least nothing worth repeating, except to the ears of the chosen"!

As the breeds gun hand left the table, Fabian said quickly, "Relax brother, the only ears worth hearing, any speculations I might or might not have are yours and yours alone, none else, for its none of their damn business as far as I'm concerned! Now if you please, raise your gun hand above the table. But you might want to drop something on the floor and as you pick it up glance under the table to see what greets you"! One Eye, looked hard at Fabian then brought his hand above the table, then removed a plug of chewing tobacco from his vest pocket, dropping it on the floor if by accident and as he went to retrieve it saw the two barrels of a sawed off shot gun, secured to the underside of the table, triggered by a knee mechanism just an inch away from Fabians knee. As he rose back up slowly he said, "Seems ya know how to take care of yourself"! Then he muttered, "So that's why you always sit in the same chair"!

"You have nothing to concern yourself about as far as I'm concerned, in fact I have something to discuss that may be of great interest to you and your boys, and I can best demonstrate this, if you'll be willing to play a simple game of cards", offered Fabian in a matter of fact manner.

"Deal the cards", said One Eye, pulling fifty dollars from his stash.

"Now I want you to pay close attention to my hands as I deal the cards and tell me if anything is amiss", said Fabian as he commenced to deal a game of five card draw poker, and One Eye looked at every movement of the cards as they flew from the deck and seeing nothing special played on.

Before the draw flew from Fabians deck, he said "Stop", when looking straight at the breed, he named each card before it exited the deck and told One Eye his exact hand This was repeated several times and after One Eye demanded that he slow down his movements, Fabian still was able to forecast the Half breeds exact hand.

"No the cards are not marked, but to prove it, I'll order a fresh deck from the bartender", said Fabian who summoned the bartender over to refill his cup of black chicory coffee and bluing a freshly sealed deck.

The activity was repeated several times over and over with Fabian dealing very slowly and still telling the breed exactly what he had in his hand.

Tiring of this and seeing that no one was looking their way, Fabian pushed his winnings back to the One Eye saying, "I've a plan that if you and some of your boys are of a mind can easily throw a fair amount of easy money our way, with just a few days' worth of effort".

One Eye nodded his head and said," Speak"!

Since One Eye controlled around a dozen hard men, and there were just four principle roads that came into and out of town, each road would have stationed a man to intercept a big winner who was flush with cash and a bit drunk on his way home. The 'Mark' would be identified by another of his men inside the saloon and the barkeep, knowing his steady customers, would indicate which way they would travel back home, to one of One Eye's men who would ride ahead and the duo would wait. Needless to say the "Mark" would never again see his home and would disappear along with any cash he had on him.

In case one of the winners wanted to go upstairs with one of the girls, so be it, for it would only delay the inevitable.

Now once a month several of the saloons in town sponsored a special night where serious players gathered round and the 'House' supplied the dealer. Now given Fabians special skills in the dealing and directing of cards without detection, anyone who chose to sit at his table, was either to be a direct loser, or an indirect loser, winning big at the table, plied with drinks at a measured rate, only to lose it all, along with his life later on in the evening. By the time bodies might be discovered, the culprits would be long gone save the bartender, who most everything depended on.

During the course of the two evenings the Dealer, the Bartender and the Road Agents stood to make a killing in every possible way.

After the first evenings activities which broke up about an hour before dawn, many people came and went from Fabians table, with Fabian never leaving his seat during the entire evening. By noon the following day One Eye entered the saloon and discretely gave the bartender a package which would be opened later, and then he sat down with Henry and slid a package to him under the table saying, "The boys are very happy and each of them is a thousand or so to the good with a minimum of sweat. Just like shootin' ducks in a barrel"!

Then he continued saying, "The barkeep is two thousand ahead and you have three thousand in your pocket Mr. Card Sharp".

As he spoke Fabian showed no emotion and kept on playing his game of Solitaire. For He had a keen sense of numbers, figuring some Twenty Thousand Dollars, traded hands on the table with all the comings and goings. He wasn't going to quibble over a few dollars, especially since his fee's for being the dealer, was to drag a dollar out of every poker pot dealt during the evening and in clear view of the entire crowd of players including the Sheriff's deputies which looked in from time to time, no one registered a single complaint. All cash money with over a hundred and fifty hands being dealt during the course of the evening, and after the sun went down it would all start over. Then sometime the following day after he met with One Eye, he would board a train and head south. Life was good…

After the second evening's activities, he met with One Eye the following day and received once more some fifteen hundred dollars in cash.

Once again being shorted by his count, but that was the price of doing business with this lot. They supplied the means to his end. Still and all, during his brief stay in Dallas he was slightly five thousand dollars to the good and he just may consider doing business with One Eye and his gang of cut throats again.

Lying low, upcountry near the Red River, One Eye and his bunch would fade away into the brush for a month then follow Fabian south towards the Waco area; just in case Fabian wanted to does this dance again. So in no particular hurry, Fabian watched the country side roll by as the passenger train moved at the speed of a fast galloping horse.

As the train was traveling south west nearing Waco, Fabian looked out the right side of the Pullman Car, and viewed a line of fully grown pine trees evenly spaced every ten yards apart sporting a continual line of wooden fencing, eventually passing a rail spur to its right with a signs that read "MHM Ranch Rail Spur Line". Just beyond that were a number of tall wooden silos flanking the rail spur.

He gave it little thought, with the vision of what lay ahead, in a little hick town occupying his thoughts. "Never underestimate the possibilities, or the attendant risks involved", was his credo. If things were just not exactly to his liking, he would know within a few days and simply get back on the train for greener pastures. More of a question of feel rather than logic was involved in the lay of the land.

As the train came to a jolting halt at the Waco Station, Fabian got off the train and immediately saw a Saloon not three blocks away and a convenient hotel right across the street. In his world convenience and an avenue for retreat were an essential commodity.

As he approached the Hotel he took scant notice of the Bank that was a block down the dusty street focusing on the hotel where he could get a bath and relax the rest of the afternoon away, before investigating the towns several saloons for action.

23

Later on in the evening, after Fabian had enjoyed a better than expected steak dinner at the hotel, he slowly wandered across the street to the first saloon that came into view as he entered town. As he entered the premises he went up to the bar and quietly ordered a drink.

"What'll ya have", growled the bartender in a gravelly voice? "Kentucky whisky straight up if ya have it", answered Fabian. The bartender nodded, reaching for a fresh glass from the back board and a bottle in full view pouring it deftly into the triple shot glass, saying "Fifty cents"!

Taking a sip, Fabian nodded his head in approval and paid the barkeep. "What brings ya to Waco stranger", asked the bartender?

As he looked up, Fabian decided to paint a picture of deception saying, "Down here from St. Louis, and am on my way to Austin then San Antonio, to investigate the viability of starting up an insurance company. Stopping at the towns along the way to get the lay of the land so to speak"!

"Interested in a little friendly game of poker", asked the bartender? The seemingly innocent question by the bartender, told Fabian all he needed to know, that there was someone about skilled in the game and the bartender was the shill. Fabian had seen it a thousand times before.

"Depends on what kind", he answered.

"Just friendly game's around here. That table over there, where the three cowboys are playing is poker straight up, while the other table that's full up with seven players is the Red Dog table, mostly comprised of the local yokels. The Pokes, sometimes 'Rowdy' things up. While the Red Dog folks are a tad more civilized"!

"Ya ever play Red Dog", asked the bartender? "I think so maybe once, a long time ago in Pittsburgh. It's one of those Yankee games isn't it"?

"A simple game really", offered the bartender. "Just high card, two of a kind and three of a kind, no draw, no straights or flushes"! Three cards dealt out and you declare whether you're in or out of that particular pot, after the standard ante of course. The winner gets the pot, while those brave souls that have the guts to stay in have to "Burn" or match the entire pot"!

"What happens if everybody drops out except the dealer", asked Fabian as if he already didn't know? "The dealer drags the entire pot but loses the deal to the one to his left," replied the barkeep! "So that means if you have the deal, you have the advantage", offered Fabian!

"You catch on fast pilgrim, but ya have the advantage as long as ya have the guts to keep it"!

"You think they'd mind if a stranger joined in", asked Fabian?

"Well, the tables full right now, but shortly some will go tap city and leave and then's when ya might ask em"?

"Thanks might prove to be fun", smiled Fabian. This was a game when spotting the players individual 'Tells' early on would prove to be profitable. Of course Lady Luck always played a large part of the outcome, but the brutal simplicity of the size of any individual pot, either brought out the foolish and greedy from hiding or kept a lid on the emotionally timid.

Fabian had learned the game while practicing his craft on the River Boats that traveled the Ohio and the Mississippi, as far as Pittsburgh and a Yankee game it was indeed. Still it was a simple game and it had always smiled on him with abundance.

As he worked his way through the second drink, he heard an exclamation of disgust come from that table, "Jesus H. Motherfuckin' Christ", and saw a man jump up, from the table and rapidly walk out of the saloon.

He waited a few hands and then wandered over to the table after the second hand and asked, "Any one mind a little fresh blood"? They all looked at him, then a few looked at the bartender, seeing him nod his head, then one of the players said, "The game is three card Red Dog Poker, pot limit. Ya ever play this before"?

"Long time ago in Pittsburgh and the bartender was nice enough to give me a quick refresher course", offered Fabian.

"Then git out yer cash, and take a seat for the cards are soon to come a flyin'! The ante is two bits, straight up"!

Fabian sat right down and tossed his ante into the pot. Since he'd only brought fifty dollars with him, he had no problem if he'd lost it all for the sake of research for future events. During the evening as the ebb and flow of the cards dictated the fortunes for some and the agony for others, Fabian quickly learned about each and every one at the table, repeating the story line for one and all as to his business in this territory.

Seven men playing in a three card game at a mere two bits ante, with an average of three men staying in each pot two of which having to match the pot, guaranteed that quite often the pot would double, then triple, then quadruple in size, depending on the cards and the bravery or foolishness of those involved.

By midnight Fabian, playing very conservatively was up some twenty dollars in cash, but had memorized each of the men's various 'Tells' that sat in and departed, for another occasion, except for a little bookish looking, well-dressed man of middling years, who played a very disciplined game, who himself was slightly up over seventy five dollars since Fabian had sat down. As the game went on the after the pot table talk, revealed that he was a clerk at the towns only bank and that his name was Mortimer Ermy. It was then he decided that for just two days more he would reconnoiter the other two saloons, before heading on down to Austin by train.

Something told him of an opportunity in this small town without him really knowing what it was. But Fabian would indeed return in the very near future. Just after midnight Fabian decided to pack it in and get a good night's rest. Bidding every one a good evening. He'd kept a low profile, arriving and departing without fanfare. Just the way he wanted to keep things, for the present.

Since he had time on his hands, the following evening he visited the other two saloons in town, finding that nothing in particular was going to happen there, other than drunks and uncommonly ugly ladies of ill virtue, he decided to head for the hotel, get a good night's sleep and catch the morning train to Austin.

He'd spent a few weeks in Austin, fleecing the politicians that fancied themselves as aficionados of "The Game", only to discover they were nothing of the sort. Fabian made it a point to play a rather conservative game, winning small and losing small, yet with just enough gleanings of the sheep to make his efforts worthwhile. All in effect marking time, till One Eye and his gang turned up in San Antonio. It was a crap shoot with no guarantee they would ever arrive, just a comment from a highly untrustworthy and unstable individual.

Further complicating things, was that this feeling that something significant and worthy of his time and efforts awaited him in this little dusty whistle stop called Waco. So he sent a letter to One Eye, care of General Delivery in San Antonio telling him of possibilities waiting in Waco.

Ten days later, he received a letter back from One Eye, care of General Delivery. As he expected, the man was barely literate, and as Fabian laboriously worked his way through the scrawl, he was able to decipher that One Eye and his boys had just arrived in San Antonio and were scouting out prospects for gain.

Fabian rushed off a reply stating that he was leaving for Waco on the following mornings train and for One Eye and his boys to expect a letter from him within ten days or so time. By that time he should be able to send a plan and a target for some big money. The following morning Fabian boarded the train north to Waco. Two things were clear. First there was a bank teller of long standing that had a penchant for the game of poker and was a better than most practitioner of the game, then second he worked in a bank. An afternoon in the privacy of his hotel room, practicing dealing seconds and bottoms, should be sufficient to hone the skill to a razors edge, sufficient to be invisible to even the most intense scrutiny.

His time in Austin proved once again his invincibility in the game, playing at the most conservative of levels and living as well as one could in the States Capitol, he was still slightly over five thousand dollars to the good, without raising a single eyebrow all the while never having to resort to his skills at table deception, just playing the game as it should be played.

The ancient goddess 'Fortuna' was indeed kind and he would have to find a way to thank her appropriately.

After reentering the very same hotel he left weeks earlier, he took a seat at the restaurant across the street from the clerks bank for a leisurely midafternoon repast', watching the comings and goings of the banks patrons. He made it a point to stay away from the Saloon for the next several days, just wandering around the town keeping a middling profile, but always taking his meals at the window seat where he could leisurely take his food and drink while observing the externals of the banks activities, intermittently.

After four days of this and gleaning nothing of apparent importance, he decided visit the saloon where Mortimer Ermy took his pleasure.

It was a Friday evening and the clock struck nine PM, the moment he entered. Seeing a different bartender than before he ordered his standard drink. A half hour later, in walked the bank teller, who recognized Fabian straight away and walked over to him saying, "Why Hello Mister DuLesseps, didn't expect to see you back here. How was your business in San Antonio"? Greeting the teller with a friendly smile Fabian responded,"Not bad. Not bad at all. This part of the country certainly could use the protection offered by a substantial and well-funded Insurance Company such as ours and the city fathers have proved most accommodating"! After another fifteen minutes of friendly yet banal, small talk, Fabian heard the words that were sweet ambrosia to his ears, "Care to while away the hours in a game of poker"? "Mister Ermy, I can't think of anything I'd rather do, with the possibility of taking a wee poke from one of the ladies of the town", offered Fabian in reply.

"Well Mr. DuLesseps, here's hoping the evening is kind to us both," said Mortimer lifting his glass in a modest toast. Then he got a fresh deck of cards from the bartender and selected a table away from the gathering throng of Friday night fellows, looking to while their spare hours away, drinking bad whiskey and trading in lies, legends and gossip. Play in few hands of five card draw heads up for a short time, one by one seat's were taken at the table until seven places were filled and a more robust game could gain ground. By ten PM the game as well as the activity in the Saloon was in full swing with soiled doves suddenly appearing from seemingly nowhere, staking out their turf, for the milking to later occur.

Once again playing a diminutive game Fabian found himself slightly over a hundred dollars ahead just after the midnight hour, with Mortimer the banker, barely breaking even. Inheriting the deal, Fabian decided to reward Mortimer by dealing him a hand that would get him to reacting. As the hand progressed the Banker was looking at a possible Kings over Tens Full house, and the big winner for the evening was a cotton farmer who was up some four hundred dollars, and was slowly working on his own full house, yet merely Jacks over Nines.

As the cards came out and the others dropped away, including Fabian, he heard one waddie exclaim as he tossed his cards in, gathering his cash and rose from the table, "That ain't a hand, it's a foot", and wandered away. Mortimer took three cards in his draw while the Cotton Farmer took two, each getting what they hoped for and hitting their respective full houses. 'Huzzah' Fabian thought, as they both registered mild surprise at their respective gifts from seemingly above, thus telling Fabian exactly what he'd been seeking.

Fabian then, his task completed placed the remainder of the deck in the center of the table and watched the two go at it, betting, raising, then raising again and again, until he heard the Cotton Farmer say "Call" and display his hopefully winning hand. Ever so slightly the unconscious facial tic briefly flickered on Mortimer Ermy's face as he quietly showed his hand for all to see.

Fabians pronouncement declared, "Kings over Tens beats Jacks over Nine"! Then he pushed his winnings over to Mortimer only to see the confirmation of the very same facial tic manifest itself still again. The cotton farmer, stood up saying, "Been playing cards with that little shit for some time now and that's the first time he's every bested me. I'll be seeing you next Monday morning' at the bank for that loan you promised and ya better come through"! Whereupon he picked up the remainder of his money, finished his drink in a gulp and stormed out of the saloon in a huff, brushing past the Town Deputy as he went through the swinging doors. By Fabians reckoning, the little banker was now almost a four hundred dollars to the good for the evening. In the aftermath of the hand, every one decided to take a brief break from the activity and consult with the painted women frequenting the bar, prompting Fabian to say, "Mortimer, well played! Well played indeed"! "Thank you Fabian", mused the little clerk as he counted his winnings. Then he pondered, "I think I've earned some time for a little companionship, don't you think."? Prompting Fabian to reply, "I couldn't agree more, my good man"!

After the interlude concluded and Mortimer disappeared upstairs, with a rather sizeable heifer, Fabian stayed yet another hour at the table playing just to break even for the evening before making his apologies and calling it an evening. As soon as he got to his room, he ripped off a brief letter to One Eye, in San Antonio care of General Delivery suggesting they'd best wrap up whatever activities they were involved in and head for Waco to arrive in Waco within ten day's time of the date of the letter, for a chance of a lifetime. He outlined where he was staying and how they were to meet. The following morning he was up early for his normal routine, but especially to get the letter in the Postal services mail bag for the eight AM train to Austin and thence by stage coach to San Antonio.

During the interim he would now set about trimming the sails of the wee little bank clerk, and setting him up for the big killing. He now had sufficient funds to play poker with the big kids. The lamb was fat and ready for its shearing.

Fabian hoped the roll in the hay with that soiled dove was worth it for it would be a long time if ever before he could ever smile again. Like a wolf scenting the kill close at hand, Fabian was ready for the golden fleecing.

Never having performed a bank robbery before, Fabian decided that it couldn't be all that difficult if one had a plan; a layout of the place inclusive of guards the cash drawers and especially the bank vault. So after his breakfast several days later, he entered the bank and stood in line waiting his turn, noting the number of teller's cages, the location of the vault and an inventory of the personnel at hand.

Apparently Mortimer was not at his teller duties, but bent over the open bank vault at the rear of the premises, working at something with two young and attractive women completely unaware of Fabian's presence, at he traded one of his fifty dollar gold pieces in exchange for a like amount in the paper currency.

'More to the good', he thought as he exited the building. Hurriedly he went back to his room and drew a layout of the bank. One or two more innocent trips to the bank should do it, in order to get a feel for the rhythm of the operation.

That evening he visited the saloon again, wondering if Mortimer was going to try and recoup he previous losses. An hour later he was not disappointed when in came the bank teller, who made a brief stop at the bar then joined Fabian and a few other 'Feather Merchants' at the table. They exchanged pleasantries as Fabian announced, "Gentlemen, the game is Five Card Stud Poker, standard ante to the table if you please. Again he was anointed as the designated dealer, drawing one Yankee dollar out of each pot for his time and efforts.

After a tepid second hand, in walked the Cotton Farmer, who previously was taken to the wood shed by the mousy looking Mortimer, taking up one of the chairs as he pulled out his bankroll. "Gentlemen, hitch up your garters for tonight's agonna be lucky for me"! From time to time he glanced at Mortimer and especially at his money. By the set of his jaw, the Cotton Farmer was determined to teach the little bank teller a thing or two.

Fabian decided that this very evening the goddess Fortuna would indeed smile on the farmer, and Mortimer was in for a comeuppance. Life indeed was a zero sum game. For every winner there just had to be a loser.

Rather than playing with his accustomed conservative mien, Mortimer upped his game betting a tad more aggressively when the cards warranted, while the Cotton Farmer did just the opposite. At the end of two hours, both men were up considerably in their fortunes by some three hundred dollars each. While others came and went, leaving their hard earned cash at the table. While the banker and the Cotton Farmer did their little prelude of the big dance together, Fabian just watched and waited dealing the cards straight as they came, without a hint of flourish. Then just before midnight Mortimer got the best of the Cotton Farmer in a hand, dragging some two hundred dollars out of his bankroll.

True to his personality, Mortimer was one who probably stood by the credo," If ya win big, keep your mouth shut and if'n ya lose big, keep your mouth shut", showing little emotion at his good fortune as he gathered his winnings.

Two hours later, after fatigue had started to make its presence known, helped along by a steady diet of warm beer and whiskey along with the entrance and exits of the Cavalcade of Fools, that eagerly left their money at the table, Fabian decided to wind the game down with his "Coupe' de Grace".

"Gentlemen, what'll it be", asked Fabian after they all returned to the table after a brief interlude to drain themselves of their bodily fluids?

"How's about some seven card stud," asked the Cotton Farmer of everyone around the table?

Hearing no dissenting opinions, Fabian announced, "Seven Card Stud Poker, it is Gents, so ante up"!

As the ante's drove to the center of the table, Fabian performed his unique feat, deftly positioning four hands of cards sequentially, to afford a progressively good hand to at least four people to butt heads over. Given that both Mortimer and one of the others had a penchant for asking for a reshuffle of the cards intermittently during the course of a given hand, played right into Fabians plan for exacting the proper position of the cards to those he wanted to last. This ability literally took thousands of hours to perfect and a superior ability to swiftly memorize, the exact positioning of any given card in a fifty two card deck, while either drunk or sober.

He'd done this so often that in his dreams, his mind performed repeated combinations, over and over relentlessly to where he could stack a deck and restack the very same deck, over and over during the course of a hand in plain view of others, without anyone being the wiser. For this he was eternally in the debt of that Mulatto Cajun Woman, from the deep swamps of Louisiana who took in this skinny white boy as an orphan and raised him up and edumacated him to the "Sportin' Life".

As the down cards flew out of the deck followed by the lone up card for each player, Fabian announced, "First Queen the bettor"! As the bets flew to table center, followed by the next round of up cards, Fabian announced "First Queen still the bettor"! One by one several men tossed in their cards, rising to leave the table and their money. Then one of the men called for a reshuffle as Fabian projected that he would. Deftly Fabian reshuffled never even bothering to look at the cards as he propositioned the hand, for the big ending.

Four people remained, each with the possibility of having a hand that they would sell their souls for. In the final four were Mortimer and the Cotton Farmer, with the latter eager for just retribution.

What lay on the table just prior to the final cards were, Aces over Kings, full house, Queens over Tens, again a full house, with Mortimer just about to draw, his fourth nine card, while the erstwhile Cotton Farmer about to draw the fifth card of a deuce through six of spades straight flush.

The trap was set as the final down card flew from the deck into the hands of each man, their various individual 'tells' flashing "Go" as the remainder of the deck was placed at center table, indicating that all cards were out and the final betting to begin. As each bet was announced and money flew to center table, Fabian could see that the Town Sheriff had wandered close to the table to witness the action. Not being a gambler and a staunch Baptist, he understood the game and had seen his share during his span of life, but never in his life had he seen so much money on a poker table with four serious men all vying for the final prize and since there could only be one winner, he gradually loosened the restraining strap, on the hammer of his Colt revolver nestled in his holster just in case.

As the betting went around the table, no one would relent; tossing their money into center ring and the various bet bumps reared their ugly head.

Once all of the visible money was out on the table, Fabian interceded saying, "Gentlemen, since all the money is on the table and eager hearts are wanting, Hoyle's rules state that if all agree, then those who elect to continue will be obligated to either draw light from the pot and should they lose will have an obligation to the winner whoever that is, or else failing in that they must leave the table and all of their money! What do you say one and all"?

As he looked around the table all nodded their heads and being that the High Sheriff was present, Fabian declared, "Since everyone has agreed with the Sheriff as a witness, the game will continue till its conclusion"!

A final round of betting and raising rose forth until everyone emotionally exhausted called. As Fabian indicated the first to show his hand, "Queen over Tens, Full House", then the next man smiled as he turned over his cards hearing Fabian intone, "Aces over Kings, a better Full House"! Then Mortimer smiling, turned over his cards, hearing Fabian exclaim, "A fourth nine card, four of a kind"!

Finally the Cotton Farmer, his prayers answered and milking each movement for its maximum impact, turned over his hole cards showing that he'd done the illogical and drawn to an inside Deuce through Six of Spades Straight Flush.

The crowd that gathered around shouted while the Sheriff helped Fabian sort out who owed what to the Cotton Farmer, by their light bets drawn from the final pot. That completed the Cotton Farmer gathered all of his winnings and written IOU's, immediately exclaiming, "Boys the drinks are on me so belly up to the bar".

"What cha gonna do with all that money Simon", asked one of the onlookers"?

"Whal de well, lemme see heah", he pondered, "Foist thing I'm agonna do is git me a bottle, then the next thing I'm gonna do it git me one of those painted whores over theah, and buy me a good long poke in the whiskers.

Then lemme see since my ole lady will be pissed I'm a gonna have at buy her a whole lotta pretties to keep her happy and finally pay cash fer the equipment I need for the farm, rather than go see Mortimer at the bank for a loan. Real nifty since some of the cash is his. But hey, don't tell anybody wouldn't wanna the man to get into any trouble"! Then as an afterthought he mused, "And if anything's left I'll deposit it in Mortimer's Bank, yeah that's the least I can do"!

As everyone rushed to the bar, to witness Farmer Simon's largesse close up and the two full house holders slinked out of the bar broke and now in debt to the Cotton Farmer for some two hundred dollars each, each dreaded going home and eventually having to explain to their wives what wastrels they were. For Hell hath no fury, like a wife done wrong.

Oblivious to everything else, there sat Mortimer Ermy, some five hundred dollars in debt, with all but six hundred dollars stashed at his abode, gone up in smoke. There'd be no pussy for him tonight, no conviviality, no apparent happiness and his clerk's salary of fifty dollars a month didn't even begin to...

Somehow he had to find a way out of this hole, but how? How does one lose with four of a kind?

What manner of celestial retribution caused his fortunes to turn so abruptly? Things were finally going so well, after years of hard work and modest living? The game was as straight and scrutinized as could be, so what went wrong?

Just then Fabian returned from the bar bringing two mugs of black coffee for them both saying, "Look at it this way sport, Fortunes ebb and flow often turning on a dime! I myself have seen both sides of the card and when I look back I find that the peaks and the valleys were all never permanent, simply a bump in the road. Why I'll wager that you'll be back in the high grass in no time at all"!

Continuing on Fabian said, "I've watched your manner of play and you play with skill and you know the cards, so I'm confident that you'll recover and sooner than you think if you keep your wits about you"!

Then almost as an afterthought Fabian added, "Besides, in your line of work, you always have access to capital whenever you wish"!

Then he rose up taking his coffee mug and wandered over to the bar to join in the celebration, of Simon the Farmers good fortune.

As Mortimer slowly went through the swinging doors, he heard the farmer bellow, "Whare's that painted Hussey I just bought me"? As Mortimer walked back to his place, the final words of encouragement from Fabian echoed in his head, 'Access to Capital', over and over again.

All of his life Mortimer Ermy had been as honest an individual as could be had on god's green earth. He took pride in his honesty and looked with supreme derision at those who took the low road. But here he was at a crossroads in his life. His only joy in life came at the poker table. The Cameraderie, and superficial fellowship, as it may be, got his heart to beating. His interaction with the Ladies of the Town, was his only source for affection, for every time he looked into a mirror and visited his scrawny body and the paucity of manliness he just knew that no woman in her right mind would ever provide him with affection, without a medium of exchange occurring. "In advance sweetie", was the usual refrain. Just once he would've liked to pay for their services, after the fact.

Mortimer had but two skills in life, one was banking and numbers and the other the poker table. Slowly he reasoned as he walked home, the monthly audit was just completed and no scrutiny was expected until twenty nine days later, when the books would again be reconciled down to the very last cent as it always had been since he arrived five years ago. He would have to think on the matter, for hasty judgments always lead to disaster.

As Fabian lay upon his bed he almost felt sorry for the little banker. He never saw it coming. No one else had either, in Fabians entire life. However just then, a scintilla of yet another scheme took root. 'Who on earth would ever suspect Mortimer Ermy of ever being a Poker Skell?' The man had a measure of skill in the game that exceeded most mortals, he knew his numbers, his manner was affable and modest, keeping a low profile, he was reasonably intelligent finally he was a forgettable entity, if taught well, could blend in anywhere. He then decided that when all the smoke cleared he see to it that Mortimer cleaved to him and perhaps they could travel out west to the gold and silver fields where the pickins' were great.

He'd planted the seed of discontent in Mortimer's mind and just knew that he'd have to tap his bank for additional funds to gain back his dignity. Mortimer might now think he was at bottom, but he had a ways to go yet. Fabian would see to that.

A few leisurely days later, Fabian received a telegram from San Antonio, from an unnamed source, which simply said, "Am leaving today. Look for me at the agreed place in five days".

It could only mean one thing; One Eye was coming with the boys, which meant he'd five days to lay Mortimer low. Every day though Fabian went through his normal routine taking his meals at the restaurant across form the bank, making two ever so brief visits to exchange money and even once having Mortimer serve him at the Tellers window, neither party serving a hint of recognition of each other.

The weekend soon at hand meant the saloon would be busy once again and Fabian again agreed to host the game for the final time, whereas he let it be known that he would soon have to leave for St. Louis and become an Insurance man once again.

Certainly Mortimer would again make a showing and sure enough there he was with a new bank roll. Fabian thought, 'Well, other people's money was always preferable to your own, unless you lose'…

The Cotton Farmer, Simon was nowhere in attendance this evening, but a fresh set of sheep eagerly arrived to be cannon fodder for Fabians machinations. All evening long Fabian intermittently steered the cards to Mortimer so that at the end of the evening he was several hundred dollars ahead. By Fabians reckoning Mortimer entered the evening with some five hundred dollars of the banks money. Thus as the designated dealer dealing some seventy five hands out during the course of play Fabian was seventy five dollars to the good.

The following evening he was certain that Mortimer would follow with an even larger influx of the banks money, given the uncharacteristic aggressive style of play Mortimer exhibited. That was when Fabian would become a participant and relinquish the chore of dealing to another.

The game started at nine PM, the following evening on a Saturday Night. The Moon was as full as a pregnant Albino, signaling that both good fortune as well as ill, would visit someone this very evening.

By ten PM Fabian was up almost four hundred dollars, when Mortimer entered the saloon. Stopping by the bar to gain a measure of courage in a glass, he wandered over to the full table, seeing Fabian sitting not in the dealers seat but strategically just to the dealers right.

Both nodded to each other in recognition as the play droned on, with Mortimer just having to wait till some poor sod buster went "Tap City", having to withdraw for the evening. Soon enough his opportunity came about and he eagerly took a seat across from Fabian as soon as it became available, still overly warm on a chilling harvest evening.

"Cards out", the dealer droned, as he announced the game as five card draw poker, jacks or better to open. Winning seventy five dollars on his very first hand seemed as a sign from the heavens that Mortimer would see a glorious evening at the tables. As the evening progressed Mortimer seemed to be blessed as his aggressive manner of play yielded rewards repeatedly. Alternatively Fabian was not far behind in his good fortune, yet being ever careful not to butt heads with Mortimer until the very end, tossing in a few winning hands and even going so far as to exhibit a visible 'tell' midway through the evening certain that all but Mortimer would never pick up on it.

Fabian knew when Mortimer was bluffing, which he did ever so rarely and when he hit his card by the ever so faint twitches he exhibited. He verified this by allowing Mortimer to bluff him out of a few modest hands later in the evening, and there it was the 'tell'. By Fabians reckoning Mortimer was now ahead some twelve hundred dollars and himself some fifteen hundred dollars to the good, as the clock struck two AM. The dealer announced, "Gents the game is straight five card draw poker, table stakes", as the cards flew around the table. The ante's were all in and the betting commenced, with Mortimer opening for twenty dollars and two souls immediately dropping out, tossing their cards to the dealer. Fabian raised the stakes a mere twenty five dollars just to keep things interesting.

All called the bet, as the dealer went around the table giving out cards and collecting the discards. Pointing to Mortimer, he asked "First bet of fifty dollars what's your poison"? Mortimer pawed at his money saying "One hundred dollars", as the bet went around the table chasing away all others who had not gotten the cards they wanted except for Fabian who said, "One hundred and see you two hundred more"!

The table went silent as well as half the saloon who recalled that Mortimer, just recently suffered the disappointment of a lifetime, when four of a kind hand came up short.

Mortimer said, "I'll see your two hundred and raise you five hundred more", as a collective sigh went out."

Fabian simply said, see your five hundred and raise you a thousand" as he reached into his vest and produced ten one hundred dollar bills that went on the table. He held in his hand clearly more money to buy the pot if need be, but he said, "Mortimer, I'm pretty sure I have you beat and I'd just hate to have you experience a repeat of last week".

Mortimer's back stiffened up as he dug deep into his pockets coming up with the thousand bet, just barely with but a few dollars to spare. Then tossing his hand on the table said "There it is, you churly scut, Four Jacks, so beat that"!

Fabian took a long look at Mortimer saying nothing but turning over four successive Queens, one after the other, letting the cards speak for themselves, while exhibiting a sad face for all to see.

Everyone around the table groaned, for it had happened once again to the little banker. A once in a lifetime poker hand, drawn a second time in short succession only to be beaten by a slightly better hand.

What made it so sweet for Fabian was that he trusted Dame Fortune to put the final touches on his exquisite plan without having to resort to his masterful manipulations. As he looked into Mortimer's eyes from across the table, he saw utter defeat. As he gathered his winnings, Mortimer started to rise after the others had retreated to the bar and Fabian said, "Mortimer, sit with me awhile"!

Meekly the bank clerk sat back down staring at Fabian with vacant eyes, seeing yet not registering.

"Right now, you are in a very bad place, but if you'll recall I asked you not to call my hand, didn't I"? Mortimer nodded his head, wanting to flee this wretched place and the sin it had foisted upon him, but Fabian's voice somehow kept him in place. No doubt to further humiliate him privately. In his mind he was responsible for his own demise, suddenly blurting out, "I'm done!"! Pausing a moment, Fabian asked, "How so Mortimer"?

"I, uh," Mortimer struggled for the words, "Borrowed the funds I used for the tables to try and reverse my fortune and I almost made it"! "From where did you borrow the money", asked Fabian although he already surmised the answer.

"From the bank", said the clerk timidly with the resignation of massive guilt. "They had just completed the monthly audit and I thought I could win the money back and then some and replace it, before the next monthly audit and no one would be the wiser and now I'm ruined"!

"Rise with me Mortimer and let's go outside and catch a breath of fresh air and take a little stroll, so I can think of a way to get you out of your situation intact and with your reputation still intact"!

As they slowly walked down the dimly lit streets, Fabian seemed to be thinking as Mortimer rambled on about the hell that awaited him, by the time of the next audit. "I might as well end things right now, but how? I'm such a coward"!

"Now, now there'll be no such talk about ending things I just won't have it", chided Fabian. "But you don't understand, I'm almost five thousand dollars in the hole to the bank and the bank is owned by the Jaeger family. They're the big dogs around here and if they ever get their hands on me, it's curtains for me"!

"So my good man we shall have to see to it that they never discover the shortage of cash", said Fabian! "I just might have a way to extricate you from your dilemma, so walk with me while I think on it some more"!

Mortimer followed his new savior hoping for anything, anything at all that would save him from a fate worse than death itself, when he heard Fabian ask, "Mortimer, approximately how much cash is on hand at the bank at this time, approximately"?

Mortimer stopped in his tracks, thinking a second, and then he blurted out, "Slightly over seventy five thousand dollars, not counting the gold and silver coinage"!

"And if one day soon if that money simply wasn't there to be counted", Fabian offered, letting that thought dangle in the night air!

"But how", asked Mortimer?

"Read the papers my boy, desperados and bank robbers are seemingly everywhere, the James Gang, the Younger Brothers and the Bass Gang, robbing banks and trains of thousands and getting away with it too", whispered Fabian.

As they continued walking, Fabian mused, "Now I know of a certain group of unsavory characters, highly skilled in the arts of robbery who've never been caught. These are serious men who ride hard, strike fast and always get what they go after. Not exactly our kind of people, but people of whom I've made an acquaintance with and most importantly there exists a mutual respect between us. Now the crucial thing is that I happen to know that they'll be in this vicinity in just a few days and I think that I can craft a way for them to rob the bank, before the next audit and in no way connecting you with the event, even leaving you with as much as, oh, say five thousand dollars to the good after the fact"!

The streets were mostly unoccupied, with most of the activity reserved for the saloons, whereas the god fearing Christian shop keepers were already fast asleep.

"I just don't know Fabian, you're forgetting the Jaeger family, they'd hunt them down to get their money back even to the ends of the earth, then where would I be"!

"Talk to me Mortimer and tell me about the daily routine at the bank"! Before too many minutes went by Fabian said, "Well there it is, a hostage will have to be taken to insure that the Jaeger family will stay at a distance and after several days the hostage will be set free unharmed"!

"This 'Esme', you say is married to one of the Jaegers and manages the bank, so it shall be her that is taken hostage. Of course you'll have to be roughed up a bit to cast any possibility of suspicion of complicity on your part elsewhere. But a wee gash on the head will serve as an appropriate wound to remind people how brave you were in trying to prevent the banks loss"!

Continuing Fabian offered, "A number men secretly infiltrating the town, then descending on the bank in a flash, removing all the cash, leaving the gold and silver, then taking a hostage as they rode out of town, which prevents any possibility of gunplay lest she gets hurt, then shortly after they leave town, they split up the money and depart in every direction of the compass? Who's gonna follow? More importantly where?

Of course what Fabian failed to mention was the myriad of things that could go awry, but in his desperate state of mind, Fabians plan seemed to be well thought out and his only possibility of emerging from this mess whole.

"So Mortimer, what say you"? "You'd do this for me"?

"Hell Mortimer, somebody's gotta do the Lord's work sometime"! "Ok, well I suppose so Fabian", said Mortimer meekly.

"Good, now you go home and get a good night's rest and don't worry about a thing. I'll connect with you sometime Monday to put the finishing touches to the final plan", said Fabian shaking hands with the meek little bank teller and sending him on his way.

The rest of the weekend went by in a leisurely manner with Fabian and Mortimer resting and contemplating their respective futures in a positive light. The following Monday Fabian went through his normal routine, taking his breakfast in the restaurant across from the bank, while reading the local paper, when he spotted a familiar face riding through town. The face belonged to a cowboy affiliated with One Eye. Paying his bill, he made his way to the local livery and rented a small carriage and a pair of horses, driving them out of town past the standing cowboy without any sign of recognition. He was seen and in due time the cowboy would follow catching up with him and guiding him to where the rest of One Eye and his gang rested, several miles south of town.

As the desperado led Fabian into the copse of trees that hid the gang, Fabian pulled his carriage to a halt, hearing the bellow of One Eye yelling, "So what's this big deal you're talking about? It better be good getting us all the way up here from San Antone'"!

"Better than good One Eye. Far better than good! The biggest payday any of you'll see in your lives. A big fat bank with over seventy five thousand dollars in cold cash, just sittin' there begging to be robbed. Now everybody gather round. The sweet part of the deal is the head clerk is in to me big time and needs to have the bank robbed to cover his ass for money he's stolen from the bank to fund a very bad gambling habit. Right now he's up shit's creek and you One Eye, are his paddle"!

With that he gave the bank a brief explanation of how Mortimer got himself in hock to the devil. Then he pulled out a paper he'd drawn as to the layout of the bank, the safe and the cash drawers. He explained the sparse security the bank offered and how to neutralize the old guard quickly.

"Now this clerk called Mortimer is expecting that one of ya is gonna pistol whip him before y'all leave with the money and did I mention leave the gold and silver alone for its only gonna slow ya down. Give Mortimer what he wants, a bullet as you leave.

The little weasel will crack under the first sign of pressure, ya follow?

But just before play along for its important the bank vault door be kept open or else all you're gonna get is chump change. Now it's very important that you capture a young girl that's the manager, her name is "Esme" and I'm told she's pretty and that's all I know, but she has to be taken hostage as y'all ride out of town, to ensure that a minimum of gunplay happens and that ya don't get followed. Now she's the wife of one of the owners of the bank, so do what you will, I really don't care, hold her for additional ransom if ya want, but I really don't recommend that."

"Why", asked One Eye?

"Because the family is full of Texas Rangers and it'll only complicate things for y'all, ya follow"? One Eye nodded his head as did everyone else.

"Now the plan is to ride to a place like this, then quickly split up the money, and if all goes well you shouldn't be immediately followed thanks to your important hostage, then everyone split up in pairs and all head in different directions. Suggest you ride hard for a half day then cut the woman loose and head for parts unknown. Where y'all meet up, if at all is your business not mine.

"So what do you expect out of this", asked One Eye?

Assuming a figure of seventy five thousand dollars, the little clerk is expecting five thousand dollars, but since he's not gonna be around to collect", the gang all nodded their heads in agreement, one less mouth to feed. "Now since it's my plan and I put this gift together for all y'all, I'm getting ten thousand dollars, which leaves sixty five thousand dollars left to split up any way you want."

Continuing Fabian said, "Leave my share in one of the bank bags and bury it under some brush under one of these trees and a few days later I'll come by and get it! Now this is important, very important, when it comes to splitting up the money, put a clock on your selves when ya get back here and allow yourselves, no more than fifteen minutes time to get that done.

Before ya slap leather and head for parts unknown. The hostage should slow any posse down following you by say a couple of hours, but one will sure be coming ya can bet on it. Any squabbling about who gets what after the fact will cut down your chances for a clean get away, so fifteen minutes is the limit, is everyone agreed"? Fabian looked around to see everyone nodding their heads in agreement.

"Now when I made up this little plan I assumed that you'd have about ten men with ya, but I see that there are but seven here"!

"More than enough to get done what needs doin'," said One Eye, "but with less mouths to feed everyone will get a little more"!

"The arithmetic I'll leave up to you, One Eye"!

Fabian continued, outlining the plan, directing how and when they were to enter the town in stages so as not to unduly draw attention to themselves.

"Now across the street from the bank is a restaurant where I'll be after my breakfast watching the whole thing and if there's anyone to soon follow, if I can I'll direct them away from where you're actually going"!

"The bank will open for business at nine in the morning, so around a half hour after they open, should be the ideal time to hit the bank, especially when the vault door is open"!

"We all clear on everything", said Fabian looking around and seeing that all were in apparent agreement.

"Remember", counseled Fabian, arrive easy, hit hard and ride out fast. The ones who enter the bank memorize the bank layout I gave ya and make the money split, quick afterwards then vanish to the four winds as only you can"!

He then got into his carriage waved them all a good bye and said "See ya all tomorrow morning", then cracked the reins as the carriage sped away.

As he rode back to town he expected that somehow there would be a change in plans from One Eye, for he was a scurrilous bastard, but worst case, he'd be shorted by any monies he'd received of possibly be left out completely. Should that happen, Fabian decided that he'd simply have to chalk it up to experience. Yet he knew in his bones the plan would work if everyone did what he said. As he approached town, he was really looking forward to the event at hand, if for nothing else than an experiment in his capabilities.

Early the next morning, he appeared at the restaurant across from the bank, for his standard breakfast of steak and fried eggs covered in gravy. He reminded himself that when this little exercise was completed, that perhaps he should go on a diet, for his normally thin waist was starting to grow.

He noticed that around eight AM, Mortimer and several women entered the bank, no doubt preparing for the days business, so far so good. A half hour later as he sipped his chicory coffee and read the local paper, he noticed the first of One Eye's men riding into town casually stopping up the street and entering the General Store. Then ten minutes later, yet another of the gang rode slowly into town positioning themselves, just waiting.

At the stroke of nine AM, two more of One Eyes men rode slowly into town passing the bank and Fabian as they went disappearing around the corner up the street, just as the bank opened their doors for the day. Yet another middle of the week lazy day for the town of Waco, with the town Sheriff coming outside of the jail to light up his morning cheroot, look around and seeing nothing awry, go back inside for his morning coffee.

Then two other strangers wandered into town Finally at nine thirty, by Fabians gold pocket watch, he viewed One Eye, accompanied, no doubt by his 'Segundo', slowly ride into town past the bank and stopping several buildings away hitching their horses to the hitching post, dismounting and giving the world a view of someone having a full stretch of the limbs after too long on the trail. Yet somehow, the few people out on the street didn't seem to pay any attention to the newcomers.

'All to the good', thought Fabian as his apparent inattention was masked to anyone who cared by the way he held the newspaper. Then he spied the Cotton Farmer who'd hit his stride the other evening at Mortimer's expense, no doubt on his way to the bank, on orders from his wife, to get his newfound wealth into a safe and secure place. An unexpected benefit that was unforeseen. More for the group to divide up when the time came. Easy come, easy go. Sure enough, there he went straight into the bank, Silas the cotton farmer carrying a sealed paper package, that surely was the cash gleaned from the tables. Then he noticed One Eye and his 'Segundo' emerge from the building they previously entered and casually walk towards the bank entrance, their eyes scanning the streets for any sign of trouble, followed at a distance by the others who were gradually making their way towards the bank entrance. Five would enter the bank while two men were to wait outside flanking the banks entrance to cover their escape. One by one the gang entered the bank, lifting their neck bandanas over their faces as they entered. Inside, Mortimer never knew exactly which day the robbery was to occur, as he was tardy each day in closing the big safe door, incurring the new bank manager Esme Jaeger's wrath, so this morning he made as if the safe door was closed, yet left it open just a crack, so apparently it would escape all but the closest scrutiny. 'The door must be left open at all costs', he thought.

Just then he saw Simon the newly rich Cotton Farmer, enter the bank with a sealed package of what have should been Mortimer's winnings, no doubt to ad visible insult to his emotional injury as Mortimer would have to account and receipt for the money. But just then he relished the thought that Simon might never have a chance to spend a dime of that money after the next few days went by.

Simon smiled as his turn to the tellers window arrived as he said to Mortimer, "Spent some of your money on the missus, but the rest is right here for y'all to take care of sport"!

Just then Mortimer spotted what he thought was divine deliverance as the first of the robbers entered the bank with covered faces and their guns drawn. Five men entered with one staying by the door holding it closed, with One Eye yelling, "Everybody stay where you are, this is a stick up"!

Mortimer looked at Silas, who seeing that his newfound fortune was about to evaporate whirled around to face the robbers while reaching for his pistol only to have One Eye, grab his gun hand before the weapon cleared the holster, while sticking his own revolver into the man's gut and pulling the trigger. The sound of the blast was muffled by the proximity of the barrel to the victim yet close enough to set the man's shirt on fire as he fell lifeless to the floor.

Esme sitting behind the cage turned her head towards the safe and seeing that it was still open just a crack, jumped up and took three steps towards the safe crashing into the heavy metal door with all her might.

Mortimer turned as the gun went off, seeing that Esme was rushing towards the safe, ran to try and cut her off, but was brought low by the gun barrel of One Eye's Segundo, who jumped over the counter going for the safe, just as he approached the safe a split second behind Esme, who's desperation was barely sufficient enough to nudge the safe door shut with a resounding "Click".

One Eye's Segundo, pushed Esme away from the door as tried to open the safe, but it would not budge as he yelled back to One Eye, "The safe door is shut and we're all fucked for fair"!

Then One Eye yelled at the other two to go for the cash drawers and stuff all the money into the bank bags. Then pushed Silas's winnings, his package partially opened and visible towards the other two saying, "Here, don't forget this", then vaulted the counter towards the safe in the rear.

As he approached the safe he addressed a frightened Esme saying, "Missy, ya better open the safe right now if ya know what's good for ya"!

"I can't", she lied "Mortimer's the only one who knows the combination". Looking at the prostrate Mortimer, he said to Segundo "Why did ya pistol whip that little booger"? Segundo looked back innocently saying, "He looked like he was going to close the safe and I tried to stop him"!

"No you dumb shit, he was supposed to keep the safe open", One Eye blurted out before he could catch himself. Then looking to Mortimer again he said, he's no good to us now, so put a bullet it the little bastard and finish him"! Segundo did exactly what he was told and fired his revolver once into Mortimer's prostrate head, ending his misery forever. The sound of the gunshot reverberated throughout the building and outside as the Town Sheriff emerged from the jail for his morning rounds just in time to hear a gunshot coming from the bank, and two riders in front looking around guarding five horses tied to the hitching post, with two people at the banks entrance starting to flee.

The Sheriff quickly got the situation and pulled his weapon firing at one of the robbers on his horse as he ran across the street towards the restaurant to get a better firing advantage. Knowing he was out numbered, his only hope was that he could keep the robbers bottled up in the bank long enough, so some of the towns people could come to his aid with additional firepower. Out of breath from the run across the street, he dodged several bullets fired his way, taking cover behind a water trough in front of the restaurant, peeking out from time to time to fire carefully placed shots at the riders in front.

Zachary was rounding the corner on his horse as he heard the gunfire and seeing the Sheriff firing at two horsemen in front of the bank, jumped off his horse, grabbing his Henry rifle from the scabbard and taking a position just to the left of the banks front, saw one of the riders get hit by the Sheriff's shooting. But the rider was apparently jus grazed and kept firing at the Sheriff, so as his father always taught him, he shot for the riders horse putting several well placed rounds in rapid fire, the rifles loading lever working at a piston like pace, in both riders horses, then aiming for the riders as they fell.

Hearing the gunfire from outside, One Eye yelled at his men, "Time to cut our losses boys and scoot"! Then he yelled at his Segundo, "See if ya can do sumpthin' right and grab the girl, cause she's comin' with us to cover our getaway"!

Cowering in the corner was Josie, crouched down out of sight of the others, seeing everything unfold before her very eyes as she tried to cry out as the robbers forcibly yanked Esme with them as she put up a valiant but fruitless struggle.

Across the street in the restaurant was Fabian as he watched all his carefully laid plans go awry as riders posted as guards engaged in a gunfight with the Sheriff and one other up the street. It would've been easy to sneak up behind the Sheriff and put a bullet in his ear, but then that would unmask his part in the whole affair, so he'd but little choice to let things play out. As One Eye and the others emerged from the bank with all guns blazing at anything that reared its head, with their lone female hostage, Fabian noticed that they were only taking a lone bank bag with them, meaning that the entire contents of the safe were secure and they only gotten the cash drawers money. 'Chump change', he thought.

Bullets were flying in all directions, when the window that was right in front of him shattered and he felt a massive shove that knocked him from his chair, taking his breath away momentarily. The errant .45 caliber bullet fired from one of One Eyes men desperately firing in every direction, struck Fabian DuLesseps in the chest cracking his breastbone and shattering right into his spinal column.

All Fabian could hear was the sound of gunfire as the robbers made their getaway, the sound of fading hoof beats growing fainter, as the gunfire became more sporadic finally stopping altogether.

He felt no pain, just a massive pressure on his chest and discovered that none of his limbs were capable of movement as he lay there flat on his back. His very last thought was, 'It wasn't supposed to happen this way' and then he died.

As the bank robbers emerged from the bank, Zachary noticed that one of them had a wildly fighting Esme, giving them all she could as they tried to mount their horses to make their escape. One of them finally knocked her senseless, throwing her over his saddles pommel then swung up onto the saddle and led the way out of town with the others behind, each horse weaving its way down the street making a moving target even for the horse hard to secure.

His rifle out of bullets, and the robbers escaping with Esme, Zack drew his revolver and carefully took aim and repeatedly fired his weapon as the horses fled from the town. He saw one of them, the very last one, rear up after he fired his very last round, indicating that he may have been hit. As he ran to the bank, he was met by the Sheriff, who was sporting several grazes in his torso, nothing apparently serious and they entered the bank, guns now reloaded and at the ready.

They were greeted by the sight of a woman who'd fainted dead away in the banks vestibule and by the dead body of Silas the Cotton Farmer with his deposit slip still in hand his chest and clothes all blackened by the fire caused by the close at hand gunshot. As they entered the banks interior they encountered that dead body of Mortimer the head clerk almost unrecognizable by the massive gunshot to his head, throwing bits of bone, blood and the remnants of his brains like all over the walls and floor.

Then Zack saw the cowering visage of his sister Josie, who was in a state of shock, trying to form words to say, but no sound would come forth.

When bullets are flying in every direction, only the brave or those with a death wish raise their heads in the midst of certain death. The Waco townspeople were certainly no exception. Once the gun fire had abated people emerged from every direction and all fell upon the bank for a host of reasons. Holding a shivering Josie, Zachary, addressed those assembled to see if their money was lost, by saying, "Folks, all they got was the cash drawer money, for the safe is closed shut, so what I'm going to ask is for a few of you to go home get your shot guns and serve as bank guards till we can get things right in a few days"!

Then the Sheriff said, "Somebody's gotta tell your old man, Zack, ya want I should go"?

"No Sheriff your wounded and ya gotta have a doc see to your wounds, besides somebody's gotta head up the protection of the bank and the best one for that is you"! Then he looked around and said "Ruben come over here" as he handed off Josie to one of the towns women to take care of, "Ya got your horse saddled". Ruben nodded his head when Zack said "Now listen up this is important. Go ride like hell to the ranch and seek out my father and tell him what just happened what with the bank robbery and all. Tell him that Rodrigo's wife Esme has been kidnapped by the robbers and that they're on the road south out of town. Tell him that shortly I'll be trailin' them loosely so's they don't get away. Further, that there's only five of em left and one of em is probably be wounded. That's all ya need to do, cause the Captain will know what to do from there. Now repeat back to me what I just said"! Ruben repeated it all back to Zack without a hitch, the Zack said hurriedly, now when ya get that done I want you to go back and get your shot gun for your now deputized under the Sheriff here to watch the bank, cause some of your money is in the safe". "Now get goin' Ruben", as Reuben ran from the bank to his horse.

The newly elected County Magistrate entered the bank and sought out Zack and the Sheriff who was being tended to by the one of the town's doctors. Both hurriedly gave him a brief rundown of what had occurred and the summoning of Henry Jaeger, with Zack saying, "I know ya ain't been here long, but leave the nasty work for us to take care of. Ya got two dead horses in the street along with two dead robbers, a dead man right here and god knows what else is around the corner"!

Just then someone came running into the bank from the restaurant yelling, "One of the men having breakfast got shot and is dead as a doornail and bleedin' all over the place"!

"See what'd I tell ya Judge, each of us has got about all we can say grace over for the time being. You do what your good at and leave the rest to us"! Then Zack went over to Josie, gave her a hug and said, "Dad's on the way Josie and no doubt Mom soon after, so keep up your spirits, we're gonna get Esme back"!

Josie looked up into the eyes of her loving brother, but then the look in his eyes switched over to a look she thought she'd never ever see, the look of complete emptiness. The look of death and it scared her. The smile was there as a comfort, but that look in his eyes spoke volumes. She immediately prayed as hard as she could for Esme's safety and if anyone could deliver her back into the bosom of the family, the boys could.

Her husband was away in Ft. Worth selling a herd of saddle ready horses to the army in behalf of the family and was as good as any of them in that aspect of the business, but for what lay ahead, only the Jaegers would do. Surrounded by some of the towns women for comfort, Josie knew that she had to get a hold on her emotions before her mother and father arrived for it just wouldn't do for them to see her in her current condition. Besides, what with Mortimer dead and Esme abducted, someone had to keep the business of the bank on an even keel and until Esme returned that someone was Josie. Besides she knew where to find the safes combination…

Ruben arrived at the ranch, riding his horse full out for time was indeed of supreme importance. Normally it took just under an hour to make the trip into town, but Ruben less than halved that in his haste as he rode through the main gate past the main house and over to one of the darkies yelling, "Where's the Captain? The bank's just been robbed and there's dead all over the place"!

Pointing over to a pasture just over the hill, he was told, "The Captain, Rodrigo and Michael are working the horses"! Ruben galloped over to where they were all assembled, yelling, "Alarm, Alarm repeatedly pulling his lathered and exhausted horse up with a cloud of dust. In a rush of words, he repeated exactly what Zachary had told him to repeat to Henry and his sons. Henry grabbed hold of Rodrigo immediately as the story unfolded.

"And Zachary said that you'd know just what to do", came the rush of words from Ruben.

"Thank you Ruben", said Henry. "I can see that your horse is just about played out so I want you to go over to Slim in the Barn and leave your horse here and borrow another. You can return him at any time later"! Then he turned to Rodrigo, who said, "We have to go home and get our guns", trying to pull away. Henry restrained him saying, "No Time! Go to the main house, there's are plenty of guns and ammunition there, but on the way Michael gather a half dozen of the wolves, for it's just gonna be the three of us and the wolves. We're keeping it strictly in the family. Rodrigo go to Slim in the barn and have him saddle up two horses apiece for the three of us and a skid on one of them. Then have him prepare the buggy for Miss Melanie and drive her into town so's she can bring home Josie. The three of us will get Esme back. We're gonna be gone awhile, so ya know what goes on the skid"! Henry rode to the house only to find that Melanie had been told the news of the robbery and of her daughters abduction and was at the front verandah as he rode up. He filled in the blanks for his wife regarding Josie saying, "Ya might want to get dressed for a ride into town and a change of clothes for Josie.

Slim is hitching up the carriage and will drive you into town", as he drew Melanie close to him.

"Zack is trailing them and were taking sufficient mounts and supplies to trail them to Mexico if need be and beyond. The bank is secure for the moment and I'm told that Josie is all right just shaken up a bit with some of the town ladies looking after her"!

"Now you get to what you need to do and I'll get about, the business of getting Esme back"! In less than a half an hour all was in readiness, six horses saddled, one pulling a drag loaded with supplies for both the men and the wolves to last a week or more if need be, saddle bags full of ammunition to lay low a force far exceeding the four desperados they were after, two canteens full of water around the saddle horns of each horse and the signature sombrero's and finally two bows and quivers of arrows for any silent work that was needed.

The men and the wolves all followed Miss Melanie and Slim as the carriage made its way towards town and in slightly under an hour they pulled in front of the bank, in time to see the remnants of this morning's carnage, with a team of mules laboring to pull the dead horses from the middle of the street and the town mortician loading all the dead away to be buried at county expense. And the county was not going to incur any great expense for these people.

As Melanie entered the bank she saw Josie taking charge working to clean up the mess created by the robbers and as they saw each other, flew into each other's arms in tears of relief. Henry and the sons entered the bank armed to the teeth, each with a look of determination to get a cherished member of the family back in the fold. Seeing that Josie was safe, Henry asked, "Is there anything of Esme's like a scarf or a handkerchief that may have her scent on it"?

Josie went through her desk and pulled out a cotton scarf that Esme wore whenever a chill came about, giving it to Henry who immediately took it out side for the wolves to imprint. Melanie and Josie followed them out and witnessed the ritual with the wolves and as Henry stuffed the scarf into his saddlebag mounting his horse, Melanie said, "Good Hunting Gentlemen"!

As the still assembled crowd of helpers and onlookers viewed the trio of riders as they placed their mounts in a slow gallop out of town after the robbers the clock struck One PM, with plenty of day light to show the way.

The trail was easy to find and follow since all the tracks were deeply made by horses that were being ridden flat out. Zachary's tracks followed just to the left of the main flock of tracks, being shorter in stride and clearly apart from the rest. Even though time was of the essence in regaining their precious daughter, the robbers were driving their mounts out of desperation while Henry was traveling at a fast enough pace to catch up with Zachary in due time with relatively fresh mounts all around. Even Rodrigo, whose mother's blood ran hot through his veins, was compelled to follow the wisdom of his father, who spent a lifetime in trailing and tracking those who would always end up dangling over the deep abyss.

Riding at a fast canter the trio followed by the wolves, were silent. For nothing needed saying between them. They were after desperate men, clearly disappointed by their partial success at the bank. With any luck they would fall upon each other like rabid feral creatures, the only hazard in this being the presence of their hostage Esme. Henry silently reasoned they would stick together, rather than split apart in every direction, for if nothing else, there was strength in numbers, which of course made it far easier to track. As they rode in silence, with Henry scanning the trail, while his two sons scanned each side of the trail for anything or sign that may indicate an ambush of their pursuers. At some point they would leave the trail and travel cross country. One thing that Josie had mentioned in passing, was that one of them was as large as Henry yet appeared in the garb of an Indian with an eye patch indicating that he was without an eye, yet appeared to be a half breed.

Henry was hearing stories of a Comanche named Quanah Parker that was apparently the son of Peta Nocona, commanding the remnants of a Comanche band, giving the US Army fits way out in North West Texas and Oklahoma Territory. He was the son of a Comanche Chieftan and a white woman. Then he recalled the Shawnee "Red Hair" of his youth, and vowed that this one eyed half breed would go the very same way. And yet, he was no longer in possession of his youth, for as he rode, he felt the aches and pains of age and endless wear and tear, with each jostle of his mount. On cold mornings, it was difficult to rise out of bed sometimes, with his back sending him painful messages that he wasn't young anymore.

Yet here he was with his two sons, shortly to be joined by the third, in a holy quest to vanquish evil and rescue Joselita's son's wife. What else could be worthy of his time and efforts? What greater quest was there than this, for the family he'd carefully crafted was in excellent hands if he never lived to see another sunrise.

As the trio droned on down the road, Henry silently recited the Lord's Prayer, over and over and then after a while, started to mouth the Holy Rosary over and over finally finishing up with him silently asking the eternal, to grant him one thing, the very thing he granted King David, when outnumbered by his enemies long ago, to obfuscate, to cloud their vision, to give him the strength of his youth and if any sacrifice was required for the safety of each member of his family, then let it be him to go to the altar as the sacrificial lamb.

Suddenly the constant drone of pain he felt in his back started to subside, and a feeling of wellbeing enveloped him as he kept scanning the trail. Then he said, "So be it"! Rodrigo heard his father and asked "What father"?

Then as they rounded the bend in the trail south, there was Zachary sitting astride his horse, pointing westward as he said, "Here's where they went cross country. I reckon their horses are on their last legs and they'll have to make camp soon"!

Just then Michael said, "Here, you can start dragging around your spare horse Zack", as he'd been dragging two saddled mounts behind him.

"We'll have to stick to the trees and away from the open fields, for they'll probably have someone to watch if anyone is trailing them", offered Henry to his sons as they well knew already.

"We'll split in two parts; I'll ride with Michael while Zack and Rodrigo can take three of the wolves and circle the open fields in the other direction. But before that happens, I want to give the wolves a last good scent of Esme"! With that he dismounted and retrieved her scarf from his saddlebag giving each animal a good whiff of her scent, then mounted his horse and went off trail following Zachary. Within a few hundred yards they mounted a rise in the land and saw an open field not twenty yards ahead of them, dividing their forces to circumvent the field, staying well into the trees and meeting up at a designated spot on the other side. By looking at the trail made by four horses going across a field of tall prairie grass, it wasn't difficult to reckon where on the other side they would meet. Henry was conflicted by his wanting to rescue Esme for Rodrigo, yet given the leader of this bunch was reported to be a half breed he has to assume a prudent course of action. Walking head long into an ambush and getting all shot up wouldn't do Esme a bit of good. On the other hand with the sun going down and perhaps another two hours of day light left, suggested urgency, but that's what the wolves were for, gaining the scent of Esme, when the human senses were rendered useless.

By the time they circumvented their third clearing, confronted by a clear trail by the robbers an noting they're horses were now slowed almost to a walk and nothing but open prairie as far as they could see, Henry picked up the pace of their pursuit. They made no apparent effort to cover their trail at any time, so by Henry's reckoning desperation to escape drove them. Soon they would have to make camp and rest their mounts for a good long while.

Henry recalled a good spot several miles ahead with good forage and a small stream for the horses, surrounded by several hillocks where a fire could be built, hidden by the cover of the terrain and the trees and by the direction the trail was going he just knew that was where they'd be for the night.

Placing their horses a about a quarter mile away down wind, he outlined his plan to everyone, taking Rodrigo with him and half or the wolves, leaving Zack, Michael and the rest of the wolves to handle the other half of the pincer. Both parties moved with the utmost stealth to envelope the robbers.

Noting that the robber's horses were sufficiently hobbled indicated they had already been watered and were grazing peacefully. As they approached the robbers campsite, Henry took notice with some pride, that his wolves had reverted to their instinctive ways crouching down as they drew closer, just as if they were about to encounter a herd of Buffalo. Occasionally they'd glance at Henry and Rodrigo staying exactly in line with them and the picket line of death drew nearer to the camp site.

The wind was favorable and blew in their faces gently from the north, signaling that even the horses were unaware of the closing presence.

Peering down into the campsite Henry could see that Esme was secured to a tree with her hands tied behind her in a sitting position, he head hanging down, no doubt from fright and exhaustion. Since her clothes were still on her, indicated that she'd not yet been gotten at by the robbers.

Whispering to Rodrigo to hand him his bow and quiver of arrows, Henry crept closer, over hearing the robbers quarrel about the paucity of their haul. He saw that one of them was clearly wounded and complaining about getting into a nearby town so a doctor could tend to his wounds, while the large half breed stood over him saying, "The wound ain't that bad and you're just agonna have to tough it out and if ya say another word I'll slit your throat right now"!

Just then another of the robbers stood up saying, "I'm tired of his bellyaching', I'm gonna go see to the horses. Cut the bastards throat if'n ya wanna One Eye, doan make me no never mind. One less to share the money with"! As he walked up to where the horses stood grazing some thirty yards away just on the edge of an open field, Henry followed him and watched him slowly roll a cigarette, then reach into his vest producing a match striking it on his pants and taking his first drag, exhaling slowly. Henry waited patiently behind a tree not twenty yards away waiting for the robber to turn away, for the best position for a throat shot. The duo was some fifty yards away from the camp site and Henry had to trust that his other two sons were in position, with their targets selected.

Slowly the robber turned watching the shadows of the open field, scanning for the unforeseen, with the horses not five yards away and as he turned some more he heard the brief whistling through the air of an arrow, just before it penetrated his body right above his breast bone and into his voice box, and into his spine. He dropped immediately to his knees trying to speak, to breathe or to move any of his limbs but nothing seemed to work, just then he felt himself roughly turned about seeing the outline of Rodrigo as he sliced his throat from ear to ear, then all went black. As he returned to Henry, Rodrigo said, "One down father"!Sensing that something was amiss, yet not knowing just what, One Eye stood up and looked towards the horses as he felt an arrow fly past him missing by an eyelash as it buried itself in one of the other robbers, just then the sounds of a hoard of snarling wolves descended on the campsite along with a volley of gunshots. Drawing his gun he fired at several of the wolves who leaped at him in midair striking out at each one as they fell to the ground mortally wounded. He raced towards Esme with his knife in his hand cutting her bonds with one swift motion and scooping her up as a human shield.

Just then One Eye heard Henry call off his wolves as they stood still their jaws clamped around the throats and the limbs of his two former compatriots, quickly suffocating before his very eyes. Then he saw determined men emerge from the shadows guns drawn with one of them making a sign for the four wolves to drop their victims and stand at the ready.

Then One Eye shouted, "I'll kill her if ya come any closer"! For the first time a very long while One Eye felt the chill of fear. Usually it was the other way around with him creating the fear in other lesser men. But his men had been very neatly overcome and there he was, at the end of his rope, or was he?

"Your men are dead, your horses are ours, the little money you stole is back with us", said Henry pointing to the saddlebag that lay near the fire, "And you are a dead man walking! You will never leave this place alive", concluded Henry calmly.

"I, I'll kill her", yelled One Eye as he tightened his grip on Esme, who looked pleadingly at her husband Rodrigo, standing just five yards away with his gun leveled at One Eye's head, the proximity of his knife at his darling's throat the only thing that kept him from pulling the trigger. He had to trust the wisdom of his father and perhaps a bit of celestial intervention at this late hour.

"Yes you can very easily get that done, but none the less shortly you will meet meet your maker, which leaves you but two choices, you can either die well like a warrior in single combat or die badly like the cowardly sniveling cur that apparently you've been all your life"!

At that Henry unbuckled his gun belt allowing it to drop to the ground, then he took off his hat tossing it away, then he slowly unfastened the bindings of his shirt removing it and tossing it away. Lastly he drew his big bowie knife and slowly started to run it diagonally across his chest leaving a trail of blood, again and again, speaking in the tongue of his ancient and long dead Shaman "You know the ways of the Apache", asked One Eye?

"And the Comanche, the Kiowa, the Cherokee and the Shawnee along with many others", replied Henry. "So just what it to be Pilgrim?

Die well in a fight to the end with an old man, or die badly and be eaten by my wolves like a common animal".

Just then Esme shouted, "Father shoot the bastard"! Henry immediately put his hands up shoulder height signaling restraint and he saw One Eye's grip tighten on Esme.

For a long minute, which seemed like eternity Henry's eyes locked upon One Eyes lone eye, measuring the man reasoning that he was as big as Henry, much younger, no doubt with more stamina that youth always brought, yet his weakness, if it could be exploited, was that he hand but one functional eye and if Henry kept to his left......Still it would have to be ended quickly which meant risks.

"I have heard stories of a man called Henry Jaeger that the old men told when around the camp fire when I was very young. They called him the 'Ghost Dancer'. The killer of many women and children of the Comanche and the Kiowa tribes. The mortal enemies of my people the Apache. Are you that man", asked One Eye?

Henry nodded adding, "What the braves forgot to tell you was that I killed many more Comanche and Kiowa warriors in every way possible and not once did they die well. Could you be the single exception"?

"I am coming to the end of my life and could you be the one to help me see my way to the hunting grounds", asked Henry his eyes pleading?

"I will show you the way", he yelled hitting Esme with the butt of his heavy pointed knife, throwing her aside and leaping at Henry with a shout.

Their knives clanged as Henry parried the blow of the Apache as he flew past, the knife barely missing his midsection. The Apache rolled, jumped up and came at Henry again swinging the blade with the swiftness of an eye blink yet wildly. The thought of Melanie flashed through his head and the words, 'Not yet', ran through his head. They both circled each other warily, each looking for an opening as Henry made it a point to circle to his blind side, each swiftly thrusting and parrying the others blows, with the sounds of steel clanging in the night, by the light of a dwindling fire.

"I will gain much coup when the news of your death echo's in the heavens", breathed One Eye.

Henry remained silent, circling, thrusting and parrying always to his left, then making a feint to his right, charged from One Eyes left grazing his gullet while catching a glancing blade as he ran by, his momentum carrying him past the Apache as he hit the ground rolling to a standing defensive position only to find the Apache quickly upon him, throwing caution to the wind as he ran head long into Henry's blade, up to the hilt. The blade cutting his heavily beating heart in two, as blood gushed from the incision.

Henry with his blade buried to the hilt in the Apaches gullet, heaved the man over on his back, with his blade still in place. With his last ounce of strength, One Eye tried to bring his blade back in on Henry, but felt the blade being kicked away by Henrys son Zack.

As the vision started to fade from his eye, One Eye heard the very last words he'd ever hear as Henry breathlessly whispered, "You will have to go to that place completely alone, but be comforted by the very last thing you will see, is me looking at you for all eternity" and with that Henry savagely twisted the blade, seeing the vacant stare of the dead as he struggled to rise.

Esme ran to Henry, her ordeal on the wane but concerned with Henry's wounds, the bloody lines across his chest relatively superficial, but the wound along his side of a more serious nature. Michael then said, "Me and Zack'll go get our horses and be back shortly, then they both disappeared as Henry directed Rodrigo to collect all the bodies and when his brothers returned hang them by the feet in the lower branches for the carrion to feed on after stripping them completely and anything not of value to be consumed by the fire.

The wolves were gathered around both of the two former family members starting to howl, in sorrow at the departure of a lost soul. Yet somehow Henry knew, that when their time came, to make that eternal trip they'd all be together once again. Chani and Akila's progeny had died well and that was all that really mattered. They would be carried back to the ranch on the skid and buried with all the dignity a warrior in combat deserved. All that mattered was that they knew they died well, those here knew of their loyal service and their story would be told to the immediate family. As for anyone else, it just didn't matter.

By the end of the following day, Henry and his clan slowly rode back into Waco, with a small armory of the robber's weapons and all the monies stolen from the bank and of course the robber's horses and saddles.

The robber's clothes fueled the fire for a time and they were left hanging by their feet in that copse of trees naked for the next evening's meal by the creatures of the air above and the ground below.

Rather than go to the ranch, Esme insisted the stolen money be taken to the bank where she and Josie spent several hours reconciling the books once again. As they worked the Sheriff made the connection between Mortimer the teller and Fabian DuLesseps the erstwhile gambler and the Cotton Farmer that had been recently lucky at the tables.

Fabian's room at the hotel was searched only to find a large amount of cash and gold coin in his 'Portmandu' bag. Factoring everything in, the Sheriff mumbled, "Insurance man my ass, why this mans a professional card sharp"! By days end the banks books were again in balance, and the towns coffers was some fifteen thousand dollars to the good, but most important, Melanie's only daughter and Henry's oldest son's wife was safe once again.

Henry, never one eager to court publicity, especially since it would trumpet the malevolent side of his personality that he wasn't exactly proud of, sometimes had little say about what others said about him. Endlessly hectored by Josie about her experience as a captive of the robbers, Esme finally relented, telling Josie all about her father, leaving not one scintilla of the story out of place. Before the week was passed Melanie was let into the chain of information regarding his heroism. Finally cornering Rodrigo, who reluctant at first, finally relented and revealed all of the exact movements moment by moment, ending by saying, "All I can do for the rest of my life is but walk in the shadow of my father! I can only but strive to life up to his name"!

"Thank you Melanie, for becoming my "Madre' dio" and do not be harsh with Papa, for he did what he had to do and it turned out well"!

Melanie sat on the porch of her home as Rodrigo rode off reaching into her apron to secretly take a small drink from the bottle of Laudanum, the oral opiate the doctor in town gave her to minimize the ever increasing pains of the growing inoperable cancer that lay within. She knew her time was shortly coming to a close and she cherished each and every one of the members of her family equally, knowing in her heart the various family units she fostered would prosper in the years ahead. In the coming days, she would spend more and more time on this very porch searching her memories of her days with Henry Jaeger. Remembering all the things she wheedled out of Juan Mendoza when he was alive of his time with Henry as his Segundo. What remained of Henry's life prior to Mendoza was a mystery, because Henry never spoke of it and Melanie never pressed him.

But it would've been nice to know of his family and of his days as a Ranger during the Republic.

Melanie had heard of Henry's overwhelming grief at hearing of the death of his first wife Joselita and thought it strange that when Josie was born that the name Josie just popped into her head from out of nowhere when it came time to name her daughter, with Henry standing right there, having a brief moment when a tear came to his eyes. Now she knew exactly why and looked up to the heavens silently thanking Joselita for allowing her to share her husband for a little while.

It had been a great deal of work and just look at what was achieved, but it indeed was a grand and glorious ride. She immediately felt sorry for the slew of women that had co joined with much lesser men, having to endure whatever came their way. But in the days she had left, she was bound and determined not to bemoan her fate, for she was made of sterner stuff, having much to be grateful for. She would meet each day as if it were her last, with great cheer for one and all, for one just should not be greedy.

She'd a number of bottles of Laudanum secreted away to dull the pain as required and would receive the town doctor every other week, for his sub rosa examinations and count the days in silence.

She had the sand and grit to endure in silence and was damned if this would dampen her spirits, and would set an example for her family to follow. Henry's wounds were healing rather nicely and no use dampening his spirit with her misfortune. She just hoped that he wouldn't grieve as much at her passing as he'd once done for Joselita.

There would be plenty of time for recollections when she entered the gates into the Elysian Fields. An eternities worth of time, when all would be rejoined in happiness.

A year later to the very day Melanie had succumbed to her cancerous malady. She'd grown so weak from her cancer that she could no longer get out of bed, her only salvation from the pain was the opiate she had by her side to alleviate her pain. When the doctor from town was called the very first thing he asked her to do was to release him from his promise to her and allow him to tell Henry that her time was near and why.

When the entire family and retinue had gathered to see her for her final time, she asked Henry to carry her downstairs placing her on the front verandah in her favorite couch facing the long front entrance way to the ranch reminiscent of the plantations in South Carolina. The Pin Oak trees they all had planted and nurtured many years ago had all grown up providing a long natural arbor providing shade for all who entered or exited the ranch as she knew it would.

Try as they all might, muffled sobs came from both the men and women of those assembled. As she entered the final stretch of her pilgrimage, Melanie looked at Henrys red and bleary eyes and said, "Henry my love, be of good cheer, for look around and see what we've wrought, for all along I've been in paradise"!

With her final breath she looked at Henry and silently mouthed, "I love you"! Then life left her body as she closed her eyes for the very last time.

The doctor took her limp wrist and finding no pulse sadly stood up and said, "This great woman has passed over"!

Simultaneously all of the wolves assembled on the perimeter of the crowd started a gradual howling announcing that a great loss had visited them all. Henry just sat there with Melanie still in his arms in the wide front porch of the verandah that surrounded the main house as sundown approached, reluctantly relinquishing his grasp of Melanie's cold and lifeless body. The doctor said, "Henry I took the Liberty of sending for the town mortician and he's just arrived to tend to your wife as she would've wanted"!

Then Henry looked up as he released Melanie to the Mortician, rising to his full height, calling out to Rodrigo to go to town and telegraph the Archdiocese in San Antonio and summon a priest to arrive with full vestments for the proper burial for a Catholic woman.

Then he and his boys went inside the house, followed by Josie to get drunk, and joined an hour later by Rodrigo. It was a onetime family event done is silence, while the mortician and his assistant did their work upstairs.

An hour after Rodrigo arrived, in walked Esme who announced, "Maddie and Elijah are taking care of the children and I'm not going to let this moment pass"! She went to the cupboard, removing a glass, then attacked the voluminous jug that contained the whiskey, filling her glass to the rim saying, "Seems I've got some catching up to do and I've never touched a drop of hard liquor before this and hopefully will never again.

But for this purpose only I'll make an exception"! Then not being an experienced drinker she took an enormous swig from the glass, choking and forcing it down in the process, compelling muffled and guilty snickers from the others gasping, "I just don't see how y'all can drink this stuff, but if Josie can do it then so can I"!

Josie, well on her way to the land of oblivion mumbled, "My first time too, but if'n ya keep at it, the taste'll sneak up on ya"!

Then the knock on the door revealed Juanita, who entered with her guitar, saying "My children are old enough to be alone this night and I just had to be with you to say goodbye with you"! She promptly was given a glass full of whiskey and being a former entertainer of sorts knew just how to treat hard whiskey, taking a small sip then slipping the guitar from her shoulder and began playing a series of plaintive Spanish ballads.

All through the night Henry regaled the family with little vignettes and remembrances of his life with Melanie, often prompting each and every one to contribute a little story of their own, some of which were known but bore repeating, while others were uniquely new.

The following day, despite a hoard of hangovers the family went to the glade that Juan Mendoza was buried in and all the sons took turns digging the burial grave to exacting proportions and prepared the site for the arrival of the priest the following day.

Father Miguel arrived the following day, his trip from San Antonio uneventful. What followed surprised the entire family for it seemed the entire town had shut down for the day and followed the priest onto the ranch, for many had a great affection for Miss Melanie, for if not for her good work many of them would not be enjoying the literacy the had today.

The odd thing was that the great majority of them were of the Baptist faith, normally not having anything to do with a priest, yet in deference to a great lady they quietly paid their last respects and rather than a quiet funeral of just family and associates, over a thousand souls made their way to the burial site atop a small hill, under a large oak tree. Many of the town's folk were taken aback at the presence of almost two dozen wolves standing at the crowd's perimeter, two of which stood atop two smaller graves occupied by two of their own.

As the casket was slowly lowered into the grave amidst the jingling of the priests bells, as he intoned the final portion of the service in Latin, the wolves all joined in with a chorus of howls, once again announcing to the heavens that a great lady's soul was soon to arrive, much to the consternation of many of the towns folk.

Early the following morning the priest fed and duly paid the stipend agreed upon was taken to town by Rodrigo for his train trip back to San Antonio de Bexar.

The coming months were hard on Henry, surrounded by loved ones yet, absolutely alone. The ladies had formed a committee to cook, wash and clean for their progenitor, the surviving patriarch of the family, not so much out of duty, but as a labor of love and respect. Each day Henry was visited by the various families children eager to hear his wonderful stories, heavily edited, of course, of his days on the frontier, the adventures he had growing up, the people he encountered, the Indian raids, the Mexican War. Stories of honor and duty and endurance against all odds, he repeated endlessly to the children. Tales of their various fathers, of how they acted in times of adversity always opting to elevate their status in the eyes of the children if necessary. Yet every evening he found himself alone, picking at his food.

His once robust appetite, now only a memory. His daily visits around the ranch, the visage of a straight as an arrow line of pine trees, long since fully grown marking the perimeter of his hard earned property, were fewer and fewer in number, with age and only memories to hold him to this mortal plane.

The ladies as they visited him each morning began to mildly chide him just as they would their children for not finishing all his food finding increasingly larger portions of uneaten food on the plate each morning.

Eventually the town doctor was summoned to examine Henry only to report, that he was in other wise good health for a man his age, yet suffering from severe melancholy at the loss of his beloved Melanie.

"Not a thing than can be done about it that y'all are not already doing! Ya see, one of the bad things about being so emotionally tied in love with someone that's been a wonderful part of your life, is that when one of you passes on, the one that has to go on, unless there's a compelling reason to go on, just seems to lose all interest. Henry has literally nothing to do, for clearly the ranch and its other businesses are doing rather well, and he'd only get in the way"!

"Josie", the doctor continued, "Remember when you told me of him sitting in his rocking chair of the front verandah looking down the front entrance of the ranch at the line of continuous trees arching over the long front entrance of the ranch? Well if you'll recall Miss Melanie's final moments, he's reliving that over and over when he repeatedly mumbles her name over and over, Melanie, Melanie"!

"Other than a back that pains him from time to time, he should normally have ten good years left, if there was a purpose, but absent that, seems to me, he just wants to get out of the way of the next generation and join Miss Melanie as soon as the good Lord will have him"! "Children all grown up, grandchildren doin' fine, stories all been told, ranch doin' fine, time to die! All there is to it. Best thing y'all can do is keep doin' what your doin', give him all the love he'll handle and let the almighty have him when he's ready"! "Oh one last thing", said the doctor, "Has he made a last will and testament"? Zachary answered, "Yes that got taken care of some eighteen months back"! "Then Henry Jaeger is in the palm of the Almighty's hand and when he decides it's time to move on, then that'll be it"!

The doctor bid all a good evening and made his way to the door of Rodrigo's house, closing it behind him. Harsh words but the truth and the logic of it hit them all as the gospel truth. All anyone could do was what they were already doing and wait for the inevitable. In a way Juanita was more understanding of the good doctors words, for she still had a family to raise which kept her busy with a purpose, her status and that of her children, in the House of Jaeger already codified in Henry's will and her place next to her husband already allotted.

She had grown to love Juan Mendoza over time and grieved as much at his loss as anyone could. But she thought, that somewhere in this Texicano was the heart of a Hidalgo, high born, a man of great accomplishment and respect, for he earned it all and now it was time for his eternal rest.

Then early one chill morning, exactly one year of the anniversary of Miss Melanie's death as she went to get his breakfast started, she climbed the steps of the main house, only to find Henry sitting in his rocking chair out on the front verandah, his sunken lifeless eyes, withered away by melancholy, staring out at the long line of trees flanking the front entrance to the ranch. Rather than die in bed, he passed just the way he wanted, fully clothed into eternity, the old Walker Colt hog leg held loosely in his lap, just in case.

She sat by him, talking to him for a while as others came up to the porch, watching her hold his hand and talking to him.

In the far distance, she could hear a lone wolf start to howl, then another, and then another as the family started to gather. Josie was the first to speak saying, "His burden is now over"!

24

Once again, it fell to Rodrigo the oldest to go into town and telegraph the San Antonio Arch Diocese, requesting a Catholic Priest to conduct funeral services for Henry Jaeger in Waco Texas. As the message had to pass through the State Capitol at Austin and be rerouted onward to its final destination, the telegraph operator noting the name of the deceased, made a copy of the message and had it delivered to the Governors Mansion, for Captain Jaegers name was well known in Austin for many years.

"Good God, Henry Jaeger's dead", exclaimed the Governor to his assistant. "Anyone know how it came about"?

"No sir, we don't and don't look for much in the way of news from that family, for they just don't cotton much for publicity"!

"As a little boy I heard stories, from the Maverick family in San Antonio about Jaeger and John Coffee Hays fightin' the Comanche, during the days of the Republic, then again some mention of him getting' even for the death of Sam Walker by the hands of a renegade Catholic priest in Mexico during the War of forty seven. The next thing we heard was that he was, for a time the only Texas Ranger in Texas and he has a spread up in Waco"!

"Well Governor", injected his assistant, "There were reports that last year he and his sons, also Texas Rangers on the rolls, ran down some bank robbers and the onliest thing that came back were their horses and all the money"?

"What happened to the robbers", asked the Governor?

"No one knows and no one's asking"!

"Well we need to do something for the man, don't ya think"?

"A full military funeral would seem to be in order, since he was assigned to General Taylor during the war of forty seven and served under the command briefly for General Worth in Mexico", offered his assistant! "Besides Governor the State and the Federal Government has been doing business with the Jaegers since before the Civil War buying saddle ready horses from them for years"!

"Splendid idea! Get hold of Colonel Rogers, for he's got nothing better to do now days and see if ya can wheedle him into sending up an appropriate company of horse soldiers by railroad by tomorrow morning and tell him to bring a bugler to blow Taps"!

Then as the Governors assistant went out the door to his office, the Governor said, "Miles, I'm going along too, for a few days so looks like you're gonna have to rearrange my appointments till I return"!

Late the following day the State contingent was met by Henry's three sons at the train station, unloading a full company of US Calvary as they made their way to the ranch. Of course news of the demise of Henry Jaeger insured that a hoard of mourners would be on hand to pay their respects.

Early the following morning the priest was met at the train station and driven to the ranch to prepare for the funeral.

In Henry's first draft of his Last Will and Testament was provision that he be cremated just as he had his parents long ago. But in protest from Miss Melanie when she was alive and from the family in general, he relented simply requesting that he be buried in a simple pine box. Melanie's protestation that if she was to be in the ground then Henry was to be right next to her. Verbally out muscled by one and all he relented, to every ones relief. But Rodrigo had plans of his own.

A year before he purchased a shipment of South Texas Mesquite wood, some the worlds hardest wood, for just such an occasion. "Damnest waste of wood there is Rodrigo", he recalled his father saying. "Takes the edge of any blade triple quick the wood's so hard", he could still hear his father fussing. But given that his father was to spend eternity next to Melanie, the effort and the expense of crafting a first class coffin made of Mesquite came to nothing as Maddie and Elijah's eldest son Joseph labored over the coffin for almost two days and nights before he was satisfied with his efforts. Then covered with multiple layers of hand rubbed shellac, his labors were completed. There it was, simple but highly practical.

Of course with the arrival of a company of US horse soldiers, replete in their finest gold braid posed a significant problem, due to the existence of the wolves. Mostly tamed to the existence of most civilized people, as long as they didn't make any sudden moves in their presence, the wolves had to be introduced to the Calvary men's horses and quickly for the wolves were as much a part of the family as anyone and there was no way they would not be in attendance at the funeral.

The funeral was basically in two parts, the Catholic religious ceremony and the secular part governed by an Army Chaplain in the proscribed military manner, with a dozen of the Cavalry dismounted, arrayed in formation, bringing up to their shoulders, standard issue Spenser Rifles, firing off the appropriate volleys, and then the slow playing of TAPS, by a lone bugler, with the Commanding Officer slowly reciting the words:

"Day is done, gone the sun, from the lakes, from the hills, from the skies. All is well, safely rest, God is neigh"!

Not to be denied their place, were the sons and daughters of Chani and Akila, who as if on cue, with the last slow note of TAPS completed, started their serenade to the heavens, howling en masse, all two dozen of them.

Of the throng of almost a thousand people in attendance, many of which were successful at fighting back tears, even at the completion of the playing and reading of TAPS, yet every single person, women and fully grown men all broke down in tears as the wolves sounded their plaintive final goodbyes standing atop the graves of their forbearers a short distance away.

The horse soldiers in particular were particularly moved by the wolves' performance. Embarrassed by the presence of their tears for someone they did not know and only heard bits and pieces about, men hardened to living on the frontier for little money and a rigorous life, they tried to quickly hide their emotions as they slowly rode away in tight formation, the wolves howling still heard reverberating in their ears.

Fifteen minutes later, as the Governor rode with Rodrigo, the wolves serenade to the heavens still echoing through hill and valley, the Governor asked, "When will the wolves stop"?

"'They will stop when father arrives in Heaven! Now you're going to want to know when that will be, aren't you Governor"?

The Governor nodded and Rodrigo then said, "Somehow the wolves will know at that exact moment. They always know"!

Then he added, we at the ranch don't expect anyone else to understand, but you can see the effect the wolves had on one and all didn't you?

Again the governor nodded, in silence. Life at the ranch eventually settled down back to some sense of normalcy and with the passage of time memories begin to fade. Stories were recanted less and less to each successive generation, as new memories begin to replace the old. Old facilities were replaced by the new, old equipment replaced by new more efficient means. The young grew old and were replaced by successive new generations. Some of which stayed to maintain the family enterprise, some of which went in other directions. Some returned to the fold, while others passed on to become distant memories.

One constant stayed for generation to generation. With each successive generation of Jaeger males, one or more of the progeny served with distinction, either in a branch of the US Military or became a Texas Ranger. Often many did both during the course of their lives, eventually returning to some aspect of the ranching enterprise in one fashion or another. With each successive generation, new bloodlines entered the family, some adding value, while others.........

The Jaeger Saga continues

25

'**N**inety days short of retirement and supposed to be approaching "FIGMO", (Fuck It Got My Orders) status and the Corps., drop's this pile of crap in my lap', thought Colonel Joe Bollinger and he reread the file of this Sergeant Jaeger. Word comes down through the ranks all the way from foggy bottom, of an American Embassy about to be under siege some twelve hours ago, (he never recalled the government wonks moving this fast) by some local war lords in Chad and he had just forty eight hours to put together an extraction team for all embassy personnel.

Seems like the CIA, the SEALS and the DELTA boys were up to their respective ass's elsewhere. A quick scan of appropriate personnel gleaned just one name "Jaeger". 'Now what kind of guy just has one name' thought Bollinger?

They faxed his file, or what passed for a file by encryption to the Colonel, here at China Lake and the Naval CID was flying him to China Lake his plane landing at this very moment, from his barracks at Camp Pendleton. He also was a short timer in the service, this Sergeant Jaeger, after some six years in the Marines, had decided that he was not going to reenlist.

So the Colonel decided that Jaeger could always say no, seeing that his time was so short, and the UCMJ could back him up should he have to issue direct orders to this grunt, but that was a nonstarter, for this extraction business was a tricky affair and he had scant time or resources to bargain with or negotiate. So he once again reviewed what he had to work with.

This Jaeger, NFN, NMI, entered the Marines when he was seventeen years of age, (some talk of his being just a step faster than the High Sheriff of McLennan County Texas, after hospitalizing his high school football coach and facing an assault and battery charge if they ever caught up with him.

His mother approving his enlistment papers and he seemed to breeze through the rigorous sixteen weeks of Marine Corps. Boot Camp down at Camp Pendleton. That's where this young man drops off the radar, as far as outsiders were concerned. The unfortunate High Sheriff discovered that his political influence just went so far and his repeated efforts to get at this young enlistee, stopped at the water's edge of the Corps. Yet after he graduated from basic training he's hustled right into the SEAL training program. A brief scan of his basic training file told him all he needed to know. Top scores in marksmanship, self-defense, endurance and not a single demerit during his entire basic training. This guy was a real stud. His SEAL training was spotless, went through with the highest marks in his unit especially his ability to endure, adapt and improvise, correctly anticipating problems that continuously arose and finding a way to complete an assignment without direction from others. His sniper school training was a mere formality, and when a brief examination of his father's time in the Corps. during the Viet Nam conflict in the sixties, revealed that he was a three timer and all of it upcountry amongst the hostiles, being a part of Force Recon, in and out of Laos and Cambodia, fourth in line to the legendary Carlos Hathcock for the number of documented sniper kills, told Bollinger of an instinct that was genetic in origin. Yet this Sergeant Jaeger's file only indicated various Embassy duty assignments, during his time in service, with large portions of his file blacked out. There were basically four types of Marines, the flyboys, the mud marines, the ship marines and the embassy marines, the latter being the cushiest duty, usually a reward for good service. Bollinger recalled his time when he was an enlisted grunt as an embassy marine, often being utilized for special assignments by some State Department wonk, escorting personnel, both dangerous and benign, from point A to point B and beyond, the epitome of the old adage, "Ten Atta Boys equal one Oh Shit". Have just one thing go awry and no matter what, the cause; it'll always be your fault. Quite often, Bollinger would go against regulations and State Department policy, when escorting important people deemed worthy by the State Department, avoiding previously agreed routes and methods of travel, trusting nothing and no one but his own instincts, always delivering his "Packages", on time and to the right people.

After discreetly getting on the phone, and delving deep into the "Old Boy" network, talking to the right people, he finally got the "Real Skinny" on Jaeger, chapter and verse.

Sure he worked for the State Department and was formally on the books as an embassy guard, but that's where all visuals stopped. He was on constant temporary assignment with the spooks of both the State and Langley; his specialty was in simply making people disappear all over Europe, South America, the Middle East, Indonesia and the southern Philippine Islands.

He'd been to jump school and had several successful lone HALO insertions under his belt and during his early years in the Corps. Desert survival, jungle survival training along with escape and evasion training and had completed assignments that tested all of his skill sets. He was immersed in language schools acquiring a passable fluency in several of the Romance languages. He was listed as being just under six feet four inches and weighing well over two hundred pounds, which made it even more remarkable that he never left a lasting impression on any one that met him, once out of the various initial training facilities the government offered.

All this and somehow the guy found time to amass a year of College Credits by correspondence with the University of Maryland's, military educational program.

'Yeah this guy should do rather nicely for what was ahead of him', thought Joe Bollinger, 'but there was less than twenty four hours to get him on board with the project, acclimated with the equipment and on site almost halfway around the world to the African Republique du Chad.

Just then Colonel Bollinger heard a metal door open and clang shut, with a trio of heavy boots walking in lockstep, the sounds echoing down thirty yards of austere hall way, then stop all at once, with a single Marine knock on the doorframe, and a baritone voice bellowing "Permission to enter, the Colonels office"!

"Come", bellowed Bollinger in return! The flimsy hollow core door opened and in came a large Navy Shore Patrol petty officer, followed by Sergeant Jaeger and another equally sizeable SP. As the trio saluted and the Petty Officer started to speak, Bollinger asked, "Are you Sergeant Jaeger"?

"Yes sir", said Jaeger!

"Then Sergeant Jaeger, you will stand at ease and you two gentlemen may depart with the thanks of the Marine Corps. All completed their salute, with Jaeger standing at ease and his escorts doing a crisp about face and departing, the sound of their brogans echoing down the halls. "Sergeant please take a seat and be at ease" said Bollinger.

"Colonel may I smoke", asked Jaeger?

"Consider the smoking lamp lit, Sergeant".

"Seems we both have a thing in common"!

"Oh sir and what's that"? "We're both on the verge of FIGMO status, me retiring after thirty and you on the verge of returning to the land of the Feather Merchants after your years of service. Yet our nation and the Corps have selected both of us for one last task before they cut either one of us loose"!

"And that task is", asked Jaeger.

"Some twelve hour ago our embassy in the African Republique du Chad is in danger of coming under fire, much like the problem in Iran several years ago, only we're not dealing with a religious problem as far as is known, strictly political. Chad is run by a dictator, who some say has a fondness for human flesh, and the only reason we're there with an Embassy is that we want a chunk of the Uranium ore deposits they have in abundance. Now the French have the edge on us as far as they've had a diplomatic presence there on and off since the end of the nineteenth century and Chad is in the French political sphere of influence. Now, the locals have grown tired of their dictator and seem to want him and everyone out of the country one way or the other. So the French are almost in the same boat as we are, except our people have started to come under fire and theirs haven't as of yet. So we have an extraction problem on our hands, with some twenty embassy personnel and about eight embassy Marines to get out and it seems that your special skills are needed for one last job"!

"And your task is to romance me into saying yes, then prep me and give me a nice pat on my ass and sent me packing", offered Jaeger.

"Something like that, Sergeant", said Bollinger hopefully.

Jaeger steepled his hands briefly exhibiting a false coyness, then blurted out, 'Well Colonel, consider me romanced, I'm in"!

Partially relieved, yet reluctant to show it Bollinger replied, "" I'll bet you're an easy target for the ladies"!

"Colonel, I'm pure as the driven slush"!

"You know the standard drill applies, right", asked the Colonel.

"Ah yes the standard drill, No one is to know, I was never there and it never happened. No one will say thanks either publicly or privately! Oh yes, and BOHICA applies at all times"!

Bollinger rose from his desk, smiled and reached over for Jaegers hand and said, "Gland to have you on board Marine and Bend Over Here It Comes Again"!

"Now if you'll follow me, we've much to do and since its mid-morning not a lot of time to do it in, I'll fill you in on the details of the insertion and extraction plan as we walk"! As Jaeger and the Colonel drove down to the flight line, the plan was hurriedly outlined.

"The whole country is in Chaos, given that several factions are fighting for control of the government. Right now the military is in control of things, with this dictator, who seems to be turning a blind eye to all except his regimes preservation. We and the French are trying to romance the rascal for exclusive rights to mine a whole pile of Uranium ore and it certainly appears the froggie's are in the driver's seat. Now they're not going to turn a blind eye towards us, because they could very well be next even though the dictator would be removing a prime source of revenue from his country.

Right now everything is in lockdown, the whole of the county's military is on alert and the only way to get you and your equipment in is by air. Yet all of their air control radar is on round the clock eyeballs everywhere. They don't have much of an air arm, just a few old prop driven fighters, and yet we gotta get you in without being seen. So a HALO jump is on the menu.

Your target is north of the Capital City of N'Djamena, close on to Lake Chad which is heavily patrolled by river craft. We bring you in and the French have agreed to bring you out, by picking you and whoever you can bring out once they cross the border into neighboring Niger so you'll be heading north across some of the southern Sahara desert.

Without entering Chadian airspace a cargo plane will be flying in a northeasterly direction and you'll be at about thirty thousand feet on full oxygen and outfitted in one of these new parasail outfits that make you look like a flying squirrel, you'll be dragging along about three hundred pounds of supplies that'll be attached to an experimental flying wing called the Gryphon Para System. We've been keeping it under wraps here at China Lake and it seems to work well. The point being that you drop and sail both at the same time traveling some fifty miles as you drop, leaving a radar cross section so small what with the ancient systems they have that the French have given them you should arrive undetected. You'll have an altimeter attached so when you're well under a thousand feet, you pop your chute and glide right in under their radar. Now you'll control the Gryphon system by an electronic joystick attached to you." Just then the jeep pulled into a hangar and Jaeger and the Colonel went with several technicians into base operations, where he was outfitted from head to toe with his new equipment.

As they exited the Base Ops building they entered an already warmed up and loaded C-130 which closed the rear hatch and taxied down the runway taking off, lumbering up to altitude.

At altitude the rear door slowly opened and the rear ramp extended, with Jaeger filled with the staccato chatter from one of the technicians read, off the check list of items, finally signaling that he was ready and lumbered over to the rear ramp and simply dropped off into the thin air, without another word.

The chase craft was closely monitoring his descent as the C130 buttoned things up, following Jaegers drop at some distance. A constant chatter traded back and forth over Jaegers earphones.

Normally those who tested this experimental equipment had well over a thousand jumps to their credit and at least some fifty high altitude, low opening jumps, but the man they were monitoring had only thirty documented jumps inclusive of a mere half dozen HALO jumps.

As Jaeger fell through the air he constantly fiddled with the mini joystick attached to his right palm, controlling the Gryphon craft that flew five yards away, with both of his arms and legs spread wide as he flew through the air. He kept close watch on his altimeter and when he reached fifteen thousand feet, he started to see a red smoke flair as his destination target. Hurtling towards earth he knew from his previous jumps, the way to defeat most Radar systems was to open his chute as much under a thousand feet as he could to not be detected. The last HALO jump he executed, his chute opened at four hundred feet in the Italian Alps. Yet with this new equipment who knew what was possible? He had to place his faith in the Naval testing wonks and hope this stuff worked as advertised.

Passing the thousand foot point in his drop he circled and counted to three, then pressed the button jointly opening up both his chute and that of the Gryphon Parasail, cutting the cord that tied them both together. Seconds later, he landed gently on the ground as the parasail with its cargo landed some several hundred yards away in a small cloud of dust. He missed his mark by some thirty yards, but so what? Close enough for Government work. What was important was that this stuff worked as advertised.

As the trucks dove him back to the flight line, he met with Colonel Bollinger and a few of the technicians over chow as Jaeger hadn't had an opportunity to eat anything yet this day and the other techs labored away setting up and re rigging the chutes for a second and final jump right after chow just to make certain that everything checked out.

By 1500 hours, with the second jump successfully completed, Jaeger felt better about getting into Chad and close to the embassy without detection.

He was to be met by a member of the French Foreign Legion, in constant contact with him by a special radio frequency the moment he jumped then signaled by high intensity flash light, intermittently as he and his cargo came to earth for their rendezvous.

Earplugs securely fitted into his ear to block out the noise of the Air Force C-130 transporting Jaeger and he team of techs and Colonel Bollinger, he tried to get some sleep amidst the cacophony of the cargo bay. He rolled over in his mind, the rendezvous points of the refueling tankers and the dangers involved by the news of a night drop. A HALO drop at night, from thirty thousand feet was not what he bargained for. The term BOHICA ran over and over in his mind, here it comes again. Well it was his own fault, he made the commitment and once in never out no matter what.

His kind was the tip of the spear, cannon fodder, for a story that would be lost in the detria of the human condition.

Everyone was still busy as the transport winged its way over the Mid Atlantic on its way over the Sahara and to its destination, for the details of plan of attack was still being cobbled together at the last moment, so many variables to fit together, that only blind luck could insure success. The long drop was only the beginning in a chain of events where just about the smallest of things could drive a monkey wrench into partially oiled gears.

As Jaeger often did, he recited the Holy Rosary over and over, for this was his mantra, his calming effect, summoning all that was seen and unseen to manifest itself and should it be the celestial will, Jaeger vowed to go down taking a number of souls into the abyss with him.

Upon his successful landing he was to meet up with a Legionnaire a certain Sergeant Thierry De Jong, of the French Foreign Legion, stationed in nearby Niger bury the cargo of the Gryphon glider, then travel some twenty miles to a well concealed opening in the ground, which was a two mile long tunnel constructed by the former owners of what was now the American Embassy on the outskirts of the City of N'Djamena the capital of Niger. The tunnel was electronically operated by the generator in the basement of the embassy, designed to glide two passengers in a prone position twenty feet underground, to and from the embassy. This would be the route of extraction.

As the sun was rising over the earth, the C-130 was crossing the Western African coast line heading in a southeasterly direction coming out over the country of Nigeria, to rendezvous with a tanker, from the base of Diego Garcia in the Indian Ocean, for its final fill up prior to the wide swing back from where it came skirting the Western Border of Niger, taking on the trappings of an air cargo plane at altitude flying from Mombasa to Algeria. A French speaking pilot was along for the ride to complete the deception if necessary.

In spite of the noise, Jaeger had slept soundly throughout the night and well into the morning, the details of the mission repeated over and over and the maps studied, committed to memory, with nothing left to do now but watch the techs go over the equipment again and again to insure that everything was to work as it had at China Lake.

Late in the afternoon the C-130 reached its rendezvous point with the tanker from Diego Garcia the pilot of the tanker asking, "Ya want regular sport, or ethyl". When the refueling was completed the normal spray of jet fuel splashed over the C-130's fuselage, with the pilot asking "Hey, what about the windows"?

The tanker driver replied, "We're a Union Shop and we don't do windows", then gently went into a gradual turn, back towards the Indian Ocean from where it came knowing nothing of why they were there.

Hours later, the Craft's engines drew back to idle speed, at thirty thousand feet to minimize the back draft of its cargo when the rear deck opened. A red light went on signaling that the drop zone was close at hand summoning all the techs to assist Jaeger to the rear of the craft as the rear deck yawned open revealing the night and the lights of the Capital of N'Djamena, far off to its port side.

The yellow light went on signaling the drop point was just minutes away and finally the green light blinked, as Jaeger received a head nod from the Air Force Load Master to fall away from the craft.

Even through the well-insulated drop suit it was as cold as a witches tit, the air rushing past him as he constantly adjusted the mini joystick that governed the Gryphon glider carrying the essentials for the extraction. His oxygen was flowing properly and since it was midsummer in this part of the world he knew he would just have to tough things out until he landed. Soon he would have all the warmth he could handle.

He knew that Colonel Bollinger was in contact with the Legionnaire on the ground via a special radio frequency and that as soon as he reached fifteen thousand feet the Legionnaire would flash his lights twice, indicating the target on the ground. The altimeter on Jaegers suit was electronically sending signals to the aircraft of his descent and at the designated altitude, a beep went off in Jaeger's earpiece and there it was, two brief flashes right off his starboard side.

At ten thousand and again at five thousand feet, a beep indicated that a flash of light would follow and right on schedule they occurred. At two thousand feet yet a final signal would occur indicating to Jaeger to prepare for separation, and right on schedule there it was.

Jaeger now had a dim visual of a person on the ground ever mindful of the altimeter that gave yet another beep in his earpiece, when the thousand foot level was reached. The beep went off signaling Jaeger for the slow three count in the aftermath when that was reached; he hit the button, summoning the chutes of both him and the Gryphon to deploy as he cut the cord tying him to the Gryphon. A quick glance at the altimeter read four hundred feet at time of separation. Cutting it a tad close, but everything was working as designed as he glided to a gentle standing landing.

Oxygen off, Helmet off, Jaeger went through the after landing checklist as he saw a lone individual approach some hundred yards away. He moved easily like a military man experienced in the ways of the desert and as he drew near sang out, "Sergeant Jaeger I presume"?

As he drew closer Jaeger replied, "Sergeant De Jong I presume"? The pleasantries exchanged, De Jong said, "Welcome to Africa Sergeant", reaching his hand out in friendship. Taking his hand in a brief exchange, he heard the Sergeant say, "That was quite a drop, especially at night"!

As Jaeger was struggling to shed himself of what he called the 'Squirrel Suit' he replied, "Thanks, every once in a while the wonks get things right"! Fortunately the Gryphon landed not twenty feet from a densely bushed area on the edge of the Sahel, the encroaching sand of the Southern Sahara as it meets vegetation.

Both men silently fell to work to stash the evidence of Jaegers arrival deep in the bush leaving a marker as to its whereabouts that only held a meaning for them, then set out for the twenty mile trek under the stars to the end of the escape tunnel to the Embassy. With steady progress they should make the trip just before dawn and appear in the Embassy's basement in time for morning chow, or what might pass for it.

Both men knew that unnecessary conversation when walking in the desert even at night drew from essential energy reserves that would be needed and in short supply for the task at hand. As they walked their eyes were everywhere, senses ever on the alert for the slightest thing that might seem out of place. However since this was the Frenchies turf Jaeger followed his lead without comment. For he knew the way in and the way out all the way to the extraction point some hundred miles away across the desert terrain to neighboring Niger where the French Government promised to have a craft fly them all to safety, from a little known landing strip just over the frontier.

Just as the horizon started to light up from the east, Thierry De Jong and Jaeger came upon the well shrouded by vegetation, metal grate that served as the entrance to the tunnel to the Embassy. Since it was so well concealed, and on the edge of the Sahel, it opened easily enough, requiring no locking mechanism and the two climbed twenty feet below to the desert end of the tunnel.

"How many know of the existence of this tunnel", asked Jaeger?

"Well I assume your Ambassador and his second, plus our Ambassador and our second and then perhaps half the UN, uh it's impossible to answer. I know and now you know Sergeant"!

The duo lay down in prone position as De Jong flipped switch lighting up the tunnel with a single bare low wattage bulb positioned every fifty yards or so casting a barely visible light down the tunnels length. The tunnel measured about four feet in height and five feet in width just enough to ferry two normal sized people in a prone position back and forth down a re-enforced concrete corridor by an electrically driven motor pulling a wire cable attached to the wooden flat cart.

Jaeger estimated the cart traveled at a speed of about ten miles an hour, which if all went well could extract everyone in the space of three hours, or so.

Both could see the tunnel coming to its terminus in the basement of the Embassy as the small cart automatically slowed its speed, eventually coming to a halt. De Jong rose up and opened the small horizontal door to the basement and finding no one around motioned to Jaeger to follow.

Both men knew that the Embassy was lucky, for if anyone knew of this tunnel on the outside and with no one to stand guard in the basement, it would be curtains for one and all.

Jaeger took the lead as they carefully mounted the steps to the main floor and seeing a Marine Guard rush by, Jaeger shouted out "Halt Marine", which caused the Embassy guard to skid to a halt, rapidly bringing his M- 16 to bear on the duo yelling out "Intruder Alert"! Then seeing that they were not in the garb of the locals, yelling, "Who are you"? "Stand at ease sport and lighten up on that trigger. Sergeant Jaeger of the United States, by gawd Marines and Sergeant Terry De Jong of the French Foreign Legion here to bring everybody out ASAP. Y'all shoot us and all is FUBAR, for we've come a very long way in a hurry, to save your skins"!

His barrel of the M-16 immediately turned aside the Marine Corporal said, "You're gonna want to know what the situation is Sergeant and I'll tell ya it's getting pretty skinny lately, with the Toureg Militia getting all fired up on the local drugs"!

"Is there a main assembly room available to gather everybody" asked Jaeger?

"Follow me", said the Corporal leading the way. As they made their way through the building, they encountered a number of people and the Corporal said to each, "Gather everyone up in the main room, we're all getting' out"!

Within five minutes, all the personnel of the Embassy were gathered together to hear from Jaeger and De Jong, with Jaeger starting out by introducing De Jong and himself, then asking what the situation on the ground was and so duly informed instructed the two Marines on the roof and the three on the perimeter wall to resume their positions and stay in touch by the radios on their belts.

Then turning to the Ambassador and his staff he asked what was being done regarding the burning and shredding of all documents, the Ambassador replying they were minutes away from completing that task.

Then he asked where the C-4 charges were and were they ready for demolition? The Gunnery Sergeant of the Embassy guards said, "We can let you inspect all the charges in place whenever you're ready Sergeant Jaeger"! Then continuing said, "There's an ignition point at the end of the escape tunnel you came in by, and we just ran an electrical test and all systems appear to be in working order"!

"Sequential ignition points", asked Jaeger? "Aye Sergeant", replied the Gunny! Now the Gunnery Sergeant outranked Jaeger by two stripes, but all that was set aside, for Jaeger was the 'Boss' for he was the one who was going to get them out in one piece.

Then Jaeger turned and addressed everyone saying, "I'm running the show, but make no mistake, Sergeant De Jong here, knows the way out and were all gonna work together as a team if we're ever gonna get out. All we have to do is schlep our way out over a hundred miles of desert, hot sand and a few hills and we have five days to get it done. Anyone who questions my or Sergeant De Jong's abilities or authority will be left behind immediately. Anyone who falls behind will be left behind without a word.

Now is anyone here have a medical problem such as diabetes that we oughtta know about raise your hand"!

No hand were raised which prompted Jaeger to say, "Good"! Now twenty miles or so from here are food, desert shoes and supplies we'll need to make the trek out. Someone will have to fill up gallon containers of water to get us to the first oasis"! Just then sporadic rifle fire broke out from outside the compound, and the Gunnery Sergeants radio blurted out, "The Toureg Militia is starting to assemble and I'm taking fire from the front wall"!

"Well fire back and hit some of those rag heads to keep their heads down", bellowed the Gunny!

One of the Marines was instructed to take one of the one of the Embassy staff and immediately evacuate through the tunnel, setting up a perimeter at the other end and send the skid back for another load of personnel, while Jaeger and De Jong went around to the various stations where sufficient amounts of C-4 explosive were strategically placed to give a very nasty and permanent surprise to any intruders to the Embassy.

Engineered for escape purposes, the last man completely out was to push the button, setting off a series of explosions designed to bring the structure completely down upon the heads of a hoard of intruders, in such a way to inflict maximum damage.

Upon occasion the Government will get things right, courtesy of lessons learned from the Iranian incursion of the US Embassy back in the late seventies.

With things set in motion Jaeger and De Jong followed the Gunny to the Armory in the basement to load up with ammunition and weapons sufficient to give the Toureg's a reason to keep their heads down while the others gradually made their way out.

It was getting to be midmorning, when on the roof a shower of grenades made their way towards the locals, who started to increase their rate of fire upon the Embassy building, followed by the Marines firing on anyone who came to the rescue of the wounded. For Jaeger had instructed the Gunny that the 'rules of engagement were suspended as of now'!

The Gunny nodded his head and passed the information to those guarding the perimeter and each and every reply was met by the word, "Cool"! Then Jaeger, De Jong and the Gunny spent the next twenty minutes ferrying ammunition to the roof top and the perimeter Marines.

That accomplished, De Jong went to the basement to see how the evacuation was going and seeing slightly more than half of the personnel were out, went back to Jaeger on the roof and said, "In about forty five minutes we need to start sequentially evacuating the Marines"!

Then the Gunny chimed in, "Perimeter guards first, then De Jong, while you and I are the last to go pal, whatta ya say! "We can hold em off from the roof should they attack"!

"Gunny, I'd say that's a plan"!

"Sergeant De Jong, we don't make it out then you're the Boss, ya follow"?

"Oui Mon Sergeant", said the Legionnaire!

From the rooftop all could see more and more of the locals running down the street, firing their weapons blindly, wasting ammo, when they clearly had no target but the embassy compound structure, while the Marines, firing short bursts from their weapons at a host of targets all scurrying about between buildings and on the street. Before too much time had elapsed, the street was littered with the wounded and the dying. Some lying there in varying stages of agony while other fired back at the embassy as best they could. The blood was up an every side, the only difference being the Marines utilizing their discipline as a well-trained fighting unit, taking a terrific toll on the untrained attackers. Jaeger noted that Hollywood movies showed that often men in combat went down and died at the very first time a bullet hit them, when reality indicated that often they would drop only after being hit repeatedly, rarely dying on the spot, but often firing back, and if all went well, they would eventually bleed out where they lay, if immediate aid was not forthcoming. Such was the case of the local militia. No time for a body count, only no neck bureaucrats did that, sufficient to say there would be a whole lot of graves dug before too long. De Jong made one more trip to the basement, then returned saying that all the Embassy personnel were away and that it was time to evacuate the perimeter Marines. The Gunny then gone on the radio and directed two of the perimeter Marines to "Dede your asses to the basement, mo hinky dink"! They didn't have to be told twice. Charging their weapons as they ran, the Marines arrived in the basement as soon as the rail mounted skid arrived back for another load, quickly taking the prone position and pushing the button that took them to freedom.

Jaeger then said to De Jong and the lone perimeter Marine over the radio, "In twenty minutes, your next"!

The rate of fire from the streets was sporadic, coming in waves rather than being a steady continuous rate of fire, as if the rag heads fired all their rounds as one then reloaded all at the same time. 'Amateur nite, thank god' thought Jaeger.

Sometimes fifteen minutes can go by at the speed of light when you're having fun, while at other times it can seem like an eternity, all depending on one's state of mind and point of view. If one has a death wish, it can certainly take the edge off things, If not...

Fear can make itself known in a host of ways. What matters, is how one deals with it. Fear is the mind killer, the great immobilizer, often freezing grown men into inaction, or inappropriate action, with the possibility of death, or even a greater disgrace, failure in the task at hand. What helped Jaeger was the mantra he repeated to himself regarding his place in the universe, when under periods of mortal danger, that he was an instrument, a mere grain of sand in the universe, that no one would know of his manner of passing, or care. He was born alone and he would die alone. He loved nobody and was loved by nobody. He cared for nobody and was cared for by nobody. It somehow gave him comfort. But what was real was his solemn vow, that when it was time to go out, he would go out in style, taking along a host of pilgrims with him.

The twenty minutes now up, he notified the Gunny who radioed the last perimeter Marine, to get his ass to the basement and meet up with the frog soldier, who replied, "Not a frog but Belgique in origin"!

After he departed, the Gunny said to Jaeger, from the middle of the roof firing as he talked, "Well sport, it's just you and me now. Ya think fifty years from now they'll be makin' up legends about the likes of us"?

"I'm told it takes a Hollywood agent to get that done now days and as one can see neither of us runs in that crowd"!

"Semper Fi", yelled the Gunny back, "Too bad I didn't get to know ya better"!

"'Well Gunny don't cash in your chips just yet, we need to make more work for the grave diggers", said Jaeger as he fired off a short burst.

The locals had now abated in their firing on the Embassy compound, as Jaeger turned around noting the gas generator on the roof was still chugging away, plugging out wattage, then hearing the Gunny holler, "Hey Jaeger, I think it's time".

Jaeger yelled back, "Fall back to the roof entrance and I'll cover you from snipers, then you do the same", the Gunny nodded and within less than a minute the exchange occurred with both disappearing into the innards of the Embassy.

Just as they arrived in the basement the skid arrived back for the final trip and needing no further prodding the duo assumed their prone positions, with the Gunny saying as he pushed the button, "Lets dede outta this rat hole"!

The skid rolled down the track art what seemed to be a snail's pace, when in reality it was moving at the same rate of speed that brought

Jaeger to the party, but inevitably it came to a stop at the end of its run, depositing its final passengers as designed.

Jaeger yelled up at the Marine up top, "Has there been any gunfire lately, from the Embassy"?

"No Sergeant, not for some ten minutes, or so"!

Then he turned to the Gunny saying," We gotta wait for the sounds of gunfire, when it stops we wait fifteen more minutes, before setting off the fireworks to insure that the Embassy is full of unwanted visitors, ya follow Gunny"?

The Gunny smiled as he said, "Ten Four Jaeger, I love how your mind works"! Up top, the civilian Embassy workers started to grow restless, when the Ambassador asked one of the Marines at the top of the escape tunnel, what the holdup was?

The Marine, keeping an ear out for gunfire, started his explanation to the Ambassador, when he started to hear repeated volleys of gunfire, shouting down to the tunnel, "Their starting the final attack on the compound Gunny", then returned to the Ambassador, completing his explanation, "We wanna get a full body count and if luck holds, get some of the leaders, who will be part of the second wave of attackers, after the first wave has made the place safe, then 'Boom', we get em all"!.

After twenty minutes the sounds of firing ceased from the Embassy as everyone looked at their watches, Jaeger and De Jong climbed the ladder emerging from the tunnel with Jaeger gathering everyone around him, repeating the explanation of why the delay in departure, then announced, "We have about twenty miles to trek to our rendezvous point where the supplies for the walkout are stashed. Which means were going to be traveling at night and on foot. Hold on to the gallons of water each of you has brought, for it's gonna be vital from getting us out of here. There will be some oases between here and the extraction point, but the whole deal is about no one knowing where we are. So if some oases are occupied, when we arrive we just might have to bypass them for the greater good."!

"Does everyone understand, please nod your heads"!

"There's more, we'll be primarily traveling at night and laying low during the day. All verbal interaction will be held to an absolute minimum for reasons that will be made obvious as we travel. We will be moving at such a pace, where each step will be around thirty inches in length, so those with a short stride will be better able to keep up. Now most important is the fact that as we move forward, everyone try their best to step in the footprint of the person in front of you and when you inhale you do so through your nose and exhale the same way. Since we're traveling in the desert with no humidity about there should be little problems with sinus allergies, but if that happens, then and only then breathe through your mouth. It's all about the retention of bodily moisture! If everybody understands then please nod your heads"!

All again nodded their heads and Jaeger returned his attention to the Embassy compound. Jaeger peered down into the tunnel and whispered, "How much time left Gunny"?

"Coming up on twelve minutes Sarge", came the response. Jaeger then turned to everyone and held up three fingers signifying three minutes to go before they all could depart. As the seconds ticked down to the zero point, Jaeger went through all the things that could still go wrong with the big bang, which was necessary to cover their getaway. Suddenly a large series of sequential explosions came from the direction of the Embassy as the Gunny hurried up the ladder saying, "Looks like everything worked. But I gotta tell ya that just five seconds before the big bang, someone on the Embassy end probably found the tunnel, and hit the button to retrieve the skid. Let's hope they went down for the full count". Jaeger then looked at Sergeant De Jong making the sign to move them on their way, which he promptly did. It was understood that Jaeger and the Gunny would be bringing up the rear.

Back into the tunnel went the Gunny anticipating what Jaeger wanted, testing the button and finding it not working as he suspected, indicating the entire Embassy was in rubble along with the diesel generator that supplied the power, he knew that anyone who may come down the tunnel would have to do it on their belly.

The Gunny looked up at Jaeger saying, "All powers gone to the skid, but just in case, give me a few minutes while I rig up a surprise for anyone who might think they're a tunnel rat"!

Five minutes later he climbed out of the tunnel for the final time saying, "Set up a little booby trap with a single grenade rigged to a trip wire. Blow to smithereens anyone who comes this way"! They both closed the tunnel grate and gathered sufficient brush and anchored it down, taking even more brush, to sweep the area clean of tracks and remove all signs of a previous presence. Didn't have to be perfect, just good enough to last five days.

What worked in the groups favor was that after the insurgents gained entrance to the Embassy; too much time was spent looking for Embassy personnel, since long gone. Then they went around looking for firearms and papers and finding the small armory mostly empty went through the entire structure room by room, looking for loot.

In the basement wandered several of the armed insurgents, eventually finding a grate that when opened revealed a deep underground tunnel.

While one insurgent climbed down the iron ladder embedded in concrete, the other remained in the basement, as peered into the lit tunnel he yelled up to his partner, just as he pushed the start button to retrieve the skid, of the existence of a tunnel when the series of explosions ripped through the embassy.

Moussa's partner was cut in half by an iron support beam that came crashing down, before he could alert anyone, while Moussa was buried alive in the bricks and sand that tore into the tunnel. He tried in vain to extricate himself from the coffin of sand and bricks that engulfed him, eventually succumbing to the inevitable suffocation. It would be some years before anyone would think to dig down below the basement, but by then.......

It was about a half an hour before before the Gunny and Jaeger caught up with the column of trekkers, but by looking at the sand, it could be seen that all were following the directive of walking in each other's footprints. The sand was that of the Sahel, gradually encroaching southward and recently superficial over solid ground, far easier than the deep sand of the Sahara proper. The footprints appeared to measure around thirty inches between them and the last man in line was one of the Marines, for they were interspersed between the travelers on every sixth person or so. Not all Marines receive the extra training of desert or jungle escape and evasion procedures, but their collective training taught them very well how to listen, take orders without question and engage in situational awareness. In time, a seasoned Marine just knew one who knew what they were about, by their manner and conducted themselves accordingly.

From the Gunny on down, neither Jaeger nor De Jong had to prove themselves to anyone. For this purpose only, their word was the 'holy writ', come down from the heavens and if anyone didn't like it they would be left behind. 'I say, you do', immediately and without question for the common good.

Every hour, the line stopped in place for a breather, for five minutes only, before resuming their pace more for the benefit of the embassy people than anything else. Of course their foot ware was completely unsuitable for the desert, but all that would change once their at the rendezvous point, once the buried supplies were reached.

At around four PM, their destination was reached and the column disbursed into the brush while the Marines set to opening up the Gryphon para sail's contents, revealing desert ware, socks and boots for each of the civilians and the Marines to help them blend in better and traverse the surrounding terrain. Salt and potable water tablets, along with hermetically sealed plastic packets of the dreaded Spam for one and all, to eat sparingly along the route at proscribed times. In the years to come, all who may have had an aversion to Spam came to view this product with a nostalgic reverence. Plastic canteens for water and most important chewing gum laden with sugar for energy.

"Everyone is allotted, ten packs of chewing gum for the trip to provide as a source of energy, You will be permitted to masticate one package of five sticks per session of travel during the night", Jaeger announced! "I suggest that you do not chew the gum but park it as one would chewing tobacco, between your check and your gum and allow the warmth of your mouth and saliva to soften the stick, so its flavor will last an hour or more. When the flavor is completely gone so will be the gums usefulness, to be discarded during the next rest break. All items of discard will be buried and covered up prior to departure, that means everything and I trust the Marines will keep a watchful eye regarding disposal"!

Continuing, Jaeger announced, "The people at the State Department were kind enough to supply everyone with clothes for the trip sized appropriately and by your name. So should anything not fit precisely, just remember this whole thing was put together by your fellow governmental employees and was put together on literally a moment's notice from the other side of the world. So now is the time for y'all not to be squeamish and hunt out your name and start changing clothes. All personal clothes will be gathered by the Marines and buried deep in the brush, for the archaeologists a thousand years from now"!

One of the very best things that are taught every grunt is how to tightly pack ones few belongings when in transit. Desert clothes and foot ware for about twenty people, first aid supplies, food, ammunition, K-bar knives for all the embassy marines, compass's a folding trench digger for each marine and a desert camo sunshade for the day.

Takes but a scant five minutes to dig a body width and length trench, from one and a half to two feet in depth, in the soft desert sand during the sunrise, then spread out and anchor the desert camo covering in the sand, then slide yourself right in for the day time slumber. Not only will you be hidden from any aerial surveillance but from the blazing desert sun, lengthening ones chances for survival. The final items from the booty of the Gryphon, was the lone flare gun to be used only if necessary and only when they reached the point of rendezvous point across the frontier in Mali to meet the rescuing aircraft. Finally, the old Soviet 'Dragunov', sniper rifle with a fifty power scope with sun shroud, to be used only when and if necessary. Should this have to be used, the barbarians were indeed at the gate, and the jig was indeed up with any chance of extraction slim or none.

By nightfall, all of the exchanges were made, some limited nourishment was taken and the evidence of old clothes was buried deep in the sand along with their method of transport. Then all were off across the desert on their first leg of the walkout, till sunup.

While most slept during the gradually building heat of the day, Jaeger and De Jong kept watch for any evidence of aerial search. As they looked back at their tracks they were grateful for the steady desert wind that did much to cover the tracks made by the group with fresh sand and by noon they could not see where any tracks existed.

Apparently Mother Nature was being cooperative for the time being.

Around 1300 hours in the afternoon, a lone single engine plane was seen, flying north for an hour then a half hour later flew back towards them in a southerly direction, clearly on a search grid pattern, then a half hour later, flying in a northwesterly direction, (their exact route of extraction) then back again, then again in the distance they could see the same plane flying in a westerly direction, on its out and back rotation.

"Apparently they've concluded that we've flown the coop somehow, finding no dead Americans in the rubble", said De Jong as they kept a keen watch on the search plane.

"Let's hope they don't have night sight capabilities, or else things could get complicated," said Jaeger!

"Should we alert the Ambassador to this", asked De Jong?

"For now only the Gunny and maybe later the Ambassador", Jaeger answered. "The civilians got all they can say grace over right now just walking in a straight line and doing what their told. Let's see how they perform for the moment. You're the man who's gonna get us all out of here Sergeant and my Marines have been on Embassy duty which ain't exactly hard duty. The Gunny appears to have his shit together and to the degree the grunts show discipline then we can bring em in the fold. So right now let the Gunny and me watch the skies all around and you keep us on the path and out of possible mine fields which would screw things up a bit, agreed"?

"Agreed", said De Jong!

De Jong then broke out his map and the Gunny was called in to view the route of extraction, and the places they could hole up during the day light hours. "Two days from now we should be able to approach the oasis of Jibril Adid, but if I were looking for us I'd have that oasis under surveillance, just in case. Now we don't know anything about the quantity or the quality of those in the Toureg militia and they really don't know that we've escaped. They suspect as much, witness the aircraft going through the search patterns, but another thing in our favor is that we could be headed in just about any direction most likely by the river route, although they will be certain to have that covered. Only a mad man would try and escape via the desert", he offered with a smile.

"What if we encounter some more search planes", asked the Gunny? "Then either they've got a very good crystal ball, or they know something they shouldn't, and to the degree we see search aircraft in our vicinity, its' a certain wager that the oasis will be under scrutiny", replied De Jong!

"Is there an alternate source for water, "asked Jaeger?

"Only miles out of the way, up in the hills, which might be a problem for the civilians", said De Jong pointing to a spot on the map.

"Now few know of this for it is a mountainous spring only used by Shepard's, so I'm told and rarely at that due to some curse placed there by an Imam, a thousand years ago and I've never been there. The oasis I've been to", said De Jong!

"What's your thoughts on bypassing all the water sources and toughing it out all the way through", asked Jaeger?

"Well, perhaps we and the Marine guards might be able to do it, but the civilians just might pose a bit of a problem. We have a brief window to be at a certain place by a certain time, to meet the aircraft that will extract us. The argument against the water spring in the hills is that it would guarantee to slow us down in finding it, for I've only an approximation of its location and if the oasis is under guard, now some sixty miles distant and we have to fight to get the water, and still cover some forty miles to extraction". Then thinking as he looked at the map, "There is a way we could circumvent the oasis if need be and still have it not slow us down, but that will require extended travel hours during the evening with us all covering some ten miles more, or traveling at a faster rate. Either way it will over extend the civilians for certain"!

At that point Jaeger summoned the Ambassador and they ran through all of the time and distance options placed before them. Then silence took hold after they finished with the Ambassador saying, "I'm a diplomat and know nothing about what you gentlemen are about. I'm not a man of robust bearing, yet mine and others lives are at stake. I pride myself of having common horse sense and realize we have to not be seen and avoid any foreseeable encounter and travel as fast as humanly possible. So my vote would be, tough it out under your respective leaderships. Get there early and unseen no matter whatever it takes.

"Then that's what we'll do Ambassador, just keep your flock in line as best you can, for any stragglers will get left behind. We have the means, if your folks have the will to live"?

"Sergeant Jaeger, answered the Ambassador, "What one man can do so can another. You provide the leadership for your flock and we will do the rest"!

"We have an hour of daylight left, and will move out as soon as it is dark. Remind your flock of the rules of extraction I've spoken of, because we're gonna be moving fast"!

When the sun went down, Jaeger reminded De Jong of the military rate of pace, which was at 180 steps per minute, which while a lively pace guaranteed leg cramps at some point along the way for those not used to it. They would still take a break every 55 minutes for five minutes or so, but perhaps the fear of death in the desert would spur some on to greater endurance.

The good news is that since they were traveling at night and there was only a quarter moon in the sky it was very dark on the ground, thus making them almost invisible to all except owls and bats. The pace that De Jong was leading was starting to take its toll on the civilians about midnight at the forth rest stop, as many of them were rubbing their leg muscles. "Look in your back packs for some muscle ointment", said Jaeger as he walked up the line, "But ya only got four minutes left, then up we go"! Come the first flickering of light on the horizon in the east, the watches all indicated slightly past 0500 hours and De Jong selected a camp site along the base of a rock outcropping shaded by the sun where the group could take sanctuary, saying to Jaeger, "My pedometer says we've covered slightly under forty five miles this evening"! As they looked around even the other Marines were glad for the respite. 'More than twice the rate projected for extraction', Jaeger thought. 'Do this one more night and they just might pull this off'! As Jaeger and the Gunny went down the line all they were met with were people who were literally exhausted. They had to be helped to drink from their canteens and have the food delivered to their mouths from their rations. The Marines were in better condition but not by much. The civilians were driven on by the fear of what would happen should they get caught by the locals.

Never to see their loved ones, and especially forefront in their minds, was the shoddy treatment afforded the hostages in the Iranian Embassy takeover, not so long ago. Their own government was inept. The UN was non responsive and the Iranians were apparently of one mind after the overthrow of the ruling royal family, "Death to all Infidels"!

The Marines all made the rounds of all the civilians applying ointments and body massages especially to the lower extremities for the trek the next day. Then when that was completed they did the very same for each other.

De Jong thought they all did exceedingly well, but the main question was, 'how would they respond the next day'?

Sentries were set out for two hour shifts, to keep a keen watch during the day light, while the others slept. Even the Ambassador, who suffered from insomnia, slept like the dead, his body as well as the others going deep into recovery mode.

Both Jaeger and De Jong tried to sleep, each drifting off for minutes at a time, waking with a start, whenever a fly or a bug would flit about.

Late in the afternoon, a low flying propeller driven aircraft could briefly be heard flying north, as De Jong followed its path east of where they were resting then a half an hour later, the very same aircraft would fly back south at a low rate of speed, in the far distance clearly searching for something or someone.

"I fear they somehow know something", said De Jong, as Jaeger drew near.

"Yeah they know something, but what"?

And the sun crossed the horizon, everyone started to wake up, their bodies and minds not used to the extreme, physical and emotional stress crying out in pain. Some mildly complained, while others suffered in silence, knowing that everyone was in the same situation.

Jaeger was silently grateful that everyone was pulling together, for often the movies portrayed civilians breaking ranks in times of stress and he honestly didn't know what he would do if someone cracked under pressure?

Leave them behind, shoot them, or cut their throats. He was sent to bring everyone out and a great many people put together a mighty effort at the task at hand, which could all be brought at severe risk if just one of those he was sent to help, didn't pull their own weight.

He forced the negative thought ought of his mind, gathering everyone together saying, "Well folks we've come a far distance, better than anticipated. But the sound of aircraft tells us that someone out there is making an effort to find us. We're all hurting, some more than others, but so far I'm proud of each and every one of you. Several of you have foot sores and we will attend to them shortly, so Sergeant De Jong will cut back on the pace a bit this evening. But nothing has changed, nothing at all. We have a certain point to be at by a certain time and if we are not there we can't expect them to wait on us. Just two more nights of sucking it up and then we just might get outta here"!

The Gunny assembled those who had problems with foot blisters, tending to them and a half hour later nodded to De Jong that everyone was ready to move out.

Jaeger nodded his head and the column moved forward with De Jong again leading the way, through the night. Carefully trudging on through the thin sand of the Sahel, leaving little evidence of a trail of frightened pilgrims by hugging the hill sides De Jong knew the worst was yet to come, for the very last stretch of land they would have to traverse, was twenty miles of deep desert sand where no shelter from above was be available. This would be a test of the civilian's intestinal fortitude and perhaps his also.

By sunrise the column stopped and found a similar outcropping of rock to shelter everyone. De Jong, gathered the Gunny and Jaeger around pointing to a map saying, "We are here and we've covered about thirty five miles. Sometime tomorrow morning we'll cross the frontier into Niger and then traverse a small group of hills before we see the old airfield. If all goes well we'll be a day early"!

Continuing he said, tomorrow morning we will have to encamp in the desert for the day, for while there exists a shorter way around" and he pointed to a spot on the topographical map, "This is the main trail for herders and years ago was heavily mined, during the last governmental problem. Few people know about this trail and I suggest we avoid it. Thus the route across the deep sand, which should be the very last place people would look for us"!

Water was getting to be a problem along with dehydration, while water discipline was going well all around with people taking a scant mouthful then rolling it around in their mouths and throats, for several minutes prior to swallowing, the gallon of water everyone started out with was halved. With the worst part of the trek right ahead. A brief swig of water then a stick of gum in the mouth to soften dispensing the much needed sugar for energy and everyone fell asleep straight away, sleeping on their sides, careful to keep their mouths shut retaining bodily moisture as much as possible.

The desert winds had been steady and helpful in covering their tracks at night with fresh sand. Jaeger briefly thought back to the legendary stories about his great, great, great grandfather Henry Jaeger, who fought the Comanche during the days of the Texas Republic and beyond. 'What would he have done'? 'Would he have done anything different'? As he lay under the rock outcropping, gathering his strength for the following evening, he summoned the images of his forefathers, asking their respective counsel, then when nothing was forth coming, he was just about to drift off to sleep, an image of an very old Indian gradually took form in his mind, looking down at him in a fatherly way, for quite some time before giving him the non-audible message from the skies, 'The problem lays within. Look for the problem within'!

Jaeger knew of no part of his family that had an American Indian in it, thus the spiritual image and the message left to, "Look within", made no sense, so sense at all. Yet the message echoed over and over in his mind as he drifted off to sleep.

As the sun went down in the west and the group started to rise from their all too brief slumber, for the next nights trek, Jaeger felt a singular uneasiness about the celestial message that still wouldn't leave his mind and he went around to each and every one of the civilians, to personally see how they were holding up and give a little moral support. He inspected their garb and equipment and gave special attention to those who had problems with their feet. The very last person he inspected was a young female clerk, apparently well educated, with dark hair, working as a translator at the Embassy. Everything seemed to be in order, yet she was wearing a leather belt holding up her trousers, rather than the cloth and metal buckle GI belt.

When asked where the Issue belt was, she answered innocently, that it simply wasn't in the kit issued.

Jaeger passed it off as highly likely, given that the government screwed up logistically all the time and with all that had gone on this was small potatoes. Jaeger let it go, what with everything else he had to contend with as darkness fell and they all moved out behind De Jong.

By 2300 hours they approached the deep sand desert they had to cross and took a break before embarking on the hardest leg of their journey.

Jaeger, De Jong and the Gunny made the rounds giving most of their attention to the cargo of civilian State Department civilians who were still hanging in there if but by a slender thread.

Then they were off, trudging into the desert sand. From time to time De Jong turned on his radio, gradually moving around the channels to see if there was any chatter and especially the channel into the airport at N'Djamena which still came in although fainter and fainter. He turned the radio off, finding nothing out of the ordinary, to save the battery.

As the hours droned on he could see up ahead the ever so faint outline of distant hills that signaled their journey was soon coming to an end. Then turning on his radio one last time tuned into the channel at the distant N'Djamena airfield. The weather report was being delivered in French for the locals and indicating a sudden weather front arriving from the Northwest. The dreaded sand storm not even the locals ever got used to. It would arise from the deep desert with scant warning blow like hell then depart as soon as it arrived.

De Jong suddenly stopped, for all his attention was in a northwesterly direction, and when he turned and saw the gathering of clouds in the northwest, he summoned Jaeger from the rear of the column and said pointing towards the clouds, "Sand storm coming over the radio from the northwest and we probably have a half hour till it arrives".

Jaeger then alerted the Marines to drop their packs, and retrieve the trench shovels and start digging trenches for the civilians, length of the body then three feet in width and at least two feet deep. With the help of the civilians who after the trench covers were retrieved from all the packs and secured to the deep sand, the appropriate instructions were given by De Jong as how to best ride out the storm.

The Marines were putting the finishing touches on their own slit trenches when the first edges of the storm came upon them. Jaeger was the very last one to climb in and zip himself up. For the next hour and a half, the desert wind howled like all the banshees that ever were.

Both Jaeger and De Jong had the similar thought, that any worries either of them may have had about leaving a trail across the deep sand were now gone thanks to Mother Nature, who was wreaking some kind of earthly vengeance on this part of the world, assuming they all didn't get buried too deeply.

After ninety some odd minutes or so, Jaeger could hear the wind start to abate in volume and made his way out of his confinement at the very same time as De Jong, the Gunny and several of the Marines. The all went around and helped the others extricate themselves from their respective enclaves, dust themselves off and prepare to continue on.

As they trudged on towards the now increasingly visible hills in front of them, one of the Marines yelled out in anger, "Not yet you bitch, not yet"!

Somehow when a goal is finally in sight a certain adrenalin kicks in from out of nowhere giving one a sense of renewed energy to continue as the burgeoning hills in front of them were now but just a few miles away.

The well beaten group of 'feather merchants' had risen to the task guided by the Marines but none of which had to be, or asked to be carried out, with their goal at last within reach. Now out of the deep desert and with the eastern horizon now starting to brighten they has but another half hour of steady gradual climbing until the summit of the hills greeted them the a day of hunkering down beneath some rocky crag, blending into the landscape until dark.

They had arrived suitably early which gave Jaeger and his charges time to rest and to then scout the terrain for the unforeseen.

Around noon Jaeger was awakened by the sound of two old Korean War vintage choppers, flying in single file crossing over head and landing on the other side of the hills in the valley below. Hustling to the top of the ridge was Jaeger, De Jong, the Gunny and two other Marines, to see why.

Slowly coming to a landing at the barely discernible edge of an old French built runway, were two vintage Guppy looking choppers disgorging between them a squad of soldiers that fanned out, with two men scanning the hill sides with binoculars directing the placement of each and every man, in the squad, except for two of the men which were eventually placed some five hundred yards away in the lower section of the hill side facing the ancient runway.

One of the two soldiers saluted the other who climber into the ancient chopper, and rose up into the sky with the other following heading in a southerly direction. A squad of men led by a man sporting gold braid in the desert, with clearly two snipers for about a five hundred yard shot between them.

Clearly the jig was up and the rag heads knew something. Since everyone was a day early prior to the extraction.....? Jaeger signaled everyone to fall back on the redoubt behind the summit of the hills to think this one out.

Arriving quickly and carefully back with the others, Jaeger searched his thoughts on just what was bothering him about recent developments, delving into the unseen to emerge with the truth. How did they know to arrive at this very place, at this very time?

He looked at each and every one, starting with De Jong and concluded that De Jong could have sold them out at any time along the route, for he was at the head of the column and had the radio, which could've been used to signal the enemy. But why? It didn't figure.

Then he looked at each and every one of the Marine Guards, straight in the face, trying to peer into the void, coming up with zero. Then he looked at the Ambassador and concluded that if he was complicit in something, anything, he hadn't the opportunity or the means of alerting anyone to his location. Well perhaps when he was in the sand storm, but that would preclude any radio transmission. Then one by one he stood in front of the embassy employees, coming to the dark haired translator.

Then he remembered, 'The problem lies from within', recalling the message from some old Indian delivered in a state of partial consciousness that he just couldn't wrap his arms around.

Then he recalled the civilian belt around the waist of the translator as he looked at her. The light bulb went on in his head as he reached for her belt stripping it from her body, holding it up to the light as she stood there in silence. His fingers traveled the length of the belt, coming to a halt by an ever so slight bulge the size of a quarter. He pulled his knife out of its scabbard and sliced the belt in two, prying out a small round disk the size of a quarter. The Ambassador stood close by watching the events unfold, as Jaeger said to him, "Any idea what this is", offering him a look at what he discovered?

After examining the object the Ambassador said, "My friends at Langley might describe this as a low power locational transmitter of Soviet design made in East Germany", as he looked straight into the face of the once trusted translator! "Why is this in your belt", he yelled?

Fear was all over her face, for she had been found out at last. But what they didn't know was the why? Perhaps the 'why', would buy her time,

Jaeger slowly pushed the Ambassador aside taking the quarter sized transmitter in his hand, placing it on a rock and crushing flat saying, "Whatever the reason for your betrayal, it makes no difference. The rest of us will get out but you will stay"!

"Any last words young lady," asked Jaeger?

"You're not going to kill her are you Sergeant" intervened the Ambassador? Jaeger looked at the Ambassador as if he were a slug, saying "She compromised this entire operation with a squad of soldiers and two snipers just over the hill. Now my orders are to bring as many of you back as is practicable and in this I'm the undisputed boss"!

"But her complicity must be brought to the bar of justice", protested the Ambassador!

"Mr. Ambassador, one more word from you and it's doubtful you'll make it back ya follow"? Then he turned to the Gunny saying, "Protect him from himself and take him away and out of sight"! The Gunny and all the Marines grabbed the protesting Ambassador, muffling his protests and hustled him around a rock outcropping away from the rest, as De Jong grabbed the now terrified translator.

Jaeger replaced his knife in his scabbard, turning to the girl and then delivered a sudden blow just below her breast bone to the heart, causing De Jong to back up a step. The girl slumped over in a heap trying to breathe then lay still.

Then one of the two other females said, "Poor girl, she just collapsed from exhaustion, didn't she everybody", as she turned to the rest. Hearing the rest of the civilians, echo the same response, with the exception of one other who said, "Yeah the poor girl, slipped and fell over that rock out cropping over there, didn't she Sergeant"?

As he and another civilian took her lifeless body out past the Ambassador and shoved her lifeless form over the ledge, turning to the Ambassador saying in unison, "Poor girl she slipped due to exhaustion and all of us will testify to that if it comes to it"!

De Jong looked at Jaeger and said, "Any Legionnaire would've done the same"!

The deed done, Jaeger then set about gathering the Gunny near to plan a way to neutralize those below before the arrival of the aircraft tomorrow.

He went straight for the Dragunov Sniper rifle, someone had the foresight to send along. Never having fired that kind of foreign made ordinance, he closely examined the weapon. Single fire bolt action long barrel, bipod equipped, fifty power scope with night vision capabilities and fifty rounds of armor piercing ten millimeter shells. So far so good.

A German range finder was included, which narrowed things down, but nowhere in the kit was there any information of the trajectory characteristics of the fifty, ten millimeter shells provided. "Scheist", hissed Jaeger in mild frustration!

"You speak Deutcher", asked De Jong? "Only on Thursdays", replied Jaeger. "An inside joke,"?

"As inside as it gets"!

"And your point of frustration is", asked De Jong?

"No drop values on the ten millimeter shells provided in the kit", replied Jaegerl

"Then you will have to do like the Legionnaires and improvise. We never receive anything near what is needed, for we are the bastard stepchildren of the French Militaire' "! Of course what you say is problematique", said De Jong understandingly.

"Soon as its dark, I'll want to get all seven of the Marines up top with me, so we can sight in with the night scope, just where each member of their squad is positioned, then your guys have all night to get in position", said Jaeger to the Gunny. In the morning as soon as it gets light enough to see and before the wind starts to kick up, the 'Go' signal will be at the sound of my first shot. Now I got two snipers to take out and so far they don't know that we're here or even if we're coming for if they had perfect knowledge that this was the place of extraction, the place would be crawling with the "Woggies", right?

Both the Gunny and De Jong nodded in agreement, with the Gunny saying, I'll go prep the men then we'll continue with the shut eye before nightfall".

"Remember Gunny tell the guys they have all night to get into position.

One sound, one rock falling down from the ridge gives everything away. All I'm gonna do come nightfall is give em a peek at their particular target through the night scope, then send em off, ya follow"? The Gunny nodded then went over to the others, to give them the drill.

Then Jaeger summoned the Ambassador over to him to give him the plan. His expression was that of a petulant child, having to be put in place by someone less adroit in the ways of diplomatic expression as he sat down next to Jaeger, legs crossed Indian style.

Before he could say anything, they were joined by one of the other male members of the Embassy who said, "Before you two get after it, I been thinking. This female interpreter was always in the habit of working late and arriving early, every day during my tour. At first I chalked it up to her being a hard worker, but she didn't have that much of a workload now that I think about it. Hell, my main duty was in cryptography and there were days when I had little to do."

"A couple of times I saw her arrive at work in a shiny Mercedes car that only the local 'Honcho's' drove, which told me that she must've had a pretty well off boyfriend. And they appeared to be more than just friendly, if ya know what I mean"!

"Now that's all I have to say, but given what's happened, recently we all have been talking and connecting the dots as best we could, and she sure look's 'Hinky', to the rest of us. Nothing of which would hold up in a court I imagine, but there's no court anywhere near where we are is there"?

The Ambassador sat there in a deep emotional quandary, for none of the rigid training he'd experienced prepared him for his current circumstances. He'd always relied on a civilized structure set forth by those who came before. Certainly what had recently occurred in such a Draconian and swift manner shook him to his very core, but the recent revelations drew every indication that this woman was an agent placed in the Embassy right under every ones nose and had to be dealt with.

"I'm not familiar with diplomatic procedures", said Jaeger, "But it seems to me that someone just didn't look into her qualifications very well, did they"?

With a deep sigh of resignation the Ambassador said, "Apparently not young man"!

"Now I'm not gonna have any trouble from you am I, Mr. Ambassador"?

"No Sergeant Jaeger and I apologize for the previous outburst"!

Then Jaeger set about informing the Ambassador what was on the menu for the evenings activities, stressing that everyone will get a good night's rest with no more marching.

"You will be in charge of the embassy personnel tonight, because all the Marines will spend all night getting in place. Tomorrow morning early I have to take a long shot that might not work out as planned. If all goes well you'll hear just before sun rise, a brief flurry of gunfire, not lasting for more than ten seconds in duration. That being the case, all the bad guys will be dead. If the gunfire persists longer than that, to that of prolonged return fire, we'll probably still be OK. But down there are two snipers that have to be taken out for the obvious reasons".

"After all the gunfire has ceased, I want you to bring everyone to the summit and you will be signaled by a mirror flash by one of us if it's safe to proceed down to the bottom. Do you understand this"!

The Ambassador nodded asking, "And when is the aircraft scheduled to arrive for our extraction"?

"Gee whiz, seems nobody told me the exact moment. After all this isn't your regular Continental Airlines flight schedule now is it", asked Jaeger with a wry smile?

The Ambassador then went back to the others and gave them what he knew, plus one other thing. As Jaeger went back to his examination of the Soviet Sniper Rifle he overheard the embassy people quietly reciting the Lord's Prayer and holding hands in unison.

'Just pray for me to shoot straight', thought Jaeger.

He sent the Gunny up top with the field binoculars outfitted with the glare shield covers, so they couldn't reflect the sunlight back at the enemy below, to try and make out the positioning of the enemy below.

An hour later he came back with a rough sketch on the back of an envelope of the approximate positions, discussing them with Jaeger and De Jong.

"Gunny, have your men rotate and keep an eye out for any new arrivals, with the field glasses this afternoon".

Then he sat down and closed his eyes, gathering into himself all that he knew of long range shooting, all his father had taught him and recalled all the stories his family had repeatedly told him of Henry Jaeger, long ago. Of the miraculous shots he garnered with nothing more than the family heirloom. The ancient twin barreled Beretta Long Rifle.

In that brief space of time between nodding off and sleep, he saw a vision of the well weathered face of a young man dressed from head to toe, in buckskin, with a strange looking, double barreled, flint-lock long rifle.

Although he heard no audible sound, the image told him to, 'be not afraid, for if I can do it then so can you'! Then the image faded away into the mists of memory. Jaeger fell asleep and any doubts of his ability with a strange rifle faded away. As night fell, He awoke to the smiling faces of the Gunny and De Jong, and immediately rose up, grabbing the Dragunov rifle and its components and departed for the ridges summit, just hoping that he was the only one that had night vision capabilities.

As he peered over the summit De Jong pointed out a position some fifty yards below the summit saying, "This would make a very good hide for you to set up on. I make it to be six to seven hundred yard shot if our snipers are still in their original positions"!

Peering through the Night Scope Jaeger followed the outline of the enemy as the Gunny had provided and saw that no one had moved from their original positions.

He was further gladdened by the fact that apparently there were a host of smokers in the ranks of the enemy seeing the brief intermittent flashes of a cigarette in almost every location. He selected each position, giving each Marine a minute long glimpse of his target, before sending him off with the admonition, "Ya have all night to get into position, so take your time". Then he sent the Gunny off down the hill and finally De Jong, without another word. He then slowly made his way down the hill to the hide De Jong had pointed out. An hour and a half later he slowly slithered into the hide, examining his newly acquired home, seeing that De Jong has a very good eye for the necessities of a hide in a rocky place. He discovered and placed a large flat rock over an outcropping that provided him an excellent prone field of fire position of the two snipers below. All he had to do was adjust his aim less than an inch for each shot. Of course he'd have to wait until light for the range finder had no night vision ability.

Now it was time for the long wait, for there would be no further communication between anybody until the sound of his first shot. All was at the ready, the Dragunov loaded and prepositioned, while Jaeger held a single round of the ten millimeter shell in his hand rolling over in his mind the estimated drop characteristics of the round, factoring in the fact that it was a downhill shot in each case.

As good a shot as Jaeger was, there were those much better than him, who never missed at even longer ranges. Those were the real pros of the business. The bullet appeared to be well made. Was it perfectly balanced like the technicians at Quantico always turned out? There was no way of knowing, but he'd examined each and every round that was loaded into the Dragunov, finding no exterior faults with each of the fifty rounds he'd been provided.

One last look into the night vision scope told him all he needed to know for at both of the sniper positions, was the brief intermittent glow of a cigarette in the night.

Every sense he had stayed alert in his conscious mind, all through the night and as the first signs of light started to make itself known over the eastern edge of the hills behind him, he estimated the light level to be reflective by the time he took the shot. A half hour later the light level was such that he removed the range finder from its cover and vectored in to the most distant sniper, reading the distance to be seven hundred ninety yards with the closest sniper ranging in at five hundred thirty yards. 'Very doable', he thought. The more distant shot first then a quick ejection and a slight barrel adjustment, then the nearest subject'. As the time drew near he went through his normal routine, of slowing his breathing down, remembering and being grateful for the two stage trigger that some thoughtful technician had built into the weapon, then over and over in his mind, the sound of the simple three note harmonica refrain that somehow brought inner peace and total concentration and focus, eventually fusing man and weapon into one singularity.

As the light gradually grew upon the horizon, Jaeger saw gradual movement in the far snipers hide. Then he saw the image of a man rise up, visible from the waist up stretching his weary bones as one would normally expect any mortal upon arising from slumber.

Then from the nearest snipers hide, arose the other form, visible from the waist up stretching his bones. As Jaegers finger slowly squeezed the trigger the distant target withdrew a cigarette and started to light it up as the Dragunov roared its disapproval, with the ejection lever moving in a flash and the brief adjustment of the barrel, landing on the second target as the crosshairs, landed on the subjects head guaranteeing the bullets landing squarely in his upper chest. As the first bullet went past the second target he was looking at his counterpart, as the point of impact and the sound arrived at his ears simultaneously. Before he could even react he felt the second round tear through his chest driving him over the edge of his hidey hole and down the hill tumbling over and over, to the ground below.

At the sound of the first gunshot, sporadic gunfire emerged lasting no more than ten seconds as each and every one of the militia tribesmen rose up to see the what and the where, only to be met by a half a clip of auto fire from the M-16's that ended their collective curiosity.

Rising up from his hide, Jaeger could see that each Marine had taken care of his assignment in text book fashion and were working their way to the target, to deliver the Coup de Gras and no doubt gather a souvenir for their efforts as a reminder of the moment in what it meant to be a US Marine.

As Jaeger approached the first hide he was met with the stench of human excrement and supposed the long confinement was too much for a tribesman with a full belly of desert rations too much to hold. He looked at the rifle to be used in their demise and saw that it was merely an old World War One issue British German Mauser bolt action, with a four power scope. Good enough he supposed for someone who knew what they were doing but worlds away from state of the art.

He went over to the other hide seeing the enemy sprawled over the make shift parapet, and once again was met by the odor of excreta, this time coming from over relaxed full bowels, letting forth its mortal load as the newly dead are wont to do..

Then he looked up to the summit seeing that his charges were making their way down the rocky hillside, very slowly and carefully, having been signaled by the Gunny by mirror, as he stood atop a rock outcropping, catching the first early rays of the sun.

A half hour later all has assembled at the bottom of the hill side, with each and every Marine, slinging an AK-47 on their shoulder as a memento for future war stories of their time in paradise.

De Jong came up to Jaeger with a Radio in his hand that he took from the squad commander saying, "At some point they will probably check in with their people and if they don't receive the expected response might well send someone to investigate"!

"Hopefully they'll speak French and since you speak French, you'll have to be the one to talk to them", said Jaeger! "Can you speak any of the local tribal gibberish"?

"Passable Toureg, but not with the local dialects", De Jong replied!

Then as your Brit friends often say, "We'll just have to brazen things out, until our ride out arrives.

As he looked around Jaeger said, "Lotza hills around here, it's a wonder they can get any signal out unless they get up top on the summit, don't ya think"!

"I think I know what you mean and we'll try it out should they call in", said De Jong!

As they looked around they saw that all of the civilians were ecstatic at their arrival, thanking the Marines for their swift and telling action.

An hour later at 0600 local time the unit commander's radio came alive, with the sound of a French specking voice coming over the radio, repeating that the recipient "Come In"! After the third attempt De Jong, went live acknowledging the message in garbled tones, saying that all was well and that no one had arrived yet and that the reception was bad.

The radio then went off air, with De Jong saying, "I don't know how convincing I was, but it was definitely some military type back in N'djamena, making the inquiry"!

"But we're clearly across the frontier in Niger aren't we", asked the Ambassador?

"Do you think that makes any difference to them? Geeze, where oh where, are helmeted United Nations troops" asked Jaeger? "Where are our pals from the Government of Niger"?

"Don't think we want anything to do with any of the locals, for they'd sell us all down the river for the price of a loaf of bread"!

"We'll just have to hunker down and wait for the next bus to come by", jibed the Gunny!

"Seems we have two future warriors in the making over there", said the Gunny!"Both of em got their man without firing a shot, by slitting their throat up close and personal"!

"But isn't the trick to do it without getting any of the spurting blood on your person", jibed De Jong"!

"Yes it is Mr. French Legionnaire, but since neither of those two have celebrated their twenty first birthday yet and aren't even old enough to vote or drink and it's their very first time, I'd think it a pretty good start for them don't ya think"?

"I would have to agree, Mon Sergeant Gunny", said De Jong with a smile!

Jaeger then thought back to the time he slit his very first throat and it was a few days past his nineteenth birthday and now he was an old grizzled veteran almost in his mid-twenties. 'My, how time flies when you're havin' fun', he thought.

Now was occasion when time passes at a snail's pace. When the anticipation of rescue is at the very forefront of everyone's mind and the sun is racing towards its zenith, showering down its intensely radiant blessing and the possibility of all going for naught looms large, due to the unforeseen.

Eventually the Gunny's radio crackled alive with a pilot announcing his arrival at the point of departure and the Gunny responding the corresponding code word that all was well and the package was ready to be airborne. "Everything just five by five", announced the Gunny as he pointed to a spot on the horizon that gradually grew larger by the moment, as it grew lower in the air swooping in for a landing.

As the plane dropped lower and lower, De Jong's radio came alive, with someone speaking in French that two helicopters were on the way to their location with an ETA of fifteen minutes.

As the rescue plane touched down, everyone could see that it was an old pre WWII Curtis C-46 cargo craft, that clearly had seen better days, as everyone ran up to the ship and it made its turn to stop and receive its new cargo, its engines still turning.

Within five scant minutes the ladder came up and the cargo door slammed shut as the single pilot, gunned the twin engines, and slowly gathered takeoff speed as the craft lifted off into the sky.

As the plane took to the air, the loudspeaker crackled over the deafening noise of the engines announcing, "Welcome to Party Airlines. Take a seat on the floor and hang on tight for it seems that we've some company a few miles back and they don't seem friendly. But up ahead is a large cloudbank that we just might lose them in. There won't be any inflight meals and the cocktails will just have at wait. Next stop Lagos Nigeria, so relax and enjoy the noise"!

Gaining altitude, the old aircrafts engines were straining to gain airspace and close the distance to the cloudbank, as the aircraft banked to its port side, and slid nicely into the lower edge of the cloud bank, as all could see as the mists flew by the window, then suddenly banking towards the starboard side as it still struggled to gain altitude, then reaching the top of the cloudbank and banking back towards the port side with a small dive that kept them well hidden from their pursuers. For the next hour the pilot banked left then right, climbing then diving slightly clinging desperately to the confines of the clouds. Finally leveling out at some eighteen thousand feet, as the intercom crackled, "Settle down folks, and put a cork in it for there just ain't any facilities on this trip. ETA into Lagos is a couple of hours, more or less and if ya don't like it, sue me"!

On the flight back to the states, Jaeger thought about the landing in

Lagos. Waiting some five hours at the far end of a taxiway, accompanied by some lower level State Department personnel from the local Embassy while watching a Gulf Oil Company private jet, swoop in and pick up the Ambassador only for a flight back to Andrews AFB, while all the rest had to wait for a late arriving unmarked C-130 to land, lower its rear deck and herd all the rest into its cargo hold and follow the Ambassador back to Andrews.

Sergeant De Jong made his goodbyes to everyone beforehand, disappearing into a privately owned Citroen motorcar. But beforehand he shook hands with Jaeger saying, "If you ever get tired of all the boredom in the Marines, fly over to Marseilles, for the Legion can use your talents", with a sly wink!

When they touched down at Andrews, all the State Department civilians deplaned while the ground personnel refueled the craft and a single passenger got on the plane just before departure.

As Colonel Joe Bollinger walked up to Jaeger sitting next to the Gunny, they both started to rise but Bollinger waved them back down saying, "As you were Marines"! "The minute I found that you'd gotten everybody out, I pulled a few strings, got some temp orders cut and got the first flight east to Andrews.

"We've been monitoring your intermittent radio transmissions from the beginning by those new satellites and the tech guys had to know if the Gryphon worked in the real world. Seems you made it work"!

Just then, the C-130's engines came to life and all conversation ceased until they were airborne.

The Colonel was eager to be debriefed about the entire mission, but Jaeger referred most of the questions to the Gunny, for he was an integral part of the mission for the most part.

They would find something for Jaeger to do once he got back to Camp Pendleton, for the next forty five days, until he officially achieved "FIGMO" status his last thirty days in the service, he recalled some noise being made by the Camp Personnel office, about assigning him to the armory or the firing range on a temporary basis. His last thirty days, Colonel Chicken Shit usually sat quiet, so one could gradually accustom oneself back to the morays and folkways of the feather merchants. Perhaps he would go work on his tan on any of the local beaches. Maybe get a little drunk a time or two, or three. But somewhere deep in the recesses of his mind was a desire to live a life of normalcy once again. He'd proven to himself that he was every bit the Marine his father was and more, far more in about the same time frame. Sure his dad had multiple tours up country amongst the 'slopes', but his son had set foot on every single continent except Antarctica and left a trail of extremely bad people rendered useless in his wake. He would just love to sit down on the front porch, back at the family ranch, just he and his dad, with a couple of ice cold longnecks of Pearl Beer and trade war stories back and forth. He'd seen just about every form of treachery that man could foist upon each other in his brief time with the Corps. learning to trust no one completely. He'd taken life from others in just about every way possible, through both direct and indirect means.

Perhaps his dad had mellowed a bit while Jaeger was away, recalling the hasty manner of his departure from the ranch one stormy evening in the dark of night, the fight between his mother and father and his final face off with the Old Man. The final words between them still rang in his head, with his father yelling, "Boy ain't how old ya are, it's how many miles ya traveled"! And Jaeger responding, casting down the gauntlet, yelling back, "You see a boy in front of you, the you kick his ass right now", standing his ground in front of a proven man who'd taken a host of lives in his time, in the service of his country.

One thing they both knew, was that if either of them struck the other in anger, 'That would be it', between them regardless of the victor. Fortunately his mother intervened, pressing the signed and documented Marine enlistment papers and five hundred dollars cash in his hands and escorted him out into the night for the long trip to Camp Pendleton and a new life in the Marines.

Admittedly Jaeger was a hot head back then, turning his other cheek to no man. But he'd mellowed somewhat during his absence from civilian life, learning important lessons such as,

"Control your passions, don't let your passions control you", "Fear is both the great motivator and the mind killer" and a host of other old aphorism's that served him well. More important he'd come far closer to his maker during this period, reasoning that the only thing that he could control in his life was how he responded to the events before him. For something, somehow kept him alive, 'but for what', he wondered?

During the flight back, he came to the conclusion that he'd take his savings, coupled with the meager mustering out stipend, go back to Texas, plop his government funded University of Maryland correspondence transcripts at the registrar's office and see if he could enroll and get a College Degree in something from the University of Texas. 'Yeah', he decided. 'He'd become a mere student and perhaps a kid again'…

26

"**H**appy New Year and welcome to the Cotton Bowl for the football game between The University of Texas Long Horns and the University of Miami Hurricanes, this very first day of the New Year"!

"I'm Porter Jolly"!

"And I'm Mike Cantrell, bringing this telecast to you courtesy of TXSN, the Texas Sports Cable Network, partnering with the Universal Broadcasting System for this Nationwide Telecast"!

"Porter, this is far more than just any football game, or a gridiron meeting between two great institutions of higher learning isn't it"?

"You're darn right Mike. This is also a story about a mystery man.

About a young man who seemingly came out of nowhere. He was a walk on last spring to the University of Texas football program, who has apparently led this team into the Promised Land avoiding a season of mediocrity. It's now just an hour before the kickoff and it'll take just about that time to tell you the tale of the "Uberballer", aka, "Jaeger"!

"So much to tell Porter, so many facets about this man that it's hard to tell where to begin"!

"Right you are Mike, so let's just plunge right in and tell all that we do know and later in the game can perhaps we can fill in the rest"!

"About this time a year ago, a young man fresh out his enlistment of the United States Marine Corps, enrolled at the University of Texas. Somehow during his time in the Marines, most of which was on overseas assignments, he managed to garner enough college credits from the military's connection with the University of Maryland's correspondence program to be accepted at UT, as a sophomore. People in the know tell us that from almost the day after he moved into the dorm, he was running the stands and when it rained he ran the stands in the field house. Now I just gotta tell ya, that anyone who's played the game at any level hates running up and down the stands"!

"Come time for the spring practice, he approached the coaches and gets a tryout for the team as a 'walk on' and that's where the fun begins, for darn few who walk on get to suit up and those who do, are usually cannon fodder for the active team players with a full jock ride. Now the thing that stands out with this individual is that he has no first or middle name. On his birth certificate he is simply known by his last name which we all know as "Jaeger", which in German means "Hunter" and fans he is every bit of that"!

"But that's not what got him on this team. Days before, when he was fooling around with some members of the Alumni on the practice field, he was seen doing the following, kicking off the ball repeatedly from the forty yard line and burying it past the back end zone marker. Then punting the ball repeatedly fifty yards with five second hang times. Then what really got everybody's attention was his standing on the goal line and throwing the ball with a decent spiral and having it hit the opposite goal line a hundred yards away. And this was what got him the opportunity to suit up, but ladies and gentlemen it gets better".

"As is with everybody else he was tested and measured, with a forty yard dash time in the four and a half second category. Very respectable for a man who measures almost six feet four inches tall and weighs a very lean two hundred forty pounds. His vertical jumps would the envy of most basketball coaches and in the weight room he surpassed all but a few linemen.

But that's not what got him on the team. During the spring scrimmages when the walk on's suit up with the rest of the last string players, was where his star shone the brightest. First he was tested as a defensive lineman and repeatedly stuffed running plays in his area for no gain. Then he was tested at the linebacker position, always either outright tackling anyone in his area, or sacking the quarterback repeatedly or intercepting the ball on pass plays and running the ball back for significant gains, time and again. "There wasn't a single practice where his efforts didn't end up with someone being in need of the team doctor, thanks to the "Uberballer".

"By the midpoint of the Spring Practice session, the stands gradually drew the attention of Alumni eager to see this wunderkind that seemingly dropped out of nowhere. Then he was tried at the tight end position and surprisingly enough proved to have soft hands that could catch any ball in his area."

"Finally he was tested at the fullback position and proved to be a devastating blocker. But the proof of the pudding, the acid test was could he run with the ball? His off the line speed was such that the quarterback wasn't able to hand the ball off to him quick enough on running plays. By the time the center had the ball in the quarterbacks hands and turned to hand off the ball Jaeger was past him and into the line".

"With some practice and adjustment, the problem now fell on the linemen many of which were trampled by a charging bull running up their backsides. In time this too was corrected. He was and is a strictly straight ahead runner who always gets yards, sure handed never fumbling and what's the best part, people just hate it when he's carrying the ball and they have to tackle him, for its gonna hurt. Gang tackling is the only thing that worked, to bring this raging bull to the ground".

"Now for some reason that no one could get to the bottom of,

Texas's starting Quarterback Trey Markland, and Jaeger had developed some bad blood between them, probably because he was tired of the repeated sacks he'd received at the hands of Jaeger when he was playing at the linebacker position. Markland had this busted pass play that he'd improvised into a running play and instead of doing the safe slide as Jaeger was closing in on him, decided to take him on".

"Roll the tape please. As you can see he tries to take him on Mano a Mano and pays the price with the helmet separating from his head, the ball squirting loose and our starting quarterback rendered unable to continue for the entire season with concussion and a fractured vertebrae".

"The head coach Vern Bachman, is more than unhappy and vents on Jaeger ala Woody Hays at Ohio State. Jaeger is told to leave the field. The head coach vows that our boy will never wear the suit of the Texas Longhorns. But later in the day, after a meeting with several influential members of the Varsity Alumni Association and the Athletic Director, certain persuasions are applied, sanity prevails and the "Uberballer", is officially a member of the team.

"Some shuffling of the roster occurs, and the rest of the team has the rest of the spring and summer, to heal before two a day practice begins at midsummer in preparation for the season opener".

"Jaeger continues with his classes the rest of the spring semester, and then enrolls in the summer semester completing both. Now Coach Bachman, we later discover has been persuaded to accept this barbarian to his team, but has no intention to fully exploit his talents unless absolutely necessary delegating him to special teams."

"Since pre game time is an issue, I'll simply say the first two games that Texas should've won were narrowly lost, by repeated turnovers by the team at large, with only five scoring touchdown in eight quarters. The only things that kept them in those two games were the play of the defense and the special teams.

But the stand out play of the "Uberballer" was spectacular, causing both of the opponents to lose the services of their runback specialists due to crushing collisions with "Der Uberballer".

"Roll tape please, then we'll pause for a commercial"!

During the commercial break Jolly looked at Mike Cantrell and said, "Ya think Texas has a chance against Miami"?

"The bookies in Las Vegas have Miami up by four TD's Porter. Of course we can't mention that over the air. After all Miami is a Juggernaut and Jaeger is just one man. He gets hurt and what was a slim chance is now zip"!

Silence then hung over the broad casting booth with the producer signaling over the headphone, "Broadcast in three, two and one"!

"Welcome back to the Cotton Bowl pre game telecast, of the game between the University of Texas Longhorn's and the Miami University Hurricanes. I'm Mike Cantrell and I'll now turn things back over to my partner Porter Jolly to continue in what is a stirring narrative of an amazing story regarding the man with just one name. Porter, take it away"!

"We left you with visual examples of what one man can do to another during the course of a brutal game and the game is American Football. I must apologize for what we should've done was alert you to the fact that any videotaped examples of plays is not for the weak or faint hearted and in the videotaped plays that will come up, we will pause for a few seconds while those who wish, may avert their eyes"!

"Continuing with the narrative, we find that by the third game of the season, something had to be done. The entire Texas campus was in an uproar, for its been an embarrassment for the Longhorns to have lost their first two games of the season, especially to teams they should've beaten, by sloppy play, turnovers and the Alumni are just about have the coach all but quartered and drawn. Not in anyone's memory has the level of play sunk so low".

"By the third game of the season significant changes have been made in the lineup, and the most significant of which is that in addition to his special team play, Jaeger the Uberballer is now playing at Defensive end and after the kickoff by Jaeger that landed well into the end zone, The Baylor Bears have the ball at their own twenty yard line and we'll slow down the tape so everyone can appreciate what happens next. Roll tape please"!

"As you can see Jaeger is playing, right defensive end and the offensive left guard gets completely upended landing on his keester, and in football parlance it's called being 'Pancaked', with Jaeger running full steam right over him, and right here, as the Baylor quarter-back drops back attempting to throw his first pass he's his squarely in the chest by Jaeger who strips him of the ball and steps on his throwing hand running into the end zone.

The quarterback had to leave the field and was out for the season with multiple bones broken in his throwing hand".

"The rest of the game has Jaeger running wild on both the offence and the defensive side of the ball with Texas eking out its first win of the season".

"We are going to skip the next two games at this point, with Texas still having problems at quarterback, throwing interceptions, and receivers unable to catch the ball with anydegree of consistency and running backs fumbling the ball at crucial times of the game. Yet they won both games not because of superior play but capitalizing on the mistakes of the other teams.

Of course in both games, the Uberballer was responsible for two running touchdowns and five quarterback sacks, two of which resulting in a Texas touchdown. Now with a record of three wins and two defeats, the team is at the mid-season mark, with all three wins coming at the expense of conference teams. Their conference record is now at three wins and a single loss, the other loss being in a non-conference game".

"Now I want to focus on the Minnesota game, where Texas travels up to the land of ten thousand lakes to take on a very difficult University of Minnesota team, the experts said have a good chance at a Rose Bowl bid, from the Big Ten Conference. Their star player is their tight end

Larson Magnusson, a bona fide All American with ten touchdowns so far on the year and over forty receptions, at midseason". "Every bit the size and stature of the 'Uberballer', a coaching decision is made to place Jaeger, at linebacker and stick to Magnusson everywhere he goes. For those football savvy fans that know the game, the game was almost an afterthought as to the battle between these two behemoths. Both seem to give as well as receive to each other, with Jaeger seeming having met his match at last".

"Jaeger can't seem to get to the quarter back with Magnusson matching his every move, yet Magnusson has caught but one pass reception, for minimal yardage with Jaeger bringing him to the ground with a savage tackle. On the very next play, 'Roll tape please'; Magnusson brings Jaeger to the ground with an equally savage cross body block, allowing the running back to gain significant yardage".

"Back and forth all game long, first Magnusson gaining the advantage, only to have Jaeger gain the advantage on the very next play. No known words pass between the two, as each know they've probably met their match in the other. Like two heavyweight fighters trading lethal blows with each other and at the end of each play nodding their heads at the other as if to say, 'How'd ya like that one stud'?"

"Now we come to the point in the game at the very end, with less than a minute to go in the game, and the play that placed two entire states in dire concern. Now we're going to roll the video tape in slow motion, while I describe the action, for at real time everything happened so fast, that few realized what happened till after it was over."

"Now Texas is ahead by a field goal and the Golden Gophers are driving down the field and have to score a touchdown and it seems like the Gophers have the momentum. The play is a swing pass to the running back out in the flats, 'Roll tape please', Magnusson runs down the field ten yards and turns as if on a button hook pass, with Jaeger with him step by step.

When Magnusson stops and turns, Jaeger slips falling to the ground. As the ball is thrown to the running back, the quarterback leads him just a bit too much and the running back catches the ball on the fingertips trying to gather it in when he is met with a jarring tackle by the Texas cornerback. The ball is now in the air as we can see, with Magnusson coming back to the ball and snatching it out of the air before it can fall to the ground. As he turns he sees Jaeger now just yards away with a full head of steam bearing down on him. Magnusson plants his feet, takes a single step in Jaegers direction, trying to brace for the collision and tuck the ball away in a split second and the two collide. Head to head like two great mountain Rams during the rutting season, both bouncing off of each other, both heads rocking back with their helmets flying off their heads and the sound of their crashing pads echoing throughout the stadium over the din of thousands of screaming fans with a single 'Thwock'. At the very moment of impact the ball squirts vertically out of Magnusson's grasp, up to chest height and the Texas safety, Dax Redbone, coming up to make a tackle was greeted with the gift of the football, snatching it out of thin air, with the surprised look of a burglar caught in the act and in midstride, ran along the sidelines seventy five yards for a touchdown".

"It took about a half minute for everyone to look back up field and see two fallen warriors that had given their all lying face down just feet away from each other. The referees blew their whistles stopping the game while the team doctors and staff came running out on the field. Jaeger was the first to come to, rolling slowly over on his stomach waving the others away and slowly coming up to his knees, then sinking forward to be held up by his two arms, struggling to regain his breath. After a few minutes he slowly rose to be greeted by the silence of a stadium full of concern. As we can see by the tape, Jaeger is in the process of regaining consciousness and usually when this happens some of the crowd cheer, but this day the entire stadium is silent, their concern is with Lars Magnusson lying face down on the turf, his right leg jerking intermittently."

"Jaeger takes a look at Magnusson, nods his head and slowly makes his way back to the Texas sidelines, fending off attempts to help him, taking one agonizing step after the other".

"Magnusson was eventually carted off the field and the game concluded with the Texas win. Both Magnusson and Jaeger were taken to the nearest hospital and kept overnight for medical observation. Both were diagnosed with concussions, yet Jaeger was wheeled out of the hospital the next afternoon while Magnusson was kept in the medical facility undergoing a battery of tests. By night fall as the Texas team winged their way back to Austin, the newscasts were full of the news that Lars Magnusson's football days were over, that several vertebra were misplaced in this neck touching his spinal column and that surgery was indicated the following day to correct the vertebral displacement. This very video tape of that final scoring play was viewed repeatedly on sports broadcasts throughout the land.

Throughout the week Jaeger was kept from suiting up for practice, but by the following Saturday he appeared in the locker room and growled to the equipment manager, "Tape the ankles", as the head coach walked by he nodded his head, in spite of the recommendations of his team's medical staff. "Texas Christian University was the next victim, of the 'Uberballers' wrath not only losing the game, but three of their starting players for the season to the seemingly unchristian actions of Jaeger, who somehow ratcheted his game up a notch flying all over the field causing fumbles, sacking quarterbacks, stopping plays dead in their tracks and with the Longhorns finally scoring multiple touchdowns on their own. Fewer fumbles, dropped passes and better blocking ruled the day". "Enrolled in the fall semester, while the season was under way, Jaeger tried unsuccessfully to make his way around the UT campus without causing a stir, but even sunglasses, couldn't hide his local celebrity. Even his laconic professors, normally unimpressed by the mindless brutes that played ball had to, ever so briefly, acknowledge his achievements on the field of battle, especially since he appeared to be a competent student". As much as Jaeger tried to avoid his new celebrity status, he was constantly hounded by the local and out of town sports media. Finally the Athletic Director summoned the campus police to place the campus off limits to the media. The lone exception was game day and that with the exception of the stadium only.

Finally the annual shootout with Oklahoma was near and a trip to the Cotton Bowl Stadium in Dallas, seemingly neutral ground for the two teams presented itself, with a sold out crowd of standing room only".

"As was and still is, Jaegers custom as part of his pregame workup, he always broke out his harmonica and sought out a place in the locker room and played repeatedly but three notes on his mouth harp".

"Remember that old western a few years back with Charles Bronson, Henry Fonda, Jason Robards and Claudia Cardinali, Porter? What was its name"?

"Right you are Mike. I believe the name of that flick was, "That was the way things were in the West", or something like that"!

"And Porter, didn't the hero in that flick go by the name of 'Harmonica', since nobody knew his name"?

"Correct you are Mike and every time he started to play the harmonica, someone soon after died, if I recall the plot line correctly! Somehow there's a parallel here, of sorts, for as we sit here and talk about the man, he's somewhere in the bowels of the stadium preparing himself, by playing those three notes over and over fixing his gaze on an object and getting deep within himself, for what lays ahead"!

"What about the Oklahoma game, Porter"?

"Ah yes, the annual Oklahoma shootout, between two institutions dedicated to higher learning, that draw the battle lines annually to engage each other in a very uncivilized manner, under the guise of civilized rules. Like a train wreck, where people want to avert their eyes, yet no one will, lest they miss the action".

"At the very last play of the game, with seconds ticking away, and the winner of this contest representing their conference in the Cotton Bowl this very day, Oklahoma finds them self on their own seven yard line, having stuffed three running plays by Texas in succession, being ahead by four points with only a single touchdown between them and immortality. Jaeger is sent in with a play from the bench, but in the huddle he gives the quarterback another play, which is a student body to the left end run, with Jaeger carrying the ball."

"Roll tape please Mister Engineer. As you can see the ball is centered and everyone is moving to the left. This play has been tried before twice, but has never worked for the Oklahoma linebackers are just too fast. Jaeger gets the ball, but after his second step plants his foot and moves to his right passing the flailing arms of the Oklahoma defenders barely and running obliquely back towards his right and by the time of his arrival at the ten yard line Oklahoma defenders start to catch up with Jaeger and by brute strength alone with his legs churning piston like, drives himself into the end zone with no less than four defenders flailing away helplessly"!

"As is his custom, Jaeger simply touches the ball down in the end zone and walks back to his bench without further ado". The game is won and Texas is going to the Cotton Bowl. The stadium erupts, with one side of the stadium experiencing the ecstasy of victory and the other the agonizing pain of defeat. Now Mike, the following day the entire

University discovers their opponent in the Cotton Bowl, which is the University of Miami, who should be playing in the Sugar Bowl, but by some freak of the NCAA is placed second in their conference to Florida State and elects to play in the Cotton Bowl"!

"Now Miami U. is almost unbeaten and their only loss was to Florida State by a single point as a result by a questionable call of the game officials and has won all their other games easily by wide margins. Quite unlike the Texas Longhorns who have struggled all season long, with an offense that is questionable at best and a defense that is mostly held together by the quiet leadership of one man."

"Now for many years, the Hurricanes have been famous for sending not only a horde of players but a gaggle of coaches to the National Football League. Almost like a training school for gladiators being sent into the arena, honing the football skills to a razors edge, with scant regard for such mundane things like academics. Yet the football program makes the University a great deal of money and pays a host of the University's bills as it does for a great many other institutions of higher learning in the land".

"Now as game time draws near, I want to say something about the man of some mystery, the Uberballer Jaeger. While many things are known, much of his recent life is a black hole.

He is in his mid-twenties, born and raised in Waco Texas, the son of Morgan and Sarah Jaeger the scions of a successful ranching and farming business along with a host of other enterprises, that sit astride a very large chunk of land northwest of Waco that's been in their family since the days of the Texas Republic and is still intact and thriving.

Jaeger's father Morgan, is a former Marine with multiple tours in Viet Nam and for some reason they haven't spoken to each other since Jaeger left high school in the greater Waco area rather hurriedly after his Senior Year."

"Now while no one is talking about it, directly rumor has it that the 'Uberballer', left the area in the dark of night with the County Sheriff on his trail and the next thing we know is that he joined the Marine's at the age of seventeen with his mother's approval, and disappeared into the bowels of the Corps. We know that apart from the many schools he attended to hone his skills as a Marine, he spent the bulk of his time overseas, ostensibly as an embassy guard, yet attempts at finding out much, more than that are met with Governmental rebuff. In short, nobody is talking about the man with but one official cognomen. Yet as we speak, the entire campus of the University of Texas, speaks as one of his accomplishments. He's not the 'Rah Rah' kind of guy, full of brag and bluster. While you'll see him lead the team out of the tunnel, you won't see him charging out of the tunnel with eyes all ablaze screaming at the top of his lungs. After each play you'll see him get up slowly and get ready for the next play, then explode off the ball. His fellow team members tell us that off the field he's a mild mannered and polite individual. But once he steps onto a football field, any semblance of civilized behavior disappears".

"The man has many recent acquaintances, but no known friends. He doesn't hang out with the team; he's not a member of any fraternity, keeping a low profile on campus. Few at the campus at Austin hold out much hope of the team winning this game. The best they can hope for is that the team puts up a good showing and keeps things close".

"Der Jaegermeister has carried the team this far by his exploits and there just has to be a limit as to what one man can do".

"I see by the old clock on the wall the kickoff is just fifteen minutes away so we'll take a pause for the cause so our producer can pay some bills. Don't go away now we'll see ya in a few ticks of the clock"!

At that very moment, Jaeger was suited up in the locker room sitting on the bench hunched over, playing the three notes on the harmonica, over and over. The team had grown used to his pregame mantra, during the course of the season, a few of which took the time to emulate his apparent solitude of the mind, readying themselves for the carnage that was a certainty.

Coach Bachman looked at his watch, and then made his way through the locker room yelling, "Saddle up people, its game time". Then he stopped in front of Jaeger saying, "Time to lead the team out"!

Jaeger looked up, tapped the moisture out of the harmonica tossing it inside the locker, slowly rose and made his way out of the locker room and down the long hall way deep inside the stadium, followed by the echoing route step clicking of the cleats on concrete. As he reached the entrance to the field he stopped, waiting for the coach to join the front of the column. His mind going deep into that sacred place where no one else was allowed to follow, repeating over and over, 'There is no yesterday, there is no tomorrow, there is only NOW'!

"Welcome back to the Cotton Bowl for the New Year's Classic between the University of Texas Longhorns and the University of Miami Hurricanes. I'm Mike Cantrell with my partner, Porter Jolly and Porter I see the Longhorns assembling at the end of the tunnel and of course, to lead them out is the Uberballer, the Jaegermeister standing there, waiting for the signal to enter the field"!

"Porter, can we get a camera close up of the tunnel? Ah yes, there he is, standing there at the head of the team, yet perhaps it's the camera angle, or the angle of the sunlight and the shade but I can't see his eyes, can you Porter"?

"Yes Mike, I can see his eyes beneath his helmet, if that's what you want to call it. I can barely make out two hot burning coals ready to ignite, with slow puffs of steam due to the cold air coming from his nostrils, almost inhuman"! "As the Longhorn band reaches the crescendo signaling the end of the pregame festivities Porter, we see Coach Vern Bachman join the head of the team leading them out with Jaeger close behind, in a slow trot followed by the entire team with determined looks on their faces and jaws set while at the other end of the Cotton Bowl, the Hurricanes come flying out of the tunnel just like the Hurricanes they profess to be"! As Jaeger set foot on the field leading the team behind the coach, he started to feel almost euphoric, for this is what he was destined to do. 'Be the instrument for the public's pleasure'. They must have their escape from the mundane and he and the others were to provide for their pleasure. 'Our tribe is better than yours, this day', he thought. For the last two weeks the team had almost lived in the field house, between practice sessions on the field, viewing endless tapes of the Miami team and their personnel looking for weakness' to exploit and finding precious few. Of course Jaeger was certain the Miami team had done exactly the same and would be on target to put Jaeger out of the game early, so they could run up the score, by half time and play their bench. He knew the Miami team was full of trash talkers at the line of scrimmage and were the most penalized team in their conference, just short of NCAA sanctions. But he had a plan which would depend on certain timing of conditions on the field.

"As the co-captains of the two teams come together at midfield for the coin toss Porter, the tension in the stadium is building to the breaking point"!

"Right you are Mike and my guess is that whoever wins the toss, Texas's strength will be on defense, while Miami's strength is on both offense and defense, but my guess is that Texas will want to kickoff, so Jaegers ability to kick the ball past the end line will negate the runback ability of the Hurricanes, which by the way, has nine kickoff run backs for touchdowns this year, along with three punt returns that went the distance for the score. Now Jaegers consistent five second hang time of punts in the air, will probably negate that advantage for the Hurricanes"!

"Here's the coin flip Porter and Miami wins the coin toss electing to receive"!

"Not exactly a win Mike, because Jaeger will boot it out of the end zone"!

As predicted, Jaeger put the ball on the tee, took his position on the Texas forty yard line and started for the ball, kicking it well past the end line and out of the field of play.

"Did ya notice Mike, how Jaeger angled the ball to the left of the receiver who was positioned on the goal line? There was no way that ball was going to be returned. Advantage to the Longhorns for the moment"!

The first three plays of the game were running plays away from Jaeger who was playing defensive end for the moment. Misdirection plays designed to see if Jaeger pursued recklessly or stayed in position. On the third play that ran away from him for a first down, the half back that ran in his direction tried a cut block on Jaegers blind side and sensing that he was about to be cut, Jaeger did a scissors kick at the last split second providing the Hurricane blocker to have nothing but air and as Jaeger came down, his elbow struck the half back luckily in the solar plexus breaking multiple ribs and leaving the runner writhing on the ground gasping for air after the play was over.

"Seems like the 'Jaegermeister' has drawn first blood, Porter, for the Miami half back is on the ground after an attempted blind side chop block coming up croppers and leaving Jaeger unscathed"!

"You can bet that came in from the bench Mike and there will be more where that came from before this afternoon is over"!

On the second set of downs the Longhorns held forcing Miami to punt the ball and the Texas receiver, Dax Redbone, the fastest man on the team, eluded the first wave of Miami tacklers and veers off to the sidelines at an angle running down the field at flank speed for a touchdown, causing the stadium to erupt in cheers.

"Jayesus Mary and Joseph, Porter, did you see that fella run"? The entire Cotton Bowl is erupting like a pregnant volcano and Texas has indeed drawn first blood"! The stadium is shaking under our feet"!

Jaeger kicked off again burying the ball well past the end line negating any runback. On the very first play on a new set of downs, Miami set in a spread formation with their flankers flooding the right side of the field. The ball was snapped and the two lines met with a mighty clash of bodies. The quarterback dropped back and let fly with a perfectly arcing pass catching the flanker in mid stride. As the ball left the quarterback's hand Jaeger crashed into him sending him into the turf at an awkward angle. Just as Jaeger jumped up to the cheers of the stadium, he turned to see the Miami receiver running across the goal line for a touchdown.

"Well Porter, Miami finally got off the schnide and scored with a great throw".

"Yes Mike, but the fact that the safety fell down, as the flanker made his break made it all the easier for Miami".

"But wait Mike, back down the field the Miami quarterback is not getting up and is writhing in pain. Rerack the replay tapes and I'm sure that Jaegers fine hand is behind this"!

The slow motion video replay showed Jaeger hitting the Miami quarterback just as he let loose of the ball, driving him to the ground with such a bone crunching force that it was almost too painful to watch on replay. Those in the stadium were focused on the touch down and only saw the aftermath with the Miami quarterback writhing in agony on the ground.

After the video replay, the announcer could only say, "Brute force Porter. Sheer brute force"!

"With less than five minutes passed in the first quarter the Hurricanes are back in the game. But with their All American quarterback being transported off the field with what appears to be a very painful shoulder separation to his throwing shoulder, I suspect that before this afternoon is finished, the medical staffs of both teams will be very busy."!

"Miami kicked off and the Long horn receiver brought the ball back to the thirty yard line. On the very first play, a full blitz of all the linebacker and a cornerback descended on the Texas quarterback as he dropped back to pass, overwhelming the linemen and three of the Miami defenders hit the Texas quarterback before he could even draw back to pass the ball, with such a force he was buried under an avalanche of angry players. As the whistle blew ending the play by the referee, two more Miami players drove into the pile, guaranteeing severe injury to the Longhorn quarterback.

"Oh my god Porter, did you see that"?

"Looks like an intentional foul by the Miami defense, and there it is a late hit flag by the refs"!

On the sidelines Jaeger standing next to the Defensive Coach muttered absently to himself, "So that's how it's gonna be, is it"?

The coach replied, "How did ya think it would be"?

As the Longhorn quarter back was carried from the filed completely unconscious, the coaches scrambled to find the red shirt substitute quarterback, a true freshman, hurriedly tossed into the fray. Back and forth both teams went to the end of the first quarter whistle came and the teams traded places. On the next running play the Hurricanes stuffed it for a small loss, as well as the next and the next, then Jaeger went on the field to punt.

The ball left his leg, and gained altitude, arcing gently skyward catching some of the breeze that had suddenly entered the stadium. As Jaeger ran down the field after it, he counted the seconds the ball was in the air in his mind. As the ball landed in the receivers hands just barely since he had to back pedal furiously to catch it, Jaeger counted slightly over five seconds hang time, giving his mates more than sufficient time to arrive.

But somehow the receiver had eluded the first wave of Texas player and veered off to the sidelines, behind a wall of Miami blockers shedding Longhorn tacklers one by one. Jaeger took a quick angle of approach at the first two blockers hoping to slow the runner down just enough so the pursuing Longhorns could catch up. He left his feet throwing himself into first two blockers and sure enough they all went down in a heap, but the nimble runback specialist simply leaped over the heap with a stride that would've done a track and field high hurdler proud, losing nary a step and continuing into the end zone for the score.

As Jaeger picked himself up, all he could say to himself was, "Damn, that guy is good", as he walked back to his side of the field.

Up in the telecasting booth high above the stadium, the sports casting team was verbally exhibiting their amazement at the display of athletic abilities of the Hurricanes. When Porter Jolly noted, "Hold on a second folks, seems the Uberballer has struck again. For yet another Hurricane player is down. Jaeger seems to have crashed into two players, and we'll roll the tape back and play it in slow motion. Roll Tape please"! As the video tape showed Jaeger crashing into the Miami blockers and the runner striding over them, another camera focused on the collision, noting that Jaeger was the first to get up slowly and as he walked back to his sidelines, the first Miami blocker started to rise, while the second lay prostrate on the side marker, face down in the turf. "Another one bites the dust, Porter", mused the announcer.

"Like I said Mike, it's going to be a long afternoon for the medical staffs of both teams"!

For the rest of the second quarter, Jaeger was played at full back, his main purpose being to block on the running plays of the Longhorns and to protect their new freshman quarterback on the few passing plays attempted. The team ran out of steam on the Miami, twenty yard line settling for a field goal. Their next set of down's yielded another field goal.

"And there it is folks, the end of the first half the score is Texas thirteen and Miami fourteen", heralded Porter Jolly up in the broadcast booth.

"What are your thoughts Porter, on how the first half rolled out"?

"Well Mike, I have my binoculars on Jaeger as he walks off the sidelines and into the locker room, being passed by the other players and the coaches and I just gotta say that he looks all but played out. I just wonder if he'll have anything left in the second half"?

"But Porter, that's just how he is, isn't he? To me he appears to be conserving his energy for the field of play, rather than the show for the fans"!

"Right you are Mike, between plays he moves at a glacial pace, but I want to focus everyone's attention on his apparent leadership skills. It would appear that he acts like another coach on the field of play, having seen him call two time outs at just the right moment apparently usurping the coach's prerogative yet being spot on it his timing and I noted not a single objection when he reached the sidelines. More important, on defense he takes over, telling certain players certain things and I've noted it's almost as if he knows just where the ball is going next"?

"Are you suggesting that he has a certain sixth sense Porter"?

"I just don't know Mike, but look at two things, how many folks are gone from the field of play in the first half? What, four, or is it five Miami players, that are through for the day thanks to him, plus haw many tackles does he have in the first half? Eight, that's the number eight and each guy he tackles, gets up real slow"!

"But what about the level of play Texas has exhibited"?

"Right you are Mike. Not a single fumble or interception for the entire first half. Not a single penalty by Texas. The very problem that's plagued the team all season long has thus far been absent from the Longhorns playbook. Miami's vaunted running game all but shut down with but fifty two yards rushing and the passing game with the exception of that one long pass in the first quarter is operating in the shadow of what the team is capable of"!

"Porter, do ya really think Texas can pull this thing off"?

"Mike common sense tells me that Miami is so deep in well trained football talent, that the coaches are at this very moment reading the riot act to the team in their locker room. With eighty yards worth of penalties in the first half of play, is a gift to the Longhorns and Miami will have to play well within them selves in the second half, or else the wagering community will take a very nasty bath by games end. Texas for the first time all season is playing disciplined football and give me discipline over talent any day"!

"So Porter, you're saying that Texas does have a chance to pull this off"?

"Texas does have a chance, although slim, to win the game, but if they lose their last quarterback and there's no one else to play the position? So let's see just what Miami does about that."?

"Do you suspect that Miami will be on a crusade to disable the Texas quarterback, Porter"?

"At this point and with what's at stake, I suspect anything. One more thing, focus on the play of both team's offensive and defensive lines. There is a brutal war going on between these people, especially in the pileups away from the scrutiny of the refs. Twice as many penalties could have been called as have been called. Hopefully the refs just haven't seen them. But anybody running into the line of scrimmage is in for a real beating. My guess is the second half of this game will stay in our memories for some time to come."

During the all too brief half time, Jaeger went to his gym bag inside his locker and to the plastic bag that contained the very last of the Dexedrine amphetamines he got while in the Corps. Great for keeping one awake and for providing a boost when all the energy to accomplish a task seemed to be gone. Hunching over the tiny glassine bag he withdrew one of the two remaining capsules, mouthing one of them and secreting the other in his helmet for the fourth quarter, out of sight of peering eyes. He walked over to the water fountain to take a gulp of water while the coach was talking to the players, when he returned he reached for his harmonica. Since his locker was the last in line away from the coach's verbal epistle, he started to softly play the three notes, over and over, each time putting a different style and tremolo to the notes, to change the level of monotony.

Coach Bachman heard the notes softly played at the far end of the lockers and as usual it irritated him, for reasons that were private, for he just didn't like the Uberballer. The guy just wouldn't fall into line. Wouldn't get with the program it seemed and the team started to copy his style, which he had to admit, turned things around thus saving his coaching ass. Here was a man in his mid-fifties, who had lived and breathed football all his adult life and in walks someone less than half his age, saying little yet leading by example his team from the abyss and possibly into the promised land. Bachman had lost control of the team last summer and he knew it. It was all he could do to put a lid on his professional jealousy but what else could he do? His talent and football savvy was taking all of them along for the ride. What got Bachman's pride the most, was the certain knowledge, that if Texas did pull this off, Jaeger would be besieged by interviews and the toast of Texas, yet take zero credit and praise the coaching staff and the rest of the team. He just had to give the guy his head and let things happen. "Hear the serenade from the Jaegermeister", said Coach Bachman!

"Hear it summon our future. Imagine the ghosts of all those who played this game on this very field, in the days gone by. Keep playing within your capabilities as you have so far and the Longhorns will be victorious. Enter back on that field of combat, with the fortitude and determination that we cannot be beaten this very day"! Then the coach looked over to Jaeger, sitting alone at the far end of the locker room playing that wretched harmonica, staring at the floor seemingly oblivious to his surroundings. "Jaeger, kommen sie heir", the coach yelled! "And say a few words to the team before we take the field"

Jaeger stopped his playing, looked in the coach's direction, stood up slowly and put the harmonica on the shelf, grabbed his helmet and walked over to where the others were. As he glanced around the locker room, making contact with each and every one, he finally said, "There is no yesterday, there is no tomorrow, there is only Now"!

Then he turned and made his way to the locker room door, his cleats marking the path on the floor and as he got to the door, the coach called out to him saying, "Is that your final word"?

His hand on the push bar, Jaeger turned and said, "The eyes of Texas are on all of us"! The steel door opened and he disappeared into the tunnel. With nothing left to hear or say, one by one the players rose up and followed him into the tunnel, their jaws set, their eyes focused, their spirits lifted somewhat, but would it be enough?

As they were walking down the tunnel towards the field one of the linemen related a story told about his grandfather, to the other linemen, about his service in the old Army Air Corps. During WWll, as they flew bombing missions over Japan in the B-29s. They knew that if they got shot down their lives wouldn't be worth a plug nickel once over enemy territory and that fear gripped each and every pilot and crew prior to every take off. The murderous flack, the swarm of fighters each flight had to combat and finally the Kamikaze tactics employed by the Japanese pilots of flying straight into bomber formations.

He related what the commanding officer said to all the flight crews prior to their mission briefings. "You're all dead men, as of this moment, every last one of you. The minute you signed up for this you became dead men. So I hope you said your goodbyes, to those who matter for you're never going to see them again. All you can do from this moment on is see just how many of the enemy you can take with you. So get over it and get the job done"!

The offensive linemen knew they had to protect the quarterback at all costs for he was the only one left. The defensive linemen knew that they had to make the Hurricanes pay dearly for every inch of ground, for they were all dead men in their minds and to make things worse 'The eyes of Texas were on each and every one of them'.

As they lined up in the tunnel, Jaegers last words rang through the heads of each and every one of them as they listened to the final crescendo notes of the school song, played by the marching band, 'The Eyes of Texas'.

The thought was branded into each man's head from that very moment.

Jaeger stood still, as the band played and wondered if this level of controlled hatred was experienced by those commanded by Sam Houston, just before the Battle of San Jacinto, when the battle cry was, "Remember the Alamo"!

His body was already tired and yet he started to feel the effects of his ingested pharmacology, bring back the effects of renewed energy. His skin started to tingle. Yeah, he was ready.

Before the final notes of the Texas anthem concluded, the Hurricanes swarmed onto the field prematurely, pouring through the ranks of the University of Texas Marching Band. A tad bit of bad form duly noted by the faithful.

"Oh that's just not going to sit well with the UT fans Porter"! "Right you Mike. No doubt polite letters will be exchanged between Chancellors and that'll be the end of it except certain people have memories that are almost eternal and I'm thinking that all the Texan's out there will now really want put the hammer down on the Hurricanes, in the second half. But that's just going to take some doing"!

"As the Longhorns prepare to receive the ball from the Hurricanes for the second half, I sense something missing Porter"!

"I sense it too Mike. Miami is one of the top dogs in college football and accustomed to winning by wide margins. Their roster is deep in talent that will regenerate in years to come. But I sense that in their locker room the riot act had been read to the team by their coaches. Reputations are on the line. Coaching contracts are to be renewed. Commercial endorsements are in the offing. Then there's the all-important Alumni Organization looming large in the deep back round. No Mike, expect the Hurricanes to live up to their name in the second half and methodically take the Horns to the meat market as they have so many others during the season"!

Jaeger stood on the sidelines as Miami kicked the ball away starting the second half. He watched the ball's graceful trajectory as it rose from the kickers foot arching gracefully up and finally giving in, to the forces of gravity falling to the earth into the waiting hands of the Texas receiver, eager to advance the ball forward. The receiver drifting to his right momentarily lost the flight of the ball as it passed through the suns glare, then panicked, lifting his arm signaling for a fair catch. Finally seeing the ball as it came down to his immediate left, started to move towards the ball as an errant gust of wind drove it even further to his left than he calculated catching the ball on his fingertips, juggling it and then losing it to the ground. The ovoid ball bouncing the unpredictable way footballs often do, away from the receiver, who gets pushed aside by one of the Hurricanes and into the hands of one of the Miami defenders who scooped the ball up without breaking his stride and high stepped in into the end zone.

"Porter did you see that"?

"I'd say everyone saw that Mike. A change of fortune for the Longhorns. The Cotton Bowl is mostly as silent as a mortuary at the unexpected turn of events. That play changes everything. For as the extra point is kicked by Miami, Texas is further behind in the game. The score is now Miami Twenty One and Texas Thirteen. Expect something else to happen within minutes Mike to break this game open"!

"Ya think an onside kick is possible, Porter"?

"The Miami coach has been known to be a real back breaker and a gambler, as well as being one of the most knowledgeable coaches in the game. This guy can smell the blood when it's in the water and the onside kick at this very time can take the very breath away from any team"!

As the two teams line up for the second kickoff, the Hurricanes gave no indication of the a possible onside kick by their formation, with the exception of the presence of their 'Hands Unit', comprised of smaller and faster players usually pass catchers used to catching a bouncing ball.

"Their 'Hands Unit' is the game Mike and I wonder if Texas will pick it up"?

As the Miami kicker approached the ball, his kick topped the ball, sending it bouncing up in that small arching bounce, clearing the first line of defenders ten yards away and bouncing erratically into the hands of one of the advancing Miami players who immediately downed the ball on the Texas forty five yard line.

Once again the entire Cotton Bowl groaned in disappointment, as Jaeger took to the field. As Jaeger took his position at defensive end he decided that now, was time to test the discipline of the Miami offensive line as the approached the ball. "As Miami approaches the ball, they're in a spread formation with no one in the back field, Porter. Miami's left tackle just leapt off the ball smashing Jaeger to the ground prior to the snap Porter"!

Signaling an off sides and as the tackle is still flailing away at Jaeger, still more flags are flying through the air signaling even more penalties as the refs struggle to separate the players on both sides of the ball"!

"The tackle in question is now arguing with the refs Mike and as Jaeger rises to his feet, he just got to have some bruises on his body from the pummeling he just received. The signal from the officials is off sides and unsportsman like conduct on the Miami player and Texas will take the un sportsman like conduct penalty and the Miami player in question is asked to leave the field by the officials"!

"Never get in a referee's face Porter"!

"Which is why several of the coaches and the players are escorting, Mackie Brennan from the field of play physically. My guess is that he had quite enough of the smaller Jaeger getting around his behemoth size almost at will, making him look very bad. What else could it be."?

"Bobby LeBeaux is running on the field Porter".

"Which means a running play Mike. He's been benched on and off the entire season for erratic play. He'll run up a two hundred yard rushing day one Saturday only to be followed by a two or three fumble game the next. Still and all if he has a good day things will indeed look bleak for Texas.

One thing to look for when he lines up is whether or not his chin strap is buckled. He just hates doing that. Says it limits him. So far so good as Miami comes up to the line. There it goes Mike, as they took their position Bobby just unbuckled the chin strap. Let's see what develops"!

As Miami came to the line, Jaeger suddenly switched places with the other defensive end, now playing on the same side as LeBeaux. As they took their position the opposing tackle growled, "Ya can call me 'Nigger' all ya like white boy and it won't bother me a bit"! Jaeger growled back, "You see a boy here Sambo, just kick his ass, if ya can"!

Just then the ball was snapped, with LeBeaux moving to his left and a fake handoff moving right for Jaeger, with the entire offensive line slant blocking towards Jaegers position. The ball was pitched towards LeBeaux moving to his left opposite Jaegers position, with two of his flanking backs running interference for him. Sweeping to his left and seeing that his path was obstructed by a slew of Longhorn players, Bobby did what he did best and stop on a dime in almost full stride, seeing a line of blockers starting to form on his right and cut back across the field. He remembered what the coached had drilled into his head repeatedly every day and switched the ball to his right arm as he moved to his right, across the field. He eyes watched what was in front of him and to his left of the opposing players.

Jaeger struggled with his two blockers, who were clearly clinging to his jersey, knowing full well that if LeBeaux ever got into the open field it was a sure score. Suddenly with great effort he broke free from their grasp, not seeing the officials flag signaling offensive holding and saw LeBeaux coming back in his direction at an angle behind a wall of blockers, with his eyes looking at the advancing Longhorns ahead of him. As Jaeger cut down the angle between them, he saw LeBeaux's eyes drift his way and grow wide just as he crashed into him.

LeBeaux hit Jaeger, just the way a small insect hits a windshield at speed, coming to a complete and instant stop, the unstrapped helmet and the ball still moving forward, giving truth to the laws of inertia, while Jaeger made certain the tackle was the final act in LeBeaux's football career. As the football bounced merrily along the field towards the sidelines The Two Miami players that were holding Jaeger trailing behind the play and the Texas players advancing towards the ball, collided just short of the sidelines with the Miami players recovering the fumble.

"Ya know Porter I don't know if that last play did Miami any good or not? They recovered the fumble didn't they"?

"Yeah Mike but they lost an outstanding running back who's out cold at midfield, thanks to the 'Uberballer' who hit him like a tank. He'll be gone for the rest of the game just another casualty of the ongoing war before our very eyes. But a holding penalty will be assessed against the

Hurricanes just as they were about to rack up some yardage which will negate everything.

So they lose yardage and a dangerous running back but they'll still have a first down and Miami is very deep in swift running backs. So it's almost an even swap. But since all play is stopped on the field, let's take a break from the action and pay a few bills"!

As Jaeger walked back to his huddle he watched the Miami team staff, summon the medical unit. "He's swallowed his tongue and can't breathe", they yelled at the sidelines as the team doctors ran to midfield. For the next few minutes, the medical staff worked feverishly on Bobby LeBeaux.

Unconscious and unable to draw a breath they quickly performed an on field tracheotomy. That accomplished, lifted his body to the gurney that was rushed to midfield and hurriedly rushed him to the waiting ambulance in the end zone.

"Looks very serious Porter"!

"Mike, I've seen a lotta football in my time, but I never saw such a savage hit like that. He ran right into Jaeger, not seeing him until the very last mille second. Way too late for the human body to respond to. I wouldn't be surprised if his lungs were crushed beyond repair"!

"Porter, I'm getting in the latest report from the field, that Bobby LeBeaux swallowed his tongue as a result of the tackle and had to have on field tracheotomy performed and being rushed to the nearest hospital"!

"There you are Mike, what did I tell you? Have the control room re rack the video tape of that last play and replay it in slowmotion............ We're ready now? Roll tape"!

"As you can see, LeBeaux unfastens his chinstrap as he gets it set position and on the left of his helmet is his mouthpiece which he just spit out dangling there. That ladies and gentlemen is probably why he swallowed his tongue as a result of that tackle. Now Jaeger is now gonna be a target of retribution as a result of the play, but it was a clean and legal tackle. The reason for the pads and helmets and mouthpieces is to limit the damage done in the game of football. If one chooses not to employ the safety devices provided by the team, how can anyone be held responsible for the damage"?

As Jaeger watched the feverish activity to revive Bobby LeBeaux at midfield, he endured the slurs of some of the Hurricane players, who were calling for his blood. "We're gonna get you muthafuckah, gonna get ya real good"! He looked at them dispassionately as he rolled through his mind every dirty thing that could be done to a player, ticking them off one by one, preparing himself for what was certain to come.

He felt nothing for the fallen. 'Fortunes of war', he thought to himself. 'Schadenfreude', 'Better him than me'. He gathered the team around him at midfield, as LeBeaux was being hurried to the waiting ambulance, saying to everyone, "Looks like things are gonna heat up a bit guys, so watch your six at all times. Expect everything and anything, because we're in the shit for fair"! As he spoke the Texas band started to play, "The Eyes of Texas" theme slowly, meant to be a salute to a fallen warrior on the field of combat. Yet as the notes of the dirge droned on, it held an entirely different meaning to the Longhorn's only emphasizing the personal importance of each and every moment on the field.

After the ten minute interlude, the referee's whistle signaled for the game to resume, with Miami taking their penalty and resuming the field of play with a boisterous resolve to bury whatever faced them that wore an Orange jersey. The very first play was a play with all the flankers out to the left flooding the zone and as the ball was centered Jaeger lunged off the ball eluding his blocker with a textbook spin move, eluding his grasping arms, counting off the two seconds he allotted himself to get to the quarterback.

Running right over the small running back, it delayed him just enough for the quarterback to pass the ball down field, just an instant before Jaeger hit him bringing him to the ground, feeling the air rush out of his lungs.

Yet to no avail, for the Miami pass receiver caught the perfectly passed ball in mid stride, eluding all attempts and raced downfield into the end zone with yet another Miami score.

"And just like that Miami scores again Porter, with the score, the Longhorn's Thirteen and the Hurricanes Twenty Seven"!

"Certainly didn't help the Longhorns that their defensive back fell over his own feet as the Hurricane receiver caught a perfectly thrown pass. But if ya look back up field the Hurricane quarterback is hurting after colliding with the Jaegermeister. If he goes out then Miami is down to their red shirt freshman, while the Longhorns are already there. If their quarterback goes down there's no one else on the team ready to play the position."! The remainder of the third quarter saw the Longhorn's close the gap slightly with a field goal and early in the fourth quarter they closed the gap a little more with yet another field goal.

"And with ten minutes left to go in the game Porter, we now have the Longhorn's down by eight points, with Miami at Twenty Eight and Texas at Nineteen"! As Miami kicked off again, the ball arched through the air and into the receiver Dax Redbone's hands as he started up the field from the goal line and at the twenty veered towards his left running at three quarters speed as he followed the line of blockers. As he ran, he saw that several of the Hurricanes had an angle on him and in an instant of inspiration, cut across their path and through them, missing their grasping arms and dashed across the field into the end zone for the score.

"And so the extra point is kicked and the score is now Miami, Twenty Eight and Texas Twenty Six and Porter, seems like the Longhorns are storming right back into the game"!

For the next seven minutes of game time, Miami and Texas each had experienced several series of three downs and out having to punt the ball down field. At the beginning of the quarter Jaeger discreetly reached into his helmet for the small baggie that contained the final 'Drexie', secretly downing it from the array of Gator Aide available.

With just over three minutes left to go in the game, Jaeger again had to punt and of course the ball hung in the air at right about five seconds allowing the Texas defenders time enough to cover the ball down field.

Somehow they had to get the ball back and time was running out. With the ball on the Miami ten yard line and them being two points up on Texas all the Hurricanes had to do was maintain possession of the ball and advance it down field.

"Well Porter, seems like all Miami has to do is grind it out on the ground and eat up the clock, make a few first downs and they will emerge Cotton Bowl Champs.

"Mike, Texas has two time outs left, while Miami is out of time outs for the game. "Fasten your seatbelts fans, we're gonna be in for a bumpy ride"! As Jaeger took his stance at defensive end, the Miami line men started back in with the trash talk as they came to the line, with Jaeger being their intended target. "Ah heah ya gots dis little sistah up near Waco boy. When dis ovah, tink I'll pay her a visit", said one of the linemen.

At the snap of the ball, it was an off tackle power run with two of the blockers working on Jaeger. Fortunately the Miami ball carrier had no place to go with the pile up gaining them only two yards. As the players untangled from the pileup Jaeger was the second last one up from the pile, leaving just one Miami lineman, the tackle who wanted to visit Waco, writhing on the ground, his knee bone sticking straight out from the skin.

As the refs whistle blew signaling yet another visit from the Miami team medical staff, Jaeger knelt down and whispered into the players ear, "Seems like you're gonna have to postpone that visit for a little while boy", then knelt down and made a very visible sign of the cross in front of the entire crown before withdrawing to his huddle.

"Seems like Jaeger has struck again Porter, but he seems sad about it making the sign of the cross over a stricken player for the opposition"!

"Don't count on it Mike, for I'm just hearing from the producer that Bobby LeBeaux has succumbed to his injuries as he was wheeled into the emergency room at Parkland Hospital. The young man has died. No news as to the exact cause, no doubt that'll come later. Don't know whether or not the news of this has reached the field of play, but if and when it does, things just might spin out of control"!

"Once again Porter, things on the field are at a halt, giving both teams time to regroup and plan. As the camera pans the stadium we can see that no one has left the Cotton Bowl and that folks seem concerned for the fallen player who seems to be in great pain"! "Great Pain Mike? I'll say he's in great pain. His leg bone is sticking out of his skin. Whatever happened, happened it the depths of the pileup, shielded from the view of the refs, the fans and the camera's. Once again' Der Uberballer' has been right in the middle of things. And there he stands, yards away with his helmet off, looking concerned, at his stricken foe. Yet I wonder just how concerned he is"?

Twenty minutes later play was again resumed as the medical staff wheeled the injured player off the field on a gurney to yet another waiting ambulance. As the two teams again approached the line of scrimmage, Jaeger felt his skin start to tingle, signaling the last jolt of meds was coursing through his body.

Miami started its march down the field. Grinding the yards out methodically as the Texas defensive backs inched closer to the line to help stop the running plays. As Miami crossed mid field with yet another first down achieved, a substitute player ran into the Longhorn huddle saying, "The coach says that all defensive backs have to play back and that the linemen and the line backers have to stop the running plays on their own". Everyone knew what the coach meant, for if the backs cheated up on the line and a speedy flanker got behind them for a quick pass play the game was lost.

Yet it was if Vern Bachman had read the Miami coaches mind, for the very next play was a double fake into the line, with the Miami quarterback dropping back two steps and tossing an almost perfect pass to the Miami wide receiver Mac Speedie. Matching the Miami receiver stride for stride as they raced down the sidelines was the Texas safety Dax Redbone, who as the ball arched down to earth reached up and snatched the ball right out of the air, inches away from Speedie's waiting hands, veering away at the Texas goal line and running back up field before he was driven out of bounds at the Texas thirty yard line.

The entire Cotton Bowl was up with a roar of the crowd, as the field clock was stopped with just twenty seconds left to go in the game.

"Porter, the entire stadium is in an uproar and Texas has just been given a new life, by that interception. But what on earth was the Miami coach thinking? All he had to do was grind it out on the ground"?

"Mike, he was going for the back breaker. He's always been a bit of a gambler, with trick plays up his sleeves and pants legs. Perhaps this time his gamble has back fired on him. Yet the odds are still long the Longhorn's will ever pull this off. For they look spent every man jack of them. They've two time outs left, with twenty seconds left to go in the game and a paltry seventy yards to go for a touchdown. Remember a field goal is a possibility to win but a very long shot. And you can bet that Miami will be in the Nickel Defense, to keep Texas from the long pass"! Just two plays left, maybe three for the Horns

"So Porter, seems like Miami is still looking long to win this one"!

"Seems so Mike, yet ya just gotta take your hat off to the entire Texas team, for all the smart money had Miami in a blow out and all game long Texas hung in there against all odds and against a team with an over flowing wealth of football talent"!

"As Texas comes up to the line of scrimmage, they're in a spread formation against the deep zone nickel defense Porter.

As the ball was hiked the Texas line was overwhelmed by a full blitz by the Miami defenders as Jaeger could only look on helplessly from the sidelines. The Texas freshman red shirt quarterback was first reached by the Hurricanes middle linebacker who lifted him up and put him flat on his back, followed by a horde of Miami players eager to end things quickly. As the clock ticked down slowly past ten seconds to go in the game, Texas called for a time out with nine seconds left.

"Well, things certainly look grim for Texas Porter, with a scant nine seconds left to go in the game and the ball now on their twenty two yard line, we see that as the Miami players arise from the pile up, that Dexter Mankiller, the Hurricanes middle linebacker, has done is work well as the last Texas quarter back is not getting up as the Texas medical staff rushes on to the field"! "Mike, this places Texas in about as bad a dilemma that can be had by a team. Almost eighty yards to go, with no one that can throw a ball except Jaeger and nine ticks on the clock left. No miracle I can conceive of is possible. So it looks like the gamble of the Miami coach will be forgotten by the performance of his team on the field"!

"Two things are happening simultaneously Porter, first the medical staff summoning yet another gurney to transport the fallen Texas quarterback to yet another ambulance and the flurry of activity on the side lines between the Texas coach Vern Bachman and his staff"!

"My guess is that Jaeger will make an appearance as quarterback for what will be the last play of the game when play is resumed. For he's the only one with the arm that can toss a 'Hail Mary' pass that far, Mike"!

"Looks like your calling that one right Porter for Coach Bachman and his staff are in an intense huddle with 'Der Uberballer' on the sidelines. But what in the world short of a tossup and prayer could they come up with"?

"I just don't know Mike. The perfect throw the perfect catch and maybe if the Miami secondary all fell down. What're the odds of that happening?"

"Things look serious down on the field Porter, for the last Texas quarterback is being lifted slowly and carefully onto the gurney and wheeled off the field into the ambulance just off the field of play"!

"Mike, something tells me that with only nine seconds left to go, there just may be yet more work for the medical staffs of both teams. I truly hope I'm wrong"!

As the eleven selected by the coach gathered about Jaeger on the field as their last quarterback was taken from the field, Jaeger said "Hap, you're gonna be the Qback on this one. You get in shotgun formation and will get the ball. Dax, you'll play as the wide out yet a yard off the line in the backfield on the right. Bobby, you and Harry will play wide outs on the left side. When we come up to the line, I'll set up at right side tight end. When Hap yells out 'down', I'll shift into the backfield and Dax you step up to the line. Everyone will think it's a deep pass play and the wide outs really have to sell this as they run down the field. Now Bruno, this guy 'Mankiller' has pretty much owned you all afternoon and he's gonna run over you again, he'll be talkin' to you, so be an actor and show him some fear, but set up your block so he comes to the inside, to your right and instead of running into a pass pattern down field, I'll drift over to the left and take care of this 'Mankiller' guy, then drift out to your left. Now Hap, all ya have to do is get me the ball, doesn't have to be pretty, just get me the ball, to your left.

Once I have the ball everyone put a hat on someone and stay with em, no penalties or else we're all screwed. I'll be busy for the next ten seconds or so and'll have a lotta company as I go down field so I'll appreciate any help I get along the way. Now Dax and the wide outs, as you run down the field somewhere around the fifty yard line you'll all become blockers, right"?

They nodded their heads in understanding. The referee's whistle blew signaling for the game to continue as Jaeger said, "OK Hap, lead us out"!

"Porter as the Longhorn's come out of the huddle for what may be the final time this afternoon, Jaeger's not behind the ball, but the freshman running back Hap Richards with Jaeger lining up at right end"!

"Spread formation Mike, gonna be a Hail Mary pass into the end zone, but wait, Jaeger just shifted into the back field".

When the ball was snapped, Jaeger took a quick step forward, then back turning to his left and just as he'd hoped caught sight of 'Mankiller' out muscling Bruno the left tackle, leaving just enough space for Jaeger to sneak his left thumb deep into 'Mankiller's throat in a quick jab as he ran by. As he cleared the line and started to turn back looking for the short toss, he saw 'Mankiller' crumble to the ground clutching his throat out of the corner of his eye as the ball lead him perfectly, with Hap going to the ground with two Miami defenders on top.

Jaeger quickly turned up field and as he crossed the fifty yard line, he saw a small phalanx of Miami defenders thirty yards away and felt the ground rumbling behind him as the jail break of Miami players desperately ran after him, each one pestered by a Longhorn eager to get between them and Jaeger, yet without a penalty.

As he drifted to his right crossing the Miami forty yard line, the first of Miami's speedy linebackers caught up with him, and then another and as a third was about to put the seal of approval on Jaeger, one of the Texas players threw a block peeling two of the players off of Jaeger. Acting purely on blind instinct, Jaeger then lurched to his left, only to run into two more Hurricanes as he crossed the twenty yard line, as he felt hands and arms reaching for his legs to bring him down, he summoned the strength to lift his legs into high stepping mode.

Crossing the ten yard line, he didn't seem to hear the throng of eighty thousand screaming fans, as his helmet was ripped off his head by the face guard by a Miami defender, or feel the desperately clutching hands or the myriad of punches, rained upon him as the thundering herd finally caught up with him, slowing his rate of advance to a crawl with Texas players trying to both push the gaggle forward and the Miami players trying to bring things to a halt.

With the field officials close at hand surrounding the glut of struggling players looking for penalties, several flags came out as several Hurricane players, desperate to bring things to a grinding stop resorted to 'un sportsman' like tactics towards the Texas players, who could not retaliate in kind.

With only the vaguest notion of direction and with his legs churning with a piston like staccato, Jaeger made a last final attempt to break free of the log jam, without the use of his arms, busy protecting the ball, he shook free, as a Lion in a fight, as he miraculously emerged from the group crossing the goal line with but one lone Miami defender hanging on blocking his vision, he kept on churning blindly on taking one step after the other gathering strength and speed, finally crashing into an immovable object and then all went blank as he fell to the ground still clutching the ball with a death grip of both hands.

"Ladies and gentlemen I see it but I don't believe what I've just seen.

Porter the entire stadium is in a state of pandemonium. And it seems the referees have signaled a Texas touchdown with the time on the field having run out and the flags on the play seem to have all been against Miami and of course Texas will decline the penalties. The public address announcer is begging the fans to remove themselves from the field of play, while the medical staffs from both teams are running towards the end zone to tend to the myriad of players injured on that last play. The police have cordoned off a perimeter around the fallen Miami safety that was clinging to Jaeger as he ran blindly into the goal post, which is still slightly moving back and forth."!

"Mike somebody had better tend to Dexter Mankiller, for there he is back on the Texas twenty yard line on his hands and knees, unable to get up. Thank fully some fans have come to his assistance and are signaling the officials and the Miami medical staff."

"Let's see if we can get our man on the field, Boyd Rainwater, who's ready to interview the man of the hour. Boyd, are you there"? "Yes Porter, this is Boyd Rainwater on the field with our field cam and I'm, on the edge of the perimeter set up by the State Police around both the 'Uberballer' and the Miami safety both of which are unconscious due to the collision with the goal post on the end line"! Both the Texas and the Miami medical staffs are hard at work to bring each man back around and as the camera can see, there is the 'Jaegermeister' out cold, still clutching the football with both arms around it. Some might liken it to a death grip. But wait it seems the smelling salts administered to Jaeger, is bringing him around and as the camera focuses on his face, let's see if the police will let us get a little closer to him to catch is first words. Can we patch this in with the stadium public address system Mike"?

"Our engineers are patching your audio feed into the PA system now Boyd, back to you"!

"Here we are, some five yards away as Jaeger's eyes begin to open and he slowly regains his senses after running into the goal post and you can hear the cheer from all the Longhorn fans rise up from the Cotton Bowl that it looks like he's gonna be OK. He's starting to rise shakily to his feet. He still looks very shaky as he asks one of the officials if he made it or not. The official nods his head and all Jaeger can do at this point is smile. Let me see if I can get him to say a few words"?

"Jaeger, Jaeger, your bleeding from your head wounds and you look pretty bad, but can you say just a few words to the National TV Audience"!

"Yeah, I'm getting a headache, but just who was that last guy that hit me? He's a real stud"!

Just then an even larger cheer went up from the entire stadium, with almost everyone jumping up and down chanting "Jaeger, Jaeger, Jaeger", over and over in salutation to a true warrior.

Boyd put his arm on Jaeger, gently turning him around and pointed to the goal post saying, "The Goal Post is, what hit you"

As Boyd's voice boomed out his message, the entire stadium again erupted into cheers as everyone was on their feet as a medical technician took Jaeger by the arm, still clutching the football he carried, saying "Time to rest my man, courtesy of Parkland Hospital and some testing that's coming your way", as they made their way toward the waiting gurney and the ambulance some yards away.

"Well Mike and Porter there you have it, from the old 'Hoss's' mouth.

As much as the 'Uberballer' gave and got all afternoon, as much as he's just gotta be hurting, no body hit him as hard as the goal post at games end.

Back to y'all upstairs"!

"Boyd, see if you and the camera man can hustle down to the other end of the field, for it seems that Dexter Mankiller is in a very bad way down there, with yet another ambulance in the wings and medical tech's working on him"!

"Porter, I've been a sports announcer for a very long time and seen many great plays, but I just can't say enough about what I've just been witness to can you"?

"Mike, I'm also struggling for just the right words to describe what I've just seen. Desperation, heroism. A mighty struggle against all odds, or a once in a lifetime celestial event. All apply here in my mind. All the stars lined up in perfect alignment for a brief moment in time? Perhaps! But my heart is still racing and I can just imagine what elation is in the Longhorn locker room at this very moment and conversely the depths of depression in the Hurricane locker room. They had the game all but won and in the last seconds of play had it whisked away by fate or ill fortune.

Still, I want to believe that what we've just seen may never be replicated in our lifetime or any other"!

"Mike and Porter, this is Boyd. The medical technicians are attempting to perform a tracheotomy on Dexter Mankiller, to allow him to breathe"!

"Everyone is waiting for the arrival of another ambulance that has been summoned from the nearest hospital. From the looks of things Dexter Mankiller is in a very bad way. His expression seems lifeless and he's not breathing"! "Back to you Mike, in the Press box"!

"Seems like an entire wing of Parkland Hospital will be necessary for the casualties of war, Porter"!

"I can tell you this Mike, video tapes of this game will be circulated everywhere, especially to every team in the National Football League and based on his one seasons body of work, both the tangibles of accomplishment and the intangibles of his hands on leadership, this young man, 'The Uberballer', is ready to play in the NFL, assuming he hasn't any lasting injuries, like brain damage after that last play. You can rest assure that the entire State of Texas will be in celebration for some time to come and after what we've just seen, I just cannot imagine whatever could top this"!

"Well said Porter. Well this is Mike Cantrell along with Porter Jolly saying good afternoon from an elated Cotton Bowl, with Texas stealing a victory, from the jaws of defeat, on New Year's Day"!

27

After a thorough examination by the hospital staff, it was determined that Jaeger had but a mild concussion. Still, he was kept overnight for close observation. The following morning, as he endured the standard visit from the ward nurses eager to say they attended the 'Uberballer', if just for a moment, his breakfast was delivered while the doctor assigned to his care was finishing up his exam.

"I trust you enjoyed your bed bath administered by three nurses last night", said he doctor!

"I never got so clean in all my life. I'm so clean I squeak", Jaeger replied sardonically"!

"The hospital administration has strongly suggested that you stay her a few more days, just so we can be certain that nothing unforeseen develops young man. It seems that you're the man of the hour, given your recent exploits. Now don't worry, the Miami injured are in another wing of the hospital, while all the Longhorns are on this floor. You'll have to endure three squares a day, endless testing and a few more bed baths by our eager professional staff before we cut you loose. Besides the University is picking up the tab"!

As he turned to leave he said, "Now enjoy you're breakfast for we've a host of people that want to see you, starting with your family sitting in the waiting room".

He hadn't seen or heard from his family since that night he fled from the family compound outside of Waco, one step ahead of the High Sheriff. He'd heard that his old football coach had died several years ago from natural causes, having nothing to do with his assault on him years ago. The cause of rift between his father Morgan and him was but a dim memory, yet he recalled the cause. Two hard headed Alpha Krauts, neither one giving way to the other. One the younger, the other older. Arbitrary words are exchanged, none of which can be taken back and the elder strikes the younger. A long standing mutual hatred emerges, as a result of the mindless 'Reptilian Response'. Parental love takes a vacation, while the younger flees the area in search of his identity. Ever since he returned to Texas, Jaeger wanted to re-establish a relationship with his family. During his absence all these years, he kept busy eagerly accepting one assignment then another, almost nonstop, avoiding his accrued annual leave from the military, throwing himself into one life and death situation after another. If he kept busy, then he wouldn't have time to think of his family and the friends he left behind. Yet something brought him back to Texas. Here he was in Austin and Waco being just a few hours up the Interstate. Yet he might as well have been on Mars. Now after all this, his family was just an arm's reach away, down the hall, waiting for an audience.

He toyed with his tepid hospital breakfast, while he thought about how to respond to their presence, concluding that he was hardly in a position to go anywhere, so he might as well relent and see them. Their presence was their attempt to make nice and if all went well reconcile. After some twenty minutes one of the nurse attendants came in to retrieve his breakfast tray and seeing that he'd hardly eaten anything said, "Yeah I know bland hospital food"!

"You think I could get my hands around a big inch thick "T-Bone steak while I'm here"?

"Well, it's against strict hospital policy, but if you don't say anything, who knows what might happens before sundown. Besides there's a higher authority, being the 'Eyes of Texas are upon you"! As she turned to the door with his tray he called out, "I think I'm ready to see my family now nurse"! The door to his room opened slowly as his mother peeked around the corner. Suddenly it opened wider as his two younger sisters, now it their early teens rushed into the room yelling "Uberballer" and flanked his bed showering him with hugs and kisses, long overdue. As he was overwhelmed by their pent up emotions, his mother Sarah approached the bedside, waiting for her daughters affections to subside and give her room to approach. Tears were in her eyes as the long years of his absence came back to haunt. "I promised myself that I wouldn't cry, but since I'm your mother", then she bent over to embrace her long lost son, finally bursting forth in deep sobs, gently touching his face, his hair, his arms, reveling in his presence.

"Please let me look at you son, for it's been far too long, far too long", she repeated!

"Our brother is the most famous man in Texas, ever", blurted Phoebe beaming with pride.

"Ya better watch out or he'll get a big head", said his other sister Melanie with a smile as wide as the Mississippi.

After several minutes of the standard small talk, loved ones who haven't seen each other in ages engage in a small knock on the door preceded, its opening and staff orderlies started bringing in bouquets of flowers, from all over the state. "These were starting to build up and we just had to bring them inside. There's more downstairs on its way up and we'll put them all in front of your room for now.

After the orderlies left, Jaeger looked around somewhat overwhelmed saying, to his sisters, "Y'all can have all the flowers as many as you want"!

"Can we take the cards and letters with us back to the hotel room, so we can read them", asked Phoebe eagerly?

"Take anything you want Phoebe"! Then Jaeger turned to his mother saying, "So how is Dad"?

"One of the heads of the Alumni Committee found us a group of seats, on the fifty yard line, about half way up and your father is about the proudest man in the world at this very moment. He loves you, you know.

He's always loved you"!

With tears starting to well up in her eyes, she continued, "He's such a hard headed Kraut, that, well you know, he's just the kind that can never bring themselves to apologize, when they've over stepped the boundaries. Their silence and the fact that they fall all over themselves to be nice in the aftermath, is their way of an apology"!

"Son, you've been away too long and we all need you to come home and be with those who love you"! All the while she spoke she had his right hand gently in her firm grip with both of her hands, mindful of the intravenous drip that was in his arm.

As his eyes drifted to the window and the world outside, he noticed his sisters gushing over the plethora of flowers and the cards accompanying them. Then turning back to his mother he said, "As Dad always said, 'A woman's first duty is to her husband', and he's the master of his domain and your first duty has and always should be to him"!

"He's in the waiting room down the hall right"?

His mother nodded her head smiling, when Jaeger said, "Well then, why don't you take the girls and trade places with him for a little bit, so we can try and get to know each other again"?

Sarah rose up beaming, as she gathered her daughters together saying, "We'll let you two alone for a little while, but try and make it as quick as you can for your sisters want to hog their big brother all to themselves"!

Several minutes passed, until Jaeger heard a single hard knock on the door. Only a Marine, knocked like that, from a force of habit. Jaeger bellowed, "Come"! The door slowly opened and there he was, Morgan Jaeger, buzz cut, granite jawed, hard cut to the bone. Once a Marine......

He slowly entered the room uncertain of his reception after all these years, closing the door behind him. Slowly his father smiled, then Jaeger saw that tears were starting to well up in his eyes as Jaeger said, "Hello Dad, long time no see"! "No shit Sherlock", his father said, with a garbled utterance.

"Well come on over here and take a seat Dad", he said pointing to a seat that was near the bed.

For well over a long minute, both of them looked at each other, scanning up and down, before his father said, "You got some miles on ya son, I can see it in your eyes"!

"Like ya always taught me, 'Ain't how old ya are its how many miles ya traveled!"

As Morgan took a seat slowly, the tears started to overflow his eyes, try as he might not to make it not so"!

"A little sinus problem there"?

"Pine tree pollen coming early this year"!

"In January"?

"Screw you and the horse you rode in on Son", uttered Morgan suddenly sniffling up the detria that threatened to overwhelm his sinus cavities, with a small grin starting to appear.

"How ya been Dad"?

"I'm better now. Tired of huntin' alone son"!

"The Ranch doin' OK"?

"It could use another experienced hand"!

Then there was a period of painful silence between the two grown men, when their gaze both drifted elsewhere, when Morgan finally spoke looking his son squarely in the eyes, "Son, I'm so sorry and I apologize for all I've said in the past and all that I've done and left undone"!

Then he asked, "Can you ever forgive me"?

Jaeger looked at his father, with his sinus's starting to feel the effects of the nonexistent early spring pine pollen in January and said, "Consider it done Dad and of this we shall never speak of it again, agreed"?

"Agreed"! Then his father arose from his chair and went over to his son and they hugged each other, their mutual sinus problems intermingling.

After a decent interval they separated, with Morgan saying, "Looks like the waiting room is starting to fill up, with Coaches, Sports Agents, Newspaper Reporters, Important Alumni, Lawyers and the like. Oh and one thing more, with all the players that went down on the field, looks like two of the players you cold cocked, Bobby LeBeaux and that guy Dexter Mankiller, well neither one of them made it and they both died in the Emergency Room downstairs"!

"Now I got our family attorney standing by in a hotel down the way just in case he's needed"!

"Well Dad, seems I'm going to have to talk to a lotta folks, will you run interference for me"?

"Consider it done and short of family you don't say a word without either me or our lawyer present, OK?

"By the way, how did Mankiller check out"?

"Well son, the scuttlebutt is that his hypoid bone in his throat somehow was broken during the final play of the game and he was unable to breathe and the Emergency Techs got to him too late", he said with a knowing wink!

For the rest of the morning Morgan Jaeger, played traffic cop, escorting the Longhorn Coaching Staff, Athletic Director, Conference Officials and various politicians of note, in and out of his room.

His doctor came back just before noon and announced that further tests would have to be made on his patient and that no one but immediate family was to be permitted to stay around.

"Der Uberballer, will be able to receive visitors, after Three O'clock this afternoon, but I must insist that visits not exceed fifteen minutes in duration or else I'm going to have to isolate our patient"!

True to form, several sports representatives were eager to represent Jaeger, as the family lawyer looked on silently in observance, keeping rigid time on each and every visitor. As the clock struck Five PM, all further non family visitors were told to return after nine in the morning and assemble in the waiting room.

"Well son, how do you think the day went", asked his father?

"Sorta overwhelmed. Looks like I have a full jock ride, from the University, according to the Athletic Director, the Sports Agents want me to sign up with them and jump right into the NFL draft and the politicians, people I never knew existed, came by to wish me well"!

"The entire State is all up in the air over your performance yesterday and expectations for your return to the gridiron next season for Texas are high, son"!

"But what if I decide I'm through with football"? "I mean, when I went out for the team, all I wanted to see was if I could still do it! Then after that, it was like, combat and I just sorta got caught up with everything and apparently I pulled things off"!

The family lawyer sitting in a corner, as the family retainer, joined in saying in an off handed manner, "I'll say you pulled things off, in rather a grand style young man"! Then he added, "Let me outline your alternatives. Your scholarship at UT will be contingent on your agreement to suit up and be a player for the Longhorns. Now should you want to continue at UT, you'll have to write out the check every semester"!

"That's alright", said Morgan Jaeger, "Money for his further education is not a problem, at UT or anywhere else he chooses. What matter's above all else, is that my son is home, with his family and that's all that matters"!

"Good", said the lawyer, "But there's that little matter of the very last play of the game and the death of the Miami players, especially Mankiller. As your family retainer, I assumed the responsibility of watching the game on television, and the tackle of LeBeaux appeared to be a clean hit, although his relatives are no doubt contacting attorneys as we speak for the obvious reasons. But the hit on Mankiller just might foster some suspicion that your son may have some exposure to a Manslaughter charge. Now I've had one of my detectives, surreptitiously review the video tapes that are known, from the media feed and they do not indicate any direct contact of your son's left arm with Mankiller's throat area, as he passed him, going through the line of scrimmage. He stated that he went over and over the video tape, in slow motion frame by frame and saw no direct contact. Now sports casters all over the nation have already scrutinized that final play and agree, with my detective. Yet something came in contact with Mankiller hypoid bone as your son passed him on that play. The tapes show his left arm elevated as he passed the line of scrimmage and unless someone comes forward with another tape or a clear picture of contact with your sons left arm coming in contact with Mankillers throat, it would seem that any question of your son's culpability will fade in due course. Of course none of the on field officials saw what happened and all of them have and are currently being grilled by their respective entities. As for me, everything happened so fast, in those last seconds, that I couldn't say what happened.

Yet if you read the sports pages or turn on the TV, for the news programs the sportscasters are already changing your son's campus nickname to 'Jaegermeister the Mankiller', and that's not exactly the kind of publicity we need at the moment"!

"Hal, I think I know where you're going with this, but spell it out anyway", said Jaeger's father! "Some years ago your son left Waco under a bit of a cloud with that dustup with the High School football coach and in time and especially with the coach's demise from natural causes, things faded away. Yet the very same Sheriff, your earthly nemesis Morgan Little, is still the County Sheriff, so each of you expect anything and everything. Next, your son is going to need all the friends he can get for the next little while, so any talk about not continuing with the UT football program, or even the possibility of taking part of the NFL draft next summer is unwise. Make no comment about anything of the sort, be vague if you must say anything, channel all inquiries through either your father, or preferably through my office. Who knows, in the coming months, you may or may not change your mind, but let it be your own decision along with some wise old heads, who can tell you when the coast is clear. Keep your thoughts just to the three of us and only the three of us and no one else. Now son, you're an ex-Marine and you know all about the concept of 'Need to know', don't you"? Jaeger nodded his head in silence.

Just then the nurse entered the room with Jaegers dinner and his father and the lawyer left the room as she delivered the evening meal, followed by his mother and his two sisters, eager to see their famous brother.

Before she allowed him to open the aluminum lid on the tray, she took his Temperature, Pulse and Blood Pressure and noted it on the chart, then said "One of the Alumni at UT came by with some inch thick Porterhouse Steaks with all the trimmings and we sorta broiled it to a medium cook.

Expect this for each of your meals tomorrow. But if word of this ever gets out, it'll be curtains for all of us. Oh, by the way, my husband like to bet on the football games and the odds against Texas were so great and I just hate it when he bets, but I made him bet against the Hurricanes. Well, to make a long story short, we made out quite nicely thanks to you and I understand the Vegas bookies took a huge bath on the game"! She then turned and went to the door with a flourish, saying "Tah, Tah"! Jaeger opened the lid and true to her word was a, still steaming, inch thick Porterhouse Steak. His family returned to their hotel around Eight PM and Jaeger settled in for a night of television. At Ten PM, the late night local news program came on and over half of the newscast was reserved for the retelling of the entire Cotton Bowl game highlights. Half way through the telecast, there it was. The local sportscaster referring to rumors that Jaegers new cognomen was, 'Jaegermeister, the Mankiller', showing slow motion of every tackle he made where it resulted in the injury of a Hurricane player, especially the hits on Bobby LeBeaux and finally Dexter Mankiller. Repeats in slow motion frame by frame, slowed proximity, but not actual contact, of Jaegers left extremity, to any portion of Dexter Mankiller's torso. Interviews with those players in the huddle, preceding the final play were unproductive, with most players stating vague recollections of Jaeger saying, "The eyes of Texas are on all of us" and generally outlining a play that had little to do with any instructions by any of the coaching staff. The final impression left on Jaeger was that Jaeger had performed heroically on the field of play in an extraordinary display of gridiron grit and effort.

The newscast ended with the TV reporters question to Jaeger, as he was just coming to his senses after the last play, "Are you all right", with Jaeger asking groggily 'Just who was the last guy to hit him' and the on field reporter turning him around and pointing to the goal post ten yards behind the goal line, with the entire stadium in an uproar.

He turned the TV off and said to himself, 'Time to sleep', closing his eyes and relived the entire last play in his mind, remembering all that transpired. Yeah, he killed the sonofabitch, straight up. Hadn't intended to kill him, just get a little payback for what he'd had done to the Longhorn players. His thumb luckily found its mark. The entire final play was a desperate effort that had somehow luckily paid off, leaving him the toast of Texas, for a little while. Yet he wondered what would the fans think if he'd have gone down short of the goal line? Close was only good when playing with hand grenades and bocce balls. If he hadn't stopped Mankiller all would've been lost. He felt no remorse for the guy; for he was a dirty player who would've ripped your heart out if he thought he could get away with it.

He'd just eliminated a predator and the world would be a better place. He knew it. His Dad knew it and the family retainer, strongly suspected it. For the man was savvy to the way of the world and Jaeger was glad he was their family lawyer. Yet as he drifted to sleep, his zeal for the game was slipping away, for however could he top this?

The following morning was a busy time, with his parents arriving at the seven AM, hospital shift change, his purloined steak breakfast arriving fifteen minutes later and Hal the family lawyer arriving just as he finished his last morsel of steak.

He asked Sarah and the children to go to the waiting area down the hallway and make nice with anyone who wanted to see Jaeger, like the media starving for face time with the family hero. "We need you to run interference for your son and in the process get interviewed about your son and brother. Get some TV time for yourselves"!

When they left the room, he turned the room TV on and the volume up so they wouldn't be overheard. Since the room had no other buildings close by he felt comfortable with the vocal security. "Within a half an hour you're going to be visited by representatives of the local county district attorney, the Texas Rangers, the interscholastic league, the Athletic Director, Coach Bachman, and perhaps a few others. Some are trying to involve your coach in the death of Mankiller, while others are out for your hide if they can get it. Now last night I secretly met with all of the guys you were involved with on the final play and all are parroting the response they gave to the TV reporters, that you made up a play at the last minute and that was it, period"!

"Now what you need to remember is that you don't remember a blessed thing. You were battered around pretty damn good the entire game and especially during the events that last play, things are a complete blank. The Medical staff will attest that you suffered a concussion and that you are still in a partial concussive state requiring medical testing and attention. Try not to appear too perky young man and perhaps all this will fade away"!

"This is that serious Hal", asked Jaegers father?

"Scholastic students died in the Cotton Bowl Morgan and almost an entire wing of this hospital is laden with injured football players, some with career ending injuries, some of which are of less seriousness. Most folks care little, while others care a great deal. It's the latter grouping that might prove a problem. Your sons a former Marine in the prime of his life and was responsible for the Lion's share of the injury's to the Miami team".

"It's all about this Mankiller fella isn't it", asked Jaeger. "Yes it is son, all about the Mankiller"!

"Yet he's not here to account for all of those Longhorn's he put out of action for dirty play during the game"!

"That's because he's dead and you are not. I grilled the on field officials about this guy asking why he wasn't tossed out of the game for egregious and un sportsman like play, since he alone racked up over eighty yards in penalties during the contest and got no response and I intend to use it as a battering ram if they start to grill you. Now it's going to start out all friendly like, but don't be fooled, these guys are on a mission and all you have to do is keep on saying 'I don't remember', or 'everything was a blur'. The burden of proof is on them and oh, expect the meeting to be recorded"!

Several minutes later, a phalanx of visitors started to enter Jaeger's hospital room, numbering over a dozen individuals. They all made their introductions to Morgan, Jaeger and Hal Latham, before the lead Texas Ranger Royce Baintree started off, "Mr. Jaeger, I'm sure you know why we're all here"!

"Actually I'm not", replied Jaeger!

"The death of Dexter Mankiller in the Cotton Bowl the other day"! "What's that got to do with me", asked Jaeger wearily?

'Well son, certain parties are eager to bring you up on Manslaughter charges at the very least, claiming that you willfully chose to target this player on the very last play of the game, intending payback for what he did to your players during the course of the game"!

While Royce Baintree was outlining his purpose, an unintended visitor slipped into the room, keeping into the background, to all except the watchful eyes of Morgan Jaeger and his lawyer. Morgan was about to speak up when Hal stopped him shaking his head, then interrupting the questioning asking, "Excuse me Ranger Baintree, but what on earth is Morgan Little doing in this room"?

Turning around to see, Baintree answered, "Sheriff Little is here as a courtesy since he's the Sheriff of the County in which you reside and pay taxes. He has no official standing in this matter and may ask no questions or make any comment pro or con"!

"Then I ask again Ranger, what is he doing here, since he has no official standing"? Those in the Waco area were fully aware of the enmity that has existed between the two men that go back decades"!

"Once again, he is here at his request, as a courtesy to his office and nothing more, now may I continue"? "On the proviso that he remain silent throughout and that any utterance from him will bring this to an immediate halt", said Baintree!

"As you might understand, some folks from out of state have questions about your conduct during the course of the game and we're all here to clear things up and I'll have to ask you some questions about that. Do you understand"?

Before Jaeger could say anything Hal Latham, started to earn his annual stipend of the family mouthpiece by interjecting, "Ranger Baintree, I think I see where this is going. You want to grill my client in front of concerned witness and others, about his recent conduct. The subject of the deceased player 'Mankiller', is the focus of your inquiry is it not? Further, if after a review of all the available video tape and any pictures, revealed no tangible evidence of culpable misconduct, for I'm certain those tapes have been gone over with a fine tooth comb, you are on a hunt to see if something incriminating can be revealed, for possible political purposes, are you not"?

Before Baintree could respond, Latham continued relentlessly, "It's come to my attention that your office and others have grilled each and every one of the Longhorn players and the coaching staff, both jointly and severally, regarding what specifically was said in the huddle just prior to the last play and you've come up croppers, have you not"?

Continuing, he summed things up, "Since we have no visual or oral evidence of misconduct and since the field officials, usually an eagle eyed lot saw nothing worthy of penalty by any member of the Texas team and I might remind everyone here that on that very final play every single field official threw a flag signaling infractions on what team? The Hurricanes, fighting desperately to prevent the final touchdown, by any means fair or foul and in this case foul, but certainly every single one of you is already aware of that aren't you"?

Every lawyer worth his salt will always know that to never ask a question during a legal proceeding, you don't already know the answer to, and Hal Latham then stepped back and waited for a barrage of questions, ready to do verbal battle in defense of his client.

"Mr. Latham, may I just ask your client a few pertinent questions"? "Fire away Ranger Baintree"!

"Mr. Jaeger, have you any recollections of the final play of the game"?

Jaeger thought a few seconds, glancing at the Intravenous Drip that still provided fluids to his veins, then said, "I don't even remember the fourth quarter, Ranger Baintree"!

At that moment Hal Latham interceded again, "And I wonder why gentlemen! Has anyone seen the complete videos of the final play and the aftermath, when asked by the on field TV reporter, how he was, and what did Jaeger ask, "Who was that last guy that hit him so hard"?

"People, it was the 'goal post' resulting in his concussive state that we all see right now"!Before anyone else could ask, Jaeger's doctor stepped forward accompanied by the Hospitals attorney saying, "This has gone on far enough. The man is still in a concussive state and I'm advised by our attorney that the hospital risks punitive litigation by others if we allow this to continue, so I'm bringing this inquiry to an immediate halt for the interests of our patient. If any review of his medical records is required please have a court order directed to our corporate attorney for execution"!

Taking charge once again, Ranger Baintree looked around at those assembled and said, "As far as the Texas Rangers are concerned, the demise of Dexter Mankiller is deemed an unfortunate accident, on the field of play, as is the demise of Bobby LeBeaux. Have our friends from the Sunshine State any further questions", he asked looking straight at them?

They all shook their heads in unison. "Then hearing nothing to the contrary, I declare this inquiry closed, with no further action deemed necessary, and to Morgan Jaeger my apologies for the intrusion"! As the visitors filed out of the room, Baintree leaned over and whispered in Jaegers ear, "Great game son, ya done Texas proud", with a slow wink.

As he left the room, still standing by the doorway was Morgan Little staring at his ancient enemy Morgan Jaeger. "You still here Morgan", growled Jaegers father?

"We're done, for now"! Then he turned and followed the entire cavalcade of interested parties to the hastily arranged news conference, awaiting them at the main entrance of the hospital.

As Jaegers mother and sister filed into the room, Morgan winked at them saying, "I think we'll be OK Sarah"!

"Not out of the woods yet Sarah. The news conference downstairs will no doubt go in our favor and let's turn on the news to see if there's a local live report since every station in the area has a camera truck on premises. I wouldn't put it past some Jake Legged local lawyer to attempt a civil suit since your family has the fiscal depth, but if there was anything out there incriminating I'm sure it would've surfaced by now"!

Just then the doctor entered the room with a nurse and said, "I think we can remove the IV from your arm and then we can spend a few hours running a few more tests on your son, and then one more night for observation, then if nothing shows up, we can probably release him by midmorning tomorrow"!

At noon the hastily prepared news conference was televised and Jaeger was given a clean bill of legal health by everyone, especially those from out of state finding no legal culpability in the accidental deaths of players, at the Cotton Bowl.

Still in the coming days, the moniker 'Jaeger the Mankiller' stuck to him like a bad tattoo.

By noon his personal belongings were brought by the team staff from the Cotton Bowl, as they all made the rounds of the Longhorns still down the hall mending their collective bodies.

One by one, the players whispered to Jaeger, a word of 'thanks' for the memories and a further 'thank you' for disposing of Dexter Mankiller in a way most appropriate. The local and national media started to reflect on the lives of both Mankiller and Jaeger with what was known, coming to a variety of conclusions on whether or not Mankiller or Jaeger was NFL material.

The conclusion was that both men were of that caliber, yet only one of them would be available for the call. The bulk of speculation then landed on whether or not Jaeger would either suit up as a Longhorn the following season, or cash in his chips and allow him to be selected in the NFL draft months away. No one had the answer and no one was talking, at the moment.

The following day the entire family pulled into the main entrance to the ranch, driving slowly down the long esplanade flanked by ancient Pin Oak trees, planted by Henry and Miss Melanie long ago that were carefully trimmed year after year, so the trees provided a complete umbrella of shade for anyone that came or departed. The old main house was dismantled long ago and rebuilt in the nineteen twenties with the standard modern amenities.

As Jaeger emerged from the family Van he said, "It's good to be home"! His mother hugged him and said, "Your room is at it was when you left son. Come let's take a look, then I'll make us all a good lunch.

"When we're through feedin' our faces, we'll take a trip around the old place so you can see what's been improved and spend some time visiting with friends and family, for there's a whole lot of folks wantin' to see you again, especially now since you're a big shot", added his father, lifting his bag and taking it into the house.

During the afternoon and long onto the evening, they spent time visiting family and friends housed in the family compound. The following morning Jaeger and his father selected a few horses and saddled them up and visited the family graveyard, still on the ranch after all the years. Each and every member of the family was buried there, going back to their original forbearers Henry and Melanie Jaeger, separated only by generations, arrayed in a circular fashion, branching out like a multi layered wheel. Next to the immediate family was the final resting place of the family retainers, once slaves when they arrived, but given their manumission of freedom, for their loyalty and hard work in building this small, but thriving conglomerate. The family retainer section was similarly arrayed as the immediate family as a multi layered wheel. Finally, came the section reserved for the family wolves, each buried with the dignity they so richly deserved, going back to the original forbearers, Akila and Chani.

"Ya know, for many years, those wolves, each and every generation of them, proved a salvation to the ranching business, Grandpa Henry developed", said Morgan! "All we had to do was feed and care for them, give them love and affection and they provided the very best security for every single one of us for generation after generation"!

Going back to the family graves, both men kneeled at the grave sites of Melanie and Henry, making the sign of the cross, with Jaeger saying, "Ya know, many times when I was in the Corps. and whenever I was in a tight spot, somehow I always felt that someone was looking over my shoulder and I always would ask myself, 'What would Grandpa Henry do'? And ya know what dad? It was as if some inaudible voice was whispering into my mind, the various options and damn if the old guy wasn't right every time"!

Morgan then answered, "Son, I know exactly what you mean, which is why something compels me to give this place a visit every so often and have a nice talk with them. During my last little visit to Nam, when upcountry amongst the hostiles, he and I talked quite regularly and the old stories he used to tell about the Comanche and the Mexican pistoleros, that were passed down from generation to generation, all came flooding back into my memory and I like to think that's what got me out of many a tight spot"!

They spent the next hour under that old tree by the grave sites, reminiscing about old times, before they got back up on their horses and rode the line. The old line of pine trees that originally marked the property line, that Henry Jaeger laid out so painstakingly long ago. While many of the original trees had disappeared and the original wood fencing was replaced by barbed wire, late in the nineteenth century, enough of the original trees were somehow still there serving as the original markers, all in a straight line.

Family and the land they held was all that mattered, everything else was a distant second. As they rode the line, Jaeger asked, "That guy Morgan Little, the High Sheriff. He's gonna be trouble isn't he Dad"? "As far as him runnin' you down for roughing up your old football coach awhile back, no. But somehow we got into this feud a long time ago regarding this woman I was seeing before I met your mother and things just got out of hand ever since. Too much bad blood between us, to apologize for and frankly it's a good thing for him that he's been the County Sheriff, for the last twenty plus years or he'd be in the ground"!

"But how does he keep getting reelected term after term"?

"Well son, it seems that he's got the county officials in various boxes. Just like J Edgar Hoover had the goods on every President during his years in office, always getting reconfirmed, well our boy Sheriff Little has is hooks in the right people, the righteous folks that like to walk on the wild side from time to time, in other places. Rumor has it that he's got a secret stash of pictures, tapes, film and those new video tapes on everyone who matters in in the City and the County Governments, so when any time he wants something, anything at all, like get reelected, all turn a blind eye, so the graveyards can vote"!

"So best I steer clear of him"!

"At best, all he's gonna do is give ya a case of worms, at the worst he's got connections with the parole board down Huntsville way, in the Ellis Unit of Huntsville prison and from time to time it's rumored, that sometimes folks can get let out very prematurely, do a job for him then disappear completely. That's strictly a rumor, but ya can bet every last dollar there's some truth there. Even to the point that he's made a few friends in the Ranger Unit downtown. As you can see by his appearance in your hospital room"!

"Not so much as to rattle me, but give you the high hat"?

"Right you are son"!

"Anything else goin' on Dad"?

"You're Uncle Don, the Real Estate developer in Dallas and Ft. Worth has wanted to break up portions of the family estate to develop into commercial and residential property and he's going around to the various relatives to put pressure on me to allow them to go into partnership with him so they can make money. But since I'm the executor and I'm saying 'No', he's soon to be off the family Christmas List. He's doing very well up there yet he wants more, like a shark always on the move and if he gets his toe in the door, next It'll be a foot then before ya know it the entire estate will be dissolved. It'll take him awhile, but that's the way he operates"!

"Now that your back in Texas and especially since the Cotton Bowl, be wary of everyone ya meet, for I wouldn't put it past Morgan Little to try and get to me through you in some way or form, so stay frostie young man"!

"Oh, got a call from the King Ranch folks this morning before breakfast and they want to meet you and have invited us down to their ranch for a hunting weekend whenever you can make it. What do ya think"?

"Set it up for this weekend Dad, for next week I got to get set up for my next semester in Austin".

As they made their way back to the main house, meandering slowly through the various pastures full of grazing cattle and horses making small talk mostly, during a sunny and mild January afternoon, a portion of Jaegers mind wondered if there would ever be any peace in his life. Ever since his late teen years, his life had raced from one crisis to another. 'Pace de Meo' was an elusive goal. Perhaps that was to be his lot in life, a reincarnation of the archangel, searching for the predators that would better their lot in life at the expense of others. But for now, he would enjoy the presence of his family and perhaps all that other stuff was an overreaction to events. As they approach the barn late in the day, Morgan asked his son, "Have any second thoughts about that Mankiller fella"?

Jaeger thought a moment before responding, and then replied, "Not a one, not a single one. Ya know how the wolves can sense evil somehow? Well, when I lined up against this guy, I could somehow sense the rot. Like a rotting corpse. Any second thoughts about the guy, no! After all it was an accident wasn't it"?

With a knowing wink of pride, Morgan Jaeger said, "An accident it was son, accident it was"! Morgan Jaeger had taken his own share of lives into his hands, both at a distance and close up and very personal, both in times of war in faraway places and at peace. Each time it was of great necessity and rational in purpose. This son of his was a chip off the old block, the seed that had not fallen far from the tree. More important, the son had made his bones, just as every Jaeger had done going back even before Henry, even before Dietrich. Somehow Morgan Jaeger had done very well in his mind with his son, a real Mensch and should something unforeseen happen to him, his son would carry on in the family name as well as Morgan if not better. As they entered the main house for the evening meal with the family, Morgan felt it necessary to silently repeat the Lord's Prayer in his head, but for now he would cherish and enjoy every single moment of his time with his son and his family.

28

"We need to meet up sometime in the next few days, for I have the solution to your expansion problem", said Morgan Little, from the phone booth at the bus station.

"How about this coming Sunday", replied Don Ryder!

"Sundays good, but how you gonna get away from your wife"?

"Mary"? "Well lemmeseeheah, that's pretty simple, I'll simply say that an emergency came up regarding a bank loan in one of my partnerships and I'll have to meet with some money guys that're flying into town. It happens from time to time, just one of the exigencies of business. We'll have some wild sex the night before and she'll be on cloud nine the entire Sunday"!

"So now comes the when and the where", said Sheriff Little!

"I've this place, called the "Snooty Foxe", just off the DFW turnpike, say about 1PM so I can have us a late lunch prepared in one of the VIP suites. Ya need directions"?

"No. The Snooty Foxe, off the DFW Turnpike. I'll find it. See ya Sunday"!

Morgan Little hung up the phone, went back to the unmarked County car and slowly drove away. He had a bit of connecting to do before his meeting with Ryder. Several more phone calls and visits during the following days put everything in position.

The next Sunday afternoon he pulled into the parking lot of the standalone edifice called the 'Snooty Foxe', and turned his car over the parking valet, entering the Club. He was greeted by an overly large but well-dressed man. The kind of man who has literally lived in a weight room all his life and was so big that if one shot him it would only piss him off.

"Can I help you sir", came the deep rumbling of his voice? "I'm here to see Don Ryder, I'm expected"!

He then lifted his massive arm snapping his fingers and bellowed, "Sheila, would you please escort this gentleman to Mister Ryder"?

He nodded at the Sheriff who was dressed in casual clothes and said, "Sheila will see to your needs"!

As Morgan Little followed the hypnotic hips of the lovely Sheila, he briefly flirted with starting a movement to allow his county to evolve from its current dry Baptist status, to one that allowed liquor by the drink. It certainly would be convenient and increase the county's tax base, yet on the other hand, the crime rate would skyrocket only making more work for the Sheriff's department. He decided that he'd leave well enough alone and allow man's hypocrisy to flourish elsewhere. Besides, the DFW Metro area was just an hour away up the interstate, why everything in Texas was 'Just up the road away's'.

Up the circular staircase they went, with Sheila's modest skirt just barely covering her cheeks, revealing her joyous distain of undergarments. It was at that very moment that Morgan Little first learned that some women could wink with their backsides.

The door opened with Sheila announcing," Your guest has arrived Mr. Ryder"! Morgan nodded at the young lady as he entered, finding Don Ryder focused on the performer in the center stage. Without looking at Morgan Little, he offered his hand out to shake, focusing on the dancer down below saying, "Her shtick, uh, her gimmick is to do the splits over a silver dollar standing on its end and then rise up without the use of her hands. As she arises the coin has disappeared! Now that my man is indeed talent"!

"So how is Mrs. Ryder Don", asked Morgan as another scantily clad waitress appeared, bringing Morgan Little his drink of choice, Jack Daniels Black Label, two fingers, neat. Now in the rest of the known world, a 'double' is known by placing the forefinger and the middle digit placed side by side against the glass, but in certain parts of Texas, a 'double' is known by placing the fore finger and the pinky against the glass, a distance of at least three to four inches and pour. Here, at the 'Snooty Foxe', the latter was the custom.

"Mister Ryder, will you and your guest be eating now or wanting to wait for later", asked the waitress?

"Let's see, two inch thick rib eyes cooked medium with all the trimmings? That about right", asked Ryder of the Sheriff?

Little nodded in agreement, signaling Ryder to say to the waitress, "Tell the chef to get to work"! Then continuing proudly he said, "As far as the Missus is concerned, everything is five by five. She fucked the lights outta me last night and saw to it that every drop out my essential fluids was drained. Why when that bitch gets in the mood, hide the livestock. When we got done, she left a wet spot on the bed, well over a yard wide and we had to go to the guest bedroom to sleep. Good thing the children were off to private school out of state, or else they'd have run into the bedroom wondering what was goin' on? That woman sure can't keep from hittin' the high note when she gets her nut. Often thought about puttin' a pillow over her face, but thought better of it. Can always tell whether or not a woman has got her nut or not by the wet spot on the bed. No wet spot and she's fakin'. Can tell it every time Morgan"!

Just then the door opened and the waitress swiftly brought the salad for both men to start on and promptly left without a word.

Both men started on their salads, with the half inch thick glass shielding them from the garish rock and roll music down below, allowing the softly lilting, staccato tones of a Vivaldi Cantata to work its wonders setting the proper mood.

"So what's this about the Jaeger estate you mentioned", asked Ryder? "You still want to gain access to the Jaeger lands for development Don"?

"Do bears shit in the woods? Does the sun always rise in the east each morning? Why hell yes I do, but as long as your pal Morgan Jaeger sits on top of that particular totem pole it's not gonna get done unless I outlive the son of a bitch. Then I'll be too old to care"!

"What if I told you of a way to bring that about with no comebacks"?

Just then the door opened and the main course arrived, with Ryder saying, "Hold that thought while we feed our faces"!

The two men ate in silence, with the relish of a condemned man taking his final meal, savoring each morsel of one of the finest cuts of steak prepared with a master's touch.

"So how'd you come to know of this place Don? I mean these people treat you like an owner"!

"That's because I am an owner or one of them anyways. One of my subsidiary companies owns ninety percent of this place. Part of a deal I did about a year ago. Remember Bruno Danziger the professional wrestler?

Well that mountain that greeted you downstairs is his nephew. The guy curls hundred pound barbells for starters.

Well a while back Danziger had this gambling problem and owed over five hundred large to some boys out west who wanted their money right away. Now these boys play rough and never take no for an answer. I got wind of Danziger situation through a mutual friend. Met with Bruno the next day and worked a deal with him that he couldn't refuse, then got his bankers together to do a deal where the four clubs he owns around the Metroplex area were refinanced and the following day delivered several cashier checks to his debtors, letting him off the hook, but giving me controlling stock in this place without it costing me a penny. OPM, my friend OPM, I own ninety percent of this club and employ his nephew as manager. This place churns seventy five thousand large a week net, cash money and Danziger has the other three places that do almost as well each month so he's hardly hurting. Of course I had to kick back some gelt to the bankers, but its pennies on the dollar in comparison"!

"So tell me Morgan, what's the deal with the Jaeger land? You say that there's a way! Show me"!

"Don, I'm not gonna show ya, but I'll tell ya. The only thing preventing you from taking control of that land is the immediate Morgan Jaeger family inclusive of him, his wife, his two underage daughters and of course the hero of the Cotton Bowl, the eldest son, the 'Uberballer'. Is that about right"?

"You forgot about the family lawyer Hal Latham, Morgan", replied Ryder with narrowed eyes"!

"Actually I didn't forget about Hal Latham at all, they all have to cease to exist"!

"You're talking some serious stuff here Morgan"!

"About as serious as a heart attack, Don"!

"So how you gonna do it"?

"You don't want to know, all you have to do is pay for it to happen! Then in the aftermath you'll know when to make your move without any further communication between us. For that's what you do best, is it not"?

Ryder thought for a moment. He knew of some people that could do what was needed to accomplish a task.

As if he were reading his mind Morgan said, "The people you think you know about, are rank amateurs that will botch the job, get caught and lead a trail right back to you. At the first sign of trouble they'll rat you out in a heartbeat. Better to render unto Caesar, what Caesar does best"!

"You're right Morgan. So what do you get out of the whole thing"?

"A quarter mill for me up front and, since it's my plan and I will be the one implementing everything. The worker bees will require twenty grand per body, Morgan, his wife Sarah, their two children and of course Hal Latham their family lawyer, who will have a suffer a fatal coronary shortly thereafter. Of course all the family secrets will die with him but he wouldn't surrender them anyway"! "You forgot about the Uberballer, the prodigal son"!

"No I didn't Don. The Uberballer will be prosecuted by the State of Texas for the murder of his family and with any luck will get the death sentence or at the very least the rest of his life in prison"! "What if he gets a good lawyer, a really good lawyer and gets off Morgan"?

"A court order will be in place through one of the judges I have in my pocket, freezing all the family and business funds for the duration of the trial and really good lawyers, I'm talking the ones with the magic cost a great deal of money. At very best Jaeger will get a public defender who will go up against a buzz saw. The only guy that could turn things around is Hal Latham the family lawyer and he'll be six feet under by that time"!

"Seems that you've thought of everything Morgan"!

"Train hard, fight easy, Don. Anything else"?

"And now to the details Morgan, what else do you want"?

"You'll of course make me a silent partner, in all your new development ventures pertaining to any and all of the Jaeger properties, which means you'll have firm documented commitments from all of the family members that are left. I'm a ten percent 'gross' partner, off the top before any expenses and that'll keep me happy. Any curve balls and I'll be unhappy and then shortly thereafter you'll be unhappy. Catch my drift"?

"Completely! Now about your front money"!

"Every other day you'll send a messenger, with five thousand dollars cash money to a private post office box and deposit the front money. When the money amount is reached, then and only then will I start to put things in motion. Should payments be late, even by one day, or stop entirely for any reason, all bets are off and any monies paid will be forfeit.

You go your way and I'll go mine. All you have to do, after all the front monies are paid is sit back and read the newspapers and watch the local evening news. Now get a pen out and write this down on one of those paper napkins"!

Ryder then wrote down the location of the private postal box in Waco and the combination of the box, saying "Just to keep the math correct, the son Jaeger is included in the front money calculations"? The Sheriff nodded his head.

"So you'll guarantee no comebacks of any kind on any of us, right Morgan"?

"None Donald, so are you in or not"?

"I'll have your first envelope in that box by the close of the business day tomorrow, is that good enough for ya"?

"Make certain your man knows there are seven days a week and the box will be visited on every other day"! Ryder nodded his head in agreement.

"So the wet spot on the sheets indicate satisfaction, eh Donald"? Ryder's face turned from grimly serious to a wide smile as he said, "Something to do with the involuntary vaginal response from a woman. Not quite certain just how their plumbing works, just that absence of the holy wet spot on the sheets, usually means she's puttin' on a show and will have to finish herself off, manually or else she'll get very cranky soon after"!

They parted company an hour later with the Sheriff begging off an offer of a freebie for the road. He could wait till afterward to satisfy his prurient interests. Currently he had the upper hand on Donald Ryder's future affairs. Should video tapes of the good Sheriff satisfying his lustful proclivities at any time, that advantage would disappear in a heartbeat. Any VIP room worth its salt would have complete videotaping facilities. He knew the likely hood of his recent meeting being taped, but since his new partner was part and parcel of his new venture, the threat factor was minimal. After all, a man doesn't stay County Sheriff for around twenty years with knowing a few things.

Late the following afternoon, he parked his unmarked County Car in the strip center across the street from the Private Postal facility and sent messenger across the street to pick up the package. He scanned the entire area to see if someone were watching. He did this three more times that week and discovering that no one had his tail, then started to make the pickups himself.

The following Saturday he got up early and drove to Houston some four hours away by interstate. Malatesta Suarez had made his pile of money as a highly successful Narco traffiker, with the special ability to make people disappear completely. Now he was completely legitimate, almost. Still dabbling in the arts, just to keep his hand in, but the running of his Mexican restraints and clubs kept him deep in the chips and busy almost seven days a week.

"Buena's Dias, Nino", greeted Malatesta as Morgan Little took a seat in one of the semicircular booths at his restaurant. The waiters descended on the duo with Morgan's 'Jack Daniel's', neatly done. "As usual we talk first and then eat, yes"?

Morgan nodded his head saying after the waiters had departed, "In about a month, I'll need you to take acceptance of two orders of beef in the usual fashion"!

"Pozole, or my specialty, the 'Mexican Stew' for my menu"?

"Exactly"!

"The meat delivery in question will be worth thirty thousand dollars. Does that meet with your approval", asked Morgan?

"The meat will be delivered to Houston", asked Malatesta?

"Mal, the shipment will be local to anyplace you say"!

"Good, no transport fees involved, so as we're old friends, lets toast to friendship", as the two clicked their drinks together sealing the deal. Then Morgan lifted an envelope from his jacket and placed it in front of Suarez, who peeked inside seeing the cash containing the down payment for his services.

"On account to show good faith Mal"!

"You will call me later with the details"!

Morgan again nodded his head, as Mal Suarez then snapped his fingers signaling his waiters to prepare the meal.

As Morgan drove back to Waco, he looked at his watch seeing that he was right on schedule for his late afternoon pickup. The two shooters would be instructed to drive to Houston and pick up the balance of their fee, where they would meet Malatesta Suarez and his merry men. Of course Suarez and his men would cut their throats in silence, dismember them and stuff each man's remains in a fifty gallon oil drum, then carefully pour carbolic acid on them. Within a few days the remains would dissolve to a gelatinous mass, un Viola, "Mexican Stew". Then the mass would be dumped down the storm drain in the rear of the restaurant and properly hosed down with water.

Once that was accomplished, Mal Suarez would get in his car one morning and be greeted with two pounds of Semtex explosive as he started his car. All trails to Waco would be expunged forever. The demise of Suarez would be chalked up to old grudges resulting from his days as a Narco..

Royce Baintree was making noises about running for political office after his retirement from the Rangers the next year. Of course he would be happy to lend an ear and exert some moral suasion to certain people on the Parole Board down at Huntsville Prison, to grant parole to two certain prisoners who would quickly find work. Further, Royce would find them Ranger uniforms, revolvers, a State Patrol vehicle and an official looking court order with which to gain access to the premises and the all-important silencer for the shooters revolver.

The two ersatz Rangers would visit the Jaeger main house late in the afternoon, gain entrance via the court order, put a well-placed silenced bullet in the wife and the two girls then, visit Morgan Jaeger who would be alone plowing one of the fields on his tractor. One or more silenced bullets in his chest as a surprise as he read the court order should do the job quite nicely, then a trip back to town to return all the uniforms and equipment equipment to Royce Bainbridge, with the exception of the revolvers that did all the damage. Then, a night time sashay over to Hal Latham's home after all had gone to bed, picking the lock on his front door and sneaking up the stairs to his bedroom and entering his room after he was fast asleep and squirting cyanide into his nostril and holding him still for a scant few minutes until it worked its magic then stealing away without a sound. Then a trip down to Austin to place the revolver in the trunk of the Uberballers car, then a short drive to Houston to pick up their money, from Mal Suarez and depart for parts unknown. Except Malatesta would be the very last one the duo ever laid eyes on.

Sheriff Little, couldn't figure out a way to cheat Suarez out of the last twenty five thousand, so he had to let that little detail go by the wayside. After all he reasoned, one had to stick to the plan and his plan was superb. He'd deliver the money, have a good meal then a pleasant drive back north. Suarez would go "Boom" soon enough after.

Morgan Little had selected the future parolees with great care. The trigger man had to be someone who relished seeing another die by his hand. One disciplined just enough to follow a well laid plan yet could improvise well enough if needed, yet motivated by money and greed. His partner also had to share many of the faculties of the triggerman yet had to be skilled sufficiently to be able to break and enter any premises at will, with the abilities of a master locksmith.

Sheriff Little had the handle on most of those who sat in judgment on the State Parole Commission, so when Pete Delano and Will Sutton came before them for their initial hearings, it was almost an automatic approval of their parole. Within a week of their release, they had done all that was required, then dropped off the face of the earth, never to have their initial meeting with their parole officer in San Antonio.

Of course, the murder of the Jaeger family occurred in Sheriff Little's jurisdiction which placed him in a central position regarding the investigation of the family's murder. What seemed to slip under the radar was the demise of Hal Latham, the Jaeger family's long time attorney. The county coroner never bothered to perform the required autopsy, pronouncing that he passed away from natural causes, since everyone knew he was hypertensive and taking medication for chronic high blood pressure.

Armed with a court order and accompanied by Royce Baintree of the Texas Rangers, several calls were placed to the Austin authorities and the University of Texas campus police, to interdict and arrest Jaeger the beloved Uberballer, for the murder of his family.

In the dead of night, the trunk of Jaegers car was forced open and there, wrapped in oil cloth was a .45 caliber pistol that later ballistics tests confirmed, was the weapon that killed the entire Jaeger family the day before.

"We're gonna need a little help here folks and I request the summoning of the SWAT team to help us in our apprehension", asked Sheriff Little of the local authorities. Within an hour, a team of SWAT operatives was on the scene ready to go into action.

"We all know the level of violence this Jaeger is capable of, especially after his performance in the recent Cotton Bowl game", suggested Sheriff Little. "After all, isn't he now known as 'Jaeger the Mankiller', he added.

All nodded their heads in agreement for everyone there had been witness to his on the field body counts.

Ranger Baintree added, "He's up on the third floor studying I'm given to understand and I suggest that we force our way into his dorm room and take him by force as a precaution"! The Rangers suggestion took its effect on the rest and as all agreed, they made their way silently up the stairway, quietly awakening students and evacuating them outside of the building.

That accomplished, Jaeger's metal door was breached and a swarm of men entered his room.

Students waiting quietly in the parking lot focused on his room above, which was one of the few rooms early in the morning that still had its lights on, witnessed from afar, the entire room breach, seeing a flickering of the lights, then seeing a form crash through the third floor window and fall to into the branches of a tree below and then yet another form wearing the dark garb of a SWAT officer follow the very same trajectory to the earth, this time missing the tree entirely and landing on the grass below. Noises and crashing from the third floor suggested that a mighty struggle was occurring and then silence.

Soon ambulances and a hoard of patrol cars, along with some late arriving media Vans arrived to bring witness to the apprehension of "Jaeger the Family Killer", as he later came to be known.

The surviving SWAT personnel dragged Jaeger manacled with his arms behind him and his feet tightly manacled, unceremoniously down the stairs bleeding from multiple head wounds, through the doors of the Dormitory, unconscious to the sidewalk at street level. Each and every member of the SWAT unit involved, suffered from bleeding wounds indicating evidence of a mammoth struggle. The only ones emerging from the third floor debacle unscathed were Sheriff Little and Ranger Baintree. Both reluctantly eager to confront the gathering swarm of media below.

Campus Police were tasked to sequester Jaegers, quarters declaring it as a Crime Scene. As he was lifted onto the Ambulance gurney still in a state of unconsciousness, Jaeger was hurriedly read his rights under the Miranda rule, a modest detail that escaped the scrutiny of those assembled in all the excitement. As for the two SWAT team members, that forcibly were ejected from the third floor, both miraculously survived the fall, but spent well over a year in the hospital at taxpayer expense, repairing the myriad of injuries suffered as well as the long and painful recuperation, eventually retiring from active duty, duly compensated by the state.

The following morning, all of the statewide media was full of reportage regarding the arrest of the former Jaegermeister and the bloody murder of his entire family. The family funds frozen by court order, Jaeger had to rely upon the State of Texas to provide a public defender, to mount a defense.

To his defense came one Elizabeth 'Buffy' Beauvoir, just a year out of law school armed with a Juris Doctorate degree and a recent bar exam graduate in the State of Texas. No matter that she came with Summa Cum Laude credentials, she was up against the State of Texas and the Media, quick to form a critical opinion, of someone who just recently was viewed as the Savior of the entire states reputation.

Prior to the run up to the trial she filed motion after carefully crafted motion attacking the circumstantial mass of evidence arrayed against her client, then a change of venue motion attacking the statewide media reportage that already poisoned public opinion against her client, then she tried to attack the court order freezing Jaeger family funds and at each and every turn she was rebuffed by the Judiciary.

All of her student life, she achieved her academic success, by self-discipline, hard work, study habits that knew few equals and a superior intellect. She studied text book court room tactics and was indoctrinated by her professors to play strictly by the rules.

Yet once she got out in the provinces and away from the professorial world of the practice of law, she quickly discovered that there was no greater teacher than experience. Further, that the world as it is, is not an entirely fair place, especially in a court room.

Her uncle, Leo Schwartzwald, was one of the old time partners of a law firm in Downtown Houston, occupying five full floors of an office building, with deep connections both in Austin and in Washington DC.

Not a great follower of collegiate sports, he was none the less aware of the recent exploits of the "Jaegermeister", and of his current legal problems germane to the murder of his family. He called Boyd Parmalee, one of his legal gunslingers in for a meeting. Over the morning coffee,

Leo asked, "Boyd, you been following' what's been goin' on in Waco, with that young man"?

"Yes Leo and of course, your niece Elizabeth is representing him, pro bono given that his family has frozen his access to any part of the family funds via court order"!

"That's why I keep you around Boyd. People like my niece should be clerking for some Supreme Court judge, while verbal pistol packers like you are what's needed when a man's life's at stake. So what do you think about the State's case against Liz's client"?

"The whole thing smells like fish gone bad. The evidence is highly circumstantial and they're moving at warp speed in getting this case to trial next week, a scant thirty days after the murder. Not near enough time to mount an effective defense. So I suppose you want me to schlep on up to Waco and worm my way into the court room every day and report back to you the supreme casual observer on a daily basis"?

Leo then reached over and filled out an office chit and signed it saying, "Please present this to Lola in accounting on the tenth floor, she'll check out one of the firm's corporate credit cards. Of course you'll shift your current case load to some of the other attorneys"!

"I already have Leo, in anticipation of your needs"! "Damn boy, why aren't you one of my sons in laws"?

"Then I'd have to become a Mormon and my current wife would give me hell, Leo"!

"Oh, just one thing Boyd, that niece of mine Elizabeth is a head strong young lady. I offered her a position here, to get her legal feet wet for a few years, before going out on her own. But that sense of hubris, that she wears like a hair shirt, will get that young man Jaeger killed. Just observe and report, don't make contact yet unless it's necessary. She wants to stand on her own two feet legally, so we'll let her"!

Several days later Boyd Parmalee called Leo after hours with a report filling Uncle Leo out on the fleshier parts of the local history, not directly germane to the case at hand.

"Interesting facts Leo, first the bad blood between the Little and the Jaeger family has gone back generations. While the Jaegers may have been the wealthiest family in these parts, Morgan Little has been the County Sheriff for over twenty years and seems he has his hooks in every body worth knowing. The politicians, judges, bankers and a slew of others. The defendant Jaeger is in the county lockup on remand and he isn't going anywhere and you realize a prior court order has frozen all access to his family funds for his defense.

Now isn't it convenient that the County Sheriff, his father's mortal enemy, is his jailer? They wouldn't even allow him out to attend his family's funeral via court order. Now interestingly enough is the convenient death of the family attorney Hal Latham on the very same day as the demise of his long-time family clients, who have had him on retainer for years. The coroner declared his death to be from natural causes of hypertension, with no mention of the possibility of foul play Leo. And if that ain't a bargain, no autopsy was ever held prior to his burial two weeks ago"!

"So what you're saying Boyd, is that you smell a rat"!

"Yeah the smell is there, it's just that I don't know from which direction Leo"!

"You think it's worth getting Rick Muscano, the firms PI up there for a look around"?

"It's the firms money you're spending Leo, but Rick does have the nose for rooting around the cess pool"!

"I'll get him on the phone this evening and tell him where you're staying and you two can meet up when he gets there and you fill him in on the details. Anything else"?

"Oh yes Leo, just one more thing. The sitting Judge has moved up the trial date by two work days, which means time is of the essence"!

After he got off the phone with his firms long time contractual PI, Leo decided to authorize two of his operatives, rather than just one to work the case. He had some explaining to do to the other partners next month at their quarterly meeting, but it was his name on the door and on all the letterheads that led the way. So they could take the expenses out of his year ending dispersions.

As Buffy Beauvoir began her jury selection, apprehension that she was way over her head with these bumpkins began to overwhelm her, for the very first time in her life, yet she suppressed her concerns and pressed on.

It certainly helped that Boyd Parmalee was a classmate of the sitting Judge for the trial, gaining him a permanent seat for the duration of the trial as a friend of the court. He had little regard for Judge Morris Womble, when they were classmates at the University of Texas School of Law and as he sat there as a mere observer, he focused on Judge Womble's every movement to try and ascertain whether or not the Judge was in the bag of someone.

His nightly reports to Uncle Leo, shared his concerns, that something was going on between the County Prosecutor and the Judge, when the majority of procedural and substantive objections by Buffy were overturned, leaving possible avenues for appeal at a later date.

Judge Morris Womble was determined to move the trial along at a break neck pace and would brook no attempts to delay or obfuscate, as a courtesy to the sitting jury. One by one all of the procedural delays and recitations of case law were ruled as, not germane to the case at hand therefore irrelevant by the Judge, time after time as the case moved on.

As it came her turn to present her case, the detectives discovered two witness's to Jaegers arrest who observed first hand that Jaegers 'Miranda Rights' were read to him while he was moving on the gurney towards the ambulance, while in a complete state of unconsciousness. The students were pre law students and had approached the DA's office previously but were rebuffed, by the prosecutor. When the two students were finished with their testimony, the prosecutor re-directed the testimony of his two SWAT officers who swore under oath that the student's testimony was 'Inaccurate". Buffy flew from desk in the court room and bored right into the testimony of both the arresting SWAT officers, boring right into them with a relentless abandon. "Do you know the meaning of perjury and the penalties a conviction carries", she asked both officers? But their response was professional and cool under fire and rendered her passions as inept, as one of the officers suggested that she ask that very question of her witness's.

In a very loud voice Buffy declared, "Well somebody around here is lying through their teeth", as she declared that she was through with her witness, gaining her a verbal admonition from Judge Womble.

She finally recognized Boyd Parmalee after the Judge declared the trial over for the day, as she filed out of the courtroom in the hall way outside.

"Uncle Leo send you up here to spy on me, Mister Parmalee"?

"Where do you think your last two witness's came from, Heaven?

Uncle Leo has spent the firm's money retaining the services of two of the firms PI's to lift the local rocks and do some nosing around at the UT campus. They stuck in their thumbs and pulled out some plumbs"!

"You might be grateful that you have an Uncle like Leo Schwartzwald, who knows his way around the street, not just relying on one's legal legerdemain. He told me to keep my hands off and listen and report and that's just what I've done. I wish he'd have let me do more"!

"I'm approaching the 'Buzz Saw' aren't I, Mister Parmalee?

"Yes you are and start calling me Boyd from now on. You've argued the facts, you've argued the law and something is going on between the Judge and the Prosecutor and I don't have a handle on quite what yet, but the hounds are still on Leo's time clock so they might yet turn up something useable, but that's a long shot right now. Right now tomorrow, when you go before the jury and make your final summation, please allow me to help you with your summation to the jury"!

"Where in town are you staying" Buffy reluctantly asked?

She had argued the law and had rebuffed. She had argued logic and the facts with apparently scant effect, now it was time to put on the show and what she knew about Boyd Parmalee, was a preview of what she was about to see.

Far into the night worked Buffy and Parmalee in his hotel room, in periodic contact with his two detectives, still hard at it trying to ferret out something useable in Jaegers behalf. But the trail had grown cold.

So together they worked on crafting her final argument in front of the jury. Boyd reminded her of his visual impressions of each and every juror and offered her pointed comments regarding what arguments just might have an effect on each juror. For all it took was to place just one seed of solid doubt in the mind of a single juror to achieve stalemate and a hung jury. Just one stubborn solitary soul had to be reached, to buy some additional time for a second trial and perhaps a change of venue and the unshackling of the family accounts for additional legal representation. Just one juror, but who?

All night long they worked, on her presentation, a lengthy examination of the circumstantial fact at hand, the implication of the rapidity of the prosecutions zeal to try this case, a redirection of the trial docket ahead of other cases suggested that something was in the air, but what? The questions of who stood to gain from the execution of the surviving member of the Jaeger family? All were questions they had to implant in the jurors collective minds, even though the dots were far from being connected.

Parmalee sat in the very last row of the crowded court room. Also in attendence on the other side of the court room sat Sheriff Little, shifting about from time to time as Elizabeth Beauvoir made a lengthy and impassioned final argument to the jury in behalf of her client, "Der Uberballer".

His two PI's were just outside the court room, their yeoman like work largely done, as Boyd reviewed his notes, ticking off one by one the aspects of the trial he felt were of appealable value. He cast yet another glance at the client Jaeger, sitting there passively staring straight ahead. What was going through his mind? What level of silent suffering was he enduring at the loss of his family?

Boyd Parmalee was a veteran of many a murder trial both as a prosecutor and a defendant's advocate and over time he acquired the ability to read people. All the aspects indicated that the defendant was on that one way railroad to perdition, skillfully done, by someone who had much to gain. He had some thoughts as to who it might be, but the dots were far from connectable. Absent hard proof, he might as well remain silent.

Short of a miracle, Jaeger was on a one way ticket to death row.

Even though this nation we live in has the burden of proof lying squarely in the lap of the prosecutors, assuming the 'initial innocence' of the defendant, once the guilty verdict came down from the jury of one's peers, all was reversed. The mountain to be climbed in reversing a verdict was daunting and almost impossible even under the most favorable of circumstances.

As Buffy was wrapping up her impassioned plea to the jury, Boyd's eyes drifted across the room stopping on each and every one of those visitors assembled, his eyes stopped at Sheriff Little as Buffy took her seat. His face was unreadable as long as she spoke; grim was his visage at best.

But as she sat down and the Judge read his instructions to the jury to commence their deliberations, the Sheriff suddenly started to smile broadly, unaware that he was under observation.

And there it was. The Sheriff was the moving force behind all of this.

But how? Why?

As the jury left the courtroom to commence their deliberations and Judge Womble declared the court in adjournment, Parmalee joined

Buffy and the two investigators in the hallway, saying quietly to the PI's, "Gentlemen, let us change our focus to the good Sheriff Morgan Little. We need to know everything about the man. Who he knows? Who he is seen with? Everything! Every jot and thistle, down to the shorts he wears, what he eats, what his blood pressure is, I'm talking everything"!

"Is your firm going to approve the additional expenditure Boyd"? "Lets all go back to my hotel room and get ring Leo up for a verbal approval of the expense"! Back at the room Leo received the conference call from those assembled, glad to extricate himself from a meeting between two of the minority partners squabbling over a petty office policy.

"So you're not angry with me for looking on at a distance Buffy"?

"No Uncle Leo, at first I was, but then….. well thanks for sending Boyd to watch and thanks for the two PI's that are here with us.

"So tell me the bad news first", said Leo Schwartzwald.

Boyd took charge in recapping succinctly all the details that preceded the jury's deliberations. "Now the good news is that your niece, can make a final jury summation with anyone, Foreman, Haines or either of the DeGurin's, she's got the makings of the magic Leo.

But that may not be enough. Jaeger is clearly being railroaded and my guess and it's only an educated guess, is that it's the long time County Sheriff Morgan Little, for there exists a long standing enmity between him and the Jaeger clan going back years. Which is why he's standing deep in the background pulling the strings like a puppet master. A complete file on him would be helpful in connecting the dots in the event of an appeal"!

Leo then asked to speak to both of the investigators, regarding what they knew and what they suspected from their all too brief exposure to the facts at hand.

The lead investigator answered each and every question asked and gave his considered opinions apart from the facts at hand and was joined in agreement with his partner adding,"I agree that something is just not right about this whole thing. Everywhere we went, it seemed that folks were reluctant to speak or form an opinion about the good Sheriff"!

"OK Boyd, tell the boys that I'll approve fourteen calendar days of their complete investigation of Morgan Little, overturn every rock no matter how insignificant"!

"Thanks Leo", said Boyd!

"Now I've got to get back to the squabble between the partners. Hugs and kisses Buffy"!

For three days the jury was out making their deliberations and on the fourth they finally assembled finding the Uberballer 'Guilty' as charged. Several days later, when they had to deliberate as to whether or not he was to be executed or serve life in prison, they retired once again to make their deliberations. For five full days the jury was deadlocked, the lone juror who held out for Jaeger's innocence redoubled her efforts to swing the entire jury into voting to spare his life, digging in her heels against the rest of the jurors.

She was torn by her caving into the pressure by the others during the initial deliberations as to his guilt and swore to herself that she'd not make the same mistake again. After five very intense days, the Jury emerged to render their verdict of life in prison rather than the death penalty.

Judge Womble then polled the jury one by one as to their verdict and as they all appeared weary from the relentless ordeal of deliberations, one by one they verbally affirmed their verdict, yet when it came to Helen Voorhees a simple waitress in a roadside restaurant on the edges of town, she was the only one to vote with a smile on her face.

The verdict read Jaeger could now look forward to a trip down the interstate to Huntsville State Prison and future associations with the dregs of society.

As for Helen Voorhees, she went home exhausted from her service to the State of Texas, only to discover that when she went to work the following day, her final check was waiting for her, for she'd been laid off from her job. The following week her husband an Interstate Long haul truck driver with a local cartage company discovered that he also had been cut loose by his employer.

Two weeks later Leo Schwartzwald, looked at the complete file of one Morgan Little. It covered every single aspect of the man's known life going back to the day he was born. A complete file of every known person he came in contact, his medical records, his shirt size, his shoe size, what he ate, where he ate, and his known bank records. Every single thing that was knowable of the man on matters both great and small was arrayed in a hundred fifty page report on the man. While this report would go a ways towards proving some evidence of political malfeasance in office, it shed little provable light on any activities engaged in regarding the Jaeger family. Those involved were no longer of this world and everything that exchanged was verbal and Cold, Hard, Train Ridin' Cash Money, leaves no audit trail. Leo called Boyd Parmalee into his office to show him the report saying, "I'm really gonna hear it from the partners next month at our quarterly meeting. Take the report home with you to go over it for a few days then return it to me. Feel free to make a copy it you wish, perhaps Buffy can use it someday if she cares to appeal. I'll need the original though to prevent the partners from starting any rumors about a possible girlfriend at my age"!

"I'll see to it that Buffy get a copy of this Leo. So tell me your thoughts about this, if you will"!

After some reflection Leo Schwartzwald ruminated, "The Sheriff is as crooked as a dog's hind leg and there is no doubt in my mind that he was a central player in the complete obliteration of the family Jaeger. My guess is that everything was done in cash, which implies someone else very behind the scene which acted as a funding source. Further it implies that the shooter or shooters are no longer with us and whoever acted as a go between is also in for a permanent visit to the Elysian Fields or perhaps some lower region. The possibilities are endless and if I had unlimited funds I'd search every possible reported death between the termination of the Jaegers life and the start of the trial. But there's always those that simply disappear"!

"It's Buffys Crusade and her responsibility, if she's the stones to grab hold"! Just then the office phone rang, Leo's secretary saying on the intercom, "Miss Beauvoir on line three"!

"Why hello Buffy, how good of you to call. How are things", shrugging his shoulders at Parmalee?

"Completely shitty, Uncle Leo. I need some further seasoning before I'm ready for prime time and I was wondering if there was still a place you could find for me at your firm", came the apparently weary voice on the other end of the speaker phone Both Leo and Boyd's eyebrows lifted in surprise, before Leo said, "Just tell me where to send the moving van young lady. I think I can find a place for a young Lioness on the prowl wanting blood"!

29

The trip down to Huntsville Prison was uneventful. Normally to save the taxpayers money and be efficient, prisoners are bundled up into a single bus and shipped to their final destination via a prison bus, but in Jaegers case he was apparently special. Handcuffed behind his back and with leg shackles, he was placed in the rear seat of a Texas Department of Public Safety Cruiser as part of a five car convoy down the interstate from Waco to the Ellis Unit at Huntsville Prison.

In the lead DPS car was Ranger Royce Baintree, as the officer in charge of the convoy, while in the very last car was Sheriff Morgan Little, while their subject of incarceration occupied the rear seat of middle vehicle.

Jaeger looked straight ahead saying nothing as the convoy pulled out of the Waco County Jail at 4AM in the morning, for there was nothing to say.

Things hadn't turned out exactly as Sheriff Little had planned, yet all and all things turned out fairly well. Jaeger was now all bottled up and no doubt would try and appeal the verdict somehow, but as a convicted felon for a lifetime sentence, the odds were very much against him. Besides, while on death row awaiting execution, there would be seemingly endless reviews of his case by the state and anything might occur to delay the execution some ten years or so distant, while as a part of the prison population anything could happen to shorten Jaegers lifespan. With time and a few connections, Morgan Little would see what could be done to hasten that last little loose end.

As far as the remnants of the Jaeger estate was concerned, he'd render onto Caesar what was Caesars, leaving all that to Don Ryder. All the good Sheriff had to do was introduce Ryder's high priced Dallas Lawyers, to the right local judges he had in his pocket, grease a few palms as far as reelection campaign contributions, perhaps forge a few signatures if needed and controlling interests in the ownership of the Jaeger estate would pass from the only surviving member, now incarcerated for life, to the more responsible members of the clan for future residential and commercial development. No doubt a Guardian Ad Leitum, with a fiduciary responsibility would be appointed by a probate court or, something of that sort to supervise the dismantling of the estate, for future development. But since he wasn't a lawyer he would leave that to others to sort out.

The only thing missing was his absence in witnessing Morgan Jaegers very last moments. The look of surprise on his face as the killer's bullets slammed into his body, caught completely unawares and yet a man who prided himself on situational awareness. He remembered the ecstasy he felt as he grilled the killers about each and every movement they made in the grand deception. He had to satisfy himself with a second hand recantation of the event prior to sending them to Houston for their payment and appointment with the ferryman. They wouldn't speak to anyone ever again.

Just after seven in the early morning the convoy pulled into Huntsville Prison and discharged their precious cargo, with Royce Baintree handling all the transfer paperwork. Jaeger stood there impassively as the handoff of custody was made. He saw out of the corner of his eye, Morgan Little standing off from the small assemblage of DPS troopers, with his hand resting casually on the weapon in his holster, eyes darting back and forth, then coming up when summoned to affix his final signature on the transfer document. That completed he slowly turned and faced Jaeger, giving him a slow and knowing wink as their eyes met.

At that very moment, Jaeger just knew that Morgan Little had something to do with all of this. But what and to what degree? He fixed Morgan Little's facial features deep in his head, for somehow he just knew they'd meet again. He knew it in his bones.

The cuffs and the leg shackles removed and returned to the departing State Troopers, Jaeger was then quickly processed into the system and issued his new prison off white garb, what passed for a small pillow, sheets and thread bare blanket, during the morning breakfast hour. As they passed through the system and on to his assigned cell block, he passed a steady stream of prisoners all going to their work assignments for the day. Each and every one of them had expected his arrival it seemed, thanks to the information grapevine that exists in every prison when someone of note arrives. Jaeger already had that level of celebrity amongst the other convicts.

As his two burly prison guard escorts, walked him towards his cell he endured the nonstop chatter of the prison policies.

"You're in luck Jaeger, the work assignment guard is out sick today, so you'll spend the entire day by yourself in the cell. Your cell mate will be at his work assignment all day. At meal time, the klaxon will sound and the cell door will open and then close. If you don't leave the cell at that exact time the cell door will close and you don't get fed. You'll have an escort to lunch and back and tomorrow morning and you'll be assigned your permanent work assignment. Give any of us some shit at any time and into the hole ya go for thirty days. You won't like it"!

"From now on you will be referred to as, number '67676'; it's written down on a card inside the pillow case, just like your prison duds. That's your number like it or not and you'll be called that from now on. By your number and nothing else"!

As they arrived at his assigned tier, one of his escorts called out, "One for cell twelve, second tier", as they climbed the steps all the cell doors opened on the second tier of cells, arriving at his assigned cell Jaeger entered, as he heard the guard say, "Be back at lunch number 67676"! The roaring in Jaegers ears grew in its intensity as he didn't hear what the guard said just prior to the iron doors slowly closing. As he measured the space, it seemed to be slightly wider than his entire arm span of 76 inches and some ten feet in length with a single commode and a sink at the rear of the cell.

The walls were high and jutting out from each wall were two metal slabs that served as bed frames that were barely long enough to fit his frame. The bottom slab was neatly made as a bunk with the three inch thick cotton mattress made up with hospital corners and a note pinned to the pillow which read; "This is my fuckin' bunk, yours is above. I don't want to have to tell you twice, mate"!

Jaeger forced a smile from his lips as he put down his stuff on the bunk above. Then something deeply and neatly etched into the concrete wall, covered over by several layers of paint over the years by a prior occupant of that cell told Jaeger how it was going to be. The etching read; "Nothing can be worth all of this"!!

At the lunch hour klaxon, Jaeger's cell door slid open and he emerged to a signaling from a guard that escorted him to the main gallery. Getting in line he went through in silence, accepting the offerings and quickly found a place at the end of one of the long tables. As he started to dig into his meal, he felt a thousand eyes upon him but tried to ignore the scrutiny. All the time he ate, within the fifteen minutes allotted to each prisoner, he kept his feet on the ground and expanded his peripheral vision. In time this would have to become a daily habit necessary for survival. For the foreseeable future, each day would become a possible prelude to combat. Those too lazy or careless would fare badly. As he quickly glanced around from time to time, he noted that with a few exceptions, people usually ate with their own kind, the Blacks with the Blacks, the Latino's with the Latino's, the Anglo's with the Anglo's. Without having to be told, referring back to his days in Boot Camp, direct eye contact with strangers is always construed as a threat whether it's meant to be or not.

Guard's and other inmates are never to be gazed upon. Never open a conversation with anyone not previously known. In time, perhaps he would be able to have someone to cover his six, but that just might be a long time in coming. One day at a time he would take it. This was an entirely new environment for Jaeger and hopefully his military training could speed up his learning curve.

As they ate, Rae asked Roy Seltzer, "Well wadda ya think Roy, of your new cell mate"? As they both were just behind Jaeger as he went through the food line, and positioning themselves to where they could casually observe him several tables away.

"He's certainly a big fella. He moves well, his eyes are constantly in motion seeing much without direct eye contact, like a shark in water. His instincts seem to be in order, by the way he contains each movement and his reputation does indeed precede him Rae. But in the end he's gonna be a hard one to get to know. He'll bear watching for some time to come, but this much I'm certain of. He's no joiner of anything"!

"Think the skinheads and the bikers will put the heat on him", asked Rae?

"Oh they'll put him to the test all right, the only question is when"? "When ya gonna break the ice Roy"?

"Either tonight at supper, if the opportunity presents or afterward when we're in the cell for the evening"! They both watched Jaeger as he arose and followed the others out of the dining hall, depositing the empty trays and the leftovers into the receptacles, under the watchful eyes of the one of the guards, to see that nothing left the dining hall with them.

His walk back to his cell was uneventful, spending the rest of the day trying to sleep in his upper bunk, but as his eyes closed, endless visions of the preceding months, prevented him from dozing off. This had been going on for each and every day since the ordeal of his incarceration and trial.

Arriving seemingly out of nowhere, without a hint of warning was a terrible series of events, that took from him all he held near and dear to his heart. He supposed that he should've been glad for the divine intervention that brought him back into the family fold.

The prodigal son finally come home, to a love he'd never hoped to experience again, only to have it all whisked away, by some unseen forces. The family estate, that had been carefully nurtured and developed by all of his forbearers, passed down from generation to generation, via a long and thus far distinguished heritage, now gone. His family gunned down by Who? A pistol suddenly appearing in the trunk of his car, that wasn't his, was all it took to convict him in record time. His sudden rise to fame, then rapid plunge into the ice cold water of infamy. His mind searched for ways to keep his sanity and self-control and thus far he was ahead of the game, thanks again to his military training, of putting his mind in a far off place and conjuring up problems and mythical solutions. Just as if he were in a POW camp. Well, he was, of a sort.

He tried to recall the biblical training he received as a child, resisting the lessons all the way, yet somehow recalling the 'Book of Job', in its entirety. How a good and successful man had it all taken away, by forces unseen, only to have the reader know that it was a silly bet between the Almighty and his fallen angel Lucifer. Jaeger concluded he hadn't lived an exemplary life thus far, he'd been many places and done many things, all of which were questionable, but in each and every case it was for the common good. Job however, was a good man that lost everything, just as Jaeger had; even his health was at issue at an old age, whereas Jaeger was still a young man. All because God had removed his unseen hand of protection, he reckoned.

What was the some of the Christ's last words as he hung from the cross, "My God, My God, why have you forsaken me"? His mortality quickly ebbing away. Gradually his eyes closed and he started to drift off, his body gradually releasing some of the tension that remained with him like a hair shirt. His mind now somehow as completely at peace, as he seemed to drift amidst little fluffy clouds, weightless without form or function, simply a thought adrift in another dimension quite apart from mere mortals.

Gradually, string wordless messages began to invade his sub consciousness, revealing the image of the biblical Job and his complete story from the beginning to the very end. Revealing the joy and the ecstasy of his pilgrimage through life, the family he'd proudly raised, and all the good and generosity he'd shown to others, throughout his early life. Then the series of tragedies he'd suffered one right after the other, coming at him from all side, one right after the other, nonstop, a Juggernaut of pain and suffering. Then in the midst of his agony, it all gradually went away, in the course of time.

The lesson perceived was that everything is cyclical, everything. Tough times never last, just as happiness never lasts, one just follows the other in an inexorable cycle of life. If he was to last the course of his naturally preordained time, he would have to endure what lay ahead, just as Job and the Christ had.

Part of Jaegers sub consciousness wanted and end to what he suspected lay ahead, yet a silent voice that lay deep within said, 'Not yet. Not until you've finished the pilgrimage I've chosen for you'! 'Quo Vadis Domine', he asked?

'I'm right here as I've always been, my son', came the response without sound or form!

'Was the sacrifice of my family, worth all if this', his mind asked?

For a seemingly long time there was silence, before the answer filtered through, 'In the course of time, ask that question again and you will have your answer'!

Then the blaring sound of the dinner klaxon occurred, followed by the opening of the cell doors. Jaeger emerged from his cell rubbing the sleep out of his eyes, feeling somewhat physically refreshed, yet mentally drained as he followed the guard to the Convict Dining Hall, finding his place in line.

As he took his seat, two other men took a seat directly in front of him, apparently at random without a glance and started into their meal.

After a few minutes had passed, Jaeger heard the in front of him say,

"Hope ya didn't mind my little note when ya arrive this morning, mate"! A slight accent, perhaps Australian, or New Zealand met his ears. Jaeger quickly wondered what a foreigner was doing in an American State run prison, before answering, "The top bunks just fine with me, pal"!

"I'm Roy Seltzer, as in 'Alka Seltzer' and this little gnome next to me is Rae, the Artist"!

Jaeger looked up briefly at the two across from him, as he met Seltzers eyes with a brief glance, then acknowledged each of them with a slight nod, saying "Back at cha, gentlemen"!

"Rae here is the facilities resident artist and runs the prison printing shop. Quite fitting since he's in for illegal currency printing after giving the Feds and the Texas Rangers fits for years, the Rangers finally put him down for the count while the Federal's gave up the ghost", offered Seltzer.

"Seems like you'd be someone worth knowing", said Jaeger as he dug into his tasteless meatloaf.

"I'm retired", offered Rae!

"For the time being, besides they watch him like a hawk. Full body search whenever he leaves the printing plant, eyes on him constantly and whenever he goes to the loo, for a whiz", countered Seltzer with a wry eye.

"And you", asked Jaeger?

"Long story mate, we can discuss that later"!

Jaeger noticed that whenever they spoke, they never looked at Jaeger, but over his shoulder, their eyes constantly on the move watching seemingly mundane events behind Jaeger, as they spoke through tight lips that barely seemed to move. He decided to return the favor.

"So how did ya draw the lucky straw and get me as a cell mate", Jaeger asked Seltzer?

"I can answer that", Rae butted in while Roy drank. "He asked for ya"! "Simple as that", asked Jaeger? "You got that kinda clout around here"? "I prefer to refer to it as 'Quid pro Quo'. A number of influential people on both sides of the coin owe me favors, and you arrive with a certain amount of celebrity and a bit of a reputation as a tough guy. Now while many of us are just trying to serve out our time with little fanfare, this microcosm of society has more than its share of certifiable crazies that should never be allowed to see the light of day. Someone has to be your guardian angel and show you just who wears the black hat and who doesn't, or else you'll end up as cannon fodder"!

Then Seltzer added, "You got a right good going over since your triumph on New Year's Day. Here it is the middle of May and you've been signed, sealed and delivered. Never in the history of modern Juris Prudence has justice moved so quickly. So some of us sense, as the crackers oft say, 'A Nigger in the wood pile, exists'. Even some of the guards, but they'll not publicly admit so. Then there are the others, a few of which made a bit of a killing on the Bowl pools long odds, while others took a rather nasty bath.

Then others will be intimidated by your performance, while some may want to sooner or later see just what you've got. Do you have the juice or are ya a mirage. So watch you six at all times mate"!

"I sorta figured that side out already, but thanks for the heads up"!

They all rose together and walked back to the cell block and as it turned out Rae had the cell next to Jaeger and Roy. In the gradual passage of time, they would become the best of friends, but that would take a gradual evolvement of events, where the trust between men would have to be hard earned, rather than taken for granted. Each man had his private space and only upon the imposition of events, or by personal invitation does another dare to intrude. Rae had his job running the facilities print shop and from time to time made extra money doing pencil portraiture of other inmates cell guards and the upper management of the facility.

Seltzer, had his function running the prison library, his intellect and knowledge of a variety of languages as well as his organizational ability served him and the other prisoners well in providing the best of a variety of magazines for their off time reading. Jaegers first job was running a fork lift and delivering metal plates to the sheet metal presses in the facility license plate plant. In the course of time Jaeger would be cross trained in the various other aspects of the plant.

One Saturday, after Jaeger finished with his workout in the prison yard he joined Seltzer and Rae up in the prison yard stands, to cool off from his exertions. While he went through his routine with the weights, Seltzer and Rae kept a keen eye on who was watching Jaeger with any interest.

"You know some people have been keeping an eye on you other than the guards. Expect the unexpected. Nothing concrete mind you, just a feeling mate. My guess is that people will be coming for you and sooner than later. You've already made enemies of the skinheads by ignoring their invitation. The Kaffir gangsters are always ready for a rumble at any cost and the Latin gangs are ready to go down for any reason for any price. My guess is that big Swartzer, that keeps glaring at you, trying to stare you down into a provocation of some sort, but it could come from the most unlikely of suspects, even Bitch Cassidy the prison whore, who'll bear his ass to anyone for any price"? Continuing on he said, "In reading the Waco and the Dallas Papers every day I discovered a little article tucked away in the Dallas paper, that indicated two whole sections of land had been released from the Waco probate courts, of the land formerly held by the remnants of your family, to be developed by a Real Estate developer named Don Ryder"!

Jaegers jaw set and he growled, "The bastard is married to my father's cousin Mary and my Dad and him fought the rest of the family to break up the estate for commercial and high end residential development, including a country club and thirty six hole golf course"!

"Well since you've had no visitors since you've arrived and no known papers had been served on you it seems to me that your signature must have been forged on one or more legal documents. I'm no lawyer mate, but something smells and while you're here sequestered, you appear to me to be a loose end that'll have to be tied up and soon. I'll make some modest inquiries and give an alert to a few chosen guards that I know have clean hands and Rae here will do what he can to have some eyes and ears out, but I'm afraid that when it comes, it'll be sudden and brutal. The dining hall, the showers, here out in the open and the going to and fro are the most likely places for attack, but it could come from anywhere"!

"My money's on Hoodoo Chile over there", said Rae. "The spade that's keeping the Voodoo Evil eye on you"!

"Rae's has a point there Jaeger. Name was Willie Patterson, until he fell in with the Black Muslim bunch of true believers, then they got him to change his name to Hassan Muhammad, but everyone still refers to him as Hoodoo Chile, but not to his face".

"He keeps the prison infirmary busy from time to time", Rae chimed in! He's one of the main contract hitters, but it's never done in the yard in sight of the bulls, always done with his hands and his victims usually end up with broken necks"!

"I'll keep that in mind Rae and thanks", said Jaeger with a frown. The following day at the lunch break, as they sat down in the Main dining hall Rae said, "Last month, two identical Mexican twins arrived for a long visit here. They're in the next cell block over from us. Seems their dining schedule is right after ours, so while we're leaving they'll be arriving for their feed bag. There's a place I'll show ya in the hallway where the video cameras have no clear view, and that's the most likely place for a hit. Their both about five foot six or seven and their heads will be the newbie clip jobs. They'll both hit you on the approach and they'll be flanking you, one on your right and the other on your left.

They'll have freshly made shivs from the metal shop and the tipoff is that they'll be wearing wraparound shades. Now the reason for that is that behind you will be someone who'll be responsible for ditching the blades"! "Any word as to when", asked Seltzer?

"Alls I know is where, but it'll be within the next few days. Cost me a carton of smokes"!

Seltzer glanced at Jaeger and Rae saying, "Not to put a wet blanket on things, but seems to me that those who are clever enough and with enough juice to put you here are equally clever enough to sew some disinformation. So how exactly did you come by this particular tid bit Rae"?

"Bitch Cassidy"!

"Bitch Cassidy, you say"!

"He was earning his daily bread by going down on his favorite client the Count of Monte Cristo"!

"A whole new meaning for going down for the count, please continue Rae", said Roy!

"While he was milking the cow, he overheard a conversation nearby, between the Count's handler and the two twins outlining the whole thing"!

"So who's this Count and isn't Bitch Cassidy in trouble if it's discovered he's the rat", asked Jaeger?

"The Count is the main prison fixer", said Roy! "He's usually the one that can get anything done for a price. A 'Dog Robber', in military parlance. A Planner and executor. He knows everyone and just about everything, inmates and guards alike. Most everything of significance flows through him. Drugs, messages, hits, etcetera ad nausiam. Now as to Bitch Cassidy, he's of course the prison whore and of his many defense mechanisms, one is that he gives the best hummers in the civilized world, or so I'm told, while the other is that he's completely deaf. Even knows sign language. Only three people in Huntsville know that he's not and you're looking at two of them"!

"So odds are that he'll not be compromised", asked Jaeger?

"He can even read lips", said Roy! "A thoroughly disgusting bloke if ya ask me, but his information is usually spot on"! "One more thing", added Rae! "One of the Mex Twins is right handed and the other is left handed, so it figures the shivs will be in their operative hands. There'll be a guard posted on either end of the hallway video blind spot, but don't really know how helpful they might be"! Then Roy described the place in the hallway where a ten yard long video cam blind spot existed. "Everybody knows where it is including the prison officials, it's been that way for years, just that it's never been a budgetary priority"!

"Would you guys mind walking several steps behind me as we go out for the next few days", asked Jaeger. "I can see what's coming up ahead of me, but I can't see what's behind me"! "In your parlance, we got your six mate", replied Seltzer! As they filed past the place where they dropped the food trays and the refuse, Jaeger noticed one of the guards posted there placing his right hand on his nose as a seemingly casual downward wiping motion. Yet his prior training taught him that is was a signal to someone up ahead the package was soon to arrive. "Heads up mate, show time", whispered Seltzer, indicating he'd seen the same thing.

Seltzer and Rae fell behind Jaeger by several steps as they slowly made their way down the hallway back to their work stations. Up ahead, Jaeger saw a seemingly loitering convict, stop, scratch his nose in the same manner then move on. The message was traveling that Jaeger was soon to arrive.

As he approached the video blind spot he paid attention to the two guards posted ten yards apart and seeing no such signaling motion from either, focused on those approaching and from about twenty yards away, he saw two short stocky Mexicans wearing sunglasses approaching. They were flanking him sure enough, one on either side him as the distance closed rapidly. With their heads down, Jaeger could see just above the top rims of their shades, their eyes focused on their target.

As the distance closed within five yards, Jaeger suddenly broke for the duo and before they could effectively bring the shiv's up, Jaeger sunk each of his thumbs into the assassin's eye sockets, wrapping the rest of his large hands around their ears gaining a quick grip on their heads and slamming them together, as their blades missed their intended mark, one sinking into his left rib at a less than lethal angle while the other grazing Jaegers right side just above the belt line leaving a large bleeding slash and disappearing in his prison shirt.

Both of the guards simultaneously saw the attack and promptly blew their whistles in alarm, while Seltzer and Rae did what they could to hold up any one coming to complete things, thus clogging up the hallway.

Jaeger was protected by Seltzer and Rae while in a few short seconds a slew of guards came running down the hallway to secure a perimeter. Both of the assassins were out cold, while it was noted that each of them was missing an eye, with one eye lying on the floor, ripped from its socket and the other in the hand of Jaeger the Mankiller.

Seeing that Jaeger had a shiv, still imbedded in his left ribcage one of the guards yelled out, "Get some of the medical staff and a few gurneys down here on the double" and stood over Jaeger while the others directed the foot traffic quickly around the scene while rerouting the rest of the lunch crowd by a different route.

"What in the hell is going on here", yelled the assistant warden William Schwelp, as he stormed into the prison infirmary?

The Floor Captain intercepted the official by saying, "Doctor Fowler has just entered surgery on prisoner '67676', who was apparently attacked as he was leaving the noon meal, Warden Schwelp"!

"Where was the attack"?

"In the video blind spot in the hallway leading out of the Dining Hall, Warden"!

"Where were the guards"?

"In their assigned positions as directed"!

"So how do we know who initiated contact"!

"Well sir, apparently it happened so fast it was all over in just a few seconds. You know how these things work. '67676' is the one who sustained the shiv damage, while the two new Mexican inmates, each lost an eye and are unconscious, apparently as a result of their attack on '67676'. Currently they're getting X-rayed for suspected concussions"!

"They're both under guard"? "Yes Warden"!

"Goddamn that Jaeger. I just knew he was going to be trouble", muttered Schwelp!

"Well sir apparently, according to the first reports, '67676' was the one attacked! All he did was defend himself and by the looks of things, just barely", replied the Floor Captain.

"That damn Federal Judge up in Tyler has been on us like stink on shit. He's going to just have a hissy fit when he reads the report I have to write"!

"Take me to Jaeger Captain"!

"But Sir the Doctor gave strict instructions not to be disturbed, whereas he's operating on '67676'"!

"Captain, Who is the Warden around here, me or Doctor Fowler"? "You are sir. Please come this way"!

As Warden Schwelp entered the small operating room he saw Dr. Fowler leaning over the prisoner Jaeger operating on his ribcage area, saying, "Doctor Fowler, a word with you please"!

"I'm rather busy at the moment warden. Nurse get that sonofabitch over to the sink and see to it that he washes up, then put him in a gown, gloves and mask then I'll talk to him while I work"!

Then as an afterthought he growled, 'Warden, you just violated a clean operating area, a violation of federally mandated medical procedure. Clean up right now and be quick about it and I'll think about 'not', including you in my monthly report to the Judge, up north. Failing in that, get the fuck out of here right now and you can deal with the judge later"!

Several minutes later a subdued and clean Warden Schwelp, approached the operating table without another word.

"Come around here William so you can see better, said the doctor. "Over there on the trey are the two prison issue 'shiv's' that were put into this prisoner by the two Chicano's in X-ray. As you leave you might want to take them with you to check for prints. They are clean as far as I can tell, since no one has touched them before he arrived here for surgery.

"How can you be sure about that", asked the warden warily?

"Odd how the prisoner had to walk all the way over here with one knife still sticking out of him and the other caught up in the back of his shirt, while the assailants were ferried over here nice as you please on a gurney, eh William? Judge Justice wouldn't think too kindly about that", he added wryly!

Continuing he said, "Now this wound just missed some of the prisoner's vital organs, while the other, that I'm going to get to shortly, was wide of the mark and will simply leave a wide scar. Usually these guys place the shiv's right up the old bread basket and twist. Clearly they were either incompetent or were hurried in their work. Had they done there work well, I wouldn't be here doing what I'm doing. I'd be doing paperwork"!

"So if I'm hearing you correctly Doctor you saying that the two Mexicans were the aggressors and Jaeger her was merely defending himself".

"The wounds on all three men are consistent with what the two hall monitors stated to me and the floor captain"! "Nurse, give me the patients vitals from the monitor please"!

After the nurse read out the numbers, Doctor Fowler continued, "Look at this patient's wounds, then trot right over to X-ray and feel free to look at the skull fractures of the other two. Then I'm certain that it will come as intuitively obvious, even to the most casual observer, that our patient here on the table, under complete sedation, grabbed both assailants by the head, sinking his thumbs in each ones eye socket and slammed their heads together in a defensive motion. A cursory examination will clearly show that one of the assailant's right side of his head, crashed into the left side of the others head, leaving both severely concussed, not inconsistent with that of a head on vehicular collision at road speed"!

"Massive brain damage as far as I can tell, but further X-rays will determine whether or not the State should expend the funds to send them off to a hospital, for surgery. Soon as I get done with this patient, in oh, say twenty minutes or so, we can look at the full set of X-rays together and make a cogent determination then. Till then why don't you go over to the X-ray room and see the two assailants for yourself"!

After some time he was joined by the Doctor, in the X-ray room and said, "The Floor Captain has taken the two shiv's over to the prison lab for prints verification and as you've said, both opposite sides of the two alleged assailants were caved in. As they both examined the X-rays the

Doctor pointed out where massive internal bleeding was occurring as they spoke.

Then he took the pulse of both men, checked their breathing and declared one of them dead, saying "The other is well past the point of no return William, only a matter of minutes"!

"Warden Murray's going to have a fit when he gets back from vacation"!

"And here we stand, both of us caught between two Masters. Warden Murray on one hand and the good Federal Judge Justice, up in Tyler by god Texas. One concerned with the sanctity of the prisoners, while the other concerned with their imprisonment and little else"!

"Look, I'm sorry I blew up a while ago, Boyd"!

"We both have reports to write, William. I suggest we work together on this, in a way to keep both Masters at arms-length. I've shown you the truth, haven't I"?

"Yes you have, Boyd"!

"Oh, my surviving patient will have to spend the next five days here in the infirmary convalescing, just to keep Judge Justice at bay, report wise"!

"And Warden Murray will be back from vacation on day six and you know his firm policy about prison altercations"!

"Yes William, any unauthorized altercations, are punishable by thirty days in the isolation wing, one meal a day, no visitation"!

"You going to fight me on this Boyd"?

"You mean Warden Murray"!

"He calls the shots, but I have to implement them"!

"Lemme think of a way we can both keep our hands clean William", said Doctor Fowler.!

"Jaeger stays here for five days convalescence and on the sixth we transfer him to the isolation unit for the next thirty days of confinement, except he gets three square meals a day rather than the one meal that you serve the other miscreants"!

"I think that's doable Boyd", said the warden.

"There's one thing more. When he's done with his solitary confinement, I'll need another hand here in the infirmary to train as a medical technician. Now since the assignment of inmate duties falls completely in your bailiwick, it should be a simple thing to accomplish"!

"Why do you want Jaeger as a trainee", asked the Assistant Warden Schwelp?

"Well for one reason he's going to be around for a long time now isn't he? Schwelp nodded his head." Next, he's clearly an intelligent individual that's highly trainable and should be able to come up to speed rather quickly, thus proving to be somewhat as an asset to this facility rather than a liability. Next, someone clearly wants this guy underground ASAP and while he's here the general prison population can't get at him. Just cutting down on the possibilities for further paperwork with Judge Justice, William"!

"And you're report to Judge Justice will make me look in a favorable light"?

"I've been known to be a very creative writer from time to time William and you should know by now that my word is my bond"!

"That you are Boyd, that you are", said Schwelp approvingly.

"Then we have a deal as outlined"?

"We have a deal"!

Upon his return from vacation, Warden Murray was not at all happy to be confronted by the attempted assassination of one of his prisoners and the death of the perpetrators. But as he waded through the reports and called in those who verified the reports, especially the copy of the monthly report of Doctor Fowler, putting the prison administration in the most favorable light, he looked over the rims of his glasses at his assistant warden saying, "'Well William, it seems you've done a right proper job tying up all the loose ends in this matter, down to the last dot and dash"!

"Thank You Warden Murray and with any luck we'll stand an even chance of getting our annual budget expanded, to allow for some additional video outlets for the facility".

"When this Jaeger gets out of isolation, see if you can't place him somewhere where the thundering herd can't get at him so easy. Don't need that pussyfooting judge Justice, writing us up any more than he already has"!

"I'll get it done as you wish Warden"!

One of the glaring loopholes in the Federal Mandate for prison reform was that all bets were off for those placed in isolation, or solitary confinement. Complete isolation and sensory deprivation for the duration of isolation, with but one hour out of every twenty four, to wander around alone, in a small courtyard. Sanitary conditions were almost nonexistent, and one had to wait until the end of confinement to enjoy the luxury of a five minute shower, or running water.

For the emotionally weak, it drove them over the brink of sanity, while for others it provided time to think, to regroup, to plot and plan, to let one's mind wander. Just before he was escorted into isolation, the good Doctor Fowler gave Jaeger a heads up as to what the future held for him as to his future work assignment. Light at the end of a very long tunnel, just maybe.

He again reviewed all that had happened to him in recent years and concluded that life, at least his life, was a cyclical occurrence. After good, came bad, and then good again and then bad again, in a seemingly relentless juggernaut of cycles.

Life was combative and the one thing he was certain of was that at least for him, life was an endless series of entering and exiting one sewer after another, with precious few ever so brief moments of peace and solitude, then back into it. It was one thing to be physically tough, but quite another to be spiritually tough. To retain and embrace those core values that were eternal.

In many of the quiet moments, he closed his eyes and allowed his mind to gently wander,

Interacting with those who had gone before, visiting as it were, with the unseen in a very private way. Then he recalled the opening verse of the Apostles Creed that he'd recited every time he attended Mass; "I believe in one God, the Father, the Almighty, maker of heaven and earth, of all that is seen and unseen".

Now, in this very dark place, away from the maddening din of the microcosmic sewer out there, able to gather his thoughts uninterrupted, and see in his mind and hear with his heart, the thoughts of those who've gone before, he started to understand the real meaning of those words, 'The Unseen'. A vision of a weathered old man dressed in frontier buckskin, carrying the ancient double barreled flintlock rifle came before his eyes.

The vision smiled, looking him over from top to bottom and unspoken message entered Jaegers mind. 'Endure, outlast them all.

When the time comes you'll do the right thing'...., and then the vision faded gradually away.

Fixed in his mind was the message that this was his time and trial for what lay ahead. This was his time for preparation. For use of his intellect, as well as his physical acumen. Somehow, he hadn't a clue as to when or where final justice would arrive at the feet of those involved with the death of his family. It was a pity they could only die once.

But perhaps, just perhaps it would be enough.

30

D r. Clever Branch, Chairman of the School of Micro Technology at Cal Tech, picked up the phone and placed a call to Boyd Fowler. They hadn't conversed in some months and he decided that it was time to see to past developments.

After the usual greetings, they got down to the business at hand, with Morris asking casually, "How's your new project coming along"? "Far better than I imagined, Clever. Of course I can't give you any details at the present, but if one of your people were to pay me a visit, in the very near future, I think a positive outcome is highly likely"!

"Good. I'll start things in motion and call you back in a few days"!

"Talk to you then Clever. Goodbye"!

Dr. Fowler had met Dr. Branch at a medical seminar some years back and discovering many professional commonalities between them had become fast friends. As part of a government grant by the Rand Corporation, the long standing think tank, Cal Tech was involved in the startup concept of Nano Technology and was developing a Micro Computer at the cellular level, that if it worked as conceived would provide a revolutionary concept in medical science, regarding a device that when implanted in an individual, would last a lifetime and add to the healing factors in the human body.

A Nano computer, the size of a dime, with micro manufacturing capabilities capable of manufacturing an army of nano robots that would circulate throughout the human body searching out viruses and cancer cells at will around the clock, relentlessly, and surgically kill them at a micro biological level. Further, any bacterial infestation would be attacked in a similar fashion in conjunction with the body's white blood cells. Further still, any coronary blockages would be set upon and eliminated in the very same way. Finally, internal injuries would be aggressively addressed.

Intrusive wounds, internal bleeding sources, would be attacked at the source and immediately cauterized allowing the natural forces with in the body to take over the healing process.

Their power source would derive from the electrical impulses of the host body. Therefore, as long as the body functioned, the computer and the mini factory would function. A very much secret pilot project gradually took form, with the first test subjects being lab mice. After five years of testing on a variety of mammals, time had come for implantation in a human subject. But who?

The relationship between Dir.'s Branch and Fowler had developed to such a degree, that one of them could start a sentence and the other would finish it. Eventually they would come together on a project and apparently now was the time.

Several days later Boyd Fowler picked up his office phone on the second ring, "Dr. Fowler here"!

"Boyd its Clever. How are you"?

"Every day above ground is a good day Clever", replied Boyd!

"Your wit knows no bounds my friend. Say that thing we we're talking about the other day, are you still up for a professional visit by two of our colleagues at your location"?

"Just tell me who's arriving and the day of their visitation, have your proper ID's at the ready for the staff to inspect and I'll alert the proper people so you'll have minimal interference at the main gate.

"There will be a Doctor Hank Murray and Doctor Anita Grabowski knocking at your door the day after tomorrow! None of us have ever been to Texas so how do we get there"? "Clever, they're going to have to fly in to Houston at either the Intercontinental North, or the Hobby airports, get a rent car and take about an hour and a half drive up I-45 and you'll run into Huntsville Texas. Only two things of interest here, other than world class barbeque. The Ellis Unit Prison and the University. Your secretary can handle the details"! "Thanks Boyd, they'll be there day after tomorrow"! Boyd then called the assistant warden Schwelp and informed him of several visitors arriving the day after next. After giving them their names he explained, "I'm helping my medical colleagues compare our medical system with that of the California Penal System William. They're having some significant problems out there and we've been talking back and forth for some time professionally and they want to spend the day picking my brain. Of course their comparisons will be published in a professional review, which after our joint review should put us in a favorable light with Judge Justice up in Tyler, once he receives a copy from our boss, don't ya think"?

"You might have made a great politician Boyd and of course we'll extend every professional courtesy for their stay. Oh by the way how's that Jaeger fella working out"?

"Hard worker, minds his own business, keeps everything spotless and a keen inquisitive mind. I have him performing most of the radiology functions, he gives all the shots like an experienced nurse and sometime in next thirty days just might start having him assist in other areas. So things are working out very well William. We keep him busy and he likes it like that"!

"Well good. I'll see to it that your visitors have smooth sailing".

"Thanks William"!

After he hung up, he got on the intercom and summoned Jaeger to his office.

"Yes Doctor Fowler, you wanted to see me"?

"Oh yes, Jaeger please sit down, for I have what just might be some good news for you, if you can keep your mouth shut"!

Jaeger nodded his head for him to proceed.

"Day after tomorrow two doctors will arrive from Cal Tech University out in California. Do you know where that is"?

"Yes Doctor Fowler I've heard of the place"!

Then Boyd Fowler launched into a long explanation of the project, what they hoped to achieve and how it would benefit Jaeger personally.

"So you're telling me, thus far no adverse side effects, no bodily rejections and I'm selected to be the first human guinea pig"!

"Since you're here every day, you'll be monitored every single work day. Thus a daily physical every day you report to work, by me. In time I'll include nurse Moran, on those occasions I'm not available, since she's highly capable and can keep her mouth shut"!

One of the things a good salesman does is make his pitch and then shut up and let the consumer decide. Boyd Fowler, aside from being an excellent medical practitioner, was a born salesman. And after a few moments of silence Jaeger looked at the Doctor saying, "You've been straight up with me, so yeah, I'm in"!

"Great. Oh by the way, I heard you've signed up for some of the classes offered by the State University for the inmates. How's that going, decided on any Major yet"?

"Well Doc, I completed my sophomore year at UT before the roof caved in, but I'm just taking courses that interest me as a way to pass the time. I'll make a decision about that sometime down the road"!

"How are things down amongst the 'Fools Parade' down there"? "Manageable. I've a pretty good cell mate that's shown me the ropes along with another in the next cell. We're pretty tight with each other. As far as the other factions down there, I'll have nothing to do with them, which is why I'd rather stay busy up here. Helps the time pass by quickly"!

"After what became of your assailants a while back one would think that you'd be off limits to even the most hostile of the inmates"!

"There's always someone who'll want to make a rep for himself, but I stay busy and try and avoid confrontation and it helps when one has someone reliable to watch your six"!

"Good. I see that the work day is almost done so why don't you knock off early and I'll see you tomorrow"!

Jaeger rose and turned towards the door and as he left said, "Thanks Doc"! The prisons video monitors only went so far. They followed the arrival of Dr. Fowler's guests, the cursory examination of their persons and briefcases, sending them on their way with a single guard escort straight to the prison medical facility. The lone camera recorded their arrival in the only entrance to the facility, recording their greeting by Dr. Fowler, then lost sight of them as they went behind closed doors.

"So Doctor Fowler, Dr. Branch has filled us in on your ongoing interest in Nano Technology as it pertains to the human host", said Anita Grabowski.

"Please, let's dispense with the formalities. May we go by our first names, since were all colleagues"?

"But of course, I go by Hank and Doctor Grabowski has been known to answer to Anita", said Doctor Murphy!

"Clever and I have known each other for many years and I've followed his work with great interest over the years, which is why I thought of your project when a certain subject came to my attention. His physical, mental and emotional attributes are of superior quality and since he will be in this facility for quite some time, especially under my direct supervision, I just had to put things in motion"!

"Based upon what Dr. Branch relayed to us we quite agree Boyd, replied Dr. Murray. "I trust the subject has been informed and is in agreement"! "Given his situation and the environment he's in and the continual threat of attack, he agrees that it's in his best interests to let us implant the devise. Oh by the way, how did you get it past the guards?

"By hiding it in plain sight", said Dr. Grabowski while reaching into her briefcase and removing a disk like devise, no larger than a dime enclosed in a Radio Shack mini package that said, 'Lithium Battery'. "In addition to the initial implantation at the base of the subject's skull, we brought along a vial of nano bots suspended in an aqueous solution, for initial injection. The injection will be intramuscular, rather than intravenous and in due course the little bots will marry up with their host automatically and set the entire process in motion."!

"So the procedure has been changed from a cranial insertion to something different", asked Dr. Fowler? "Yes Boyd and for several reasons, first of which, Cranial insertions come with certainhazards and we weren't sure of the depth of your facilities, plus the subject would have to be bed sequestered at the facility which would eventually shed light on our little project. At the base of the skull, deep implantation should afford us two advantages, first of which, it will be close enough to the spinal column to afford access to the bodies electrical impulse supply and of probably greater importance, given the subjects physical proclivities and his environment, the Mini Computer, the brain as it were, would have greater protection, from sudden jarring out of place, in the event your subject should be involved in a violent altercation, which given his environment and his natural proclivities is likely to occur"! Plus this way, we can affect the implantation on an outpatient basis, with minimal invasiveness and the subject can resume his normal duties within scant hours of the procedure"!

Doctor Grabowski chimed in, "Given the fax you sent the other day, we saw the subject has a low iron count in his body, so he'll need iron supplements on a measured daily basis, to enhance the electromagnetic interaction of the bots with their base, since the little beasts, will be constantly be roaming around at all times"! "Thanks for the heads up

Anita and if there's nothing else I'll summon the subject and we can begin"!

Jaeger was in the X-ray room just finishing up developing some film for the Doctors review when he was summoned.

While they were waiting for him, Anita Grabowski ran over the mental file she had of the prisoner Jaeger. Since she worked directly for the funding entity The Rand organization, this was technically her show and within the hour of Clever Branch's phone call she found out all that could be known about the subject Jaeger. His mostly obfuscated time in the Military suggested the Government had much to hide, while his brief but glorious Collegiate football career, suggested the capability for massive brutality, yet underlying all that suggested a superior intellect that clearly was going to waste. Then there was the cause and manner in which he ended up in this facility which did not square with someone with his demonstrable assets.

As Jaeger entered Dr. Fowler's office he was introduced to the two visitors who spent the next half hour going over all of the details of the operation and the benefits that were possible for mankind.

"So we assume that you're in complete agreement with what is to occur and will keep the appropriate security within all in this room", asked Anita Grabowski? Jaeger nodded his head in agreement. "Good", she replied. "Doctor Murray will be in charge of the surgery and will handle the initial insertion, I'll assist him and Doctor Fowler will handle the anesthesia. It's now ten AM and by noon the procedure should be completed and you'll probably just be able to make the noon meal after you wake up."

By twelve thirty he was making his way down to the Main dining facility, just forty five minutes later than usual, missing his pals Roy and Rae. Since each inmate was afforded an scant fifteen minutes in which to consume their meals, that was OK with Jaeger, since the dining facility without someone trustworthy to watch your back wasn't exactly a healthy place to be. As he went through the chow line, as it was every single day, he felt the glances of hundreds of eyes on him constantly. His permanent moniker was now Jaeger the Mankiller, for the inmates as well as the bulk of the non-supervisory guards.

As he ate, he felt the numbness of the anesthetic wearing off and a dull ache began to occur at the base of his skull an inch above his hairline. The devise was implanted, surgically about an inch deep, nestled between the muscles and the tendons adjacent to his spinal ganglia. After the surgery they showed him, via a mirror the site of the incision and one could hardly tell that anything had occurred, since no bandages were applied, the wound surgically bound with medical super glue like substance that would dissolve within ten calendar days of the surgery. No telltale stitches and minimal scarring occurred.

As he ate, thousands of submicroscopic bots lining up entering the 'Dime', getting their marching orders and going out to do battle with a host of germs, viruses, infestations, blood clots, and searching his entire vascular system scrubbing away any and all blockages. Not a bad thing, if it worked as designed. He decided not to concern himself with it and go about his business.

As he made his way back to the medical facility, he noticed two of the inmate electricians installing an overhead video camera in the hallway blind spot where he was attacked. Yet another good thing, as long as the monitors weren't catching some nap time. Still there was always the video tape.

For some of the inmates time passed at an agonizingly slow pace, for others it moved a bit faster, depending on how busy one kept oneself.

Eventually the first year came and went, with no further attempts on Jaegers life. Still, every single day there were the possibilities. He made it a point to converse to only a chosen few, living a borderline existence of constant paranoia, every waking moment. His only real refuge was after lights out, the cell doors slammed shut and eventual sleep took hold.

People will tell you that when experiencing the last stages of REM sleep, you dream. Probably so, Jaeger reasoned, but he was never able to recall any of his dreams the following morning. But all that was prior to his incarceration and subsequent conviction. In the county jail, just prior to and all during the trial, he finally started to remember his dreams. Not all at once, but gradually, in bits and pieces. Sort of a gradually accelerating process like opening up the petals of a torpid rose, petal by petal, only to find the last petal revealing a horror beyond verbal description. In each of us lay a certain Hell, unleashed by circumstance. His only lifeline to sanity was an almost daily prayer to that invisible spirit that defied quantification.

He often wondered what his father would do in the same circumstances.

Morgan Jaeger former patriarch of the family fortunes, former Marine, former scout sniper hard as nails in almost all aspects of life. Multiple tours in Viet Nam, up country operating mostly alone deep on Indian Country always returning with multiple scalps hanging from his kit. FormerTexas Ranger and finally a successful rancher and farmer. How would he handle the current situation?

All these things and much more rolled around in Jaeger's subconscious while he was asleep each night. He always recalled what his father said about handling adversity. The myriad ways one twisted, "When the going gets tough", "The tough get going", "The weak get screwed", "The weird turn pro"! Each of which contained a certain truth, fitting an occasion.

As the dream sequences progressed in intensity, he recalled with remarkable detail all of the events of his speedy trial, begun on a Monday and concluded that very Friday. His rookie, public defender lawyer out maneuvered at every step, by both the prosecution and the presiding Judge at every turn. She might have been a whiz at law school, but in the legal trenches she was spanked. Only the actions of a single juror, he later found out kept him from the death penalty, at the penalty stage of the trial. Each morning he'd wake up in a cold sweat, gradually remembering what had gone on inside his head while he was asleep.

Everything he'd valued was gone, taken from him by some unseen force. Yet he must endure, survive and eventually return to society, whole. But how? The legal presumption of innocence was gone, the very moment the foreman of the jury announced his guilt. Now the burden of proof of his innocence was squarely on his shoulders. The only tangible thing Jaeger had on his side was time. Yet he was not completely alone. He'd somehow lucked into a few people that just might be reliable over time and he was in a work position where he was acquiring skill sets he'd never imagine he'd need.

His quick dispatching of the assassins, early on was apparently a blessing, for the other inmates gave him a wide berth and kept the internecine squabbling to themselves and others.

Gradually he concluded that he indeed had a few precious assets. Then there was the subject of revenge. But against who? The subject would have to be set aside, until the very day that he was set free, with nothing hanging over him. His conscious mind constantly repeated, 'Fat Chance', for his sentence was life imprisonment, with no possibility of parole.

He concluded that he would endeavor to stay busy, every waking moment, doing, learning, and sharpening the blade of his mind, for that time when the walls would be tumbling down.

Every night before he went to sleep, he glanced at that inscription etched deeply the wall of his cell which read, "Nothing can be worth all of this"! Jaeger wondered, what must have the author of that message experienced? Did he survive his time in Huntsville or succumb to its horrors?

31

olonel Bollinger landed at Bergstrom AFB on the outskirts of Austin Texas, now in its last days of being a viable Air Base due to Federal budget cutbacks. He caught a ride on one of the General Staffs jets on its way to shut down Kelly AFB in San Antonio. The others on the craft were the usual civilian crew from the Department of Defense along with some staff higher echelon of the Air Force doing Pentagon duty as part of their career path obligations.

Upon landing he made straight away for the motor pool and upon showing his orders, checked out a blue staff sedan for his trip to Huntsville Prison. Of course his orders determined that he was supposed to liaison with local Marine Corps. command personnel in Austin and Houston regarding reserve training activities, but a little side trip was certainly his prerogative considering his rank as a full Colonel stationed at Quantico. He would meet with the locals in due course after the real business at hand was concluded.

He'd previously written ahead to the Warden of the facility, on Official Marine Corps stationary and received a phone call from the warden to discuss the purpose of his visit to see Prisoner #67676, aka Jaeger and received official permission both verbally and via official letter days later. So upon his arrival he was greeted by the Assistant Warden Schwelp, who guided him through the initial visitor procedures.

True to his letter, the purpose of his visit was to give Jaeger a football, a harmonica and pictures of an ancient firearm, all family heirlooms from the now dissolved Jaeger Estate. As they made their way to the visitor's facility, both made the usual small talk, with Warden Schwelp asking, "Why is an important man such as you, talking his time to visit a convicted criminal"?

"The man served under my command just before he was mustered out. His actions were directly responsible for saving the lives of a number of Americans serving their country in a foreign land. When it was brought to my attention that he'd been convicted of the murder of his entire family, you can imagine the shock inflicted on all of us who knew him. His time served as a Marine was without blemish. We respect the decision of the Texas Courts, but the least we could do was retrieve what we could that was clearly purloined from his families estate for him which was precious little Warden"!

"Well Colonel, I suppose your right and since you've come a long way and the convict in question hasn't caused any problems during his first fifteen months with us, I'm going to extend a courtesy to you not normally done and extend your visiting time from the usual fifteen minutes, to a half an hour. You will be the very first visitor he's received since he's been here. There will be a guard in the same room as the both of you watching you're every move. At no time are you to touch the prisoner, in any way. At no time are you to pass anything to the prisoner other than what has been approved. Do we have an understanding Colonel"? "We do Warden", replied Bollinger "and thank you for your courtesy"!

Schwelp handed the gym bag containing the approved items to be handed to the prisoner, back to Bollinger with the mild caveat, "The gym bag is not part of the approved items and will be taken with you upon your departure Colonel"!

Bollinger nodded his understanding entering the visitor's room and took the proffered seat at a table far apart from the few other families there visiting the other inmates. Several minutes later after frisking Jaeger, he was escorted into the visiting room and offered a seat across the table, from Bollinger by the Warden who disappeared into another room to view the meeting on Closed Circuit TV. Some five yards away out of earshot, stood one of the guards scanning the room for anything untoward that may happen.

"So how ya doin sport", asked Bollinger?

"Seen better days Colonel, but I've got three hot's and a cot, a roof over my head and meaningful work to do, so things could be worse"!

"Never explain, never complain, eh Marine"?

"That's about right Colonel! By the way I thought you were gonna be retired by now and here you are in full uniform, what with that if I may ask"?

"Well son I did retire. For about a year, but the wonk that replaced me had zip operational experience, commanding a desk somewhere and screwed things up to biblical proportions so bad, that I'm told the Secretary of State demanded I be recalled to duty with the promise of a

General's star in the near future, if I get things back to normal, mohinky dink"!

"FUBAR Colonel", asked Jaeger?

"That's right son, Fucked Up, Beyond All Recognition. But that's not why I'm here. How are ya doing son"?

"Like the Mafia dons always say, Every day above ground is a good day, just keeping my head down and my ass up, trusting few, questioning all. This is a good environment for the practice of 'situational awareness', almost to the point of constant paranoia. Look forward to going to work every day at the prison's medical facility, for that's about the only place I can relax a little bit"!

"Well son a little bit of paranoia is not a bad thing, just remember that 'Paranoia is simply the flip side of complete awareness'"!

At that Bollinger opened the gym bag slowly reaching in and retrieving Jaegers old harmonica, slowly sliding it over to him saying, "Retrieved this from some souvenirs thief that took part in stealing your things. They still tell stories about how you used to play just three notes on the mouth harp to get in the mood for bad times ahead. They say that you played it repeatedly at half time at the Cotton Bowl just before you kicked ass, it's a legend now"!

Jaeger just sat there looking at the harmonica, the repressed past forcing itself back into his conscious memory.

Bollinger then reached back into the gym bag, retrieving a football and placed it on the table saying, "This is the game ball awarded to you for your efforts in the Cotton Bowl. Some of the guys caught up with this guy trying to sell it and persuaded him to relinquish possession for the common good.

He protested and was duly convinced that he'd never see another sunrise unless he did the right thing. Clearly he made a wise decision"!

Reaching for the final time into the gym bag, he withdrew a folder and placed it in front of Jaeger. "Open it Sergeant, for the most important thing"!

Jaeger, turned the cover over and was greeted by an 8x10 glossy picture of the old Beretta double barreled rifle that occupied an exalted place over the fireplace at the main family mansion, since the days of the Texas Republic. The emotions that were deeply buried inside for many months began to well up as the tears would not be denied. As he sniffed them back he made the excuse, "Goddamn'd sinus problem"!

He gently reached for the picture and the many memories of their forbearer, Henry Jaeger confronted his memory. Tales of heroism repeated verbally many times over as a lesson to every generation that came after, as something to live up to. Honor, Common Sense and Wisdom, the ability to endure, no matter what. "You must believe this son; you have many friends amongst those in the Corps. People you've never met. Men who would gladly form an armed assault on this facility to secure your freedom. But this will not, cannot happen for then you'll always be on the run and no matter how good you are at what you do best, you'll never truly be free"!

"Then Colonel I suppose there is no hope"!

"Something better exist's son and it's called Faith and the other thing, Confidence. Some have been nosing around and a full transcript of your so called trial has been acquired and is in the hands of some friends of mine in the Naval JAG office in Quantico. Now these boys have taken a preliminary look at your trial transcripts and given their full workload of cases promise to put their heads together from time to time to see what can be done on appeal, if anything. Current thinking is that things smell to high heaven, but no apparent judicial errors are apparent, for the moment"!

"Now I've taken the opportunity to have an appointment with your former lawyer who's working in Houston for her uncle's law firm and whose doing very well I'm hearing. Our meeting is to occur tomorrow morning 10:00 hours at her office. I will provide her and her Uncle with a full copy of the trial transcript along with the preliminary notes from my friends at the Quantico JAG office. I will appeal to their sense of moral integrity, via a little bit of moral suasion."!

"Colonel, I've little faith in lawyers as you can understand"!

"Oh before I forget, the Musket heirloom was in the possession of a Ft. Worth Real Estate developer named Don Ryder, do you know anything about him"?

"Don Ryder", exclaimed Jaeger wide eyed? "Why he married my Aunt May"!

"Which explains how he neatly came into possession of the weapon", replied Bollinger.

"My dad had absolutely no use for Ryder! Both him and Sheriff Morgan Little. Dad used to call them Pond Scum"!

"Back to the point being your heirloom. It's in my possession and it's in a secret place and secure. Now you're gonna ask how I persuaded Don Ryder to relinquish the weapon aren't ya"?

Jaeger nodded. "Well I can't take direct credit, let's just say that mortal fear is a great motivator", the Colonel whispered.

"You have other friends you don't even know about on the outside and if you'll recall you've already been visited by those with a vested interest", whispered the Colonel! Just then, the guard approached saying, "Colonel, you have ten minutes left"!

"Thank you son", Bollinger replied, waiting for the guard to step back out of earshot.

"Sergeant, to accomplish what needs to be done and do it right will take time. Thus patience is what will need to be evident at all times, coupled with a little bit of faith. You will have visitors again in the future", said Bollinger through clenched teeth.

"Now just in case you think you're the only one this has ever happened to, I suggest you get a copy of the Bible, and thumb through the pages till you get to the 'Book of Job', now that's a guy who had problems"!

Bollinger then stood zipping up the gym bag, "Stay healthy Sergeant, we'll be seeing each other again, but it'll be awhile"! Jaeger stood up and nodded saying, "Thanks Colonel" and watched as Bollinger turned crisply and followed the guard out of the facility. The gym bag was re-examined upon the Colonels departure and the guards finding it completely empty of contents allowed Bollinger to depart.

Upon leaving the visitors facility, Jaeger was greeted by Warden Schwelp who demanded to re-examine the football, harmonica and the file containing the picture of his family's Musket and the notarized document relinquishing ownership of the Biretta Musket heirloom into Colonel Bollinger's custody in behalf of the prisoner Jaeger and establishing complete ownership provenance to the prisoner Jaeger. Finding nothing amiss he handed everything back to Jaeger and directed him to go back to work in the prison's medical facility.

Upon reaching the medical facility he checked back in with Nurse Moran who directed him to the Xray room to develop the preceding days x- rays for Doctor Fowlers perusal upon his return the following day.

Bollinger had an uneasy feeling as he departed the Ellis Unit parking lot. Driving through town he saw the sign that indicated the entrance to I-45 South and the direction sign to Houston southward. Several cars back there was another sterile looking bureaucratic car similar to the one he was driving that followed him on to the entrance ramp to the Interstate. There were two people in the car, which was careful to follow at a distance, several vehicles behind and staying right at Bollinger's speed. When several miles later Bollinger changed lanes so did the other car. As Bollinger approached the outskirts of Houston's suburbs, he saw a sign that read "Greenspoint Mall", and taking the very next exit took note of the trailing vehicle and there it was, still several cars away. He trailed back to the Mall complex and finding a convenient office building he entered its parking garage going up several levels parked his car and waited. Ten minutes later when no car followed, he took off his Marine Blouse and completely examined the car he was driving, the engine compartment, the entire underneath, looking for any electronic tracking monitors, or explosive devices, then satisfying himself the vehicle was clean put his blouse back on.

Then he went to the garages parapet and after having spotted the two on the ground from above parked very near the parking garage's exit, he decided to have a leisurely afternoon late lunch, then when he went to his vehicle, again going over his car from stem to stern and finding nothing amiss drove down to ground level and back to the Interstate to his next appointment, the Marine Corps. Reserve unit in Houston for a brief chat with the head of the local weekend warriors.

And there they were, parked across the street in a strip centers parking lot, one car amongst many with his vehicle in full view. Bollinger briefly toyed with the idea of treeing his pursuers and hoisting them on their own petard, yet thought better of it. They were just locals put on his trail by those unknown. If they were really serious people his vehicle would have a tracking device attached somewhere on the chassis. Thus since there was none, he'd make a note and play along.

Oh he would lose his pursuers well enough, but he must do it in such a way that would make it seem that it was their incompetence rather than his skill. Two hours later he left the Marine Corps Reserve facility and joined into the early phases in the evening rush hour traffic. Searching for just the right situation for about a half an hour, he went through an intersection just as the light was changing, with a Houston Police Car, sitting right at the light that was about to change to green. To follow him further his pursuers would have to risk running the light right in front of the police. The police would be compelled to apprehend, allowing Bollinger to leisurely get away. To stop at the light would allow him to get away. Either way he was golden.

His pursuers took the road of caution and waited at the light. A scant city block away Bollinger turned right then worked his way through the various neighborhood's back to the freeway and back into Houston's Central Business District in the center of town pulling into the parking garage of the Downtown Sheraton Hotel and checked in for the evening.

The following morning he decided to walk the five blocks to the high rise building that housed the offices of Schwartzwald and Associates LLC, discovering they occupied multiple floors in the building. From the looks of things these people were clearly not light weights. The elevator door opened into their lavish reception area and Bollinger went to the receptionist offing his official card and stating, "Colonel Bollinger, here to see Leo Schwartzwald, for our ten o'clock meeting". Duly acknowledged, the receptionist offered him a seat and alerted someone on the office intercom.

Several minutes later, a man walked up to the Colonel offering his hand saying, "Colonel Bollinger I take it? I'm Boyd Parmalee one of Mr. Schwartzwald's partners. He's just winding up an important call and will be with us shortly. If you'll be kind enough to follow me to the conference room"!

Bollinger followed Parmalee down a long hall, elegantly attired with various works of art, festooning walls of subdued wall covering, while the lilting strains of Vivaldi played 'sotto voce', in the background emanating from the offices PA system. While they walked, Parmalee offered, "I hope you don't mind if I sit in in the meeting, for all during the trial of your Sergeant Jaeger, I was lurking in the deep background, being what help to his niece that I could. Now Buffy's running a tad late and will join us shortly."

After accepting the proffered coffee by one of the staff and making several minutes of small talk with Parmalee, in stormed Leo Schwartzwald and hurriedly introduced himself to Bollinger. "Colonel

Bollinger, I'm Leo Schwartzwald and I trust you and Boyd here have gotten acquainted"?

"The preliminaries have been exercised Mr. Schwartzwald", replied Bollinger!

Just then the phone buzzed, with Parmalee picking it up and listening, then after he put it down he said, "Ms. Beauvoir is in the elevator on her way up." Schwartzwald then said, "She's been working all night on a difficult case and has to deliver her summation down at the County Court House at One PM, so I hope you'll accept our apologies on her behalf"!

"I'm grateful for the time you've allotted and the courtesy you've extended", said Bollinger. He then reached inside his briefcase and removed a large sheath of papers saying, "I've taken the liberty to acquire complete copies of Jaeger's trial transcripts and ran them by some friends of mine in the JAG office in Quantico and here they are for your perusal with some notes in the margins. Now they're military lawyers, and good ones, but they realize that various state laws are in play here, plus the various subtleties that may come into play in certain Juris Dictions. Thus their reference to your organization"!

Just then, in breezed Buffy Beauvoir, looking somewhat worse from wear, via her late night efforts in crafting a summation to the jury in behalf of her client, yet still able to turn the heads of both mortal man and women, appearing as an almost exact double for the actress, Elizabeth Taylor, in her prime. She appeared without a word, sliding into a seat across from Bollinger, saying simply "Sorry I'm late please continue"!

Continuing, Bollinger added, "Now no one is going to fault you Ms. Beauvoir, for your defense of Sergeant Jaeger, for the boys back at Quantico that looked at the transcripts found it full of passion and truth and none of them is eager to come up against you in a courtroom. Yet up in Huntsville prison sits a man, found guilty of murdering his entire family, on what everybody feels is rather thin circumstantial evidence. I visited him yesterday and discovered that he's had no other visitors, other than me, since day one of his incarceration"!

Bollinger again reached into his briefcase pulling out another file, "This is a full copy of his record in the Corps., from day one and it makes for some very interesting reading, but it only reveals part of what Jaeger was up to. Most of which he was involved with was of a highly classified nature and will never be part of his dossier. But I'll tell you this much, he was attached to various State Department assignments on the continuum of his service and each assignment was a dangerous assignment, all over the world. He carried out each assignment successfully especially the last one of which I directed him in. This involved the complete removal of Embassy personnel from a Central African Nation and he pulled it off"!

Several moments of silence ensued, before Bollinger again spoke; "This is not a man that goes off half-cocked, this is a high trained and talented man, full of discipline and self-restraint, the epitome' of what a Marine should be. The epitome' of what all men should be and he needs all the help he can get"!

"So you visited him yesterday Colonel", asked Schwartzwald?

"Yes I did"!

"How did he appear"?

"He, he looks healthy enough and he appears to be holding up well enough, but somehow I sense that there's a war going on inside of him"!

"Understandably Colonel, given the overwhelming nature of what's happened, but did he relate to you the attempted assassination on his person a few months after he arrived"?

"Assassination attempt? Why no he didn't"!

"Not a word Colonel"? Bollinger shook his head in the negative.

"Interesting", Schwartzwald mused aloud.

For the next hour Uncle Leo brought Bollinger up to speed relating their peripheral involvement in Jaegers trial, in complete detail, inclusive of the various superficial reports of the detectives involved. Bollinger in turn related his visit to Jaeger and the subsequent tailing by persons unknown.

"What's your schedule after you depart us Colonel"?

"I drive back up to Austin, look in on the local Marine Reserve unit, check into the BOQ for the evening, then catch a flight out of Bergstrom early the next morning for Langley Field, in Washington, then back in my office at Quantico by midafternoon"!

Schwartzwald then looked at his niece and asked "Any break in your schedule you can foresee in the very near future Buffy"?

"Should have some time in a few weeks to squeeze in an afternoon for a trip to the Ellis Unit Uncle Leo"!

Schwartzwald then looked at Bollinger, nodding his head, then returned his gaze back to his niece saying, "Good make it so"!

"Colonel, could I interest you in a fine lunch in our executive dining room"?

"Going to ask for a rain check on that Mr. Schwartzwald, just let's see what can be done for this man and if I can be of any help, please let me know. I have access to certain unofficial resources if the need arises"!

At that, the meeting concluded, business cards were exchanged and Parmalee escorted Bollinger to the elevator and as they waited for it to arrive offered, "We will make thing right Colonel Bollinger, for a whole host of reasons, you have our word on that"!

After that he joined Leo in the executive lunchroom, saying "Well Leo seems we have a Tom Clancy potboiler right on our doorstep"!

"What do you think of our Colonel Bollinger Boyd"!

"All military, squared away, a pro and a serious man not to be taken lightly by anyone. Seems like a guy that would be good to have on our side down the road sometime Leo"!

32

Morgan Little picked up the phone in his office at the second buzz, punching the button that was his private line that lit up at the base of the receiver that did not run through the office switch board. Only a handful of close people knew that number.

"Sheriff Little", he answered.

"Morgan, its Bill Schwelp"!

"How are ya Bill? So tell me what happened to our boy and his visitor"! "Well, everything went off on schedule. The Colonel Bollinger came to the meeting in full Marine Corps. Uniform displaying his rank and all his medals, showed his bona fides, and followed the rules to a tee, then left"!

"So Bill, what did they say to each other"?

"As you know, the CCTV system is monitored for video only, so I've not a record of what was said"! "But Bill, you're an experienced lip reader"! Not when both parties speak through clenched teeth, Morgan. I could only make out a few words maybe, but nothing that could be put in any tangible context. How did your boys do tailing the Colonel"?

"Not worth a shit, I'm sad to say. He visited a Marine Corps. Reserve unit in Houston, apparently on Government business, then they lost him after he left in rush hour traffic"!

"So Morgan, what's to be done now"?

"Any new blood worthy of recruiting in your facility Bill"?

"Several months ago, this big guy arrived, a first degree manslaughter case from the Odessa oil fields. He's already been recruited by the skin heads. Done a turn in the segregation unit for roughing up one of the sissies when he rode the Hershey Highway. The guys massive and lives for his yard time with the weights. Rips up the yellow pages just to rile up the other inmates and the guards. Took three shots of the stun gun to get him to calm down before we put him in segregation. So maybe he can be persuaded"!

"Good Bill. See to it. Oh before I forget there will be several envelopes arriving in your private post box day after tomorrow. Understand"!

"I understand and thank's Morgan"!

"Good, hopefully the next call I receive will be the good news, certain people are waiting"!

As he hung up the phone, Bill Schwelp knew that one of the envelopes would contain a significant amount of cash for his efforts, while the other would be of a lesser amount for one of his unit captains. It paid very well to know folks who could get a job done and keep their mouths shut.

Prison Guards are usually the bottom feeders of the law enforcement establishment, receiving little training compared to other law enforcement officers, underpaid, highly unionized, and mostly bored, with a career path that offers few means of advancement. Their daily work environment offers little incentive for humanity for each day they have to surround themselves with the dregs of society, knowing that at any moment the inmates could turn on them with or without reason. Every incarceration facility on the planet has men who, in the words of Johnny Cash, "Shot a man in Reno, just to watch him die"! Every perversion known to man was experienced to greater or lesser degrees in prison life. The Texas Prison system was one of the better managed state facilities in the nation and yet, things happened, every day. Horrible things. A microcosm of what is called humanity. If one knew the right people and if favors were owed, then all manner of things could find their way into the right hands, in spite of all the security procedures put in place. The best thing a convict could do was to keep as low a profile as possible, yet from time to time circumstances would make that impossible.

Yet for a variety of reasons, usually money, some guards could be easily persuaded to look the other way and allow things to happen.

The time was just about right for another shot at prisoner #67676. A year had passed, he was doing as well as could be expected and perhaps his guard would be relaxed. He'd made a few friends, unaffiliated with any of the other thugs and perhaps soon his days would be at an end.

The instrument of that termination was a massive man straight out of the West Texas oil fields, who answered to the name of Cloyd Elsasser. At approximately six feet seven inches and weighing just under three hundred pounds of pure grit and muscle, the joke was not to shoot him with anything short of double ought buckshot, or you're liable to simply make him mad.

He had a nasty habit of taking anything he wanted, anytime and anywhere. The reason was simple, because he could. The only time he was ever caught in a smile, was when he was crushing some poor souls skull. Everywhere one looked all you could see was massive muscle and sinew. The only thing that was ever known to bring a smile on his face was to witness someone else's misfortune either at his hands of that of another. The greater the injury the greater the smile.

Once out of solitary confinement he found a small measure of contentment out in the yard, settling in as the prince of the free weights.

While there were a number of gangs in the yard, all making their moves on each other, the only ones Cloyd Elsasser would allow to approach were the Nazi skinhead pretenders and even those he kept at arm's length.

Jaeger could either ignore him or not, but it was clear that it was only a matter of time, until Elsasser and Jaeger would have cause to collide and when that time came it was certain to be a deadly collision.

One of the things one learned early on when out in the yard lifting weights was never to work to your maximum, for eyes were always on you and others were always sizing you up, looking for weaknesses and ways to get over on another, when the time came. Such was the case with Jaeger and Elsasser. The word was quietly out on the two amongst all the inmates and the guards as to when and where the two would do the 'Man Dance'. Bets were made between parties, with cash money being but one of many mediums of exchange. The bets took two distinctive angles, 'The When' and 'Who would win'?

Early on when Jaeger had quickly dispatched the duo of Mexican killers, he'd earned a certain measure of respect amongst the others, yet while Elsasser was still an unknown, he was seen to be not only the strongest man in the yard, but as quick as a cat.

One sunny afternoon when Elsasser was working out, Jaeger, having finished a shift on the prison medical facility casually walked over to the bench press area and asked, "Mind if I work in"?

Elsasser at first eyed him warily then said, "Sure pal, let's see what ya got"? Jaeger reset the weights down from the three hundred pounds to his approximate body weight of two hundred and fifty pounds, settling in to position and started lifting a set of normal number of repetitions, comfortably finishing, then got up and repositioned the bar to its former setting for Elsasser.

As Elsasser settled in for his set he said, "Good to see ya got good gym manners. Gonna be too bad the day I crush ya"! Then he proceeded to double the number repetitions than Jaeger, at the higher weight, sending a subtle message as to who was the stronger.

Every guard and inmate in the ground was keen to pay attention to the duo, wondering was this the time or not. After several sets between them Elsasser wandered away to where the dumbbells were and started working on his biceps, without another word between them. Each man had taken the measure of the other, of sorts and palpable electricity was clearly between the two, neither of which negated the other.

When Jaeger had finished with his final set, he wiped the sweat from his body with his small towel, putting his prison blouse back on and joined Roy Seltzer and Rae on the top riser of the wooden stands adjacent to the playing field to watch a soccer game between two of the Mexican gangs.

"Ya disappointed a lotta of yer mates out in the yard just now, for they all had money down on the when and the where of you two getting into the Big Dance".

'Well it couldn't be helped Roy. Can't let the guy get under my skin"! "Just so's ya know there'll be a time coming soon when he's gonna come for ya and it'll be outta nowhere, all of a sudden with no warning. The word has gone out that he's got you in his sights, no rules, complete annihilation. I'm guessing that your friends on the outside are behind this.

Time has passed, things have settled down and they have their own reasons and resources"!

"So what're you hearing Rae", asked Jaeger? "Pretty much the same, thing according to Bitch Cassidy. He overheard the Unit Captain talking to Elsasser this morning. Didn't hear everything but he's definitely been contracted to put your lights out. Don't think they worked out the when and the where of it yet"!

"Seems to me mate, that if they wanna dance, ya need to have em dance in your ball park, and use your equipment, don't cha think"?

"Keep it goin' Roy"!

"Well just thinking, if it were me plotting and planning it can't be in the yard amongst the great unwashed. Guards on the walls with guns, CCTV cameras all around, even in the wee places"! Just then Seltzer fell silent thinking. Then he came to life saying, "Just thinking out loud", he mused with his hands shielding his mouth from the cameras, "He's larger and stronger, a very quick boy and wherever you two tangle it has to be in such a place where he feels superior. Such a place where he has confidence that whatever he brings to the game will make it certain that he'll come out on top"!

Suddenly Seltzers face grew into a smile saying, "And that place would be in an empty closet"! "A closet", mumbled Rae?

"Something measuring around four feet by four feet. Just big enough to fit in two very large blokes standing up. Brute strength only all other forms of martial arts useless, no room to maneuver, no room to fall. Ya hit the deck and you're a dead man. Once the doors are closed and a large desk placed in front with everyone sittin' on it so a bloke can't emerge. The two get after it for a time not exceeding three or four minutes, or until thirty seconds after all has gone quiet. As for any rules, there aren't any"!

"Wouldn't that be playing right into Elsasser's hands", asked Rae? "A long, long time ago, on a planet far, far away, I once made the acquaintance of a bloke who was in the employ of the Soviet Spetsnaz. We did a joint piece of work together. Now he wasn't much bigger than me, but he took out a guy a head taller than he was, silently in less than a minute in an enclosed space with a rather simple move"!

"Yeah, the Spetsnzaz", mused Jaeger, "Came across them a few times when I was in the Corps. And they're some pretty nasty fellas"!

"That they are mate, but ya wouldn't want at come across this guy. The last I heard he's in a Gulag deep in the heart of Siberia. No doubt he's running the whole place there. But as it is, it's an elegantly simple move and I've even had an occasion to use it myself and this evening after vespers and with our belly's full, I shall teach you the move Mate"!

"Now as to the where", Roy continued," Rae, you shall employ Bitch Cassidy to find us a snug closet measuring as close to four feet by four feet as possible and allow the prison grapevine to discover only that an secret encounter between the parties is possible, with details to come at a later date. Of course selected witness's to the event will be permissible, several from the Guards, one from the skinheads, the Spics and of course the Kaffirs"! "What's a Kaffir", asked Rae?

"A Woggie. A word for one with very dark skin, usually used in the pejorative sense"!

"Oh, a Nigger"!

"Shush son, or the PC police will come and snatch you away"!

From across the prison yard a parabolic microphone was directed at the trio by Assistant Warden William Schwelp. Not normally known for working on weekends, but since he was deep into preparation of the annual budget for the Ellis Unit, he was hard at work until word reached him that Jaeger and Elsasser were working out together in the yard. He ran to his favorite room and connected the parabolic mike in the direction of the duo, only to be disappointed by the result. Across a distance of a hundred and fifty yards, there was too much additional noise from the activities of the other inmates to get a clear indication of the scant conversation between the duo. As Jaeger joined his friends up in the stands, the very same thing held true, with the addition of the subjects of his surveillance masking their mouth's with their hands while conversing. Still all was not lost, for the meeting between Elsasser and Jaeger and the subsequent intensity of the conversation told Schwelp that something was in the making. He'd just have to be patient and allow things to develop. Still, he'd have to include in next year's budget an upgrade of his parabolic mike system.

Later that evening after supper and after the lights went out and the cell doors slammed shut, Jaeger and Seltzer slipped out of their bunks and in just a few minutes Seltzer took Jaeger to school on the simple 'off the books' Sambo martial arts move that could kill or disable anyone, if executed with speed and strength within a minute at the longest, with a minimum of noise. Whispering in the dark, Seltzer slowly placed his flat hand horizontally into Jaegers mouth until Jaeger began to engage his gag reflex then withdrew his hand. Then he placed his hand again deep into Jaegers mouth and said, "Now try and bite down on my hand as if your very life depended on it"! Fighting the gag reflex Jaeger tried to bite down, but was unable to get any leverage into his bite, as Seltzer patted him on the shoulder and withdrew his hand.

"Now me boy you see what a nasty bit of work this move is once properly engaged and held lock tight. The subject is fighting the gag reflex, which is normal; he cannot get any air at all and no matter how big or strong he is, he can't get enough leverage to bite down on your hand in anything approaching a significant manner. Now your subject doesn't know it yet, but within seconds, his air gone and him gagging, he's about to upchuck all of the contents of his innards", whispered Roy. "Naturally he will panic. So would any of us in that position. Along with all else he is soiled of his own making and risks drowning in his own vomitus. Now I've watched this guy during his workout sessions and his mouth is open at all times of exertion to gain the maximum amount of air into his lungs. The trick is to move on him as soon as the door is shut, with your hand, face to face and it must be flat and into his mouth up almost to your wrist, for the duration. Your left arm must be well within his guard and around his neck holding rock solidly onto his right clavicle, or else all may be lost, but once the hold is in then start a slow count past thirty seconds he will pass out as sixty seconds approaches, so does the grim reaper, but once the hold is locked in your subject is yours to do with what you will".

"Now to keep from getting bored, while counting, I've discovered, the subject's right ear was upon my lips and my desire to leave him with a lasting reminder of our encounter was to bite the bloody bugger off completely. But whether or not to go that far is entirely up to you mate"!

Climbing into the lower bunk, Seltzer whispered, "Sweet dreams mate"!

By the end of the following day, the silent buzz around the entire facility was when Jaeger and Elsasser would dance? The Mexican and the Black gangs relished the thought of two white hombre's beating each other to a pulp, just one less to worry about, but just who was to be the survivor was the question and most important, what was it worth?

Assistant Warden Schwelp had gotten word of the buzz and silently gave his assent suggesting a long dormant room that was mostly used for storage, in an obscure wing of the facility. His unofficial reasoning was that it was a way to take the pressure off the convicts. Give them something else to think about other than their confinement.

The entire week every one gave both Jaeger and Elsasser the guarded once over multiple times, at their every waking moment, especially during meal time in the dining hall. The convicts would peer up, over and around each other to steal a guarded glance at the subjects as if they were important personages, which they were, if but for a brief moment in time.

The word eventually made its way back to Elsasser of the pending fight and in one of the rare moments he actually smiled, growling slowly, "I'll eat his flesh and drink his blood", then ambled away. Word of this comment made the rounds the following day and no one doubted that things would be otherwise. The following Saturday the entire prison yard was a buzz of activity, with meetings between groups going back and forth and when Jaeger appeared in the yard striding to the weight lifting area he came upon Elsasser just finishing a set of bench presses, with one of the convicts acting as his spotter, helping him up with the last inch of stretch, the bar bending slightly from the weights it bore.

"Mind if I work in a few sets", asked Jaeger casually? "Ain't no skin off my ass", replied Elsasser sarcastically!

Jaeger removed his shirt, then started removing a number of the plates from the bar, getting it down to his standard two hundred and fifty pounds, saying to no one in particular,"Four hundred pounds eh, impressive. How many reps ya push"?

"Normally about fifteen reps but today I'm doin' around twenty. How come you got such a puny amount on your bar", asked Elsasser?

"Well, I suppose like you I'm just not feelin' it today"!

By this time a crowd gathered at a distance, to see the two big men size each other up, with one guy commenting, "Elsassers so big, ya can't even see his collar bones"! With another convict answering, "That's because he's got a solid inch of muscle coverin' em up Nigger"!

"He's got no neck, just solid muscle, from his ears on down", offered another. All of these comments went far to drive up the odds for the Big one.

Normally Jaeger limited his repetitions at the bench press to fifteen at his approximate body weight, but as he started he decided to ramp things up a bit, eventually passing the fifteenth mark, then the twentieth without much apparent strain, then the thirtieth, then the fortieth, then at the forty fifth he began to strain a bit finally leveling out at fifty repetitions at completion without need of the spotters assistance. As he rose from the bench everyone saw the sweat covering his body, but he didn't seem extraordinarily winded.

He went and placed the additional plates back on the bar to the four hundred pound limit so Elsasser could resume his set without a word, only to hear him drawl, "Put another fifty pounds on the bar pard, I'm feelin' it today"!

Stepping back from the bar after adding the additional plates, Jaeger stood witness along with the others as Elsasser went through his routine, reaching the fifteenth rep then struggling through the last five, setting the bar back in its place, but just barely.

They alternated back and forth for several sets, setting their sights back to their normal workout limits as before, each having taken the measure of the other strength and stamina wise. A small thing possibly, but Jaeger noted that Elsasser's mouth was wide open as he went through his routine, grabbing the air, while Jaeger inhaled through his nostrils and exhaled through his mouth. A slight weakness? A sinus problem? Or just a bad workout habit? He mulled it around in his mind. 'Seltzer was right', he reckoned.

The guy was not only a bully, but unlike most bullies, this one had the juice to back it up. His eyes indicated a deep seated malevolence towards all and the very likely possibility that Jaeger was soon to join his ancestors, summoned a very real fear of failure, down to his very bones. Only a fool would not be afraid of Cloyd Elsasser. This would have to be overcome.

As he finished his last set before moving on Elsasser leaned in the weight bar wiping the sweat from his body and said, "Word has it that ya wanna do the 'Man Dance' with me in a closet"! Jaeger careful to stay just out of the reach of Elsasser's long and powerful arms replied, "Y'know, I've been hearing the very same thing"!

"So whadda ya say pard"?

"Gee whiz, I might just be needin' a little romancin' to get me in the fuckin' mood"!

"We could do this right now", growled Elsasser!

"Look around sport, the guards on the wall, with rifles and shot guns, the guards in the yard, the close circuit TV and don't forget the others who're already calculating the odds. The disappointment would be massive and the troops would be pissed at both of us, not to mention the warden who would have to do something about it"!

"No Cloyd, let's let the event unfold when it will and not disappoint the others", replied Jaeger, grabbing his towel and slowly backing away, his eyes never flinching from Elsasser's for an instant. After a few steps backward, he slowly turned and joined Rae and Seltzer in the stands to view the soccer game with no rules between the Mexican gangs.

Elsasser's eyes followed Jaeger into the stands as he mumbled absently to himself, "I'm really gonna enjoy killing this guy. I think I'll do it slow like and talk to him as he dies"! "Geeze, that was close", offered Rae as Jaeger sat down, "Thought he was gonna jump ya right then and there"!

"Apparently I talked him out of it"!

"Did ya notice anything about him as he worked out", mused Seltzer. "Yeah, he keeps his mouth open as he inhales"!

"Precisely", answered Seltzer. Most likely a severe sinus problem. Now listen up mate there's several things I forgot to mention about the forthcoming tango. Once inside the closet, remain as close to Elsasser as possible and do not wait for the door to shut before springing into action, but pounce as the door shuts. The guys clever but not very smart, he's going to rely on his strength alone, as he always has, rather than thinking things through. You must be upon him and locked in place in the blink of an eye or faster or all may be lost. Now he will going to try and wedge one or both his arms up between you and him. If he does all may be lost and any possibility of retribution in behalf of your ancestors will be lost because you'll be dead"!

"What do you know about my ancestors", asked Jaeger gruffly? "Why you told me mate"!

"What"!

"Yes every night in your dreams. Well not every night, but usually around three in the morning, if the muse paid a visit while you were asleep fighting world war three, you would alternate between mumbling and semi articulate conversation with some bloke named Henry Jaeger, Indian fighter, one of the original Texican Rangers fighting the Mexicans and the Comanche Indians. Oh, from what I've been able to gather, that bloke must've been some piece of work. I'd really like to have met the fella. Then you'd have conversations with a couple of pet wolves, named Chani and Akila. Now before you accuse me of peering into your privacy, I'm usually asleep at that time and you are the one who interrupts my sleep, so what can I do but listen"?

For the next hour and a half Roy Seltzer recanted a slew of conversations that Jaeger had with his ancestors, going all the way back to the family of Detrich Jaeger and his settlement in the Cheviot Hills of southern Ohio. A Miami Indian medicine man and the wanderings of one, Heinrich Jaeger. Each and every story rang true, for these tales of the Jaeger family had been repeatedly passed down from generation, to generation and finally to Jaeger himself by his father Morgan, on the evenings during their numerous hunting trips, when he was young. "Now they're all gone, everyone that matters, and you're the only one left. The only one that can settle things eventually and right the wrongs that have been committed"!

As Seltzer talked, Jaeger stared silently out upon the prison yard, with that thousand yard stare, seeing everything yet seeing nothing, knowing that what Seltzer recanted was true enough. "In a way I truly envy you mate.

Your family history far exceeds mine by light years. Which is why you must prevail, not only in the short run but all the way to the bitter end"! Jaeger then set his jaw, somehow feeling the presence of those long past, somewhere close at hand, finally saying, "It's good to have friends such as the both of you, no matter what happens I'll remember who my friends are"!

Just then a shout from the bottom of the stands brought the trio out of their reverie and they all looked down at a new face shouting at Seltzer. "Hey, you slimy, limey son of a nasty Sheila"! As the intruder slowly mounted the stairs to where they were seated. Seltzer slowly stood up with a huge smile spreading across his face replying, "You mealy mouthed son of a diseased toad, your mother blows dead bears"!

As the slim figure approached, he shouted back, "And yo momma runs around with a mattress on her back yellin' Curb Service"! Finally the two came together in an embrace of fellowship, with Seltzer turning to Jaeger and Rae saying, "Mates, I wanna introduce to the both of you a bank robber extraordinaire, Duke Vultee, from parts unknown"!

Rae extended his hand saying, "Been awhile Duke, good to see ya"!

Then Roy turned to Jaeger saying, "And Duke this is Jaeger"!

"Der Uberballer, the savior of the Cotton Bowl" said Vultee as he offered his hand in friendship. "If you're a friend of Rae here and this Aussie Kiwi, then you're a friend of mine, no questions asked"!

"He's my cell mate Duke", offered Seltzer!

"So how'd you guys get to know each other", asked Jaeger?

Glancing briefly at Seltzer, Vultee casually said, "I think it goes back to the New Moon whorehouse in Inchon, if my memory serves. A cold winter might and both of us drunk as monkey's, from cheap Korean whiskey, then attacked by a gang of slickee boys as we walked back to what passed for civilization. We made it back and they didn't. Simple as that. From that point on a lifelong friendship. But in all the years he never rid himself of that strange accent, or learned to drive on the correct side of the road. Plus the fact that he joined me in a project or two over the years"!

"Well it's good to make your acquaintance Duke, I'm sure we'll be seeing each other again. Now if you'll excuse me I think I need a little alone time"! Then Jaeger grabbed his sweat towel, rose up and went down the wooden stands some dozen rows, sat down by himself, taking his old harmonica out and started playing the three notes, over and over, his gaze on the yard, seeing everything and nothing.

Seltzer and the group watched as Jaeger settled in at the bottom of the stands and started playing his harmonica. Then Rae chimed in, "They say he did the exact same thing at half time of the Cotton Bowl and we all know how that turned out"! "Mate, he always did that, just to get himself all fired up and in the mood", replied Roy!

Some fifty yards away, Cloyd Elsasser was just completing his final workout set, with massive muscles gleaming with perspiration, when the repetitive sound of a harmonica came to him. Turning in the direction of the sound, he saw Jaeger sitting alone in the lower section of the wooden stands, playing the harmonica.

He turned to his black workout spotter and asked, "What's that all about"? Mr. Tat, named for the plethora of tattoo's adorning his body simply said, "It means somebody's gonna die soon"!

Vultee asked pretty much the same question of Rae, who replied, "We just got the word this morning that the 'Closet Fight' is on tonight about an hour after lights out. Jaeger and Elsasser. Two enter the closet and only one comes out. No rules. No questions asked. Five minutes inside a four by four empty closet. The door is locked and big roll top desk is pushed in front of the door and the witness's all sit on it, till either all sound from within stops, or five minutes are up. The witnesses are to be from the various gangs here, the Texas Mafia, MS13, The Aryan Brotherhood, The Crips, The Bloods and the Prison staff. Mr. Crib, Nigger Tom, El Loco, Sally Speed and Cave Man, along with the

Assistant Wardens section Captain and his armed contingent, just to see things run smooth as far as the winnings of the bets being fairly distributed afterwards. The Prison staff will be responsible of getting rid of the body of whoever loses. Haven't a clue as to how that'll get done, but since nothing can get in or out of this place without the help of the guards, I'm sure they got that covered"!

"Yeah that's all everyone has been whispering about as I got processed in", asked Vultee? "Any one to look after Jaegers interests or that of this Elsasser guy", he added?

"I get to attend only for the reason to see to Jaegers body after it's over and as far as Elsasser is concerned, he needs no one", replied Roy. "The winner is to receive five thousand dollars, in 'Cold, Hard, Train Ridin' Cash Money' out of all the bets made"!

"Seems our boy has all he can say grace over for the time being"! "Duke, me boy, you just don't know the half of it. But rest assured it'll be explained in due time no matter the outcome"!

The evening meal passed without much fanfare, with everyone paying close attention to what Jaeger ate and that of Elsasser. Jaeger ate sparsely while Elsasser consumed all on his plate and that of several others, without a single complaint.

When the announcement of 'Lights Out' came and the doors slid shut in unison, few of the prison population were able to sleep, each already counting his winnings. Of course by bed time all the bets were booked and the odds lay clearly in the favor of the mountain of a man named Elsasser.

Ninety minutes after lights out, a trio of guards each, came for Jaeger and Seltzer, cuffing them and escorting them as quietly as possible to the largely unused storage area. As they entered the room they were greeted by a single light bulb hanging from the wooden ceiling that provided illumination. The night captain was there along with several other witnesses' from the various contingents, all in leg irons and cuffs. The last to arrive was Elsasser, who viewed all those assembled, with complete distain.

As the guards were busy frisking and removing the cuffs from both antagonists, the Captain called them together and announced what was going to happen for the benefit of one and all, "Over there is an empty closet, measuring approximately four feet by four feet. Both y'all will enter and upon the closing and the locking of the door, will get after it.

Everything is legal, for only one of you will emerge in one piece. The only way the door will be opened, before five minutes has elapsed is if all sound has ceased from within the closet. Either one of you will emerge alive or the both of you will be dead. In the unlikely event of both parties being killed at the hands of the other, all bets will be considered off and the monies bet returned to each bettor as if this never took place. We will now toss a coin to determine who enters the closet first. Now remember, no one may attack before the door is shut"!

The coin was flipped and called by Elsasser who called "Heads"! It came up "Tails". "Jaeger enters first", declared the Captain!

Jaeger entered the closet, felt the wall behind him and quickly turned to see Elsasser enter behind him, as he turned to greet Jaeger with a sneer, Jaeger closed to within a foot of his antagonist, just as the door slammed shut, moving his right hand palm flat straight into Elsassers open mouth simultaneously with his left arm wrapping around the back of Elsasser's head and his four fingers buried inside of the left side of his opponents mouth. Immediately Elsasser felt the gag reflex take hold, as he tried to breathe while flailing about, slamming Jaeger against the walls, his stomach eventually giving up its full contents, spewing the vomitus full force against the walls of the closet. As Elsasser tried to draw breath, his airway was blocked by the presence of Jaegers entire hand which was deeply buried in his throat almost to the wrist, thus triggering yet another upheaval of the remnants of the evening's meal.

Those outside had now settled on the overly large roll top desk that was placed hurriedly against the locked closet door, expecting to hear the sounds of punches landing, yet hearing the sounds of bodies slamming against the wall and retching and muffled gasping.

As Seltzer had stated, Elsasser in his vain attempts to draw breath, started to ingest some of the vomitus, back into his lungs, now almost completely devoid of air. He tried to force his massive arms between Jaeger and himself and Jaeger countered by wrapping both his legs around Elsassers torso.

Yet after some twenty seconds of effort Elsasssers massive strength began to make some small headway, in his arms coming between them. With Jaegers hand stuck still deeply as possible down Elsassers throat, and his mouth hard against his antagonist's right ear, Jaeger opened his mouth and bit down as hard as he could, almost completely crushing the flesh and cartilage of Elsassers ear.

His arms dropped away momentarily to grab for Jaegers hair, he tried to scream for the pain, but nothing would come out. He was coughing and choking and as he started to weakenfrom the lack of oxygen, much less the foreign objects already in his lungs, Jaeger stopped his count having passed sixty seconds and breathlessly whispered in Elsassers almost severed ear, "Your time is soon at an end and the very last sound you will hear is me"!

At that very moment Jaeger felt the life go out of Elsassers flailing arms and the man go completely limp, yet he wouldn't let go. His very existence on this earth depended upon it. He waited and waited, then something deep in his mind shouted "Let him go NOW" and Jaeger complied immediately. Then there was silence.

By Jaegers rough reckoning half of the time allotted had passed and he then bellowed, "Elsasser's out and it's over. If ya want him dead then wait awhile, but then think of all the explaining the warden'll have to do"! He wanted to sink to the floor for he was exhausted, yet he couldn't, for the floor was occupied. The last statement rang a resonate tone in the Captain of the guards, who ordered the convicts to remove the desk so the guards could open the closet door. Jaeger staggered out of the closet covered in Elsasser's vomit and smelling foul. The convicts were ordered to enter the closet and drag out the body of Elsasser. They reluctantly complied, with the Captain explaining they all would receive extra shower privileges this very evening and while he was at it proclaimed Jaeger the winner.

But what to do with Elsasser? Was he dead? Jaeger dropped to his knees and felt his jugular and finding a weak pulse said, "Get him on his feet right now just maybe we can save him"? Once he was erect, Jaeger went around to his rear wrapping his arms around him and performed the Heimlich maneuver, over and over, until Elsasser started to sputter and exhale portions of his evening meal that he inhaled. Then Jaeger directed that he be placed on all fours by the others while he was still atop him forcing air into his chest, as Elsasser started to choke and wretch slowly coming back into the land of the living.

"He's slowly coming around Captain" wheezed Jaeger "And ya might wanna think about reapplying his leg irons and cuffs"! The Captain nodded his head and two of the guards immediately reapplied the leg irons while Jaeger was still atop a now coughing mountain of a man. Finally Jaeger withdrew after seeing that his former antagonist and erstwhile patient was starting to gradually recover, albeit much weakened from his recent brush with death.

Turning to the Captain Jaeger said, "Might have broken a few of his ribs Captain, couldn't be helped, so ya might want to have someone clean him up tonight and keep a close watch over him and then bring him around to the medical facility early in the morning so he can be X-rayed by the nurse on duty."

"Might prevent a lot of explaining," added Jaeger absently.

"Well son, seems you got a fist full of money coming your way", said the Captain.

"Do me a favor Captain, if you will"?

"Depends on what it is convict"!

"Take the five large and give it to Roy here, then give Roy a list of all those who bet against me, so it can be divvied out as best as possible. Can ya do that Captain"?

The room was quiet except for the still retching and gasping of Elsasser.

With all the witness's awaiting the Captains decision. He then gave the large envelope to Seltzer full of his winnings in full view of the others saying, "You'll have a list of all the losers by mid-morning. Anything else"!

"A shower would be great right about now"!

"I suppose your right. After all you smell so bad; you'd knock a buzzard off a shit wagon"!

33

Every night after lights out, a supply of small swabs of cotton would be needed in ones ears, to lessen the noise continuing from the other convicts. People yelling with or without a purpose, then howling like a wolf just for the sake of howling. Eventually things would settle down after a while.

Prisons everywhere mostly are filled with those beyond redemption and need to be isolated from society in general. Some enter incarceration beyond any hope of redemption, while some others are driven to that point by either circumstances or their environment. From time to time, cellmates would get into a fight over a wide variety of causes from the serious to the mundane and the guards would fall upon the area to bring things to a swift conclusion. Often as not, that conclusion would be reached just prior to their arrival, with the facilities population having one less individual to feed.

Many new arrivals will be eventually be tested by someone, as to his manhood. Is he a punk, or not? Will he stand up, or not? Experienced guards will usually be the first ones to sort that out and depending on the circumstances word will precede the prisoner as he works his way through initial induction. From time to time, its determined that some semi feminine additions be made to a certain section of the prison, just to take the edge off of things for certain members of the population. Sometimes it works out, sometimes it doesn't.

The average prison is a microcosm of any society at large, with many of its inmates formally garaged for a certain duration depending on the crime of which one is convicted. To greater and lesser degrees any prison is in a constant state of turmoil. It's easy to gain enemies for even the slightest offence whether it was meant or not. To apologize for anything to most others was usually considered a sign of weakness to be immediately exploited by others. Jaeger was in a constant state of emotional suppression during most of his waking hours. The only people that gained a measure of trust with him were Seltzer, Rae and eventually Duke Vultee, but even that was incomplete. Yet the measure of dependable trust is only achieved with the passage of time and circumstance. Violate that trust even once and it's gone forever, never to return.

From time to time prisons will conduct random contraband shakedowns of a cell block at random, examining every nook and cranny for weapons, drugs and anything unauthorized, even to the point of full body cavity searches. Sometimes it will occur during the evening after meal time, the sometime in the dead of night. The guards always find a treasure trove of contraband, if they really want to. There wasn't a day that went by that Jaeger or Seltzer did not witness an act of malevolence from one inmate to another to greater or lesser degrees. If one wanted another killed, and one had the 'juice', then it was only a matter of time until the subject would meet his destiny. If one was fool-hardy enough to incur the wrath of another influential individual and word of his death sentence reached his ears, he would then be wise to not attend his daily meals, or his thrice a week communal showers, (a strictly limited period of five minutes per inmate) where his vulnerability would be the greatest. A story is told where an inmate was so shaken by the news of his impending death that he refused to leave his cell, surviving for a time by drinking the water from his sink and washing himself by the water in his toilet. Eventually the prison administration forced the convict to rejoin the population. After several weeks went by and no apparent attempts on his life occurred he relaxed his guard. One evening during their shower period, he entered the showers along with a host others never to reemerge. He was discovered amidst the steamy environment with several dozen knife wounds, with a prison shank deeply embedded in the back of his skull.

He was not missed by anyone. He had nothing but enemies of his fellow convicts, having ratted many of them out to gain favor with the guards and of the guards by being a constant complainer and pain in the ass. When news of his demise reached what passed as his family, no one shed a tear, for this was the way the man led his live, or what passed as a life. He died badly and completely alone.

Normally most have to earn special privileges for the simple things by good behavior on the continuum and one simple mistake could wipe out years of continual good will amongst the prison administration. As a rule, simple things like pencils or pens, that could be utilized as weapons were forbidden to the population at large, with the exception of specific written permission from the floor captain and that was inserted into ones record.

When each convict entered the population he was given a list of what was forbidden, should a sweep of his area or search of his person find contraband, it was confiscated and the offender was immediately shipped off to solitary confinement for a specific duration.

The easiest way for anyone to get into trouble was to return from their shower session and during the wee hour of the morning get swept up in a search of their area to find unauthorized contraband in their area.

Regardless of who was responsible in the cell unit, both convicts were considered as guilty and both were shipped off to the segregation unit for a minimum of thirty days. One can imagine the anger of a cellmate if he was unaware of the presence of contraband in his cell by his cellmate, then assumed as guilty as the offender having to suffer the consequences just as well. Many people have died for less.

Several weeks after Jaegers confrontation with Elsasser, as he and Seltzer came back from their midweek shower session, which usually required only fifteen minutes in which their cell was completely open, Seltzer stopped and said, "Something's not right". They immediately dressed and set about taking apart their cell unit, bit by bit, examining everything in minute detail, clothing, shoes, personal kit, pillow, sparse blanket, finally they flipped, Seltzer's four inch mattress examining it for anything untoward, any recent penetrations in the seams and finding nothing then went to work on Jaegers mattress and there it was, a very neat slit not over an inch and a half long made right into the under seam of the mattress almost invisible except to the utmost scrutiny. As Jaeger looked on, Roy poked his finger deep inside and after some manipulation removed a small retractable orange penknife, with segmented blades, sufficient enough to cut a throat from ear to ear.

"Seems like someone wishes both of us a measure of ill will matey. Go keep a casual eye out for any nosey parkers while I dispose of this". Jaeger moved to the doorway of their cell and watched, turning occasionally to see Roy, dismantle the penknife, break apart the blade into small manageable bits along with the plastic form and gradually flush them down the toilet in small increments.

"Looks like this will have to be a constant ritual with us for the foreseeable future, from now on mate. Agreed?"

Jaeger nodded his head and asked, "Any ideas as who"?

"Any numbers of sods mate, starting with the guards and ending with anyone who lost money betting against you last week, not to forget any number of rat finks that might be quick to curry favor with the powers that be"!

Continuing he added, "Me thinks this entire wing will be tossed in its entirety before the Cock crows"! They made a complete second sweep of their area just in case and finding nothing else, set everything right and waited. Both discussed alerting Rae and Vultee the following day, and Rae was two cells down yet up on the second level, while Vultee was in another wing entirely. Rae had commented from time to time about his cell mate, that he was the nervous type in the extreme. Like Jaeger he mumbled in his sleep from time to time and that his dirty little secret that was never discovered, since he was convicted of grand larceny was that he had a lifelong penchant for the flesh of little children.

Sure enough, at the stroke of two thirty in the morning, all the lights came on to the entire wing and an announcement came over the PA system directing all prisoners to immediately get out of their cells and into the common area.

The guards were all dressed in black divided into four groups of three individuals, two groups searching each side of the upper tier cells and two searching the ground level cells. Two guards to toss the cell and the third to bag and tag any contraband discovered. Plus two others to secure and escort the offenders to the ground level for immediate disbursal to the segregation unit. Each unit worked quickly and methodically, for they were all old hands at discovering and removal. Every inmate had to submit to a body cavity search. Not to do this was considered an admission of guilt and off to segregation they went, usually kicking and screaming.

By the time they came to Jaeger and Seltzers unit they seemed to spend an extra long time going over everything twice as if they were expecting to find something, which of course was not there. As the two guards emerged, pronouncing this cell as clean, both Jaeger and Seltzer looking straight ahead never making eye contact with the guards seeing that one of them went immediately to the next cell while the other gave both of them an ever so brief glance of what appeared disappointment. He moved his head indicating for them to reenter their cell, which was done without a word. As they made to set things straight having to restructure all that was tossed about and remake their beds, Jaeger said, "You see that last guard when he glanced at us"!

"Yeah Mate, seemed a bit disappointed, don't ya think"!

"Now the only question is, who's the rat fink who planted the pen knife"?

"Only two possibilities Mate, either one of the staff or one of the convicts"!

'We might never know Roy"?

"Just gonna have at stay on top of things, for the duration Mate"! "From appearances, looks like the staff has gotten quite a haul this morning"!

"Oughtta keep em happy for a bit, but on the other hand there'll be a lot of pissed off blokes, heading off to a place where they really have something to scream about"!

"From the looks of things, Roy about a quarter of the wing is headed off to segregation, so things oughtta quiet down for a while"!

Several days later during the breakfast meal Rae mumbled, "I think I know who the rat is"? "Well spill what ye know mate"!

"Saw my cell mate, speaking to the guard, yesterday evening after supper, the both of you pointed out as the one who apparently had a great interest in your cell the other night. Just caught them in passing as I walked out, but he sure looked about as nervous as a whore in church and the guard was giving him a quiet hell. Then I decided to stay awake last night to see if he said anything in his sleep and lo and behold he did. He was the guy who slipped into Y'all's cell while you were showering and he was mumbling an excuse that he made the slit in your mattress exactly as the guard said. But the guard kept saying that he must've fucked things up or else you'd never have discovered it. Seems our boy is scared shitless of what the guard has in store for him"!

"And we know who the guard is", asked Jaeger?

"We know who the guard is", replied Rae emphatically!

"Can't do anything to the guard except keep eyes out", offered Roy. "As for your cellmate, let it rest awhile. We retaliate now and others can connect the dots eventually, so we lie doggo in the tall grass and allow the bloody events to unfold. However me boy, the more we hear of what his somnambulistic tendencies are the better off we all will be, don't ya think?

"For Christ sake Roy, when will I get any sleep"?

"Son, it's his REM sleep that we're interested in and REM sleep is when most dreaming occurs during the last few hours of your sleep cycle. Ya simply make it a point to awaken sometime around three AM and listen quietly and carefully. You will be our secret spy and that will benefit us all, since clearly this cretin is the guard's private bitch, ya follow"?

Several days later Jaeger was summoned to the visitor center. "Ya have a visitor number '67676' and she sure is a looker", said the guard. As he entered, he was greeted by the sight of his former public defender, Elizabeth (Buffy) Beauvoir, who was clearly looking nothing short of spectacular.

Like a super magnet the sight of this woman drew the glances of all the guards and the other visitors alike.

Jaeger sat down in front of her, without as much as a hello, striving to control his emotions, saying through tightened lips, "This whole room is videotaped from almost every angle, but without the audio and some of the staff I'm told is adept at lips reading, so the softer one speaks, with a minimal amount of lip movement assures privacy"!

"Understood", she softly mumbled!

"It's been awhile Buffy"!

"My fault entirely", she replied. "Embarrassed by the way I let you down and when Colonel Bollinger paid us a visit it sort of built a fire under me to pay you a visit at long last and to let you know that certain people aren't forgetting about you. But how are you doing Jaeger"?

"Seen better days. I make it a point of not complaining about anything, because it will not do any good, nobody wants to hear it and I attract enough attention as it is. After all I'm a convicted felon, pronounced by a jury of my peers and a murderer of my family"!

"Bollinger brought copies of the court transcripts of your case, that had already been gone over by some of his people at Quantico with notes, but we already had copies of the court transcripts along with PI investigations by my uncles law firm. Been working for him, ever since your trial, trying to get enough experience in street layering as it's practiced every day in the courtroom. I think I know where the mistakes I made are. As an afterhours project I and some members of the firm have gone over the transcripts with a fine tooth comb for errors on appeal on a pro bono basis along with monitoring activities in the Waco area. As to court errors for appeal, there are a few and they are minor, not sufficient to warrant a new trial, much less overturn a verdict!"

Then Buffy leaned in towards Jaeger by a few inches saying, "However the way things are moving forward towards the dissolution of your family's estate, by a group led by Don Ryder, and various lesser members of your family, we suspect a connection between him and Sheriff Morgan Little and a former Texas Ranger named Royce Baintree, who spearheaded the initial investigation against you. Just wanted to let you know that eyes are on, these various people and there appears to be a connection between them and your incarceration, nothing of which is provable in a court of law with what we have currently"!

"Really now", said Jaeger sarcastically.

"All you had worth anything had been egregiously taken from you and I'm here to let you know that no matter how long it takes, I and others will find a way to secure your freedom and perhaps a small measure of Justice", whispered Buffy through tight lips. Continuing she said, "You will be visited from time to time by a variety of people most of whom you'll not know. It'll be awhile before I visit you again. Don't wish to set up any discernible pattern for your jailers to latch onto just in case a connection reaches into the Ellis Unit"!

"And what if you discovered that it's did reach all the way into here", whispered Jaeger?

For several moments there was silence as Buffy arched an eyebrow in response. Just then the guard said, "One minute to go Ms. Beauvoir"! She nodded her head at the guard, before turning back to Jaeger saying, "Before I forget, seems like the former ranger Royce Baintree is running for the Governorship of Texas and one of his main contributors is of all people, Don Ryder. Just thought you'd like to know"!

As she rose to leave she added, "We'll be in touch, Uberballer"!

Later on in the day, Assistant Warden Schwelp phoned Sheriff Morgan Little on his private line saying, 'Well Morgan she's departed and no doubt is back in Houston"!

"Jaegers former attorney, Beauvior"?

"The very same Morgan"!

"Well what did you glean"?

"Not much, since they've somehow figured out a way to whisper and mumble making my abilities almost useless. Think I'll make another run at getting the visitors facilities audio capable in my next state budget presentation"!

"Bill, the civil liberties ladies will only shoot ya down in flames once again, like many times before. Ya need to do what I did several years ago, hide the costs elsewhere and then have it installed on the QT, with only you and perhaps one other trusted soul knowin' about it. That's what I did in all the county's lockups and other important places of interest and if such as a mouse farts I'll know about it"!

"And if Warden Murray discovers what has occurred, then what"? "Then you'll have a whole lotta tall explainin' to do son and it just might be your ass on a stick, which is why ya gotta get your visitors center in the twentieth century, by hook or by crook, we need to know just what's goin' on with our boy"!

The following Saturday afternoon was bright and sunny as Jaeger joined, the trio up in the top row of the prison yard bleachers after his workout, he asked Seltzer, "Is it me or do I sense that something is about to blow"!

"Yeah sport", chimed in Vultee"! "Word around is that several hits are in the wind this weekend some time. One rumor is that "Cave Man" has a hit out on someone who ratted out one of his members of the Aryan Brotherhood. Some little weasel who never gave it a bit of thought that one of the staff might have loose lips. Then another is that" Nigger Tom", of the Bloods has had just about enough of "El Loco's", Texas Mafia bad mouthin'! Some of his boys are driving him to that place called "Do Something", or else his leadership role, with the Bloods is history, which means he will be history unless he turns his boys loose"!

"Now the good news is that Warden Murray is on one of his extended vacations to parts unknown and Warden Schwelp is in charge", offered Rae! Which meant nothing more than the status quo would be maintained.

Almost everyone knew that William Schwelp did all of the heavy lifting as far as this facility was concerned and has his nose right up the ass of his boss, the Warden.

"So when is all of this action supposed to go down", asked Jaeger?

"Sooner or later sometime this weekend", answered Vultee!

"So how's your friend 'Elsasser' doin' Mate", asked Seltzer? "Noticed that he was struggling with his weights and having trouble breathing. Also noticed that he's giving you a wide berth, Mate"!

"I suppose that ingesting large quantities of stomach acid in your lungs along with various chunks of undigested food just can't do any good for your ability to breath. A few days after our little spat, the bulls brought him into the infirmary to see Nurse Moran and I took a series of X-rays of his lungs and I gotta say they didn't look good. The nurse put him onto some inhalation therapy for the last two weeks and next Monday Doctor Fowler returns from his medical sabbatical, he's to examine Elsasser. But it looks like a large portion of his lung tissue has been compromised"!

"Seems you've tended to your task well enough. He's keeping to himself these days after having cost a whole lotta blokes a great deal of money. Which reminds me, that last weekend when I paid all of the losers of the wagers a pro rata share of your winnings which you foolishly directed me to do, expecting some good will outta the yard birds, not all of the blokes were grateful, especially "Cave Man" and I believe his words to me were, "That's the second time your pal has cost me money. There ain't a gonna be a third time"!!

"Now Roy you just had to have a snappy comeback for the Cave Man", said Vultee!

"I did Mate. Gave him the 'Tough Shit', standard answer"! At that they all laughed as they set to watching the Cavalcade of Fools wander about the yard, forming their respective cliques and ever on the watch of all the others. Just then one of the guards yelled down from one of the nearby towers at the group, "Some shit is about to go down boys and I expect to see you boys stay put or else I'll have to run some lead your way. Ya unnerstand"!

Seltzer responded for the group, "Thanks for the heads up Tom" and they all nodded in agreement.

"Well old Tom apparently sees and know something's up so apparently the shows just about to begin, let's just see who's been naughty and who's been nice", mused Seltzer!

"Been quite a while since I've been in a bar fight, not since Singapore back in the early sixties", mused Seltzer. "Dirty business that. A swirling melee of blokes and whores, knives, broken bottles, people coming at you from every direction, one can't make out who is friend from foe and eventually someone has brought a gun. Don't quite reckon which is worse, getting' gutted with a knife or being on the receiving end of twelve gauge buckshot at close range"!

"All I can say is stay clear from Algiers in the early morning hours, especially the bars. The Bubba's and the Huey's and the guys with long greasy hair done up in pony tails with tats and earrings with those long Cajun names, that always end in 'Eaux', that reek of day old shrimp, don't rightly cotton to those they don't know early in the morning'. Hell, they don't even cotton to folks they do know", mused Vultee.

A hundred yards across the prison yard, Rae pointed out what seemed like the opening act of the epic event that was about to unfold, "Look over there" he pointed, as a small group of skin heads started to gather around a single convict while he was walking around the track. While simultaneously a group of blacks belonging to the Bloods edged casually closer and closer to a crowd of the Texas Mafia. The air tingled with apprehension as the various groups jockeyed into position, aware only of what was in front of them, oblivious to the mortal danger in the guard towers and on the walls.

Seeing the entire picture slowly unfold Seltzer said, 'We see only what we want to see and hear only what we want to hear, Mates"!

"Situational Awareness", offered Jaeger!

"Precisely me boy, precisely! Everyone heads up now I think the shows about to begin"! Several minutes passed as the various parties positioned themselves. Suddenly all of the various groups coalesced upon their various targets to try and correct the apparent egregious sins committed upon their various groups. The white 'Skinheads' falling upon the hapless one who ratted one of their own to the guard staff, with homemade shanks plunging deep into the hapless cretins body with a ferocity not seen since the death of Caesar. simultaneously with that event, a small group of 'Bloods', plunged into a group of the 'Texas Mafia', razor sharp prison shanks plunging deeply into anyone that bore the richly illustrated image of their kind with a rapid staccato motion inflicting multiple deep wounds in their targets with a twisting motion guaranteed to bring mortality on the run. "Looks like MS13 is gonna sit this one out", mused Vultee! No sooner the words left his mouth, the entire gaggle of 'MS13' charged en mass into the swirling group of

'Bloods', who by this time had been joined by the rest of their group who enjoyed but a brief instant of numerical superiority. Upon seeing that his former enemies the 'Bloods' were being overwhelmed by both the Latino groups, Mr. Crib, the leader of the prison 'Crips', signaled his men to join the party. This was accomplished with a sudden rush of bodies that brought a certain equality of numbers to the swirling melee of slashing and plunging of blades of every possible kind. All this happened within the space of thirty some odd seconds.

The prison yard public address system echoed forth the message to the convicts to cease and desist, over and over and by the third time, one by one the guards on the wall one by one started to select targets and opened fire.

The various doors to the yard opened as prison klaxons blared their harsh message to one and all signaling a riot in progress, spewing forth a contingent of armed guards, who tried their best to contain the struggle, but finding the white Aryan Brotherhood square in their path, who were at the time not a part of the existing melee between the Latin and the Black groups, would not be bullied or shoved by the newly arrived 'Yard Bulls' fought back with a vigor venting all of their collective pent up grievances upon the prison staff.

Although the heavily armed two dozen of the 'Yard Bulls' fought hard, they were gradually being overwhelmed by the white skinheads as the guards on the wall increased their rate of fire upon all those below.

As the swirling groups suffered casualties and began to disburse into smaller groups spreading out to eventually encompass most of the prison yard, it became more difficult for the guards on the wall to selectively choose targets that were not their own. By the ones and the twos bodies began to litter the prison yard, the convicts seemingly unfazed by the gunfire from the walls, but completely taken by the passing of their fallen comrades, choosing other targets as they came to bare plunging and ripping their shanks deep into others and in many cases, succumbing to others at their very moment of triumph.

Deep into the stands was the quartet of Jaeger, Vultee, Rae and Seltzer, staying low between the seats as Jaeger mumbled to Vultee, "Charon the ferryman is going to be very busy tonight"!

Seltzer shot back, "Just so none of us takes the final trip quite yet" As the melee spread out and the gunfire from the wall increased, many of those not directly involved were swept up in the deadly activity.

"There goes my cellmate", said Rae as one of the 'Crips' took a swipe at his throat slashing an artery, which prompted an endless pulsating spurt of blood from the wretched being who was only scant minutes away from that final trip.

"There goes Elsasser", prompted Seltzer, as Elsasser held up two frantic Mexicans by the necks, their legs dangling high above the ground, squeezing the very life out of them while they repeatedly stabbed him with a shank in each of their hands. For a short while it was a question as just who would go down first as they pummeled him with thrusts of their blades.

Each thrust finding a home deep in his body and as each blade withdrew, ready for another thrust, it tore out flesh and sinew, along with the attendant loss of bodily fluids. But eventually the life bled quickly away from Elsasser as he sunk to his knees, his massive hands in a death grip around the now silent Mexicans who hung lifeless in his grip. He filled his weakened lungs for a final time and bellowed forth a loud roar that echoed over the din, finally falling over face down into the dirt"!

"One less problem for you Jaeger", mused Vultee.

As the gunfire from the guard towers increased, it seemed the prisoners took little notice, venting months and years of pent up rage at the other gang members and any guards foolish enough to enter the fray.

Then a second wave of guards burst forth from the prison into the yard, led by Warden Schwelp himself, directing squads to various clots of activity armed with shotguns and clubs. After several minutes things still seemed not to settle down as the level of violence defied abatement. Then 'Sally Speed', leader of the 'MS13' gang noticed that Warden Schwelp was out in the yard, in full battle regalia, replete with helmet, flack vest, pistol and bull horn, barking orders. Yet his back was turned to Sally Speed, who saw an opportunity and peeled off a half dozen of his people and closed the fifty yards to Swelp and his contingent of body guards at a rapid pace. They closed the distance almost at the speed of a sprinter and fell upon Schwelp and his group with a vegeance.

Schwelp was the second to fall as he suffered a thrust from Sally Speeds shank deep into the back of his neck, severing his spinal cord instantly. As Schwelp fell to the ground, Sally Speed, let forth with an old Mayan yell of triumph only to be immediately cut down by Schwelps assistant and Captain of the Guards along with his Lieutenant via four rounds of buckshot tearing through Sally Speeds body. He was dead before he hit the ground. As the Captain and his assistant turned they were immediately met by the surviving MS13 members who ripped the shotguns from their hands while others delivered slashing blows to the guards unprotected body parts with their shanks. Now armed with several shotguns and the Wardens pistol, they went back to work trying to whittle down the numbers of the "Nigrito's". As they tried to reload, several of the wall Guards took aim with their high powered rifles and fired upon them at will, eventually killing them all.

From time to time other members of various gangs tried to scoop up the unused firearms. Yet the wall guards took aim with their bullets finding their mark by the ones and the twos.

After just under an interminably long twenty minutes, the surviving guards slowly brought the riot to an end taking notice that almost half of the population of the yard lay dead or dying. The local police had been alerted, arriving on scene just as the melee started to wind down, followed an hour later by several units of the National Guard who ringed the Ellis Unit Prison serving as an auxiliary force, to the various local law enforcement entities.

As the locals swarmed into the prison yard putting the survivors under restraints, a few noticed Jaeger and his group sitting all alone and ran to their direction, ordering them at gunpoint to come down and surrender.

The guard on the wall, yelled back at them saying, "These people are noncombatants and had nothing to do with this and I had them in sight all along. Now ya might want to put them to work caring for any survivors because Jaeger here works in the Prison medical Unit"!

"Jaeger did ya say"? Jaeger the Uberballer, the Mankiller"?

"Yup, he's the very one", said the wall guard reloading his weapon as he talked. Continuing, he said, "See if you can find the prison nurse. Her name is Moran and she will vouch for him, so they all can be put to work, but ya might wanna peel off four of yourself to keep an eye on things fella's"! Then Jaeger and his group came down from the stands, looking relatively clean compared to the survivors of the riot, accompanied by four of the Huntsville City Police and searched for nurse Moran eventually finding her as she greeted Jaeger, "Oh good you're not part of this mess," then she took charge directing Jaeger and his new assistants to various triage assignments accompanied by the City Policemen.

Within the hour, the various elements of the media made a beeline to Huntsville Texas. Helicopters swarmed overhead while Jaeger and his people finished their triage assignments. Nurse Moran then directed Jaeger and his people and the guards to go to the dispensary, giving him the keys to all the medical cabinets and bring back supplies with which to tend to the wounded.

Within a half an hour Jaeger and his group accompanied by the city police attached returned with the supplies and set to trying to save some lives. Eventually as the afternoon progressed the entire prison yard was a swirl of secured prisoners, doctors from the local hospitals, guards, soldiers and various members of the state and local police units. Seeing the Assistant Warden dead along with his assistant the questions lingered as to where, was the Warden of the facility? Fortunately Doctor Boyd Fowler had just returned from his sabbatical that very morning and upon hearing of the riot made a bee line for prison and was on hand to direct medical activities an hour after the riot had subsided.

The dead were all tagged and neatly placed in body bags at one end of the prison yard, by the rest of the guards who by this time had all come to the prison to join in for the task at hand, witnessed by the circling media choppers overhead. As night fell the prison lights all came on illuminating every square foot of the facility, swarming with politicians, soldiers, guards, law enforcement officials and the ever present media asking all of the embarrassing questions that no one wanted to answer directly.

Not only was the entire prison placed into complete lockdown, but the entire Huntsville area was placed under temporary Marshall Law, by the Governor. Several days later when all of the prisoners had been accounted for be they dead or alive, was the Military lid on the city lifted. Hearing of the riot from afar, Warden Murray hurried back to Huntsville cutting short his respective sabbatical, only to be greeted by a horde of reporters and politicians asking the embarrassing questions and eventually demanding his resignation.

Through all of this Jaeger, Seltzer, Rae and Vultee worked silently and tirelessly with Doctor Fowler and Nurse Moran, doing exactly what they were told, for hours on end, silently building up points of goodwill. Within days of the event, video tapes of the prison yard were reviewed constantly by key prison staff that survived the conflict and the perpetrators and participants in the riot were identified be they dead or alive and the survivors were harshly dealt with by the prison staff in the months to come.

The good news for all of this was that a temporary mortal blow had been done to all of the various gangs housed at the Ellis Unit of the Huntsville State Prison. Cave Man, Nigger Tom, Mister Crib, El Loco and Sally Speed along with their respective seconds in command all met the ferryman and crossed the river to the great beyond, leaving their gangs leaderless, for the time being.

The unheralded good news for Jaeger was that Assistant Warden Schwelp and several of his staff henchmen all met the very same fate, departing this mortal coil. For the foreseeable future Sheriff Morgan Little had no clout inside of Huntsville Prison. Many of the prison staff had little reason to shed a single tear for Warden Schwelp and his merry crew. Oh, they would attend the various funerals to be held, but many would relish being on the work schedule that very day. The following week, the clamor for Warden Murray's resignation was so strident that he was called to the Governor's mansion in Austin and before he left his office the Governor had, in hand, the Wardens immediate resignation.

During the evening meal some days later, the quartet of Jaeger, Seltzer, Rae and Duke Vultee, noticed the dining facility seemed to be more spacious than previously. Prisoners actually seemed to be happy since the bulk of the predators and trouble makers were no longer with them. The solitary confinement section of the prison was full to the hilt, with those involved taking their meals alone for a good long while.

"See how the almighty works", said Rae reflectively! "How's that pal", asked Vultee?

"The Lord passes his hand over a crowded space full of very bad people and eventually the overcrowding is a thing of the past. Those who unjustly oppress us simply disappear, making room for others that shall eventually come forth"!

"Save the taxpayers a lotta money in the process Mate", offered Seltzer through a mouth full of food.

"The world is round", said Jaeger!

"Or, what comes around, goes around", Vultee chimed in!

"Ya know, I gotta admit, that when we all saw Elsasser go down, say what ya will about the man, he went down as a true warrior to the very last", said Jaeger through steepled fingers. "I examined his body along with Dr. Fowler" said Rae and he crushed the necks of the two Latinos with just his hands and I counted up all the stab wounds for the doctor and there were over fifty nine penetrations in his body between the front and the back of his body"!

"The very first day I arrived and met you Roy, I recalled in the middle of the fracas what's etched in our cell wall by a prior occupant and is still there"!

"Yeah mate it reads, 'Nothing can be worth all of this' "! "Yeah, though I walk through the Valley of Death, I still fear evil", chimed in Rae, wiping his mouth.

"Well pals we can all thank the guard on the wall that gave us the heads up and didn't toss us into the hot grease with the rest of them when it was all over", said Vultee!

"Oh ya mean Tommy Boy", asked Seltzer? "That his name Roy", asked Rae?

"Yeah Rae, Tommy Boy's the guard on the wall. Seems we have our pal the Uberballer to thank for that. Seems Tommy was a former US Mud Marine, a ground pounder and since the Jaegermeister is an ex-Marine a tad bit of affinity is in play. Now Tommy Boy briefly attended the University of Texas and as a result of the Cotton Bowl game that Jaeger played in.

Tommy Boy won on the sneak, some Eight Thousand dollars from the bookies that very day in cold hard train ridin' cash money. Now time passes and the Uberballer is now housed in this very facility, but Tommy Boy remembers him and when the word leaks out about his erstwhile pal tangling with Elsasser, he scrounges as much gelt as he can lay his hand on, waits until the very last minute for the best odds available then plunks it all down on the Uberballer, then crosses his fingers, toes and eyes. He's on duty the night of the event walking the wall as it were. Later in the evening before his shift is up, he receives word of his investment from one of the other guards in the form of an envelope full of some five thousand dollars. Now if the Uberballer had lost, he'd be dead and Tommy Boy would be in debt, but since he got five large in an envelope, seems he has a very good reason to give a fellow Marine some slack. But don't sell Tommy Boy short, he'd stick a round or two in any of us, should the situation call for it"!

"The Lord acts in mysterious ways don't he", chimed in Rae! That said they all rose up from dinner after saying in unison "Amen"!

<h1 style="text-align:center">34</h1>

Weeks later after the Governor made top down sweeping changes to the State Prison System, by appointing a new hierarchy, a new Warden and his assistant took charge of the Ellis Unit facility. Many behavioral changes were implemented, designed to be more 'user friendly' and well within the parameters sought by various liberal elements in the States body politic.

Gone were the Draconian measures taken by the prison staff for the most minor of infractions. Various restrictions on the prison population were relaxed. The thinking was that, since the riot had inadvertently gotten rid of the vast majority of the most violent elements of the convicts, in an overall sense, then a new day of opportunity could take hold.

Various elements of educational enhancement were upgraded and offered the prisoners on a voluntary basis at both the most basic level and the College Level, all flowing through Sam Houston State University, located nearby. In addition various medical programs were upgraded for the prisoner's welfare, such as a program of continual inoculations for the prevention of the most common of diseases, which was mandatory for all prisoners.

A few other medical procedures were offered on a strictly voluntary basis, one of which was medical circumcision.

One evening at supper time, Jaeger and his friends were just sitting down to their meal when Duke Santee asked Jaeger, "Hey Sport, what's going on in the medical front? I hear they got you pretty busy"!

"Dr. Fowler's got me doing circumcisions"?

Seltzer then howled with glee, "Circumcisions, eh mate! You mean they got you cutting' on the convicts weenies"? "Yep, all part of the Wardens new program to enhance the cleanliness of the prison population. You remember the flier we all received four weeks back? Well, it apparently was Dr. Fowler's idea and was blessed by the Warden. At first there were only a few takers and Dr. Fowler did the procedures, roping me into assist him.

Which meant I had to prep all of the new patients beforehand, involving shaving all the body hair from the subject from the rib cage to mid-thigh, on the entire supine portion of their bodies"!

"Does that mean that ya gotta shave their weenies", growled Seltzer?

"Yep, inclusive of the entire scrotal area"!

"Scrotal area", asked Vultee?

"Yes again Duke, which means the Weenie and the balls"! Everyone cringed in mock horror, stifling giggles.

"So how's that working out for ya mate", giggled Seltzer?

"Well we have a medical straight razor, which has to be kept at a fine edge, but even at that, the scrotal area is tough to shave without the occasional nick here and there of a sensitive body part"!

"Ooh I'll say", grimaced Rae!

"So ya can imagine the bitching the Latino's and the Blacks put up whenever the slightest scratch occurred. Seems the South of the Border crowd almost to a man aren't circumcised while about half of the Blacks are"!

"Got off to a rough start did ya", asked Vultee?

"Yeah, but eventually it got smoothed out. Seems that when word got out that ya had the procedure, ya had to have an ice pack over your privates for the first five days and have a minimum of physical activity for the first five days, which meant that the guards were kept busy bringing ice bags to the convicts every three hours round the clock and the convicts were confined to their cells with their meals delivered to them just like they were in solitary. The meals had to be heavily laced with salt peter', so to keep any possibility of swelling down"! "One boner and all the stitches would be ripped out eh," laughed Seltzer.

"Excactamundo Roy"!

"Then what happens" asked Rae?

"Well, after the initial five days of lying around the patient returns and is examined by Dr. Fowler and if all is well, he authorizes the patient to perform light duty functions for the next thirty days. The patient comes back and is reexamined and if all is well, the patient is considered healed and goes back to his previous function"!

"Lemmesee if I got this straight asked Vultee? Ya snip the guy, he lays around for the first five days, doing zip, then goes on light duty for the next thirty, standin' around with one finger up his ass, and the other in the air, swapping off every thirty seconds, then goes back to work"?

"A vacation", mumbled Seltzer!

"That's about it", said Jaeger!

"Ya still shavin' the mates", asked Seltzer?

"Not anymore. Too many complaints, from the Mexicans. So Nurse Moran gets this neat idea to apply a depilatory on the entire area a day prior to the surgery, we make sure all the body hair is removed the second day, then Dr. Fowler does the surgery and Nurse Moran handles the paperwork with the guard staff"!

"So how come they got you doing the circumcisions", asked Rae/

"Seems they all misjudged the demand and it was eating up too much of Dr. Fowlers time at the prison and at the University where he teaches in town, so he had me observe the procedures and then he cut me loose on several of the patients while he observed and supervised, then he directed Nurse Moran to have me perform all of the circumcision procedures"!

"And ya been doin' them ever since right bubila", mused Seltzer with a grin?

"Not very difficult at all Roy. Ya check the patient to insure that all body hair is removed, then ya swap the guy with disinfectant, usually Wescodine, then ya lift his soft member and draw a dotted line around the ridge of his penis, you inject a measured amount of local anesthetic around the base of his penis and wait until it takes hold, usually no longer than five minutes, then ya apply an Alice forceps to each end of the foreskin and then ya take a surgical scissors and ya snip the forskin. Snip, snip. Then you suture anywhere between four to eight stitches to connect the two pieces together, depending on the size"!

"So what happens if the crud gets a hard on during surgery", asked Vultee?

"Never had it happen yet Duke, because the local anesthetic while deadening all sensation also keeps the schwantz from receiving additional blood. The guards administer pain pills every four hours along with providing the ice for the ice bags, for the first five days.

"Then ya cut em loose to the guards", asked Rae?

"Nurse Moran handles all that and she never fails to giggle when she tells of how they walk out of the clinic"! "Lemme guess", said Vultee.

"Bowlegged"? "And very slowly", added Jaeger with a wry grin.

"So how many are ya doin each day Sport", asked Vultee? "Oh about three or four in the morning, then a like number in the afternoon for now. Keeps me busy and makes the day go by faster"! "If that don't beat all", snickered Seltzer! "Your resume grows along with the number of your monikers. First its 'Der Uberballer', then it's 'Der Jaegermeister', then it's 'Der Mankiller' and now it's gonna be, 'Der Meister Schwantzstucker Nipper'"!

"Any of the staff take advantage so far", asked Rae?

"Not really at liberty to say"!

"Which says volumes", added Vultee!

Just then one of the guards walked up to the quartet, motioning with his head that their allotted meal time was in excess of the normal fifteen minutes and to make tracks. Ever since the riot the knowledge of the quartets actions during the riot went a long way with most of the guards towards a given amount of latitude in their actions. Still, they were convicted criminals according to statute and there were limits to the exercise of prison policy.

Sheriff Little made the trip up to Ft. Worth, to meet with Don Ryder at his Gentlemen's Club, for the purpose of calming him down. As the luncheon was served by the buxom hostess, they made innocuous small talk, until she had left the VIP room.

"So Morgan, what are we gonna do since our men down in the Ellis Unit are gone? As long as Jaeger is alive, we'll always have that threat hanging over our heads"!

"Don, now settle down. There is nothing that fella can do. Sure he seems like he's got the nine lives of a cat, but the legal action against him is solid or else there would have been an appeal of his case filed by now. He's there for the duration and that's a fact. Sure my people are in the Happy Hunting Grounds and a new Warden is in place with a new supervisory staff. But since Royce Baintree announced he's running for Governor, it would seem prudent that you and the rest of us do whatever is necessary to get behind him and see that he gets elected. Now I have his word that should he get elected he will appoint me to the regulatory body that governs the State Prisons, ya get what I'm saying"?

"So I'm gonna have to pony up with some cash to accomplish this Morgan"? "You and as many of your friends you can muster and then some. You're the principle recipient of the Jaeger Estate and you're doing a fine job in the dissolution and development of that land thus creating wealth, which is trickling down to the rest of us"!

"It's just that as long as Jaeger is alive, I just can't see how any of us can get a good night's sleep. You know what his father was like and by all accounts, he's cut from the same cloth and even more so"!

"Don, Jaeger is in a place where he can do us no harm and he's gonna be there a good long while. Now once Baintree is elected he can appoint me to a position where I can do us some good and eliminate this threat forever"!

"What about this Colonel Bollinger or his former lawyer this Beauvoir woman. I hear that she's tearing them up in Houston. Jaeger has already received them as visitors at the Ellis Unit"!

"One visit apiece Don, does not make a conspiracy, so cool your jets. I'm keeping an eye on her from afar, while Colonel Bollinger is not gonna do anything to jeopardize his pension with the Military after all this time in service. Baintree is a solid man as you well know spending all that time as a Texas Ranger. He's a savvy as they come and he doesn't break under pressure. So we all should relax and see to it that he gets elected then I can be in a position to solve our little problem. So let's enjoy this Prime Rib and let things develop at a natural pace"!

Ryder then cracked a smile and said, "Of course you're right Morgan. Please pardon me for being concerned"!

As Morgan Little drove back to Waco down the Interstate, it became abundantly clear that Don Ryder was the weak link in the entire scenario. Further, he'd been following the newspaper accounts of the progress of Elizabeth Beauvoir's legal career in Houston and by all accounts it was meteoric. In such a short time she had become the premier defense attorney in all of Texas, especially of the egregiously wealthy. The elite list of clients she brought to her uncles firm was literally around the block, indicative of the adage that word of mouth was the best of all advertisements. She indeed would bear watching.

As far as Colonel Bollinger was concerned, there was nothing he could do about it. The man was clearly busy up in Quantico, doing god knows what for his country. Perhaps random chance and circumstance could solve that end of the problem. For the time being he would have to push every button he could to see that Royce Baintree was the next Governor of the Great State of Texas.

35

Elizabeth R. Beauvoir, aka Buffy from her College days, had made quite a name for herself in the intervening years since her first debacle in Waco.

She hadn't lost a case since. Her drop dead gorgeous looks accompanied by a crisp, almost accent less command of the kings English, belied the fact that in any aspect of a legal venue, her opponents were in for a nasty learning experience. She relished in the fact that her detractors often commented that she was like a veritable "Black Hole" of the American System of Justice. Her ability to frame any argument effectively held even the harshest of her critics in awe. Living modestly in a town house in Houston's upscale west side, her life was her clientele which had rapidly grown during the years since Waco. Those who few knew her best saw that she was on a quest to become the very best lawyer in the land. As for any social life, it virtually nonexistent, save for the few social country club and political soiree's, her uncle arranged through the firm, always furnishing a carefully selected escort for her arm.

The partners of the firm, eventually grew accustomed to her sometimes 'Prima Donna' attitudes, but seeing that she brought an ever increasing number of well-heeled clients, thus increasing the billable hours for the firm in general, put up with her various behavioral inconsistencies with a guarded smile, for she was an earner. A 'Rainmaker', in the legal parlance. One of the first in the office each day and one of the last to leave, six and often seven days a week, she was a juggernaut of activity. As her client list grew, so did her support system, keeping two and sometimes three legal secretaries busy, along with their attendant legal researchers, gleaning the law books for legal precedent with which to bludgeon, prosecutors, judges and other lawyers severely.

"The bitch is like a tidal wave a hundred feet tall", commented one attorney after having his litigious head handed to him. On her desk were two small sand vertical hour glasses, one of which measured out three minutes of sand precisely and the other five minutes. When most people entered her office she quickly flipped the three minute glass over. Should your point not be made within that allotted time, she would dismiss you with a flip of her hand. For more important personages, like her Uncle Leo, or Boyd Parmalee, they were blessed with the five minute sand timer, but always with a smile. With everybody else, you were lucky if you escaped with an arch of her eyebrow.

Yet when the results of her deft hand on an article of litigation were announced, who could argue with success? When the annual Christmas Bonuses were handed out, her section's employee's always had reason to smile, yet describing the offering as, "Combat Pay"! She watched her diet like a hawk, having her one of her secretaries bring a repast to her desk from the executive dining facility as time warranted, only taking time each day do to a hard hour in the executive gymnasium. Eventually she had almost unfettered access to the firms, 'Off the books' private investigators, which always seemed to unearth things and events thought long buried.

They came from the ranks of retired Texas Rangers and the Houston Police Department. All of which were both book and street savvy. As she passed her thirty third birthday with a half dozen years at her uncles firm, she began to grow restless, wanting to branch out, yet wanting a private life of sorts. Of course, she was approaching the dreaded burn out without knowing it. She would look into the mirror from time to time deeply, searching for the lines of age, especially after artfully applying her modicum of war paint on a daily basis and seeing none yet, wondered if there would ever be a time when she could ever sleep late, make love to a worthy man and even have children. Then something deep inside always whispered, 'Not yet…unfinished business lay ahead'. Of course, that silent voice was always correct, for somewhere in Texas was someone of substantive worth that had great need for her legal skills, either from a criminal or a potentially costly civil transgression. Since unlike most women, she functioned well with only six hours of sleep, she soldiered on winning cases like the unstoppable force that she was.

Every other year, she'd drive up to the Ellis Unit and spend fifteen minutes of visiting time for Jaeger and she gladly supplied what books he'd requested care of the prison library, eventually discovering that he'd completed his studies while incarcerated and gained an undergraduate baccalaureate degree in business from Sam Houston State University and was enrolled in the prison's off campus program for a master's degree.

Always nagging in the back of her mind, was the feeling that she must do something to set this man free. But what? She and others had gone over the trial transcripts with a fine tooth comb to find anything substantial with which to file an appeal. Yet nothing surfaced.

She prayed for little in her life, more dependent on her ever growing formidable legal skills and her indomitable work ethic to carry the day, yet this one thing eluded her. Of course she dreaded her occasional drive up and back to Huntsville, for the round trip forced her to confront the lone failure in what was an almost flawless career, yet she went. She had to. She owned this man, things she could never repay. Always on the way back she prayed that the eternal would somehow show her the way to set him free.

He always seemed to be in good spirits, yet closely guarded in their all too brief conversations, never once sharing with her the almost daily turmoil that occurred deep within. She was completely unaware, (as were most others) of the battle with the unseen that came to fruition many nights when he was deep in slumber, only to subside with the coming of every work day. How could she know? How could anyone know? Except for Roy Seltzer, a light sleeper out of many years habit, who was the lone chronicler of what lay deep within. But who better than Roy to keep sacred the life story of Jaeger? Their time as cell mates, proved as mutually binding as brothers in combat. Each taking care of the others six o'clock without fail, thus earning a bond that would last for past either of their lifetimes.

"There's a little fund raising soiree', for Harrison Townes I'd like to escort you to at the Raveneaux Country Club, this coming Saturday evening. The man is one of our more important clients and he's running for Harris County Commissioners Court Honcho", said Leo Schwartzwald. "Can you find time on your schedule, to socialize with the rich kids in town"?

"Might take some doing Uncle Leo, but seeing that it's you, I'll make the time"!

"Good, I'll tell Maggie to put it on your calendar and remind you daily. George and I will be by with the Limo around eight PM and I know you'll look spectacular"!

All of this ran through Buffy's mind as she returned on the Continental red eye flight from Minneapolis after guiding through her very first corporate merger with two budding Computer firms. She's pulled out all the options in her legal bag of tricks, in getting the two parties together and finally at the stroke of four pm, a binding deal was struck between parties.

Throughout the evening and all during following the day, she and the other lawyers waded through the legal papers and finalized the deal, with Buffy acting as prime steward, seeing to it that all the loose ends were neatly tied.

She was a day early in her estimation of return and decided to surprise her husband. She looked forward to a lavish, unrepentant night of lovemaking with Artie Snyder. As she looked at her watch she estimated her arrival into Houston's Intercontinental Airport at just past eleven PM, so she closed her eyes and allowed her mind to drift.

Uncle Leo and George the chauffer had picked her up right on time at her town house and as George rang the doorbell, Buffy opened the door, as George's eyes grew wide in wonder.

'Well George, waddaya think", asked Buffy as she displayed her evenings adornments?

George thought a long second, before saying, "Missy, I can't rightly say anything about how you look, afore it might cost me my job and I got a wife and kids to feed"! "George, you rascal. You said exactly what I wanted to hear", as she grabbed her small matching bag and trotted on down to the firms Limo leaving George to lock the door to her home. As she approached the Limo, the rear window electrically came down as she approached, with her uncle whistling a slow tweet as she took a slow turn, saying "There oughtta be a law"!

As she entered the Limo, she was careful to make certain that her feminine charms didn't spill out inadvertently from her bodice, prior to settling in her seat saying, "A law against what"?

"A law against women looking like you", he added with a wry grin. Then he said, "In that attire you just might get us arrested Buffy, or even worse give some of our more elderly clientele a coronary, which would be bad for the check books of our clients election campaign"! Buffy returned the comment with an arched eyebrow as he continued, "Still all in all you look spectacular. Too bad Emma can't be here to see how wonderful you look"!

"How is Aunt Emma doing? "Well, she's holding her own and the

Doctors at MD Anderson are doing all they can I'm sure, but they don't give me much to bite on as far as her recovery is concerned. She sure would appreciate a visit from you when you can find the time"!

"I'll make the time Uncle Leo, for the both of you, early next week and you have my word on it"!

"One thing I know Buffy, is that your word is golden"!

Forty five minutes later the Limo slowly pulled into the Raveneaux Country Club driveway and stopped to discharge its passengers at the entrance. As Leo and Buffy slowly made their way into the Grand Ball Room, the sounds of one of the local big bands echoed its music throughout as Leo worked the room with Buffy on his arm, introducing her to much of the cream of Houston's upper crust society. Eventually they came to the subject of the evening, Harrison Townes. "Leo, good of you to come", said Townes continuing, and I see the best arm candy a man can ever have, offered Townes subject of his fourth Vodka and Tonic of the evening.

"Harrison Townes, this is my niece, Elizabeth Beauvoir. She's one of the finest lawyers in our firm"! Townes deftly took her hand and proffered a chaste kiss, then said "'Beaviour? You're not the very same Buffy Beauvoir, that's the terror of the downtown court system, are you"?

"The very same Harrison", said Leo in her behalf. "Unless there's a clone running around that I don't know about"! "Leo, where on earth have you been hiding her"? Plunging into the conversation, Buffy injected, "Not been hiding at all Mr. Townes. I usually can be found most days at the Harris county court house, joining the legal battle, righting wrongs and doing god's work in behalf of our clients", she added cheerfully.

Leaning slightly forward, Townes added while stealing an ever so swift glance at her bodice, "Some in this room might refer to you as the 'Princess of Darkness', my dear"!

"A title she's no doubt earned, Harrison. Now if you'll allow us to take our leave, so we can mingle, so we can take part in loosening up the checkbooks for your campaign, we'll leave you to the task of doing social work amongst the rich", offered Leo graciously.

As they moved through the room, Leo introduced Buffy to only those who really mattered, the ones with either money, or influence, or both, some of which who hadn't heard of her and were pleasantly taken aback and others who had heard of her, or crossed legal swords with her and were grudgingly impressed.

Moving from group to group seamlessly Buffy said, "You certainly know how to work a room Uncle Leo"! "The art of the twenty four carat schmooze young lady. Many of the men here, trot their wives out for a tad bit of the social, while their girlfriends languish in their hide out spots, ready for that three in the morning knock on the door and a session of slap and tickle. Still this is the world we live in and all we can do is what we can with what we got"! As Buffy and Leo moved through the room, all eyes were on the duo, fleetingly. Buffy had to chuckle, when one of the wives nudged her husband for leering too much, as sign that Buffy had it all working in her favor. Whatever doubts she may have had as to whether or not she still 'Had the Juice', quickly evaporated. Still she felt a bit ill at ease for some strange reason as if someone was mentally undressing her, as she moved through the room, she caught sight of an uncommonly handsome man, clearly unescorted who constantly had her in his sights. When she mentioned this to her uncle, 'sotto voce', without a single glance he said, "Oh yes, you must be talking about Archie Snyder"!

"The redheaded guy"!

"Yep, that's Archie Snyder"!

"So what's the skinny on this Archie Snyder, Uncle Leo"!

As they approached the bar for a refill of their drinks Leo mused, "Well lemmeseeheah now Archie Snyder an uncommonly successful man. He's got his fingers in many pies around town, Construction companies, with both city and county construction projects, upscale homes, dabbles in some midrise office projects, has a string of car washes around town, schmoozes with the right professional jocks as partners in his joint ventures, is a scratch golfer, so if you've a client that plays golf with him you'd be wise to tell him not to. An avid gambler and I'm told he's an adept at counting cards in blackjack, oh and one last thing, he's never been married as far as anyone knows, he's a world class dancer, ladies' man aka, 'Swordsman'!" "Oh really" mused Buffy.

"Yup, left a long line of broken hearts and crushed egos in this town, not to mention, ducking out on two weddings at the very last minute, prompting several lawsuits for alienation of affection, all of which cost him more than just a few shekels in out of court settlements. Oh yes I forgot, he's majority partner in several of the most successful upscale Gentlemen's Club's in town and I'm told at times he personally auditions his dancers, if that's what one wants to call them, meaning he's an seemingly endless supply of 'Boujin', to coin the phrase as delicately as possible. Other than that, the man's a mystery"! "So you're saying the man's not a keeper. That what you're saying Uncle Leo"? "If this were a hundred fifty years ago, in the days of the Texas Republic, when the legal system we know have and enjoy did not exist, I'd do all in my power to have the man lynched and never lose a night's sleep"!

"So how do you know all this, about the guy"?

"Ten years ago we were engaged, by a certain prominent San Antonio family, who spent a ton on a lavish wedding at the old Shamrock Hilton on South Main. He never made it to the alter, and was seen emerging from one of the all night massage parlors on Montrose Boulevard an hour after the wedding was supposed to commence. Then he was seen at the Astrodome later that afternoon, watching the Astros ballgame with a "dancer", in tow. We were engaged straight away and I got the boys to follow him day and night for a week. Took a variety of depositions, filed suit, met with his lawyers and Boyd Parmalee, hoisted him on his own petard. His lawyers settled out of court and we got a nice fee for our troubles, end of story"!

"Is that all"!

"Oh my not by a long shot. Two years later the very same thing, this time with a local girl of significant means. He always gets his hooks on the rich girls. Always leaves her cooling her heels at the altar. This time a different firm went after him with the same result, an out of court settlement. But apparently this swordsman has learned a lesson of sorts, never to get engaged or even look like it. He's an aficionado of the principle of the four "F's".

"Oh, you mean, find em, feed em, fuck em and forget em"! Leo nodded asking wryly, "Do you eat with that mouth, young lady". "Well, Uncle let's get back to doing some social work amongst the rich", as they turned to face the crowd, Buffy pulled a cigarette slowly out of her purse, only to hear her Uncle exclaim softly, "We have company"!

"Quick on the mark there he was just steps away, Archie Snyder pulling out an expensive gold plated lighter and as her cigarette approached her lips, there was the lit lighter at the ready to serve her needs"!

"Why hello Archie, I didn't know you attended these things", said Leo! "And why not Leo? I'm a member of the Country Club and I live right across the street on Cypress Wood Drive"! Smoothly transitioning to another subject he said, and I must admit I find it extremely difficult to take my eyes off of this young lady. May I introduce myself? I'm Archie Snyder and you are"?

"Rotopearl Baja", replied Buffy with a serious face!

"Rotopearl", asked Snyder with a bit of a smirk?

"You have a problem with that name sport"? Quickly taken aback by her assertiveness, he quickly countered, "Uh, no. Not at all, it's simply that it's such a unique name"!

Deciding that she'd drawn enough of his ego out to dry, Buffy countered, "Well it might be if it were my right name"?

"So your name isn't Rotopearl? May I know just what your name is "? "It'll cost ya a C note Archie"?

Snyder gave her a long look, then a short glance at Leo, who was doing all he could to keep a straight face, then seeing no comfort there, glanced back at Buffy and reached into his wallet removing a hundred dollar bill, handing it to her as she said, "Uncle Leo you may do the honors"! Heaving a small sigh, Leo said, "Mr. Snyder may I introduce Elizabeth Beauvoir my niece. She is an integral part of our law firm"! Snyder's eyes grew even wider in surprise as he exclaimed, "A lady lawyer and your niece"?

"There are those in this room who might not think I'm much of a lady", she retorted.

"All that and a hand full of whoop ass too", he exclaimed as Buffy blew a thin stream of smoke out from between her lips in his general direction.

It didn't take a sledge hammer for Leo to see the percolation of simmering passion bubbling between his niece and Snyder as he said, "Well I'm going to leave you two and see what I can get into for a little while. I'll give this C note to Harrison's election campaign. Try and be gentle to Archie will you"?

Buffy nodded her head, her eyes never leaving that of Archie Snyder for an instant, with him saying to Leo, "I'll take good care of her Leo"! As Leo departed with a fresh drink in hand he said, "Rotsa Ruck cowboy"!

"They say that your 'All hat and no cattle', Archie!

"Well I don't really know who 'They' are but that's not true! I do own some cattle, along with a few quarter horses which I race up on Spring Cypress Road not far from here"! With that said they gradually traded banal banter back and forth, with Archie growing in awe of this woman with every passing moment. Clearly she was like no other woman he had ever met in his entire life. Eye candy, ear candy, arm candy, a rapid fire quick mind and a lawyer to boot.

She had this hypnotic way about her, that was addicting and oh what a visual sight she was. He'd boffed his way through the finest looking women available anywhere in the world, always having his way eventually and then losing interest sooner or later, but this woman before him, was the key to his lock. As they conversed he would start a sentence and she would quite easily finish the sentence as he would for her, striking a commonality of interests.

After almost an hour, the band drifted into the song, "The Lady in Red", as he led her to the dance floor, they slid into the slow lilting rhythm of the melody, "and nobody's here, just you and me", came the lyrics, with others on the dance floor taking note of the two as discretely as possible. Her musk drifted up to his nostrils as he felt himself start to get hard and then slightly pulled away, concerned with too much too soon. First rule in life, "Don't spook the livestock". This Philly would have to be handled with kid gloves and reeled in gradually. Buffy briefly felt him grow between them signaling that he was hooked, but not trying to impress as he adjusted the space between them.

'This guy is really smooth, but so am I', she thought. Time will tell just who succumbs to whom. After all she reasoned, 'All work and no play, tends to make one cranky'. She knew that a good oil change was long overdue and she'd have to tend to that sooner or later, but it would be strictly on her own terms. She had the gold and thus made the rules.

As she rode home in the Limo with her Uncle, they exchanged small talk, with her saying, "We may have just gotten a new client"! "Let me guess, hmmm, could it be Archie Snyder"?

"He has my card"! After a moment he said, "Want to hear an old Chinese Curse"?

"Which is, uncle"? "May you live an interesting life"!

It's common knowledge that woman love to receive flowers, anytime, anywhere especially at their workplace, but expensive bouquet's delivered thrice a day, five days a week, each with a simple card saying; "From an ardent admirer", gets to be a bit much going into the second week"!

After a few days, Buffy started to give them away to the other secretaries in the firm replete with the attendant card, which was unsigned, to use them as they saw fit. "If one of our girls doesn't come in for work one morning, done in by a jealous husband or boyfriend as a result of these shenanigans, they'll be hell to pay young lady", growled Leo Schwartzwald as he walked past her office with several of the firm's partners on their way to a meeting in the conference room, pausing a bit in front of Buffy's office.

"Place is starting to look like a funeral home", mused one of the partners!

"Archie Snyder is my guess young lady", said Leo as Buffy came out of her office!

"And you know this how, Uncle Leo"?

"You forget, I've seen this dance before my dear. Has he contacted you yet"?

"He certainly does appear to be working it Uncle, but in answer to your question, No"!

"Well he will, if he's running true to form. Expect a slew of expensive chocolates starting in a few days and then in about ten days or so for an unannounced visit insisting the both of you have lunch on one of his boats docked in Kemah"!

"With my workload it's impossible", said Buffy as she handed several legal briefs to her secretary, with the appropriate notes for changes.

"Besides too much chocolate is bad for the complexion and the hips", she said as she made a bee line to the secondary conference room, on the floor below.

Going into the third week, the thrice daily delivery of flowers was accompanied by large boxes of imported Belgian chocolate, which was promptly disseminated to the female staff, but not before undergoing an ever so brief quality control check, by the object of Archie Snyder's attentions.

She carved part of an afternoon out to visit her Aunt in the hospital, appropriating the firms Limo and the driver, burdening him with the task of carrying several bouquets of Snyder's flowers to her room while she struggled with the singleton box of chocolates. Her Aunt was dying from a very aggressive case of intestinal cancer, that wasn't responding to the various regimens of treatment.

Some of the very finest medical minds were to be found at the MD Anderson Hospital, with an enviable list of lives saved from that dread malady. Yet sometimes Mother Nature throws a screwball and this was one of those times.

After a pleasant hour spent with her Aunt, she looked at Buffy with weak eyes and with a weak voice, that taxed her waning abilities to communicate she said, "Now Buffy, next to Leo, I'm probably going to miss you most of all. The doctors say that it just a matter of probably weeks that I'll be around, if that much. Of course Leo will be crushed and will not probably be his normal gracious self around the office. Other than Boyd Parmalee, there's no one that he respects or cherishes more than you, so I'm going to ask that you keep a keen eye on him in the coming months."!

She paused for a moment to catch her breath fighting off a tear that began to form in her eye, then continued, "Now come here and give your Aunt a final kiss, so I'll have that to think about in the coming days". Buffy did as she was told and took that as a signal that it was time to depart for what may be the last time. As she embraced her Aunt she whispered into her ear, "I'll pray for you Auntie"! "And I you Buffy, never forget that!

On the drive back to the office, Buffy was quiet, for in many ways her Aunt was like a mother to her, cherishing her very existence ever since she was a child. No doubt she'd lived a full and rewarding life and seeing that she was in her late seventies and had lived well, being one of the Grande Dames of Houston's River Oaks old money community, she'd be sorely missed by both the great and the small. Buffy struggled with the tears, deciding to get it out of her system during the ride back, for she still had a slew of time sensitive contracts to review before her day was done and had to focus on what lay ahead. There was time enough for additional crying when she got home later in the evening.

A week later, the spirit of Emma Schwartzwald left her body for that celestial journey. Her long struggle with cancer had taken its toll on her frail body. Once the toast of Houston society, she gradually evolved into the status of unofficial 'Grande Dame'. Rather than bury her in any one of Houston's grand cemeteries, Leo decided to erect a Mausoleum in the back yard of his two acre estate, deep in the heart of the River Oaks community. After all he had the space, he knew the right people, it was out of sight of any view of friends or strangers and he could afford only the finest of sculptured Sicilian Marble for his Emma.

The services were held on his estate and all of the invited guests were closely scrutinized by selected off duty members of the various local constabularies.

As the services droned on, various selected members of Houston's upper crust, took their place at the well shaded podium on the Schwartzwald Estate and added a small vignette to illustrate the sanctity and generosity of Emma Schwartzwald to the community at large.

In the rear of the seated assembly stood Archie Snyder, appropriately attired in a somber dark gray suit, his eyes fixated on that of Buffy Beauvoir, hearing little of the ceremony at hand. The services concluded the entire assembly then wandered around on this sunny day, a string quartet playing somber music softly in the background. Buffy, true to her word, was on the arm of Uncle Leo as the various personages filed past Leo, saying endless words of comfort, to Leo who was putting on the brave face, the eminent front, for his guests. Something in the corner of her eye caught Buffy's attention and that something that made look twice was the image of Archie Snyder standing just out of her direct line of sight, shifting ever so slightly from one foot to the other holding a proffered drink by one of the attendants that catered the affair. Their eyes met and Buffy acknowledged his presence with an ever so slight nod of her head, her glance lingering perhaps a moment too long, sending a message that this intruder to a very private affair was perhaps not so unwelcome after all. An hour later after those assembled began to gradually depart, having done their duty, Buffy grabbed a drink from the proffered tray and excused herself from Leo's side replaced by another of Leo's nieces and mad her way slowly towards an ever patient swain. "Don't recall you being on the list of invitee's", mused Buffy casually!

"That's because I wasn't invited"!

"So how'd you get in"? "One of the County's Constables, who I happened to know owed me a favor and since he needed a little help out with his kids college fund", his voice trailing off to nothing. "I hope you realize that you are trespassing as we speak and if I wanted to, life could become instantly uncomfortable for you", said Buffy pulling out a cigarette from the small hand bag she carried.

As the cigarette came to her lips, it met up with the proffered flame of Snyder's lighter. Taking her first drag and blowing it slowly between her lips for effect, Archie offered, "That you can Ms. Beauvoir and god only knows that I'm no stranger to litigation, especially at the hands of women, but I just had to take the risk of intrusion. I sincerely apologize if the moment is inopportune but I meant well. If my fate is to be to spend a night in the Harris County Jail, then I place my future willingly in your hands and will bother you no more"!

An old sales adage is that you make your point as concisely and convincingly as possible, then you shut up and Archie Snyder was a great salesman, standing stock still as Buffy slowly paced back and forth contemplating his fate, drawing something other than smoke from her cigarette.

Just then one of the Sheriff's deputies came up to her asking where her Uncle was. "Getting close to time allotted Ms. Beauvoir and we need to know how much longer your Uncle is going to need us"!

She turned and pointed to where he Uncle was receiving one of the last of a dwindling line of well-wisher's and as the Deputy departed, turned towards Archie saying, "Well Archie seems you're not going to spend the night in Harris County Jail. At least not this night. Be too bad for you to have to spend time with all the vermin there, after all you do smell rather nice and you're dressed rather well, all that would change very quickly"!

Snyder then shifted into his patented expansive smile that guaranteed to make the bodily fluids in most any female churn saying, "If that makes me forgiven, then please allow me to make amends and have dinner with me this evening"!

"On one condition pal"!

"Anything", committed Snyder!

"The flowers and the chocolates stop as of now"!

"Done", agreed Snyder, then adding quickly, "Now when and where shall I pick you up"?

"You don't! I'll meet you at Eight Thirty this evening at the Rainbow Room on Wood Way Drive. Standard suit and tie will be the uniform for the evening. If you're a minute late, I book, ya savvy"?

Lifting her proffered hand lightly to his lips, he whispered, "Your slightest word is but a command", smiled again then departed.

She watched him as he walked away and just before he arrived at the entrance space between the two large hedgerows, he turned his head to glance back then disappeared. That turn around told Buffy all she needed to know about the current state of mind of Archie Snyder. He was smitten. As he approached his flaming Red Ferrari Testarossa, Archie understood her watching him depart meant that she was hooked for fair and that all of his efforts had thus far paid off and now was the time to reel this prize in ever so slowly, no matter what the cost. Beauty, brains and grit was just what he had been searching for. He must capture her heart!

The initial rendezvous went well that evening with each searching the other verbally for points of commonality and as the time raced by and the bottles of vintage Champaign arriving and departing they began to settle into each other's rhythm in comfort. As the midnight hour passed and they discovered their waiter patiently looking past them out the windows onto a well-lit Buffalo Bayou, Archie summoned him over to settle the bill with an over generous tip. As he summoned the lot attendants to get their cars he asked, "Elizabeth, I must see again"!

Pulling out a cigarette which met Archie's eager lighter, gave her time to collect her thoughts as the lot attendants brought their cars around, with Archie pulling a fifty dollar bill for the smiling attendants motioning with his head for them to scram, then holding her car door open, she went up to him and whispered softly in his ear, "From now on you can call me Buffy and ring me up at the office next week and maybe we can take a ride on that big Sea Breeze Cigarette boat people talk about, but enough with the flowers, Ok sport"? Then she gave him an ever so chaste kiss on the cheek, lingering just enough to allow her amply subtle scant, laden with pheromones to do their work.

As she entered her car, she allowed just enough of her well-muscled leg to show almost to the entrance of the sacred garden, then put her BMW in gear and sped off into the night, leaving Archie and the lot attendants some yards away, with visions of sugar plumbs and unicorns dancing before their eyes.

The following weekend found Buffy on Archie's boat as its twin sixteen cylinder engines roared through the NASA lake estuary and out into Galveston Bay and then out into the open waters of the Gulf of Mexico. The late spring day was mild, sunny and the waters with but a mild chop as the craft sped along at speed, chopping through the miniscule waves as they weren't there.

After a half hour and well out of the normally traveled sea lanes, Artie spotted a distant oil rig barely visible on the horizon and turned his single side band Coast Guard radio off as he throttled down the engines and turned the FM Radio on, to be greeted by the West Coast Jazz offerings of Gerry Mulligan to be heard wafting over the waves softly lapping on the sides of the boat with the occasional sea gull circling overhead then speeding off. As his boat approached trolling speed, he yelled back at Buffy, "In a minute I'll put down the sea anchor and break out something to eat"! As he turned off the engines and the boat began to drift, he went to the bow and let loose the anchor. Coming back he noticed that Buffy had shed her clothes down to a very brief bikini and was already applying sunscreen to her alabaster skin.

"You do wonders for that bikini" said Archie admiring the view!

"Oh, this old thing? Hadn't worn it since law school, when a bunch of us went out on Long Island sound for the day, but hey I'm gonna need your help with my back when you return with the refreshments"!

Minutes later when he emerged from the cramped forward cabin with catered entrees and the pre-made margaritas in spill proof containers he was surprised to see Buffy's bikini top tossed on the back of one of the sea chairs.

As he approached he commented, "Ya know, with you top off, you're making it very difficult for me to be a gentleman Buffy"!

"Can it sport, you're no gentleman and everyone knows it and its nothing you haven't seen before isn't it. Besides, apparently I've grown a bit in certain areas since I'd last worn it and it was doing a lousy job covering up the particulars and now that it's over there I'm much more comfortable"!

"Far be it for me Buffy to argue the point", said Archie as he put down the tray on the fold down table, reaching for the Margarita and positioning the straw for her to sip upon. As she rose up from her prone position on the back bench to take a sip, she revealed the entirety of her well-formed breasts, noting that Archie was smiling.

"Great Margarita Arch, now how about you're getting to work and putting that sunscreen on my back and I hope you enjoyed the view"!

"Makes my heart sing Buffy", he replied as he set to work on Buffy' back and all the places only a contortionist could reach. Ten minutes later he was still at work kneading her muscles, repeatedly with the well-practiced motions of previous encounters, occasionally offering her yet another sip of his warlocks frozen brew, the returning to his anointed task of eliciting the occasional moan.

"Feel free to untie the bottoms Archie and work on the old tushie, for I've been sitting on my ass too long as of late and it also has its needs"!

Without a word Archie followed her directives, revealing two glorious mounds of gluteus maximus, continuing his work as before. Several more sessions of Buffy and her margarita, left the container empty and Archie withdrew to the cabin for a refill. Upon his return, he noticed that Buffy had turned over, shedding the last vestige of her virtue, with the bikini bottom lying on the boat deck. As he slowly approached with drink in hand he knelt before her and offered her yet another long sip, enjoying the moment with a relish he never thought possible. When she had enough, Buffy said, "Secure that drink Mister and do continue on", as she spread her legs, gently forcing his head between them, with her left hand while reaching under his shorts with her right and securing his throbbing member.

All afternoon on they enjoyed the raging intimacy between them, reaching clashing crescendos of passion, then laying breathless in each other's embrace. Moving to the bow of the boat and laying supine to gather every bit of the sun's rays, before falling victim to the passions that raged within them both. The third go around, several hours later, found them so deeply intertwined they lost their balance precisely at the moment of truth, falling into the water, emerging gasping for breath and laughing intermittently. Treading water they again came together in an embrace only for Buffy to spot a fin in the water some thirty yards away and immediately yell "Shark" as she kicked away from Archie and swam for the ladder at the stern of the boat.

Archie had been struck in a very sensitive spot by Buffy's inadvertent kick, painfully making his way to the boats stern and pulling himself aboard. He saw Buffy scanning the waters from where they came and pointing out to that very spot, her normally alabaster skin starting to show a tinge of pink. As Archie followed the point of her hand, he tried to smile as what appeared to be a shark, turned out to be the fin of a sail fish as it leapt from the water. "Sail fish, not shark Buffy he groaned, as he painfully sat down upon the rear deck". "Your hurt", said Buffy as she looked to where Archie was covering. "Did I do that"? "Yes you did as you kicked off, but we'll just chalk it up to friendly fire"! "Let me see where it hurts, so I can make things right, as she reached down between his legs and gently massaged his now flaccid member and the appropriate attachments. Several minutes later with the pain of his injury in remission, Buffy said, "Have to keep your equipment in good working order, for I'm not yet finished with you. Not by a long shot mister", she said defiantly! As the sun worked its way towards the earth, Archie made Buffy don her shirt and floppy hat after liberally applying another layer of sunscreen, with her saying< but can I keep the hat on mister"?

"The hat stays", said Archie with a huge grin. "After all we can't have you turning into a lobster can we"? They ate and drank some more during the leisurely afternoon, serenaded with the finest Jazz music that FM radio could provide, the gentle Gulf breezes, the waves lapping against the boat and eventually Archie said, "The suns going down and in a little bit we have to start back. Night navigation is a pure bitch and I need to take very good care of you"!

"Point well-made Archie, but before we depart you've one last task ahead of you", as she took hold of his much used and currently flaccid member and placed it gently between her lips performing that age of miracle of rejuvenation.

As his member reached its point of diminishing returns, she mounted him facing her newfound lover and inserted his valuable key into her insatiable lock and went to work with what seemed like the thrusts of life designed to drain the essential bodily fluids to the very last drop.

When they reached the summit of passion together, they stayed as if glued together, both breathing heavily from their exertions, as she felt Archie's member gradually withdraw, from whence it came. And there was Buffy, squatting in a very unladylike fashion astride this beast of a handsome man, completely satiated. Never in either of their lives had they any expectation of the heights of passion possible as on this very day, this magic day of days. Archie Snyder the well-practiced purveyor of passion mounted by the lawyer Buffy, who hid behind text books for so long, sacrificing her best years for the sacred halls of juris prudence, only to discover true passion that transcended anything she's ever imagined.

Archie finally stood up weakly saying, "I'm on empty, the tank is dry.

But I'm not complaining, not by a long shot Buffy", as he gave her yet another long look drinking up the visual beauty of her completely unadorned body, perfect in every aspect. He reluctantly reached for his clothes and shoes, went to the bow to secure the sea anchor and made them both another margarita and started up the twin engines, noting that Buffy had made no move to retrieve her clothing. Artie went back and got her clothes and offered the bikini to her of when she immediately tossed it overboard, "My gift to Neptune", she jibed and placed the rest of her clothes in a bag, adorned only with an open shirt and her floppy hat, saying as the engines idled, "Full Speed Ahead Captain"!

As the craft gained speed, the hat was caught by the wind, flying off into the briny deep, with Buffy, eagerly standing in all her glory clad only in a wisp of a shirt. All this, plus intelligence too.

The following days for them both were full of thoughts of each other. Dinner every Friday night at both Archie's home and Buffy's town house, followed by night long struggles to climb the mountain of passion. They always reached the summit together.

After several months of this and both of them having to make time for the other, given their mutually busy professional schedules, Archie announced during dinner one evening, I'm thinking of selling my interests in my Clubs Buffy and I'd like your thoughts on the matter. I've already turned over all of the decision making to my general manager.

"All, of the decision making? Even that of the selection of the dancers and staff"? "The decision to turn over the entire selection of all staff was made the very night that I met you Buffy"!

Enduring the several moments of silence he continued, "Somehow owning the finest Gentleman's Clubs in Houston, in spite of the fact that they're pure cash cows, somehow seems no longer interesting to me"!

Buffy finished her meal, put her utensils up astride the plate saying, "And your contemplating all this for little old me, aren't ya sport"!

"It just isn't going to get better than you Buffy. We'd make a great team together in every way possible", said Archie his face devoid of that winning smile and completely serious.

"Now I suppose this is the place where you ask me to marry you"! "Took the words right out of my mouth Buffy"!

"Seems you've trod that path before, not only once but twice in the past and it cost you a chunk of money"!

"I've changed Buffy and it's all your fault", he answered with a weak smile. "You're a lawyer, so craft any document you want to hold my feet to the fire. Set any terms you like and I'll sign it, without question"! Buffy gazed at Archie for the longest of moments and longer, thinking quickly of the pros and the cons of their official union. Of course she could craft such a legally binding document that would in effect inure him to bonded servitude for the rest of his natural life if she wanted to, but eventually that would drive them apart, bringing them both to grief and making them mortal enemies. After all, the man had his pride to consider. Then there was the fact that his digs were indeed a step up from her townhouse and in intro into the Country Club set, but then she'd no doubt that she'd eventually get there anyway and it wasn't an urgent priority in her life. But if he was sincere, really sincere in his ardor?

"It's down to this, you want to marry me, but ya got a bad track record in appearing at the altar, which is a concern to me. I can draw up a legally binding agreement that will compel you to perform with no possibility of exceptions and you will execute said document of your own free will, witnessed by several of this towns finest jurists and it will be legally binding, with a financial penalty that you don't even want to think about, which will be due immediately, should you not appear, for any reason whatsoever"! Archie nodded his head and said, "I'll do it, anything else? A prenup agreement perhaps"?

"No prenuptial agreement sport. There has to be some element of trust that develops between parties after all and I'm not after your money or your country club status. You will get me a simple diamond engagement and wedding ring with a simple flawless stone set in each ring not being larger than a single carat in size. Then after we do the necessaries at the courthouse with the marriage license, etcetera, we will have a civil ceremony conducted by a judge of my choosing. Agree to that and I'll willingly be your wedded wife and partner for the rest of our natural lives. And if all goes well, we'll grow old together sitting on our front porch watching the world go by. We got a deal Archie"?

"Darling, we have a deal", said Snyder beaming with joy. "Oh yeah and you don't have to sell your upscale titty bars, just keep your wick in your own pants, and I'll make certain that your well never runs dry. Besides they all turn a very nice profit"! Over the next thirty days, all of the necessaries were tended to, the "Performance Agreement", duly executed and bonded, the rings selected as directed, the judge and the place of the ceremony, being at the Schwartzwald estate in River Oaks, the caterer, flowers, string quartet for the baroque music all attended to courtesy of Uncle Leo. In the interim, Uncle Leo made certain that Snyder was under close surveillance during every moment of the day and night, via their contract detectives, who even went as far as wiring his home and places of business for sound, of such a quality that would match that of the Federal Government. If Archie screwed up, the performance bond would pick up the tab, if not then Uncle Leo would have a measure of peace of mind and he could afford it.

The only bubble was that it was agreed that only the employees of the law firm would be permitted to attend along with key personages in the city and selected neighbors of Uncle Leo. Key management people in Snyder's construction organization were invited, but under no circumstances were anyone else considered for invitation from any one of Snyder's entertainment enterprises.

Topless dancers were not on the guest list.

At the magic day, all went off as planned. The various bookies in town that tossed out long odds against Archie Snyder's attendance, took a bath. The nuptials mention in the local papers was minimal, which suited all parties' right down to the ground.

As time went on, Archie gradually shifted all of his legal affairs to Uncle Leo's firm, against all counseling against it. Their corporate tax division took over his affairs eventually restructuring his investments tax wise, thus saving him a large chunk of money. They counseled him as to which of his business interests were on the brink of disaster and provided farmed out auditing facilities to keep all of his known business affairs above board legally.

Lacking a formal education in business, everyone positively commented on Archie's overall business acumen, simply polishing off the rough edges. Many of the City and County palms that were greased to obtain valuable construction and service contract's, were gradually restructured in such a way to limit any unfavorable legal entanglements. As an offshoot of all of this, many of Archie's business partners were current professional athletes, who eventually shifted their contract negotiations with the various local teams, to Uncle Leo's firm, thus compelling him, with his partner's unanimous approval, to branch out and create another aspect of Sports Agentry, which proved very profitable.

After two years of wedded bliss, Archie had in every conceivable way turned a corner, concentrating on his various business interests during the day and paying homage to Buffy every evening. One evening as they concluded dinner, Archie asked, "Something I want to run past you, for your professional and personal opinion"!

"Fire away Archie"!

A competitor of mine and I were talking the other day and this guy builds upscale homes north of town in gated communities and for years he's been trying to cut costs at every turn to expand his bottom line. Now the guy has been in business since Moses went to Law School and he's been sued many times in the past for a variety of things, some of which he was admittedly responsible for, some of which he wasn't. Yet for the last ten years he hasn't been taken, to court even once and ya know what he told me was the reason why"?

Buffy shook her head, "No I don't but I think you're going to tell me, aren't ya"!

"He formed several shell corporations and named his wife as President of each and sold her each and every one of his companies to her for a, cents on the dollar transaction. Everything is on record, but deeply buried in the Harris County Courthouse, for no public announcement was ever made.

Now during the last ten years a number of people have tried to sue him, but have come up 'Bupkus' during discovery and eventually dropped the case and his legal fees are minimal. Everything, including the clothes on his back is owned by his wife and they been married for thirty five years. So tell me what ya think"!

"So how long, has this been going on? Ten years you say"?

Archie nodded his head. "Well, yes I supposed that would insulate him to a certain degree, from much legal liability, but if the legal transferal documents are in the court house of record, with some time, effort and cost, legal ownership could be established and by inference traced back to him"!

"Now Buffy his wife is only the figurehead, she's just a housewife and knows nothing about the construction business"! "Well Archie, my guess is that only private individuals with limited financial budgets have had a beef with him, right"?

"Yeah along with a few small subcontractors"!

"And they also being small companies didn't have deep pockets in which to fund a decent lawsuit"! Archie nodded his head in agreement, "So what do you think of his plan"?

"Well if it's worked for him that's one thing, but the very first time her gets in a snit with someone with deep pockets, he's screwed for they will spend whatever is necessary to find out where the gold is buried, depending on the level of their potential loss. If the legal documents are there they will be found eventually"!

"He's counting on that Buffy and from what I can gather the records section of the Harris County Court House is a mess going back to the early part of this century"!

"Yeah Archie, but they are talking about full computerization of the records section of the County facility"!

"They've been talking about that for years, but each time it's brought up in session it gets voted down because it's a very expensive proposition so nothing ever gets done. Their halfhearted efforts of putting everything on micro fiche have completely screwed things up down there"

"Who signs all the checks for his business"? "He does", Archie answered.

"What if he gets a heart attack and croaks? Who has check signing authority to continue the business"?

"Only him and none else", said Archie already seeing the folly of the man's plan.

"Well I hope he has a Registered Will naming his wife as full controller of his estate, that could be the binding entity in case of the unforeseen other than that he better take good care of his wife, or else she could have his ass if she ever wanted to. He should've given his wife complete power of attorney over all his business affairs, in the event of his incapacitation, with complete check signing authority, in the case of emergency, so his various enterprises could continue without interruption", said Buffy wondering where Archie's fertile and devious mind was taking him. "That would be infinitely simpler legally and much more malleable if ever the unforeseen should occur. Now if one has deep pockets they will discover eventually where your money is and go after it legally, which is where you are business wise. The way your friend has worked this only applies to the small potato's folks with whom he deals with. If the county ever computerizes their record section, then his plan is unworkable for all can be brought up at the push of a button, but I'll bet that he's counting on that very thing being far in the future and if it ever comes to pass, then he'll have enough lead time to sell his business at whatever he can get for it, retire, then fold his tent and silently steal away to some retirement community in Arizona of Florida"!

"I'm certainly glad I married you Buffy in more ways than one"! "Artie, I don't like that look in your eyes. What are you thinking"? "Have the papers drawn up Buffy", said Archie!

"What papers"? "The papers giving you complete and full power of attorney along with check signing authority on all of my business accounts. Then I want a silent transfer of all of my business, holdings into a newly formed Nevada holding company. Of course it'll be a shell company with no tangible assets except for the preferred share stock in each of my private companies and the President of the holding company will be you"! "Archie Snyder, have you taken leave of your senses? "Look at it this way if something ever happens to me, anything at all, you're immediately taken care of right"?

"That in and of itself doesn't shield you directly from any liability lawsuits"!

"That's not where my mind is right now, but I'll slow down potential litigants a bit wouldn't it and if that should happen, one needs all the time one could get to, uh, rearrange things right"?

"I'm not at all legally comfortable with what you propose Archie. For one thing, I would own your very soul legally. I'd have you by the short and curlies should we ever have a serious disagreement of any kind and I just don't want that"!

"Which is exactly why I want you to set things up this way", appealed Archie. "Look, we're good together, in fact great. Over the last two years have we had even one significant disagreement? No! Plus the fact that your legal skills have made my companies far more efficient, finally you've earned my trust completely and I hope I've earned yours"!

Buffy then got up and went to the kitchen where she kept a hidden pack of cigarettes just in case she fell off the wagon. Then she poured several fingers of Wild Turkey into a shot glass and returned to the dining table.

"And you're responsible for pushing me off the wagon"; she said as she took a long puff and tossed half of her whiskey down the hatch. "Soooo", crooned Archie?

All right, all ready, I'll run the idea past Uncle Leo and get his input, but I think I can already tell you what he'll say"!

"And that is", asked Archie?

"The man is completely crazy"!

"Yeah babe, crazy like a fox"! "He wants what" asked Uncle Leo when Buffy approached him the following day with Archie's reorganization ideas. "Why, that man is crazy", Leo said emphatically! "That's exactly what I told him you would say Uncle Leo, but that's what he wants and before you say anything else, I spent a very long time over dinner going over all the reasons against it, but that is what he wants done"!

"And you agreed to it", said Leo looking out plate glass window upon the haze of the city below!"Only on the proviso that you said it could be legally accomplished"! "And he agreed that it was billable time Buffy"?

Buffy nodded her head. Then said, "I told him that my schedule is so full I couldn't handle it, which it is, but that I'd prevail upon you to have someone competent in the firm see if such a concept could be crafted and that it would be billable time on his account"!

"And the man's answer Buffy"?

"He said whatever it takes"! Leo grimaced, then got on the office phone to Boyd Parmalee. "Yes Leo", he answered!

"Boyd, didn't we bring onboard some youngster from TCU, with a specialty in corporate law recently? This young man had some off the scale IQ and I think his name is Polk"!

"Oh you must mean Polk Moon III. They call him "Pokey"!

"Yes, yes, that's the man I've in mind. Is he on anything pressing at the moment? I may need him for a special project, billable time if you please, that entails a private corporate restructuring, germane to Buffy's husband, not to exceed two weeks in duration"!

"Well, he's currently on a project, but nothing of any pressing importance, that he can't be missed for a fortnight Leo"!

"Then send him here right quick, so we can get started", ringing off. "There now are you happy my dear"?

"I'll be happy when my conference room is finished" said Buffy.

"You took the words right out of my mouth, my dear. The final touches were completed last night and as you know the room has been on lockdown ever since. They wouldn't even let me in, but in my hand is the key, so if you'll follow me"? At that Buffy followed her Uncle to the other end of the floor, walking past her office and stopped in front of the newly constructed small conference room adjacent to her office.

As the large double doors opened, what was revealed was a massive marble conference table, flanked by the buildings windows to the left and a wall to wall set of specially built in book shelves filled with law books.

Finally at the end of the room was a giant wall covering photo mural of the curved surface of the moonscape, complete with the pockmarked craters, revealing the thousands of stars in the sky. The original photo being taken by the low orbiting moon craft as it traversed the moon.

As she walked around the room inspecting everything she gradually started to smile, tossing first one thumb then gradually the other upwards, finally sitting down at the head of the conference table and settling back in the large black leather padded chair and put both feet up on the table crossing them at the ankles.

As Leo looked on he asked, "Why the expensive wall covering of the moonscape? A little gaudy isn't it"?

"It'll pay for itself in no time Uncle"? "How's that", asked Leo?

"During the litigation process, I'll invite both parties to engage with each other in this very conference room and I will sit here and the opposing counsel will sit at the other end of the table facing me and the wall covering. Now during the process of back and forth, the question will always be asked, if not implied, "What is it we want"? Thus the opposing counsel will know, having faced me and the wall covering for every minute he's there and of course the subtle answer will be, 'The Moon and the Stars'. That, my good Uncle is the reason for 'that', particular wall covering"!

"Seeing the subtle wisdom that matched her track record of accomplishment so far, then Leo turned to leave the room saying, "Remind me never to lock horns with you in this room and especially to stay out of that chair", pointing to the leather chair at the end of the marble conference table facing the moonscape. A week later Polk Moon had laid before, Leo, Buffy and Boyd Parmalee, his proposal to structure all of Archie Snyder's various business interests to be lawsuit proof, while still conforming to all the state statutes in both Texas and Nevada. Archie's general concept was in play, but in order to polish off all of the rough legal edges, the skill of a competent and more over a creative corporate lawyer, was required craft the various corporate documents, to be error free.

All three followed Polk closely as he led them through the maze of corporate legalities that serendipitously tied both states together inadvertently. "You see, it's like we invent a light bulb and someone else also invents a light bulb, that fits in each other's sockets, yet are demonstrably different in design"!

The plan completely followed Archie's idea, on many points, differing only where the laws of each state might clash. Polk's concept carefully merged both states statutes into a cohesive concept.

"Brilliant my boy", said Leo after the presentation. "Anyone see any problems in his concept"? Boyd and Buffy shook their heads in the negative without a further word.

"Again well done my boy. So how long will it take for us to review the finished product"?

"Well sir, Ms. Beauvoir has the originals of all of his business and accounting documents along with all of his banking information, so if I could exclusive access to one of the legal secretaries, I could probably have the completed product ready for your final review in say, ten working days"!

"Excellent", said Leo. "Boyd, can this this young man have access to one of our ladies for the next two weeks"? "Consider it done Leo"!

Two weeks later the final product was reviewed by the trio and finding it without flaw, Archie was brought in to formally execute all of the germane documents. They provided no surprises to Archie, where as he was eager to get a daily progress report from Buffy each night. He was greatly pleased when he was initially told that his plan was legally workable and she took him to school somewhat into a few of the legal intricacies involved in accomplishing what he wanted.

Within an hour, of the day of their meeting, Archie had executed all of the required documents, required to turn over complete power of attorney, to his wife for all his affairs, both corporate and personal, should events of her determining prove necessary.

As he rose from the chair beaming he said to Leo as they shook hands, "Best money I ever spent on lawyers Uncle Leo"! He gave Buffy a brief kiss and a hug, then shook hands with all involved, thanking them all for their work then said, "Well, I have to get down to city hall and rub butts with the politicians. See ya tonight Buffy", then flew out of Buffy's office.

"So it's done", said Leo as he watched Archie rapidly make his way down the hall to the elevator. As Leo and Parmalee, left Buffy to meet with another client, Boyd said, "They'll be Ok Leo, as long as Archie remains righteous in her behalf"! "And if he back slides Boyd, then what"? "Then Leo, the earth will open wide and Archie Snyder will fall into the deep abyss"!Tired and eager to get home, Buffy had fallen asleep during the flight and was awakened, by the rumbling of the Continental Jets landing gear, the engines having gone into idle mode as the craft descended into Houston. She gathered her things and fastened her seat belt, eager anticipating her transference from the Alpha Lioness to lover of Archie Snyder, silently slipping into their bed au natural, and pouring out her passion to her supreme recipient her husband and lover, a day earlier than expected.

She and Pokey had worked well together, working the various disparate corporate entities together, he with his creative legal machinations, melded closely with her guile and charm, brought the parties together. Not to mention the merger fee brought into the firm would be a cause for celebration for all the partners. Pokey had stayed behind in Minneapolis for one final day to tend to the niggling details, so things went smoothly.

Life was treating her very well these days, with her greatest accomplishment yet behind her. The announcement of the merger would be media wide in two days, and in the words of the singer, 'Peggy Lee', "The best was yet to come and babe won't it be fine". She was grateful for two things in life, as of late, her union with her Uncle Leo and her marriage to Archie Snyder. Yet something was missing and it wasn't the lack of a child in her life, she still had time for that later.

It was the nagging thought of her only legal defeat, sitting there up in Huntsville Prison, his life, if one could call it that, wasting away through her legal naiveté at that time. Jaeger was still in prison and there wasn't a damn thing she could do about it legally, with any reasonable chance of success. Unfinished business nagged at her from time to time and every time it did, she was compelled to say a brief prayer for Jaeger's sanity and safety. That was about the only time she ever took time to talk to 'the man'. She hadn't seen him in a few years and it was high time she rectified that venial error. Sometime within the next thirty days she promised herself.

But tonight she resolved to be good to herself, very good to herself and to sole the object of her desires. As Archie always said good-heartedly, 'When she was good she was very good, but when she was bad, she was Bettah'.

As she drove west from the airport through the fog shrouded early morning hours on Cypresswood Drive, a deep physical longing for Archie somehow took hold and she felt herself grow damp, in the area of her other 'Money maker'. 'Odd', she thought, 'how the subconscious takes over at times'. Passing the intersection, replete with shade trees that danced with the street lights, she viewed the shopping center in her rear view mirror and the Country Club coming up on her left just a minute left and she was home. They had given Maria, their live in maid the week off. She tended to them during the week keeping the place spotless, preparing their meals and giving hell to the grounds keepers, spending her nights in the small apartment above their detached five car garage. But she was to be back early in the morning, so maybe Buffy could spend the day catching up on her snooze time after Archie went into town for the day.

As she turned her BMW into the side street across from the country club, she made an immediate left going up the driveway into the garage that opened automatically via her clicker. She decided to leave her bags and briefcase in the car and retrieve them late tomorrow morning.

Walking out of the garage, she passed Archie's three Ducati motorcycles and his precious Fire Red Ferrari Testarossa and exited stage left crossing the covered breezeway and went right into house, shutting the door after her, putting her keys down on the kitchen counter.

She opened the refrigerator and brought out an inexpensive bottle of chilled Lambrusco wine, pouring it into one of the glasses and as she took her first sip, she had this sudden feeling that something was wrong, very wrong. She walked around into the wide open space and turning on one of the area lights, immediately saw what it was. An empty wine glass, with fresh lipstick on it. Looking around, she saw an ash tray full of cigarette butts with the same color lipstick on it, then her nostrils kicked in when a whiff of cheap perfume assaulted her sinuses. On the dining table half eaten plated full of cold food. Her mind reeled, with anger as she remained motionless, then moving towards the front of the house and the stairway to the second floor, she stopped at the sight of a woman's skirt, then halfway up the dimly lit stairway was a blouse, then a bra. Then she slowly started to climb the stairs, passing the intruding articles of clothing strewn along a path leading straight to her and Archie's bedroom. As she approached the door to the bedroom, she stopped and listened for any sounds and heard only the ringing in her ears. Buffy slowly opened the door and was met with that all too familiar scent of the aftermath of a man and woman, performing heated combat in her bed. Her bed, her sanctum sanctorum and there both were, the scent of another woman, the cheap perfume and the blonde hair in a state of complete disarray peeking out from under the large quilt that covered them both, deep in the arms of a drunken stupor guaranteed to leave them hors de combat for a number of hours to come.

She lifted one end of the quilt revealing the presence of the secretary Archie said that he fired almost a year ago, in all of her bare glory. Putting the quilt down, she silently went around to the other side of the bed and lifted the quilt, hoping that it would be someone other than her beloved Archie, but there the bastard was dead to the world and deep in a drunken stupor. He'd be out for a good long while.

With the anger building deep inside of her, she turned and silently left the bedroom, gathering the intruders clothes as she made her way downstairs, trying to clear her mind as she went. Then she entered Archie's den and went to his desk dropping the offending clothes on the floor. She opened his drawer and there it was, the .380 automatic he always kept loaded just in case of intruders. Pondering about how simple it would be to stick around in each of their ears, thus ending their misery on this earth, would create endless misery for Buffy, so she carefully wiped her prints from the weapon with her blouse and placed it back in the desk.

This was not the time to think like the typical woman, so she pushed the button in her head and went back into the garage, started her car and backed down the driveway and drove off down the street. As she drove in as trying to clear her mind, she eventually found herself coming to the main intersection of FM 1960, and entered an all-night diner, finding herself hungry, not having eaten since lunch the previous day.

Waiting for her order to arrive while drinking her coffee a plan was starting formulate in her mind. As she absently picked through her breakfast, the plan started to come together and in a rush to put the plan into motion and finding the food tasteless, she quickly paid the bill and left. As she drove down the northern most main drag, her eyes came upon the sign of an all-night Walgreen's pharmacy. Roaming the aisles not certain of what she was looking for, or why her eyes came upon a Polaroid Camera Kiosk, prompting her to grab one of the camera sand an extra package of film. As she continued he quest, she came across her unknown quest several aisles over. A kiosk full of tubes of, "Super Glue". Standing there was the Holy Grail, as she viewed it which immediately brought the entire plan together. Quickly gathering up, every single tube of glue, which totaled several dozen in total, she quickly but calmly took her purchases to the counter and was checked out by the sleepy attendant, who wanted to ask why she was buying all the glue, but thought better of it reasoning that it was a sick world, but he was a happy guy. Taking all her purchases, she drove with all deliberate speed back to her house checking the time on her watch, wondering if she had the time prior to sunrise to effectively bring everything together. Driving quietly into her garage, she entered the house and, poured all the tubes of the glue out on the counter and prepared them for use upstairs.

Climbing the stairs quietly she went down the short hallway and into the bedroom. Standing at the foot of this now unholy bed, she surveyed those who were soon to be the objects of her attention and finding them deep in the embrace of drunken sleep, checked her watch one more time, finding it just short of two in the morning quickly setting to work, gently positioning the two bodies to face each other, placing Archie's hands around his partner for the evening in such a way to clasp her buttocks and carefully opened the tubes of glue and liberally applied the glue to his hands, placing them securely on her buttocks. She was pleased with the effort seeing that each of his hands required three tubes of the witches' brew, to achieve the desired effect. Then she gently placed his partners' hands upon his back and shoulder repeating the same procedure. Seeing that she had still a dozen tubes of glue remaining, she used the remainder carefully cementing their fronts together.

She thought, 'They want to be together, so now they can be together. Only doing God's work here'!

Her work done, she gathered up all the empty tubes of glue and put them bathroom trash can, then went to Archie's closet and started her main task of removing all of his clothes and carrying them out onto the front lawn and placing them in a pile. Everything went, to the pile including hats, coats, boots, shoes, socks, undergarments, everything.

Eventually after several dozen trips, she had everything in the pile, inclusive of his wallet and his partners garments and her purse. All the time thinking, over and over, 'They want to be together, so they shall"!

Exhausted, she checked her watch as she closed the front door and entered the kitchen to pour herself a glass of cold wine from her refrigerator, pondering the next move as the time closed in on four in the morning. Deciding that it was time to go all in, she went to his den on the first floor and quickly selected all of his truly personal effects, birth certificate, passport and a host of other business documents germane to his ability to continue as before, then gathered them all up and after several trips added then to the pile in the front yard.

Noting the time creeping up to four twenty in the morning and the early morning traffic was about to commence in earnest within the next half hour, she reentered the house and went into the garage and after a bit of searching discovered the grounds keeping crews five gallon gas can, three quarters full and took it back to the front yard and carefully emptied it all around the pile, then took it back to the garage and placed it exactly where she took it from. She went back into the house and removed any signs of her presence, taking her wine glass and cleaning it putting it back in the overhead cupboard.

Finding all in readiness, she went back outside to the front lawn scanned the streets of any signs of activity and finding none lit a cigarette she'd removed from her hiding place inside the house, took two long puffs, taking note, of the front entrance of the Country Club being right across the street, then tossed her cigarette at the gas soaked foot of the pile, a monument to one man's perfidy. Seeing that it was lowly catching fire turned, reentered the house, locking the door. As she left the rear of the house, she engaged the security system, locking the rear door, entered the garage, started her car and backed out of the drive way and off into the still darkened night. Soon, sunrise would beckon the traffic on Cypress Wood Drive and a passing motorist would notify the local county volunteer fire Department, which would no doubt summon the local county law enforcement entities. Then many of the neighbors would wander from their homes in their night clothes, covered by their robes and a crowd would gather in wonder.

If the gods were still with Buffy this day, the outside commotion would wake up the two love birds inside the house and then the fates would have their fun. As she drove off she noticed the lack of head lights anywhere on the street as she made her way back to the all night eatery, this time to have a hearty and enjoyable breakfast. As she drove down the street she called her secretary to alert her to get to the office within the hour and put in action plan 'A', which entailed the removal of fully executes divorce papers that Archie had signed without reading as Buffy had shoved under his nose along with a host of other documents that were time sensitive, since he had a golf outing that he just had to attend.

Along with these documents were a cease and desist order that forbade one Archie Snyder from coming anywhere near his former home, wife, or various listed places of business's. The only thing missing was the name of the Judge giving issuance and the date.

"Oh yes, and call Pokey, find out when he'll return today, should be sometime this morning and then get with me and I'll give him directions as what to do next. When Uncle Leo arrives at the office, fill him in on the QT letting him know that Plan "A" is in effect, he'll then know what to do.

Sorry for this early call, I'll make it up to you"!

Then she had one more call before breakfast. 'Odessa Robillard', formerly of the Houston Post newspaper, now the self-anointed "Queen of the Baghdad on the Bayou Gossip"! Her tag line on her daily column for the Houston Chronicle, her new employer was, "If I don't know about it, it's not worth knowing"! Her sources of information were everywhere, especially amongst the elite of Houston's high society. She always found great humor, when someone of the local social crowd, ratted out secrets of another told in confidence, careful, never to betray a source, by employing the phrase, "A little bird told me…" She and Buffy grew into a fast and lasting friendship over time, whereas Buffy used her as a conduit from time to time to bring low a number of deserving personages. Yet this Creole lady always found her way into the vast majority of societal soiree's, for to deny her entrance would incur her immediate wrath, which was eagerly read by all those who mattered, along with a hoard of those who didn't.

As the phone rang it was picked up by a sleepy Odessa who as a matter of course always answered her personal phone, "Dave's not here"!

As was Buffy's custom, she always yelled into the phone with Odessa, "Odessaaaah"!

Jolted awake Odessa sweetly answered "Mus be that slut Buffy on the other end! You evah get about running off that snake of a husband Archie", she asked in a still groggy voice?

"Ah love you too Cher", said Buffy sweetly! "Funny you should ask for why else would I be so rude and disturb yo precious sleep"? Suddenly wide awake, Odessa asked Buffy to repeat herself, "You telling me that you got the goods on Archie Snyder"?

"Odessa, all's I'm gonna say is how soon can you get a camera man up to my house and Tomball Hospital, for the inside scoop of a ball buster of a story, of course leaving my name out of it"?

"Is it about Archie, Cher"?

"Sure tis Odessa"!

"Hell's fire I'll do it myself"!

"No please send someone else, someone reliable, for I need you for something else, that should make the front page about a week from now, under your byline, babe"!

"What you talkin' about Cher"?

"Do you still have those pictures of Judge Raymond Lodestone, in a Montrose Boulevard Massage Parlor the one's he's never want his wife and children to ever see"?

"You know I do Cher"!

"And you agree that its way time for him to be doing something else, rather than sit in judgment of his fellow man"?

"You know I do, but get to the goddamned point Cher"!

"And if you had bullet proof and unassailable proof, that just recently surfaced last week, of his taking kickbacks from certain lawyers in town for favorable verdicts, directed into his reelection committee, handed to you by midmorning, no questions asked"!

"I'd give a year off my life for that Buff and you know it"!

"That will not be necessary Cher, just get the ball rolling at my house and Tomball Hospital, so it can make tonight's papers and be ready to meet me in Judge Lodestone's chambers late this morning"! "So get off the phone Buff so I can get things rolling"!

"See yaw later Odessa", said Buff ringing off just as she pulled into the restaurants driveway, noticing the sky in the east starting to get brighter.

Now it was time to stoke the furnace, for she was going to have a very busy day ahead of her.

Finishing up her breakfast and looking at her watch, seeing that it was now around five thirty in the morning and the sunrise was making itself known, she paid her bill and went to her car for the trip back to her house.

As she approached he house, she noticed the traffic begin to slow down apparently caused by some commotion up ahead. Drawing nearer to her house she parked her car some fifty yards away from the Volunteer Fire truck that had just finished putting out the fire on her lawn in front of the house. Walking down the street to join the onlookers and neighbors that had gathered, she noticed one of her neighbors standing at the corner and asked, with wide eyes, "Ethyl, what in the world is going on at my house"?

"Oh Buffy good god it's you. We all thought it was you in the house screaming, what with the fire and all on your front lawn"!

"I just returned from an out of town business trip and what's all this about a woman screaming in my house"?

'We all thought it was you inside screaming and the County Constable's office was called and the volunteer firemen just destroyed your front door to gain entrance and the alarm just was disabled minutes ago", said a distraught Ethyl.

The stream of neighbors and onlookers was growing with cars parking on the road and People streaming down the side street where the house was located. Just then Buffy saw Mack the stringer that worked for Odessa, with camera in hand and walked up to him saying, "The houses front door should be the place where all the action is, so you can get the best shots and if ya do a great job, maybe Odessa'll pull some strings to get you on the Chronicles payroll full time"!

"Who's she got up at Tomball Hospital Mac"? "Little Janie"!

"Good, she's a terror. Heads up now I think some people are coming out"! No sooner the words left Buffy's mouth, the hoarse, yet strident sound of female screaming, was heard by the crowd outside and a long minute later the collapsible gurney was seen manned by four struggling firemen who wrestled the gurney down the staircase.

As the gurney was wheeled out down the front walkway to the waiting ambulance in the street, the crowd was greeted by the sight of a blonde woman atop Artie Snyder, both covered by a single white sheet. As the firemen carefully negotiated the front walkway down to the street, the gurney passed two flanking rose bushes, with the sheet snagging upon one of the thorns quickly revealing the unclad bodies of Artie and his part time lover.

Well positioned at the bushes was Mac the stringer, firing away with his camera as the gurney and its revealed contents passed him by, heightened by a loud gasp by the assembled crowd. For some inexplicable reason Artie's male member suddenly became erect as the covering left them exposed, causing his partner to scream even louder, spooking the firemen, who inadvertently hit a bump in the walkway, toppling the gurney and its contents over on the grass, just scant feet away from the awaiting ambulance.

The accident caused yet another gasp of revelation from the crowd as Mac moved around the sprawled co joined bodies lying on the front lawn, with the attendant firemen rushing to their rescue, struggling to lift the squirming mass back on to the gurney. Unsuccessful they were, summoning others to come and join them in their efforts.

As the prostrate Archie lay helpless amidst the melee of people trying to help him, he heard a woman in the crown yell, "Hey, that's not his wife", prompting the assembled crowd to howl with unbridled laughter, causing Archie to shut his eyes momentarily. When he opened them again, he was greeted by the sight of Buffy, standing there expressionless just scant feet away. As his eyes grew large at the sight of her, his expression drew into that of a pleading prisoner, moments away from execution.

As the struggling firemen finally brought the duo back upon the gurney, Buffy drew near and said to Archie, "That's a long ride, for such a short slide pal"!

Knowing that he was in for a world of hurt for his egregious perfidy, Archie had no idea as what he was in for, for in a few short hours he would discover that he had lost everything in the world that mattered, everything, including the very clothes on his back.

As the ambulance drove off, Mac said, "I gotta get back to Odessa down at the Chronicle, she's gonna want to see these pics, soon as I can get them developed"!

Struggling through the crowd of neighbors, all of which peppered her with questions, Buffy announced, "Folks read it in the evening Chronicle to night"! Then catching sight of her housekeeper who had also come back early, driven back by her brother who also handled the weekly landscaping chores, she quickly explained to a partially shocked, but not surprised woman who had been Archie's housekeeper for years and had seen it all.

She addressed her by asking her to call the locksmith and have him change all of the locks in the house, even to the point of recalibrating the automatic garage door openers.

"You are now the mistress of the house, Senora Buffy"?

"That I am Maria, and Archie is never to set foot in this house ever again"!

"You sign my paychecks Senora"?

Buffy nodded her head in affirmation. "Then I be loyal to you from now on, but look what happened to that beautiful front lawn", she said in dismay"!

"Which is why I'm glad your brother is here"!

"Juan, can you make this front lawn beautiful again and remove all the burnt stuff and re-sod the burned area like it was before before five o'clock this evening"!'

"Si Senora, I will get my crew on this muy pronto and all will be made right"! Then he rushed off to get his crew together.

As Maria and Buffy walked into the house the crowd began to fade away back into their own homes, chattering amongst themselves about the early mornings events. Just before they entered the house via the crushed front door, a man rushed up to them and introduced himself as a carpenter, handing Buffy his card saying, "Seems you're gonna need a new front door and I'd like to be the one to handle the work"!

"Can you come close to matching the door that was busted and get the work all done by five o'clock this afternoon? Money is no object and if the door you select is not an exact match it doesn't matter, just so your done by five this afternoon"!

"I'll have the door or one very close to it on your property by ten this morning and installed by late this afternoon"!

"Come by my office tomorrow morning with your bill and I'll pay you in cash. Maria here will give you the address"!

As the newly discovered workman left, Buffy looked at Maria and said, much has happened this morning, with much left for me to do. I'll explain everything tonight when I get back"! At that both women embraced and Buffy made for her car for the long trip into town.

While on her way she called Odessa once again, reporting that her stringer Mac was on his way back to her office with many revealing pictures. Then she called her office and talked to her secretary, who informed her that the files she requested were on her desk awaiting her arrival.

"Judge Lodestone usually arrives at his office by eight AM, so call his office and ask his girl, if he can fit me in to his calendar for ten quick minutes around midmorning. I'm currently en route to the office"!

As Buffy hurriedly entered her office, passing her secretary in a rush, she quickly reviewed the documents regarding her soon to be former husband. First, the pre executed Divorce petition, relinquishing full and free title and ownership of all that he possessed, inclusive of homes, vehicles, business interests, partnerships and bank accounts. That coupled with a fully executed Power of Attorney in all things business and personal, alreadyregistered in the court house several years ago, guaranteed that Archie Snyder was an instant pauper. In addition was the prepared restraining order that required Judge Lodestone's approval, prohibiting Archie Snyder from entering any of his afore mentionedbusiness's or the home on Cypress Wood Drive.

Multiple copies were prepared for all of therelevant parties.

As Buffy completed her review of all the documents, her secretary stuck her head in her office saying, "Judge Lodestone can find fifteen minutes for you Buffy at ten AM"!

"Splendid. Now has Pokey landed yet"!

"Just fifteen minutes ago at Hobby Airport and he should be in the office sometime before Eleven AM, traffic permitting boss"!

"Good, have him stay close for I'll need him to walk the executed Judges orders through the court house and distribute them by hand to the appropriate parties prior to night fall, Oh and get hold of George and have him pick me up in front of our building in forty five minutes, for I'm going to need him for a few hours"!

Then Buffy called Odessa at her office at the paper. "Dave's not here", she answered as a matter of form.

"Odessa, Buffy here"!

"Chile', whatever did you get into"?

"The pictures get developed yet, Odessa"? "Yeah", she slowly drawled, "And some of them will never make it past the editor. Girlfriend. What on earth have you done? It's marvelous. Super Glued Archie Snyder, the world's greatest cocksman, to another woman, buck nekkid, 'Flagrante' Dilecto' with a hundred or more witnesses, how did ya ever do it"!

"If all goes well the next two hours, we'll have dinner together tonight and I'll fill you in on all the details Cher. How are things going at Tomball Hospital"?

"Oh just the standard stuff, with more salacious pictures and could you believe it those ambulance folks dropped them from the gurney again, this time breaking Archie's girlfriends arm in several places, but it even gets worse. Just before you called, we discovered the only thing that'll dissolve super glue, is the chemical 'Acetone'. Well the hospital searched their pharmacy only to discover they're plumb out of the stuff.

So now they got people running to all the pharmacy's to get some Acetone. Seems like Archie's new girlfriend has lost her voice and has been placed under sedation, while the doc's in Tomball try and tend to her broken arm, but it's tough going since she's still tethered to Archie"!

"You have the pics of Judge Lodestone getting his oil changed at the Oriental MassageParlor in Montrose Odessa"?

"Copies and originals in two separate folders, in living color Cher. Now do you have your files, with names or the crooked lawyers that bought verdicts from the honorable Judge"?

"Copies and originals Odessa in two separate folders. Can you be in front of your building in about forty five minutes so George and I can pick you up in the Limo"?

"Just call me when you're leaving and I'll be there, but I just gotta say, I been just about every where there is to be on God's green earth. Been from Maine to Spain, ever seen goats fuck in the market place in Marrakech, but Cher, I ain't never and I'm talkin', never seen no shit like this"!

The line went dead as Buffy could tell by the very tone of Odessa's voice that she was having a grand time of it all. Just as she hung up the phone, Uncle Leo stuck his head inside her office door saying, "Hear you've appropriated George and the Limo along with a certain file and are paying a visit to that wonderful Judge Lodestone"!

"He's approaching checkmate, Uncle Leo along with that wonderful Archie, but don't worry, the firms tush is protected. I'll fill you in when I get back"! With that Buffy scooped up the files and documents loading them all into a large legal brief case and gave a brief kiss on the cheek, to her Uncle as she ran past him to catch the elevator stopping briefly at her secretary's desk to move all of her appointments till tomorrow. As Odessa and Buffy waited in the Judges Ante room, his secretary opened the door to the Judge's chambers and said, "Judge Lodestone will be happy to see you now"! Buffy and Odessa entered the Judge's chambers and were greeted by old and grizzled looking Raymond Lodestone who greeted them, "Buffy, it's wonderful to see you and whom have you brought with you this fine morning"?

Judge, may I introduce you to Odessa Robillard, of the Houston Chronicle"!

"Somehow that name rings a bell, but I currently can't place the name, have we ever met before"? "No sir Judge, I can't say that I've ever had the pleasure"!

"Well then, Buffy how can I help you"?

As she went to her briefcase she pulled the various documents out and placed them before the judge saying, "Your honor, time is of the essence and I'm calling in a favor if you'll recall. I require your approval on these documents, right now and I'll see to it that all of the distribution to the concerned parties is taken care of saving this court the time and the money knowing that you've a very busy schedule", she said sweetly!

"Well my dear I'll at least have to peruse these documents prior to my approval", replied Lodestone. "Judge, all of the documents are fully executed and witnessed according to state law and just require your signature and date"! "Still I never approve something that I've not at least perused, even as a favor to you, my dear"!

"And that is your final word Judge", asked Buffy still the model of judicial decorum?

"It is and if you'll leave these with me I'll review them this evening", said Lodestone testily! Buffy then nodded to Odessa, who rose up and approached the judge reaching into her folder and producing the copies of the pictures, taken while in the throes of ecstasy at a Montrose Massage parlor saying, "Then perhaps you can review these Judge, whereas it's in the best interests of your social reputation"!

As the Judge reviewed the embarrassing pictures of his perfidy, his normally florid face grew flushed and he wheezed, "This is blackmail"!

"Call it what you will Judge", said Odessa calmly, but if word of this ever got out, you'd be in a world of judicial hurt, quite apart of what your lovin' wife might say"!

"You'd publish these at the Chronicle"? "In a heartbeat Judge"!

"Now I remember you. Didn't you have a gossip column at the old Houston Post paper"?

"Yup, that's me and I bring down the mighty when they deserve it"! Lodestone stammered flustered, "I won't do it; I simply won't give into blackmail"!

"Well Judge, if ya won't save your reputation, then maybe you'll save yourself some jail time, up in Huntsville Prison. Buffy, it's your turn", said Odessa!

Reaching once again into her voluminous legal briefcase and brought forth the large file, with copies of all of the Judges various monetary relationships with various criminal attorney's that came in front of him going back over a dozen years and laid them before the judge saying, "I suggest you take a deep breath Judge and summon your common sense"!

As Raymond Lodestone quickly reviewed what lay before him, his very life passed before his eyes. Here before him was chapter and verse, were a series of financial transactions clearly linked to his favorable decisions from the bench, in behalf of lawyers representing their clients.

After several minutes, Buffy then said "Tick, tock, Judge, Time is of the essence and if you don't respect our time, then respect yours along with your reputation and your career. There's a man I know up in Huntsville, a former client of mine, unjustly convicted for a crime he didn't commit, who once related to me on his very first moment in his cell, what he saw etched on the cell wall. It read as follows; "Nothing can be worth all of this"!Now if you don't care about yourself of your career, or your reputation, think about how you will spend the twilight of your remaining years Judge"!

Lodestone then looked up at both of them, his mind racing to find a way out of the fix he'd made for himself and finding none made the feeble comment, "I'm executing these documents under severe moral duress, I hope you know"!

"Judge believe us when we say, we feel your pain, now sign the fucking documents just as Buffy wants", said Odessa with that Creole edge to her voice that was just the thing to strike mortal fear into the jurist.

For the next ten minutes Buffy guided Raymond Lodestone's hand onto each of her documents and the copies, before they were completed. By this time the Judges face was florid and he'd loosened his tie before saying, "When do I get the originals and all of the copies of what you've presented"?

"Well Judge, it'll be sometime tomorrow, late in the day by special messenger after the relevant documents are registered in the court house and disseminated to all concerned parties", said Buffy in reply sweetly.

"What guarantees do I have that you'll do exactly what you say"? "Why none Judge. Just my word as an officer of the court. We'll leave all the copies of your malfeasance in office for you to mull over, for the next day or so. Once we complete the courts directive, then you will receive all of the originals by special courier and our business will be done. Won't it Judge"?

Hanging his head in defeat, Raymond Lodestone, nodded his head and weakly mumbled, "Yes it will"!

"Then we are concluded. Have a wonderful day Judge", said Buffy as she and Odessa walked swiftly out of his office. As they walked out of the court house to the waiting Limousine, Buffy commented testily, to no one in particular, "Nobody fucks with Buffy and survives"!

"Amen to that Cher, added Odessa!

Dropping Odessa off at the newspaper before heading back to the office, Odessa said, "Gonna have to hustle to make the evening edition, but I'll drift on by your house later this evening, so you can fill me in on all the details, but don't worry I'll heavily edit the piece and keep you in a very low profile. The good stuff will come later when I write a book about the downfall of the mighty, but I just gotta say, that all through the time in the judge's chambers, I truly was afraid the old coot was gonna croak from apoplexy before he got finished"! "The thought entered my mind also Odessa, but now that it's done, if some day next week the old fart has a seizure, the world just might be a better place"!

As the limo came to a stop in front of the Chronicles building, Buffy added with a sly wink, "But we both still have copies that just might mysteriously surface in the very near future, don't we"? As the elevator opened on her floor, Buffy caught sight of the newly arrived Polk, saying "Walk with me please", as they made their way to her office. Opening up her briefcase, she collated all of the fully executed court documents in front of Polk, asking, "Darlin', can you spend the afternoon running around town delivering these executed court orders, but walk them thru the court house first and get them registered. The Limo and George are downstairs and are at your complete disposal. Then around eight this evening will you join me at my house for dinner? There will be friends in attendance. But picking up two of the copies, she said, "I'll save you a long trip out to Tomball and deliver these personally"!

"Worked my way through, law school as a process server Buffy, I know the drill and I'll see you tonight"!

As Polk left her office with an armload of papers, Buffy looked at her watch and saw that it was now eleven AM, and all the wheels were turning at speed. By the close of the business day Archie Snyder was kaput. But she did let him keep his precious cigarette boat. How he was going to obtain a copy of his title was going to prove a problem, but that was not Buffy's concern. He'd have to sort that out on his own.

After a round of returning her calls, she decided to pay a rare visit to the executive dining room. As she entered she approached her uncle's table as he was seated with Boyd Parmalee and asked, "Gentlemen, may I join you"?

"But of course Buffy", said Boyd as he rose to pull out her chair.

"Seems you've been busy putting in effect plan 'A', this morning", mused Boyd slyly with a wink. "How did the Judge Lodestone take it"?

"As expected", Buffy replied. "But with a tad bit of moral suasion,

Odessa and I persuaded the good Judge to do as he was told. Polk is now running around town with George making the appropriate deliveries", she said as her salad arrived.

"In about an hour I'll go home and see to the repairs to the house, caused by the firemen, early this morning, then pay a visit to Tomball Hospital and deliver Archie's papers in person"!

"I hear that someone glued Archie together with his 'Ad Hoc' paramour in the wee hours of the morning and they're both in the hospital awaiting some sort of separation surgery", said Leo, between chews. "Know anything about that young lady", he continued?

"Seems that Tomball Hospital, was completely out of Acetone", replied Buffy saying nothing more, trying unsuccessfully to hide a weak grin on her face, turning her attention to her salad.

"Both Boyd and Leo gave a brief glance at each other, with a brief smile of pride on their face, with Boyd adding ruefully, "Well whoever concocted this has the blood of the Machiavellians running through their veins, for it was artfully executed"!

No mention of the corporate merger occurred since they already knew it was cast in stone, but Buffy added, "Seeing since tomorrow is Friday, I'm going to take a sick day off and be back at my desk Monday, my schedule has been rearranged"!

"Of course Buffy, you've earned it", replied Leo! As she pulled into the driveway of her home, she looked at her watch and it indicated just short of two PM. She said to Maria, can you throw together one of your wonderful Mexican Buffets this evening for about a half dozen friends, say, oh for about eight o'clock? And I'd like you to join us also"!

"De nada Senora", replied Maria smiling! "Muy Gracias domina"! She then sought out the carpenter who was putting working on installation of the massive front door, who said,"A little frame damage was done by the firemen early this morning, but we're on the downside of getting that fixed and your door over there will be installed in about an hour, for the locksmith to do his work"! Buffy walked over to examine her new door and while it wasn't an exact match, was close enough to fit in the ambience of her neighborhood, giving the craftsman her card and saying, "I'll be here for another hour, so before I leave get with me so I can write you a check"!

She then went over to the landscapers who had neatly cleared all of the burn debris from the front lawn and were busy positioning the new sod skillfully, so it would be difficult to tell how it looked just hours before. "In about a month Senora, the new grass will mix with the old and all will look exactly the same"!

"Muy Gracias", replied Buffy smiling. Finally she went to the garage where the locksmith was finishing up working on the garage door openers. "Had to install a new door opening system, because the old one, the company went out of business and it was easily defeated by burglars. The new system will work much better. Be done here in about an hour and then the only door I'll be waiting on is the front door"!

"Leave your invoice with Maria when you leave and I'll write you a check first thing in the morning. And thanks for your quick response"!

As she slowly made her way upstairs to the scene of the crime earlier in the day, she entered her bedroom and surveyed everything. What was once the supreme inner sanctum and the altar of prurient and puellent bliss, now seemed to be cursed forever. Tomorrow, she and Maria would go shopping for a new bed and the old bed would fall into the hands of others, with scant memories to haunt their souls.

Adding up in her head the day's activities, had cost her in excess of six thousand dollars, but on balance, she had gained so much more. Now all she had to figure out was what she was going to do with a slew of upscale "Titty Bars"? Time enough to sort that kind of thing out later, but at the very least she'd gained additional closet space.

As she pulled into the visitor parking space at the Tomball Hospital, she noticed that apparently word had somehow gotten out about two lovers, being glued together, in an embarrassing fashion, witnessed by the slew of local Radio and TV reporters and their attendant remote telecast vehicles on premises. Asking about the condition of Archie Snyder from the main receptionist, well within earshot of one of the reporters, she was told that he was still in surgery but should be out within the hour.

Passing the time working a crossword puzzle from a leftover newspaper, she casually eyed the gaggle of reporters gathering about for the story, some of whom were keeping a wary eye on Buffy, still attired in her traveling business suit, now a bit rumpled, sitting there, working her crossword puzzle, with a legal briefcase on the floor next to her feet.

After about an hour one of the hospitals spokesmen emerged to confront the media about the two lovers saying they had just emerged from surgery and continuing on, which allowed Buffy to elude the gaggle of reporters and wander about the hospital and make theappropriate inquiries, at to Archie's location.

As she stealthily walked into his room, the ward nurse being unaware of her intrusion, Buffy closed the door, seeing that Archie was under heavy medication. As his eyes opened to the sound of Buffy's approach to his bed, she said, "How ya doin' sport"?

Archie drowsy from his medication said, "Buffy, I don't know what to say except I'm so sorry. I just don't know what came over me. Please forgive me"!

Stow it sport, way too late for all that"! Reaching into her briefcase she produced a legal sheaf of documents saying, "As of late this morning I am divorced from one Archie Snyder"! Then she reached back into her briefcase and removed yet another sheaf of documents saying, "As of about the very same time, this is a fully executed Court Order, ordering you to stay away for your former abode on Cypress Wood Drive, any bank that you have accounts with and any of the business's you own, or partnerships you've an interest in, because as of around noon this day they no longer are yours sport! All signed sealed and delivered"!

"But Buffy", Archie weakly started to plead. "Hush now Cher", she drawled. "You signed away ownership a few years back if you'll recall of your own free will, not being under duress of any kind. In fact if you'll recall, I and several others strongly advised you against such an action, in your zeal to be lawsuit proof, but you wouldn't listen. So it was done your way. All you had to do was to keep your schwanz in your pants and none of this would be happening. So piss and moan if ya wanna, but before you do look in a mirror"!

Buffy then closed her now empty briefcase with a snap and walked out of his room. As she made her way past the reporters in the front of the hospital, she announced, "Mr. Snyder is now in room 210 and is ready to answer any questions you may have"! As she got into her BMW she turned around and saw that the reporters had all disappeared from the front of the hospital.

Later that evening as her company was digesting their sumptuous meal and had received Buffy's tale of woe, a chapter and verse recitation of her early morning discovery and the events that followed, the local station was announcing the ten PM newscast. The lead in story was of a delirious man, clad only in a hospital gown, running through traffic on the Tomball Parkway and having been run over by a tractor trailer truck and killed. As of this reporting, his identity is unknown, but the staff at the local hospital has been notified. Everyone looked at each other, wide eyed with surprise, with Maria making the sign of the cross, for she knew immediately. Odessa also connected the dots, saying during the commercial, "One less problem to confront, eh Buffy? But at least he had the decency to wait until after my story in the evening papers came to press"!

Thirty days later a front page story emerged in the Houston Newspaper with the byline by Odessa Robillard, announcing a Harris County Grand Jury being convened regarding the criminal purchase of one Judge Raymond Lodestone, by well over a dozen prominent local criminal attorneys in Harris County, going back well over a dozen years, complete with names, dates, case numbers and bank account data.

The following day, the very same paper reported the death of the wife of Judge Raymond Lodestone, having suffered a massive coronary after receiving the news of her husband's Grand Jury Indictment.

Days later, the Six PM newscasts announced the suicide death by gunshot of Judge Raymond Lodestone. The following morning, the sun made its usual appearance and the world still turned on its axis.

36

I t had taken Buffy some eight months of working through her busy court calendar, before she could make time in her schedule, to make the ninety minute drive, up I-45 from Houston to Huntsville prison. Rare as it was her appearance there, she was always greeted with open arms by the guard staff, for after all she was a lawyer of some accomplishment, along with being a very charming eye full.

As she sat down in front of Jaeger, he covered his mouth in an off handed fashion and silently mouthed, 'Big brother is watching and listening', before indicating with his eyes, where the small cameras were mounted.

"So how ya doin' sport", Buffy asked cheerfully?

"Thanks for the care package, but please look over the list of what's permitted and what's not permitted for us cons to receive, for all they'll do is confiscate the items, marking them contraband"!

"Are the books you requested getting through to you", she asked as Jaeger covered his mouth once again, mouthing 'Directional Mikes', then answered, "The books you sent are fine and I received them all and thanks"!

"So how close are you to getting your Master's Degree from Sam Houston State University"?

"Just received a note from the head of their program, saying they've accepted my Master's Thesis and that I'll be receiving my Degree in the mail in due course. Of course I'll not be permitted to attend any of the graduation ceremonies, but none the less, the profs say their collectively proud of me and that I'm the very first one to be awarded a Masters certification under this state sponsored program"!

"Well, I suppose congratulations are in order, too bad prison regulations won't permit any hugs, but let's see here, an undergrad degree in, ah, what is it Business Administration and a graduate degree, in Classical Management Theory? Well done"!

"Fat lot of good it's gonna do me Buffy since I can't even hang it on the wall of my cell or ever have a chance to put it to use. Just a way to pass the time productively"!

"So where do they let you keep the books I send you sport"?

"The warden was nice enough to allow me to keep them in the prison clinic where I work every day. A special privilege he calls it"!

"I heard that yet another assassination attempt occurred last month. So how are you"?

"Four newly arrived Mexican nationals jumped me when we were in the showers, all armed with homemade prison shanks. If it wasn't for my pals Seltzer and Duke Vultee and some 'Schvoogies', from the Crips I didn't even know, they might've gotten the job done. As it was, one of em took a slice outta my side", as Jaeger lifted his prison shirt to show Buffy the four inch long bright red scar, that matched yet another scar experienced years ago by others, shortly after his arrival, "I call them my racing stripes", he grinned!

"So what's the administration going to do about these four killers"? "Slight correction Buffy, three of them now, for one of the guards had to put a choke hold on one of them, after he sliced one of his pals up who interceded and the guy didn't make it. But in answer to your question, the surviving assassins are in the "segregation unit", awaiting the in house adjudication which should start tomorrow sometime, for attempted murder. Their probably going to get a life sentence, is my guess, spend some time in segregation, then if they're good eventually be released back into the general population"!

"Which means you'll eventually probably have to deal with them again", mused Buffy!

"More than likely that's how it'll come down, Buffy"!

"Let's see, that's four attempts on your life in the last eight years", asked Buffy?

"Five", Jaeger corrected!

"Any additional information as to who's behind this"?

"Other than those you already have, No! The Mexicans know how to keep their traps shut tight"!

Just then one of the guards approached, leaned over and said,

"Two minutes left Miss Buffy", as she nodded her head towards him. She then leaned towards Jaeger, shielding her mouth and whispered, 'Sotto Voce', "Keep the faith Jaeger, some things are starting to finally come together, admittedly far too slowly, but they are and it'll take some time, but there'll be a good out come on the horizon, I haven't ever forgotten about you"!

As they both rose for Buffy to leave, Jaeger said, "Thanks Buffy, I'm appreciative of all you can do"! Driving back to Houston she examined her feelings toward Jaeger, Seeing the various scars he'd acquired, revealed that he was in excellent shape in spite of his incarceration. He'd accomplished much during his time there educationally and his spirits seemed to be far better than one would warrant given what happened to him. Yet somehow she sensed that far more was churning deep inside the man, tightly controlled, waiting patiently for the unseen opportunity to burst forth. Somehow she just had to provide that opportunity.

Then there was the fact that he was a ruggedly attractive man, replete with an array of skills and the good sense to know when to apply them and when to hold them at bay. She concluded that it must've been his former military training, or his genetic makeup or both.

Regardless, this man must be made free, for she feared that his patience and his resolve would eventually erode caused by the cavalcade of circumstance and the passage of time and the world at large would be worse off.

Arriving back at the office, the first thing she did was place a call into Quantico to Colonel Bollinger.

"General Bollinger's office", came the over the speaker phone, with Buffy asking to speak to the General.

"The General is out on an inspection tour, but he'll be back in the morning. Can you leave a message", said the secretarial voice on the other end.

"Buffy left the message with the secretary leaving all of her phone numbers saying, "And please tell the General this is concerning a certain Sergeant Jaeger who served under him. He'll know what that means"!

The following morning Buffy received the return call from Bollinger. After the niceties, she got down to brass tacks, reporting of her recent visit to the Ellis Unit, to visit Jaeger and inform him of his academic achievements, his general demeanor and of the numerous assassination attempts on his person.

"He's been in that place going on nine years General and recent developments have surfaced that start to connect the dots as to reasons germane to his unjust conviction. I'm talking about a conspiracy at the highest levels of State government. Now I have some access to some very capable local people and am in a financial position to fund an in depth exploratory investigation, to gain evidence as to his innocence and I'm in need of some additional competent manpower. Can you be of any help"?

"So you want the assistance of some very capable people with certain expertise, who just happen to be between things at the moment, to join up with some of your locals, to gain information, is that about right Miss Beauvior"?

"Hit the nail right on the head General"!

"Since you're a lawyer I have to ask you, are you particular as to how this information is gleaned"?

"General, if you're asking if the data collected will ever see the light of day in a court of law, the answer is, highly unlikely"!

"I assume that you might want them to be former members of the Corps"?

"Couldn't hurt General"!

"And you'll pick up the tab for their time and expenses"?

"Completely General"!

"How many operatives will you require"?

"Roughly speaking about a half dozen, give or take General, but I must emphasize, they must be competent"!

"Give me a day to make some inquiries and I'll call you back with contact information with certain selected people I've in mind and you can do the rest if that meets with your approval"!

"That'll be just fine General", said Buffy!

"I might even find some time to visit the Marine Reserve facilities in your neck of the woods before too long, if you don't mind"!

"Should you do so, let me know upon you your arrival and I'll see to it personally that your sheltering needs will be met"!

"Call you tomorrow Buffy"!

As she hung up, she went to her personal files and pulled out the accounting files of Archie's, three Gentlemen's Clubs and looked at the account balances, which were brimming with money. 'Good thing I never sold those clubs yet, for they were all indeed cash cows', she thought. 'That should be more than enough to pay not only for Uncle Leo's PI's, but the additional manpower they would have at the ready'.

"Looking at her pending court schedule for the coming week, she saw that she would have the time to invest in the coming events. Then she removed the old file of notes of information gleaned by Uncle Leo's investigators regarding Jaegers trial long ago and their personal assessments.

Anticipating the newly arrived manpower's needs she made a list of what their needs might be; A comfortable place to stay locally, individual transportation, advance money, ongoing expenses, any armament requirements, money to pay for existing living conditions, et al. After some minutes she completed her list, for she wanted nothing to concern her new arrivals, but the ability to focus at the task at hand, along with her locals.

Over time she'd used these former local retired law enforcement officers, now applying their experience as private investigators. They knew the lay of the land, local and state ordinances and laws, had contacts with other competent affiliates in other localities and most important, weren't squeamish about when to turn the screws and when not to. They always found the weak spots, one way or the other and when they furnished information, it was always reliable.

The following day General Bollinger called her back and the faxed contact information as to the selected operatives to her office.

"I've already talked to each of them briefly giving them a rough outline of what is involved, leaving the details to you Buffy"!

"Thank you General, I'll take it from here and remember if you're headed this way let me know your ETA and I'll see to it that your picked up and appropriately sheltered"!

"Will do Buffy"!

After she hung up, she fell to the task of calling each of the names on the list supplied by the General. Explaining to them what was involved and filling out some of the details the General left to her. As she talked to each, any questions of their competence faded quickly as she learned of the unique talents each individual was able to bring to the table and as a group she concluded the General had selected well, each having served under the General in various capacities in the very recent past. It appeared these operatives were professional and would work well with her locals.

She made arrangements for each of them personally to fly to Houston, had them picked up and housed them at two furnished rental homes in Houston's Northwest side, as they trickled in over the next three days. Then assembled them at her home for dinner with three of her local detectives and over dinner went into complete detail as to what was needed, with the help of Uncle Leo's detectives that took part in the initial investigation prior to the trial.

"Gentlemen, this might last thirty days or it might last ninety days or more, I don't know? But one thing is certain, you will all leave here well paid. I asked each of you to bring along contact information as to your landlords or mortgage company, utilities and so on, so your monthly obligations can be met by me in a timely fashion. Before you leave, give it to me so it can be handled. Any additional equipment or armament required will be immediately paid for by me, so look to your local partner for direction. Finally gentlemen, this is a full court press, for a fellow Marine, that's been victim of an egregious plot, which I've given you all the details of and I've been led to believe the Marines take care of their own", as she then poured each of them another shot of expensive whiskey and held her almost brimming glass up asking "Semper Fi fellas"?

At that each of them, including the locals who just happened to be former 'Mud Marines' themselves all rose in unison saying, "Semper Fi" and tossed the whiskey back as did Buffy stifling a brief cough.

One of them then said, "Maam, we like your style. Don't worry, we'll get it done"!

An hour later she cut them all loose, confident that before too long, that which was buried long ago would surface and provide that which would free her from the memory of failure.

The following day was spent by the men outfitting each of them, with whatever was required, armament, transportation, electronics, body armor, and the all important component, cold, hard, train riding cash.

She had let loose the dogs of war, to operate with stealth and a sense of 'delicatesse', to find the secrets that lay hidden. Her targets, the new Governor of the State of Texas and former Texas Ranger, Royce Baintree, the longtime Sheriff and now additionally Head of the Texas Pardons and Parole Commission, Morgan Little and Ft. Worth Real Estate Developer, Donald Ryder, for starters. By the end of the first month of operation, not much was seemingly resulting, except for the escalating costs of the operation, easily paid for, as a stream of temporary technical help was hired to perform a task, then paid in cash and cut loose. But at the end of the first month, all parties were under round the clock surveillance and all known forms of telephonic communications were under a non-judicial wiretap.

The team leaders and their charges proved to be real pros, whereas none of those who were surveilled had the slightest clue they were being watched and recorded. Every week each team leader made a report to Buffy and sent any pertinent documents to her by fax. Over the course of time, evidence gradually began to build, revealing that indeed a conspiracy to incarcerate the last direct survivor of the Jaeger family and appropriate by illegal means the land of his family began to grow. Had many of these things come to light years ago, Jaeger would've never seen a day of prison and his family's estate would be intact.

One by one the dots started to connect, with Buffy slowly assembling the jigsaw puzzle of information, every night at home well past midnight. Her agents in the field exceeded her every expectation and they wanted for nothing.

During the weekdays she tended to her court activities, ripping off a rapid fire string of victories in behalf of her grateful clients, revealing technical flaws in the prosecutions various cases in some cases, causing them to be dismissed and in others turning certain defeat into victory, by a series of impassioned arguments worthy of celestial praise by none other than the mythical 'Merlin', obfuscating the facts at hand, thus creating a cloud of doubt in the minds of the merely mortal jurors, many of which were secretly eager to get back to their everyday lives.

As the third month of the operation drew to a close, she was completing her report to the various media outlets statewide, as yet to be revealed, thus having connected all the dots in the jigsaw puzzle as she saw it concerning her former and continuing client Jaeger. On the surface she thought as she typed, a single word echoed through her mind and that word was "Checkmate"! From time to time she brought her secretary to the house to help her prepare and assemble all of the information that started to flow into Buffy, but she had her own familial needs to attend to, so on this Friday night, Buffy worked alone crafting what she thought were the finishing touches of her statewide Apocalypse, certain to bring all of the guilty into the light of day for public scrutiny.

When that was concluded, she would work on the Pardon papers for Jaeger, but as she turned her computer off, she heard the television set in the other room announce the Ten PM nightly local newscast. Mostly pleased with how things were going, she and others had assembled a body of irrefutable evidence that proved a conspiracy to defraud, judicial misconduct by a sitting trial judge, perjured testimony by governmental officials, but most important politically, her relentless efforts had revealed, the unseemly underside of the lives of the wealthy and privileged governmental officials at the most senior positions of state government, starting with Royce Braintree, the Governor of the Great State of Texas. Yet something seemed to be missing. What it was she didn't know? Trained in the efficacies of logic, facts that were irrefutable, she came to believe fervently that logic never lied. In fact it can't lie, for facts are facts, provable in every way, like the sun rising in the east each morning. It does so and has done thus, since before the dawn of man, due to the certain balance of the celestial forces with unbridled regularity. One can depend on the sun rising in the east every morning as a provable fact.

Yet facts, germane to the dynamics of mankind, are unable to reveal the entire truth of a matter or event, given the fluidity of those very same dynamics and that is where onesfeelings, or intuition comes into play, be it a the stored sum of one's life experiences, or a genetic anomaly, that worked its way up the ladder from generation to generation, never getting blunted by education or civilized society, Buffy viewed it as the icing on the cake and any cake worth its substance is incomplete without an accurate peek at seemingly random inference.

Something was indeed missing from this puzzle, one last ingredient, but what? She asked that of herself repeatedly as the local news droned on at a low tone, from the TV set. Just then the phone rang and on the second ring, Buffy picked up the receiver and said "Pronto"!

"Buff, that you? It's Randall and are you sitting down"!

"She could tell it was Randall White, one of her local team leaders and former HPD detective, by the quality of his mobile phone unit.

"While I'm sitting down Randall please dial the volume down a touch on that Stevie Ray Vaughn music on your radio, ok"?

"Sorry Buffy, but I think we just struck gold. Do you recall the Judge that signed the original search warrant that Royce Baintree used when he was a Ranger and the boys used it to bust into Jaegers campus dorm room"?

"Remember it well Randall, only too well. Looked at that thing and found it flawless. Signed by Judge Myron Brown if I do recall one of the local Austin Judges at that time"!

"Well Buffy, that warrant always bothered me for the longest time and why? Because, it was too neatly done. Served a slew of them myself in the course of time and when done after hours and in a rush, there are inevitably corrected errors that can be found on most all search warrants, rushed signatures etcetera, but this warrant was pristine, as if it were done during normal working hours, which was not the case at that time"! "And the point is Randall"? "I'm getting' there Buffy. The point is the search warrant on your man Jaeger at that time didn't exist"! "What", Buffy exclaimed.

Repeat that real slow"!

"When Royce Baintree and his campus police along with Sheriff Morgan Little, burst into the room of the 'Uberballer' and got into that scrape and arrested him, they had no, let me repeat, no warrant in hand at that time. Nothing at all signed by a local magistrate. It wasn't till just before noon the following day, after Jaeger had spent the night in lockup and sweated by the locals, without benefit of counsel, which was another perjured testimony you already know about. Anyway, they put the cart before the horse and went to a friendly Judge the following morning, who granted them the warrant, after the fact to cover their asses and back dated the warrant date and time wise"! "Randall, I'm cleaning out my ears for there must be a wax buildup. No judge in his right mind would", then her voice trailed off to silence. "Now I'm sure you have proof"!" I certainly do. For I've just left the hospital room of Judge Brown, where he's in the final days of a struggle with colon cancer and he's pushing eighty years of age.

We ran him down on a sheer hunch and he volunteered, on the pain of eternal damnation I suppose to get this all off his chest. We have it all tape recorded and transcribed by a local court reporter I know that owed me a favor and witnessed by the attending nurse.

The judge implicates Royce Baintree, then a Ranger and arresting officer and Sheriff Morgan Little, as the two peace officers who approached him on the morning following the arrest, in his chambers. Of course the promise of ten thousand dollars occurred and was delivered a few days later personally by Sheriff Little. It's all on audio tape and in writing signed sealed and soon to be delivered, by me to you"!

"Somebody pinch me" said Buffy blandly!

"I knew you'd be pleased, young lady", said Randall"!

"That's the final link in the chain Randall, tell everyone to wrap things up and head this way as soon as reasonably possible and to drive safely.

When can you place this in my hands Randall"?

"Well, I can be at your place in about three and a half hours, but it's starting to rain"!

"No Randall, go back to your motel and get a good night's sleep.

Tomorrows Friday and I have to wrap some things up in court here, so use it as a travel day, so let's all meet up at my place tomorrow evening and I'll have Maria work on a wonderful Mexican Buffet for us all. Tell the mud Marines, I'll have airline flights first class booked for the weekend back to their homes and Randall take care of yourself for your carrying the Holy Grail"!

"I'll call your office when I get in tomorrow Buffy"!

After she hung up the phone she went to the liquor cabinet and made herself a double vodka and tonic and sat in front of the television set thinking. In her thoughts she included the almighty for handing to her, this mighty sword. Or course she'd review what Randall gave her and if it was well documented, something he always did unfailingly, it would be the final nail in the coffin for some very bad and sleazy fellows.

Of course nothing in this world could right the wrongs committed and she was conflicted as to whether or not trust the court system or not. All her legal training directed her as to litigation as the way to a complete and total Pardon, yet that would take time, perhaps several years and time neither she nor especially Jaeger had to spare. As she mulled around the problem, helped by the smooth bite of imported Russian vodka, she concluded that speed was her and Jaegers ally and that the fun was truly about to begin.

Jaeger would have his parole within in about a month. Of course she would help him get settled when he was free and give him a running start on life again as best she could, but she sure wouldn't want to be in the shoes of those who were responsible for the murder of his family or his imprisonment. Were she Jaeger, the end of their lives would only be a matter of time and she sensed that it would be anything but pleasant.

She'd already paid into the accounts of each of her operatives a sum of five thousand dollars a month for the three months they were in her employ and in the subsequent months ahead she paid into each of their accounts a similar monthly amount until the agreed amount of fifty thousand dollars was met. All of the money came from the three accounts of the three clubs she had a majority interest in. Each of the clubs managers remained silent for in the very near future, they were guaranteed to gradually take ownership of the clubs at favorable terms to their liking. Of course any and all technical equipment acquired by them in the course of their activities was considered theirs to keep. Everybody was happy, everybody was content and everybody left the message that should Buffy ever again require there services, all she had to do was whistle. Just put her lips together and blow.

37

"**S**o tell me Dr. Meister, how did all the tests I took the other day, come out", asked Seltzer anxiously"?

Jaeger kept his head down saying as he ate his evening meal, "I can't tell you much Roy, because that's the responsibility of Dr. Fowler and Nurse Moran, all I am is the hired help. But what I can tell you in confidence, is that starting tomorrow, you'll be on a selective dietary plan for the duration and that each day you'll be escorted by one of the guards to the prison clinic, for receipt of medication for your intestinal pain right before the start of your shift and immediately after and you'll be placed on a physically non taxing task for the duration of your stay"!

"Well mate, I suppose that's somewhat good news, but I've been round you long enough, to know when you're holdin' back the bad news, which is, is this thing I got a serious matter or not"?

Jaeger put down his utensils and said, "Roy, it's serious"!

"Well, thanks for the heads up. I'll just have at wait till I hear the official word tomorrow", Seltzer replied in a matter of fact manner that fit his stoic nature precisely.

"Changing the subject mate, congratulations are in order for our mate Rae here, for the news from the parole board is that he'll be released sometimes in the next ten days, so he can go back to Houston and hob nob with his eclectic pals on Montrose Boulevard"!

"Congratulations Rae", said Jaeger, "Any restrictions on your parole, other than not to associate with criminals and felons"?

"Other than the obvious one, not to engage in my former profession of printing counterfeit currency, or the crafting of the plates, I cannot have anything 'directly' concerning with the business of printing, during the term of my parole"!

"Sorta leaves ya high and on the outside mate don't ya think", asked Seltzer?

"Well that might be the case for some, but my old girlfriend is gonna take me back and put me up in an old rent house a block away, then run off her current delivery service, get an assumed name certificate, from the county and put me in as the owner of a delivery service and just between us, I'll give y'all just one guess who my prime customer will be", Rae offered with a big wink"!

"Neatly done, neatly done", repeated Seltzer, with a grin and additional nod from Jaeger.

"Of course, my terms of parole will only last for three years, so after that I can get back to printing and hire a driver to deliver the printing. In addition to her other customers, she does all the printing for several of the area small newspapers, so she's kept very busy most of the time"!

Just then Duke Vultee, showed up running late for his evening supper, "Sorry I'm late fella's did I miss anything"?

"Yeah Duke, we got good news and bad, so which do ya want first mate"?

"Gimme the good news Roy, said Vultee diving into his tray hungrily.

"First the bad news. Our mate and friend Rae will be leaving us, in short order, due his approval of his parole, by the quacks, in Austin"!

"Aw shit Rae", said Vultee, "Who'll be around to give us all grief each day"?

"Now the good news! I'm gonna die", said Seltzer with a grin.

"We're all gonna die Roy, eventually", Vultee replied with a wry look back.

"No Duke, apparently the tests he took last week at the clinic came back and apparently he's got some real bad 'Juju' in his stomach and the prison Doc is putting him on light duty, a special diet and daily medication"!

"Aw fuck", exclaimed Vultee in visible disgust, "Just when I was startin' to like you"!

"Doan worry mate, I'll still be round for a little while and while Rae here is enjoyin' the good life in the big city, I'll make it a point to take up where he left off", said Seltzer with a grin!

When they got back to their cell, Jaeger said to Roy, "Ya know as long as we've shared this cell together, you know just about everything about me, while I know almost nothing about you, other than you're here for twelve years for illegal weapons smuggling. Isn't it about time you opened up Roy"?

Seltzer thought a bit then started, "Born in Christchurch New Zealand, almost sixty years ago. Never knew me pa, but me Mum took proper care of me the best she could I suppose, given that she had little formal education.

She never talked about her parents, so I suppose I never knew who they were".

"Sometime around mid-nineteen and forty she up and died on me, after a long illness. Sometimes when I go to sleep, I can feel her presence somehow. Got the municipality to bury her since we had no money to speak of and I had a decision to make, as to how to make my way in this world, since I had nobody. So I hitched a ride to Wellington, sorted things out for a few days and stowed away on a freighter to Sidney Australia. Lied about me age, like a proper Kiwi and enlisted in the Australian army. They were takin' in blokes at that time with few questions, other than is the bastard fit enough! I was fit enough. The pacific war was on the horizon and everyone was nervous about the Japanese"!

"Fortune placed me in the Australian Marines, and those limey blokes worked us hard, but when Pearl Harbor hit and later when the Philippines went belly up, then Singapore, everyone in Australia was sittin' on the very edge"! "General Mac arrives in the subcontinent and takes over and plots and plans. Next thing I know I and some Brits that 'dee dee'd' early out of Singapore, found ourselves in a god forsaken place called "Guadalcanal", just there to help out the first contingent of your Marines, that arrived".

"Our task was to be the eyes and ears for your Marines. To see where the Nip's were and radio back their location, with a heads up. We all we're mostly green behind the ears and sometimes we we're successful and at other times we weren't. Along with your jolly blokes we had our share of dust ups, mostly with the jungle critters and the mosquito's. I was there from the beginning to the end. The US medics were nice enough to treat me for Malaria, a nasty bit of stuff it is. But I can't help but think that no matter how bad we had it, the Nippo's had it worse. They were on a one way trip, while we at last had a few options".

"For the rest of the war, I kept me nose clean and was mostly relegated to training the new recruits into the Aussie Marine Corps. And the boyo's at the time even saw fit to promote me to Sergeant. Was nice tangling with the willing Sheila's that roamed about at that time, for the aspect of war does wonders in opening up a woman's legs at precisely the right time"! "After the war, I decided the Corps was the place for me, she was me mum, me dad, she put a roof over me head, put grub in me belly and clothes on me back, fortunately the Corps agreed and in around 'forty seven', the Communists were trying to take over Malaya, and Great Britain sent down some of their SAS blokes, what had jungle experience and rounded up a bunch of us and we spent the next two years forming militia groups and eventually drove the little buggers north out of the country"!

"We killed everyone we could find for the place was a target rich environment"! "The SAS blokes, somehow thought that I'd make a good instructor at Sand Hurst, the Royal Military Academy on the great island, giving me another stripe and shipped me out, where I spent, the next ten years teaching escape and evasion tactics along with teaching the Royal Marines, how to be proper snipers"!

"Got in a bit of a dust up with me commanding officer, whereas his girlfriend, at that time failed to tell me that she was also carrying on with my commanding officer and I was just a wee bit of activity on the side.

Eventually me commanding officer's wife discovered his ongoing dalliances with what I thought was my sole girlfriend and all might've kept 'sotto voce', except perhaps in a fit of feminine pique, she reveals that she's been keeping me on the side, just like he'd been keeping her on the side"!

"Now he's in a bit of a pickle and cuts orders for me to be transferred to Ottawa Canada, to teach the Canadian blokes how to shoot properly at some distance. Later found out that my former Commander was cashiered out of the military and divorced while his ex-girlfriend met her end walking into the front end of a speeding Lorry, in mid-town Nottingham"!

"So the world is indeed round, eh what"?

"By this time, I've acquired dual British and Australian citizenship and decide to saddle up and get me pension after some twenty years of service. Do a bit of Mercenary work on the African Continent, mostly in Nigeria, working for Mike Hoar during their long civil war and emerged relatively unscathed, finding myself in Hong Kong where I'm hired on by some wealthy Taiwanese businessmen as their head of security. At this point life is very good to me, whereas I'm traveling everywhere they are and have access to the finest food and pussy the world has to offer. I do my work well, keeping the Triad's off their back only to discover that they are a part of the Chinese Triad's and everybody's trying to assassinate each other all the time".

"Ten years of this leaves me on the outs, especially when the old mandarin's I'm guarding die of natural causes and their son's take over the families various business's and want their own people guarding them".

"It wasn't a friendly parting of the ways, since the way they usually discharge people is to have them killed and knowing this, I thought it prudent to disappear from sight, but not before leaving a little present for the ones sent to take me out in my own apartment. The following day, on a flight to Singapore, I read in one of the Hong Kong papers a story about how an apartment exploded in Kowloon and four mangled and burned bodies, of unknown origins were discovered. The bodies were all male and had no means of identification as to origin or nationality. The apartment in question was mine"!

"So now, I find that I have a multitude of international connections, in the world of arms trafficking and that is how I make me living, henceforth"! For several seconds Roy fell silent. Then Jaeger broke the silence asking, So how on earth did you ever end up here"! "Broke rule number one, boyo, which is never fall in love with a woman and if ya do make certain that you know everything there is to know about her and I do mean everything, both great and small. Oh, and if ya do fall in love with some Sheila, make certain you're in a legit business and even then there's no guarantee's.

"She was a Cuban dancer, what had a dance studio in San Antonio. We knew many of the same people on the other side. We became lovers in almost every sense of the word. Tall, with the legs of a dancer, she was. She taught me how to Tango, Mambo and I developed a taste for Latin music, over the course of time. Well, through her contacts I met some very nasty sorts, in Columbia that were in need of AK-47's and ammo that I happened to have stashed in a warehouse in Corpus Christi. Took three shipments to get everything to Bogotá and I got well paid for the first two, but on last shipment somehow the Texas Rangers had gotten onto her, put her in the box, applied pressure and she gave us all up. The third shipment was intercepted with meself right in the middle of things. The Rangers and the local law rounded us all up and then a trial and here I am"!

"Last thing I heard was that Marcella had turned state's evidence for ratting me and the others out, in turn for a lighter sentence in a female facility. She had little to fear from me, but the Columbians that got caught up in this have long memories and are a bad lot, so she just might not be with us any longer. More the pity, for she was a magnificent woman, especially between the sheets"!

"Your life story reads like a novel Roy", said Jaeger. Ya oughtta write it down"!

"A novel that's soon to reach its ending me boy by the looks of it. Been a long ride it has, had its ups and its downs but on balance, I've had me moments and memories to last an eternity"!

"But you, Boyo, have some brave memories also and over the years, I just gotta say that my time served with you has been memorable and of all the blokes I've ever served with the world over, you're right in the top drawer"! "Back at ya Roy", replied Jaeger!

The following day Roy met with Doctor Fowler and got the formal news of his apparent cancer of the lower intestines.

"If we could get you to one of the state of the art Medical facilities in Houston, Dallas, or San Antonio, perhaps we could get you treatment in time to reverse your condition. But you won't be eligible for parole for another six months and the state budget doesn't provide for treatment of this kind. The medication you're under should slow down the growth rate"!

"So that's it, right Doc", asked Seltzer?

"In my report, I'm going to fudge a bit and say that your estimated time left is about six months and hope it lands on the right desk of the Pardons and Parole Commission. You've kept your nose clean while you were here and perhaps a conditional pardon can be obtained, but there's guarantee's other than a release on conditions of compassion in a timely manner.

"But even if you're released, the treatment is very expensive and you don't qualify for any governmental programs because you're not an American citizen. But I'll try my best to make your case known to the right people and maybe they'll listen. In the meantime stick to your regimen I've proscribed and perhaps you can be comforted"!

"Thank you doctor, I appreciate all your efforts", said Roy before he left. As he made his way back to his cell, his mind was suddenly filled with the image of Marcella. He'd not seen her in many years. Didn't even know if she was alive or not. Nor would he ever most likely, but since the medication he'd just received was starting to take effect, his nagging pain started to diminish and as he lay down in his bunk, memories of her gradually started to return as he drifted off into a late morning slumber, with a smile on his face. After all was said and done, he did have his memories and they were grand.

The following day, some familiar faces greeted Jaeger in the prison clinic. The people from Cal-Tech that visited him long ago secretly implanting the dime sized nano particle factory at the base of his skull.

While Dr. Fowler and nurse Moran monitored Jaeger on a monthly basis, in effect giving him a full physical and taking blood specimens, then issuing a report on a monthly basis, the word was that they wanted to eyeball Jaeger with the possibility of upgrading the dime sized factory unit implanted, deep in the base of his neck.

As far as Jaeger knew, the implant was working very well. He experienced no aftereffects and all he knew was that any bruises he suffered were gone the following day. His attack by others in the shower's, was treated by Dr. Fowler in the standard way, by suturing the shank wound at that time. But by the following day, the superficial but none the less large wound was over half healed and by the second day, only a large red scar remained.

Jaeger recalled Dr. Fowler commenting in amazement, that it was abundantly clear, the sutures were unnecessary and that a simple butterfly bandage would've sufficed. So apparently those tiny bots that swirled around were working very well.

As Jaeger sat with Dr.'s Murphy and Grabowsky, along with Dr. Fowler in his officer, Anita Grabowsky started off, "Mr. Jaeger as you know we've been following your progress thanks to Dr. Fowler"!

"Over the years", she continued, "Our nanotech research has grown by leaps and bounds and we've brought along some mini testing equipment and wish to remove the mini factory from you, test it and possibly replace it with what our tests have proven to be a far longer lasting and more efficient platform, lasting the rest of your lifetime"!

"So we're talking a technical upgrade, eh Doc"?

"That's about it"!

"Last a lifetime"?

"Well then let's do it", agreed Jaeger!

"Just one thing more", said Doctor Grabowsky!

"While all those around you suffered from the effects of the variety of influenza strains, via their symptoms treated and the effects usually lasted from ten days to two weeks. Did you ever wonder why those few times, you experienced the first stages of the flu malady several times, not once did it ever advance past that and that usually by the third day, you were free of all symptoms"?

"The little bots came to the rescue right doctor", asked Jaeger?

"The little robots as you put it, under the direction of the, what we'll call the 'mother ship'. Now as you know, influenza strains are mutating from time to time and usually the body's white blood cell protective system is often hard pressed to overcome these mutations through standard processes. Yet we have every indication that, our new upgrade will be ably effective in coping with just about any malady that may come your way, throughout the balance of your lifetime"!

"Just one thing more. While we don't exactly know why this works yet, in the labs, we've discovered a remarkable enhancement of the senses in our test animals, hearing, sight, taste, smell and the reaction time process's. Our current theory is that all of the animal protective senses that we've genetically inherited over time, that have diminished with the acquisition of homo sapiens ability to think and reason, should be gradually restored in you in a relatively short period of time"! Jaeger thought a moment, then asked, "So if I'm hearing you correctly, there is a possibility that I could achieve the sensory acuity of, oh a timber wolf"?

Dr. Grabowsky, looked at her colleague's Drs. Murphy and Fowler before answering, "Although that specifically hadn't occurred to us, now that I think about it, it seems to be well within the realm of things possible"!

"Might it also be able to deal with an existing and ongoing malady? "It depends on what it is! We've had some modest success with the treatment of certain forms of cancer in our lab animals"?

"In what stages of development, Dr. Grabowsky if you will"?

"If treated in the initial stages, total regression occurs at a one hundred percent rate. In various stages of advancement, the success rate diminishes, while in the extremely advanced rates of progression the success rate slides down to zero"!

"Thank you doctor", said Jaeger continuing, "I'll be glad to do it, with one single condition"! "There is another here in this facility that would serve very well as a platform for your work. Dr. Fowler knows who I'm referring to and if you will give me your word to return very soon, to make the very same implantation in this individual, then I'll be happy to let you folks have at it with me"!

"I know exactly who Jaeger is referring to and the subject is in a semi advanced stage of lower abdominal cancer that if treated, may well save his life, but since state regulations do not provide standard medical treatment it appears the prisoner will expire in this facility. He's currently under treatment for pain only but I'll be happy to have you people examine his file and perhaps take copies with you upon your departure, said Dr. Fowler"!

"The deal is they return soonest, say thirty days from now and implant", said Jaeger!

"Mr. Jaeger, please, we're all on the same page here and of course we'll agree to your conditions. The only thing is that we will of course take that individuals file back to Cal-Tech and may have to slightly re-engineer the mini factory, worst case scenario to achieve the desired results. We might not have to, best case, is all I'm saying. But we feel confident that we can be back here in thirty days latest and perform that function regardless. Will that assurance be sufficient"!

Jaeger then made a motion to spit in the palm of his hand as an age old universal sign that the deal had been agreed upon saying, "Done"! In turn Doctor's Grabowsky, Murphy and Fowler performed the same procedure saying, "And done again, and again, and again"!

An hour later, Jaeger sat up on the operating table as Dr. Grabowsky handed him the old dime sized factory saying, "She sleeping. She's in a state of stasis, since she's no longer feeding on the electrical impulses from your body, ready for reimplantation. It's working really well and can be still reused on another subject. Our gift to you Jaeger", she said handing it over to him. "We've a lot of them back at the lab, so consider this a spare"!

"Where's Doctor Murphy" asked Jaeger?

"Copying medical files to take back with us, since time is apparently of the essence regarding the other subject, that'll be our reading matter on the flight back this evening. I assume the subject is a very good friend of yours"?

"Better than a friend, way better", mused Jaeger absently?

"Don't worry, we'll be back sooner than you think, because as we operated on you we we're discussing doing something that didn't occur to us and if this works, it'll advance our research by leaps and bounds. So we too have a vested interested in this"! As they worked their way through the evening meal, almost a month later Seltzer asked Jaeger, "So that thing they put into my head, is going to help me get better mate"?

"As they told you Roy, it's all very experimental", said Jaeger in a hushed voice amidst the normal din of the prisoners during their evening meal.

"All very hush, hush, stuff with the prison staff completely unaware of what's going on, so say nothing to nobody not even in your sleep. Doctor Fowler has gone out on a very long limb here along with nurse Moran. As far as anyone knows nothing has changed. It's all experimental pal, with no guarantees, but if it works, many things may change for you and they all will be for the good"!

"So Rae, when's the magic day you get sprung outta this hole", asked Jaeger?

"It should be day after tomorrow. They kept pushing it back as you know, but this morning, I got the final word from the bulls. Day after tomorrow"!

"Normally pal, we'd toss ya a party, but as you can see our collective style's a little cramped, so a simple toast of this bug juice will have to do", said Duke Vultee smiling. At that they all modestly raised their containers in a mini toast.

"As far as your old lady, do ya think you'll get any your first night out", continued Vultee?

"Dunno. It depends on what side of the plate she's batting on when she comes and gets me. Sometimes she gets on this jag for the women and the only time I get any is when that little switch in her head, turns the other way and then life is great, until it switches back then the only use she has for a man is to do the heavy lifting and maybe keep her warm on a cold winter night"!

"Well, sport since she's bigger than you, that accounts for the heavy lifting and since electric blankets are cheap and everywhere, not to mention that in this part of the world cold winter nights are a rarity", said Vultee leaving the sentence unfinished.

"Look fella's, neither one of us are much to look at and on balance we seem to click together. So I'm very grateful for the hand I've been dealt and I'm not complaining"!

"Then neither, should any of us", said Jaeger!

Leo Schwartzwald looked in on Buffy just before leaving the office for the weekend saying,

"Have a few minutes for an old man"?

Buffy looked up from her desk having just finished roughing out her summation for the jury tomorrow morning saying, "Of course Uncle Leo, Me casa e su Casa"!

"How's your summation coming Buffy"?

"Just reviewing it, seeing if I missed any points"?

"Well did you"?

"Not that I can see, upon my third reading"!

'Well I've been following his case in the papers and going into the trial is seemed to me the DA had an airtight case against your client, but as the case progressed, it seemed that you just might pull his rear out of the fire"!

"Isn't that what the rich pay us for, Uncle Leo? Doing the impossible?

Creating doubt is all we have to do, while the DA's office has the heavy lifting in creating absolute certainty in the weak minds of those they serve. We've already collected a smooth million in legal fees billed and paid and when we receive the 'Not Guilty' verdict, Ten million in stock options in his company will automatically be transferred into the brokerage account of your law firm, with an automatic sale order with your broker. All I gotta do is obfuscate the facts tomorrow"!

"Thus blinding the jury to reality and the DA goes home with severe 'Agida'"!

"So shifting gears Buffy, how are things going with your 'Big To Do' with our dear Governor Baintree"?

"I'm scheduled to have lunch with him next Monday at the Governor's mansion in Austin. As far as he's aware, I'm going to be there to advocate for the Texas Children's Hospital for additional state funding. As you know I'm on the Board of Directors for the foundation. All of the file's and tapes have been copied and Odessa is prepared to see to it that all the copies of the files, video and audio tapes will be distributed to every media outlet in the state, inclusive of the Feds just down the street from us. The bastards are in checkmate, they just don't know it yet"!

"But why did you include this Australian gun runner and Vultee the bank robber, to make things more difficult"?

"Because the Aussie has a terminal illness according to Jaeger and Vultee is his friend and simply because I'm certain that I can. All parties have an immaculate prison record, with Seltzer getting a Compassionate Pardon, due to his inoperable Cancer condition, with less than a year left on his clock and as far as Vultee is concerned, he's eligible for parole next month and all I'm doing is accelerating the schedule. Baintree's pal the good Sheriff Little is concurrently running the State Pardon and Parole Commission so with his connections, he can have everything signed sealed and delivered within a week and I'm giving them thirty calendar days"!

"We have Judge Womble, the sitting Judge in Jaegers case, balls in a vise, for Jury Tampering, said Buffy continuing. We have both Baintree and Sheriff Little skewered in their post-acquisition of the Warrant for Jaegers arrest. We have Baintree in a vise for perjured testimony at the trial and I've a host of other goodies of a more personal and telling nature. So like you showed me when I was a child uncle when we spent a weekend on your ranch in Ft. Bend County, the cattle will soon be entering the long chute and at the very end of the chute will be some simple waddie with an electric prod to their heads. My luncheon with the good Governor should be over before the entrée is served and I dare say that I'll ruin his appetite for the rest of the day. Don't anticipate that I'll finish our luncheon with the good Governor and should be back in town by afternoon's end"!

"So what does Jaeger and his friends know of what you're planning"?

"Not a thing Uncle, Nada'?

"Why haven't you told Jaeger of this"?

"The man's had way too many bad surprises in his life. I owe him a positive surprise. To restore his faith in humanity and society. Everything in this world that he held near and dear has been torn from him, violently by the acts of evil men. I owe him that Uncle Leo"!

"But there is the law Buffy. There is society and a sense of order to consider, the legal constraints that we all must work with and embrace"!

"Yes Uncle Leo there is that to consider and consider it I have and do every day. I think about it every time I step into a court of law and tomorrow when I give my summation to that jury and weasel my way into their minds and hearts, knowing full well that slimy son of a bitch murdered his wife, with malice and forethought all for another win and a hefty fee for our wonderful services, I'll remind myself of how much of a whore I am as I walk past her grieving family, who's gaze I'll have to deal with. Then when I walk out of that courtroom victorious, I'll see that statue of the woman with a blindfold on holding the scales of justice in one hand and"…her voice died out not completing her sentence!

"I understand Buffy, for this is the profession we chose to make a living at", said Leo. "I'm just playing devil's advocate for a moment. I know you've done a great deal of work on your own on this mission of mercy and justice. I also know that you've planned this with almost military precision and can find no flaw with the way all the pieces have united. But do this one thing for an old man that loves you"!

"Yes Uncle Leo" said Buffy?

"Let me call Randall White and one of his operatives to shadow you up and back from your drive to Austin and the Governor. They will place a small tracking device on your vehicle and have a small portable radio in your Beemer just in case, while they form a very loose tail in their vehicle. You'll hardly know they're there. Do this for me"!

"OK Uncle, I'll let them be my keepers on the road"!

"Good Night my dear, I'll see you in the morning", said Leo as he made his way to the elevator.

As George, drove him home in the firms Limousine, he dialed Randall Whites number on the limo's mobile phone and as they connected Leo told him what he wanted to do regarding Buffy's trip to the Governor's Mansion in Austin the following Monday. Randall assured him that he could rearrange his schedule to accommodate Buffy's needs.

"Oh and Randall, one other question"?

"Yes Mr. Schwartzwald"?

"Are those ears you previously installed, can they be resurrected for a short period of time"?

"One phone call this evening and they can start hearing by noon tomorrow. If that's what you want. Do you want all of them to come to life or just certain ones"?

"All of them Randall and can they be remotely monitored"?

"Yes sir they can, for the ears are all externally affixed"!

"Good, let's say for now the next thirty days we'll need to take a listen and if it's any longer than that I'll let you know"!

"Anything else sir", asked Randall?

"Yes, I'll need a daily heads up on everything you hear, via fax to my private number and when it's all over send your time and expenses to me directly and this is between just you and I unless I tell you otherwise"!

"Yes Sir, anything else", asked Randall?

"No, that's all for the moment. Oh, just one thing, of course you and your associate will be armed won't you Randall"?

"Sir, we're always carrying, during every waking hour"!

"Fine. Have a good evening Randall and thank you"!

38

As Buffy rolled along State Route 290 on her way to Austin, from Houston, she marveled at the rolling hills and the intermittently heavily wooded scenery as the miles flew by. She wondered what the early Texan settlers must have thought as their wagons slogged through the wilderness on their way to a new life. A life of hardship to be sure, replete with the uncertainties of nature coupled with the ever present hostilities of the Indians on one hand and the Mexicans on the other. No money to speak of in circulation back in the day. No judicial system to speak of to meet out justice. No doctors around to cure the sick. Nothing but the promise of free land for the taking, if one could hold on to it. The promise naught but hard times for people with grit and endurance.

'That was the way it must've been in those early days before civilization as we know it evolved gradually over time. Through trial and error generation after generation built one on top of the other, to render what we have today', she thought.

Buffy glanced at the portable radio Randall White, had given her laying on the front passenger seat of her BMW 745i, loping along at the posted speed limit, its engine purring along effortlessly. As she glanced in her rear view mirror, she could barely see Randall's car far behind her and even farther back was his associate. But the electronic direction finder they'd secreted in her trunk along with the portable radio which was to be 'On' at all times she was driving, gave her the comfort that they'd never be far away.

Her luncheon with the Governor just a few hours away was billed as a simple meet and greet, in behalf of a local charity she represented and they could take care of that business within the first five minutes of their luncheon, then the real business of her trip would begin.

It was the return trip that Uncle Leo was concerned about, for Royce Baintree, over time, had proven to a very clever man, who'd risen quickly in the ranks of the Texas Rangers, through a combination of guile and cunning. Making and maintaining the right friends at the right time, having risen to the Governor's Mansion. Yet over time he'd been known to do oddly impulsive things. One of which was invading Jaegers campus quarters without a warrant of any kind, which would eventually serve to bite him in his ass. It was the drive back to Houston that concerned Uncle Leo. Most likely nothing would happen, but just in case it wouldn't hurt to have some armed company along for the ride, monitoring events.

As for the present, Buffy would sit back in her seat and enjoy the scenery, while a cassette tape of Carlos Santana serenaded her to the sounds of 'Bella'.

At eleven thirty on the dot Buffy pulled her car into the Governor's mansion and after showing her invitation to the guard was directed to the visitor's parking spot. As she opened the door, she turned off her radio that kept her in touch with Randall and his associate, putting the radio in the glove compartment. As she emerged from her car, dragging her legal briefcase with her, she looked around to see if she could catch sight of Randall's vehicle and finding that he was nowhere in view, was none the less comforted that he was close at hand.

As she approached the entrance to the mansion, she was greeted by one of the Governors assistants, who asked, "Ms. Beauvior I presume", and before she could answer he continued, "Governor Baintree is just finishing up his meeting and will be with you shortly. So if you'll be so kind to follow me to the dining room you can be seated to await the pleasure of the Governor", said the assistant.

Buffy was glad the tall willowy looking assistant didn't offer his hand in greeting, for he looked every bit the type who would leave a slimy film upon ones palm, after shaking his hand. No doubt, one of those public policy majors who wrangled a sweet soft governmental job after college as a resume' builder prior to seeking either state level political office or an appointment to some state agency, building his career as a professional bureaucrat.

Ten minutes later, the very same assistant stuck his head inside the door and announced Royce Baintree's arrival just seconds before he breezed into the dining room saying, "Ms. Beaviour, I'm very glad to meet you", as he approached her and offered her his hand in friendship. "We've heard a great deal about you down in Houston and it appears that you're doing great work down in Houston in behalf of the Children's Charity you represent"!

'Well, thank you governor, I'm just here to do God's work in furthering the never ending cause to seeing to it that the little tykes get the very best medical care that this great state can provide"!

"Well, young lady lets enjoy the salad and wine and discuss how we can be of help to you. I do hope you like prime rib of beef for that's what's on the menu today"!

As the wine and the salad arrived, Buffy reached into her briefcase and pulled out the paperwork that would allow the Governor, by executive order to direct the State Department of Human Services, to allocate additional funding for the Children's ongoing medical care in the coming fiscal year.

All the governor had to do is sign the order. As he quickly perused the prepared directive, he quickly glanced at Buffy from time to time, ever the man to appreciate a beautiful woman, while he turned to the second page, quickly scanning the official epistle to the very end, finding it all in order then taking pen in hand and quickly affixing his signature on both copies, before returning the copy to Buffy and giving the original to his awaiting assistant saying, "See that this gets into the hands of Mrs. Gandy within the hour"!

Then he returned back to Buffy saying, "One of the rare benefits of being the Governor is when a woman of your beauty and grace adorns the Governor's Mansion. So tell me about yourself Ms. Beauvior, or may I now call you Elizabeth"!

Seeing that all too familiar male leer, that surfaced from time to time, Buffy acted just a bit flustered, drawing things out as she sipped her wine and took an additional bite of her salad, before saying, "Governor, the word is that you're a happily married man and while you cut a rather fine profile, I think it would be wise for you to refer to me by my formal cognomen.

Besides, there is one other subject of great importance that begs your total attention, she said sweetly"! "And that would be what", asked Baintree with a slightly pained look on his face, his delicate attempt at flirting being deftly swept aside? "His name is Jaeger and he's a prisoner at the Ellis Unit in Huntsville"! She then reached into her briefcase, removing the large portfolio she'd deftly prepared and handed it to the Governor.

"It's in your best interests and in the best interests of several others, that you read what's at hand, view the tapes and listen carefully to the cassette recordings, for in all this is direct evidence of your complicity and that of others, in his tainted trial and his illegal conviction of the murder of his entire family and his illegal incarceration. You will discover the names of not only yourself but Sheriff Morgan Little, Judge Morris Womble and Ft. Worth Real Estate Developer, Donald Ryder as being complicit in the plot to not only murder his family but frame the only surviving son Jaeger to life sentence in the Huntsville facility without any possibility of parole. Now in that offering your will find the papers of a full and unconditional pardon for prisoner number 67676, known only by his cognomen as Jaeger. Now there exist other copies of these evidentiary papers, video tapes and cassette recordings, ready to be delivered to every media outlet in every city in the state, should you fail to comply with my wishes. Governor, as of this moment, you have thirty calendar days in which to comply, or else your ass is grass and I'm the lawnmower. Oh I almost forgot, an additional package is slated to be delivered to the Federal Prosecutors in Houston, Dallas and San Antonio, who I'm certain would find them more than interesting. Now before you make any excuses, we all know that a full pardon by the Governor is a rare and time consuming event, but since Sheriff Little who in addition to his long standing responsibilities as the High Sheriff in Waco, is the Head of the States Department of Pardons and Paroles, appointed by you Governor upon your taking of office and a central party to this, can easily cut through all of the red tape involved in granting Jaegers pardon within the time frame I've indicated"!

Catching his breath Royce Baintree said, "Young lady this is blackmail an I just won't"! Buffy quickly interrupted his intrusion by saying forcefully, "Baintree, call it anything you like, but what will your wife say when she see's proof of your continual infidelity, by your pimp Don Ryder, in one of his VIP suites at his club on the Ft. Worth turnpike on the nightly news, or what will the media make of things when they see video tapes of your daughter during her European sabbatical, having oral fellatio, with a naked male dancer in a Hamburg Exotic Club"?

Quickly continuing she finally said, "Or what will your political enemies make of things when they read and view the well-documented testimony of Judge Myron Brown. The testimony of a dying man, in one of your local hospitals, that will be the final nail of all of your coffins, that you and a contingent of Texas Rangers invaded the campus room of

Jaeger without a warrant of any kind, only obtaining that warrant after the fact the next day from Judge Brown"!

"As I gaze into my crystal bowl", said Buffy now toying with the Governor, "I see political impeachment in your future, followed by a trial and your incarceration somewhere in the Texas Correctional System. Not to forget the federal authorities that no doubt will fight over your carcass as to who has the appropriate Juris Diction"!

As Baintree tried to respond, Buffy cut him off once again, "Now not only will you sign every document I've provided germane to the Unconditional Parole of Jaeger, but you will sign the papers regarding the conditional release of one Roy Seltzer, since he has a case of inoperable cancer and may not be around a year from now and the release of one Duke Vultee, on parole, since he's up for consideration next month anyway. You will comply in every way given the terms. If so much as a comma is altered, all bets are off and the earth will swallow both you and everyone associated with you"!

"Governor, I will expect your complete compliance and nothing more, nothing less. I suggest that you spend the rest of the afternoon reviewing what's been placed before you"!

At that she rose to leave, looking at her watch, the entrée arrived, with Baintree yelling at the steward as he entered the room, "Get Out"!

As the door closed Buffy then spoke one last time, "And should anything happen to me other than a hangnail, the wheels of justice will be placed in motion immediately and you and the others will be ground into dust Governor, by a shit storm, beyond your reckoning"!

"And if I make this happen Ms. Beaviour as per your demands, what will happen then"? "Then Governor you will receive all of the copies that have been made, except one. You will not run for reelection and Sheriff Little will relinquish his post from the State Pardon and Parole office he holds and will not run for reelection of Sheriff, quietly retiring and finally Judge Womble will retire from his office immediately due to reasons of health. Once the final office has been relinquished, then and only then will you receive the very last copy. Now should anything happen to Jaeger or his friends at the Ellis Unit prior to their release, anything at all, then all bets are off. Que sabe cabrone'"?

"What assurance do I have that you'll keep your end of the bargain", asked Baintree?

"Assurance? Why none at all, other than my word Governor as a member of the Bar and an officer of the court! Have a nice day Governor and remember, time is of the essence"! With that Buffy grabbed her briefcase and departed the Governors presence, with a sweet smile on her face thinking, 'They want to screw with me, they can eat shit and die'!

As she drove through Austin's streets she thought to herself, 'Not a bad day, not at all. The wheels have been set in motion for Jaeger and his friend's freedom, as well as the kiddies getting some additional funding'.

As she reached the suburbs on her way back to Houston, she caught sight of Randall Whites sedan in her rear view mirror, a half a city block away in another lane. She reached into her glove compartment and removed the special radio and flicked it on just as Randall said, "Are ya there"?

"Ten four pal", answered Buffy!

"Everything go as planned"?

"So far, so good"!

"What do ya say we take another route back just for grins", asked Randall?

"I'm in no hurry, just lead the way, but what about your pal"?

"He's a block behind me and he has his ears on"!

"Lead the way pal"!

The following morning, while Buffy was in court, Leo Schwartzwald received a call from Randall White saying, "Good Morning Randall.

Anything of interest, going on"?

"More than just a little bit Leo. Apparently it didn't take long after Buffy left the governor, till he got on the horn. She apparently didn't get too terribly deep into her luncheon and by twelve twenty, in the afternoon, she was walking out of the Governor's Mansion with a big smile on her face.

Apparently the governor is a swift reader, for the phone chatter started at one thirty. His first call, on his private line was to Sheriff Morgan Little, who as luck would have it was in Austin conducting a Parole Committee determination. The call just asked that the Sheriff call the Governor back later in the afternoon, which he did".

"Next he called Judge Womble in Waco, giving him chapter and verse of what happened in his meeting with Buffy. They talked for about a half an hour"!

"Finally he called Don Ryder at his office in Ft. Worth. He wasn't in and the Governor raised holy hell with his secretary to have him call the Governor back. Fifteen minutes later Ryder called him back and that's when all hell broke loose. After Baintree, gave him the skinny on what happened with Buffy, Ryder hit the ceiling, even to the point of sobbing on the phone"!

"Well clearly Randall, seems that our weakest link is Don Ryder, wouldn't you say", asked Leo?

"Oh it gets better Leo. Afterwards they agreed to meet have a conference call, later last night at Nine PM and you could tell by the tone on everybody's voice that all were as nervous as a whore in church. Of all the parties, Sheriff Little is the hard case telling them to pull out all the stops, kidnap Buffy and sweat her good so she'll reveal the locations of all the copies of her little story, then afterwards make her disappear forever. He claimed that he knew of reliable people who could do that very thing Leo and I have it all on tape"!

"I swear Randall, Buffy's got herself into something this time"!

"But get this Leo, Ryder then jumps in and says, 'No more of that', to the Sheriff, 'For that's how the Sheriff took care of the shooters that did in the Jaeger family', and again I have it all on tape, which I'll bring to your office in a few hours. But to continue Leo, apparently sanity prevailed, because the Judge, Ryder and the Governor all took turns in persuading Sheriff Little to do exactly what Buffy said and turn whatever wheels and grease whatever palms and cut loose, Jaeger, Seltzer and this Vultee character, within the next seven days, with absolutely zip fanfare"

"Randall, what is your opinion of the six former Marines that recently worked for you"?

"Top notch Leo. Wouldn't mind working with them again"!

"Do you think they'd be available to do some shadowing work again for us"!

"I'll look into it for you Leo and get back with you tomorrow.

"I'm thinking about two teams, one to stick to Buffy like glue and one to do the very same for Sheriff Little, at least until Jaeger and his friends get out of Huntsville"!

"I'll drop off the tapes to you this later in the morning then if I can borrow an office, get the boys on the horn", said Randall who then hung up.

By the end of the following day, two teams of men, each driving a separate vehicle, connected by radio, shadowed Buffy and Sheriff Little everywhere they went, without their knowledge, without event.

By the middle of the following week, Buffy received a call, her secretary saying on the phone intercom, "Buffy, line three is a man very insistent on talking only to you.

"She punched the button to the speaker phone, whereas Boyd Parmalee was with her in the office, "Ms. Beaviour speaking, so how can I help you"?

"The subjects of the luncheon last week will be available by noon tomorrow as you've directed, with all documents prepared and fully executed as you've directed. If you'll be so kind to arrange transportation at the previously agreed location, all interested partied will be grateful"!

Smiling at Parmalee as the voice over the phone droned on and watching his eyebrows rise, Buffy replied, "Tell your party, the message is received and that I will be there personally to receive the package and that payment will be forthcoming with in the time constraints indicated", then she pushed the button ending the call.

As Buffy was smiling in anticipated relief, Parmalee offered, "Interesting that Governor Baintree, a former Texas Ranger, hadn't quite put together that it was you that was the defending counsel of Jaeger years ago, until Sheriff Little admonished him on that conference call last week"!

"And these are the very people we elect as our leaders", Buffy replied.

"I think Leo will approve of George driving the firms Limo up and back for the trip. I'll see to it Buffy", said Parmalee as he rose from his chair and left the office.

At the very same time, the Assistant Warden received the Pardon papers issued by the State Pardon and Parole office in Austin by special delivery, indicating the pending release of prisoners, Jaeger, Seltzer and Vultee. The papers were verified via a phone call by the Warden, to Sheriff Little in his office in Austin. The very nature of the alacrity and the surprise of this took the Warden off guard, since pardon and parole procedures are usually long and cumbersome events.

"I can have the Governor call you personally if you like Warden", said Morgan Little testily, indicating his ire that his directive be called into question.

"No sir that will not be necessary. I'll be happy to comply on your say so"!

"Are you not convinced of our signatures"?

"No sir, it's just that this is all very sudden and that I'm simply doing my due diligence. Your and the Governors directive will be duly seen to by me personally"!

"Thank you Warden, just see to it that those indicated are ready to go by noon tomorrow. And warden, speak to no one except those of your staff on a need to know basis. Am I understood Warden"?

"Yes sir, need to know basis. Anything else sir"?

"No Warden, we're done here"!

"Thank you sir and good bye"!

The Warden hung up the phone and reexamined all of the papers regarding the release of the prisoners. Finding once again, them all in order, he had no reason but not to comply. As he turned the tape recorder off, he was secure in the knowledge that his hind end was indeed covered.

Knowing Sheriff Little and his long relationship with the governor and what an enemy the good Sheriff could be when provoked, to question him further would be indeed a career ender.

The Assistant Warden was tasked with the duty of seeing to it that the prisoners were notified and that the appropriate work station supervisors were alerted to the fact that they were to lose a worker.

"Well son seems that today will be your very last day in this facility", said Dr. Fowler to a surprised Jaeger. "It seems that you're to be pardoned tomorrow. A full and complete pardon"!

"Doctor Fowler, please don't joke like that with me" said Jaeger."

"Well then son, read this for your self. It was hand delivered to me by the assistant warden just thirty minutes ago"!

And there it was, a memo signed by the warden, notifying Dr. Fowler that his charge, prisoner number 67676, aka 'Jaeger' was to be released as of noon tomorrow. Jaeger was stunned to say the least.

"I've never said this before, but I'm really going to miss you son", said Dr. Fowler, and I'm certain that Nurse Moran will join me in that sentiment. Of course I'll have to notify our friends out west that you're going to be released and that our little experiment will apparently come to an end. Do you have any idea where you will be"?

"Doc I haven't a clue, but if you'll give me your campus and home contact information, as soon as I settle some place I'll be happy to let you people poke and prod"!

"I was hoping you'd say that".

Just then the Assistant Warden knocked on the doctor's door saying, "Well Jaeger, did the doctor break the good news to you"?

"Yes he did Warden", replied Jaeger"! "Good. Normally when a prisoner is released he's given the clothes he entered with back to wear on the outside, but when you arrived, you were clothed in Travis County jail attire. It seems that all of your belongings somehow disappeared prior to your arrival. My guess is the souvenir hunters and scavengers from you're playing days at UT. I think I join the doctor when I say, that over the years I followed your story and especially since you've been here say how well you've done with yourself, and I just have to say that I never have, and still do not believe that you had anything to do with the death of your family"!

"Now if I can borrow you from you duties in the clinic for a little bit, we need to get you to the prison tailor shop to get you a new suit of clothes and some shoes to wear for your release tomorrow. Then you can grab some lunch and then back to the clinic in the afternoon"!

As Jaeger went through the chow line to get his lunch, he caught sight of Vultee and Seltzer ahead of him. Eager to share his good news with them he had mixed emotions. Over time he'd develop solid relations with them and each of them. Yet his pending freedom trumped everything else and deep in the dark recesses of his mind a plan of retribution started to grow.

As he sat down to join them they both seemed to be in a state of shock, with Seltzer saying, "Well mate seems that I have one final appointment with your boss this afternoon, for tomorrow I'm gonna be cut loose. I suppose the state doesn't want to have the responsibility of burying me and is going to give me a compassionate pardon, from my crimes"!

As Vultee and Jaeger's eye's widened, Vultee asked, "Roy, when are you gonna be released tomorrow"? "Well pal, me too! The assistant warden came by this morning and told me that my pardon had been granted and they'd be cuttin' me loose at noon tomorrow. Kinda strange since I'm not up for parole for another few months and I've never sat before them and answered their stupid questions"!

They both looked at Jaeger, with some sadness, for if any of the three deserved to be cut loose from this place it was him, as Seltzer said, "We're gonna miss ya mate"!

Jaeger then started to laugh as he said, "Just got back from the prison tailor shop, where they measured me for a new suit of clothes to wear at noon tomorrow"!

Vultee and Seltzer then looked at each other saying "What's this", incredulously?

"It appears that I've been granted a full and complete pardon signed by the governor himself. I'm not to say anything to anyone not concerned about this apparently a very hush, hush event and I'll receive my papers at noon tomorrow"?

"Ya think Rae can put us all up at his place in Houston asked Vultee"? "Haven't thought that far ahead", replied Jaeger. "Just concerned with getting free from this place"!

"As we all are Boyo, as we all are", mused Seltzer.

"Just crossed my mind, what Einstein once said about the passage of time", thought Vultee out loud"! "Well, spit it out boyo", said Seltzer. "Tonight, I'll bet none of us will get much sleep, in anticipation of our getting' out and time will pass at a snail's pace. But once we walk through those gates, time will speed up 'Muy Rapido' "! After lunch Seltzer visited the clinic and received a thirty day supply of his medication and a complete and final physical along with copies of all his medical records to take along with him. The recent implantation of the nano device was far too soon, in his opinion to evaluate and he asked Seltzer to stay in touch with him for future evaluation. It never occurred to the good doctor that recent phone calls from the state board of pardon and paroles, regarding the physical conditions of Seltzer, Vultee and Jaeger had any connection, until this very moment.

"Fella's something's happening here. What it is, isn't exactly clear.

Let's just chalk it up to good fortune and perhaps a confluence of the stars and be thankful"!

The afternoon drug by slowly for all three and by the time of the dinner meal, they had little to say to each other. In the morning Jaeger would make one last visit to the clinic to retrieve his harmonica, the game football and some other personal papers and say some final farewells to the good doctor and Nurse Moran, prior to visiting the prison tailor shop for his new duds.

Later that evening, while in their cell for the final time, Jaeger and Seltzer spoke with Jaeger asking, "So what are you going to do tomorrow Roy"?

"Think Duke and me will take a bus to Houston and look in on Rae. Boy won't he be surprised and see if he'll put us both up for a couple of days. What about you mate"?

"Nothing left for me in Waco, so do ya mind if I tag along with the both of you to Houston on the Bus"?

"Sure mate. In for a penny, as Rae always says"?

"I gotta get a job of some kind, to pay the bills. The couple of hundred bucks they're gonna give me won't last long"!

"Well, how long do you think it's gonna take Duke, to hit the banks once again, mate"?

"No telling, but that's off the plate for the time being. Besides, I just gotta get used to civilization once again and get my bearings. I've got a lotta thinking to do Roy and my mind just has to be clear about where I'm going from here and what I'm gonna do"!

"I think I know just what's rolling around in your mind and it's gonna take some doing, so if ya need any help, someone to cover your six, just sing out and I'm down with ya, besides I won't be exactly broke. A wee bit of a stash, what I call get out of jail gelt is waitin' for me in Houston, the Bulls don't know about it. So if you and Vultee need a few bucks to get ya over the hump just sing out, ya follow"?

The following morning at Eleven AM, found Jaeger, Seltzer and Vultee in the waiting room awaiting their formal release from prison. To Jaegers great surprise, in walked the Warden accompanied by Elizabeth Beaviour aka, Buffy who said, "Gentlemen and Mr. Jaeger, the Warden and I have met. I've examined the documents of your pardons and your parole Mr. Vultee and the good Warden is ready to release the lot of you into my custody. Oh, Mr. Jaeger you can close your mouth now. So if you will all follow me I've arranged transportation to Houston"!

As they all approached the gate, the warden said after them "Hey fella's, we don't want y'all back, ya heah"! As they went through the gate and to freedom, they caught sight of a back Lincoln Continental Limousine, with two men at an opened rear door. Open wore the livery of a Chauffer while the other was a well groomed man, older man with an expensive haircut, gray in color, rapidly approaching white.

He offered his hand and introduced himself, "Gentlemen, my name is Boyd Parmalee an Associate of Buffy's and this is George our firms Chauffer and if you don't mind we'd like to drive you to Houston, where we have a place for y'all to stay until you can find accommodations suitable for you. But first I think Buffy will want to take you to her home, where she has prepared a small party in your honor"!

As they all entered the Limousine and settled in Seltzer was the first to comment, "Certainly beats a Greyhound Bus, Miss Beauviour"!

"That it does Roy and my friends call me Buffy"! "Then Buffy it is my dear", said Roy smiling Parmalee then opened the mini refrigerator and said, "Think you gentlemen might use a beer while we go down the road", as the Limo made its way through downtown Huntsville on its way to the interstate and south to freedom"! As the men savored their first taste of the beverage denied them, lo these many years, Parmalee said, "You can all thank Buffy here, for your release and especially you Mr. Jaeger, for she has been relentless these many years in her efforts, hitting brick walls and it wasn't until recent fortunate revelations surfaced that she was able to gain the upper hand in the whole affair and procure your release, for you were the principle cause, while you Mr. Seltzer and Vultee had the good fortune to be close and trusted associates of her client and who were included in the deal"!

"In addition, we're being accompanied by former associates of your Mr. Jaeger, following in unmarked cars in our wake, just doing Shepard duty in case of the unforeseen. No doubt you've never met them before, but you have one thing in common, The Marine Corps. And thanks to one General Bollinger, in Quantico Virginia, that I believe had the good fortune to have you briefly serve under him. I believe the last time I talked to him; he said to me something I've never forgotten, "Once in, never out"!

"That's a bloke I'd like to meet", said Seltzer.

"And meet you will", said Parmalee, "For before we arrive at Buffy's home, we have to make a brief detour to Intercontinental Airport to pick up the General, for the evening. For the rest of the day and deep into the evening, all will be revealed and friendships made and renewed"!

True to her word, a celebration was on tap at Buffy's home, with all of the ex-Marines, General Bollinger, the detectives and Leo Schwartzwald himself in attendance to pay homage to the 'Uberballer', emerged at long last from his incarceration. Over the course of the afternoon, all of the facts, that were currently known, regarding the murder of his family and Jaegers arrest, trial and conviction came to light.

Vultee and Seltzer took their turns in revealing stories of their experiences with him, at the Ellis Unit and especially interesting was their joint recantation of his struggle with the giant, Cloyd Elsasser and the aftermath of his death during the riot. Of course his brief time at the University of Texas and his exploits there, over time would become that of legend, especially the final play of the of the Cotton Bowl, which enshrined him for generations to come.

Finally General Bollinger rose to speak, telling all those assembled of Jaegers very last mission of mercy and his successful rescue of the entire Embassy staff, while under siege by Toureg tribesmen in Africa.

"He didn't and will not receive a medal, or at least formal recognition, of any kind, from our government, for this heroic selfless action, but we assembled this day know him for the man he is. So raise your glasses in salute to a real 'Ubermenchen', a man's man, Jaeger, for the world at large, may not know, but we who matter do! Glasses up"! At that all rose and downed their drinks, in homage. "Finally, I wish to thank Ms. Beauvior and all the rest of you that tirelessly persevered in the pursuit of justice, albeit outside of the normal course of events"!

Then one of the former Marines spoke up asking, "General Sir. Does this mean that the 'means', sometimes justify the ends"?

Buffy then rose up and said, "Marine, you bet your sweet ass it does"!

After the laughter settled down, the very same Marine said to Jaeger, "I think I can speak for the rest of us by saying that we all are happy that we were involved in your getting sprung and from what I can see, you just might have some 'unfinished business' ahead somewhere down the road. Ya ever need someone to cover your 'six' Marine, just sing out and we're there"! He looked around at the others and they all nodded their heads in agreement, while Jaeger lifted his glass in acceptance saying, "Thanks fellas, I'll keep that in mind, but for the time being, I've got to get about the business of adjusting to civilian life and find a way to make a living"!

The rest of the afternoon and evening was spent exchanging war stories between military men and as Boyd Parmalee made his way around to each and every man, an envelope was passed to them containing a significant amount of cash along with an airline ticket back home.

Buffy later got Jaeger, Seltzer and Vultee aside and offered each of them an envelope saying, "Here's a little something to tide each of you over and I've a client with an auto dealership who owes me several favors, and you'll each be in need of reliable transportation, so late tomorrow morning, I'll have George come by and drive you over to the dealership to get some suitable wheels. Now you know before you leave this evening, that I've access to a three bedroom furnished house that all of you can use for several months and I've three clubs that just happen to need an assistant manager in each, for as long as each of you wish to stay. So each of you will be gainfully employed in the interim"!

So the deal was done as each of them accepted her largesse. But after the other two drifted off to refill their glasses, Seltzer went up to Buffy and slipped the envelope back into her hands saying, "Thanks Buffy, but I won't be needin' this, for I've a wee bit of a rainy day fund lying about, but as to all the rest I'm ready willing and able"!

Buffy pushed back the envelope into Seltzers hand saying, "Please, take this from me as a favor, for you've helped keeping a good man alive, during his dark days, which bought me time, with which to right a wrong. For me, please, as a favor"!

"Well my good woman, I was never one to disappoint a lady, but tell me, if you will, are there any other Sheila's like you lying about"?

"Dunno mate, she said flashing a smile. "Think they broke the mold after I popped out"!

39

Days later as soon as they all got settled in, discovering that they were all assistant managers of three of Houston's finest upscale Gentlemen's Clubs, Seltzer commented, "Mates, pussy everywhere, wall to wall", and that was indeed the case. Some of the finest examples of feminine pulchritude, uniformed in next to nothing every single day, turning every single device and angle to separate a patron from his hard earned cash was there for the asking. Like in everything else that operated around the clock, there was the day shift and then the night shift. Single women and married women with children in some cases all working to do whatever it took to turn a buck.

Of course, the average blue collar workman was turned away from entering via a loosely defined dress code, that mostly hosted the coat and tie crowd. Whoever worked the door enforced this criteria. Which is precisely what the intrepid trio, found themselves doing initially. Fortunately the reputation of these clubs didn't encourage the hard core working class, to even try to enter. Primarily the expense account crowd accounted for the bulk of their clientele, with very little cash trading hands.

Early on it was agreed by all, that the 'dancers' were, a rather untrustworthy group, using their charms at all times to gain advantage, with Vultee commenting one evening, "Never shit where ya eat"! All eventually agreeing that should ever any of them become in serious need of serious feminine company, never to indulge at their particular club, but to pay a visit to one of the other clubs, where their needs would be met!

After a few months, the managers eager to gain help in the food and beverage aspect of each clubs operation, taught each of them the rudiments of food and beverage purchasing and management. In short order each one gradually took over much of that aspect of the operation. Thus inside of six months, each of them acquired an intimate knowledge of what a cash cow, the 'Club' business was.

Of course, like any gynecologist will tell you, after daily viewing of women in all aspects of their naked enterprise, and hearing their nonstop complaints and oft times sheer whining about the smallest grievances, their allure gradually diminished and it just became another job.

One day when they all found themselves together, they decided to pay a visit to Rae, the printer at his 'Old lady's' printing company. At first Rae just couldn't believe his eyes, thinking that they all had escaped and we're on the run. But later on in the day, they all went to dinner and Rae was filled in, chapter and verse on the details of their getting sprung.

"So what finally happened fella's", asked Rae eagerly?

"Well sir", answered Jaeger, "A week after our release Governor Baintree announced that he was not running for re-election and would serve out the balance of his term. The following week, Judge Brown, the one who dummied up their arrest warrant after the fact, died in his hospital bed. The week after that Sheriff Little resigned from the Department of Pardon's and Parole's, indicating that both jobs were too much for him to handle. Now he hasn't made any announcement as to whether or not he'll run for re-election as of yet, but I'm sure that Buffy'll hold that bastard to it"!

"And the judge in Waco, what's his name", asked Rae eagerly?

"Womble, Morris Womble. Just last week he announced his immediate retirement, from the bench, due to reasons of his health that recently surfaced.

"What about the Real Estate Developer in Ft. Worth" asked Rae?

"No plans for him according to Buffy. I suppose she's going to let him sweat for a good while, besides not all of the packages were delivered to the Governor, apparently a few are being withheld, for possible use in the future"!

"Do you think that Buffy'll ever use them", asked Rae?

"She gave her word to Baintree that after he and Sheriff Little, officially leaves office, she'll deliver the 'last' package to the Governor"!

"Do you believe her"?

Jaeger looked at Rae, saying with a wink, "She gave her word as a lawyer and a member of the Texas Bar Association"!

At that they all laughed, with Seltzer saying, "When the sun rises in the west. That bit of Sheila has a good deal of grit and sand about her and I for one intend to stay on her good side. The sword of Damocles, hangs ever about their collective heads and she's got em by the short and curlies"!

Rae then added, "Still and all, it just don't seem near enough, for what they done to ya"!

"They could still be indicted and go to prison, for a long stretch. The Boys at the Ellis unit would just like to get their hands on em", said Vultee!

"And the powers that be know it, so they'd probably end up at some country club, minimum security facility, mopping floors all day long, so they would escape having to travel the 'Hershey Highway', to satisfy some Bubba", said Jaeger!

"Ya ever have plans to visit your old home in Waco", asked Rae? "Been thinking' about it and puttin' it off. I hear that not much is left that once was and so far I've been able to contain things and try and put them in perspective" said Jaeger. "I've been doin' that for a long time now. But I suppose that sooner or later I'm goin' to have to confront things.

Maybe next month, I'll drive up to Waco and have a look around"!

Vultee than said, "And when you do, you'll need the three of us along for the ride, and I want your word on that pal"!

"Duke you have my word and I'm not a lawyer", said Jaeger with a weak smile!

True to his word, Jaeger and his pals drove up to Waco early one morning, three weeks later in Seltzers newly purchased Jaguar sedan, purchased at the local auto auction northwest of the city. They had been moving steadily along state route six, on a parallel route, of the Brazos River traveling northwest. It was a sunny fall morning late in November, with the warm weather still hanging on with grim determination. But as they drove north with the windows open, the normally humid air of the Gulf Coast, began to give way to the cooler, drier prairie air.

"I hear about this cop that that initially arrested you Duke, looking in on you periodically"!

"Everything is copasetic between me and this guy Roy. He visits me on a monthly basis at the club and each time I comp his drinks and his meal.

Other than that nothing. Once and awhile I intro him to one of the girls and what happens between them is their business. The only question he ever asks is if I've robbed any banks recently"?

"And what do ya tell him mate"!

"I always answer, with a wink, "Not yet"!

"But while we're on the subject, aren't you supposed to be at deaths door step by now? How's that implant working for you"?

"Must be doing some good, for I haven't needed the pain meds for some weeks now and the pain has all but vanished. Called up Dr. Fowler at the Ellis unit last week and let him know. Just yesterday I got a letter from him inviting me to meet with him and his out of town friends next Wednesday at the Methodist Hospital so they can poke and prod, me innards"!

"I got the same letter too Roy", said Jaeger?

"Good. So we can both go to see them together mate", said Roy! "By the way, how's that piece of shit '63' Ford Galaxie restoration coming along"?

"Takin' almost every dime I can scrape together to get it running. Good thing I live on the bus route. But the rebuilt engine should be finished next week and it'll be up and running, from there on out it'll be a rolling restoration and I'll still be broke for awhile, but after that, I'll have a supreme ride"!

"If ya need any money to tide ya over mate, just sing out mate", said Seltzer!

"I'll keep that in mid if I get desperate"!

"We just passed through 'Marlin' and should be in Waco in about thirty minutes Jaeger. Are ya getting' nervous", asked Rae.

Jaeger just sat in the passenger's seat, in silence, watching the land pass him by, with memories of the past starting to return, one by one, eventually answering Rae's question with a nod of his head.

The old homestead straddled the county line between McLennan and Bosque counties with the Brazos and the North Fork of the Bosque River flanking the land as they worked their way through the streets of Waco, continuing on highway six and out the other end. One by one Jaeger pointed out land marks, until at last they came upon the entrance of Lancaster Estates. Turning through the massive stone entrance that fronted the estate, the Jaguar slowly made its way down the long two lane boulevard, separated by great old oak trees that over hung the pavement providing shade.

Jaeger absently commented as they drove on, "My forbearers planted those tree's sometime around 1850"! As they drove on, eventually they came upon a large, newly constructed building, that appeared to mirror an old nineteenth century English Manor House, with a well-crafted sign in front that read, "Lancaster Estates sales and information office".

The Jaguar stopped and they all got out, with Jaeger walking halfway to the front door looking at the building from stem to stern and turned to them saying, "They tore my parents' home down and replaced it with 'This'"!

He then sunk into a squat hiding his face from the others fighting back the tears that had been building up for years. Then suddenly gaining control of himself he said, "Let's get back to the car, there is more to see"! The old massive barn was, of course, gone replaced by a series of tennis courts and pools. As they drove down the newly installed streets, they all saw that a hoard of upscale home were constructed and occupied, as they drove on, guided slowly by Jaeger who was searching for something uncertain of which way to go, he finally said, "Stop the car over there", pointing to a partial grove of trees, that intersected a newly constructed homeowners property, and a water well storage facility. As they all got out of the car, they walked up to the edge of the grove of trees, as Jaeger searched and searched for something, finally saying, "The bastards dug em all up"? "Dug what up Jaeger", asked Vultee? "Right here was the family grave yard and every member of the family was buried here, every single one", he said as he walked along the fence line of the adjoining homeowner's yard.

As he walked further, he then said, "And right over there, is where my ancestors buried 'Chani and Akila', the wolves that followed my ancestor Heinrich Jaeger all the way from Southern Ohio, when he was but a kid.

"This was sacred ground to each and every one of us, from generation to generation and tales of all of my forbearers were told to each and every one of us, by our parents when we were young, under these very trees. It got so that we could all feel the very presence of all those who came before us, as the stories of the family unfolded before us when we were little kids. Every single one of us memorized those stories, to tell to the next generation and now it's gone" said Jaeger as he slowly walked, to the few surviving trees that remained. Still searching for something on the ground, but finding nothing but a smooth section of replanted grass of a different type from the old prairie grass that had been in place for centuries.

Just then a woman walking her dog on a leash came upon them saying, "Hello, may I help you", as her dog eagerly sniffed each and every one of Jaegers friends.

"My name is Helen Trent and I live here" she said. Each of the party introduced themselves to her in turn except Jaeger, with Seltzer talking the lead saying, "We're all thinking about building a home here and we're just taking a little look see to get the lay of the land. Mind if we ask a few questions"?

"Why no, just fire away"!

"How long have you lived here"!

"Well, my Howard the kids and me moved out here from the City about two years ago. Howard, my husband teaches at Baylor University in town.

"How do you like it here"?

"Oh we like it very well, although it's a bit pricey, but when Howard gets to be the Dean of his department, which should be soon, we'll be better able to afford it"!

Searching for something else to ask, Roy gave way to Vultee, who asked, "Any trouble with the developer, during construction"?

"Oh you must mean that son of a bitch Donald Ryder, pardon my French. You just gotta watch him like a hawk. We were very specific during closing, as to the quality of the construction and we discovered that he was cutting corners to no end, giving us substandard materials, and quality, to such a degree we finally had to file a lawsuit to get him to comply"!

"Appears he had the county building inspectors in his hip pocket and when we filed a complaint, he set Sheriff Little's boys on us to make us back down. Now my Howard just wanted to walk away, but I held to my guns and we eventually forced Ryder into settling out of court. We got the quality of materials we signed up for, which meant that Ryder's subcontractors had to tear out a lot of what was installed and redo almost everything. Took an extra nine months with me coming out here most every day it wasn't raining, with a punch list that was forwarded to the court for approval. So I can' say that Don Ryder and the Sheriff has not much use for us, but neither do we for them"!

Jaeger then asked, "Since you all have moved in have you noticed anything unusual going on"? Helen thought a moment before saying, "Now that you mention it yes we have. Now I'm not a superstitious woman, but there has been some strange goings on since we moved in. Just before the construction began, there used to be a little grave yard over there", she said pointing to the edge of the remaining copse of trees. Seems that a family called Jaeger used to be buried there and on part of our property. I asked Ryder's people about that and they assured me that all of the graves would be disinterred by the state and that all permits were obtained, to that effect, then never gave it another thought, for I had a lotta other things on my mind. But that's before we all got cross ways with Don Ryder and his people. Now that I think about it, something's very fishy about that, for two days later when we visited our property, everything was gone, a lotta trees and the ground was smoothed over and replanted and we saw a front end loader and one of those, oh, uh looks like a big ground scoop on tracks being loaded large truck, like they were in a hurry to get this done. Now I don't know anything about graves and what they contain, but I would think that with all those graves, it would take some time and all of them would have to be dug up by hand very carefully"!

"Anything else ma'am, you can think of", asked Jaeger?

"Like I said, I'm not a superstitious sort, but ever since we've moved in, little 'Fluffy' gets all nervous from time to time and she's never done that before when we lived in town. Usually happens at night, when she'll wake us all up and start barking at a spot in the house or outside of the house. We'll all run downstairs, turn on the lights and Fluffy will stop her barking. Then we'll go back upstairs, turn off the lights and just about the time we start to fall back to sleep, she'll start barking again. Then days and weeks will go by without a problem and then it'll start up again"!

She stopped briefly then continued, "One more strange thing.

Sometimes after we go to bed at night, either one of my kids will enter our bedroom wake us up, saying that something, little Hank calls it the boogie man, while Josie thinks it's Fluffy jumping up on her bed to sleep with her. Now when she wakes up, she see's nothing and figures that Fluffy has gone back to her little bed down by the fireplace and little Hank has never seen anything. When we look in on Fluffy, she's there in her bed each time. But every once in awhile, when I'm asleep, I'll feel a presence at the foot of our bed, while I'm half awake, think it's Fluffy and drift off back to sleep.

Strangest thing though. Do y'all think this might have anything to do with any of those graves"?

"Not for us to say maam, but you've been very helpful and informative" said Vultee as he turned back in the direction of the Jaguar"!

Helen then looked back at Jaeger and asked, "Pardon, but I never got your name", offering her hand in friendship"?

Jaeger thought a second then said, "My name is Jaeger, ma'am, Jaeger", he repeated, shaking her hand gently before joining Vultee. Seltzer then bid his goodbye to the woman, followed by Rae, who saw the look of bewilderment of the woman who while saying goodbye to Rae was looking in the direction of Jaeger as he walked away.

"If you're wondering if who that man called Jaeger is who you think he is, of might be, You'd be correct and if your questions about what's in your house from time to time is a figment of your imagination, or not, all I can offer is that they pose no threat to you or your family, they're probably just curious", he said before joining the rest.

As the Jaguar drove off, they eventually made the circuit of much of what was the old homestead, before departing the development with Jaeger pointing out various places of interest.

As they all drove back down highway 6 into Waco, Jaeger was silent with a passive look on his face, then after they'd driven through town and were on their way back to Houston, Jaeger finally broke the silence in the car saying "Her name was Helen"!

"Yeah I agree, her name was Helen" said Vultee.

"Not the Helen at the Estates that we met. My grandmother. Her name was Helen also and she was buried under the trees with all the rest, when I was around ten years old. She was buried some five yards from Chani the wolf. She used to take me up to the grave yard, when I was a little tyke, she'd make a picnic lunch and while I was playing she'd be keeping an eye on me and talking to someone. She'd always be sitting next to the grave of Chani the first female wolf. I'd drift off to sleep in her arms, tired from chasing bugs and dandelions and hear her calling Chani and even Akila, by name, talking to them both, usually about what was going on in the family. Never was quite sure before, but now I am, she was talking to their spirit.

Whenever I'd ask her about it she's always say that she was talking to herself.

But now I know better"!

Half way back to Houston, as they were passing through College Station, Seltzer offered, "There's someone I think you might want to meet mate. I met him last week at the club. We talked a bit and he needs some help with his business. He's in a rather specialized business and while our paths have never crossed professionally, I know him by reputation and he's very good at what he does. Given what's ahead of you, I think a bit of a chat could be useful to the both of you in the coming days"!

'What is he looking for Roy"?

"He's looking for a hunter. A hunter of men and that's who you are, or certainly can be. Jaeger, is German for 'hunter', is it not? And for generations gone past, that's precisely what your family has done, is it not? By my reckoning, all you need is a few of the rough edges polished off, besides you can make a great deal of money fast in the coming days and he needs a man with the talents"!

The Jaguar went yet another mile down the road, before Jaeger interrupted the silence, saying, "Set it up Roy", with a grim look on his face.

"Did ya catch the look on that lady, Helen's, face when Jaeger told her, what his name was", asked Rae with a laugh?

"Sure did", said Vultee! "By the time we get back to Houston, it'll be all around the subdivision, and the housewives will all have their tits in lather"!

40

Midafternoon is always a quiet time for restaurants and clubs, after the lunch rush on weekdays, when men have to get back to work and try and function after a slew of martini's and having their blood pressure rise as a result of the undulations by desirable unclad women.

Seltzer and Rafferty sat in the almost empty confines of the Palomino Club waiting for Jaeger to arrive while performing their quality control checks, on Wolf Schmidt and Ulanskya Vodka's both served chilled and neat. They conversed at some length, randomly about the feckless nature of Houston's professional sports teams, agreeing that it just might be a cold day in hell before the city would field a champion, when Jaeger came through the entrance doors of the club. The girls cloistered at the other end of the long bar all turned their heads then turned back seeing that it was only Jaeger. 'No money to be made there', they all concluded.

"Sorry I'm late gentlemen, but just as I was leaving, had to put out a little female fire. Roy, you know how that can go", said Jeager!

"Nary a week goes by when that doesn't happen mate", agreed Seltzer nodding to Rafferty. Then he turned to Jaeger saying, "Me boyo, this here is Chips Rafferty, owner of the largest Bonding company in these parts and at that I'll leave you two alone to see if there's anything in common between ya, while I go up to me office and tend to some paperwork"!

As the bartender brought Jaeger his standard Gin and Tonic, Jaeger slowly spun around in his barstool, with the bar behind him and the club before him, a subtle move not lost on Rafferty, who always was for sitting with one's back to the wall at all times and keeping all visuals in front of him. Rafferty started out by saying, "Roy tells me that you're thinking about making a change in the way you make a living"!

"Thinking about it Chips, just thinking, for the moment", said Jaeger! "Did Roy tell you about what we do", asked Chips?

"Most everyone knows what a bail bonding company does Chips. Someone screws up, the cops put the cuffs on em and you guys get em their get outta jail card, but at a cost, thus guaranteeing their appearance in court.

Should they appear all goes well, but if they don't then ya gotta go find em. That about right"?

"More to it than that, but you hit the high points"! "So why are we talking, Chips"?

"Been following your story for quite some time and we seem to have a few people in common, for example, your mouthpiece 'Buffy'. I do quite a little business with her, in fact most all of her clients, that get their tits in the legal wringer, she send to me exclusively. Thus far, few problems. For the high risk ones she sends elsewhere and the really high risk usually gets remanded to jail for the duration of the trial at the Judges orders"!

"You came onto my radar years ago when you played ball for UT and not being a college type myself was really impressed by the trail of broken bones you left in your wake, not to mention, the money I made off you in that Cotton Bowl game, betting against the odds. That last play still gives me the Willies whenever I think about it"!

"Now since I've come to know Roy, we got to talking shop and he's told me quite a bit about your time at the Ellis Unit, just up the road and I'm impressed with how you've conducted yourself. Got an education, chose carefully when you decided to confront people, making sure that it was in your ball park with your ball, bat, gloves and rules. The very fact that we're here talking says that you're not only very lucky but good and that combination, suits me right down to the ground. So here tis. I'd like you to come and work with me. There's be a lot for you to learn tracking down felons who skip their bail and a significant part of this would be out of country and you'd not be just tracking down the low renters. Quite a few of my skip's, are costly and if all goes as I think it will you'll be making six figures in no time"!

"I know nothing at all about the art of skip tracing Chips"!

"But the very fact that you know what the word means tells me that I've got a lot to work with. Listen, I was damn good at what I did for years before I opened my own shop and over the years built a damn good and profitable business. By the way I'm still damn good at tracking down the critters, but time has slowed me down. Now I got this guy named "Hondo" that I'd like to team you up with. Trained him myself and he lives well.

Now between us both, we could have you up to speed in no time. And making money lots of it, legitimately. With what you've been through, I think and Roy agrees that you'd make an excellent tracker"!

"Besides, Roy and I have already talked with Buffy about it"! "Talked with Buffy about it", exclaimed Jaeger.

"We ran the concept past her, to get her thoughts"!

"And what did she have to say"? "She said that she thought it was, a good career move for you, seeing what you had laying ahead of you, but that it was your decision". If you said yes, OK, if you said no, it was still OK. Either way the two of you would still maintain contact"! Jaeger remained silent, lighting up a cigarette; to gain time thinking things rapidly through, then finished his drink, saying, "Done, I'll do it. But give me a few days to wrap thing up at the club. Don't want to leave my boss in a lurch.

The club business is getting boring and repetitive, starting to feel like a gynecologist. How about I show up next Monday and we can start fighting crime, sorta"?

"Monday it is, mid-morning'll do", beamed Rafferty, who fished out a business card and gave it to Jaeger saying, "I'll team you up with Hondo first thing. Glad to have you on board"!

As Jaeger exited the Palomino Club, he said to himself, 'Yet another page turns, in the passage of time'! The following Monday as Jaeger and Hondo selected three 'skips' to track down, Hondo plunged into the DMV data base, the a host of other little known avenues of research to determine a 'skip's' whereabouts, saying, "If a guy has enough cash and transacts by cash only it makes it harder, then we gotta get on the phone and become actors and actresses to track em down. Now if the guy starts writing checks on his accounts or uses credit cards, then it gets easier to get a line on em"! "Now when he leaves the country, that's when the real fun begins"! By early afternoon Hondo had a good idea where each of their 'skips' might be. They had to drive into Waller County, the next county over and within an hour, came upon their skip; sound asleep on the front porch of his girlfriend, sitting in a rocking chair, with a six pack of consumed empties on the floor, mouth open, catching flies and breathing heavily. As they wrestled him into the trunk of Hondo's old Chevy Malibu, with hands cuffed behind him and leg irons affixed, still groggy from his rude awakening, Hondo said, "Now that was a gimme.

They all won't be that easy. But the next stop is the Harris County Jail for booking, and we're both five hundred bucks to the good.

By the close of business the following day, the other two 'skips' we're in custody, drugged and secured in Hondo's trunk, on their way to the Harris County Jail and their destiny with justice. As they drove back into town Hondo was a nonstop Thesaurus on human behavior saying, "What these clowns never seem to realize is that, in order to really skip bail, you have to completely reinvent yourself. Ones habit's is what always gets em caught, almost every time. Identify a man's habits and you got your finger on most men and women. Most felons are just plain stupid, making the same mistakes over and over, getting them arrested repeatedly for the very same screw ups. Now in the movies, you'll see an actor brag and tell the dumb ass, just how they got caught. But in the real world, we ain't no school teachers."!

"Five hundred bucks, for just tagging along. You mean your splitting your end with me", asked Jaeger? "Yup, that's the way it works pal. On the job training. So the sooner you get brought up to speed, the sooner I can get back to making my full amount. But hey that's how I learned at the knee of the master. Chips Rafferty. I was suckin' on his tit for a full six months before he cut me loose. By the way, the way you covered the rear of the last guys apartment window without me having to tell ya, says to me you got the right instincts for this work and I'll be back on my own in no time. You disarmed him right nicely and the way you hit him behind the ear, was a work of art.

"Thanks", said Jaeger passively! The world these people concerned themselves with were comprised of several different types of people, 'Runners' and 'Trackers', and then everyone else. As time wore on Jaeger found, that patience, guile, speed and the ability to be all things to all people, were the principle arrows in the quiver of a tracker.

If one wants a regular work schedule of forty hours a week, then look elsewhere, for a 'trackers' work schedule spans the time and date spectrum.

A lot of a tracker's best work is done at night, and especially in the wee hours of the morning. From time to time a successful tracker will have to engage in activity clearly illegal. Wire taps, breaking and entering, kidnapping, or hijacking are all a part of the agenda. The trick is not to get caught. Actions must be well thought out in advance, with a multiple of escape route planned in advance, with above all, Murphy's Law being in constant attendance. Cameras, tape recorders and a host of technical equipment all were part of Jaegers repertoire before the year had come to a close. In time he developed to ability to change his appearance and acquire various regional and international accents. When one day he walked into the office, in the guise of an old man hobbling about on a cane and asked for Rafferty. When Wanda escorted him into Rafferty's office, Jaeger sat down in font the old man after introducing himself in an affected, eastern European accent, asked if Rafferty had seen Teo Valdez?

Knowing that Jaeger was in Alexandria Louisiana to bring him back, Rafferty asked what the strangers interest was in Mr. Valdez?

Jaeger answered in heavily accented English, "Perhops you should investigate the trunk of the car parked outside in front of your place and see what is inside", tossing weakly Rafferty the keys to his car.

While Rafferty and Wanda went outside and opened the trunk of Jaegers 63 Ford Galaxie sedan, Jaeger removed his disguise and walked to the front door. As they opened the trunk, Jaeger saw the surprise on both their faces as the inert body of Teo Valdez lay in the trunk.

As Wanda and Jaeger turned to look at each other, they caught sight of Jaeger standing in the front doorway smiling, now standing fully erect, in the very same clothes, but with the facial disguise in tatters.

Wanda then exclaimed, "Well if that doan beat all", as Jaeger went down to the trunk to lift an inert Valdez from the trunk. "Have to give him a bigger dose of relaxant than normal, so it might be prudent if we take him inside till he comes around, then I'll take him over to booking at the jail"!

As they all went inside, Jaeger unloaded his cargo on a long wooden bench, then looking at his watch said, he oughtta be waking up in a few hours. Then he turned to Rafferty and Wanda seeing their jaws agape saying, some flies are about to enter into your mouth's"! As Wanda went away mumbling repeatedly, "Damn, if that doan beat all", repeatedly and taking care of the paperwork on Teo Valdez, Jaeger gave Rafferty an after action report on the capture of his 'runner', saying, "I remembered what Hondo always said about a man's habits, so I had to get a bit inventive, so I could approach him. Every day he walked his dog in the park, so who would figure, an old man would be lying in wait? Parked my car on the street, waited a few hours and here he came walking that damn Chihuahua. Played like I was ill as he walked by the park bench. Since no one else was nearby, as he bent over me out came the syringe and into his neck. He tried to go for his gun, but he let his dog loose, as I grabbed his gun hand and some twenty seconds later he slumped in my arms. Last thing I saw as we drove off was his dog chasing us down the street. Checked on him twice on the way back and he was breathing normally and here we are. Nothing to it"!

"Son, ya had us fooled, for fair", said Rafferty

"Sorry to play that little trick on ya both, but it's one thing to be able to fool a runner, but to fool the both of you told me that I'm onto something", said Jaeger.

"Oh while you were gone, Buffy called to tell you that rumors are your friend Sheriff Morris Little, is about to announce he'll not going to be running for re-election as county Sheriff, come next fall", said Rafferty, noticing a peculiar look come on Jaegers face when he mentioned that name. By this time the full story on what had happened to Jaegers family became known to Rafferty and being a perceptive individual connected most of the dots and then knew of the unfinished business that lay ahead. For well over a year, Jaeger had worked almost nonstop, clearing the backlog of skips along with Hondo and had allowed himself to be farmed out to other bonding agencies in town, always chasing the hard cases, sometime with Hondo, sometimes alone.

Sometime in the future ya ever need some time off, just sing out, but let me know about certain things, so I can cover your six. Ya follow", said Rafferty. Like maybe that you're out of the country for a certain period of time on Company business, like the little trip I want you and Hondo on next week. Go home and get some rest this evening, I'll get Valdez booked into the County lockup when he wakes up"!

As Jaeger drove back to his apartment, thoughts of Sheriff Morgan Little flooded his mind. Memories of his family back in happier times and to know that Sheriff Little was behind all of it was almost more than he could stand. He'd stayed in control of himself for far too long and prayed to whatever entity that would hear, to keep him alive until all was made right. Then the names of "Little, Baintree, Womble and Ryder", came into his head. Soon, quite soon, he'd have to find a way to get them all together in the same place.

The following day Jaeger met with Rafferty and Hondo at Rafferty's office. Wanda was up to her eyeballs doing the paper work for a family that wanted their son bailed out on an auto theft charge. "Let's go to the café across the street, where we can talk", said Rafferty over the commotion!

As they went out the door, Wanda glared at Rafferty saying, "Y'all will bring me back some lunch now won't ya"! Prompting Rafferty to stick his head back in the door saying, "Yes Wanda. Will the Philly Cheese Steak with all the fixin's, be OK"?

She busily nodded her head, waving them all away, prompting Chips to say, "Damn women, can't do with em an ya can't do without em"!

As the trio settled in to the café booth deep in the rear of the restaurant, prior to the lunch rush, they all ordered coffee and after it arrived, Rafferty started out, "Got a call from Buffy, last night and she asked me to look into something and nose around to see if I could come up with a solution"!

"What's the problem Chips", asked Jaeger stirring his cup?

"Well ya know we all got this internet thing going round, where just about everything is connected by telephone, especially banking transactions. Don't quite know how they do it, but seems like everything's being put on computer these days and there are some folks in Mexico, very smart folks that are able to hack into a computer system and have money transferred to offshore accounts, in the early morning hours and they can do this while thousands of miles away".

Continuing on Chips said, "There are four separate groups in the world that are scamming the banks. One is in Helsinki Finland, as far as anyone knows, another is in Lagos Nigeria, another is in Hong Kong, and the one that's hitting our country hard is in Nuevo Laredo, Mexico, specifically Boys Town. In case one doesn't know, Boys Town is wall to wall whore houses and the only reason that place exists is the purveyance of pussy.

Generation after generation of whores going back farther than anyone can remember spread their legs, to milk the bull, so to speak. Now two clubs in particular are Papaguyo's and the Miramar are the premier establishments and as we all know, they are essentially walled compounds and on top of these walls are embedded glass and nails, that'll give anyone a surprise trying to go up and over".

But that shouldn't concern you except to point them out as landmarks. Both are a few city blocks from each other, but in between them is a single building. A two story building, that's bustling with electronics and that's where some enterprising people, some very smart eggheads are secretly hacking into our banking system. Buffy can get all of the details, if needed"!

"Now your gonna ask why isn't our State Department trying to put the quash on these guys"? And the answer is, they've tried but seems no one on the other end is listening, since they're all on the pad. 'Mordida', the bite.

Now seems the drug honcho's down there would be interested on getting in on some of the action, but not for some strange reason. Seems that some folks, in our government will pay very handsomely to get their hands on the two guys who are the brains of this outfit for prosecution and if somehow along the way, the building and all of its hardware goes up in smoke, all the better"!

"The price tag for all this", asked Hondo?

"Half a Mill", said Rafferty.

"Cash Money", asked Jaeger?

"What's the split, this end", asked Hondo?

"If you guys are all in, I get ten percent for a finder's fee and certain contingencies like running the show, and the rest is divvied up by whoever is involved. You do the math"!

"All anticipated expenses fronted, as usual", asked Jaeger?

"That's what I'm for", nodded Rafferty? Jaeger and Hondo both nodded their heads at each other, saying simultaneously, "Vultee, Duke Vultee"!

"Duke Vultee? He's out", exclaimed Rafferty?

"He came out with me and Roy Seltzer, almost two years ago and he and Roy are running two of Buffy's titty bars in town"!

"Damn, Duke Vultee on the loose, why that guy can make explosives from stuff ya get in the drug store or any supermarket"?

"So we hear", nodded Jaeger.

"Here's the way it's gotta be", said Jaeger emphatically. Work it up the line that the price'll be 750 k, plus 75 more for working capital, vehicles, bribes, weapons, ect. The money will be in a safe deposit box in a bank here in town. You know the drill, old bills etc. Buffy'll be the transfer agent. The working capital will flow thru you as we need it, in advance. We bring the bodies in alive and breathing hopefully, but if something happens to any of them in transit across country, it doesn't change the terms of payout. They furnish us all the information they have on the subjects in advance, pictures, maps, personal histories, everything with the seventy five K working capital. Then we'll know we have a deal. When we bring in Mr. Lucky and his partner, deliverable to Buffy or her designated agent, then the dough will be immediately payable on demand. Now Chips, I know and trust Buffy, but I don't know who she's involved with so it's imperative we know who she's talking to, catch my drift"? Rafferty nodded in agreement.

"The plan'll be simple. We all go down there separately, check the lay of the land. Take up different residences within walking distance of the building. We'll give you a laundry list of things we'll need before we leave, then you'll mail them down by Fed Ex. We pick them up and go to work.

My guess is that their building'll be guarded by locals of some sort. We ring the building with homemade Semtex, enough to turn it into one big pile, but not until an hour after we do a snatch and grab, on your two Honcho's. Fill em full of Thorazine and stash em in the vehicle, for the long trip back. All goes well; it should take about thirty days".

"Sounds simple enough Jaeger", said Rafferty.

"It won't be Chips"!

Later that afternoon, they visited Vultee at his club and filled him in about the possibilities, with Vultee saying, "Three days out of pocket can be explained but any longer? But I know just what you'll need and It'll take me, in stages, about five days in my spare time to put enough together, along with the detonation devices and anything else you'll need. I'll lay it all out in advance for ya and give ya written directions"!

Three days later, Rafferty received the front expenses required and called Jaeger to a brief meeting between court sessions at the Harris County Court House. He met up with Buffy as she was going from one court room to another hurriedly as she reached into her pocket and slipped him a name and contact information of her contact, saying "This guy is a lobbyist for the Bankers in Washington and his cousin is a Federal Prosecutor on the make for a smash mouth case to make his rep. One of a bunch of young Turks in Washington. They don't know you or anyone you may be affiliated with. A lotta people want this thing solved, without soiling federal hands. I don't know these people all that well, but seeing that you've your expenses in hand, it must be an indicator that they're serious people. Should they prove not to be in any way, I'm certain you'll know what to do, Jaeger", she whispered. Just then the elevator door opened and she stepped in with a gaggle of others, as the door closed, she gave Jaeger a wink and a nod of good Luck.

The entire file on the two subjects was studied repeatedly by Jaeger and Hondo, along with the grainy pictures taken at some distance. Approx. height, weight and all the known vitals. Gonna need a small to midsize truck, said Hondo. Used, with a good engine, I'm thinking full sized Ford Bronco or Chevy Blazer, four wheel drive. Within two days they had their vehicle, a light brown 85 Ford Bronco four wheel drive truck, in need of a paint job, but all else was in good working order. Next they went to the metal working shop, where an old friend of Jaeger from his Ellis Unit days, patiently welded the prefabricated rectangular metal containers with a door to the vehicles undercarriage, out of sight to all but the most curious.

When Luke had finished he said, "goin' over and empty won't be a problem, but comin' back another thing", as he handed them each a beer. Then Hondo slipped him an envelope and as Luke peered inside, he said, "A tad more than we agreed upon isn't it Hondo"?

"A little Lagniappe for a bad memory, ya think?

"Up and under all tucked away. Should hold around three hundred pounds each, with twenty four inches ground clearance", mused Luke. "But right now I can't rightly remember a thing".

As they all bid each other good bye and Luke going back inside his shop, Hondo said, "Luke was right, goin' over the International Bridge to Nuevo Laredo will be the easy part, but coming back is another thing"!

"We won't be going back the same way. There's another way a ford, that during the dry season, the river won't be higher than eighteen to twenty inches in height", said Jaeger.

On successive days each of the trio, visited the Federal Express office in town, depositing a foot locker sized container to be shipped to Nuevo Laredo, Mexico, general delivery. After the third day all was in readiness for their departure south of the border, with Jaeger taking a Trail Way's bus, followed the next day by Hondo driving the Ford Bronco and, the third day followed by Vultee taking the bus.

Jaeger procured a rented room, not one half block from the subjects building, across the street, on the second floor of the building, then Hondo another room a half a block away in the other direction, the following day. Two days later Hondo picked up Vultee, in the Ford Bronco. What helped things immeasurably was the theft of Mexican License plates, from two different cars for the Bronco the very first thing, by Jaeger, during the dark of night, anything to help them blend in.

By the time that Vultee arrived, Jaeger and Hondo had surveiled the subject building, for two days, purchased yet another used car in Mexico and then waited. Hondo drilled them repeatedly in the placement of the specially prepared Semtex explosives.

"How come you chose to make Semtex rather than C-4 detonations", asked Hondo?

"Oh, one is pretty much as good as the other, it's just that C-4 is known worldwide as American issue, while Semtex, being of a different explosive, is usually of Soviet issue and is the explosive of choice by the Soviets and the Rag Heads. Just another way to confuse those hot shots trying to figure out who blew it up. Both are 'Le Plastique'"!

At the end of their second day of surveillance both subjects were sighted, entering and departing the building. All access and egress was done in the darkness of night. The was no sight of any external guards and during a gradual extensive look see at night, the front of the two story building was well lit by a single street lamp, with the sides partially lit with areas of deep shadows and the rear of the building completely dark at night.

"Look for cameras, especially night vision and then there are always motion detectors" said Vultee.

"Wouldn't motion detectors be set of by any movement even those of dogs, cats, or birds", asked Jaeger"?

"We know of a front entrance", said Vultee. "But what about a rear entrance"? "If critters are setting off their motion detectors, then someone will have to come outside and investigate. Failing in that, night vision CATV will be the ticket for the sides and the rear of the structure. You'll have to gain entrance to the top of surrounding buildings and look through your high powered telephoto day/night binoculars and cameras, to see everything that might be available to them. I'll hang around an extra evening and scope out the front of the building, while each of you select a higher structure nearby with a good view of the rear And a given side of the structure"!

As he glanced out of the front of Jaegers window, Vultee pointed out two buildings with a good vantage point of the rear and a side of the building.

The following morning they all met in Vultee's room and both Vultee and Jaeger agreed that while camera's we're mounted on the roof, they were poorly mounted, for the very sides of the building were completely blind for about six feet, given the angle of where the lenses were placed, plus the fact that various places around the structure had a combination of bushes, wild untended weeds and trash piled up against the building.

"Given the age of the building and what I believe their quality of constructions is, it's probably of wood brick and mortar construction, with zip rebar placement. Which means that it is of poor quality and any kind of significant earthquake will bring it down 'muy pronto'. Bad for them, good for us"!

After a morning of sleep, Jaeger brought back some food and drink and the all set about constructing twenty explosive devices apportioning the Semtex into twenty separate blocks, with twenty battery operated detonators and timing devices. They went over precisely where the devices were to be placed all around the building. Unlike the movies, no external blinking lights were visible, so once they were placed, all one had to do upon departure was press a single button on a miniature master hand held detonator and a separate clock would start, giving the others an hour to be somewhere else with their cargo.

His work done, Jaeger took Vultee back to the Nuevo Laredo Bus station the following morning and dropped him off. By nightfall Vultee should be back at work tending his flock of barely clad ladies, doing social work amongst the lax and horny.

The following week, Jaeger and Hondo worked separate and apart from each other chronicling the comings and goings of the partners and the few helpers in the building, discovering that each of them had a girl friend at the ready, and that both had become very lax in their security given the magnitude of what they were gleaning.

Before they had left Houston, they learned that the Mexican

enterprise had made off with over two hundred million dollars of American depositors money spread out over twenty some odd banks. No doubt immediately placed through Panamanian banks then wire transferred to a slew of off shore bank accounts. Ten thousand here, fifty thousand there. As fast as the various banks were able to repair their internet firewalls, they would be again be breached within the week and great American banking whore was again available to suckle the needy.

After two weeks of around the clock surveillance, a pattern of activity began to surface, every Tuesday one of the Honcho's would visit his girlfriend and every Thursday, the other would visit his girlfriend, each spending the entire night. Then every Saturday night, they would visit a different night spot, for the world to see, them on display. For the pedestrian level female mind just had to show the world how lucky she'd been, sporting some round shouldered genius around for the others to see and be envious. While the object of her affections was showered with all of the usual public displays of affection, he'd never imagined as a child prodigy coming up through the ranks of academia. Then later when they were duly satiated, his bought and paid for inamorata, would make it a point to introduce him to the inner wonders of femininity, completely and in full measure. By four in the morning they both would be deep in the arms of Morpheus, not to awaken until the sun had reached its zenith. Sometimes they would spend the Sunday together, sometimes he would beg off, drained completely of his inner essences, returning to his cash cow with renewed zeal, only to return on his appointed weekday evening for yet another session of slap and tickle.

Once their routine was firmly established in the minds of Jaeger and Hondo and appropriate means of silent entry was established into each mini harems abode. Jaeger and Hondo set out to lay in wait for the two teams of lovers to land. At the appointed time, here they came the first of the two teams, early on a Sunday morning. Waiting an hour for the first duo to spend themselve's into deep oblivion, Jaeger and Hondo entered, quickly injecting a measured amount of Thorazine into the musculature of their subject, then a much smaller amount into the buttocks of their willing Houri. Their cargo would be hor's de combat for at least the next twenty hours, while his partner was assured of the deepest of sleep, almost until the following day's sundown.

An hour later they repeated the exercise, extracting their cargo and leaving his girlfriend deep into her dreams, only to awaken the following afternoon arrayed, naked in all her glory, her meal ticket gone forever, with the certain knowledge that she would once again have to ply her wares at Pappa Cats or the Miramar, to the dregs of the world.

Their respective rooms previously wiped clean of any signs of their presence and their cargo safely loaded, inert in the inner bowels of the Ford Bronco, Hondo ditched his car on a side street and joined Jaeger in the Bronco. They made their way past the two story building in question, with Jaeger at the wheel and Hondo pressing the button of the triggering device. Twenty previously placed explosives all timed to sequentially explode, a split second apart all around the facility, in one hour's time, guaranteed to be an exciting Sunday Morning for the residents of the neighborhood, and a rather nasty surprise, for the few occupants of the building weary from their all-night vigil.

As Hondo pressed the button, each sequential red light flashed on his receiver. Twenty devices, twenty flashes, then Hondo said, "Were good to go pal. Let's head north"!

Driving the back streets of Nuevo Laredo, Jaeger quickly found himself on the east side searching for that singular place in the Rio Grande River and driving slowly through the brush with his lights out, as not to draw any undue attention as to their presence, for the fording point where during the dry season, his ancestor Henry Jaeger set out with twenty head of longhorn Mexican cattle and started the legend. As he searched his memory in the darkness of night, the stories of the first of the American Jaegers, crossing the Rio Grande returned, for the legend had been repeated so many times when he was a child, that every word was deeply imprinted into his skull.

After almost an hour of searching, he stopped the Bronco and briefly turned on his head lights, seeing the small ripples of the water of the river as they passed over the high point in the river that lay ahead. Charting the exact path across, he then turned off the headlights saying, "Cross your fingers pal", to Hondo and put the vehicle into four wheel drive mode, shifting into first gear and slowly made his way across the river.

"Keep an eye out on your side for the water level, and sing out if it gets near the door level of the cab. Wouldn't want to deliver our cargo all drowned", to Hondo. Thankfully the Rio Grande at that point of the river, was a scant hundred yards wide and as they made slow progress across the fording point, eventually the vehicle came to the American side of the river and made its way up and over the gradual bank in that very same spot that his ancestor re-entered the State of Texas over a hundred and fifty years ago.

As they stopped at the rise through the rivers embankment, looked at their watch, then turned around and within seconds saw the flash of a distant explosion in Boys Town, then some ten seconds later heard the explosion.

Hondo then said, "Damn that boy Vultee does do good work! Put her in gear pal, if we hustle we can be in Houston by supper time"!

A half hour later, while refueling at a gas station on US 59 in Freer Texas, Jaeger got on the pay phone and dialed Rafferty's private number.

"Now who in the hell is callin' me up this time of morning", said the cranky voice on the other end of the phone!

"Drop your cock and grab your socks pal", bellowed Jaeger into the phone. "Sometime around supper time, your package will be delivered and you'll be busy getting all concerned parties rounded up and at your office. Oh, and one more thing you're buying dinner tonight at a place of our choosing", then he abruptly hung up!

The drive back to Houston was long and they weren't in any particular hurry. Enjoying the scenery as they leisurely made their way back to the big city staying under the posted speed limit.

Around four in the afternoon the old cranky Ford Bronco pulled up to the front of Rafferty's Bail Bonding and pulled into the small parking lot that adjoined the structure. Within seconds, Rafferty, Buffy and several US Marshall types, along with a few others surrounded the vehicle looking inside and finding nothing. Rafferty said, "Where's the beef"? Jaeger and Hondo wearily poured out of the vehicle saying, "S'cuse me and promptly scooted underneath the Bronco, loosening three hand turned external screws allowing the long rectangular doors to flop open, then both men said, "A little help here", as they wrestled both of the still inert and drugged captives to drop to the ground, naked as the day they were born.

As Jaeger and Hondo stood erect turning both captives over to the Federal Marshals for disposition, Jaeger said, "No one will be getting into the banks for quite awhile from that location. Ya might wanna check the Laredo and the Nuevo Laredo News Papers for the details, folks"!

Just then Buffy looked at one of the 'Suits' that accompanied them and received his nod of approval then handed Jaeger, Hondo and Rafferty three large bulging manila envelopes holding a forth envelope by her side.

Jaeger then said, "You might as well hand that envelope to me, for it'll be delivered to the right hands within the hour"!

"Of course Jaeger", said Buffy, handing over the envelope, without even looking at the accompanying suit. The delivery made and the Federal Marshals on their way to the lockup with their cargo, Jaeger, Rafferty, Buffy and Hondo made their way, uptown to deliver the last of the packages and celebrate for the evening, the wheels of Justice turning one more cog in the circle of life.

An hour later they all huddled at one of Buffy's clubs called 'Strangers', where a monster repast was laid out, to celebrate, Jaegers victory. The club was sparsely attended on Sunday evenings, so a skeleton staff was on board. The girls in the club were completely unaware that a woman was the majority owner of the establishment and when Buffy entered the club, with all of these men, looking every bit as wonderful as the other girls, yet fully attired in slacks and a loose fitting blouse, with scant makeup, the others looked on her as an intrusion, to their turf.

But since this was Roy Seltzers club, to partially manage, he showed; once again that he could serve as a wonderful host, keeping the girls at bay, while serving the finest Prime Rib of Beef, with all of the accoutrements.

As the evening drew on, Buffy was seated next to Jaeger, while Hondo regaled the others with a blow by blow account of their Mexican adventure. She leaned close to Jaeger, saying, "Next week, Sheriff Little will announce that he will not run for reelection and in six months after he formally leaves office, the very day, Odessa will release to every media outlet in the state, all of the material we have on Baintree, Ryder, Little and Judge Womble.

Now I hear that Judge Womble is in ill health and the news of his participation in your conviction, just may be too much for his poor old heart, so I expect the old fart will croak under all of the scandal"!

"Interesting news Buffy, but that won't undue what's been done.

They'll get indicted, hire some hot shot lawyer, drag the cases out, spend a lotta cash and in the end there's no guarantee that they'll spend one day in prison, much less return any of my family's property. Hell, we went up to Waco a few months back and much of the family homestead has already been developed over the years. How do you undo that? Besides, their all high profile figures, not like those eggheads we just brought back. Even if they do get convicted, I kinda doubt they'll spend any time in anything like Huntsville Prison"!

"And if they could all be gotten together in one spot, for one evening", asked Buffy? "Could you work your magic then and find a way for them to disappear"? She continued on,"Since Don Ryder and his family holds title to the vast majority of what's left, should he no longer be available to fight any litigation for restitution of your property, since all the other members of your family have given their voting proxy's to him. It might take a while but I'm certain that restitution could be effected. Remove the soiled trinity and all things are possible! Think about it then tell me what you want to do. We have some time"!

41

It had been years since Jaeger had entered a church and celebrated the word of the almighty. He strained his memory, to the last week he spent with his parents in Waco, when they attended Mass, to give thanks for the safety of their son after the Cotton Bowl game. But more important, the rift between Jaeger and his father was miraculously healed, with the prodigal son back in the family fold once again.

As he made the sign of the cross, before taking a seat in the pew of the empty church, the old liturgy of the profession of faith, eventually came flooding back into his consciousness, as he silently mouthed the words, "I believe in one God, the Father, the Almighty, maker of heaven and earth, of all that is seen…. . and unseen"!

When he was finished, he just sat there, looking up at the figure of the Jeshua Christo, hanging on that cross, concluding quickly, that were it not for the grace of the unseen, he'd not be sitting right there at this very moment. His thoughts then drifted to that of his two sisters long gone.

They'd no doubt be married by now and have a passel of children of their own, doted over by Jaegers mother and dad on a daily basis. He imagined the sounds of children's laughter, permeating all over the great house. Then he thought of his loving mother. What horror must have passed before her eyes, as she saw her children gunned down by inhuman creatures? What were her last words?

What about his father? The trial indicated that he was the very first to be gunned down. What was going through his mind as he slipped the bonds of life, helpless in his prime filial duty to protect his family. Just at the very moment, where old insults were forgotten and father and son could become one, it was all horribly whisked away.

Then the tears started to come. He tried to fight them back, but it was no use. If he had just one wish, he'd gladly change places with them all, but that was not to be. What was done, was done. Over the years, he'd concluded the shooters, met their end, soon after the event, and the proof of their complicity vanished with their disappearance. But there were four people left that were indeed culpable. Living the good life all these years, while Jaeger languished in prison.

He's taken other's lives before a number of times, never once giving it a second thought, but just a part of his job. What he was trained to do, amongst other things. Hardened by his years in the 'Corps' and during his time at the 'Ellis Unit', he reviewed what had gone past, concluding, that it was all in preparation for what lay ahead. The lives he'd taken in the past were mostly a preemptory action, in defense of himself or others in his charge. Yet now, things were different. Unfinished business lay ahead and he must divest himself of all foolish notions, of civilized action. What lay ahead was premeditated murder, straight up. Required to right a wrong that could never be restored.

As he sat there in the pew thinking, trying to summon reason and enlightenment, he knew he was losing the battle. Why, after all was he here, in this place? He could have this conversation with himself any old place.

What brought him here, into God's house? Eventually it came to him. Simply to ask forgiveness for what was about to come. The wheels were set in motion long ago and the inertia of the Juggernaut was about to begin.

'Please God, forgive me for what I'm about to do', he implored silently.

The conundrum of the Commandments, between whether or not it was, 'Thou shalt not kill, versus, Thou shalt not murder', seemed inconsequential, since soon he was to set about taking the lives of four men, slowly and very painfully, regretting but one thing, that all of them could only die once and the very last thing they would ever see, is Jaeger looking them straight in the eyes asthey breathed their last. As he rose to leave the church, he stepped out of the pew, kneeled, making the sign of the cross and turned to leave, thinking all the while of what actions the unholy trinity would plan. In several months Sheriff Little would retire from his office, then Buffy would return several envelopes of their activities to them and hopefully they would think that it was all over and they were home free.

But she'd see to it that Odessa Robillard, would announce the news publicly of their complicity in his family's murder and the framing of him. So what would he do if he were them?

The hard case would be Sheriff Little and the weak link would be

Don Ryder, he concluded. Now he had the time and the means with which to plan coming events. 'It was time he took some time off from Rafferty's and tended to his own business', he thought as he drove out of the church's parking lot, but not too much time. The stack of 'Runner', files had diminished to a point, to where Hondo could handle it on his own, he concluded. He'd call Rafferty this afternoon and tell him that he was taking some time off and that he'd check in with him from time to time, in case he was needed.

For the next three months, he shadowed each of the subjects of his interests, Governor Baintree, Sheriff Little, Donald Ryder and finally Judge Morris Womble. He discovered that Royce Baintree had a mistress, a dancer in one of Austin's pricier Gentlemen's clubs. EveryThursday evening, like clockwork he would arrive at her apartment, spend three hours or so, then depart, with a smile on his weathered face.

Likewise was the situation with Donald Ryder. Once again a local stripper in his club, yet with Ryder there was no set time that he visited his main squeeze. He visited Ryder's club on the Dallas, Fort Worth Turnpike, in disguise, on multiple occasions, assessing the layout and the girl in particular and even at one point Ryder came in the club and passed right by Jaeger without a hint of recognition.

That completed, he then spent over a month in the Waco area, shadowing Sheriff Morgan Little and Judge Womble, discovering little of value, except that both lead apparently mundane lives, following very rigid habits of their comings and goings. Of the two, Judge Womble was the least wary, going about his daily routine completely oblivious of his surroundings. He would be the easiest to approach.

As for Morgan Little, Jaeger gave him the closest scrutiny one could give at a distance. From time to time, Jaeger flirted with the idea of shadowing him up close, to test his ability to disguise himself, but thought better of it. A man like Morgan Little, wouldn't have survived and prospered this long, without some sort of sixth sense that danger was close at hand.

Having planted a miniature radio transponder on the Sheriff's personal as well as his County patrol vehicle, Jaeger settled for shadowing the Sheriff at some distance, to determine his comings and goings.

As Jaeger took his well-earned sabbatical, Chips Rafferty called Buffy Beauvior at her office to tell her that Jaeger was going to be 'out of pocket' for a while. After hanging up the phone, Buffy placed a call to Randall White, asking him to awaken the offsite telephone bugs on the Governor, Don Ryder and Sheriff Little, until told otherwise.

Several days a week Morris Womble drove to the Baylor University Campus, to walk his little Yorkshire terrier and mull over the happier times he spent pursuing his undergraduate studies at his alma mater, always alighting on the very same park bench. After all, his doctor said that with his medication and an adjustment in his dietary regimen along with some modest exercise should go a long way in bringing down his blood pressure to more moderate levels now that he was in retirement. However the caveat was clear, he was to avoid any activity that created an over exertion of any kind. Moderation in all things was the order of the day if he was to enjoy any reasonable quality time while in retirement.

Judge Womble, particularly enjoyed spending the lunch hour, while sitting on this one particular bench under a spreading Pin Oak tree, for it was at this very tree, long ago, where he first proposed to his wife of many years. When she relented and said a tearful "Yes", it was one of the happiest days of his life. Sometimes he would spend the entire time alone on that bench watching the next generation of citizens, scurrying about oblivious to his existence, while other times someone would join him on that bench, under the generous shade of the old tree and they would engage in small talk for a time.

He'd usually arrive sometime around eleven thirty in the morning and depart sometime after one in the afternoon, waiting until the afternoon classes had commenced. He'd always be nattily attired, in a sport coat and tie of a sort, every mindful to keep his container of Nitro Glycerin pills, in his coat pocket, at the ready, just in case of emergency.

One fateful day Jaeger decided to join him on that park bench, attired in a hop sacked sport coat and loosely knotted tie, wearing horn rimmed glasses and a Texas Rangers baseball cap, looking every bit the College Professor, carrying a portfolio presumably full of books and papers. Jaeger had decided to test the extent of Wombles alleged heart condition and to raise a little dust in the process.

Judge Womble had just settled in to his favorite park bench when Jaeger approached him, leaning heavily on a cane as he approached the park bench asked, "May I join you sir", in his finest Chicago accent?

"Why of course young man", replied Womble!

As Jaeger sat down on the far end of the bench, he placed his bulging portfolio between them saying, "Just the place where one can have a peaceful repast away from the gaggle of students"!

"Do you teach here", inquired Womble?

"Why yes I do sir! I'm so sorry where's my manners", Jaeger said absently! "My name is Mark West and I just joined the faculty last semester and your name is sir, he said reaching out his hand, in greeting.

"Morris Womble, and I'm glad to meet you young man", he said reaching out his hand in friendship.

As Jaeger fumbled abound his portfolio to retrieve the sandwich, bag of chips and chilled can of soda he'd purchased from the Student Union, he heard Womble ask, "So you just joined the Baylor faculty"!

"They enticed me away from the bosom of my Alma Mater, the University of Chicago, where, I taught Classical Management Theory and I'm trying to bring a degree of enlightenment to these fine students at Baylor", replied Jaeger as he opened his can of soda, eagerly taking a drink.

"And you sir. Are you a graduate from this institution"?

"Yes I am. Performed my undergraduate matriculation here, later received my Juris Doctorate in Law from Texas Christian University, practiced law for a while, then became a circuit judge here in Waco for many years and I've recently retired", replied Womble proudly!

"Interesting", replied Jaeger absently while chewing eagerly his BLT sandwich. "I wonder what would happen if Fredrick Taylor, that father of Classical Management Theory and Salmon P. Chase, ever met", asked Jaeger absently in a feeble attempt at making small talk. "What would they have in common to discuss"?

As Jaeger and Judge Womble continued their small talk, Jaeger took note of the Judge's physical posture, indicating the Judge's relaxed positioning and started to subtly mirroring his positions to that of the Judge. Within a very few minutes of random conversation, he and the Judge were laughing about the most mundane of things, with the Judge saying, "It's been far too long, Mr. West, since I've met someone of our intellectual level that I could have a pleasant level of verbal discourse with"! "Likewise Judge and please call me Mark if you will"!

The conversation briefly drifted into the realm of politics, again with Jaeger matching the Judges views with his own bringing them closer and closer attitudinally. Then the conversation drifted into the realm of economics, with both of them exchanging similar views on the state of macroeconomics as it existed in the United States today, with Jaeger offering, "You know Judge, I briefly toyed with the idea of becoming an economist in my undergraduate days, but as my studies continued, I concluded that economists in general haven't a clue".

"Oh Mark", asked the Judge, "Why is that"?

"Since you asked", offered Jaeger with a wry wink, "Seems to me that little has advanced ever since Adam Smith wrote the 'Wealth of Nations', in the late seventeen hundreds" he said, continuing. "Since the man is pretty much universally acknowledged as the father of modern day economics by the world's intellects, there is a plethora of diverse economic theorem, very little of which coincides, much like your world of Juris Prudence, don't you think"?

"Well, young man, I agree that the body of laws that govern man is subject to vast schisms of diverse interpretation from time to time summoning vast and spirited debate, but that is the burden that society places upon us"!

"However shouldn't there be a commonality as to what is right and what is wrong", asked Jaeger"?

The Judge pondered a moment, then answered, "Years ago, as a student in pre law, I asked the professor, why lawyers and judges always answered when asked what they did for a living, "I practice Law", or a derivative of that term. Those words always troubled me, for if I were a common man and I was in a legal bind, and upon engaging the services of a learned member of the bar, to find me a viable way out of my predicament, I wouldn't want someone to 'practice', I'd want someone who could deliver the goods. Well the good professor placed things in proper perspective for me when he answered, "Given the never ending dynamics of human interaction and the world as it is, one never can master ones craft for it is ever changing and dynamic"!

"So that might also apply to the disciplines of, Medicine, Science, Architecture, Engineering, et al", asked Jaeger quickly?

"Precisely young man"!

"Well what did it for me against Economics was one day, the Dean of the Economics Department, threw a little get together at his Campus residence, for his best students and in the middle of some ribald economic debate, brought the house down with the ultimate definition of an 'Economist', which is quote, "If one takes every bona fide economist in this world and lays them end to end at the equator, they will circle the globe eight times and point in all directions"!

This summoned a huge series of almost uncontrollable laughter from Judge Womble, who eventually started to choke, finding it hard to catch his breath.

As Jaeger, leaned over seeming to comfort the Judge who appeared to be in some minor distress, he asked, "Judge are you alright"?

Appearing to regain some of his normal coloring and breathing normally once again, the Judge said, "I must be careful, for I've a bit of a heart condition, that requires that I not become over excited, but I'm feeling better now"?

Casually noting the time was nearing One PM and the students were now going into the various buildings for afternoon classes, leaving the campus in general almost deserted, Jaeger decided that it was time for the grand Apocalypse.

"Speaking of the law Judge I wonder if you could answer something for me that's been rather troubling as of late" and before the Judge could speak continued, "The other day, while I was at lunch at the Student Union, I overheard some of the students quite perplexed about an apparent miscarriage of justice that occurred a while back. Seems that an entire family had been murdered and the eldest son, just back from his days in the military, was enrolled at the University of Texas, was framed for their murder and incarcerated for life, in Huntsville"!

As Jaeger droned on he casually removed his ball cap and placed it on the bench continuing, "Now apparently a little while back his pardon was secured by his lawyer and he's a free man, but the question is Judge, will this man ever forgive those responsible for the death of his family and the theft of his family's estate"? At that, Jaeger removed his horn rimmed glasses, removing the last remnants of his thin physical disguise.

"Now I hear this man is loose in the world and that he's been known to do terrible things to people. Unspeakable things"!

As Womble listened, Jaeger noted that Womble was now sitting more erect and his eyes were flicking around. "Then the students mentioned the name of a local Judge who was responsible for the man's egregious imprisonment, and the name the mentioned was a certain Judge Womble", said Jaeger absently.

He let that sink in for a moment, then continued, "My god, could it be?

Your name is Womble and you're a retired local judge. Could you be the infamous Judge Womble", Jaeger asked in mock surprise, his Chicago accent returning to that of his native Texas.

At that point Womble was beginning to tremble uncontrollably as Jaeger then said, "Turn your head Judge and look into the eyes of the man you sentenced to prison many years ago"!

Grasping his arm Jaeger growled, "Look at me"! As the Judge turned his head, he was compelled to look into Jaegers eyed and he saw the look of death, that of a shark, without forgiveness or remorse, for the past, the present, or the future"!

As the Judges blood pressure escalated uncontrollably, he tried to pull away, but Jaegers firm but apparently relaxed grasp held him in place. As Morris Wombles eyes met Jaeger's unadorned face, he finally recognized Jaeger as not the collegial professor, but the man he conspired against so long ago and croaked a weak, "You", in grudging recognition.

"That's right you fucking weasel, now you recognize this face. The face that's going to haunt you every moment that you spend in hell, with Baintree, Ryder and you're palMorgan Little"! Summoning up the feeble strength to jerk his hand free and fumble around in his coat pocket for his container of 'Nitro' pills, his hand emerged and struggled amidst the mounting pain of the coronary he was experiencing, to open the container, momentarily forgetting in his panic to push the lid down before turning, Jaeger placed both of his massive hands over the Judges saying, "Here, let me help ya", and pressed down and turned the lid slowly. As the lid slowly opened, the Judge felt his arm jerk just once and saw his precious pills flying out of the plastic container and onto the ground.

Then he heard a "Whoops, let me go get one of those little boogers for ya", as he saw Jaegers form go to the ground ever so slowly in search of just one pill, just one. As the pain grew, and his breath became even more labored, he wondered what was taking the man so long to find just one of those damnable pills?

Eventually Jaeger came back up to sit next to the Judge saying,

"Seems this isn't going to be one of your better days Judge", in a matter of fact way. "Apparently the ground has swallowed your pills all up! All gone. Kaput"!

"Looks like you'll be taking the down elevator, but don't worry, soon you'll be in the company of friends, three of them in fact, as Jaeger turned his head gently in his direction by placing both hands gently on the side of his head, wiping his prints from the pill bottle.

"Soon the lights will go out and all your earthly worry's will vanish, only to be replaced by others, but before you go, remember my face for its gonna be the last thing you see on god's green earth and it'll be with you every, single, moment."! Just then he felt Judge Womble, grow limp.

Feeling for a pulse at his throat and finding none, then twisting his finger as he removed it, as to not leave a good imprint for the autopsy that was sure to follow, he left the man as he was, gathering up his trash and putting it in his bulging portfolio. Then putting on sunglasses and his ball cap, he slowly rose making his way across campus through the trees and back to his car.

All through the afternoon, classes started and concluded, with the occasional passerby paying little heed to the old man on the bench, looking down with sightless eyes, an empty pill container in one hand and its cap in the other, its contents on the ground in front of him. Concern only briefly by the occasional bird that landed, then quickly flew away. It wasn't until the dinner hour when a member of the campus security staff, on foot patrol passed him by, noticing that a chipmunk was sitting atop a slumped over man, while another was on the ground trying to make a meal of all these little pills on the ground.

The following afternoon, Sheriff Little stood beside the county coroner as he conducted the autopsy of Morris Womble's cadaver. Following every move with a well-practiced keen eye, there was no evidence of foul play regarding Judge Womble's untimely death. His heart and surrounding arteries displayed various massive blockages that had taken years to accrue, due to a faulty diet and lack of physical activity. An earlier phone consultation with Judge Wombles private physician verified that very fact.

The complete examination of the cadaver produced no evidence of physical harm, either internally or externally. Yet something was wrong in Morgan Little's mind, so he had his people reassess the park bench site, later in the afternoon. The entire bench was dusted for prints. For several days students were surveyed, yet revealed nothing, of value. Bulletins were posted on the campus bulletin boards, yet it seemed that no one even noticed or would acknowledge the periodical visits of the Judge to that location. Various prints showed that the bulk of the prints on the park bench were that of the Judge.

42

"Yeah Morgan I heard about the death of Judge Womble. But it didn't raise a stir outside of Waco", said Don Ryder. "So what of it"?

"I smell a rat Don, that's what of it. For about a few weeks now I been getting' this feelin' that I was being followed. Would go through the various counter measures to see if someone was tailin' me, but came up empty"!

"So", asked Ryder impatient for the Sheriff to continue?

"I'm getting' to it, don't rush me", a clearly angry Sheriff spat back! "So, on a hunch I go over my patrol car with a fine tooth comb and what do I find"?

"Dunno Morgan but I'll bet you're gonna tell me, aren't ya"!

"A magnetic transponder, neatly attached to the undercarriage of my patrol car. Way back in one of the recesses where it's not easily found. Then later on I go home and give both my personal car and that of my wife's the once over and I discover that someone has fit a transponder, neatly away on my personal car just like that of my patrol car"!

"Now Don, with a transponder, one can follow you at a distance, without your even knowing it"!

"Sounds pretty much like James Bond like stuff", said Ryder weakly. "Ryder get your head outta your ass and listen up! The average guy can't get ahold of stuff like this. Very hi tech material. This call is a warning to you to check every vehicle you own for a bug, twice. I mean put it up on a lift if ya have to, flash light, get dirty and scour every inch. Your car, your wife's car and that of your kids. Tomorrow, I'll send someone up there to sweep your office and home for any phone bugs"!

"OK Morgan, anything else"?

"Yeah, give Baintree a call and alert him to what's happened and tell him to do the same and while I'm thinking about it, have the same thing done for both of your girlfriends, cars and apartments. Then have Baintree call you back with what he's found and then you call me with the overall results, so I can plan a strategy, ya understand"?

"Call you this time tomorrow", said Ryder before hanging up!

In the time following his beloved wife's death, Leo Schwartzwald gradually lost interest in the day to day affairs of the law firm that he and his partners built up over the course of time. He would attend the necessary meetings of the partners and various groups, yet his mind was prone to wandering from time to time, from the subject at hand, with an increasing frequency. Oh, the ever so keen legal mind was still there, with the ability to recall legal precedent, but he was increasingly seen to stare out of the high rise window during meetings, still listening, but only with half a mind. Something that he never had done before and that no junior associate of the firm would dare to do. When asked, he would always jump back into the fray with a mild apology, and then pick back up the gist of the discussion, giving the appropriate opinion or direction as to where to discover binding legal precedent. Over time, as a trial lawyer, one had to give him very high marks as a litigator in behalf of his client and a highly skilled negotiator, but where he excelled above all, was his extensive recall of even the most obscure legal precedent, anywhere in the land. His legal library being simply for show, since it was all neatly tucked away and sorted in his head.

Gone were the days of seventy hour work weeks experienced in his youth as well as the standard forty hour weeks, most mortals experience in the course of their careers. His work schedule had diminished to a mere part time status of several mornings a week.

Gone was the sparkle in his eyes as he roamed through the office. In the early days of the firm, he was usually the first one in the office, each day and one of the last to leave. His penchant for legal research and advocacy, as necessary to his body and mind, as the air he breathed.

One lazy afternoon Boyd Parmalee, his most senior partner and who had been with Leo almost from the beginning, visited his home in the exclusive River Oaks area of town. As Parmalee exited from his shiny black 1987 Lincoln Continental, he could see Leo sitting on the side verandah of his vast two story home, watching congressional testimony on his portable TV, plugged into the outside cable outlet.

In the back he spotted George the firms Chauffer, working faithfully on the Lincoln Limousine, belonging to the firm, with the hood in the upright position. As he approached Leo, his presence was acknowledged by George with a cheery, "Hey, Mr. Boyd"!

"Back at ya George"!

"Can I get ya anything sir"?

"Oh perhaps a can of brew from the fridge if ya don't mind"!

"Comin' right up sir"!

"Ave, Boyd", said Leo absently, keeping close watch on the testimony on the CSPAN hearings!

"Hello, back at you also Leo", said Parmalee as he settled into one of the chairs next to Leo.

"Things slow at the office"?

"Nope, things are humming along as usual, just thought I'd pay you a personal visit, to see how you're getting along"!

"Goddamn career politicians. Preening for the cameras. Most of them lawyers, but not a damn one of them worthy of employment in the real world. Sucking at the tit of the body politic, living on a steady diet of half- truths, or outright lies, each ogling for an angle and damn few with any thought about the common good"!

"Thank you George", said Boyd as his can of cold beer arrived.

Just then as George went back to working on the Limo without a word, Leo said, "Other than you and Emma, no man ever had a better friend than that darkie George"!

"Yes I remember Leo, when you first brought him into the firm. What was it, some twenty years he's been with us"!

"Twenty three, next month", said Leo.

"Long odds were the partners concern that a convicted felon could ever serve the firm as well as he could"!

"Well, Boyd no matter what it was, a stretch in Huntsville apparently was his come to Jesus moment. A big roll of the dice that over time paid repeated dividends. Emma loved him as if he were a member of the family"!

"So how're you doing Leo"? Leo reached for the TV remote and turned the volume on mute, allowing the subtle sounds of afternoon jazz, coming from George's radio back in the multi car garage. "KTSU, Texas Southern University, the black spot on your dial, with the finest in jazz music, is their tag line Boyd! Never much cared for jazz music before George arrived, but thanks to him I've developed an appreciation for jazz and rhythm and blues music. Before Emma, I couldn't stand classical music, but thanks to her steady tutorials over the years, I became to appreciate the classical arts"!

"Seems that we've all been mutually blessed by the sure presence of each other", offered Boyd. "For example, your wise guidance at the helm of the firm, your ability to see what many others couldn't, in the selection of associates, allowed the firm to not only survive during the lean times, but prosper greatly during the times of plenty"!

"Thanks Boyd, but are you trying to butter me up for some reason"? "Just stating the facts Leo just the facts. And the fact is that everyone at the firm is worried about you, right down to the mail room clerk. You're not your old self and you haven't been ever since the passing of Emma. Oh the show is going on as usual, but folks are genuinely worried about you"!

Leo simply looked across the street, his mind somewhere else for several minutes, before saying, "I loved that woman about as much as any man could love a woman. When we discovered that she could never have any children, after years of trying, she almost had a breakdown, from the grief. As if somehow, she'd sinned against God somehow, but our love for each other stood strong, for I adored her, every scintilla of her being. You know, in all the years we were together, I can't recall either of us having a single argument about anything"?

"Your joint interests coincided completely", offered Parmalee!

"We lived in this great house with the expectation the walls would ring with children's laughter and when that wasn't to be, somehow it seemed far too much, too ostentatious. Then years later, when Buffy's parents died in that horrible auto accident when she was but a teenager, we went up to New Hampshire to help settle the family affairs and seeing that Elizabeth had no relatives able to care for her adopted her into our family"!

"I remember the time well Leo as if it were yesterday", said Parmalee! "Especially the first six months were rough going for a girl in her early teens. But she smoothed out splendidly, don't you think"?

"Never did acquire a Texican accent, but in all other things, she was a Texas woman through and through, Boyd", said Leo proudly. "Then when she went off to college back east we worried about her coming back deeply influenced by the liberal culture of elitism and universal entitlement"!

"But that didn't happen, did it Leo"!

"No by God it didn't Boyd. She came back to us, educated full of sass and sand as well as a well-rounded young lady able to stand on her own two feet, beholding to no one and by god Boyd you had a great deal to do with it in your own right and I have to thank you for that"!

"De nada Hombre, de nada", said Boyd with a chuckle as he sipped his beer. "Her presence with the firm has been nothing short of a blessing, her work ethic almost exceeding yours and as a legal advocate; she'd be able to stand against the likes of Percy Foreman in his prime or even Dershowitz. Her ability to mold a jury's opinion, in the final moments, as great as any of the renaissance Italian masters and we both can take some pride in that Leo"!

Continuing on Boyd offered, "Emma's niece became your daughter by an act of the eternal, placing her squarely in your midst as a blessing. Now what I'm concerned about is you Leo. Since Emma's passing, seems to everyone that your zest for living, much less the practice of law, has diminished. We need you back at the firm. We need you at the helm, to guide us through the shark infested waters and you need us Leo, for we are all family in case you haven't noticed"!

Again looking across the street and allowing his gaze to pass from tree to tree, following the birds and the squirrels going about their business, Leo eventually said, "Emma, was the one who gave my heart a reason to keep beating each day and now that she's gone", his voice trailing away into nothing.

There was silence between them, as the sounds of Miles Davis's horn echoed the lilting strains of "Killer Joe", in the background as George closed the Lincoln Limo's hood in triumph.

Then Leo spoke, "As you know, after I join Emma, whenever that is, I've provided well for George and the house maid Agnes, for as long as the firm exists or until they pass"! "And as you know that's been voted on and approved by the partners without a single dissenting vote"!

"And this house is to go to Elizabeth in its entirety"!

"Again signed, sealed and all but delivered, hopefully not for a very long time Leo"!

"And a variety of provisions to key 'non partner', members of the firm, who've been with us since the dark ages"!

"Again Leo, signed sealed and all but delivered, along with a brief amendment the partners universally agreed upon, that you were unaware of until this moment, the partners will match you dollar for dollar in this regard"!

"Not exactly a thrifty move Boyd"!

"We can well afford it Leo"!

"And Buffy will see to it that the rest goes to the Texas Children's Hospital, Boyd"!

"She's on the board Leo, as you well know"!

"Oh yes I forgot"!

"We need you back Leo, bright and shiny so the troops can smile once again"!

"Let's shoot for a Monday morning meeting Boyd. How about Nine AM, with the partners"!

"Done. I'll set it up! Now I'm going to nose around and see what George was up to before I leave and steal another one of your beers from the garage fridge if you don't mind and leave you to kvetching about those damn Washington politicians"!

As Boyd went towards the garage area to see George and grab another beer, he heard the volume of the TV set return to normal.

"George I'm gonna swipe another of those beers if you don't mind. Now stay as you are I'll get it"! As he returned he asked George, to open the hood and show him just what he was working on. As the hood of the firms Limo opened, Boyd was greeted with the sight of the cleanest engine he'd ever seen. Show room clean. Each part of the engine glistening, prompting Boyd to ask, "This Limo is over ten years old isn't it George"?

"Yessir, sure tis, fifteen years old to be exact and it's almost got over eighty thousand miles on the clock and doesn't burn a drop of oil", he beamed proudly.

"So how do you keep it in such great shape George"? "Hard work Mr. Boyd, hard work. The moment this Lincoln was converted into a Limo the Ford factory's warranty was cut back sharply what with all that was added to it. Mr. Leo sent me to mechanics school, bought a complete set of factory tools in the garage and said to me, that it just wouldn't do to have this fine car broke down on the side of the road. Besides, if I had my druthers, I wouldn't allow those factory mechanics to get anywhere near this vee hickle"!

"Excellent George, excellent! Now I want to ask you about Mr.

Schwartzwald, as to how he's doing? As we all can see he's still grieving over the passing of Miss Emma and doesn't seem to be improving and what you say will be held in the strictest of confidence"!

George reflected on this awhile and then said, "Miss Agnes and me are really worried about Mr. Leo"!

"In what way George"?

"Well sir, as you know she's a great cook and she gets here each morning by bus before any of us is awake, and the meals are ready on time. She tends to the laundry and keeps the house spic and span. But since Miss Emma crossed over, he just sits there, during his meals. On a good day he'll eat only part of his food and on a bad day he'll just push the food around on his plate. Then after its cold it becomes dog food. Now nobody does grits and biscuits better than Miss Agnes, or southern fried breaded pork chops with all the trimmings, which Mr. Leo never failed to enjoy to the last crumb. But now"?

"Which squares with his gaunt looking frame as of late, George. Anything else"?

"From time to time, I'll see him sittin' in that old rocking chair, in front of Miss Emma's mausoleum in the back yard, just sittin' there whispering 'Emma, Emma'. Sometimes he cries, sometimes he don't! Reminds me of my aunt Bea, when her husband died. They been together almost sixty years. Raised a family, had a pile of chilren, grand-chilren and great grandchilren. When my uncle's heart just gave out from old age, she spent the next year just waistin' away. Sittin onna front porch all day long, wouldn't eat much, lost a lotta weight and she had a lot to lose, just watchin' the world go by and every once in a while would say his name softly over and over, askin' him to wait up, that she was gonna join him soon"!

"And Mr. Boyd, a year later to the very day of her husband's death, the very hour, she joined him up above! She just didn't want to live anymore. She'd sit on that front porch and softly sing, 'Wade in the Water' and 'Amazing Grace', over and over and it just plain broke all of our hearts, to see her this way and there was no way any of us could talk her out of it. She was gonna get out of the way and make room for the rest of us. She'd done her work and now it was someone else's turn and she would be damned if she would take any charity from any of us. All her life she was a giver, Mr. Boyd. That's all she knew, or ever wanted to know. There was enough of us around to see to her needs, but she just plain wouldn't have it Mr. Boyd", said George with tears starting to form in his eyes, "And I see the very same thing happening to Mr. Leo and it breaks Miss Agnes and my heart, because Mr. Leo has been so good to us over the years and it's just not our place to say or do anything and we feel helpless"!

"Well George, if it's any comfort, you're in good company and what you've just related to me makes a lot of sense and I thank you for that.

Please tell Miss Agnes that no matter what the future brings and none of us want Mr. Leo to depart this mortal coil any time soon, both you and Miss Agnes are to continue as before and are considered part of the family and are not to worry about anything. Now for the present I'm not at liberty to say anything else, but the both of you will be well provided for. Do we understand each other man to man? The both of you have been a great and continuing service to all of us. Now try and buck up and hope for the best George"!

"Thank you Mr. Boyd, I'll pass that on to Miss Agnes, if it's ok with you". At that Boyd nodded his head turned and made his way back to his car. As he passed, Leo on the verandah, he yelled, "Damn fine Chauffer that George is. Why that engine 'shines like a whores belly' Leo. See you Monday morning, Nine AM"!

Later on in the afternoon Leo, completely disgusted with the goings on of the congressional committees, turned off the TV, got up and went into the back yard, to sit in front of Emma's mausoleum as was his custom each day it was not raining. Several months before he'd caught a chill, from sitting out in the rain, just talking with his precious Emma, as if she were really there, oblivious to the rain. Both Agnes and George ran from the house and hustled a reluctant Leo inside. Agnes called the family physician that came right away to tend to Leo's chills. Since Agnes had missed her bus, George drove her home, pressing a fifty dollar bill in her hand saying, "This is from Mr. Leo, who asked me to say that he was sorry for keeping you so late"!

By the following afternoon, Leo was on the mend, with either George or Agnes constantly at his side. But as Leo sat this sunny afternoon, under the shade of the old magnolia trees that surrounded the large back yard, his mind began to wander. He was weary of life. He longed to be, once again at his precious Emma's side. He was simply tired of the mundane struggles of mankind. He kept up the brave front in the time since Emma's departure, but now he felt that he was losing ground in the battle.

He briefly thought about the firm he'd so carefully built over the years, concluding that it would in the very capable hands of Boyd Parmalee. Then he thought about Agnes and George, his loyal retainers over the years, praying for their continuing health and welfare. Then his thoughts drifted over to his niece/daughter Elizabeth. If ever in his life, he was proud of anything that had crossed his path, it was Elizabeth. He wondered if he could have done more for her, in their all too brief time together, concluding that it was time to let go. After all, she'd made but two mistakes in her life, the first of which was marrying that scoundrel, some years ago, but the magnificent way she'd extracted herself from that debacle, made him proud. The only other egregious error she'd made was her representation of Jaeger, in a Waco courtroom. Her refusal to join the firm to get her feet on the ground, before handling the big cases, probably caused this man a great personal loss of his humanity. But in her defense, she recovered gained experience and stature, finally freeing him from a horrible fate.

Then his thoughts went to Jaeger for some strange reason. Though he only met the man once, he thought he knew him as well as he'd known anyone. For never in his experience had one man suffered such a grievous loss at the hands of his fellow man, as Jaeger experienced.

Most mortals would be broken forever spiritually, yet this man seemed to be well contained within himself, with a sense of self discipline that ran deep. Yet when one looked deeply into his eyes, one saw the deep abyss.

He'd heard little about him since his freedom was obtained, but he seemed to be doing very well as a bail enforcement agent, working for Chips Rafferty downtown. Leo decided to say a prayer for Jaeger and his family up above, for that was all he could do these days.

These moments of complete clarity were indeed rare, so he decided to ask the eternal for one last favor, to allow him to join his beloved Emma. He looked at his watch noting that it read six thirty in the evening.

Somehow, his evening meal had been delivered neatly and quietly on a tray, no doubt by George, while he was in a state of reverie and

Agnes was on her bus, soon to join her family for the evening. All was in readiness.

Leo simply closed his eyes and let his mind drift. Time to die!

A half hour later, George went into the back yard to pick up the dinner tray, finding Leo just sitting in his favorite chair, staring straight ahead with his eyes closed. Immediately he knew that his beloved benefactor had breathed his last and had joined Miss Emma up above. He felt for a pulse and finding none ran into the main house and called Boyd Parmalee.

Within the hour, most of the firm's partners had assembled along with members of the Houston Police Department, with a wide assortment of vehicles lining both sides of the exclusive River Oaks Street. The driveway was occupied by the local EMT ambulance. A quick investigation was entered into and the arrival of the family physician confirmed that Leo had indeed died simply of old age and nothing more.

The arrival of the county coroner at nine PM, concluded a very rapid coroner's inquest, concluding that death indeed came from old age and was not as a result of anything else. Of course, there was some talk about a cover up in the media, that that soon came to nothing. Absent any proof of foul play, absent any proof of disease or mistreatment by those trained to ferret out anything out of the ordinary, the unasked question by those not intimately acquainted with the facts was, "How does one put down on an official document, Tired of Life"?

So there sat Leo Schwartzwald, eyes closed, completely at ease, his spirit having already left his body, briefly observing the gaggle of important personages keeping their distance, while the authorities did their work, then bidding them all a silent goodbye as he made that final trip up the long alabaster tunnel to his beloved Emma.

Buffy had arrived at eight PM, soon followed by Jaeger, who had just arrived back in town, the first phase of his quest completed. Within minutes, they were followed by Rafferty, Seltzer and Vultee, all in turn beholdin' in one way or the other to the deceased patriarch.

Upon seeing the arrival of Jaeger, Buffy went up to him, grabbing his hand and made their way through the exclusive crowd and walked around the front of Leo, who sat there peacefully in quiet repose. "I might have been the one who got you pardoned Jaeger, but without the guidance and resources of this man you see, you'd still be in the Ellis unit", said Buffy, her eyes welling up in sorrow!

Kneeling down with her and looking at the man, Jaeger replied, "Only met the man once, during that night at your house and I remember him as a dignified man, quiet and refined, but with an apparent inner strength. As I met him, it was as if his eyes saw right through me. I hope he was pleased with what he saw"?

"He was Jaeger, believe me, he was"!

By ten PM, the coroner's conclusion reached, that foul play was not at issue in the old man's demise, the body was released by Buffy as his only living relative, to the selected mortuary for preparation for entombment on the property, next to his beloved Emma, in the very same tomb, three days hence. By midnight Leo had departed to the selected mortuary, for his preparation.

As they walked to their cars, Buffy and Jaeger were amongst the last to leave. Buffy asked, "Do you have anything pressing on your calendar, for the next few days"?

"No Buffy, why do you ask"? "I don't quite know, but somehow I'd feel a great deal better if you were close at hand, in the coming days, at least until Uncle Leo is interred. I have several extra bedrooms in my house"!

"Buffy, I owe you and Uncle Leo my life. Anything you want, that I can provide, all ya have to do is ask and it's done"!

"Good, you can start by following me home just until I get into the house and locked up for the night, because I'm feeling a bit mortal. Then while I'm at the office tomorrow move several day's worth of clothing tomorrow. I'll give Maria a heads up that you're going to be a guest for the next few days and one more thing, bring along a suitable suit of clothes for a funeral"!

<h1 style="text-align:center">43</h1>

A few days after Sheriff Little talked to Don Ryder over the phone regarding the death of Morris Womble and of his concerns, he received a call back from Ryder, stating that their friend in Austin had all of his vehicles examined and the Governor's Mansion swept as well as that of his special friend and that nothing untoward was discovered. "What about you and yours", asked Little?

"Your guy came up, swept the house, the office and the club. We checked all of the vehicles and nothing was discovered. Think you're getting' a case of the willies Morgan"!

"As long as Jaeger and his pals are walking the streets, we've all got sufficient reason to be concerned"!

"I think you're seeing substance in places where there's only shadows Morgan"!

"Dammit Don, I been in office a very long time and one of the reasons I remain in office is my nose for sensing trouble and I'm telling you that trouble is just around the corner. Can't see it but I can smell and taste it!

Besides I just made a decision to solve all of our problems, once and for all and you get to pay for it"!

"What"?

"That's right Don, you get to keep your hands clean while others do the dirty work and be very thankful that I'm a friend and can get things done"!

"Soon as I ring off with you, I'm gonna reestablish an old friendship.

We'll meet up somewhere, develop a plan of action I've in mind, a cost figure will be arrived at. You and I will meet, money will be handed over. The next day that action will be repeated and then you and I sit back and watch the fur fly"!

"Morgan, what's wrong with simply waiting"?

"You believe that bitch in Houston will really keep to her word"?

"Why wouldn't she"?

"Tell me Don, when did you ever keep your word to someone, when there was never anything forcing you to keep your word"?

"I'll tell you when. Never. Not once in your entire life. So just sit back and await my call"!

At that Little hung up abruptly, then lifted the receiver and placed another call.

On the third ring Little heard a furry sounding voice say "Yeah"!

"Bomber? Bomber Abrams"!

"Who wants to know"?

"Morgan Little"!

"Well lemmeseeheah", growled the voice? I seem to remember a certain Sheriff of that name? But he's an old fart and most likely dead by now"!

"Heard you got outta the Corcoran unit about two years ago and that you're back to your old tricks"! "Now who the fuck you hear that from"?

"Oh, a guy you and me both know. A guy you stash a variety of things for in a new storage warehouse, built west of Waco. Of course, this guy doesn't know that we know each other from before and this guy doesn't know that I know that the both of you are partners with some Muy Malo hombres in Matamoras. And this guy doesn't have a clue just how nasty you can be, does he"?

"So Morgan Little is still alive after all", said Abrams! Heard he wasn't running for reelection"!

"Decided to retire. But before that's done, there's a little job for you to do that'll pay you very well. Ya still up to it"!

"How well it gonna pay"?

"Search your memory. You ever have a reason to complain before"?

"Nope"!

"And you still got your connections across the Rio Grande"!

"Si Hombre"!

"Then what say you let me buy you lunch were we can discuss the who, what, where and when"? "Long as your buyin'"!

The following day they met for lunch at a truck stop in Corsicana Texas, on Interstate 45.

After the usual preliminaries Little asked Abrams, "How come you served the full ride at the Corcoran unit"?

"Didn't want anybody looking' over my shoulder once I got out. Been free for the last two years, on the street and makin' my moves"!

"Ya still got the edge for the wet and nasty", asked Little?

"It's what pays the best still ain't it"?

Little nodded his head smiling, remembering just how good this guy had been in the past. He was good at killing people, not necessarily for the money, but for the sheer enjoyment. It was what indeed paid the best.

"How well you know Houston"?

"Well enough Morgan. We done some work for ya down that way before if you'll recall"!

"That you did Bomber"!

"So what's on the plate"? Little handed Abrams an envelope and invited him to open it. As the single sheet of paper was unfolded Little said, "You will notice several names, the first of which is a high yellow gossip columnist for the Houston Chronicle, named Odessa Robillard. Don't have a picture of her, but all ya have to do is by a copy of the paper, turn to the entertainment section and her picture will be right there fronting her column. She lives somewhere off Montrose Boulevard"!

"I'm thinking a two man team should do, waste the bitch, torch the place in the early hours of the morning then fade away"!

"No problem. She live alone"?

"As far as I know she does"!

"Need a day to nose around, then poof the magic dragon. What's next"?

"A bitch lawyer named Buffy Beavior. Lives in a fancy house on Cypresswood Drive across from the Raveneaux Country Club. You have the address written down. I'm thinking a team of four hitters, two vehicles, two RPG launchers; each man's outfitted with Tech 9's with four clips each and will need about six RPGs each. Flank the house in the early hours of the morning, then start firing away when every ones asleep. It would be better if both attacks went off as close to the same time as possible, for both know each other"!

"That's it. Anything else"?

"You pull those two things off and I got one more job for ya, that'll really lite ya up"!

"Lemme borrow your cell phone hombre'. I gotta few calls to make", said Abrams as their lunch arrived. As he ate, Abrams made several calls south of the border, where his connections in Matamoras held sway. After a number of calls, between bites of his burger and fries, with him writing on the back of several napkins, he said, "I can have seven men in Houston by tomorrow morning. Seven first rate pistoleros, who know how to dance with the RPG's. No teenagers, but proven pro's, two of which speak passable English. I'll supply the hardware, you supply the dinero'. Each one'll cost ya five thousand each and their padrones can spare them for a week max"!

"How much for the hard ware"?

"Another ten thousand"!

"And for your efforts"?

"Another fifteen thousand for my planning and personal supervision"!

"Any incidentals"?

"Let's say another two hundred each man for expenses"!

"And you're the paymaster"?

"But of course. Payable upon successful completion only, for that's the only way it's done"!

"Good my friend. Make the call. Well meet up here later tonight and I'll have the money"!

As desert arrived, Abrams hung up the phone saying, "Tomorrow morning I'll be meeting seven men at the Ramada Inn on US 59 South in Houston and it begins"!

"Good, then we will meet up right here around nine tonight for dinner"! "Pleasure doing business again with you Morgan"!

Little nodded his head as he grabbed the check and rose to leave.

By ten PM, money had been exchanged and both men had been fed and Morgan Little was some twenty thousand dollars to the good, having marked up the tally by that amount. For wet work always paid good.

As he drove back to Waco he reviewed the day's work. Don Ryder as usual always squealed, like a newborn pig any time he had to shell out cash and of course he was a weasel, but the money always came. The man had no other choice. Soon after this was all over he would have to find a way to make Ryder disappear, then Baintree, but first Jaeger. He'd think up a way to make Ryder pay for Jaegers disappearance. He'd employ Bomber once again and then he could retire in peace. For the last day and a half Jaeger had dutifully shadowed Buffy to her office, to the court house, then back to her office, keeping an ever unobtrusive eye on her from a distance. Of course he had to do this unarmed. As he shadowed her home, he noticed every car that passed them, but it really wasn't that much a problem since she rarely left the office before Seven PM when rush hour traffic was on the wane.

The first night passed uneventfully, with Maria, preparing a magnificent Tex Mex meal fit for the gods.

What they couldn't know, was the fact that Bomber Abrams passed their block several times, pointing out the home in a ten year old Green Ford Van, to two of his passengers and later in the day, two different vehicles took turns charting the comings and goings of everyone on the other side of Cypresswood Drive. Parking never for more than an hour in a single spot then leaving only to be replaced by the other car, in a different spot. Its occupants apparently clean cut in appearance and clean shaven, never once causing anyone to give it a second look.

While things up north were progressing apparently on its own, Bomber Abrams and three of his counterparts staked out the entrances of the Houston Chronicle. Each was armed with the latest edition of the paper, turned to the entertainment section and there she was, Odessa Robillard, plain as day in picture. At seven forty five in the morning, in she walked to the main entrance, noticed by two of the killers. At noon she went to lunch at a local bistro on old market square, sitting with several others at a shaded sidewalk table. At One PM she walked the two blocks back to the Chronicle, passing someone with a keen interest in her appearance as she entered the building.

Now the rules in trailing someone's comings and goings is whenever possible, always use multiple people, never look directly at someone, never be noticeable in any way and never make eye contact, ever. Especially with a sensitive and Odessa was every bit a sensitive. She had that inexplicable sixth sense, when things were right and when things were wrong, very wrong.

As she entered the Chronicle building, she felt uneasy. She started to feel uneasy during lunch with some friends at the sidewalk. All of a sudden through her sunglasses, there were several men she'd previously seen earlier in the morning reading the paper and in various places out across the street, there were two men, who seemed to resemble some she'd previously seen, again reading the newspaper, but what raised the hair on her head, was when she entered the Chronicle building after lunch, seeing a man, previously seen, reading the paper and then as she passed, making eye contact with her and quickly looking away.

She immediately placed a called to Buffy at her office and was told that she was in court and would be back later in the day. As she hung up, Odessa thought of rescheduling her much sought after interview, with the grand maven of the local Junior League. The prestigious entity that local women of significant means belonged to. She was about to get a scoop about the woman's philandering husband, the very day prior to his being served with divorce papers.

At three forty five Odessa's phone rang and it was Buffy. For a half hour they exchanged the feeling that both felt. Then Buffy said, "Look here Cher. I have Jaeger staying with me at the house and he's sleeping in the guest bedroom".

"In the guest bedroom Cher? Damn girl, why ain't that hunk in your bed"?

"I'm going to call Randall White. He's a very good PI that does work for our firm. You stay put until he calls you then do everything he says, understand Cher"?

"I'll stay put girlfriend"!

"Good. Now Randall has some friends in one of the Constables offices and between them they'll keep an eye on you tonight. After your interview, go straight home and lock the door"!

After all had been put in place with Randall White, Buffy summoned Jaeger inside her office and told him all that had happened with Odessa. Now a woman's intuition is not the most reliable barometer of perceived danger in most cases, the female chemistry being as dynamic as it usually is. But when two different women, usually reliable in every way, not easily susceptible to panic sense that something is amiss, it would be wise to listen very carefully. At the very end of Buffy's exposition she asked Jaeger, "Well what do ya think sport"?

"I think that we should shower early, sleep fully dressed and keep the coffee pot full, for the next several days. Of course, Maria is keeping a look out during the day isn't she"?

On the way back to Buffy's home, they entered into an Academy Super Store, each separate from each other, meeting up at the ammunition counter, with Jaeger directing her to purchase a .357 Ruger Police six

Revolver along with two boxes of .357 Glaser safety slugs for her personal protection and a separate box of .380 safety slugs for Archie's old Beretta for Maria to use. As they all sat down to dinner later, Jaeger unveiled his masterpiece.

"This ladies, is a shot gun. But not an ordinary shot gun. It's a street sweeper. A twelve gauge shot gun, loaded with ten rounds of double ought shot shell, just aim in the general direction of your target and pull the trigger. Each time you pull the trigger it will go BOOM, sending nine balls of nine mm shot at your target. Your target will go down. Now Buffy, I'm loading your revolver with these Glaser safety slugs, advertised as having one shot stopping power, each shell containing shot. The revolver will not jam nor malfunction, just aim and pull the trigger. Now Maria, I'm loading the .380 with Glaser slugs also and while it won't have the stopping power of the shot gun or Buffy's Ruger, just aim slightly below the belt buckle and you'll be fine, should the need arise. Now Ladies shall we eat and afterwards I'll instruct you on some of the finer points. It not difficult at all"!

Maria, decided to sleep on the big leather couch, in the main living area, the small automatic nestled in her hand, under her pillow. Facing the rear entrance door, through the laundry area, all she had to do was shoot anything that came through that doorway and she had seven little decision makers, nestled in the clip, with one in the chute, ready to go.

Buffy lay atop her bedspread in her bedroom, looking at her newly purchased Ruger revolver. 'One shot stopping power', Jaeger had said. 'Aim for just below the belt buckle', Jaeger reminded them, 'for if they're wearing Kevlar vests, they will not extend to that area'! She wondered whether or not, if it came to it, could she ever take another's life?

'Silly girl', she thought. 'Other than Odessa's somewhat tangible concerns and her innate feelings, she had absolutely no evidence that anything was wrong. Not a blessed thing'.

And yet she sensed a growing evil, gathering unseen, ready to pounce.

All the precautions had been taken. It was now up to each of them to act appropriately. If it came to it, Buffy would pull the trigger and damn whatever consequences that came after.

Then there was Jaeger. Dear Jaeger. So quietly confident and certain.

An Archangel Michael ready to defend those dear to him. She hadn't given the eternal much thought lo these many years, at least not consciously, but now she said a silent prayer for all in this house and her dear friend Odessa, to get them all through this night and whatever lay ahead. That completed, she again thought of Jaeger downstairs, ever alert through the night. That would give her tangible strength and assurance.

Bomber Abrams had done what he could, with the two teams up north of town. At around three in the morning when all were asleep, two vehicles would make several random drive by's of the location, then agreeing that all were asleep; both vehicles would stop at each end of the house, unloading an RPG operator. The driver was to keep the engine running and serve as the shell carrier, ready to immediately reload, the launcher. Six RPG rounds into the home should be sufficient to bring the structure down on their heads with the resultant fire to occur in the aftermath. The Mac-10's were strictly insurance against the unforeseen. The whole thing was sure to be over in less than two or three minutes. But now Abrams was busy tailing Odessa as she left her interview around nine in the evening. He had one of the Mexican shooters with him in his Van, while the other two were in the other car, running a loose tail on their subject. So intent were they on surveilling Odessa, they failed to notice Randall White and Roy Seltzer in White's Beige Ford LTD, or Duke Vultee, accompanying Clyde Mack an off duty Harris County Constable, following them in leap frog fashion back in the shadows of the roadways.

As she drove back to her Montrose residence, a small single level brick home, built some fifty years ago, nestled tightly in between others of its vintage, she almost forgot about the feelings she'd been having all afternoon. Her interview had gone extremely well with the society maven and during the evening edition of the Chronicle; she'd have a blockbuster of a story certain to have the local chapter of the mythical four hundred, chattering for weeks.

Try as she might she was unable to spot any one following her, but she was assured by Randall White, that two vehicles would be close at hand, shadowing her every move, throughout the evening and well into the following day.

As Odessa pulled into her drive way, she emerged from her car, locked it, looked around, then unlocked the rear door and went into the house locking the door behind her. Since all her windows had burglar bars installed into the frame, as had many others in this crime prone neighborhood, she had little worry that anyone was going to enter through the windows. As she tentatively went through the house, turning on each room's lights, she searched all her closets and under her beds and only then did she begin to feel at ease.

'Perhaps it was all nothing but her hormones', she thought. 'And yet Buffy was going through the very same thing and neither of them spooked readily'.

After she entered the house, Bomber Abrams, slowly drove down the street she entered and eventually saw her car parked in the driveway. Seeing the lights gradually turning on in the house, told him that someone was in the home and he knew exactly who that someone was. He made note of the address and slowly drove off to meet the rest of the team at the all night diner at Montrose Boulevard and lower Westheimer Road. They'd grab a bite, kill some time, stoke up on coffee, then return, blow up the place, scoot on down the street, he'd pay the shooters and Vamanose'.

Randall decided to follow the Van to the all night diner, while Clyde Mack and Vultee took position silently down and across the street some fifty yards away, in Mack's vehicle. Secure that both teams of shooters, were going to be in place for the next several hours, White and Seltzer drove back to Odessa's street, taking up a position some forty yards away from Odessa's home on the other side of the street backing quietly into a residential driveway, turning off the engine and waited.

White called Buffy on his cell phone and she went downstairs to have Jaeger hear from White what was occurring in town. "Ain't no goddamn phantom Buffy, it's the real thing, Two teams, two different vehicles. One of em is a Ford Van and the passengers are an Anglo and a Mexican, while the other vehicle has that south of the border look and it carries two Mexican looking shooters. We've got Odessa's house flanked and are waiting for them to return. My guess, they'll be back around two or three in the morning"!

As White and Buffy rang off from each other, Jaeger said, "Two teams in town, tells me that the same drill is gonna happen here. Two hits simultaneously, early in the morning. The only question is what kind of hardware will they be bringing", asked Jaeger to himself speaking to no one in particular!

"Ladies, please try and get some rest as best you can", asked Jaeger politely. Throughout the entire house, there only burned one area lamp, dimly in the back portion of the open common area that could not be seen from the street. As far as anyone outside knew, all inside were fast asleep.

At around two AM, the two teams assigned to Buffy's house, sat in two different all night diners, glances at their watches, settled their bill, went to the restroom, took care of their personal business and departed.

At around the very same time sat two pairs of men in the Silver Dollar Café, not six city blocks from Odessa's home. Each sat quietly at either end of the Café, neither acknowledging the other. Abrams glanced at his watch signaling his partner that it was time.

He rose, paid the bill and walked out of the restaurant, with his partner close behind. A minute later the other duo did the same, neither paying heed to the other. As Abrams pulled out of his parking space on the street, he noticed an HPD patrol unit parking across the street in the empty strip center parking lot and a weary looking officer taking his early morning coffee break on his way to the Silver Dollar Café. He pulled very carefully away from the curb and hoped the other team would also. 'Didn't need no hassle with John Law, not now', he thought. Up in the north part of the county, one team pulled away from the Copper Kettle, passing a County Sheriff's cruiser, pulling in the parking lot, for his morning coffee. As the cruiser approached the shooter sitting in the passenger seat ducked down for a minute as the other vehicle passed by. One Mexican driving at night was far less likely to draw unwarranted attention from the law, than two. While at the Waffle House, a fifteen minute drive away, the very same thing happened, pay your bill, leave a decent tip for the waitress, get in the car, see the County Constable cruiser enter the parking lot, duck your head, look straight ahead, use your turn signal and drive away into the night all normal like.

As Bomber Abrams drove down Odessa's street past her house, he noticed nothing out of the ordinary except an empty lone Ford Ltd. parked in a driveway some distance away. As he reached the end of the street, he turned around and slowly drove back up the street, peering into the darkness, with his lights out and seeing nothing out of the ordinary, stopped at the entrance of her street to discharge his passenger into the trailing car saying, "Three RPG's into the Casa, then slowly drive off the way I showed ya. We meet up later at the Ramada Inn after I inspect what happened up north". Then he drove off parking a block away, in strip centers parking lot on Westheimer Road. As the shooters slowly drove to Odessa's house, with their lights off, two of them got out. One with a locked and loaded RPG and the other with two spare rockets for a quick reload. Just as he started to quickly take aim, both Clyde Mack and Seltzer emerged from Mack's car, while White and Vultee came out of their car, drawing their weapons, with Mack yelling," POLICE! Stay right where you are". In a split second the Mexican driver jumped out of his car with his Mack-10 blazing away at Mack who was straight ahead of him, while the RPG shooter, pulled his trigger, his aim a bit off, hitting Odessa's roof. His loader, quickly shoved another rocket into the tube, while firing wildly his Mac-10 in the direction of White and Vultee, who were taking careful aim and squeezing off rounds, one of which hit the RPG shooter spinning him around as he squeezed the trigger hitting a house across the street. While the Mexican driver struggled to change clips in his Mac-10, two rounds his him from Mack and Seltzers weapons. His weapons reloaded he struggled to his feet and sprayed his weapon in Mack and Seltzers general direction, hitting nothing but air, dirt and the other homes down the street. Taking aim Seltzer did a double tap in his Sig Sauer automatic, with both rounds hitting home, while Clyde Mack, reached for a quick reload, and resumed firing at the others. Somehow, the RPG shooter managed to reload the remaining rocket, while His partner already hit, kept up a steady rate of fire at the others. As he stood up to fire at Odessa's House, he ran into a steady hail of bullets from the attackers combined firearms, squeezing the RPG's trigger, firing wildly over all the houses into the air and landing hundreds of yards away right in the middle of the intersection of Westheimer Road and Montrose Boulevard, mortally injuring a sleeping vagrant on a bus stop bench.

The neighborhood now awake flooded the 911 switchboard, while Clyde Mack got on the radio and summoned the Constables office to his location saying "Patrolman under fire" and giving the location.

With nowhere to hide and nothing but their Mac-10's in their hands, and severely injured themselves, the two remaining shooters went out firing wildly as round after carefully aimed round slammed into them, until they both lay inert.

After the shooting ceased, the silence of two long minutes echoed down the normally quiet street. Only Seltzer had his hearing left unimpaired, for years of experience had taught him to bring balls of cotton to stuff into your ears just before a gunfight, if you want to have any hearing left in the aftermath.

Seltzer and Vultee, both handed their weapons to Randall White, then plunged into Odessa's wreckage of a house, ripping apart drywall and old support beams as best they could searching for Odessa, as the first sirens started to make a distant sound. Soon the neighbors, started to tumble out of their homes, attired in their nightclothes. Within five minutes the street began to fill with police and fire trucks all busy as could be.

Suddenly Randall White grabbed for his cell phone and after the forth ring to Buffy, with no pickup called out to Clyde Mack, to get on the radio and sent a few county patrol units to Buffy's home just in case.

With a crowd gathered across the street, out of the ashes emerged a shaken Odessa, jointly carried by Seltzer his arms wrapped around her ample chest and Vultee, his arms wrapped around her hips, struggling to emerge through the wreckage of her home, into the arms of awaiting firemen, struggling to retain her modesty and tend to her injuries.

As Seltzer and Vultee joined White and Clyde Mack, Seltzer removed the cotton from his ears as the others struggled to regain their hearing, with White saying, "Now there's a real pro for ya", while the others smiled in understanding.

Noting that Seltzer was beaming with pride, Mack asked, "Why are you so happy"!

"Mate, aye ain't had so much fun since Malaya, back in forty eight and nine. That was a real shootout, to make the OK Corral look like child's play"!

"Except the Clanton bunch are toast", offered Vultee lighting a well-earned cigarette.

"What about Jaeger and Buffy", asked Seltzer?

Called her mobile number five minutes ago, with no answer, then had Mack call his dispatcher and send a few units out to their house and hope for the best"!

"How can we help them", asked Vultee?

"Look around sport, the street is clogged with cop cars, fire trucks and EMT vehicles. Unless you can find a way for us to fly, were all grounded for the next few hours", said Mack as he drifted away to get together with arriving investigators to give them an after action report.

The rest went down to the street to look in on Odessa who was being attended to by the EMT techs. Finding her with nothing but cuts and a hoard of bruises, she saw them all saying, "Y'all could've started shooting earlier, don'tcha think"!

"Probably so, probably so", said White smiling.

"So who am I to thank for haulin' my ass out of my house", asked Odessa?

Just then Vultee pushed forward Seltzer saying, "Here's the culprit ma'am, he's the one"!

"Say you look familiar, haven't we met before", asked Odessa?

"Doubt it lass, for we run in quite different social circles I fear"?

"Damn, if it ain't an old man Brit that saved me"1

"Watch yer mouth Sheila, I'm not a Brit, but an Aussie, of Kiwi extraction"! "An Aussie with an attitude, my, my", she exclaimed. "Well I might not look like much now, but some day very soon, I insist that we get together so I can thank you proper"!

"I'll wager that a fine looking' Sheila, like yourself oughtta clean up right proper! I'll look forward to it at your earliest convenience", said Seltzer reaching out and kissing her hand.

"Lordy lawd", said Odessa, "I imagine I'm gonna swoon"! Just then she perked up saying,

"But what about Buffy"?

"White rang her up on his mobil but no answer, so Mack called his dispatch to send a few units her way Pronto. Hopefully they've arrived by now. But as you can see this place is a mess and there's no way we can get out. But she's with Jaeger, so all we can do lass, is cross our fingers and hope the other shooters are just as inept, if there are any, as these blokes are", as he pointed to the dead bodies lying on her lawn.

Jaeger was growing uneasy just sitting inside the house, so he grabbed his Street Sweeper, and slipped out the back door after telling Maria, what he was going to do, keeping to the shadows of the house and moving slowly behind the manicured bushes, kept fifteen inches away from the house. He parked himself at the corner of the house, where the bushes afforded him a good view of not only Cypress Wood Drive, but the side street that ran past her home. Something told him that time was close at hand. He could see the streets but no one could see him unless they had night vision optics and that was unlikely. The street lights at the intersection would defeat that technology rendering it useless. No, at this time of morning damn few vehicles would be going back and forth, all he had to do would make a mental note of each vehicle that passed by and if the same vehicles transited back and forth, then the show was soon to begin.

He figured that one vehicle would attack from the main street and another from the side street. Since the fenced and gated properties on both sides of her home had dogs on the outside, only Ninja's would dare approach from the rear. 'No', he thought, 'front and side it is'.

After a half hour he felt his legs start to cramp up, so he slowly changed positions and fought the pain, massaging the affected areas until the pain subsided. When the show started, he'd have to be mobile as possible if he were to be any use at all.

The vehicular traffic was at best sparse as he scanned the Country Club's parking lot across the street and finding it deserted, focusing back on the street again. Then he saw a twenty year old Datsun sedan drive slowly past the house, east to west, occupied by two men. Several minutes later he saw an old Plymouth pass slowly by the house in the opposite direction, west to east, again occupied by two men. Minutes later the same Datsun, slowly passed by the house in its opposite direction, west to east, occupied by two men, then minutes after that the very same old Plymouth passed by east to west again occupied by two men.

That was all Jaeger needed for it was soon to be 'Show Time' as he set himself in position. Ten minutes passed without a single vehicle passing either way along Cypress Wood Drive, then slowly both vehicles converged from opposite directions, east to west and west to east with the latter doing a U turn and facing west, but with both stopping in front of Buffy's next door neighbors home, immediately west of her property. Two men jumped out of their cars, followed by two others carrying what appeared to be two feet long rockets and before Jaeger could react the first two quickly brought to bear an RPG launcher on Buffy's neighbor house and fired away simultaneously at the house from the edge of the homeowner's lawn. The rockets each penetrated a front window, exploding deep into the interior of the large ornate structure. Quick as a wink, the drivers reloaded the RPG tubes and the RPG's again erupted, this time penetrating windows on opposite ends of the second floor, again with massive explosions.

Moving out from the bushes and behind a tree, some thirty yards away from the shooters, Jaeger took aim as the loaders were loading the third rocket and let the Sweeper speak. From Thirty yards away, two quick blasts from the vaunted shot gun took the legs out from under one of the shooters and one of the loaders, before the rockets could be properly reloaded, then one of the shooters and the other loader brought to bear their Mac-10's, unloading a withering hail of bullets in Jaegers general vicinity. With only the massive front oak tree to provide him shelter, Jaeger peeked around and fired off two more blasts at the shooters, hitting one of them in the chest, as his finger closed on the trigger spraying the trees and Buffy's home in the process.

As Jaeger peeked out from the tree again, one of the wounded shooters had successfully reloaded his RPG and fired off a shot in the direction of Buffy's second floor bedroom hitting the brick side of the home and blasting a massive hole in the side of the house. Just then Jaeger heard screaming behind him and saw Buffy and Maria emerging from the front door firing wildly at their assailants. Jaeger bolted from behind the tree and knocked them both down, just as another hail of bullets from two operative Mac-10's flew past their heads and into the house. Just then another 'Whooshing' sound came from the street, quickly followed by yet another explosion, behind Jaeger as the second and final RPG rocket hit Buffy's second floor window penetrating to the deep interior of the structure with a crippling explosion.

One of the shooters was dead, while two of the others, were badly crippled by Jaegers blast and were hurriedly trying to reload their Mac-10's with fresh clips as Jaeger rose up and pulled the trigger of his Street Sweeper dropping them both like a stone. As Jaeger approached the final shooter only partially wounded, but struggling with a fresh ammo clip he saw Jaeger coming fast and giving up his weapon as a lost cause, reached into his pocket for his butterfly knife and in a blink of the had the blade at the ready, lunging at Jaeger who easily parried the blow with his all metal assault weapon, breaking the attackers wrist, causing the blade to fly free from his grasp and quickly Jaeger grabbed the sparsely built attacker by his neck and his legs pressing him up in the air and dropped him on his knee, while in a supine position breaking his spine in two.

Then all went silent, except for the ringing in his ears, for he forgot his bits of cotton in all the rush.

Buffy, still recovering from Jaegers cross body block, looked up with an ailing Maria, to see Jaeger dispatch the final shooter, in such a personal way, with Maria whispering to herself "Muy Malo Hombre", as a sign of respect. Now Buffy as well as Maria knew why Jaeger was freed from his captivity. In a matter of just a few minutes the man had more than earned his keep for a very long time. Jaeger then picked up one of the Mac-10's made certain a full clip was in the weapon, then went around to each of the shooters and squeezed off a few rounds in each of their heads. As he approached Buffy and Maria, he simply said "Insurance". Then he kneeled down and said, "I'm sorry I had to slam you ladies, but it just wouldn't do for the both of you to get gunned down. Besides who could replace Maria's cooking"?

As neighbors began to emerge from the surrounding homes and in the distance sirens were beginning to be heard, Jaeger went over to his Street Sweeper and casually scooped it up and went around to the garage and put it in his car all wrapped up, then went to the homes main breaker and shut down the power. Finally found the main natural gas line and closed it off.

After all of that it just wouldn't do to have the house blow up. He went around the front of the house just as the Volunteer Fire Department trucks arrived along with a veritable gaggle of Sheriff Deputies and County Constables arrived to do what they could, which wasn't much.

None of the Buffy's neighbors had ever seen a single dead body if their lives and now this. Four dead Mexican shooters lay dead on Buffy and her next door neighbor's front lawn and the saddest thing of all is that her next door neighbor's entire family perished in the onslaught all because of a simple error. As the county investigators dug through the wreckage of both homes, Buffy overheard Jaeger whisper a single word, 'Schadenfreude'!

She asked him asides what that word meant and after a brief moment he replied, "It's Kraut speak and loosely translated means, 'Better them than us'", showing no emotion in his voice.

"But how are you feeling, Jaeger, right now"?

"Apart from my ears still ringing, I'm feeling pretty good right now. Oh if you're referring to those out on the lawn, I'm feeling nothing for them, except 'Schadenfreude'. There no better than rabid animals. Now if something had happened to either you or Maria, then I'd feel badly, very badly"!

As the sun rose in the east several hours later, Boyd Parmalee, finally arrived along with several of the partners, to intercede with the county authorities. "About time you arrived", said Buffy testily!

"Now young lady, if you'll just calm down a moment we've all been pretty busy down in town, for Odessa's house got hit by two teams, with her home gone up in flames and she's been injured, but Randall White and his crew have dispatched all of the assailants"! "How's Odessa", asked Buffy?

"She and Roy Seltzer suffered some injuries, but they're being tended to at the Herman Hospital emergency room. White, Clyde Mack and Willis Voorhees are still with the HPD investigators giving them an after action report"?

"Voorhees is there", asked Buffy?

"The man is a bit cranky after being jerked out of bed so early, but he's the best of the partners to intercede with the Police"!

"I agree, Willis is indeed a 'Hoss' downtown"! "So what happened here", asked Parmalee?

"Ask Jaeger, he can tell you best", said Buffy pushing him forward. "Tell Boyd what happened"!"Two teams, two vehicles as you can see", said Jaeger pointing to the street. "Two men with RPG's and apparently they initially mistook the next door neighbor's house for Buffy's and each of them put two RPG's into the home for bringing it down. I took out one of the shooters, but then they put their last two RPG's into Buffy's home and as you can see, it's mostly in splinters"!

"Any survivors in the house next door", asked Parmalee?

"Don't know yet Boyd, for as you can see, they just got the fires put out and now the firemen are combing through what's left for any survivors", said Jaeger, but we're damn lucky they couldn't read street address's properly or else Buffy and Maria wouldn't be here"!

"Any survivors here, to be questioned," asked Boyd?

"Nope. All out on the front lawn in body bags" said Jaeger! "What about at Odessa's place in town"?

"Same thing. Yet three men all dead as far as I know. Just who could've done such a thing"?

"I think we all know the answer to that one Boyd", said Buffy.

"You're meaning Baintree, Little and Ryder of course", replied Parmalee

"But where's the proof of their complicity"?

"There is none", said Jaeger!

"Apparently they didn't think I'm a woman of my word", said Buffy!

"Well are you", asked Parmalee lifting an eyebrow?

"Only when it counts"?

"Well Jaeger, do you have any plans" asked Parmalee?

"Not for the moment and if I did, you wouldn't wanna know"!

"Well, there's the media remote trucks, up the street to contend with, I'll have to go down and talk to them, so you all stay put and after all of this is settled down I'll get hold of the insurance people and get them out here, to start the claims procedures"!

"Oh Boyd", asked Buffy, "Could you find some time to put off Uncle Leo's funeral services for just a few days"!

"Already on the agenda, called your secretary on the way out here and she's seeing to it"!

Across town sat a dejected Bomber Abrams in the motel room viewing the aftermath of his efforts. 'How could they have possibly known' he wondered over and over. For this way the very first time he'd ever failed in a hit. His reputation in certain circles was sure to suffer unless he made things right. The early morning local television programming preempted all of the other programming throughout the morning and it wasn't until late morning that he had some sort of grasp on what went wrong. Still it was clear that all of the imported shooters went down to the last and they weren't about to say anything.

At noon Abrams left his room and drove over to the restaurant in one of the motels down the street and got a roll of quarters from the cashier, going to the phone booth outside and placed a call to Morgan Little on his private line.

"You fucked up son", said Little, as he picked up the phone, expecting Abrams call sooner or later. To not get the call meant that Abrams was dead.

"They were waitin' for us. It was an ambush straight up", said Abrams testily.

"You know you just gotta make things right, don't ya. How much of the money I gave ya is still unspent"?

"A little over seventy thousand", said Abrams.

"So what are ya gonna do next", asked Little? "You left a lotta strings hanging in the wind. That bitch Robillard is still alive and under heavy guard. Buffy is still with us, we both saw em on the television and no doubt that son of a bitch Jaeger is somewhere in the shadows. Seems all you did is get your hitters killed"!

"Isn't there supposed to be a funeral of some kind for this Buffy's Uncle" asked Abrams?

"It's been postponed for several days with announcements for its rescheduling soon to follow, said all the news reports. Got the local news on now. No doubt your handy work will be nationwide news by suppertime", said Little testily. Seems to me that you're gonna have go down south for some more manpower, or else your rep is gonna suffer somewhat"!

"I'll do just that, but it's probably gonna cost some more money. I'll make up what has been spent, but the cost of additional shooters will drive up the cost's, that's all. I'm thinking about an even dozen shooters. There's gonna be a shipment heading north via an eighteen wheeler tomorrow and there will be four cars accompanying the shipment. All I have to do is talk Papa Mondragon into adding another four or five shooters into the mix and we'll have more than enough fire-power to get things done. Either way I'll be back in Waco by tonight"!

"So how much more", asked Little.

"Just guessing here, but probably around fifty large would do the trick"!

"And every dime will go to the shooters right", said Little.

"Every dime"!

"I'll see what I can do. Call me tonight when you get in. And oh, in case you haven't already guessed, this time things better work, for if it don't, then between Papa Mondragon and myself, I wouldn't wanna be you if things didn't work out"!

44

The phone call to Papa Mondragon at his encomienda in Villa Hermoso was not one Bomber Abrams ever wished to repeat, wiping out years of successful dealings between them. A textbook rendition of that old adage, "Ten attaboys, equal one Oh Shit"! The men he sent north had a long history with him and in his mind, to see them squandered the way they were was almost akin to a mortal sin. Some shout and wave their arms when very angry, but the old man Mondragon, would get very quiet when he was very angry, his voice never exceeding that of a whisper, which meant the object of his attention at that point, was literally on the razors edge of existence.

"They will come back with not one less centavo than one hundred thousand, or joo might as well cut jour wrists somewhere Vato! Que sabe"?

Abrams drove back up to Waco late that afternoon and by Nine PM met up with Sheriff Little who handed him a large manila envelope with the remainder of the hundred thousand of course after marking up the amount with a little stipend for himself, reminding the Bomber that further failure was not an option guaranteed for a long life.

Early the following morning, the Tractor Trailer truck and its escorts pulled into the storage warehouse complex, on what used to be the Jaeger Ranch, and the shipment of South American Cocaine and Mexican Marijuana, coupled with Brazilian fire arms to be sold all over America, was unloaded and secured by midmorning.

The shipment had been escorted by Ricardo Moscante, aka 'El Morro', the dark one. Short and powerfully built, El Morro was the kind of man with a rapid and violent temper, the kind of man who after shaving in the morning, by noon his face was covered with a dark five o'clock shadow and whose back and barreled chest was a black mat of fur.

"Phase one of our business is finish and now we continue with phase two in Houston. But amigo, there are just two small changes in your agreement with Papa Mondragon"!

"Changes, what changes" asked Abrams nervously?

"Change nomber one, is you will pay our fee in advance not afterward as before, before we do anodder thing"!

"Wait just a minute, all the time I've done business with your boss, we've had a level of trust between us, so why the change"?

"An change nomber two, is that this time joo go wid os to da very end as insurance"!

"El Morro, this is not right and you know it"!

"Be that as it may, that is the way things will be. Now before joo say anodder thing, I gotta tell joo that joo hab no choice. We will hab our dinero in right now and then we all go down to Houston, to do a job, then we go home and joo go home an that is the way it gonna be"! Seeing that he was in a no win situation, Bomber went over to the trunk of his car, opened it and reached in removing several manila envelopes and tossed them over to El Morro saying, "Here, count it if you want"!

"No need amigo, for we are all friends here. Now we go hab lonch, den come back and select the weapons and ammunition from joor warehouse, den we drive to Houston and see what we can see. We gonna enjoy joor company, da next couple days"!

The tragedy of the previous day's joint attack was that an entire family, Buffy's next door neighbor had been wiped out by a simple mistake in the early morning. The father, a successful surgeon in Houston, the wife and mother to their children, and their four children all taken while asleep in the dark of night. Not exactly on a fast friends basis with the family next door, Buffy recalled that every Sunday at ten in the morning, the entire family all piled into the family station wagon in their Sunday finest and trundled off to church as a family unit, to receive the Lords blessing. 'We gather together to ask the Lord's blessing', she thought. Fat lot of good that got them. When she looked at things objectively, it probably should've been her in the body bag, rather than the charred remains of a once righteous family sacrificed on the altar of sheer chance. She promised herself not to dwell on the subject too long for there was no possibility of a rational answer in this lifetime.

The answer as to 'why', would simply have to be, 'because'!

There was the funeral of Uncle Leo to attend to and the majority of the firms activities had to be rescheduled, far into the following week. For Leo Schwartzwald would have his propers attended to.

Jaeger was kept busy running errands mostly and when that was through, remained at Buffy's side every minute of every day. She could function like the whirlwind she was, with him by her side, and during the interim stayed at Uncle Leo's home in River Oaks, with Jaeger in the adjoining bedroom. The second evening after the attack, when Jaeger was in the shower, he heard the bathroom door open and shut seeing the shadow of a female form shedding a bathrobe and the misted sliding glass door opened and closed and he was joined by the familiar face of a completely unadorned goddess, who simply said, "There's a water shortage going around and I hope you don't mind if we conserve water"!

Shortly thereafter each tended to the others physical needs repeatedly through the evening and every possible moment in the days ahead, especially making certain that the other was squeaky clean at all times, whenever possible. The day after tomorrow was the day when Uncle Leo would be removed from the mortuary and transported under heavy guard back to the mausoleum to spend his final resting place with his beloved Emma for all eternity.

The following day while in her office, Buffy had been putting the finishing touches on a contract for one of her clients, when the inter-office phone buzzed, "Buffy, Randall White on line three", came the voice of her secretary.

"Hello Randall, I just have to say thanks for your fine work with Odessa, the other morning. How is she and how are you"?

"Well let's see heah, Odessa is in the company of Roy Seltzer day and night and I understand that he's in possession of a huge smile. As for me, just a few nicks and scrapes which will be accounted for in the next billing cycle"!

"Duly noted, Randall"!

"But that's not why I called. I wanted you to listen to a tape of something we gleaned from the offsite taping of Sheriff Little's private office line". At that he played the tape of the conversation between Sheriff Little and Bomber Abrams. When it was completed he said, "Buffy they're planning an even bigger hit at the River Oaks home during the services for the old man"! "Announcements made and invitations sent, the funerals going to go forward Randall, so it just seems like we're going to have to plan a little surprise for them don't you think"?

She summoned Jaeger into her office and related what she'd heard from the taped conversation saying, "Well sport, what're you thinking"?

"You're Uncle needs to be buried quietly with but a chosen few mourners, tonight. Tomorrow latest"!

"The revised guest list of the chosen few is over three hundred people of Houston's finest citizens, who would feel slighted if they were not permitted to pay their last respects, Jaeger"!

"How tight is that guest list? I mean, can it be discreetly whittled down to a more manageable number"?

"The partners made the list together and some of them are out of town at the moment. Uncle Leo touched the lives of a great many people over the years in a positive sense and he is due his final moment, for posterity.

Besides, you and I both know who the real target is don't we"! "That's the whole point Buffy, I'm suggesting we limit your exposure"!

"I'm a risk taker Jaeger, for if I wasn't, you wouldn't be standing here right now. Am I right"? Without acknowledging her last statement Jaeger said, "I imagine the partners voted on a security detail for the event"?

"Yes, a half dozen off duty, HPD officers and County Sheriff's deputy's, will provide security and the will be in full uniform, armed with black armbands"!

"I'm guessing that Boyd Parmalee is running the show hereabouts", said Jaeger!

"He and Willis Voorhees are sharing that duty, until the partners can get together for a vote, after the funeral"!

"I'm trying to get into that beautiful head of yours and its damn difficult, but let's see about this, the killers were slain in their very first attempt at your life and you want to set up a killing field and get all of the rest at one time, at the home of your Uncle, never mind that the lives of innocent people are at stake. You've got the dice in your hands and you're planning to make your point. Have I got that about right"?

Buffy just stared at Jaeger, saying nothing for he'd seen right into the very heart of the matter.

"Your silence says volumes Buffy, so here it is, "You're setting yourself up as the stalking horse, waiting for the wolves to arrive, creative but not very wise. So a half dozen locals, with only side arms and maybe a few Kevlar vests, wouldn't last very long under a professional attack by pros.

You need at least twice that number of uniformed officers along with a fully armed SWAT team close by, just in case. So the question is can you get this done? For if not, I hope everyone has their will made out. We got very lucky the other morning and I for one don't trust my luck"!

Buffy later ran Jaegers concerns by Randall White, who agreed with Jaeger adding, "These people are the kind that likes to advertise. An intended massacre if pulled off is intended to implant fear in others and once mortal fear is implanted, it never goes away. So listen to Jaeger, he's got the skills and the smarts to set things up"!

Later in the afternoon Boyd Parmalee had concluded his phone conversation with the mayor. Then walked into Buffy's office saying, "The Mayor's onboard with your concerns and will see to it that a dozen off duty patrolmen will serve as security for the event and a fully armed SWAT unit willow profile be at the High School just minutes away"!

Then continuing, Parmalee said, "We really need to arrest this Sheriff Little right away Buffy"?

"On what exactly? What proof do we have? You talked to White; you heard the taped conversation with this guy 'Bomber', or whoever he is. The whole conversation is tangential and wouldn't hold up in a court of law",

Buffy shot back! I'd feel a lot better about things if Jaeger was heading up the security detail Boyd"!

"My thinking exactly, which is why he's to be at a meeting tonight with the officers selected for the detail, at the Police Chiefs office downtown, for a security run through.

Funerals are for the living, not the dead. The dead are gone and not part of this plane of existence. The funeral ritual the world over is to celebrate the passing of a life, no matter how it may have been lived. In the case of Leo Schwartzwald, the list of those awaiting their turn to sing his praises was a long one. Over time he had amassed a fortune in the business of practicing the law, giving a great deal away to local charities and institutions during his life. Not too shabby for a simple country lawyer he'd always portrayed himself as. He'd made the right friends and steered clear of any scandals in his long life and was slated to be laid to rest, next to his beloved Emma, in a twilight ceremony conducted by the rector of St. Mark's church which he'd long been a member.

All of the firm's partners were to be the Pall Bearers and the Bella Rosas Catering Service, long a reliable caterer for the elite of Houston, was selected to provide victuals and refreshments to the attendee's. As the catering vehicles were passed through the security cordon with but scant inspection, George and Agnes were busy helping them set up their stations on the grounds. As the caterers were unloading their gear, Hondo went over to Jaeger saying, "I dunno pal, but I just gotta a bad feeling about those caterers that were hired"!

"How so Hondo", said Jaeger as he gave them the once over? "They all seem to be working hard to get things set up for after the services and they all seem to know what they are doing. They got their heads down and their asses up"?

"Don't quite know, but the lone white guy, his face somehow seems familiar, but I just can't make out where and that squat dark one over there, well something just seems to be wrong with that one and I just can't tell you why"!

"Keep an eye out for them without being obvious OK", asked Jaeger The second line of security was comprised of Jaeger, Rafferty, Seltzer,

Vultee and Hondo, all neatly attired in somber suits, smiling and escorting the many guests to their prearranged seats, while keeping a keen eye for anything that looked out of place.

As they finished setting up all of the tables, steam trays and the refreshments all iced down Abrams said to El Morro in passing, "Great idea how we got in, hombre', but how do you think we're gonna get out"?

"Hostages hombre'. Nebber fail me before"! The unspoken message was that, just one mile away was the strip center on Westheimer Road where their cars were randomly parked. All they had to do after shooting the whole place up kill the security detail down to the last man, with their Kevlar penetrator rounds, then steal whatever cars they needed for their get away, leaving a number of them to block access or egress from the area, drive to the strip center lot change cars, then drive to the Tractor trailer truck in the motel parking lot on the South West Freeway, drive two of the vehicles into the truck, then slowly drive off into the night to Mexico.

Whether or not the hostages survived or not was of little consequence to El Morro, just a means to an end"! All of the intruders were smart enough to know, that above all, blend in to the frame work. Never make eye contact with anyone. Appear subservient at all costs, that is until the signal was given by El Morro, then on the underside of each table was two Mac-10 machine pistols,

With a dozen fully loaded magazines all taped to the underside of the tables with duct tape. Something no one, not even Jaeger, gave a second thought to investigating. The Mac-10 machine pistol was a wonderfully compact way of generating a maximum amount of firepower, for short range work and would work reasonably well at a right down to the ground cost factor. If fired in relatively short bursts, the weapon would work as advertised. But if fired in prolonged bursts, thus heating up the weapon past its design limits, the weapon was prone to jamming and thus useless. As Seltzer escorted Buffy and Odessa to their seats, he reminded both of them that if gunfire was to erupt, they were both to hit the ground immediately and become one with the grass. Then he returned to his duties escorting guests as best he could with his left arm in a dark gray sling and hidden in that sling was his trusty WWII Webley breakfront revolver with the three inch cut down barrel. It was every bit as nasty as the American .45 Caliber weapons.

As Odessa and Buffy looked around at the growing assemblage, they spotted Jaegers inner security detail, busy smiling and being helpful escorting people to their seats, while subtly eying each and every one they helped.

On the far end of the vast back yard well lit by the area lights positioned in the trees long ago, which provided a waxing and waning series of shadows and light, throughout the property, Abrams whispered to El Morro, "How come we're waiting until after the old man is set in the mausoleum until we hit em"? "We got nossing against the dead, only da living. We get paid for killing da living. Besides, none of em gonna get to da frijoles, dey all gonna die hungry. Beside it would be a sin to interrupt da services in da eye ob da church. We wait until everything over, then we hab fon"!

Odessa then looked at Buffy asking, "How you and your man getting along Cher"? That question brought a twinkle to Buffy's eye as she simply said, "Passable, just passable. But how are you and that old Australian getting along Cher"?

"A twinkle then came to Odessa's eye, as she cocked her head and said, "Passable, Mon Cher, really passable and besides that old tiger ain't so very old. He gives as well as he gets and I ain't complainin', not one little bit and neither is he"!

"Besides that old man can really cook, and I mean in the kitchen also"! Just then the somber music, supplied the string quartet hired from the Houston Symphony changed their music, indicating the arrival of the casket borne by all of the firm's partners, placing it on the temporary platform, in front of all. St. Marks rector, entered into an abbreviated funerary service reading from the scriptures, then turned the podium over to Boyd Parmalee, who made several brief but glowing remarks as to the life of Leo Schwartzwald, then the microphone was turned over to Willis Voorhees, who dutifully did the same, then a string of important personages, from every aspect of Houston's society made their way to the podium, for several brief remarks praising Leo Schwartzwald.

As each speaker in turn took to the podium, something told Buffy to turn her head to the left and as she raised her eyes, she saw several Vultures sitting in the half shadows, high up in the trees. She nudged Odessa to glance in the same direction and when seeing the very same thing whispered, "Oh Cher, now I'm truly worried. Ain't no buzzards ever been in the trees of River Oaks, since the Civil War"!

Seeing both Buffy and Odessa glance into the trees, Jaeger was barely able to make out what they both were seeing. Then by chance his gaze swung around and as it passed the roof of the garage, there were another four vultures equally spaced along the entire apex of the roof. He then recalled what that old Miami Indian Shaman taught Heinrich Jaeger so long ago, passed down orally from generation to generation, that when vultures were in attendance, people had either died or were going to shortly and they were just patiently waiting their turn. Jaeger would be willing to bet that vultures had not been to River Oaks in anyone's memory, as he made his way through the crowd slowly pointing at the vultures, to all of his inner security. As for the rest of the assemblage, no one else noticed the uninvited winged guests, with the lone exception of El Morro, who smiled inwardly.

For nothing in his life gave him more pleasure, than to see the look of sheer terror in someone's eyes in their final moments. Although he'd never admit it, this he would do for free. Only two things would compel his neither region to expel its bodily fluids, one was brutal sex, while the other was just minutes away.

The services concluding with the last of the speakers having has their say, Jaeger and Seltzer gradually made their way along the periphery, flanking the assemblage, to the front, each with their pistols neatly tucked away into their shoulder holsters. The only thing left was for the partners to lift Leos casket and place it in the Mausoleum next to his beloved Emma, behind the podium and seal the Mausoleum, which they dutifully did.

Signaling St. Mark's rector to address the crowd saying, "May the Lord watch over me and thee, while we are absent one from the other, Amen. The services are at an end, be with God"!

Then one by one starting with El Morro, the assailants dropped to their knees and retrieved their weapons and the magazines, from the draped tables, un noticed by all except for Jaeger and Seltzer and as El Morro and Bomber Abrams were the first to raise up with their weapons at the ready followed a split seconds by the others. Jaeger and Seltzers hollered in unison, "Guns", pulling their weapons as the first rounds poured out of the dual Mac-10's in unison.

Now .45 caliber bullets are bad enough, but when the rounds are Teflon Penetration rounds, designed to defeat a Kevlar vest, it not at all unlikely that a given bullet will penetrate two or more individuals before coming to rest after breaking a bone or two.

At the first sounds of the boys yelling "Guns", both Buffy and Odessa hit the ground unceremoniously, just as the very first of El Morro's and Abrams bullets came speeding over their heads, slamming into those poor souls behind them. Both Jaeger and Seltzer's rounds found their mark as they fired at the assailants in front of them working their way towards Buffy and Odessa. Seltzer was only partially hampered by his arm sling, being the repository for a half dozen speed loaders, as he sped them into the waiting cylinder, to continue its cycle of death. Two bullets slammed into him, just as he arrived at Odessa's side, he jerked, stumbled and squeezed off two well-placed rounds, hitting this short and dark looking Mexican waiter squarely in the chest, knocking him back, his finger locked in a death grip as the Mac-10 fired wildly into the trees overhead. Odessa immediately threw herself over Seltzers body as he carefully fired the last of his rounds, most of which hit was he was aiming at. Seeing that the lone Anglo waiter was running towards the front of the property along the side of the garage, Jaeger flipped a speed load into the cylinder of his .357 Ruger and jerked off a double tap of, two quick rounds as Bomber Abrams was fleeing to escape with the other five surviving shooters. The rounds struck Abrams in the side as he pulled the trigger of his Mac-10 at Hondo just five yards away as Hondo fired a single round, the bullet finding its way into Abrams chest knocking him back, as his finger stayed locked on the trigger spraying rounds past Hondo only one of which spun his thin body around breaking his collar bone.

As the five remaining assailants fled into the front yard they were greeted by a half dozen of the local law enforcement security detail who ran into a hail of the penetrator rounds, the whole encounter taking a scant five seconds. From that just two of the assailants, fled into the darkness, across the street and into the night followed closely by the lone K-9 German Shepard who caught several rounds just as the dog planted its teeth in a death grip deep into the throat of the shooter. The final shooter was pursued down the dark street by three of the Houston officers who caught up to him just as he was struggling with his jammed Mac-10, completely out of breath.

With the SWAT unit vehicle just a block away and coming fast with its lights flashing, each patrolman looked the other, and one by one fired a mortal round into the front of the final assailant, who died with his hand on the trigger of his jammed Mac-10.

As Jaeger made his way back to Buffy and Odessa, he saw Odessa keening over the prostrate body of Roy Seltzer and a bleeding Buffy trying to comfort her. His weapon still smoking from its exertions, Jaeger quickly looked around for another assailants then dropped to one knee, to examine Buffy saying, "Buffy, you're hit"!

"A scalp wound and one in the leg. I'll get by so go tend to Seltzer and Odessa, the ambulances will be here shortly", said Buffy sitting up on one of the folding chairs.

Prying Odessa away from her newfound love, Jaeger placed her in the hands of Buffy just feet away as they both watched Jaeger kneel down over his prostrate friend. Using his medical training he soon discovered four fresh wounds all leaking fresh blood, onto the lush grass of the estate.

Grabbing Jaeger by the shirt Seltzer wheezed, "Mate we ain't got much time left, so here tis. Member what we talked about when we were in stir"?

"As if it were yesterday Roy, every word"!

"Good, now in my pocket are my keys, all of em. Several of which are the keys to Donald Ryders club up in Ft. Worth mate. You'll know what to do with it, right"?

Jaeger, somberly, nodded his head.

"Next", he wheezed coughing up some blood, and struggling for breath, "" My will is in my flat, leaving every bloody thing I own to you, turn the place inside out and you'll be glad what ya find. Lastly the way I check out, we discussed it at length, right"!

Jaeger nodded his head.

"Well I'm holdin' ya to it"!

Jaeger spit in his palm, saying "Done", while Seltzer did the same weakly and wheezed, "And done again mate", having a look of relief in his eyes saying, "Now let me gaze at Odessa"! He exchanged places with Odessa, as the night grew alert with the sirens of ambulances and fire trucks.

"Oh darlin' Odessa" he wheezed, each breath taking one more measure of his life off the table, "Many thanks for bringin' the sweet life back to an old man, fer one moment with you was like a thousand years in eternity.

And the one thing I'll cherish is the very last thing I see, is your sweet face looking' back at me"! Before Odessa could say another thing, she saw the life slide gracefully from his eyes as she held his head in her arms, looking up at the heavens and whispering the unintelligible through clenched teeth.

As Jaeger rose up he saw that he was joined by Vultee and Hondo, who had holstered their weapons, under their coats looking down at their fallen comrade, held in the arms of a blood stained Odessa, keening softly into the night, refusing to relinquish her long lost lover.

Jaeger then took a swaying Buffy into the house, sitting her down at the kitchen table and running upstairs and quickly returning with the first aid kit examining her for wounds and finding a scalp wound deep into the hairline and another slow bleeder in her left thigh.

When he was finished, he said, "That ought to hold ya until we get you to the emergency room", as first Agnes then George found their way into the kitchen and seeing that their new mistress of the house was alright ran back outside to help with the wounded.

"It's all my fault. I should've listened to you", mumbled Buffy wearily. "Buffy, look at me", said Jaeger grabbing her gently by shoulders, "Be no more of that talk, now or ever, ya understand. You're a lawyer and never forget that. Hell even I can figure out that an admission like that would bring a flood of lawsuits down around everybody you hold near and dear, so snap out of it and soldier on, like the Texican woman your Uncle Leo knew you to be. The broad that got me sprung outta Huntsville"!

Two evenings later, Jaeger, Odessa, Buffy, Rafferty, Vultee, Hondo and Rae stood by the banks of Buffalo Bayou as Jaeger attired in that of a Comanche warrior, his bare chest displaying freshly made wounds, by his knife, seeping stripes of blood and placed the freshly wrapped and cleansed body of one Roy Seltzer in a wooden row boat, washing the entire body with five gallons of gasoline, then coming ashore and commencing the old Miami Indian ritual of burial, chanting in the old and almost forgotten dialect learned many generations past by his forbearer, Heinrich Jaeger, passed down from generation to generation. Rarely used over the years.

It had had just stopped raining, with the air still pregnant with humidity, so the possibility of the overhanging trees catching fire was nonexistent.

When the ritual was concluded, Jaeger, Vultee and Rafferty, all put the prepared arrows in their bows, while one by one Odessa Robillard lit each whispering her own silent goodbye. Then each man in turn, fired a flaming arrow into the boat as it gently floated down stream.

As the flaming boat floated downstream, the group followed the wooden structure for almost a mile as it worked its way down the center of the slowly moving bayou, never drifting from one side to the other, but right down the middle of the bayou, as if guided by some unseen hand.

Then as if by the same unseen hand, the body now consumed of its flesh by the conflagration, the boat slowly sank, Seltzers charred bones finding a final resting place in a foreign land. In the years to come, Odessa having marked the very spot in her memory where the old row boat sank, would take a picnic basket to that spot on a sunny afternoon and tell seemingly nobody the events of the week and the day and have a grand old time. This she would do for the rest of her days. In the coming days, first the local news media took hold of the story as if by storm, with investigative reporters storming their usual sources for information, but nobody seemed to know anything. Then the National media had a go at things, spending their vast intellectual capital deep into the unknown coming up with nothing, for all of the assailants perished. With no one alive to prosecute or find culpable, the story finally withered away into nothing soon enough.

Fortunately the small legion of well-seasoned lawyers guided by the ever skill full hands of Boyd Parmalee and Willis Voorhees, steered attention away from the firm or any of its Associates, by a combination of timely obfuscation and legal guile.

Jaeger, still the honored houseguest at the Schwartzwald residence, enjoying all of the prerequisites of the wealthy, long denied him, and the bed of a fabulously beautiful woman in dire need of him in every way imaginable, sat in front of the mausoleum of Emma and Leo Schwartzwald, sipping the occasional beer George kept coming, smoking the occasional cigarette and playing his harmonica, with that three note refrain he played over and over, slowly, running as a counterpoint with Gerry Mulligan and his west coast jazz ensemble, echoing over the garage radio as George worked on the firms Limousine.

Buffy had left the office early, as was her want these days, to make more time for her and Jaeger, allowing herself to be catered to by this impenetrable diamond in the rough. As she approached him sitting there in the back yard, she sat down silently in one of the yard chairs placed in front of the mausoleum. Jaeger feeling her presence said, "Ya know I'm slightly jealous of your relationship with your Uncle Leo. Would've liked to get to know him better, for I sense there was a mountain of wisdom just there for the asking and it's that which I'm in short supply of"!

"Wisdom's in short supply the world over darlin', for that's what keeps our firm in business"! Buffy then lit a cigarette and took a swig of the bottle of Pearl beer, she grabbed from the garage refrigerator saying, "I just got a call from Randall White this afternoon before I left the office"!

"Oh really? What's Randall got to allow"?

"The phone tap on Donald Ryder is still operative and according to Randall, the trio will be getting together for a Pow Wow, at his club, in Fort Worth, tomorrow night"!

"No doubt planning the future", answered Jaeger in an off handed manner.

"Plus the news report at noon, said that HPD had discovered an abandoned Tractor Trailer rig in a parking lot next to a Roadway Inn on the South West Freeway, and in it was two cars with Mexican plates, they traced back to a Mexican Drug Honcho. Inside the trailer was six dead bodies traced back to those missing from the catering service the firm contracted with for Uncle Leo's Funeral. Now in the parking lot they discovered two other cars, with stolen Texas license plates once the additional search warrant arrived, they gained entry into the vehicles and discovered almost a hundred thousand dollars in cash, with the vehicles being traced back to the same source in Villa Hermosa Mexico just south of Matamoras. Although it's not in the media, the shooters belonged to a Papa Mondragon, head of a Mexican drug smuggling crime family. The lone white guy you killed was a certain Bomber Abram, from Tyler. Finally Odessa is going to press with her expose of the Governor, Sheriff Little and Donald Ryder, the day after tomorrow. Should give folks something exciting to sink their teeth into. Murder, corruption deep in the bowels of State Government all of the juicy stuff for the great unwashed"!

"So maybe I should take a road trip up north for a few days and soon while the fish are jumpin'", said Jaeger.

"I'm just sayin'", muttered Buffy. "You do what you need to do whatever that is. As far as I'm concerned, you've been here all the time. Ya follow"?

"Ya know that Roy was a real warrior and he checked out exactly as he would want", said Jaeger absently staring at the Schwartzwald mausoleum.

"Too bad he and Odessa didn't have more time together", mused Buffy.

"I could see it in their eyes, they were made for each other"!

"I sure would've liked to get to know your Uncle Leo a whole lot better", said Jaeger repeating himself.

"You were busy doing God's work darlin'!"

Just then George approached saying, "Miss Agnes has left for home and she's made Chicken Fried Steak with all the fixin's. It's in the warmer in the kitchen and it's the best yet".

"By gawd, Agnes's chicken fried steak", said Buffy affecting he finest Texican accent, "With cream gravy and smashed taters", she asked George in a theatrical way?

"Yes ma'am, God Almighty's food with all the fixins. Just letting y'all know", he said turning on a dime and going back to the garage.

Then Buffy got up and sat on Jaegers lap saying, "Y'all do what you have to do, only come back to me in one piece, ya hear"?

Jaeger looked deeply into her eyes for a long moment, and then said, "Your lightest touch is but a command"!

That night after a candle light dinner of Agnes's 'Gawd Food', they watched TV huddled together on the sofa and after an hour or so, went upstairs and made a slow passionate love together as if it were their final time. By midnight Buffy was in a deep sleep, only to awaken at five in the morning to the blaring sounds of the alarm clock. As she rolled over sleepily in her bed reaching for her man, she found the bed empty for he was gone.

Tears started to well up in her eyes, but she fought them back by sheer willpower, for she knew that Jaeger was in the process of taking care of long overdue 'Unfinished Business'.

45

s Jaeger drove the old Ford Bronco, up to Ft. Worth, he quickly reviewed all the necessaries he brought along. The disguises, three prepared syringes of Thorazine and his two sound suppressed revolvers. Then, of course there were the keys, Seltzer said, that would gain entrance into Don Ryder's club. He just hoped that Randall Whites information was correct. If not, it would prove but a bump in the road, but things would be done and soon. He arrived in Ft. Worth late in the morning and as he drove by Ryder's Club, he wondered what size of the crowd, would be drawn with the dual headliners announced on the Turnpike's oversized marquee announcing the limited engagement of; "Tondalayo Strokahontas and the inimitable, Molly Badcock".

As he took his seat in a corner booth, dressed as a modest businessman, in a suit and tie, he had a very good view of those entering and leaving the club. Since the headliners were to perform starting this evening, he didn't expect overwhelming crowds until then. As the one o'clock hour approached and the lunch crowd had to get back to work, in walked Sheriff Morgan Little in full uniform. As he stood in the entranceway to the clubs main room, he was seen talking to the clubs massive manager at some length and pointed to one of the VIP rooms that partially ringed the second level of the club, then quickly scanned the room and the departing guests, then abruptly left.

Jaeger surmised that Little was preparing the manager for the meeting this evening and he made note of the room at the very end of the upper hallway, the meeting would be held.

Later on in the afternoon, after changing from his business suit into that similar to a county health inspector, he entered into the rear of the club through the kitchen entrance, replete with preprinted Tarrant County Health Inspector Credentials and clip board and met briefly with the head cook, inspecting the kitchen, while the cook tended to his business preparing for the dinner hour. Pretending to inspect every aspect of the kitchen, he went into the kitchen staffs dressing room and after some rummaging, found some kitchen whites that came close to fitting him, stuffing the shirt and pants inside his shirt. Then he discovered the back stairwell leading up to the VIP suites. As he ducked his head inside one of the suites he guessed was the one the meeting was to occur, he saw that a table was set for only three people.

As he departed smiling, he quickly had the head cook sign one of the forms approving the health status of the kitchen, leaving a copy.

Several hours later Jaeger returned, dressed in the white trousers and button up the front smock of the kitchen staff, walking in the very same rear kitchen entrance, unnoticed and made his way up the rear stairwell to the VIP room, set for three guests later in the evening. Now all he had to do was wait, as he checked his watch which indicated six thirty in the afternoon. The headline performers wouldn't start until ten in the evening and the special guests probably wouldn't arrive until nine, have their meeting and meal. The club would close sometime after two in the morning and if this club was like all the others, the manager would depart an hour after closing after tallying up the evening's business.

The three syringes of Thorazine were only good for twelve to fifteen hours of sedation, depending on the subject and the drive to Brewster County would take at least twelve hours of hard driving to accomplish. He would wait until they had completed their meal and drinks, before making his appearance. He would direct Ryder to close the drapes, which would signal all below that the room was not to be disturbed.

Finally, there was an extra thirty CC's of Thorazine in his first aid kit, to be used if needed, but he had to be careful for he didn't want them dead, at least not yet. So for now all he had to do was wait and that's what closets were for. Time passed ever so slowly, when one had to wait, especially when so much was at stake, so Jaeger entered into the standby mode and let his mind drift back to the last time he spent some time in a closet. There was a lot at stake then. Life and death. For the rest of his life, a closet would always remind him of life and death. In his partial reverie, his mind played the three notes of the harmonica, repeatedly, echoing again and again, until the sound of a door opening and Don Ryder's voice telling one of his staff, when to serve the drinks, dinner and then not to disturb them unless summoned. Minutes later Royce Baintree arrived saying, "Where's Morgan? We've much to discuss"! "Morgan's running late. County business he said on the mobil phone on the way over here. Should arrive any minute now"!

Just then the wait staff arrived with the drinks and entrée's and then Morgan Little arrived somewhat winded, as they immediately sat down to Prime Rib of Beef and whiskey all around. Jaeger looked at the luminous numbers on his watch, which read nine forty five as the men talked amongst themselves about the recent debacle in Houston. With Ryder complaining the most about well over a hundred thousand dollars paid, for services to be rendered, as money down the drain.

"Morgan, you told me that all was guaranteed", said Ryder!

"Now Don, it's no time to panic. The guy I contracted with has always delivered the goods in the past", said Little chewing on his salad.

"Well he certainly didn't this time", muttered Baintree!

"The good news is that dead men tell no tails and he as well as the other shooters are dead"! "That's this Bomber Abrams, from Tyler, the papers are talking about", asked Ryder?

On this, Morgan Little remained passive, only saying, "This Pocahontas is about to start her show. Let's enjoy her awhile and get back to cases later"!

Over the next three hours, the trio filled their glasses repeatedly with the finest of whiskey from the bar and around midnight; Ryder got up and pulled the curtains to the VIP room shut indicating to all, that the room wasn't to be disturbed.

As they started to discuss as best they could their current mess, Jaeger peered though the slats on the closet door, reaching for his silenced .22 caliber revolver and one of the syringes. Morgan Little sat with his back to the closet door as it swiftly opened. With his right hand, Jaeger fired off a silenced round at Ryder's shoulder, shattering the drinking glass full of whiskey and with his left hand, plunged the syringe of Thorazine into Morgan Little's neck, then pistol whipped him into immediate unconsciousness.

As he placed the cap on the syringe and placed it in his jacket pocket, he withdrew a second syringe and plunged it straight into the neck of the Governor, without a word, then clubbed him to the ground also.

Recapping the syringe, he then summoned the wounded Ryder over to the couch saying, "Had a good meal? Now we wait for things down stairs to settle down". For several minutes they waited, with terror in the eyes of Donald Ryder, who eventually mouthed the word, "Jaeger"?

"You've been running up quite a bill these past years and soon it'll be time to pay the tab", for what you've done. As well as those slumped over the table"!

For the next twenty minutes, he took his time, telling Ryder what was to break in the media all over the State the following day.

"Now I can either kill you all and save you the embarrassment of what's to come down on you all, or I can let you live. What you do next will determine which way I go", said Jaeger casually!

"What do you want me to do", asked Ryder meekly?

"You're gonna call the club manager on the house phone next to you and tell him to tell your man, the governor's driver, as well as the body guards to take the evening off and go to the house, that y'all will be awhile. And you'll be casual about it and convincing. Say that Sheriff Little will see to it that everyone gets to where they need to be. Then we wait"! Ryder then picked up the house phone and called the manager saying exactly what Jaeger had instructed him to say, then hung up.

For several minutes they sat in silence, with Ryder starting to sweat profusely in the air conditioned room. The silence being too much for Ryder to bear, prompted him to ask, "What're we waiting for"?

"For the club to close", replied Jaeger. The VIP room was sound proofed, so it was not possible for anyone inside the room to be able to tell when things were over in the club, but as the Jaeger looked at his watch, he noticed the hands indicated ten after two in the morning, just as they heard a knock at the door.

Jaeger indicated to Ryder to answer. "What do ya want"?

"The clubs closing Mr. Ryder and I gotta lock up", said the Manager. Jaeger mouthed instructions to Ryder to have the manager come in,

"Come on in, we're just wrapping up", he said as the door opened, the massive manager entered the room only to be greeted by the partially muted sound of Jaegers pistol, slamming two quick rounds into the managers head, dropping him like a stone. Jaeger then went over to the couch taking one of the table napkins and placed it over the manager's head and fired once again. He folded the napkin up and placed it into his jacket. He quickly glanced down the executive hallway and seeing no one, was convinced that all had gone home.

Then he returned into the room and removed the last syringe and plunged it into Ryder's neck savagely saying, "Time to sleep". Within a minute Don Ryder joined the rest. Jaeger went down to the club and to the manager's office and eventually found the security room where all of the various aspects in the club were videotaped during all the hours of operation.

He turned off the recorders, and removed all of the tapes of the day's activities. He then went to the external alarm system, to assure himself that it was not engaged. Then, he turned off the outside rear security lights.

Within the next thirty minutes, he'd carried out each of the men, securing their wrists behind them and legs with plastic heavy duty tie wraps, placing Baintree in one of the undercarriage storage bins and Morgan Little in the other, while Ryder was curled up behind the rear seat. He then went over to the rear door of the club and nudged it shut. He had touched nothing while inside the club, thus he was never there.

As he drove off into the morning he looked at his watch, surmising that by sunrise he could be pulling into Brady Texas for gas. The final destination, a desolated mountaintop in Brewster County overlooking the Rio Grande River, sometime around sundown.

He made fairly good time, keeping to the posted speed limits all the way and made his final fuel stop in Marathon Texas, late that afternoon. By sometime around midnight he should be somewhere near the crest of Talley Mountain looking straight into Mexico, in the desolated heart of Big Bend country.

By eleven in the evening, he found the exact place he was looking for on Talley Mountain, overlooking the Rio Grande, after having driven a little used trail, without benefit of his headlights, just lit by the light of the soon to be Full Moon, just days away. He got under the Bronco and removed his secured cargo checking their pulses and it appeared the Thorazine was starting to wear off as they were coming slowly back to the world.

He then went to the First aid bag and refilled all three syringes, a third full, injecting the trio and leaving them under the truck inert, so he could get some much needed rest.

The following morning he ate the first of the sandwiches purchased at the gas station in Marathon. Soon enough he found the tiny copse of trees he'd recalled, chasing down a runner, some months ago with Hondo. Then he found some trees with branches sufficient for his purpose and by noon he'd dug three holes in the ground the width of the branches, three feet deep, neatly crafting three nine foot long poles.

By his reckoning, all three should be coming awake, within the next two hours. Something then told him to look up and there atop the ridge sat four vultures, in attendance, waiting patiently.

"Not just yet my friends, not just yet", he said to them softly. He then gathered brush together and cut off all the trio's clothing and shoes rendering them ready for their final mission in life. Final atonement for sins long past.

The entire trip down to the valley was consumed with the manner of their final demise. Thus his final decision of impalement, facing west into the setting sun. The engorgement of their final meal, being the deciding factor.

As the last of their clothes burnt to a crisp, Jaeger stirred the ashes.

Then he one by one wrestled the still inert bodies upon the poles in their available cavities and hoisted each one carefully into the slot on the ground. To properly do this would take some assistance from several others, but as he set the poles into the ground, he removed the bonds of each of them, for when they soon came to their senses, they weren't going anywhere. Yet he did keep the gags in their mouths, for in Jaegers mind they had nothing to say of interest.

Just minutes after each man was gently slid into place, they came awake painfully as to their predicament and Jaeger said, "Now folks, try not to wiggle as best you can, for that'll only shove the pole deeper into your innards. Let the gravity of your situation do all the work"!

He then sat on a rock facing them as they painfully gazed into the afternoon sun, the Rio Grande River to their left. He tried to think of something fitting to say, as this very moment was a long time in coming, but he let his eyes rest on that of Morgan Ryder, naked and yet in good company as he struggled to raise himself from the pole that slid ever deeper into his body cavity, with each passing moment.

Jaeger again glanced up at the vultures, who had since grown in numbers by two more, saying, "Not yet my children, not yet"!

His talking to the winged dinner guest's, compelled all three to look in the direction of the vultures, prompting a muffled scream of terror from each of them at the prospects that awaited them.

As Morgan Little's head lolled around in pain, the pole inching ever deeper into his body cavity, his glance landed squarely upon Jaeger who stood below him. His eyes filled with a combination of hate and terror. Here was the son, taking silent revenge, for the murder of his family long ago.

Then he glanced once again at the vultures waiting patiently for his passing, wondering whether or not Jaeger would let them wait or feast upon him before he died. He then looked back at Jaeger pleadingly for mercy, something long ago he swore never to do.

All he saw in his remaining moments, the pole sliding ever deeper was a dispassionate look of a man disposing of refuse.

Throughout the night, Jaeger sat in attendance, of the three impalee's. Watching as gravity forced them lower and lower. Eventually he felt the unseen presence of another. 'The Ghost Dancer' of days gone by. Unseen but felt, he sensed the approval of the other and knew it was the spirit of his ancestor and then it was gone. By dawn, he stood up and considered his work completed, thinking that it was a shame, they could only experience this event but once, in this plane of existence, but that an even greater accounting was ahead for all eternity. Eventually he looked up at his winged visitors, patiently waiting, he took some comfort of the events soon to occur upon his departure, and then there was always the final resting place for their tormented souls, in the aftermath.

Taking a large branch he swept the area clean of any sign of his presence, announcing to his guests, "Breakfast is served"!

As the Ford Bronco drove down the mountain, Jaeger rolled over in his mind, his final task across the Rio Grande, before to returning to Houston.

46

s Jaeger was driving eastward towards his rendezvous in Valle Hermoso Mexico, the morning edition of the Houston Chronicle ran a front page headline, "Texas Governor Guilty of Murder". During the morning, a series of detailed audio and video taped were released to the media, detailing the Governmental conspiracy concerning the Murder of the Jaeger family years ago and the illegal appropriation of the family estate, along with the conspiracy to try and convict the only surviving family member.

Sheriff Morgan Little and Real Estate mogul Donald Ryder were completely implicated, along with the deceased Judge Morris Womble. In addition to the attempted murder of Houston Attorney, Elizabeth Beauvior and Newspaper Columnist Odessa Robillard. The authorities in Houston, Austin, Waco and Ft. Worth attempted to contact, those implicated by the weeklong series of articles and media reports, yet all the key parties were missing. All of the State law enforcement agencies were placed on a state wide alert. Family members and close associates were questioned as to their whereabouts.

The death of the manager of Donald Ryder's Club in Ft. Worth and the last known sighting of the three individuals, meeting far into the night, caused the authorities to descend on the club, in force. Yet apart from evidence of a final meal for the trio, in one of the VIP suites, some broken dishes and some blood spatters, that matched the same blood type as Don Ryder, the Clubs owner, all clues as to their disappearance ended right at the clubs doorstep, with the exception of the bullets recovered from the body of the clubs manager, which matched no known weapon in the States registry.

Yet after some days of inquiry it was feared that either they had all fled in fear of prosecution, or somehow had met with foul play, at least in part.

Examination of their personal affairs showed no financial activity or that anyone matching their description had left the country. Proving or disproving nothing one way or the other except they were all nowhere to be found. As if they had completely disappeared from the face of the earth.

Several days later, headlines appeared in the Matamoras Mexico newspaper, of the disappearance of Drug Smuggling kingpin, "Papa Mondragon. The following day it was reported that a body had washed ashore at the very southernmost point of South Padre Island, on the US side of the border, devoid of its head or any of its extremities, simply the torso.

Forensic examination of the torso indicated that it was the body of Papa Mondragon, by the plethora of tattoos on the body. Further examination also revealed a significant residual amount of the drug Thorazine in the cadaver.

Jaeger returned to Houston quietly telling no one except Buffy of his return by phone. "Are you OK", asked Buffy?

"Almost! Gotta pay a visit to Waco and visit what's left of the family burial site, and have a talk with my people, but after that I should be fine"!

"Well, when you get back, set up shop at my place for a while, for the authorities are all over the place and we need to establish your alibi as air tight. Ya follow"?

"Be seeing you, the day after tomorrow" said Jaeger.

By noon the following day, he drove his now completely restored 63 Ford Galaxie, into the subdivisions main entrance. The same entrance that used to be that of his family's ranch. He drove until he got to the copse of trees that used to be the family's collective burial plot. As he got out of his car, he slowly approached the site, his mind flooding with fond memories of a far better time.

He walked around the now diminished site for yet another time, then kneeled down in prayer, asking the eternal for forgiveness for what he decided needed to be done and explaining his reasons for his actions.

An hour later, as the sun passed its zenith in the sky, a car pulled up next to his and a man emerged, seeing the kneeling figure under the shade of the old trees. The man bore himself erect, replete with his civilian clothes and a severe military haircut displaying a graying head, rapidly turning white.

He went to the trunk of his car and removed with great care, what appeared to be a long tubular frame wrapped and well padded, shutting the trunk and walked up the short dead end street towards the kneeling figure in the trees.

He stopped some ten yards away holding the heavy parcel, for some minutes then said "Jaeger. It's General Bollinger"!

"I was wondering when you'd show up General", said Jaeger still with his head bowed.

"May I approach son? I've something for you"!

Jaeger nodded his head, still kneeling under the tree, in supplication as he felt the General approach, kneeling next to him.

"I've been reading and hearing about the Shit Storm that been swirling around you as of late. Two recent attempts on your life. A State wide political and judicial scandal, concerning people responsible for the murder of your family and your imprisonment. Then to find out the perpetrators have gone missing and everyone is beating the bushes, trying to find them. The morning news says the FBI has been called in to investigate"!

"So how did you find me General"?

"Met with your lady lawyer yesterday and she got me together with some bounty hunter that answer's to Hondo and he told me where you could be found today only and only because I have something for you long overdue"!

Jaeger then turned and faced the General, who then unwrapped the Jaeger family heirloom, the ancient Beretta Flintlock/Cap and ball dual barrel rifle that was brought to America by Dietrich Jaeger long ago. As the General handed the rifle to Jaeger, tears again came to Jaegers eyes, as he felt each inch of the priceless family heirloom.

"My family used to tell endless stories of Heinrich Jaeger in his early days in Texas and this rifle was what kept him alive in part and put food on the table, for a lot of people", said Jaeger. "Thank you General. You have no idea what this means to me"!

"Oh I have an inkling of what it means. But this is my way of saying to you, it was great having served with you and I take great pleasure of having known someone like you"!

"So what's next for you General"?

"In two weeks, the jarheads up at Quantico are going to toss me a final going away party, whereupon the Commandant will attend, to award me a second star upon my final retirement. This time, no more and I can sleep late every morning and go fishing any time I please"!

"Oh yes, that lady lawyer of yours says to get your ass back to town so she can cover it and sometime tomorrow, you're to meet with some Doctors from Cal Tech University for a once over. She said you'd know all about it"!

Jaeger then nodded his head, looking back at the rifle fondly and then said, "Before I return, General, how about a nickel tour of the ranch, should take a while"!

Bollinger nodded his head as they both rose up in unison and headed for Jaegers car. The rifle rewrapped and placed in the massive trunk.

As they drove across what they could of the ranch, Jaeger gave General Ballinger a running commentary of the history of the Jaeger family, pointing out various places where events occurred important to his forbearers.

"There's still a lot of undeveloped land here", said Bollinger. "Can't someone locally do something legally to restore it to you"!

"Perhaps. Buffy says that she'll work on it as her schedule permits. But I'm not holding out much hope that ranching or being a landsman is in my future. I'm sure it'll be a legal nightmare to undo what's been done"!

The following day found General Bollinger flying back to Washington to suffer his last days in office and on his very last day, he entered to ready room at Quantico, to see an assemblage of Marines, in mid celebration under a large sign with the acronym "FIGMO", for his retirement bash, to hear them hold their glasses on high and yell "Fuck It, Got My Orders"!

Jaeger met with the doctors from Cal Tech and the Rand Corporation for his annual exam and directed them and a team of divers to the very spot in the middle of Buffalo Bayou, where the charred bones of Roy Seltzer lay in quiet repose. Using an electronic detector, they eventually recovered the still functioning implant that somehow still lay near his skull, leaving the rest of his remains undisturbed The following evening, during dinner at the Schwartzwald mansion, Buffy and Jaeger were visited by several members of the FBI and the Texas Rangers and interviewed for several hours as to the events of the preceding days. Finding nothing to be overly concerned about and gaining corroborating testimony concerning Jaegers whereabouts, from George and eventually Agnes, they left abruptly never to return. The mystery of the whereabouts of a soon to retire Governor, County Sheriff and Commercial Real Estate Developer still hanging in the air.

They put the dishes into the sink for Agnes to attend to in the morning then went upstairs to rejoin with each other with a passion that was both intense and gentle.

With no one culpable to prosecute, the entire affair drifted into memory.

47-Epilogue

Some three years later, a small group of hikers, seeking the perfect view of the Rio Grande River, deep in a desolate region of the Big Bend Country, hiked a little known goat trail up Tally Mountain.

As they rounded a bend they came upon a small copse of hardy trees and decided that this would be a splendid view of the river. As they entered the secluded spot they came across three weathered poles stuck into the ground and at the base of each pole, was a pile of bones, bleached white by the sun. As they struggled to make sense of what they were looking at, they heard a screech from above and saw four buzzards looking down at them warily.

"I don't think the buzzards want us here", said one of the hikers.

"I think you're right" said one of the others.

"You think this place might be one of those old Indian burial grounds", asked another?

"I think this place and the buzzards are giving me the creeps. Let's try Mule Ear Peaks. It's only a day's hike away"!

As the hikers hurriedly made their way back down the mountain, not one of them looked back, for if they had they just might have caught sight of one of the buzzards smiling.